HANS FALLADA

Alone in Berlin

Translated by MICHAEL HOFMANN

With an Afterword by GEOFF WILKES

PENGUIN BOOKS

PENGUIN CLASSICS

Published by the Penguin Group
Penguin Books Ltd, 80 Strand, London WC2R ORL, England
Penguin Group (USA) Inc., 375 Hudson Street, New York, New York 10014, USA
Penguin Group (Canada), 90 Eglinton Avenue East, Suite 700, Toronto, Ontario, Canada M4P 2Y3
(a division of Pearson Penguin Canada Inc.)
Penguin Ireland, 25 St Stephen's Green, Dublin 2, Ireland (a division of Penguin Books Ltd)
Penguin Group (Australia), 250 Camberwell Road, Camberwell, Victoria 3124, Australia
(a division of Pearson Australia Group Pty Ltd)
Penguin Books India Pvt Ltd, 11 Community Centre, Panchsheel Park, New Delhi – 110 017, India
Penguin Group (NZ), 67 Apollo Drive, Rosedale, North Shore 0632, New Zealand
(a division of Pearson New Zealand Ltd)
Penguin Books (South Africa) (Pty) Ltd, 24 Sturdee Avenue, Rosebank,
Johannesburg 2196, South Africa

Penguin Books Ltd, Registered Offices: 80 Strand, London WC2R ORL, England

www.penguin.com

First published as *Jeder stirbt für sich allein* 1947
This translation first published in the United States of America
by Melville House Publishing and in Great Britain by Penguin Classics 2009
Published in paperback in Penguin Classics 2009

4

Copyright © Aufbau-Verlagsgruppe GmbH, Berlin, 1994
Translation copyright © Michael Hofmann, 2009
Afterword copyright © Geoff Wilkes, 2009
All rights reserved

The moral right of the copyright-holder and translator has been asserted

Set in Dante MT
Printed in England by Clays Ltd, St Ives plc

978-0-141-18938-3

www.greenpenguin.co.uk

Penguin Books is committed to a sustainable future
for our business, our readers and our planet.
The book in your hands is made from paper
certified by the Forest Stewardship Council.

ALONE IN BERLIN

'Has a journalistic clarity and a thriller writer's pace'
Ian Brunskill, *The Times*

'A novelist I've always loved . . . now, thrillingly, Penguin have put the authority of the translator Michael Hofmann behind his heartbreaking tale of futile resistance in Nazi Berlin . . . He's a unique novelist, a writer of great sweetness and charm whom historical circumstances forced to take an interest in violent historical turmoil' Philip Hensher, *Independent*

'A vibrant translation by Michael Hofmann . . . sprawling, dark and densely observed' Matthew Shaer, *Los Angeles Times*

'Gritty, unpolished realism . . . *Alone in Berlin* is a credible thriller, but its stark portrayal of fear and the effects of persecution is disturbing on another level' Charlotte Bailey, *The Times Literary Supplement*

'This novel is far more than a literary thriller. Fallada's vivid novel gives us the true, concentric circles of lives in a Berlin apartment block under totalitarianism. Michael Hofmann should be congratulated for bringing this work with all its immediate clarity to the English language'
Hugo Hamilton, *Financial Times*

'Hofmann is a complete literary professional . . . he gives this tough and shady author his all' James Buchan, *Guardian*

'A readable, suspense-driven novel . . . the characters – and what characters they are, the good, the bad and the ugly of the Berlin working class during the war – are drawn from life. They are alive . . . a one-of-a-kind novel . . . Fallada can be seen as a hero, a writer-hero who survived just long enough to strike back at his oppressors' Alan Furst, *Toronto Globe and Mail*

'The perspective afforded by his decision to [remain in a devastated Germany] makes *Alone in Berlin* one of the most immediate and authentic fictional accounts of life during the long nightmare of Nazi rule'
James Martin, *New York Observer*

'Magnificent . . . hammered out with such passion that it is painfully convincing' Caroline Moore, *Standpoint*

ABOUT THE AUTHOR

Hans Fallada was one of the best-known German writers of the twentieth century. Born in 1893 in Greifswald, north-east Germany, as Rudolph Wilhelm Adolf Ditzen, he took his pen-name from a Brothers Grimm fairytale. His most famous works include the novels *Little Man, What Now?* and *The Drinker*. Fallada died in 1947 in Berlin.

Michael Hofmann is the author of several books of poems and of a book of criticism, *Behind the Lines*, and the translator of many modern and contemporary authors, including Joseph Roth. Penguin publish his translations of Kafka's *Amerika* and *Metamorphosis and Other Stories*, Ernst Jünger's *Storm of Steel* and Irmgard Keun's *Child of All Nations*.

Contents

PART I
The Quangels

I

Some Bad News

The postwoman Eva Kluge slowly climbs the steps of 55 Jablonski Strasse. She's tired from her round, but she also has one of those letters in her bag that she hates to deliver, and is about to have to deliver, to the Quangels, on the second floor.

Before that, she has a Party circular for the Persickes on the floor below. Persicke is some political functionary or other – Eva Kluge always gets the titles mixed up. At any rate, she has to remember to call out 'Heil Hitler!' at the Persickes' and watch her lip. Which she needs to do anyway, there's not many people to whom Eva Kluge can say what she thinks. Not that she's a political animal, she's just an ordinary woman, but as a woman she's of the view that you don't bring children into the world to have them shot. Also, that a home without a man is no good, and for the time being she's got nothing: not her two boys, not a man, not a proper home. So, she has to keep her lip buttoned and deliver horrible letters from the front that aren't written but typed, and are signed Regimental Adjutant.

She rings the Persickes' bell, says 'Heil Hitler!' and hands the old drunk his circular. He has his Party badge on his lapel, and he asks, 'Well, what's new?'

She replies, 'Haven't you heard the bulletin? France has capitulated.'

Persicke's not content with that. 'Come on, Fräulein, of course I knew that, but to hear you say it, it's like you were selling stale rolls. Say it like it means something! It's your job to tell everyone who doesn't have a radio, and convince the last of the moaners. The second Blitzkrieg is in the bag; it's England now! In another three months, the Tommies will be finished, and then we'll see what the Führer has in store for us. Then it'll be the turn of the others to bleed, and we'll be the masters. Come on in, and have a schnapps with us. Amalie, Erna, August, Adolf, Baldur – come in here. Today we're celebrating; we're not working today. Today we'll toast the news, and in the afternoon we'll go and pay a call on the Jewish lady on the fourth floor, and see if she won't treat us to coffee and cake! I tell you, there'll be no mercy for that bitch any more!'

Leaving Herr Persicke ringed by his family, hitting the schnapps and launching into increasingly wild vituperation, the postie climbs the next flight of stairs and rings the Quangels' bell. She's already holding the letter out, ready to run off the second she's handed it over. And she's in luck: it's not the woman who answers the door – she usually likes to exchange a few pleasantries – but the man with the etched, birdlike face, the thin lips, and the cold eyes. He takes the letter from her without a word and pushes the door shut in her face, as if she were a thief, someone you had to be on your guard against.

Eva Kluge shrugs her shoulders and turns to go back downstairs. Some people are like that; in all the time she's delivered mail in Jablonski Strasse, that man has yet to say a single word to her. Well, let him be, she can't change him, she couldn't even change the man she's married to, who wastes his money sitting in bars and betting on horses, and only ever shows his face at home when he's broke.

At the Persickes' they've left the apartment door open; she can hear the clinking glass and rowdy celebration. The post-woman gently pulls the door shut and carries on downstairs. She thinks the speedy victory over France might actually be good news, because it will have brought the end of the war nearer. And then she'll have her two boys back.

The only fly in the ointment is the uncomfortable realization that people like the Persickes will come out on top. To have the likes of them as masters and always have to mind your p's and q's, that doesn't strike her as right either.

Briefly, she thinks of the man with the bird face who she gave the letter from the front to, and she thinks of old Frau Rosenthal up on the fourth floor, whose husband the Gestapo took away two weeks ago. You had to feel sorry for someone like that. The

Rosenthals used to have a little haberdashery shop on Prenzlauer Allee that was Aryanized, and now the man has disappeared, and he can't be far short of seventy. Those two old people can't have done any harm to anyone, they always allowed credit – they did it for Eva Kluge when she couldn't afford new clothes for the kids – and the goods were certainly no dearer or worse in quality than elsewhere. No, Eva Kluge can't get it into her head that a man like Rosenthal is any worse than the Persickes, just by virtue of him being a Jew. And now the old woman is sitting in her flat all alone and doesn't dare go outside. It's only after dark that she goes and does her shopping, wearing her yellow star; probably she's hungry. No, thinks Eva Kluge, even if we defeat France ten times over, it doesn't mean there's any justice here at home . . .

And by now she's reached the next house, and she makes her deliveries there.

In the meantime shop foreman Otto Quangel has taken the letter from the front into the parlour and propped it against the sewing machine. 'There!' he says, nothing more. He always leaves the letters for his wife to open, knowing how devoted she is to their only son Otto. Now he stands facing her, biting his thin underlip, waiting for her smile to light up. In his quiet, undemonstrative way, he loves this woman very much.

She has torn open the envelope, and for a brief moment there really was a smile lighting up her face, but it vanished when she saw the typed letter. Her face grew apprehensive, she read more and more slowly, as though afraid of what each next word might be. The man has leaned forward and taken his hands out of his pockets. He is biting his underlip quite hard now, sensing that something terrible has happened. It's perfectly silent in their parlour. Then the woman's breathing comes with a gasp.

Suddenly she emits a soft scream, a sound her husband has never heard from her. Her head rolls forward, bangs against the spools of thread on her sewing machine, and comes to rest among the folds of sewing, covering the fateful letter.

In a couple of bounds Quangel is at her side. With uncharacteristic haste he places his big, work-toughened hand on her back. He can feel his wife trembling all over. 'Anna!' he says, 'Anna, please!' He waits for a moment, and then he says it: 'Has something happened to Otto? Is he wounded, is it bad?'

His wife's body continues to tremble, but she doesn't make a sound. She makes no effort to raise her head to look at him.

He looks down at her hair, it's got thin in the many years of their marriage. They are getting old; if something serious has happened to Otto, she will have no one to love, only him, and there's not much to love about him. He has never had the words to tell her how much he feels for her. Even now, he's not able to stroke her, be tender to her, comfort her a little. It's all he can do to rest his heavy hand on her hair, pull her head up as gently as he can, and softly say, 'Anna, will you tell me what's in the letter?'

But even though her eyes are now very close to his, she keeps them shut tight, she won't look at him. Her face is a sickly yellow, her usual healthy colour is gone. The flesh over the bones seems to have melted away – it's like looking at a skull. Only her cheeks and mouth continue to tremble, as her whole body trembles, caught up in some mysterious inner quake.

As Quangel gazes into her face, so familiar, and now so strange, he feels his heart pounding harder and harder, he feels his complete inability to afford her the least comfort; he is gripped by a deep fear. A ridiculous fear really, compared to the deep pain of his wife, but he is afraid that she might start to scream, more loudly and wildly than she did a moment ago. He was always one for peace and quiet; he didn't want anyone to know anything about the Quangels at home. And as for giving vent to feelings, no, thank you! But even in the grip of his fear, the man isn't able to say any more than he did a moment ago: 'What is it in the letter? Tell me, Anna!'

The letter is lying there plain to see, but he doesn't dare to reach for it. He would have to let go of his wife's head, and he knows that her head – there are two bloody welts on it from the sewing machine – would only slump once more. He masters himself, and asks again, 'What's happened with Ottochen?'

It's as though the pet name, one that the man hardly ever

used, recalled the woman from the world of her pain back into life. She gulps a couple of times; she even opens her eyes, which are very blue, and now look bled white. 'With Ottochen?' she says in a near whisper. 'What do you think's happened? Nothing has happened, there is no Ottochen any more, that's all!'

'Oh!' the man says, just a deep 'Oh!' from the core of his heart. Without knowing what he's doing, he lets go of his wife's head and reaches for the letter. His eyes stare at the lines without being able to decipher them.

Then the woman grabs it from him. Her mood has swung round, furiously she rips the letter into scraps and shreds and fragments and she shouts into his face: 'What do you even want to read that filth for, those common lies they always write? That he died a hero's death for Führer and Fatherland? That he was an exemplary soldier and comrade? Do you want to hear that from them, when you know yourself that Ottochen liked nothing better than fiddling about with his radio kits, and that he cried when he was called away to be a soldier? How often he used to say to me when he was recruited that he would give his right hand to be able to get away from them? And now he's supposed to be an exemplary soldier, and died a hero's death? Lies, all a pack of lies! But that's what you get from your wretched war, you and that Führer of yours!'

Now she's standing in front of him, the woman, so much shorter than he is, her eyes sparkling with fury.

'Me and my Führer?' he mumbles, stunned by this attack. 'Since when is he *my* Führer? I'm not even in the Party, just in the Arbeitsfront, and everyone has to join that. As for voting for him, I only did that once, and so did you.'*

He says it in his slow and cumbersome manner, not so much to defend himself as to clarify the facts. He can't understand what has induced her to mount this sudden attack on him. They were always of one mind . . .

* The Arbeitsfront was a vast, Nazi-run umbrella organization of all German labour unions, instituted after Hitler outlawed the free and diverse labour unions of the Weimar Republic. Membership was voluntary but it was nearly impossible to get a job without joining, and the Reich made a considerable income from its compulsory fees.

But she says heatedly, 'What gives you the right to be the man in the house and determine everything? If I want so much as a space for my potatoes in the cellar, it has to be the way you want it. And in something as important as this, it's you who made the wrong decision. But then you creep around everywhere in carpet slippers, you want your peace and quiet and that's all; you want never to come to anyone's attention. So you did the same as they all did, and when they yelled: 'Führer, give us your orders, we will obey!' you went with them like a sheep. And the rest of us had to follow you! But now Ottochen's dead, and no Führer in the world can bring him back, and nor can you!'

He listened to her without answering a word. He had never been a man for quarrelling and bickering, and he could also tell that it was her pain speaking in her. He was almost glad to have her scolding him, because it meant she wasn't giving in to her grief. The only thing he said by way of reply was: 'One of us will have to tell Trudel.'

Trudel was Ottochen's girlfriend, almost his fiancée; she called them Mother and Father. She often dropped in on them for a chat in the evening, even now, with Ottochen away. By day she worked in a uniform factory.

The mention of Trudel straightaway set Anna Quangel off on a different tack. She glanced at the gleaming clock on the mantel and asked, 'Will you have time before your shift?'

'I'm on from one till eleven today,' he said. 'I've got time.'

'Good,' she said. 'Then go, but just ask her to come. Don't say anything about Ottochen. I'll tell her myself. Your dinner'll be ready by midday.'

'I'll ask her to come round tonight,' he said, but he didn't leave yet, but looked into his wife's jaundiced, suffering face. She returns his look, and for a moment they look at each other, two people who have been married for almost thirty years, always harmoniously, he quiet and silent, she bringing a bit of life to the place.

But however much they now look at each other, they can find no words for this thing that has happened, and so he nods and goes out.

She hears the apartment door close. No sooner is she certain he is gone than she turns back towards the sewing machine and sweeps up the scraps of the fateful letter. She tries to put them back together, but quickly sees that it will take too long now. She has to get dinner ready. She scoops the pieces into the envelope and slides it into her hymnbook. In the afternoon, when Otto is at work, she will have time to fit them together, glue them down. It might all be lies – mean, stupid lies – but it remained the last news she will ever have of Ottochen. She'll keep it safe, and show it to Trudel. Maybe she will be able to cry then; just now it still feels like a flame in her heart. It would do her good to be able to cry.

She shakes her head crossly and goes to the stove.

2

What Baldur Persicke Had to Say

As Otto Quangel was going past the Persicke apartment, rapturous shouting mixed with chants of 'Sieg Heil!' greeted his ears. Quangel hurried on, anxious not to encounter any of that company. They had been living in the same building for ten years, but Quangel had always been at pains to avoid the Persickes, even at the time old Persicke was just a little loud-mouthed publican. But now the Persickes had turned into important people, the man held all sorts of Party posts, and the two older boys were with the SS; money didn't seem to be an issue for them.

The more reason to be wary of them now, because people like that had to keep on good terms with the Party, and the only way they could do it was if they did things to help the Party. 'Doing things' meant reporting on others, for instance: So-and-so was listening to a foreign radio station. Ideally, Quangel would have packed up all the radios in Otto's room and stashed them in the basement. You couldn't be careful enough in times like these, when everyone was spying on everybody else, the Gestapo had their eyes on all of them, and the concentration camp in Sachsenhausen was expanding all the time. He, Quangel, didn't need a radio, but Anna had been opposed to getting rid of them. She still believed in the old proverb, 'A good conscience is a soft pillow.' Even though it was all bunk now, if it hadn't always been.

With these thoughts going through his mind, Quangel hurried down the stairs, across the courtyard, and into the street.

The reason for the cheering at the Persickes was that the darling of the family, young Bruno – who now goes by Baldur because of Schirach* and, if his father's string-pulling can get

---

* Baldur von Schirach was head of the Hitler-Jugend – the Hitler Youth.

him in, is even going to one of the party's elite Napola schools – well, Baldur came upon a photo in the Party newspaper, the *Völkischer Beobachter*. The photo shows the Führer with Reichsmarschall Göring, and the caption reads: 'After receiving news of the French capitulation.' And the two of them look like they've heard some good news too: Göring is beaming all over his fat face, and the Führer is smacking his thighs with delight.

The Persickes were all similarly rejoicing when Baldur asked, 'Doesn't anything strike you about that picture?'

They stop and stare at him in consternation, so convinced are they of the intellectual superiority of this sixteen-year-old that none of the rest of them even hazards a guess.

'Come on!' says Baldur. 'Think about it! The picture was taken by a press photographer. He just happened to be there when news of the capitulation arrived, hmm? Probably it was delivered by phone or courier, or perhaps a French general brought it in person, though there's no sign of any of that. It's just the two of them standing in the garden, having a whale of a time . . .'

Baldur's mother and father and sister and brothers are still sitting there in silence, gawping. The tension makes them look almost stupid. Old Persicke wishes he could pour himself another schnapps, but he can't do that, not while Baldur's speaking. He knows from experience that Baldur can cut up rough if you fail to pay sufficient attention to his political lectures.

So the son continues, 'Well, then, the picture is posed, it wasn't taken when the news of the capitulation arrived, it was taken some time before. And now look at the Führer's rejoicing! His mind's on England, has been for ages now, all he's thinking about is how to put one over on the Tommies. This whole business here is a piece of playacting, from the photo to the happy clapping. All they're doing is making mugs of people!'

Now the family are staring at Baldur as if they were the ones who were being made mugs of. If he hadn't been their Baldur, they would have reported him to the Gestapo right away.

But Baldur goes on, 'You see, that's the Führer's greatness for you: he won't let anyone see his cards. They all think he's so pleased about defeating the French, when in fact he might be assembling a fleet to invade Britain right now. We need to learn that from our Führer, not to tell all and sundry who we are and what we're about!' The others nod enthusiastically: at last, they think, they've grasped Baldur's point. 'Yes, you're nodding now,' says Baldur crossly, 'but that's not the way you act yourselves. Not half an hour ago I heard Father say in the presence of the postwoman that we were going to turn up at the old Rosenthal woman's flat for coffee and cakes.'

'Oh, the old Jewish cow!' says Father Persicke, in a bantering tone of voice.

'All right,' the son concedes, 'I daresay there wouldn't be many inquiries if something should happen to her. But why tell people about it in the first place? Better safe than sorry. Take someone like the man in the flat above us, old Quangel. You never hear a squeak out of him, and I'm quite sure he sees and hears everything, and probably has someone he reports to. And then if he reports that you can't trust the Persickes, they're unreliable, they don't know how to keep their mouths shut, then we've had it. You anyway, Father, and I'm damned if I lift a finger to get you out of the concentration camp, or Moabit Penitentiary, or Plötzensee Prison, or wherever they stick you.'

No one says anything, and even someone as conceited as Baldur can sense that their silence doesn't indicate agreement. To at least bring his brothers and sister round, he quickly throws in, 'We all want to get ahead in life, and how are we going to do that except through the Party? That's why we should follow the Führer's lead and make mugs of people, put on friendly expressions and then, when no one senses any threat, take care of business. What we want the Party to say is: 'We can trust the Persickes with anything, absolutely anything!'

Once again he looks at the picture of the laughing Hitler and Göring, nods curtly, and pours himself a brandy to indicate that the lecture is over. He says, 'There, there, Father, don't make a face, I was just expressing an opinion!'

'You're only sixteen, and you're my son,' the old man begins, still hurt.

'Yes, and you're my old man, but I've seen you drunk far too many times to be in awe of you,' Baldur Persicke throws back, and that brings the laughers round to his side, even his chronically nervous mother. 'No, Father, let be, and one day we'll get to drive around in our own car, and you can drink all the Champagne you want, every day of your life.'

Old Persicke wants to say something, but it's just about the champagne, which he doesn't rate as highly as corn brandy. Instead Baldur, quickly and now more quietly, continues, 'It's not that your ideas are bad, Father, just you should be careful not to air them outside the family. That Rosenthal woman might be good for a bit more than coffee and cake. Let me think about it – it needs care. Perhaps there are other people sniffing around there, too, perhaps people better placed than we are.'

He has dropped his voice, till by the end he is barely audible. Once again, Baldur Persicke has managed to bring everyone round to his side, even his father, who to begin with was offended. And then he says, 'Well, here's to the capitulation of France!' and because of the way he's laughing and slapping his thighs, they understand that what he really has in mind is the old Rosenthal woman.

They shout and propose toasts and down a fair few glasses, one after another. But then they have good heads on them, the former publican and his children.

3

A Man Called Borkhausen

Foreman Quangel has emerged on to Jablonski Strasse, and run into Emil Borkhausen on the doorstep. That seems to be Emil Borkhausen's one and only calling in life, to be always standing around where there's something to gawp at or overhear. The war hasn't done anything to change that, for all its call on patriots to do their duty on the home front: Emil Borkhausen has just continued to stand around.

He was standing there now, a tall lanky figure in a worn suit, his colourless face looking glumly down the almost deserted Jablonski Strasse. Catching sight of Quangel, he snapped into movement, going up to him to shake hands. 'Where are you off to then, Quangel?' he asked. 'Your shift doesn't begin yet, does it?'

Quangel ignored the extended hand and merely mumbled: ''m in a hurry.'

And he was off at once, in the direction of Prenzlauer Allee. That bothersome chatterbox was really all he needed!

But Borkhausen wasn't so easily shaken off. He laughed his whinnying laugh and said: 'You know what, Quangel, I'm heading the same way!' And as the other strode on, not looking aside, he added, 'The doctor's prescribed plenty of exercise for my constipation, and I get a bit bored walking around all the time without any company!'

He then embarked on a detailed account of everything he had done to combat his constipation. Quangel didn't listen. He was preoccupied by two thoughts, each in turn shoving the other aside: that he no longer had a son, and that Anna had said 'You and your Führer.' Quangel admitted to himself that he never loved the boy the way a father is supposed to love his son. From the time Ottochen was born, he had never seen anything in him but a nuisance and a distraction in his relationship with Anna.

If he felt grief now, it was because he was thinking worriedly about Anna, how she would take the loss, what would now change between them. He had the first instance of that already: 'You and your Führer.'

It wasn't true. Hitler was not his Führer, or no more his Führer than Anna's. They had always agreed that after his little carpentry business folded, Hitler was the one who had pulled their chestnuts out of the fire. After being out of work for four years, in 1934 Quangel had become foreman in the big furniture factory, taking home forty marks a week. And they had done pretty well on that.

Even so, they hadn't joined the Party. For one thing, they resented the dues; they felt they were contributing quite enough as it was, what with obligatory donations to the Winter Relief Fund and various appeals and the Arbeitsfront.* Yes, they had dragged him into the Arbeitsfront at the factory, and that was the other reason they both had decided against joining the Party. Because you could see it with your eyes closed, the way they were making separations between ordinary citizens and Party members. Even the worst Party member was worth more to them than the best ordinary citizen. Once in the Party, it appeared you could do what you liked, and never be called for it. They termed that rewarding loyalty with loyalty.

But foreman Quangel liked equality and fair-dealing. To him a human being was a human being, whether he was in the Party or not. Quangel was forever coming up against things at work, like a man being punished severely for a small mistake whereas someone else was allowed to deliver botched job after botched job, and it upset him. He bit his lower lip and gnawed furiously away at it – if he had been brave enough, he would have told them where they could stick their membership in the Arbeitsfront!

* Winter Relief Fund was a Nazi-organized charity collected during the winter months. Pressure to contribute was considerable, and armbands and pins were distributed for public display to identify donors – and thus, non-donors. Much of the money was syphoned off by the Party, and scholars have noted that it kept the populace short of extra cash and acclimated to the idea of privation.

Anna knew that perfectly well, which is why she should never have said that thing: 'You and your Führer!' They couldn't coerce Anna the way they could him. Oh, he could understand her simplicity, her humility, and how she had suddenly changed. All her life she had been in service, first in the country, then here in Berlin; all her life it had been Do this, do that. She didn't have much of the say in their marriage either, not because he always ordered her about, but because as the principal breadwinner, things were run around him.

But now Ottochen is dead, and Otto Quangel can feel how hard it has hit her. He can see her jaundiced-looking face in front of him, he can hear her accusation, and here he is off on an errand at a quite unusual time for him, with this Borkhausen fellow trotting along at his side, and tonight Trudel will come over and there will be tears and no end of talk – and Otto Quangel likes order in his life and routine at work; the more uneventful a day is, the better he likes it. Even a Sunday off is a kind of interruption. And now it looks as if everything will be topsy-turvy for a while to come, and maybe Anna won't ever get back to being her old self again.

He wants to get it all clear in his head, and Borkhausen is bothering him. He can't believe it, here's the man saying, 'And is it true you got a letter from the field today, not written by your Otto?'

Quangel throws a sharp, dark glance at the fellow and mutters, 'Chatterbox!' But because he doesn't want to quarrel with anyone, not even such a waste of space as that idler Borkhausen, he adds, rather in spite of himself, 'People all talk too much nowadays!'

Borkhausen isn't offended because Emil Borkhausen is not an easy man to offend; instead, he concurs enthusiastically: 'You know, Quangel, you're right! Why can't the postwoman Kluge keep her lip buttoned? But no, she has to blab it out to everyone: There's a letter for the Quangels from the field, and it's a typed one!' He stops for a moment, then, in a strange, wheedling, sympathetic voice, he inquires, 'Is he wounded, or missing, or . . . ?'

Silence. Quangel – after a longish pause – answers indirectly. 'The French have capitulated, eh? Well, it's a shame they didn't do it a day earlier, because then my Otto would still be alive . . .'

Borkhausen pulls out all the stops: 'But it's because so many thousands have died heroic deaths that the French have surrendered so quickly. That's why so many millions of us are still alive. As a father, you should be proud of such a sacrifice!'

Quangel asks, 'Are yours not of an age to go and fight, neighbour?'

Almost offended, Borkhausen says: 'You know perfectly well, Quangel! But if they all died at once in a bomb blast or whatever, I'd be proud of them. Don't you believe me, Quangel?'

The foreman doesn't give him an immediate answer, but he thinks, Well, I might not have been a proper father and never loved Otto as I ought to have done – but to you, your kids are just a millstone round your neck. I think you'd be glad if a bomb came along and took care of them for you!

Still, he doesn't say anything to that effect, and Borkhausen, already tired of waiting for an answer, says, 'Just think, Quangel, first Sudetenland and Czechoslovakia and Austria, and now Poland and France – we're going to be the richest country on earth! What do a couple of hundred thousand dead matter! We're rich!'

Unusually rapidly, Quangel replies, 'And what will we do with our wealth? Eat it? Do I sleep better if I'm rich? If I stop going to the factory because of being such a rich man, what will I do all day? No, Borkhausen, *I* don't want to be rich, and much less in such a way. Riches like that aren't worth a single dead body!'

Borkhausen seizes him by the arm; his eyes are flickering, he shakes Quangel while whispering fervently into his ear, 'Say, Quangel, how can you talk like that? You know I can get you put in a concentration camp for defeatist muttering like that? What you said is a direct contradiction of what the Führer says himself! What if I was someone like that, and went and denounced you . . . ?'

Quangel is alarmed by what he has said. The thing with Otto
and Anna must have thrown him much more than he thought,
otherwise he would certainly not have dropped his innate caution
like that. But he makes sure that Borkhausen gets no sense of
his alarm. With his strong workingman's hands Quangel frees
his arm from the lax grip of the other, and slowly and coolly
says, 'What are you getting so excited about, Borkhausen? What
did I say that you can denounce me for? My son has died, and
my wife is upset. That makes me sad. You can denounce me for
that, if you want. Why don't you, go ahead! I'll come with you
and sign the statement!'

While Quangel is speaking with such unusual volubility, he
is thinking to himself, I'll eat my hat if Borkhausen isn't a snoop!
Someone else to be wary of. Who is there anywhere you can
trust? I have to worry what Anna might say, too . . .

By now they have reached the factory gates. Once again,
Quangel doesn't offer Borkhausen his hand. He says, 'All right,
then!' and makes to go inside.

But Borkhausen grabs hold of his shirt and whispers to him,
'Neighbour, let's not lose any more words about what's just
happened. I'm not a spy and I don't want to bring misfortune
to anyone. But do me a favour, will you: I need to give my wife
a bit of housekeeping money, and I haven't got a penny. The
children have had nothing to eat all day. Will you loan me ten
marks – I'll have them for you next Friday, I swear!'

As he did a moment earlier, Quangel shakes free of the man's
clutches. So that's the kind of fellow you are, he thinks, that's
how you make your living! And: I won't give him one mark, or
he'll think I'm afraid of him, and then I'll never see the last of
him. Aloud he says, 'Listen, mate, I take home thirty marks a
week, and we need every penny. I can't lend you a thing.'

Then, without a further word or glance back, he passes
through the factory gates. The security guard knows him and
doesn't stop him.

Borkhausen stands there staring and wondering what to do
next. He feels like going to the Gestapo and denouncing Quangel,
that would certainly net him a couple of packs of cigarettes at

least. But better not. He had got ahead of himself this morning, he should have let Quangel speak; following the death of his son, there was every chance he would have done. But he got Quangel wrong. Quangel won't allow himself to be played like a fish. Most people today are afraid, basically everyone, because they're all up to something forbidden, one way or another, and are worried that someone will get wind of it. You just need to catch them at the right moment, and you've got them, and they'll cough up. But Quangel, with his hawk's profile, he's different. He's probably not afraid of anything, and it's not possible to catch him out. No, Borkhausen will let him go, and perhaps try to get somewhere with the woman; the woman will have been thrown for a loop by the death of her only son! She'll talk, all right.

So, he'll keep the woman in reserve for the next few days, but what about now? It's true that he needs to give Otti some money today, this morning he secretly scoffed the last of the bread in the box. But he has no money, and where is he going to get hold of some in a hurry? His wife is a real nag and can make his life a misery. Time was, she was a streetwalker on Schönhauser Allee, and she could be really sweet. Now she's the mother of five children – most of them probably nothing to do with him – and she's got a tongue on her like a fishwife. And she knocks him around too, him and the kids, in which case he hits her back. It's her fault; she doesn't have the sense to stop.

No, he can't go back to Otti without some money. Suddenly he thinks of the old Rosenthal woman, who's all alone now, without anyone to protect her, on the fourth floor of 55 Jablonski Strasse. He wonders why he didn't think of her before; there's a more promising victim than that old buzzard, Quangel! She's a cheerful woman – he remembers her from before, when she still used to have her haberdashery, and he'll try the soft approach with her first. If that doesn't work, he'll bop her over the head. He's sure to find something, an ornament or money or something to eat – something that will placate Otti.

While Borkhausen is thinking, envisioning what he might find – because of course the Jews still have all their property, they're just hiding it from the Germans they stole it from in the first place – while he's thinking, he nips back to Jablonski Strasse, pronto. In the stairwell, he pricks up his ears. He's anxious not to be spotted by anyone here in the front building; he himself lives in the back building, in the 'lower ground floor' of the 'garden block' – the back basement, in other words. It doesn't bother him, but it's sometimes embarrassing when people come.

There's nobody in the stairwell, and Borkhausen takes the stairs quietly and quickly. There's a wild racket coming from the Persickes' apartment, laughing and shouting, they must be celebrating again. He really needs to get in touch with people like that – they have proper contacts. If he did, things would start to look up for him. Unfortunately, people like that won't even look at a part-timer like him, especially not the boys in the SS, and that Baldur is up himself like you wouldn't believe. The old fellow's different; when you catch him good and drunk, he's good for five marks.

In the Quangels' apartment everything's quiet, and at Frau Rosenthal's one floor up, he can't hear anything either, though he presses his ear to the door for a good long time. So he rings the bell, quick and businesslike, like a postman, say, someone who's in a hurry to move on.

But nothing stirs, and after waiting for a minute or two, Borkhausen decides to try again, and then a third time. In between, he listens, but can't hear anything, and finally he hisses through the keyhole, 'Frau Rosenthal, open up! I've got news of your husband! Quickly, before someone sees me here. I can hear you, Frau Rosenthal, open the door!'

He keeps ringing, but without results. Finally, he falls into a rage. He can't go home empty-handed – there'd be an almighty scene with Otti. The old Jewess should just hand back what she stole. He jams his finger into the bell and yells through the keyhole, 'Open the goddamned door, you Jewish bitch, or I'll smash your face in so badly you won't be able to see out. I'll haul you off to the concentration camp today, if you don't open the door, you fucking kike!'

If only he had some gasoline, he could torch the bitch's door.

Suddenly Borkhausen goes all quiet. He's heard a door open downstairs, and he presses himself against the wall. No one must see him here. They're bound to be going out, he just needs to keep really quiet.

But the steps are coming closer, ever closer, even if they're slow and halting. It's one of the Persickes, and if there's anything Borkhausen doesn't need, it's a drunken Persicke. Whoever it is is making his way toward the attic, but the attic is secured with an iron door, and there's nowhere to hide. Now he's only got one hope, which is that whoever it is is so drunk, he'll walk straight past without seeing him; if it's old Persicke, it could happen.

But it's not old Persicke, it's the loathsome boy, Bruno or Baldur or whatever he calls himself, the worst of the lot. Prances around in his Hitler Youth uniform all day long, looking to you to greet him first, even though he's a little snot. Slowly Baldur climbs up the last few steps, gripping the banister – that's how drunk he is. His glassy eyes have spotted Borkhausen against the wall, but he doesn't address him till he's standing directly in front of him. 'What are you doing hanging around in the front building? I'm not having you here, get down to your basement hole with your whore! Get lost!'

And he lifts his hobnailed boot, but quickly puts it down again: he's too unsteady on his pins to kick anything.

Borkhausen simply can't cope with a tone like that. If he gets barked at, he curls into a frightened ball. He whispers back, 'Terribly sorry, Herr Persicke! I was just looking to have a bit of fun with Frau Rosenthal!'

Baldur furrows his brow, thinking. After a while he says, 'Stealing is what you came to do, you sonofabitch. Well, on your way.'

The words are crude, but the tone has something a little more gracious or encouraging about it. Borkhausen has a sensitive ear. So, with a grin that craves indulgence for the joke, he says, 'I don't do theft, Herr Persicke – at the most I might do some spontaneous reorganizing from time to time!'

Baldur Persicke doesn't smile back. He won't sink to the level of people like that, even though they have their uses. He cautiously follows Borkhausen downstairs.

Both of them are so preoccupied with their thoughts that they fail to notice that the Quangels' door is slightly ajar. And that it opens again once the men have passed. Anna Quangel darts over to the balustrade and listens down the stairwell.

Outside the Persickes' door, Borkhausen extends his arm in the 'German greeting': 'Heil Hitler, Herr Persicke! And thank you very much!'

He's not sure what he has to be thankful to him for. Maybe for not planting his boot on his backside and kicking him downstairs. He couldn't have done anything about it, little pipsqueak that he is.

Baldur Persicke doesn't return the salute. He fixes the other man with his glassy stare, until he starts blinking and lowers his gaze. Baldur says, 'So you wanted to have a bit of fun with Frau Rosenthal?'

'Yes,' answers Borkhausen quietly, not looking at him.

'What sort of fun did you have in mind?' comes the question. 'A bit of smash and grab?'

Borkhausen risks a quick look up into the face of the other. 'Ach!' he says, 'I would have given her a good beating-up!'

'I see,' Baldur says. 'Is that so?'

For a moment they stand there in silence. Borkhausen wonders if it's okay for him to go, but he hasn't yet been told he can. He continues to wait in silence with his eyes averted.

'Get in there!' says Baldur Persicke, suddenly, in a thick voice. He points through the open door of the Persicke apartment. 'Maybe we're not finished yet! We'll see.'

Borkhausen follows the pointed index finger and marches into the Persicke apartment. Baldur Persicke follows, a little unsteadily, but still upright. The door slams behind them.

Upstairs, Frau Quangel lets go of the banister and sneaks back inside her flat, softly letting the lock click shut. She's not sure what prompted her to listen to the conversation between the two men, first upstairs outside Frau Rosenthal's, then downstairs outside the Persickes'. Usually she does exactly what her husband says, and doesn't meddle with the other tenants. Anna's face is still a sickly white, and there's a twitch in her eyelid. Once or twice she has felt like sitting down and crying, but it's more than she can do. Phrases go through her head: 'I thought my heart would burst,' and 'It came as such a shock,' and 'I felt as though I was going to be sick.' All of them had some truth about them, but also there was this: 'The people who are responsible for my son's death aren't going to get away with it. I'm not going to let them . . .'

She's not sure how she's going to go about it, but her listening on the stairs might be a beginning. Otto's not going to decide everything by himself, she thinks. I want to do what I want some of the time, even if it doesn't suit him.

She quickly prepares dinner for him. He eats the lion's share of the food they buy with their ration cards. He's getting on a bit, and they always make him work past his strength, while she sits at home with her sewing, so an unequal distribution is perfectly fair.

She's still wielding pots and pans when Borkhausen leaves the Persickes' place. As soon as he's on the steps, he drops the cringing posture he adopted in front of them. He walks upright across the yard, his stomach has been pleasantly warmed by a couple of glasses of schnapps, and in his pocket are two tenners, one of which should be enough to sweeten Otti's temper.

As he enters the parlour of the so-called lower ground floor apartment, Otti isn't in a foul temper at all. There's a white cloth on the table, and Otti is on the sofa with a gentleman unknown to Borkhausen. The stranger, who is by no means badly dressed, hurriedly pulls away his arm, which had been thrown round Otti's shoulder, but there's really no need for that. Borkhausen's not particular in that regard.

He thinks to himself, Well, will you look at that! So the old bird can still pull in a john like that! He's bound to be a bank employee at least, or a teacher, from the look of him . . .

In the kitchen, the children are yelling and crying. Borkhausen cuts them each a slice from the loaf that's on the table. Then he has himself a little breakfast – there's sausage and schnapps as well as bread. He throws the man on the sofa an appreciative look. The man doesn't seem to feel as much at home as Borkhausen, which is a pity.

And so Borkhausen decides to go out again, once he's had a bit of something to eat. He doesn't want to chase the john away, heaven forfend. The good thing is that he can keep his twenty marks all to himself now. Borkhausen directs his strides toward Roller Strasse; he's heard there's a bar there where people speak in a particularly unguarded way. Perhaps he'll hear something. There's always fish to be caught in Berlin. And if not by day, then at night.

When Borkhausen thinks of the night, there seems to be a silent laugh playing around his drooping moustache. That Baldur, those Persickes, what a bunch! But they're not going to make a mug of him, no sir! Let them think they've bought him off with twenty marks and two glasses of schnapps. He can see a time coming when he'll be on top of all those Persickes. He just has to be clever now.

That reminds Borkhausen that he needs to find someone called Enno before nightfall – Enno might be just the man for the situation. But no worries, he'll find Enno all right. Enno makes his daily rounds of the three or four pubs where the little punters go. Borkhausen doesn't know Enno's full name. He only knows him by sight, from a couple of pubs where everyone calls him Enno. But he'll find him all right, and it could be he's exactly the man Borkhausen is looking for.

4

Trudel Baumann Betrays a Secret

While it might have been easy for Otto Quangel to get into the factory, getting Trudel Baumann called out for a moment to see him was an entirely different matter. They didn't just work shifts as they did in Quangel's factory, no, each individual had to produce so and so much piecework, and every minute counted.

But finally Quangel is successful, not least because the man in charge is a foreman like himself. It's not easy to refuse a favour to a colleague, much less one who has just lost his son. Quangel was forced to say that, just for a chance to speak to Trudel. As a consequence, he will have to break the news to her himself, whatever his wife said, otherwise she might hear it from her boss. Hopefully, there won't be any screaming or fainting. Actually, Anna took it remarkably well – and surely Trudel's a sensible girl, too.

Here she is at last, and Quangel, who's never had eyes for anyone but his wife, has to admit that she looks ravishing, with her dark mop of curls, her round bonny face that no factory work was able to deprive of its healthy colour, her laughing eyes, and her high breasts. Even now, in her blue overalls and an ancient darned and patched sweater, she looks gorgeous. But maybe the most captivating thing about her is the way she moves, so full of life, every step expressive of her, overflowing with joie de vivre.

Strange thing, it crosses Otto Quangel's mind, that a lard-ass like our Otto, a little mama's boy, could land such a girl as that. But then, he corrects himself, what do I really know about Otto? I never saw him straight. He must have been completely different to how I thought. And he really understood a thing or two about radios; employers lined up for him.

'Hello, Trudel,' he says, and holds out his hand, into which she quickly slips her own warm, plump hand.

'Hello, Father,' she replies. 'What's going on at home? Does Mother miss me, or has Otto written? You know I like to pop by and see you whenever I can.'

'It'll have to be tonight, Trudel,' Otto Quangel says. 'You see, the thing is . . .'

But he doesn't finish the sentence. With typical briskness, Trudel has dived into her blue overalls and pulled out a pocket calendar, and now starts leafing through it. She's only half listening, it's not the moment to tell her anything. So Quangel waits while she finds whatever it is she's looking for.

The meeting of the two of them takes place in a long, drafty corridor whose whitewashed walls are covered with posters. Quangel's eye is caught by the one over Trudel's shoulder. He reads the jagged inscription: *In the Name of the German People,* followed by three names and *were sentenced to death by hanging for their crimes of treason. The sentence was carried out this morning at Plötzensee Prison.*

Involuntarily he takes hold of Trudel with both hands and leads her away from the picture so that he doesn't have to see her and it together. 'What is it?' she asks in perplexity, and then her eyes follow his, and she reads the poster in turn. She emits a noise that might signify anything: protest against what meets her eyes, rejection of Quangel's action, indifference, but then she moves back to her old position. She says, putting the calendar back in her pocket, 'Tonight's not possible, Father, but I can be at your place tomorrow at eight.'

'But it has to be tonight, Trudel!' counters Otto Quangel. 'There's some news of Otto.' His look is sharper now, and he sees the smile vanish from her face. 'You see, Trudel, Otto's fallen.'

It's strange: the same noise that Otto Quangel made when he heard the news, that deep 'Ooh!,' now comes from Trudel's chest. For an instant she looks at him with swimming eyes and trembling lips, then she turns her face to the wall and props her head against it. She cries, but cries silently. Quangel can see her shoulders shaking, but he can hear no sound.

Brave girl! he thinks. How devoted she was to Otto! In his way Otto was brave, too, never went along with those bastards, didn't allow the Hitler Youth to inflame him against his parents, was always opposed to playing soldiers and to the war. The bloody war!

He stops, struck by what he has just caught himself thinking. Is he changing too? It's almost like Anna's 'you and your Führer!'

Then he sees that Trudel has rested her forehead against the very poster from which he just pulled her away. Over her head he can read the jagged type: *In the name of the German people*; her brow obscures the names of the three hanged men.

And a vision appears before him of how one day a poster with his own name and Anna's and Trudel's might be put up on the wall. He shakes his head unhappily. He's a simple worker, he just wants peace and quiet, nothing to do with politics, and Anna just attends to the household, and a lovely girl like Trudel will surely have found herself a new boyfriend before long . . .

But the vision won't go away. Our names on the walls, he thinks, completely confused now. And why not? Hanging on the gallows is no worse than being ripped apart by a shell, or dying from a bullet in the guts. All that doesn't matter. The only thing that matters is this: I must find out what it is with Hitler. Suddenly all I see is oppression and hate and suffering, so much suffering . . . A few hundred thousand, that's what that cowardly snitch Borkhausen said. As if the number mattered! If so much as one person is suffering unjustly, and I can put an end to it, and the only reason I don't is because I'm a coward and prefer peace and quiet, then . . .

At this point, he doesn't dare to think any further. He's afraid, really afraid, of where a thought like that, taken to its conclusion, might lead. He would have to change his whole life!

Instead, he stares again at the girl with *In the name of the German people* over her head. If only she wasn't crying against this particular poster. He can't resist the urge to pull her shoulder away from the wall, and says, as softly as he can, 'Come away from that poster, Trudel . . .'

For an instant she looks uncomprehendingly at the printed words. Her eyes are dry once more, her shoulders no longer heaving. Now there is life in her expression again – not the lustre that she had when she first set foot in this corridor, but a darker sort of glow. With her hand she gently and firmly covers the word 'hanging'. 'Father,' she says, 'I will never forget that when I stood crying over Otto, it was in front of a poster like this. Perhaps – I don't want it to be – but perhaps it'll be my name on a poster like that one day.'

She looks at him hard. He has a feeling she's not really sure what she's saying. 'Girl!' he cries out. 'Stop and think! Why would your name end up on a poster like that? You're young, you've got your whole life ahead of you. You will laugh again, you will have children.'

She shakes her head stubbornly. 'I'm not going to bring children into this world to be cannon fodder. Not while some general can say "March till you drop!" Father,' she goes on, clasping his hand firmly in hers, 'Father, do you think you can carry on living as before, now that they've shot your Otto?'

She looks at him piercingly, and once again he tries to fight off the alien influence. 'It was the French,' he mumbles.

'The French!' she shouts indignantly. 'What sort of excuse is that? Who invaded France? Come on, Father!'

'But what can we do?' Otto Quangel says, unnerved by this onslaught. 'There are so few of us, and all those millions for him, and now, after the victory against France, there will be even more. We can do nothing!'

'We can do plenty!' she whispers. 'We can vandalize the machines, we can work badly, work slowly, we can tear down their posters and put up others where we tell people the truth about how they are being cheated and lied to.' She drops her voice further: 'But the main thing is that we remain different from them, that we never allow ourselves to be made into them, or start thinking as they do. Even if they conquer the whole world, we must refuse to become Nazis.'

'And what will that accomplish, Trudel?' asks Otto Quangel softly. 'I don't see the point.'

'Father,' she replies, 'when it began, I didn't understand that either, and I'm not sure I fully understand it now. But, you know, we've formed a secret resistance cell in the factory, very small for now, three men and me. A man came to us, and tried to explain it to me. He said we are like good seeds in a field of weeds. If it wasn't for the good seeds, the whole field would be nothing but weeds. And the good seeds can spread their influence . . .'

She breaks off, deeply shocked about something.

'What is it, Trudel?' he asks. 'That thing with the good seeds makes sense. I will think about it. I have such a lot to be thinking about now.'

But she says, full of shame and guilt, 'I've gone and blabbed about the cell, and I swore I wouldn't tell a soul about it!'

'Don't worry, Trudel,' says Otto Quangel, and his calm is such as to immediately help to settle her agitation. 'You know, with Otto Quangel a thing goes in one ear and out the other. I can't remember what you told me a moment ago.' With grim resolve he gazes at the poster. 'I don't care if the whole Gestapo turns up, I don't know anything. And,' he adds, 'if you want, and if it makes you feel more secure, then from this moment forth, we simply won't know each other any more. You don't need to come tonight to see Anna, I'll cook up some story for her.'

'No,' she replies, her confidence restored. 'No. I'll go and see Mother tonight. But I'll have to tell the others that I blabbed, and maybe someone will come and see you, to see if you can be trusted.'

'Let them come,' says Otto Quangel menacingly. 'I don't know anything. Bye, Trudel. I probably won't see you tonight. You know I'm rarely back before midnight.'

She shakes hands with him and heads off down the passage, back to her work. She is no longer so full of exuberant life, but she still radiates strength. Good girl! thinks Quangel. Brave woman!

Then Quangel is all alone in the corridor lined with posters gently flapping in the draft. He gets ready to go. But first, he does something that surprises himself: he nods meaningly at the poster in front of which Trudel was weeping – with a grim determination.

The next moment, he is ashamed of himself. How theatrical! And now, he has to hurry home. He is so pressed for time, he takes a streetcar, which, given his parsimony that borders sometimes on meanness, is something he hates to do.

5

Enno Kluge's Homecoming

Eva Kluge finished her delivery round at two o'clock. She then worked till four totting up newspaper rates and surcharges: if she was very tired, she got her numbers muddled up and she would have to start again. Finally, with sore feet and a painful vacancy in her brain, she set off home; she didn't want to think about everything she had to do before getting to bed. On the way home, she shopped, using her ration cards. There was a long line at the butcher's, and so it was almost six when she slowly climbed the steps to her apartment on Friedrichshain.

On her doorstep stood a little man in a light-coloured raincoat and cap. He had a colourless and expressionless face, slightly inflamed eyelids, pale eyes – the sort of face you immediately forget.

'Is that you, Enno?' she exclaimed, and right away gripped her keys more tightly in her hand. 'What are you doing here? I've got no money and nothing to eat, and I'm not letting you into the flat either.'

The little man made a dismissive gesture. 'Don't get upset, Eva. Don't be cross with me. I just wanted to say hello. Hello, Eva. There you are!'

'Hello, Enno,' she said, reluctantly, having known her husband for many years. She waited a while, and then laughed briefly and sardonically. 'All right, we've said hello as you wanted, so why don't you go? But it seems you're not going, so what have you really come for?'

'See here, Evie,' he said. 'You're a sensible woman, you're someone a man can talk to . . .' He embarked on a long and involved account of how he could no longer extend his sick leave, because he had been off for twenty-six weeks. He had to go back to work, otherwise they would pack him off back to the army, which had allowed him to go to the factory in the first place because he was a precision toolmaker and those were in short supply. 'You see, the thing is,' he concluded his account, 'that I have to have a fixed address for the next few days. And so I thought . . .'

She shook her head emphatically. She was so tired she could drop, and she was longing to be back in her flat, where much more work was waiting for her. But she wasn't going to let him in, not if she had to stand outside half the night.

Quickly he added, in a tone that immediately struck her as insincere, 'Don't say no, Evie, I haven't finished yet. I swear I want nothing from you, no money, no food, nothing. Just let me bed down on the sofa. No need for any sheets. I don't want to be the least trouble to you.'

Again, she shook her head. If only he would stop talking; he really ought to know she didn't believe a word of it. He had never kept a promise in his life.

She asked, 'Why don't you get one of your girlfriends to put you up? They usually come through for something like this!'

He shook his head. 'No, Evie, I'm through with women, I can't deal with them any more, I want no more of them. If I think about it, you were always the best of them anyway, you know that. We had some good years back then, you know, when the kids were still small.'

In spite of herself, her face lit up at the recollection of their early married years. They really had been good years, when he was working as a machinist, taking home sixty marks a week, before he turned work shy.

Immediately Enno Kluge saw the chink. 'You see, Evie, you see, you still have a bit of a soft spot for me, and that's why you'll let me sleep on the sofa. I promise I'll be quick dealing with the management, I'm not bothered about the wages, I just want to go on sick leave again and stay out of the army. In ten days I'll have my medical discharge, I promise!'

He paused and looked at her expectantly. This time she didn't shake her head, but her expression was opaque. He went on, 'I don't want to do it with stomach ulcers this time, because then they don't give you anything to eat when you're in hospital. What I'm trying for this time is inflamed gall bladder. They can't prove you're lying, all they can do is X-ray you, but you don't have to have gallstones to have the inflammation. You might, but you don't have to. That'll work. I'll just have to clock in for ten days first.'

Once again she didn't say a word, and he went on, because it was his belief that you could talk your way into or out of anything and that if you were persistent enough, in the end people would just give in. 'I've got the address of a doctor on Frankfurter Allee, he writes medical excuses just like that, he just doesn't want any trouble afterward. He'll do it for me, I'm sure; in ten days I'll be back in the hospital and you'll be rid of me, Evie!'

Tired of all the chat, she spoke at last: 'Look, Enno, I don't care if you stay here till midnight talking, I'm not taking you back. I'm never doing that again; I don't care what you say or what you do. I'm not going to let you wreck everything again with your laziness and your horses and your hussies. You've done it three times, and then a fourth, and then more, but I've reached my limit, and that's it. I'm going to sit down on the steps, because I'm tired, I've been on my feet since six. If you want to, you can sit down, I don't care. You can talk or not, that's up to you: as I said, I don't care. But you're not setting foot in my apartment ever again!'

She sat down on the same step where he had stood and waited for her. And her words sounded so determined that he felt no amount of talking would change her mind. So he pulled his cap slightly askew and said: 'Well, Evie, if that's the way you feel about it, and you won't even do me a little favour when you know I'm in trouble, the man you had five children with, three of them in the ground, and the other two away fighting for Führer and Fatherland . . .' He broke off. He had been talking mechanically to himself, going on and on as he was used to doing in pubs, even though he had grasped that there was no point in it now. 'All right then, Evie, I'm going. And let me tell you, I've no complaints against you, I'm no better than I ought to be, Evie, you know that, but at least I don't bear grudges.'

'Because you don't care about a thing in the world except your races,' she retorted, in spite of herself. 'Because nothing else interests you, and because you don't feel an ounce of affection for anything else, not even for yourself, Enno Kluge.' But she stopped right away; she knew it was useless talking to this man. She waited a while, and then she said, 'Weren't you going to leave now?'

'I am going, Evie,' he said surprisingly. 'Be a good girl. I don't hold anything against you. Heil Hitler, Evie!'

She was still firmly convinced this leave-taking was a trick on his part, a prelude to a new and stupefying bout of talk. To her limitless surprise, he said nothing further, but really did start walking down the stairs.

For one or two minutes more she continued to sit on the stairs, as though numb. She couldn't believe she had won. She heard his footfall on the bottom step, he hadn't stopped anywhere to hide, he really was going! Then the front door banged shut. With trembling hand she unlocked her apartment door; she was so nervous, she couldn't get the key into the keyhole. Once inside, she put on the chain and slumped into a kitchen chair. Her arms dropped; the struggle had taken the last of her strength. She had no more energy. If someone had prodded her with a finger, she would have fallen out of the chair.

Gradually, as she sat there, strength and life returned to her. She had done it at last, her willpower had defeated his obstinacy. She had successfully guarded her home, kept it for herself. He wouldn't be sitting around here any more, banging on about horses and stealing every mark and every piece of bread that crossed his path.

She leaped up now, full of renewed courage. This little bit of life was what remained to her. After the endless work for the post office, she needed these few hours here to herself. The delivery round was hard for her, harder with each passing day. Earlier in her life she had suffered from female troubles, and that was why her three youngest were all in the graveyard: they had all been born prematurely. Now her legs were giving her trouble. She wasn't cut out to be a working woman was what it came down to – she should have been a housewife. But when her husband suddenly stopped working, she had been forced to go out and earn money. Back then, the two boys were only little. It was she who had brought them up, she who had kept this little home going: two rooms, kitchen and bedroom. And, on the side, as it were, she had pulled a man along as well, whenever he wasn't staying over with one of his fancy women.

Of course, she could have divorced him long ago; he wasn't exactly discreet about his adulteries. But divorce wouldn't have changed anything. Divorced or not, Enno would have gone on clinging to her. He didn't care – there really wasn't a speck of pride in him anywhere.

She hadn't thrown him out of the house until the boys had gone off to war. Till that time, she'd always believed she had to maintain some semblance of family life, even though the boys had a pretty shrewd idea what was going on. She was reluctant to let others in on her struggles. If someone asked after her husband, she would say he was off on some installation job. Even now, she paid the odd visit to Enno's parents, took them something to eat or a few marks, to pay them back, so to speak, for the money that Enno filched from their pathetic pension.

But inwardly, she was long done with the man. Even if he had changed and started working again, and become what he was in the first years of their marriage, even then she wouldn't have taken him back. She didn't hate him – he was such a nonentity you couldn't hate him – he was simply repulsive to her, like a spider or snake. He should have just left her in peace – all she wanted for her contentment was not to see him again!

While Eva Kluge was thinking of these things, she put her dinner on the hob and tidied up the kitchen – she did the bedroom in the morning before going to work. As she listened to the soup bubbling, and the good smell of it spread through the kitchen, she got out her darning basket – stockings were always such a bother; she ripped more of them in a day than she could mend. But for all that she didn't resent the work, she loved those quiet half hours before supper, when she could sit snugly in the wicker chair in her felt slippers, her aching feet stretched out and crossed – that was how they seemed to rest most comfortably.

After dinner, she wanted to write to her favourite, older boy, Karlemann, who was in Poland. She had rather fallen out with him of late, especially since he had joined the SS. A lot of bad rumours were flying around about the SS. They were supposed to be terribly mean to the Jews, even raping and shooting Jewish girls. But she didn't think he was like that, not the boy she had carried in her womb. Karlemann wouldn't do that sort of thing! Where would he have got it from? She had never been rough or brutal in her life, and Enno was just a dishrag. But she would try to put some hint in her letter to him to remain decent. Of course it would have to be very subtly expressed, so that only Karlemann understood it. Otherwise, the letter would wind up with the censor, and he'd get in trouble. Well, she would come up with something – maybe she would remind him of something from his childhood, like the time he stole two marks from her and spent them on sweets, or, better yet, when he was thirteen and went out with that little floozie, Walli. The trouble there had been then, to get him out of her clutches – he was capable of such rages, her Karlemann!

But she smiled as she thought of it. Everything to do with the boys' childhood seemed lovely to her. Back then, she still had the strength, she would have defended her boys against the whole world, she worked day and night so that they didn't have to go without what other children got from their fathers. But over the past few years, she had got steadily weaker, particularly since the two of them had gone off to the war.

Well, the war should never have come about; if the Führer really was all he was cracked up to be, then it should have been avoided. Danzig and that little corridor outside it made a reason to put millions of people in daily fear of their lives – that really wasn't so very statesmanlike!

But then they claimed he was illegitimate or all but. That he'd never had a mother to look after him properly. And so he didn't understand how mothers felt in the course of this never-ending fear. After each letter from the front you felt better for a day or two, then you counted back how many days had passed since it was sent, and then your fear began again.

She has let the stocking fall from her grip, and has been sitting in a dream. Now she stands up quite mechanically, moves the soup from the stronger hotplate to the weaker one, and puts the potatoes on the better one. While she is doing that, the bell rings. She stands there, frozen. Enno! she thinks, Enno!

She puts the saucepan down and creeps silently in her felt slippers to the door. Her heart calms down: at the door, a little to the side so that she can be seen more easily, stands her neighbour, Frau Gesch. Surely she's come to borrow something again, a little fat or flour, that she always forgets to return later. But Eva Kluge nevertheless remains suspicious. She tries to scan the landing as far as the peephole will allow, and she listens for every sound. But everything is as it should be: there is only Frau Gesch occasionally scraping her feet in impatience or looking into the peephole.

Frau Kluge makes up her mind. She opens the door, though only as wide as the chain will permit, and she asks, 'What can I do for you, Frau Gesch?'

Straightaway, Frau Gesch, a wizened old woman worked half to death, whose daughters are living very nicely thank you off their mother, launches into a flood of complaints about the unending washing, always having to be doing things for other people, and never getting enough to eat, and Emmi and Lilli doing nothing at all. After supper they just walk out of the house and leave their mother with the washing-up. 'Yes, and Frau Kluge, what I came for, I think I've got a boil on my back. We only have the one mirror, and my eyes are bad. I wonder if you'd have a look at it for me – you can't go to the doctor for something like that, and when do I have time to go to a doctor? You might pop it for me too, if you wouldn't mind, though I know some people just are squeamish about that sort of thing . . .'

While Frau Gesch goes on and on with her lamentations, Eva Kluge quite mechanically undoes the chain, and the woman comes into her kitchen. Eva Kluge is about to shut the door, but a foot has slid in the way, and Enno Kluge is in her flat. His face is as expressionless as ever; a degree of excitement is betrayed by the trembling of his almost lashless eyelids.

Eva Kluge stands there with her arms hanging down, her knees shaking so hard she can barely stay on her feet. Frau Gesch's speech has suddenly dried up, and she looks silently into their two faces. It's perfectly still in the kitchen, only the saucepan goes on bubbling away gently.

Finally Frau Gesch says, 'Well, Herr Kluge, I've done as you asked. But I tell you: this once and never again. And if you don't keep your promise, and you start the laziness and the pub-crawling and the gambling again . . .' She breaks off after looking at Frau Kluge's face, and says, 'If I've done something stupid, then I'll help you throw him out right away, Frau Kluge. The two of us together can do it easy!'

Eva Kluge gestures dismissively. 'Ah, never mind, Frau Gesch, it's all right!'

Slowly and cautiously she goes over to the cane chair and slumps into it. She keeps picking up the darning and looking at it vaguely, as if she didn't know what it was.

Frau Gesch says, a little offended, 'Well then, good evening or Heil Hitler, whichever you prefer!'

Hurriedly Enno Kluge says, 'Heil Hitler!'

And slowly, as though waking from a dream, Eva Kluge responds, 'Goodnight, Frau Gesch.' She pauses. 'And if you've got something with your back . . .'

'No, no,' Frau Gesch says hastily, from the doorway. 'There's nothing the matter with my back, it was just something I said. But this is the last time I'm getting mixed up in other people's affairs. I get no thanks from anyone.'

With that she has talked her way out of the apartment; she's pleased to be away from the two silent figures – her conscience is pricking her somewhat.

No sooner is the door shut behind her than the little man springs into action. With an air of routine and entitlement, he opens the closet, frees up a coat hanger by bunching two of his wife's dresses together on one, and hangs up his coat. He drops his cap on top of the dresser. He is always very particular about his things, he can't stand being badly dressed, and he knows he can't afford to buy himself anything new.

Now he rubs his hands together with a genial 'Ah!' and goes over to the gas and sniffs at the saucepans. 'Mhm!' he says. 'Boiled beef with potatoes – lovely!'

He stops for a moment. The woman is sitting there motionless, with her back to him. He quietly puts the lid back on the pot and goes to stand over her, so that he is talking to the back of her head: 'Oh, don't just sit there like a statue, Evie. What's the matter? So you've got a man in your flat for a few days again, I'm not going to make any trouble. And I'll keep my promise to you as well. I won't have any of your potatoes – or just the leftovers, if there are any. And those only if you freely offer them to me. I'm not going to ask you for anything.'

The woman says nothing. She puts the basket with the darning back into the dresser, sets a bowl out on the table, fills it from the two pans, and slowly starts to eat. The man has sat down at the other end of the table, pulls a few sports gazettes out of his pocket, and makes notes in a thick, greasy notebook. From time to time he casts a swift glance at the woman eating. She is eating very slowly, but he is sure she has refilled her bowl a couple of times, so there won't be very much left for him, and he is ravenous. He hasn't eaten anything all day, no, not since the night before. Lotte's husband, returning on furlough from the field, drove him out of their bed with blows and without the least regard for his breakfast.

But he doesn't dare to talk about his hunger to Eva: her silence frightens him. Before he can feel properly at home again here, several things need to happen. He doesn't have the least doubt that they will, any woman can be talked round, you just need to be persistent and take a lot of nonsense from her first. Eventually, usually quite suddenly, she will cave in, because she's had enough of resisting.

Eva Kluge scrapes both saucepans clean. She's done it, she's eaten the food for two days in one single evening, so now he can't beg her for any leftovers! Then she quickly does the little bit of washing up, and embarks on a wholesale removal. Before

his very eyes, she moves everything of the least value to her into
the bedroom. The bedroom door has a lock; he's never yet
managed to get into the bedroom. She lugs the provisions, her
good coats and dresses, her shoes, the sofa cushions, yes, even
the photo of their two sons into the bedroom – all before his
watching eyes. She doesn't care what he thinks or says. He tricked
his way into the flat, he's not to profit from it.

Then she locks the bedroom door and puts the writing things
out on the table. She's dog-tired, she would much rather go to
bed, but she's decided she's going to write Karlemann a letter,
and so she does. It's not just her husband she can be tough with,
she's tough on herself as well.

She has written a couple of sentences when the man leans
across the table and asks, 'Who's that you're writing to, Evie?'

In spite of herself, she gives him an answer, even though she'd
intended not to speak to him. 'It's to Karlemann . . .'

'I see,' he says, and puts his sports papers away. 'I see. So you
write to him, and for all I know you send him food parcels, but
for his father you don't even have a potato and a scrap of meat
to spare, hungry as he is!'

His voice has lost a little of its indifference; it sounds as though
the man is seriously offended because she has something for the
son that she refuses to the father.

'Forget it, Enno,' she says calmly. 'It's my business. Karlemann's not a bad lad . . .'

'I see!' he says. 'I see! Then you've obviously forgotten the
way he was to his parents when he became a pack leader. How
everything you did was wrong in his eyes, and he laughed at us
as a stupid old bourgeois couple – you've forgotten all that, have
you, Evie? A good lad is he, Karlemann!'

'He never laughed at me!' she feebly protests.

'No, no, of course not!' he jeers. 'And you've forgotten the
time he didn't recognize his own mother as she was lugging her
heavy mailbag down Prenzlauer Allee. Him and his girlfriend
just looked the other way, what a charming piece of work!'

'You can't hold something like that against a boy,' she says.
'They all want to look good in front of their girls, that's the way

they are. In time, he'll change, and he'll be back for his mother who nursed him from a baby.'

For an instant he looks at her hesitantly, as if he had something he wasn't sure whether to tell her or not. He's not a vindictive man usually, but this time she's offended him too badly, first by not giving him anything to eat, and secondly by carting all the valuables into the other room. Finally he says, 'Well, if it was me that was his mother, I wouldn't ever want to take my son in my arms again, not after he's turned into such a thorough-going bastard!' He sees her eyes grow wide with fear, and he says pitilessly right into her waxen face, 'On his last furlough he showed me a photograph that a comrade took of him. He was proud of it. There's your Karlemann, and he's holding a little Jewish boy of about three, holding him by the leg, and he's about to smash his head against the bumper of a car.'

'No!' she screams, 'No! You're lying, you're making it up! It's your revenge because you didn't get anything to eat. Karlemann wouldn't do anything like that!'

'How could I have made it up?' he asks, calm again after dropping his bombshell. 'I don't have the imagination to make up something like that. And if you don't believe me, you can go to Senftenberg's pub, which is where he showed the photo round to anyone who cared to see it. Senftenberg and his old woman, they saw the picture themselves . . .'

He stops talking. He's wasting his breath talking to this woman. She sits there with her head slumped on the table, crying. That's what she gets, and her a postwoman and therefore a member of the Party, who's taken an oath to support the Führer and his deeds. She can't be too surprised at the way Karlemann's turned out.

For a moment, Enno Kluge stands eyeing the sofa doubtfully – no cushions, no blanket. This isn't going to be a comfortable night! But perhaps it's the moment to take a chance? He hesitates, looks at the locked bedroom door, and then he acts. He reaches into the woman's apron pocket as she sits there crying hysterically, and pulls out the key. He unlocks the door and starts rummaging about in the room, not even quietly . . .

And Eva Kluge, the exhausted, downtrodden postwoman, hears it all too; she knows he's robbing her, but she doesn't care. What's the point of her life, why has she had children, taken pleasure in their smiling and playing, when in the end they just become monsters? Oh, Karlemann, what a sweet blond boy he was! She remembers how she took him to the Busch Circus, and the horses were made to lie down in the sand, and he felt so sorry for the poor hossies – were they ill? She had to comfort him, promise him the hossies were only sleeping.

And now he is going around doing things like that to the children of other mothers! Eva Kluge doesn't doubt for a second that the story about the photograph is true: Enno really isn't capable of inventing such things. No, it seems she has now lost her son as well. It's much worse than if he had merely died, because then at least she could mourn him. Now she can't take him in her arms again, and she must keep her doors closed against him too.

The man rummaging around in the bedroom has found the thing he has long suspected was in his wife's possession: a post office savings book. Six hundred and thirty-two marks in it, thrifty woman, but why so thrifty? One day she'll get her pension, and with her other savings . . . He'll start tomorrow by putting twenty on Adebar, and maybe another ten on Hamilcar . . . He flicks through the book: not just a thrifty woman, an admirably tidy one. Everything in its place – at the back of the book is the card, and there are the credit slips . . .

He is about to put the savings book in his pocket when the woman shows up. She takes it out of his hand and drops it on the bed. 'Out!' she says. 'Get out!'

And he, who a moment ago thought he had victory in his sights, now leaves the room under her furious glare. Silently and with hands shaking, he gets his cap and coat out of the wardrobe, and without a word he slips past her into the unlit stairwell. The door is drawn shut, and he switches on the stair lights and climbs down the stairs. Thank God someone has left the street door unlocked. He will go to his local; if push comes to shove, the landlord will let him bed down on the settee. He trudges off, reconciled to his fate, used to receiving blows. Already he's half forgotten the woman upstairs.

She, meanwhile, is standing by the window staring out into the night. Fine. Awful. Karlemann gone, too. She'll make one last attempt with her younger son, with Max. Max was always the colourless one, more like his father than his dazzling brother. Perhaps she can win Max over. And if not, then never mind, she'll live by and for herself. But she will keep her self-respect. Then that will have been her attainment in life, keeping her self-respect. Tomorrow morning she will try to find out how to go about leaving the Party without getting stuck in a concentration camp. It will be difficult, but maybe she'll manage it. And if there's no other way of doing it, then she'll go to the concentration camp. That would be a bit of atonement for what Karlemann has done.

She crumples up the tear-stained beginning of the letter to her older boy. She spreads out a fresh sheet of paper, and writes:

Max, my dear son, it's time I wrote you a little letter again. I'm still doing all right, as I hope you are, too. Father was here a moment ago, but I showed him the door – all he wanted was to rob me. I am also breaking off relations with your brother Karl, because of atrocities he has committed. Now you are my only son. I beg you, please keep your self-respect. I will do all I can for you. Please drop me a line or two yourself, if you have a chance. Kisses, from your loving Mother.

6

Otto Quangel Gives up His Official Function

The part of the furniture factory where Otto Quangel was foreman once employed eighty male and female workers and turned out single pieces to order; all the other sections of the factory made only mass-produced articles. At the beginning of the war, the business was put on a war footing, and Quangel's workshop was assigned to make large, heavy crates that it was thought were used to transport bombs.

As far as Otto Quangel was concerned, he didn't have the least interest in the destination and function of the crates; to him, this new, mindless labour was simply ridiculous. He was a craftsman, whom the grain of a piece of wood or the finish on a nicely carved wardrobe could fill with a deep satisfaction. He had found in such work as much happiness as a person of his cool temperament was capable of finding. Now, he had sunk to being an overseer and a taskmaster who only had to make sure that his workshop fulfilled, and if possible overfulfilled, its quota. In accordance with his nature, he had never spoken to anyone about such feelings as he might have, and his sharp, birdlike face had never betrayed anything of the contempt he felt for this wretched matchwood carpentry. If someone had observed him, he might have noticed that the laconic Quangel had stopped speaking altogether and that in his role as overseer he tended simply to wave things through.

But then who was there to attend to such a dry and flinty character as Otto Quangel? All his life he had seemed to be no more than a drudge, with no other interest except the work in front of him. He had never had a friend at the plant, never spoken a kindly word to anyone there. Work, nothing but work, never mind if it was men or machines, so long as they worked!

For all that, he wasn't disliked, even though his job was to supervise the workshop, and to exhort the men to greater effort. He never swore, and he never went running to the management. If production wasn't proceeding properly somewhere, he would go to the trouble spot and with a few deft movements silently fix the problem. Or he would go and stand beside a couple of chatterboxes and stay there, his dark eyes fixed on the speakers, until they no longer felt like talking. He seemed to spread an aura of chill. During their short breaks, the workers tried to sit as far away from him as they could, and in that way he enjoyed a sort of automatic respect, which another man could not have won for himself with any amount of shouting and ordering about.

The factory management was perfectly well aware of what an asset they had in Otto Quangel. His workshop achieved the best scores, there were never any personnel issues, and Quangel always did whatever he was told. He would have been promoted long since if he had only consented to join the Party. But he never did. 'I've no money to spare for that,' he said. 'I need every single mark. I have my family to feed.'

They might very well smirk at what they termed his money-grubbing attitude. Quangel really seemed to feel every ten pfennig piece he was forced to contribute at collection time. It cut no ice with him that joining the Party would earn him much more in terms of an increased wage than it would cost in contributions. But this hardworking foreman was politically a hopeless case, and so people didn't mind leaving him where he was, holding a moderately responsible job, even though he wasn't in the Party.

In reality, it wasn't Otto Quangel's miserliness that kept him out of the Party. It was true, he was dreadfully pernickety about money matters and would be annoyed for weeks by the tiniest needless expense. But just as he kept scrupulous account of his own affairs, so he did also with the affairs of others, too, and this Party seemed to him to be anything but precise in the way it enacted its so-called principles. The things he had learned from his son's years at school and in the Hitler Youth, the things he heard from Anna and those he directly experienced himself – for instance, that all the best-paid jobs in the factory were held by Party members, who exercise authority over the most able non-Party members – all reinforced in him the conviction that the Party was not scrupulous, was not just, and that therefore he wanted none of it.

That was another reason why he was so hurt by Anna's accusation this morning, about 'You and your Führer'. It was true, thus far he had been a believer in the Führer's honest intentions. One just had to strip away the corrupt hangers-on and the parasites, who were just out for themselves, and everything would get better. But until such time, he wasn't taking part in it, not him, and Anna, who was the only person he really talked to, knew that. All right, she had said it in the heat of the moment, he would forget it in time, and he wasn't the sort to bear grudges.

Now, standing in the din of the workshop, head slightly raised as he scanned the room from the planing machine to the band saw to the nailers, drills, and conveyor belts, he can feel the news of Otto's death, and in particular Anna's and Trudel's reactions to it, continuing to affect him. He doesn't really think about it, but he knows instinctively that that layabout of a carpenter, Dollfuss, has already been gone from the workshop for seven minutes, and that the work on his part of the line is grinding to a halt, because he's popped out either for a smoke or a political harangue. Quangel will give him another three minutes, and if he's not back then, he'll go looking for him in person!

And as he glances up at the hand on the wall clock and sees that in another three minutes Dollfuss will have skipped all of ten minutes, he thinks of the hateful poster over Trudel's head, and what treason means, and how he might learn more about it, but he also thinks about the fact that he has in his jacket pocket a curt note given him by the porter, summoning Foreman Quangel to report to the office canteen at five o'clock precisely.

Not that the note unduly bothers him. Earlier, when the factory still made furniture, he was often summoned to the boardroom to discuss the production of some item or other. The office canteen is an unfamiliar venue, but that doesn't bother him so much as the fact that it's only six minutes till five and he'd like to have Dollfuss back at his saw before he has to go. So he sets off to find Dollfuss a minute earlier than he'd intended.

But he finds him neither in the toilets nor in the corridor nor in the adjacent workshop, and by the time he's back in his own workshop, the clock is showing one minute to five and it's high time to go to the meeting, if he's not to be late. Quickly, he brushes the worst of the sawdust off his jacket, and then he heads for the administration building, the ground floor of which houses the office canteen.

It's clearly been made ready for a lecture. A speaking platform has been set up, and a long table for committee members, and the whole room is full of rows of chairs. The layout is familiar to him from the meetings of the Arbeitsfront that he's had to attend, only these are always held in the works canteen. The only other difference is that they sit on rough wooden benches, not cane chairs, and that most of those present wear workman's blue, like him, whereas here the majority are in uniforms, brown or grey, with a few people in civilian suits sprinkled among them.

Quangel takes a chair right by the exit, so he can get back to work as soon as possible after the end of the talk. The room is already pretty full, and some of the audience are already sitting down, others are standing in the aisles or along the walls of the hall, talking together in little groups.

But all of those who are gathered here are wearing the swastika. Quangel seems to be the only one present without the Party badge on his lapel, except for the people in Wehrmacht uniforms, and they have army insignia. He's probably been invited here by mistake. Quangel turns his head alertly from side to side. He knows a few of the faces. The pale fat fellow already sitting at the committee table is Director Schröder, whom he knows by sight. The little one with the pinched nose and the pince nez is the cashier who hands him his wages every Saturday evening, and with whom he's had a couple of arguments about deductions. Funny, thinks Quangel, he never wears his Party badge when he's standing by the till!

But most of the faces are completely unfamiliar to him. They're probably all managerial or white-collar. Suddenly, Quangel stares hard: in one group he has spotted the man he was just looking for in the toilets and corridors, the carpenter Dollfuss! But Carpenter Dollfuss is not wearing his work clothes, he's wearing a dark suit and is talking to a couple of men in Party uniforms as though among equals. And Carpenter Dollfuss, the fellow whose incessant chitchat already has drawn Quangel's attention in the workshop, is also wearing a swastika. So that's it! thinks Quangel. The man's a spy. Perhaps he's not a carpenter at all and his name isn't Dollfuss, either. Wasn't Dollfuss the name of the Austrian chancellor, the man they murdered? It's all rigged – and I didn't even notice!

And he starts to wonder whether Dollfuss was already in the workshop at the time that Ladendorff and Tritsch were suspended and there were rumblings about them having been put in a concentration camp.

Quangel tenses. Careful! he feels his instinct warning him. And: I'm sitting among murderers here. Later on, he thinks: I won't let them get me. I'm just an old foolish foreman, I don't know anything about anything. But I'm not going to join them, for all that. I saw the dread that came over Anna this morning, and Trudel; I'm not going to participate in something like that. I don't want a mother or bride to be put to death on my account. I want no part in this business . . .

So Quangel tells himself. In the meantime, the room has filled to the very last chair. The table is occupied by brown jackets and black uniforms, and on the podium is a major or colonel (Quangel has never learned to distinguish different uniforms and badges of rank), speaking about the state of the war.

Of course it's going splendidly, victory over France is duly proclaimed, and it can only be a matter of weeks before England is crushed. Then the speaker gradually gets to the point he wants to make: with the front making such great strides, it is all the more urgent that the home front do its duty. What now follows sounds as though the major (or captain or colonel or whatever he is) has come directly from HQ on behalf of the Führer to tell the workforce of Krause & Co. that they will have to up their productivity. The Führer expects them to increase it by 50 per cent within three months, and to have doubled it within six. Suggestions from the floor as to how the target could be reached are welcome. Anyone not participating will be viewed as a saboteur and treated accordingly.

While the speaker pronounces one final *Sieg Heil* to the Führer, Otto Quangel is thinking, So England will be defeated within a few weeks, the war is done and dusted, and we're going to double our productivity inside six months. Who comes up with this nonsense?

But he sits down again and looks at the next speaker, a man in a brown uniform whose chest is thickly bespattered with medals, orders, and decorations. This Party speaker is a completely different sort from his army predecessor. From the get-go, he speaks in a sharp and aggressive way of the poor attitude that still prevails in some industries, in spite of the tremendous victories won by the Führer and the Wehrmacht. He speaks so sharply and aggressively that he seems to scream, and he doesn't spare the moaners and the pessimists. The very last of them are to be eradicated. They will be ridden over, they'll get smacked so hard they'll be looking for their teeth. *Suum cuique*, it said on the belt buckles in the First War, and To each his own over the gates of the labour camp. There they'll be re-educated, and anyone who helps get a defeatist man or woman put away will have done something for the German nation, and will be a man after the Führer's heart.

'But all of you sitting here,' roars the speaker in conclusion, 'foremen, department heads, directors – I make you personally responsible for the healthy condition of your works! Healthy condition means National Socialist thinking, and nothing else! Anyone who is weak-willed and mealy-mouthed and doesn't immediately denounce anything and everything wrong will wind up in a concentration camp himself. I swear, whether you're directors or foremen, I'll get you knocked into shape, if I have to kick the feebleness out of you with my own boots!'

The speaker stands on the rostrum a moment longer, his hands clenched with fury, his face is purple. At the end of this outburst the auditorium is silent. Everyone looks sheepish, all those who have effectively been asked to spy on their fellow workers. Then the speaker stomps off, the decorations on his chest tinkling slightly, and Director Schröder gets up and inquires palely whether anyone in the audience has anything to say.

The assembly draws a deep collective breath, shifts about in their chairs – it's as though a nightmare has come to an end and the day can begin. No one seems to have anything to contribute, everyone wants to leave the hall as soon as possible, and the general director is about to close the meeting with a *Heil Hitler!* when a man in a blue work tunic gets up near the back and says that as far as the productivity of his team goes, there is a perfectly simple remedy. They just need such and such machinery, and he lists the items and explains how they have to be set up. Yes, and then six or eight people will have to be laid off the team – unproductive wastrels and layabouts. If he were given those conditions, he would be able to reach the productivity targets in three months, not six.

Quangel stands there, cool and calm: he has taken up the fight. He can feel them all staring at him, the simple worker, out of place among these natty gents. But he has never cared about them especially, and he doesn't care that they are staring at him now. Now that he's said his piece, they put their heads together on the rostrum to talk about him. The speakers are asking who the fellow in the blue shirt is. Then the major or colonel gets up and tells Quangel that the technical directors will discuss the machines with him, but what does he mean about the six or eight people who ought to be thrown out?

Slowly and obstinately Quangel replies, 'Well, there's some who can't work, and some others who don't like to. There's one of them sitting there!' And with his big stiff index finger he points directly at Carpenter Dollfuss, sitting a few rows in front of him.

A few people in the hall burst out laughing, among them Dollfuss, who has turned his head round to look and is now laughing at him.

But Quangel goes on, not batting an eyelid, 'Yes, talking and smoking cigarettes in the lav, and skipping work, that's all you're good for, Dollfuss!'

On the rostrum, they have put their heads together about this peculiar eccentric. But nothing can hold back the speaker in the brown uniform, who leaps to his feet and shrills: 'You're not in the Party – why are you not in the Party?'

And Quangel answers the question the way he has always answered it: 'Because I need every penny for my family to live. I can't afford to join any Party.'

The man in brown roars, 'Because you are a selfish dog! Because you won't do anything to help your Führer and your nation! How many are in your family?'

Coldly Quangel answers to his face, 'Listen, mate, don't talk to me about my family today. I've just had news that my son has fallen.'

For an instant there's a deathly hush in the room, the brown official and the old foreman stare at one another across rows of chairs. Then abruptly, as though everything was settled, Otto Quangel sits down, and a little later the Nazi sits down, too. Once more, Director Schröder rises and offers the *Sieg Heil!* to the Führer. It sounds a little thin. With that, the meeting is at an end.

Five minutes later, Quangel is back in his workshop; with raised head, he slowly allows his eyes to travel from the planing machine to the band saw and then on to the nailer, the drills, the conveyor belts . . . But it is no longer the old Quangel standing there. He can sense it, he knows it, he has outfoxed them all. Maybe he did it in an ugly way, by capitalizing on the death of his son, but where does it say you have to play fair with those monsters? No, he says to himself, almost aloud. No, Quangel, you'll never be the same again. I'm curious what Anna'll have to say to all this. Perhaps Dollfuss won't return to his workstation? Then I'll have to take on another man, we're shorthanded . . .

But no need to worry, here comes Dollfuss. He's even accompanied by a junior manager, and Foreman Otto Quangel is instructed that, while he will technically remain in charge of the workshop, he will be replaced in the Arbeitsfront by Herr Dollfuss, effective immediately. 'Understood?'

'You bet I understand! I'm glad you're taking the post off me, Dollfuss! My hearing is getting worse, and having to keep my ears peeled the way the gentleman told us to a little while ago, I don't think I can do that in all this noise.'

Dollfuss nods curtly and says, 'What you saw and heard a moment ago, not a word to anyone, or else . . .'

Almost offended, Quangel replies, 'Who am I going to talk to, Dollfuss? Have you ever known me talk to anyone? I'm not interested in all that, I'm interested in my work, and I know we're significantly behind today. It's high time you were back at your machine!' And with a look up at the clock: 'That's one hour and thirty-six minutes you've missed already!'

A moment later, Carpenter Dollfuss is back at his saw, and in no time, no one knows from where, a rumour has started up that Dollfuss was given a carpeting for his incessant smoking and chitchat.

But Foreman Otto Quangel walks alertly from machine to machine, takes a hand here, glowers at a chatterbox there, and thinks to himself, That's the end of that, for good and all. And they haven't got a clue: as far as they're concerned, I'm just a doddery old fool! When I called that Nazi 'mate', that did it for them! I wonder what I'm going to do next. Because I will do something, I know. I just don't yet know what it will be . . .

7

Break-in at Night

Late in the evening, almost night-time, and properly speaking far too late for the matter in hand, Emil Borkhausen did indeed run into his Enno in an establishment called the Also Ran. (The righteous fury of the postie Eva Kluge may have had something to do with that.) The two gents sat down at a corner table over a beer, and whispered and whispered – all over that single glass of beer – till the landlord brought it to their attention that he had called for last orders a long time ago, and didn't they have wives to go home to?

The two men continued their conversation outside in the street; first they went in the direction of Prenzlauer Allee for a while, and then Enno wanted to go back the other way, because it occurred to him that it might be better to try his luck with an old flame of his who went by the name of Tutti. Tutti the Gorilla. Better off staying with her than pulling some cowboy stunt . . .

Emil Borkhausen almost leapt out of his skin at so much fool-ishness. He assured Enno for the tenth, for the hundredth time, that this was not a cowboy stunt. It was an SS-approved and prac-tically legal confiscation, and the victim was an old Jewish woman that no one cared what happened to. They would make enough to tide themselves over for a while, and the police and the courts would have absolutely nothing to say on the matter.

Whereupon Enno again: No, no, he had never got involved in business like that, it wasn't his thing at all. Women, yes, and bets any time, but he had never done anything crooked like that. Tutti had always been pretty good to him, despite being called the Gorilla, and she surely wouldn't hold it against him that she had helped him out previously with a little money and a few ration cards, without knowing it.

And with that they were on Prenzlauer Allee again.

Borkhausen, always veering between enticements and threats, says crossly, tugging at his long, wispy moustache, 'Who on earth asked you to understand this operation? I can do it all by myself, if need be, and you can just stand and watch with your hands in your pockets! I'll even pack a case for you, if you like! The only reason I'm taking you, Enno, is for insurance, in case the SS doublecross us, as a witness that we've divvied up everything properly. Just think of the riches we can find at the house of a wealthy Jewish businesswoman, even if the Gestapo must have picked up the odd item when they took away the husband!'

All at once Enno Kluge said yes. There was no more wavering, no more demurral. Now he couldn't get round to Jablonski Strasse quickly enough. What changed his mind was neither the arguments advanced by Borkhausen, nor the prospect of a rich haul, but plain and simple hunger. He suddenly imagined Frau Rosenthal's larder, and he remembered that Jews had always liked to eat well, and that he had probably never enjoyed anything so much in his life as a stuffed neck of goose that a Jewish clothier had treated him to once.

Suddenly he is thoroughly in the grip of hungry fantasies: he is convinced Frau Rosenthal will have a stuffed neck of goose in her larder. He can see the porcelain dish, the neck lying in congealed gravy, stuffed to bursting like a big fat sausage, and both ends tied with thread. He will take the dish and heat the thing up over the gas – nothing else is of any interest to him. Borkhausen can do whatever he wants; he doesn't care. He will dunk bread in the rich, spicy gravy and he will eat the goose neck with his fingers, the juice running all down his wrists.

'Would you mind getting a move on, Emil, I'm in a hurry!'

'What's the rush?' Borkhausen asks, but in fact he's more than happy to get a move on, too. He'll be only too glad when the thing is over and done with; it isn't his line of work either. It's not the police or the old Jewish lady he's scared of – what's going to happen to him for Aryanizing her property? – but the Persickes. They're an unscrupulous bunch all right, and he wouldn't put it past them to put one over on a freelance like himself. It was purely on account of the Persickes that he picked up this goofy Enno, he'll be a witness, someone they don't know, and that will cramp their style.

In Jablonski Strasse, everything went smoothly enough. It will have been about half past ten when they unlocked the front door with Borkhausen's key. Then they listened in the stairwell, and when there was no sound, they switched on the stair light and pulled off their shoes, because, as Borkhausen said with a grin, 'The property is entitled to peace and quiet.'

After the light clicked off, they tiptoed swiftly and silently up the stairs, and then everything went like clockwork. They didn't make any beginners' errors, like bumping into anything or dropping a shoe with a clatter, no, they tiptoed silently up four flights of stairs. So, that was a good bit of stair work, even though neither of them is a proper burglar and they're both in a state of fair excitement, one over his stuffed neck of goose and the other over the booty and the Persickes.

The door to her apartment was something Borkhausen imagined would be fifty times harder than it proved: it was not even locked, merely closed. What an irresponsible woman, and as a Jewess she really should have known better than that! So the two of them slipped into the apartment, they couldn't even say how, that's how easy it was.

Now Borkhausen, bold as brass, switches on the light in the corridor. In fact, he's all boldness now. 'If the old bitch screams, I'll smack her in the chops!' he announces, just like he did in the morning to Baldur Persicke. But she didn't scream. So they took a relaxed gander round the small corridor first, which was fairly stuffed with furniture and boxes and cases. Well, the Rosenthals used to own a large apartment near their shop, and if you have to leave in a hurry and move into two rooms with bed and kitchen, then that's bound to create a bit of clutter, isn't it? Stands to reason.

Their fingers were itching to begin prying and poking and packing the loot away, but Borkhausen thought it would be sensible to find Rosenthal first and tie a hanky over her face so she wouldn't make any trouble. The bedroom was so piled high they could hardly move, and they understood that there was so much plunder here that they wouldn't be able to move it in ten nights – they could only try and pick the best stuff. In the other room, same story, and in the cloakroom as well. Only there's no Rosenthal anywhere. The bed hasn't been slept in. Borkhausen checks the kitchen and the toilet, but there's no sign of the woman, and that's a huge stroke of luck, because it saves them trouble and makes their work considerably easier.

Borkhausen goes back into the first room and starts digging around. He doesn't even notice that his partner, Enno, has gone missing. Enno is standing in the larder, bitterly disappointed at not finding any stuffed neck of goose, just a half a loaf of bread and a couple of onions. But he starts eating anyway, slices up the onions and lays them flat on the bread, and he's so hungry, it tastes pretty good to him.

While Enno Kluge's standing there chewing away, his eye falls on a lower shelf and he suddenly sees that while the Rosenthals may not have much in the way of food in the house, they do keep a cellar. Because down on the lower shelf are rows and rows of bottles – wine, but also schnapps. Enno, a moderate man in all things except horses, picks up a bottle of dessert wine, and starts off by drizzling his onion sandwiches with it from time to time. But God knows why, suddenly the sweet stuff is sickening to him. (Ordinarily, he is perfectly capable of nursing a glass of beer for three hours.) He opens a bottle of cognac and takes a couple of slugs from it, and within five minutes the bottle is half empty. Perhaps it's the hunger, or the excitement, that makes him act so out of character. For the moment he's stopped eating.

After a while the schnapps no longer interests him, and he trots off to find Borkhausen, who is still rummaging around in the big room, opening wardrobes and cases and chucking everything on the floor in his quest for something better.

'Wow, they must have moved their whole haberdashery here!' Enno says, awestruck.

'Stop talking and get cracking!' is Borkhausen's reply. 'There's bound to be some jewellery hidden here, and cash – the

Rosenthals used to be well-off people, millionaires – and you, you prize fool, go talking about cowboy stunts!'

For a time the two of them work together silently, which means they chuck more and more stuff on the floor, now so covered with clothes and linens and stuff that they're trampling it underfoot. Then Enno, feeling the worse for wear, says: 'I can't see anything any more. I need a drink to clear my head. Get some cognac out of the larder, will you, Emil!'

Borkhausen doesn't fuss but does as he's asked, and comes back with two bottles of schnapps, and then they sit down together companionably on the piles of linen, drink slug after slug, and talk through the situation earnestly and thoroughly.

'You know, Borkhausen, we're not going to clean this stuff out very quickly, and we don't want to sit over it too long, either. I vote we each take a couple of suitcases and clear off. Tomorrow, we can think about a return visit.'

'You're right, Enno, I don't want to sit here too long, either, on account of the Persickes.'

'Who're they?'

'Oh, these people . . . But when I think of leaving with a couple of suitcases full of linens, and leave behind a box full of money and jewels, that drives me crazy. You'll need to let me look a while longer. Cheers, Enno!'

'Cheers, Emil! And why wouldn't you go on looking around a while longer? The night is long, and it's not us paying the electricity bill. But what I wanted to ask you is where are you going to take your cases?'

'How do you mean? I don't understand the question, Enno.'

'Well, where are you going to take them? Back to your flat?'

'Do you think I'm going to take them to the lost property office? Of course I'm taking them home to my Otti. And tomorrow morning off to Münzstrasse and flog the lot so the birds sing a bit.'

Enno rubs the cork against the bottleneck. 'Here's birdsong for you! Cheers, Emil! If I was you, I wouldn't do it your way, and involve your apartment and your wife. What does she need to know about your little earnings on the side? No, if I was you

I'd do it my way, namely take the suitcases to the Stettiner
Bahnhof and leave them at the station's checked baggage department, and send myself the receipt, but poste restante. That way
there'd never be anything on me, and no one could prove
anything against me.'

'That's pretty sharp, Enno,' says Borkhausen admiringly. 'And
when do you go back to collect the goods?'

'Well, whenever the coast is clear, of course, Emil!'

'And what do you live off in the meantime?'

'Well, it's like I said, I'll go to Tutti's. When I tell her what
I've done, she'll throw open all her arms and legs!'

'Very good,' Borkhausen agrees. 'Then if you go to the Stettiner, I'll go to the Anhalter. You know, less attention that
way.'

'Not bad, Emil. You're a pretty sharp cookie yourself!'

'Oh, I pick up a few tricks here and there,' says Borkhausen
modestly. 'You hear this and that.'

'Well, right! Cheers, Emil!'

'Cheers, Enno!'

For a while they gaze at each other with mute fondness, taking
the odd swig from their bottles. Then Borkhausen says: 'If you
turn round, doesn't have to be right away, there's a radiogram
behind you, must be at least ten valves. I wouldn't mind picking
that up.'

'Go on then, Emil, take it! A radio's always a useful item, to
keep or to sell!'

'Well, let's see if we can stow the thing in a suitcase, and pack
it in clothes.'

'Shall we do that now, or shall we have a drink first?'

'Ach, we can have one first, I say. Only one, mind!'

So they have one, and a second, and a third, and then they
gradually get to their feet and try to pack the large ten-valve
radiogram into a case that might have managed at best a portable radio. After some considerable struggle, Enno says, 'Oh, it
won't go, it won't go. Leave the damned thing, Emil, take a
suitcase with some suits in it.'

'But my Otti likes listening to the radio!'

'And I thought you didn't want to tell your old lady about this whole deal. You must be pissed out of your mind, Emil!'

'And what about you and your Tutti? You're pissed yourself. Where's your Tutti in all this?'

'She sings. I tell you, how she sings!' And again, he moves the moist cork in the bottleneck. 'Let's have another!'

'Cheers, Enno!'

They have a drink, and Borkhausen continues: 'You know, I do want to take the radio after all. If I can't get the damned thing in a case, then I'll tie it on a string and wear it round my neck. Then I'll still have both hands free.'

'Go on then, mate. Well, shall we pack up?'

'Yeah, let's. It's getting late.'

But they both stop and stare at each other with silly grins.

'All things considered,' Borkhausen begins, 'life is really pretty good. All these nice things here,' he gestures at them, 'and we can take our pick of the lot, plus we're doing a good deed because we're taking them off a Jewish woman who only stole them in the first place . . .'

'You're right there, Emil – we're doing a good deed for the German nation and our Führer. These are the good times he has promised us.'

'And our Führer, you know, he keeps his promises, he keeps his promises, Enno!'

They gaze at each other, eyes welling with tears.

'What on earth are you two doing here?' comes a sharp voice from the doorway.

They jump, and see a little fellow in a brown uniform.

Then Borkhausen nods slowly and sadly to Enno. 'This is Herr Baldur Persicke, whom I spoke of to you, Enno! This is where our troubles start!'

Small Surprises

While the two drunks were talking together, all the male members of the Persicke family had filed into the room. Nearest to Enno and Emil is the short, wiry Baldur, his eyes glinting behind his highly polished spectacles; just behind him are his two brothers in their black SS uniforms, but without caps; next to the door, as though not quite sure of himself, is the old former publican Persicke. The Persicke family has had a bit to drink as well, but the alcohol has a different effect on them than on the two housebreakers. Far from becoming emotional and dull-witted, the Persickes are even sharper, greedier, and more brutal than in their normal condition.

Baldur Persicke barks, 'Well, out with it! What are you doing here? Or is this where you live?'

'But Herr Persicke!' Borkhausen whines.

Baldur pretends only now to recognize him. 'Ah, it's Borkhausen from the basement flat in the back building!' he exclaims in mock astonishment to his two brothers. 'Herr Borkhausen, what are you doing here?' His surprise takes on an edge of sarcasm. 'Wouldn't you be better advised to look after your wife, the lovely Otti, a little bit – especially at this time of night? I've heard tell of convivial gatherings with well-placed gentlemen, and your children rolling around the courtyard at all hours, drunk. Don't you think you should put your children to bed, Herr Borkhausen?'

'Trouble!' mutters Borkhausen. 'I knew it the moment I saw the spectacles: trouble.' He nods sadly at Enno.

Enno Kluge is no help to him at all. He is swaying slightly, his brandy bottle dangling from one hand, and he doesn't have a clue what's going on.

Borkhausen turns back to Baldur Persicke. His tone is no longer plaintive so much as accusatory; all at once he is deeply offended. 'If my wife does behave in a certain way,' he says, 'then I'll take responsibility for it, Herr Persicke. I am a husband and father – by law. And if my children are drunk, well, you're drunk yourself, and you're no more than a child yourself, for Christ's sake!'

He looks angrily at Baldur, and Baldur glints back at him. Then he gives his brothers a discreet signal to get ready.

'What are you doing in the Rosenthals' apartment?' the youngest Persicke barks again.

'But it's all according to our arrangement!' Borkhausen assures him, eagerly now. 'All agreed. Me and my friend here, we're just on our way now. We're running a bit late, in fact. He's going to the Stettiner, I'm going to the Anhalter. Two suitcases each, plenty left for you.'

He's practically falling asleep, the last few words are mumbled.

Baldur fixes him with an alert stare. Maybe it'll pass off without violence – the two men are completely sloshed. But his instinct warns him. He grabs Borkhausen by the shoulder and barks: 'Who's that man with you? What's his name?'

'Enno!' Borkhausen barely manages to say. 'My friend Enno . . .'

'And where does your friend Enno live?'

'Don't know, Herr Persicke. Met him at the bud . . . drinking pubbies . . . at the Also Ran . . .'

Baldur has made up his mind. Suddenly he swings his fist into Borkhausen's midriff, causing him to fall into the piles of clothes. 'Bastard!' he yells. 'How dare you refer to my spectacles, and call me a child. I'll show you!'

But his shouting serves no purpose, for the two men can no longer hear him. His SS brothers have jumped in and knocked their opponents cold with a couple of brutal blows.

'There!' says Baldur happily. 'In an hour or so we can hand the two of them over to the police as burglars caught in the act. In the meantime we can move down whatever things we want for ourselves. But quiet on the stairs! I haven't heard old Quangel come back from his late shift.'

The two brothers nod. Baldur looks down at the bloodied, unconscious victims, then at all the cases, the clothes, the radio-gram. Suddenly he breaks into a smile. He turns to his father. 'Well, Father, how did I do? You and your anxiety about every-thing! You see . . .'

But that's as far as he gets. His father isn't standing in the doorway, as expected; his father has suddenly disappeared. In his place is Foreman Quangel, the fellow with the sharp, cold bird-like face, silently staring at him with his dark eyes.

When Otto Quangel got home from his shift – even though it had grown very late, because of the meeting, he had refused to take a tram, saving his pennies – he saw that in spite of the blackout there was a light on in Frau Rosenthal's apartment. On closer inspection he saw that there were lights on at the Persickes' as well, and downstairs at Judge Fromm's, shining past the edges of the blinds. In the case of Judge Fromm, of whom it wasn't certain whether he had gone into retirement in '33 because of old age or the Nazis, this wasn't surprising. He always read half the night. And the Persickes were presumably still celebrating their victory over France. But he couldn't believe that old Frau Rosenthal would have the lights on all over her apartment – there was something amiss there. The old woman was so cowed, she would never light up her flat like that.

There's something wrong, thought Otto Quangel as he unlocked the front door and slowly went up the stairs. As ever, he had forborne to switch on the lights in the stairwell – he didn't just economize for himself. He economized for everyone, including the landlord. Something's up! But what's it to do with me? I want nothing to do with those people. I live for myself. Me and Anna. The two of us. Anyway, perhaps it's the Gestapo conducting a search of the place. And I walk in! No, I'll just go to bed . . .

But with his scrupulousness, almost his sense of justice, sharp-ened by the 'You and your Führer' gibe, he found this decision rather unsatisfactory. He stood outside the door of his apart-ment, key in hand, head cocked. The door must be ajar there, there was a little light filtering down, and he could hear a sharp voice giving orders. An old woman, all alone, he thought suddenly, to his own surprise. Without protection. Without mercy . . .

At that moment, a small but forceful male hand reached out of the darkness and grabbed him by the scruff and faced him toward the stairs. A cultured voice said: 'Why don't you go on ahead, Herr Quangel. I will follow and appear at the correct moment.'

Without hesitating now, Quangel went up the stairs, such persuasive force had been vested in that hand and voice. That can only have been old Judge Fromm, he thought. What a secretive so-and-so. I think in all the years I've lived here, I've seen him maybe a score of times by day, and now here he is creeping around the stairs in the middle of the night!

So thinking, he mounted the stairs unhesitatingly and reached the Rosenthal apartment. He just caught sight of a squat figure – certainly old Persicke – retreating hurriedly into the kitchen, and he caught Baldur's last words about the thing they had done, and that it was wrong to be afraid all the time . . . And now the two of them, Baldur Persicke and Otto Quangel, stood silently confronting one another, eye to eye.

For an instant, Baldur Persicke thought the game was up. But then he remembered one of his maxims, Shamelessness wins out, and he said a little provocatively, 'I can imagine your surprise. But you got here a bit late, Herr Quangel, we've caught the burglars.' He left a pause, but Quangel didn't say anything. A little less brightly, Baldur added, 'One of the two villains appears to be Borkhausen, who lives off immoral earnings at the back of the house.'

Quangel's eyes followed Baldur's pointing finger. 'Yes,' he said curtly, 'that's Borkhausen.'

'As for you,' broke in Adolf Persicke of the SS, 'what are you doing, standing there staring? Why don't you go to the police station and report the crime, so that the police can arrest the culprits? We'll keep them pinned down in the meantime!'

'Will you keep out of it, Adolf!' hissed Baldur. 'You can't issue orders to Herr Quangel. Herr Quangel knows what he has to do.'

But that was just what Quangel at that moment did not know. If he had been alone, he would have decided spontaneously. But there was that hand grabbing at his shirt, and that cultured voice, and he had no idea what the old judge had in mind, or what he wanted from him. But whatever it was, he didn't want to spoil his plan. If only he knew what it was . . .

And that was when the old gentleman appeared on the scene, though not, as Quangel had expected, at his side, but from the interior of the apartment. Suddenly he stood in their midst, like an apparition, and gave the Persickes a further, deeper shock.

He did look rather singular, the old gentleman. Of frail build and average height or less, he was swathed in a lustrous black silk dressing gown trimmed with red and secured with large red toggles. The old gentleman wore a grey imperial and a white moustache. The very fine, still brown hair on his head was brushed carefully across the pale scalp, but was unable to hide its bareness. Behind the delicate gold-rimmed spectacles lurked two amused, sardonic eyes.

'No, no, gentlemen,' he said smoothly, seeming to continue a conversation begun long ago to the edification of all. 'No, no, Frau Rosenthal is not at home. But maybe one of the junior Persickes would take the trouble to look in the bathroom. Your father appears to have been taken ill. At any rate, he seems to be trying to hang himself with a towel there. I was unable to persuade him to desist . . .'

The judge smiles, but the two elder Persicke boys storm out of the room so fast that the effect is rather comical. Young Persicke has turned pale and quite sober. The old gentleman who has just set foot in the room and is speaking with such irony is a man whose superiority Baldur effortlessly senses. It's not a seeming, jumped-up superiority, it's the real thing. Baldur Persicke says almost beseechingly, 'Please understand, your honour, father is, to put it bluntly, very drunk. The capitulation of France . . .'

'Oh, I understand, I quite understand,' says the old judge, and makes a little deprecating gesture. 'We are all human, only we don't all try to hang ourselves when we're in our cups.' He stops for a moment and smiles. He says, 'Of course he said all sorts of things, too, but who pays any attention to the babble of a drunkard!' Again he smiles.

'Your honour!' Baldur Persicke says imploringly. 'I beg you, take this matter in hand! You've been a judge, you know what steps to take . . .'

'No. No,' says the judge firmly. 'I am old and infirm.' He doesn't look it. Quite the opposite, he looks in flourishing health. 'And then I live a very quiet, retired life, I have very little contact with the world outside. But you, Herr Persicke, you and your family, it's you who took the two burglars by surprise. You must hand them over to the police and secure the property in the apartment. I have taken a cursory look. There are seventeen suitcases and twenty-one boxes here. And more. And more . . .'

He speaks more and more slowly. Then he says casually, 'I imagine that the apprehension of the two burglars will bring substantial fame and honour to you and your family.'

The judge stops. Baldur stands there, looking very thoughtful. That's another way of doing it – what a wily old fox that Fromm is! He must see through everything; certainly his father will have blabbed, but this man's retired, he wants his peace and quiet, he doesn't want to get involved in a business like this. There's no danger from him. What about Quangel, the old foreman? He's never bothered himself about anyone in the house, never greeted anyone, never chatted to anyone. Quangel is a real old workingman, scrawny, wizened, not a single independent thought in his head. He won't make any needless trouble. He's utterly harmless.

The only ones left are the two drunks lying there. Of course you could hand them over to the police, and deny whatever Borkhausen might say about your having tipped them off. They'll never believe him, if he's up against members of the Party, the SS, and the Hitler Youth. And then report the case to the Gestapo. That way you might get a piece of the action perfectly legally, and without risk. And you'd get some kudos for it, too.

Tempting. But it might be best to handle everything informally.

Patch up Borkhausen and that Enno fellow and send them packing with a few marks. They won't talk. Lock up the apartment as it is, whether Frau Rosenthal comes back or not. Perhaps there'll be something to be done later on – he has a pretty certain sense that policy against the Jews is going to get tougher. Sit tight, relax. Things might be possible in six months that aren't possible today. As things stand, the Persickes are somewhat compromised. They won't suffer any consequences, but they'll be the subject of gossip within the Party. They'll lose a little of their reputation for reliability.

Baldur Persicke says, 'I'm almost tempted to let the two rascals go. I feel sorry for them, your honour, they're just small fry.'

He looks round, he's all alone. Both the judge and the foreman have vanished. As he thought, neither of them wants anything to do with this business. It's the smartest thing they could do. He, Baldur, will do the same, no matter what his brothers say.

With a deep sigh for all the pretty things he has to say goodbye to, Baldur sets off into the kitchen to restore his father to his senses and to persuade his brothers to put back what they've already earmarked for themselves.

On the stairs, meanwhile, the judge says to Foreman Quangel, who has silently followed him out of the room, 'If you get any trouble on account of Frau Rosenthal, Herr Quangel, just tell me. Goodnight.'

'What do I care about Frau Rosenthal? I barely know her,' protests Quangel.

'Very well, goodnight, Herr Quangel,' and Judge Fromm heads off down the stairs.

Otto Quangel lets himself into his dark apartment.

9

Nocturnal Conversation at the Quangels'

No sooner has Quangel opened the door to the bedroom than his wife Anna calls out in alarm: 'Don't switch the light on, Papa! Trudel's asleep in your bed. I made up your bed on the sofa.'

'All right, Anna,' replies Quangel, surprised to hear that Trudel has got his bed. Usually, she got the sofa when she stayed. He asks, 'Are you asleep, Anna, or do you feel like talking for a bit?'

She hesitates briefly, then she calls back through the open bedroom door. 'You know, I feel so tired and down, Otto!'

So she's still angry with me, thinks Otto Quangel, wonder why? But he says in the same tone, 'Well goodnight anyway, Anna. Sleep well!'

And from her bed he hears, 'Goodnight, Otto!' And Trudel whispers after her, 'Goodnight, Papa!'

'Goodnight, Trudel!' he replies, and he curls up on his side to get to sleep as soon as he can, because he is very tired. Perhaps overtired, as one can be over-hungry. Sleep refuses to come. A long day with an unending string of events, a day the like of which he has never experienced before, is now behind him.

Not a day he would have wished for. Quite apart from the fact that all the events were disagreeable (aside from losing his post at the Arbeitsfront), he hates the turbulence, the having to talk to all kinds of people he can't stand. And he thinks of the letter with the news of Ottochen's death that Frau Kluge gave him, he thinks of the snoop Borkhausen, who tried to put one over on him so crudely, and about the walk in the corridor of the uniform factory, with the fluttering posters that Trudel leaned her head against. He thinks of the carpenter Dollfuss, the smoking-break artist, he hears the medals and decorations jingling on the breast of the Nazi speaker, he can feel the small, firm hand of Judge Fromm, clutching at him in the dark and propelling him up the stairs. There is young Persicke in highly polished boots standing in the sea of clothing, looking greyer and greyer, and the two drunks groaning and gurgling in the corner.

He is on the point of sleep when something jolts him awake. There's something else that bothers him about today, something he knows he heard but put from his mind. He sits up on the sofa and listens attentively. That's right, he wasn't inventing it. In a tone of command he calls, 'Anna!'

She replies plaintively, which isn't her style, 'What are you bothering me about now, Otto? You're not letting me sleep. I told you I didn't want to talk any more.'

He continues, 'What am I doing on the sofa, if Trudel's in your bed? In that case, surely my own bed is free.'

For a moment there's complete silence, then his wife says, almost imploringly, 'But Otto, Trudel's in your bed. I'm here alone, and I have such aches and pains . . .'

He interrupts her: 'I don't like it when you lie to me, Anna. I can hear the breathing of three people quite clearly. Who's sleeping in my bed?'

Silence, long silence. Then the woman says stoutly: 'Ask me no questions, I'll tell you no lies. Just pipe down, Otto!'

And he, insistent: 'This apartment is in my name. I'm not having any secrets kept from me. What happens here is my responsibility. For the last time, who's in my bed?'

Long, long silence. Then an old, deep woman's voice: 'I am, Herr Quangel, Frau Rosenthal. I don't want your wife and you to have any trouble on my account, so I'll just get dressed and go back upstairs.'

'You can't go into your apartment now, Frau Rosenthal. The Persickes are up there, and some other fellows. Stay in my bed. And tomorrow, early, at six or seven, go down to old Judge Fromm's on the first floor and ring his bell. He'll help you, he told me.'

'Oh, thank you, Herr Quangel!'

'Don't thank me, thank the judge! All I'm doing is throwing you out. There, and now it's your turn, Trudel . . .'

'You want me to go, Father?'

'Yes, you have to. This was your last visit here, and you know why as well. Maybe Anna can go and see you from time to time, but probably not. Once she's seen sense and I've had a chat with her . . .'

Almost yelling, his wife protests, 'I'm not putting up with this! I'm going as well. Stay in your flat by yourself, if you want to! The only thing on your mind is your peace and quiet . . .'

'That's right!' he interrupts. 'I don't want any funny business, and above all I don't want to be dragged into other people's funny business. If it's to be my head on the block, I want to know what it's doing there, and not that it's some stupid things that other people have done. I'm not saying that I'm going to do anything. But if I do anything, I'll only do it alone with you, and with no one else involved, even if it's a sweet girl like Trudel or an old, unprotected woman like you, Frau Rosenthal. I'm not saying my way is the right way. But there's no other way for me. It's how I am, and I'm not going to change. There, and now I'm going to sleep!'

And with that, Otto Quangel lies down again. Over in the other room, they go on whispering for a while, but it doesn't bother him. He knows he will get his way. Tomorrow morning, the flat will be empty again, and Anna will give in. No more irregular episodes. Just himself. Himself alone. All alone.

He goes to sleep, and whoever found him sleeping would see a smile on his face, a grim little smile on that hard, dry, birdlike face, a grim and stubborn smile, but not an evil one.

10

What Happened on Wednesday Morning

All the events related thus far took place on a Tuesday. On the morning of the following Wednesday, very early, between five and six, Frau Rosenthal, accompanied by Trudel Baumann, left the Quangel apartment. Otto Quangel was still fast asleep. Trudel left the petrified Frau Rosenthal, the yellow star on her coat, outside Fromm's apartment door. Then she went back up half a flight of stairs, resolved to defend her with her life and honour in case of a descending Persicke.

Trudel watched as Frau Rosenthal pushed the doorbell. Almost immediately the door was opened, as though someone had been standing behind it, waiting. A few words were quietly exchanged, and then Frau Rosenthal stepped inside, and the door shut. Trudel Baumann passed it on her way down to the street. The front door of the building was already unlocked.

The two women were lucky. In spite of the earliness of the hour and the fact that early rising was not among the habits of the Persicke household, the two SS men had passed down the stairs not five minutes before. Five minutes prevented an encounter that, given the routine brutality of the two fellows, could only have ended badly, certainly for Frau Rosenthal.

Also, the SS men were not alone. They had been instructed by their brother Baldur to take Borkhausen and Enno Kluge (whose papers Baldur had examined in the meantime) out of the house and back to their wives. The two amateur burglars were still almost completely out of it, what with the amount they had had to drink and the ensuing blows. But Baldur Persicke had managed to persuade them that they had behaved like pigs, that it was merely due to the great philanthropy of the Persickes that they hadn't been handed over to the police, and that any subsequent blabbing would land them there double quick. Also, they had to promise never to show up at the Persickes' again and never to admit knowing any of the family. And if they ever set foot in the Rosenthals' apartment again, they would be handed over to the Gestapo forthwith.

All this Baldur had dinned into them, with much abuse, till it sank into their befogged brains. They had sat opposite each other across the table in dim light in the Persicke flat, with the incessantly swaggering, threatening, flashing Baldur between them. The two SS men had sprawled on the sofa, a threatening, dark presence, for all that they seemed to be smoking cigarettes nonstop. Enno and Borkhausen had an awful impression that they were in a kangaroo court facing imminent death. They swayed back and forth on their chairs, trying to grasp what they were supposed to understand. From time to time they nodded off, only to be wakened by painful blows from Baldur's fist. All they had planned, done, and suffered seemed to them like an unreal dream, and they longed only for sleep and oblivion.

In the end, Baldur sent them away with his brothers. In their pockets, without their knowing it, Borkhausen and Kluge each had fifty marks in small-denomination notes. Baldur had decreed this further, painful sacrifice, which for now turned the whole Rosenthal scheme into a loss-making operation for the Persickes. But he reminded himself that if the men went back to their wives penniless, shattered, and incapable of work, that would give rise to much more fuss and questions than if they showed up with a little money. And he imagined it would be the women who found the money, given the condition of their men.

The older Persicke, who was charged with getting Borkhausen home, accomplished his mission in ten minutes flat, during which time Frau Rosenthal had disappeared into Judge Fromm's apartment and Trudel Baumann had emerged into the street. He simply grabbed Borkhausen by the scruff of his neck – he was barely capable of walking – and dragged him across the courtyard, dropped him on the ground outside his flat, and woke his wife by banging on the door with his fists. As she recoiled from the dark figure looming in her doorway, he yelled: 'Here's your

man back! Put him to bed! He's been lying around on our staircase, puking over everything . . .'

And all the rest he left to Otti. She had quite a bit of trouble
getting Emil out of his clothes and putting him to bed, and the
elderly gentleman who was still enjoying her hospitality was
roped in to help. Then he too was sent away, despite the early
hour. Also he was told he mustn't on any account come again
– perhaps they might arrange to meet in a café or something,
but not here.

Otti was seized by panic on seeing the SS man Persicke at the
door. She knew of some colleagues who, instead of being paid
for their services by these gentlemen in the black uniforms, had
been pitched into a concentration camp for being immoral and
work-shy. She had imagined she had a completely invisible existence in her gloomy subterranean apartment in the back building,
and now she made the discovery that – like everyone else at this
time – she was the object of unceasing surveillance. For the
umpteenth time in her life she swore to reform herself. This
prospect was made easier by her discovery of forty-eight marks
in Emil's pockets. She put the money in a stocking and decided
to wait to hear what Emil told her of his adventures. She, at any
rate, would begin by denying all knowledge of any money.

The other Persicke's task was much harder, especially as the
distance to travel was a lot further, for the Kluges lived on the
other side of Friedrichshain. Enno was no more capable of walking
than Borkhausen, but Persicke couldn't take him by the arm or
the collar in the public street. It was embarrassing enough anyway
to be seen with this battered-looking drunkard, because although
Persicke had little regard for his own honour or that of his fellow
men, his uniform demanded respect to a unique degree.

It was equally unavailing to order Kluge to march a step ahead
or a step behind, for he always had the same insuperable inclination to sit down on the ground, to stumble, to grab hold of
walls and trees, to walk into pedestrians. Hitting him was useless,
so was barking at him: the body just wouldn't obey, and the
streets were too busy already for the good seeing-to that might
just sober him up enough. The sweat stood out on Persicke's

brow, his jaws were working with rage, and he vowed to tell his odious little squirt of a brother to his face what he thought of such assignments.

He had to keep off the main roads and make detours down quieter side streets. Then he would grab Kluge under his arm and lug him for two or three blocks until he couldn't do it any more. He got some grief from a policeman who had noticed this compulsory form of transport, and who trailed after him through the whole ward, forcing Persicke to adopt a gentler and more concerned manner than he would have liked.

But once they arrived in Friedrichshain, he was able to get his revenge. He put Kluge on a bench behind some shrubbery and beat him so hard that he lay there unconscious for ten minutes at the end of it. This little chump, who cared about nothing in the world except his horses – and all his knowledge of them was through the tabloids – this creature that was capable of feeling neither love nor hate, this idle creep who had devoted every winding of his pathetic brain to the avoidance of real exertion, this pale, modest, colourless Enno Kluge developed such a fear of uniforms from that time forth that meeting any Party member was enough to paralyse his brain.

A couple of kicks in the ribs roused him from his stupor, a couple of thumps on the back set him on his feet, and then he trotted along like a beaten dog in front of his tormentor till he reached his wife's apartment. But the door was locked. The postwoman Eva Kluge, who had spent the night in despair of her son Karlemann and her whole life, had set off on her usual daily grind, the letter to her other son in her pocket, but very little hope in her heart. She delivered mail as she had done for years, because it was still better than sitting idle at home tortured by gloomy thoughts.

Once he'd persuaded himself that the woman really wasn't home, Persicke rang next door, as luck would have it at the door of that same Frau Gesch who with her lie had helped Enno gain entry to his wife's flat. Persicke simply shoved his hapless victim into the woman's arms as she opened the door, said, 'Here! Look after him, you know where he belongs!' and then left.

Frau Gesch had firmly resolved never again to take a hand in the affairs of the Kluges. But such was the authority of an SS man, and such was the universal fear of them, that she took Kluge into her flat without protest, sat him down at the table, and plied him with coffee and bread. Her own husband had already gone to work. Frau Gesch could see how exhausted little Kluge was, and she could also see from his face, his ripped shirt, and the filth on his coat evidence of protracted mishandling. But since Kluge had been handed over to her by an SS man, she didn't dare ask a single question. Yes, she would have rather put him outside the door than listened to an account of what had happened to him. She didn't want to know anything. If she didn't know anything, she couldn't testify to anything, blab, get herself in trouble.

Slowly Kluge chewed his bread and drank his coffee. Thick tears of pain and exhaustion dribbled down his cheeks. From time to time, Frau Gesch cast a sidelong look at him. Then, when he had finished, she said: 'Now where do you want to go? Your wife's not taking you back, you know that!'

He didn't answer, just stared straight ahead of him.

'And you can't stay here with me either. For one thing, my Gustav wouldn't have it, and then I don't want to have to keep everything under lock and key on account of you. So where do you want to go?'

Again, he didn't reply.

Frau Gesch said crossly, 'Well, in that case, I'll leave you on the staircase! I'll do it right away. Or?'

He said with difficulty, 'Tutti – old girlfriend of mine . . .' And then he was crying again.

'For goodness sake, what a baby!' she said contemptuously. 'If I always folded like that the moment something went wrong! All right, this Tutti: What's her real name, and where does she live?'

After many further questions and some threats she learned that Enno didn't know Tutti's real name, but thought he could find his way to where she lived.

'Well then,' said Frau Gesch. 'But you can't go on your own

in that state – any traffic policeman would arrest you. I'll take you. But if you're wrong about the apartment, I'll leave you there on the street. I've got no time for looking around, I've got to go to work!'

'Could I have just a little nap?' he begged.

She hesitated briefly, then decreed, 'All right, but no longer than an hour! In an hour we're off. There, lie down on the sofa, I'll find something to cover you with.'

He was asleep before she came back with the blanket.

Old Judge Fromm had let Frau Rosenthal in personally. He had led her into his study, whose walls were completely lined with books, and let her sit down in a chair there. A reading lamp was on, a book lay open on the table. The old gentleman himself brought in a tray with a pot of tea and a cup, sugar, and two thin slices of bread, and said to the terrified woman, 'First have some breakfast, Frau Rosenthal, and then we can talk!' And when she wanted to bring out a word of thanks, he said kindly, 'No, please, I insist. Just make yourself at home here, take an example by me!'

With that, he picked up the book under the reading lamp and calmly carried on reading, all the while mechanically stroking his beard. He seemed entirely oblivious of his visitor.

By and by, a little confidence returned to the frightened old Jewess. For months she had lived in fear and confusion, with her bags packed, always ready for a vicious attack. For months she had known neither home nor ease nor peace nor calm. And now here she was sitting with the old gentleman whom before she had never seen except on the stairs, and very occasionally at that; the light and dark brown leather bindings of many books looked down at her, there was a large mahogany desk by the window (furniture the likes of which she had once owned herself, in the early years of her marriage), a slightly worn Zwickau carpet was under her feet. And then, add in the old gentleman himself, reading his book, stroking away at his not un-Jewish-looking goatee, and wearing a long dressing gown that reminded her of her father's kaftan.

It was as though a spell had caused a whole world of dirt,

blood, and tears to fade away, and she was back in a time when
Jews were still respected people, not fugitive vermin facing extermination.

Unconsciously, she stroked her hair, and her face softened. So
there was still peace in the world, even in Berlin.

'I am very grateful to you, Judge,' she said. Her voice sounded
different, more certain.

He quickly looked up from his book. 'Please drink your tea
while it's hot, and eat your bread. We have a lot of time, there's
no hurry at all.'

And he was reading again. Obediently, she drank her tea and
ate her bread, even though she would much rather have conversed
with the old gentleman. But she preferred in the end to obey
him in all things and not disturb the peace of his apartment.
She looked around again. No, everything had to remain as it
was. She wasn't going to endanger it. (Three years later, a high-
explosive bomb would blow this home to smithereens, and the
sedate old gentleman himself would die a slow and agonizing
death in the cellar . . .)

Replacing her empty cup on the tray, she said, 'You've been
very kind to me, Judge, and very brave. But I don't want to
endanger you and your home to no purpose. It's no use. I'm
going to go back to my flat.'

The old gentleman looked at her attentively while she spoke,
and when she got to her feet, he led her gently back to her chair.
'Won't you remain seated a little longer, Frau Rosenthal!'

She did so, reluctantly. 'Really, Judge, I mean what I say.'

'Won't you kindly listen to me, first. I, too, mean what I am
about to say to you. Let's start with the question of danger. I
was in danger, as you put it, all my professional life. I had a
mistress whom I had to obey: one that rules over me, you, the
world, even the world outside as presently constituted, and her
name is Justice. I always believed in her, I made Justice the guiding
light for everything I did.'

While he spoke, he paced back and forth, his hands behind
his back, always in Frau Rosenthal's sight. The words passed his
lips calmly and unexcitedly. He spoke of himself as in the past,

a man who really no longer existed. Frau Rosenthal listened to him, gripped.

'But,' the judge continued, 'I am speaking of myself, instead of speaking about you, a bad habit among people who live alone. A little more now on the matter of danger. I've received threatening letters for ten, twenty, thirty years . . . And now I'm an old man, Frau Rosenthal, sitting reading his Plutarch. Danger means nothing to me, it doesn't frighten me, it doesn't engage my head or my heart. Don't let's speak of danger, Frau Rosenthal . . .'

'But people are different nowadays,' Frau Rosenthal objected.

'And if I tell you that those earlier threats were issued by criminals and their accomplices? Where's the difference!' He smiled. 'They are not different people. There are a few more of them, and the others are a little more circumspect, a little cowardly even, but Justice has remained the same, and I hope that we both live to witness her victory.' For an instant he stood there, rather erect. Then he began his pacing again. Quietly he said, 'The triumph of Justice will not be the same thing as the triumph of the German nation!'

He stopped for a moment, then went on in a lighter tone of voice: 'No, you can't go back to your flat. The Persickes were there last night, you know, that Nazi family that lives over me. They have your keys in their possession, and they will keep your flat under constant observation. You really would be putting yourself in unnecessary danger.'

'But I must be there when my husband comes back!' begged Frau Rosenthal.

'Your husband,' Judge Fromm said in a kindly tone, 'your husband will not be able to visit you any time soon. He is currently in Moabit Prison, accused of having secretly passed property abroad. He is safe, therefore, at least as long as he is able to keep the state prosecutors and the tax authorities interested in his case.'

The old judge smiled subtly, looked encouragingly at Frau Rosenthal, and then went back to his pacing.

'But how can you know that?' exclaimed Frau Rosenthal.

He made a dismissive gesture, and said, 'Oh, even if he's retired, an old judge gets to hear this and that. You will be interested to learn that your husband has a capable lawyer and is being reasonably well fed. Of course I can't tell you the name of the lawyer, he wouldn't welcome visits from you . . .'

'But perhaps I can visit my husband in Moabit!' Frau Rosenthal cried. 'I could bring him clean clothes – who's looking after his laundry? And some toiletries, and perhaps something to eat . . .'

'My dear Frau Rosenthal,' said the retired judge, laying his veined, liver-spotted hand firmly on her shoulder, 'you can as little visit your husband as he can you. Such a visit would not be useful to him, you would never get in far enough to see him, and it would only harm you.'

He looked at her.

Suddenly his eyes were no longer smiling, and his voice sounded strict. She saw that this small, gentle, kindly man was following some implacable law, probably the law of that Justice he had referred to earlier.

'Frau Rosenthal,' he said quietly, 'you are my guest – as long as you obey the conditions of my hospitality, which I will go on to explain to you. The first law of my hospitality: as soon as you do anything without consulting me, as soon as the door of this apartment has closed behind you a single time, one single time, you will never be readmitted here, and the names of you and your husband will be wiped from my mind. Do you understand?'

He touched his brow with his fingertips, and looked at her piercingly.

'Yes,' she breathed.

Only then did he take his hand off her shoulder. His expression lightened again, and he slowly resumed his pacing. 'I would ask you,' he continued, a little more easily, 'during the daylight hours not to leave the room I am about to show you, and not to stand by the window. My cleaning woman is reliable, but . . .'
He broke off a little irritably, and looked across at his book under

the reading light. He continued, 'Try to do as I do, and make your nights into days. I will give you a sleeping pill every day. I will supply you with food at night. Now would you kindly follow me?'

She followed him into the corridor. She was feeling a little bewildered and frightened, her host seemed so changed toward her. But she told herself perfectly correctly that the old gentleman loved his quiet life and was no longer accustomed to the presence of strangers. He was tired of them, and longed to be back with his Plutarch, whoever or whatever that was.

The judge opened a door for her and switched on the light. 'The blinds are down,' he said, 'and I keep it dark. Please leave it that way, otherwise someone from the back building might be able to see you. I hope you will find everything you need.'

He allowed her to take in the bright, cheerful room with its birchwood furniture, a side table well stocked with toiletries, and a four-poster bed upholstered in flowered chintz. He looked at the room as at something he hadn't seen for a long time and was now revisiting. Then he said, with deep seriousness, 'This was my daughter's room. She died in 1933 – no, not here, not in this room. Don't be alarmed!'

Quickly he took her hand. 'I'm not going to lock the door, Frau Rosenthal,' he said, 'but I would ask that you bolt it immediately from the inside. Do you have a watch? Good. I will knock on your door at ten o'clock this evening. Goodnight!'

He left. In the doorway he stopped and turned to her once more. 'Over the next few days, you will be very much alone with yourself and your thoughts, Frau Rosenthal. Try to accustom yourself to it. Solitude can be a very good thing. And don't forget: every single survivor is important, including you, you most of all! Now – bolt the door!'

He went out so softly, shutting the door so gently, that she only realized later that she had neither thanked him nor said goodnight. She walked quickly to the door, but stopped and reconsidered. Then she turned the bolt and dropped on to the nearest chair. Her legs were trembling. In the mirror of the dressing table, she saw a pallid face, swollen with crying and sleepless nights. Slowly, sadly, she nodded at her face in the mirror.

That's you, Sara, she said to herself. Lore, now called Sara. You were a good businesswoman, always working hard. You brought five children into the world, and one of them is in Denmark, one in England, two in the USA, and one is lying in the Jewish cemetery on Schönhauser Allee. It doesn't make me angry when they call you Sara; it's not what they meant to do, but they made me a daughter of my nation. He is a good and kind old gentleman, but so distant . . . I could never talk to him properly, the way I talked to Siegfried. I think he is cold. For all his goodness, he is cold. His goodness itself is cold. That's on account of the law he serves, the law of justice. I have followed only one law, which is to love my husband and children and help them in their lives. And now I'm sitting here with this old man, and everything I am has fallen from me. That's the solitude he mentioned. It's not quite half past six in the morning, and I won't see him again until ten at night. Fifteen and a half hours by myself – what will I discover about myself that I never knew? I'm afraid, I'm so afraid! I think I'm going to scream, I'm going to scream in my sleep! Fifteen and a half hours. He could have spent at least the half hour sitting with me. But he wanted to get on with his old book. For all his goodness, human beings don't mean anything to him, the only thing that has meaning for him is his justice. He does it for that, not for me. It would only matter to me if he did it for my sake!

Slowly she nods at the suffering face of Sara in the mirror. She looks round at the bed. My daughter's room. She died in 1933. Not here! Not here, she thinks. She shudders. The way he said it. Surely the daughter also died because of – them, but he'll never talk to me about it, and I'll never dare to ask him, either. No, I can't sleep in this room, it's awful, inhuman. Why doesn't he leave me his servant's room, a bed still warm from the body of a real person sleeping in it? I can't sleep here, I can only scream . . .

She picks up the tubes and boxes on the dressing table. Dried-out creams, lumpy powder, verdigrised lipsticks – dead since

1933. Seven years. I have to do something. The way it runs through me – the fear. Now that I've landed on this island of peace, my fear comes out. I have to do something. I can't remain so alone in my thoughts.

She looked through her handbag, found paper and pencil. I will write to the children, Gerda in Copenhagen, Eva in Ilford, Bernhard and Stefan in Brooklyn. But there's no point, the foreign post no longer goes, it's wartime. I will write to Siegfried; somehow I can smuggle the letter to him in Moabit. So long as the servant is indeed reliable. The judge doesn't need to know, I can bribe her with money or jewels. I still have enough left . . .

She took these out of her handbag as well, and spread them out in front of her, the money in little bundles, the jewels. She picked up a bracelet. Siegfried gave that to me, when I had Eva. It was my first birth, it was hard. How he laughed when he saw the baby! His belly shook he was laughing so hard. Everyone had to laugh when they saw her with her tight black curls and her thick lips. A white Negro baby, they said. In my eyes Eva was beautiful. That's when he gave me the bracelet. It was very expensive; he spent a whole week's earnings on it. I was so proud to be a mother. The bracelet didn't mean anything to me. Now Eva has three girls herself; Harriet is nine already. I wonder how often she thinks of me, over in Ilford. But whatever she does think, she won't imagine her mother sitting here, in some dead girl's room at Judge Fromm's, who only obeys Justice. And all alone . . .

She laid down the bracelet and picked up a ring. She sat the whole day over her things, muttering to herself, clinging to her past. She didn't want to think of herself as she was today.

In between came outbursts of wild panic. Once, she got as far as the door, and said to herself, If I could only be sure they wouldn't torture me, that it would be swift and painless, then I would give myself up to them. I can't stand this waiting any more, and in all probability it is futile. Sooner or later, they'll catch me. Why does each individual survivor matter so much, myself most of all? The children will think about me less and less, the grandchildren not at all, Siegfried will die soon in Moabit. I don't understand what the judge meant, so I had better ask him about it tonight. Probably he will just smile and say something I won't understand, because I am just a woman of flesh and blood, a Sara grown old.

She propped herself on her elbow on the dressing table, and gloomily studied her face with its network of creases. Creases drawn by anxiety, fear, hatred, love. Then she went back to the table, to her jewels. Just to pass the time, she counted through her money again and again. Later on, she tried ordering the notes by serial numbers. From time to time she wrote down a sentence in the letter to her husband. But it wasn't really a letter, just a series of questions. What was the accommodation like, what did they give him to eat, couldn't she help with the laundry? Small, banal questions. And: She was fine. She was safe.

No, it wasn't a letter, it was silly, useless chatter, and not even true at that. She wasn't safe at all. Never in the last ghastly months had she felt herself in such danger as in this quiet room. She knew she would have to change here, she wouldn't be able to escape herself. And she was afraid of who she might turn into. Perhaps she would have to endure even more terrible things to come, she, who had already changed from a Lore to a Sara.

Later on, she did lie down on the bed after all, and when her host knocked on the door at ten, she was so fast asleep that she didn't hear him. He opened the door quietly with a key that turned back the bolt, and when he saw her asleep, he nodded and smiled. He brought in a tray with food and set it down on the table, and when he moved aside her jewellery and money, he nodded and smiled again. He tiptoed out of the room, turned the bolt once more, and let her sleep . . .

So it came about that Frau Rosenthal saw no human being during the first three days of her protective custody. She slept through the nights, and woke to anguished, fear-tormented days. On the fourth day, half-crazed, she did try something . . .

11

It is Still Wednesday

In the end Frau Gesch wasn't so hard-hearted as to wake the little man after an hour on the sofa. He looked so pitiable lying there in his exhausted sleep, the purple bruises slowly coming up on his face.

He had his lower lip pushed out like a sad child, and sometimes his eyelids trembled, and a deep sigh shook his chest, as though he were about to begin crying in his sleep.

When she had got her dinner ready, she woke him and gave him some food. He muttered his thanks to her. He ate like a wolf, looking at her from time to time, but not saying a word about what had happened to him.

In the end she said: 'All right, that's all I can give you, otherwise I won't have enough left for my Gustav. Why don't you lie back down on the sofa, and have some more sleep. I'll talk to your wife . . .'

He muttered inaudibly; whether in agreement or disagreement was unclear. But he went back to the sofa willingly enough, and a minute later he was asleep again.

When Frau Gesch heard her neighbour's door open in the late afternoon, she crept over quietly and knocked. Eva Kluge opened right away, but stood squarely in the doorway. 'Well?' she asked defensively.

'Excuse me for bothering you again, Frau Kluge,' began Frau Gesch, 'but I've got your husband lying next door. An SS man brought him in early this morning. You must have just left.'

Eva Kluge persisted in her defensive silence, and Frau Gesch continued, 'He's in quite a state, I think there's no part of him that's not bruised. I don't know the ins and outs between you and your husband, but you can't put him on the street as he is. Why don't you have a look at him, Frau Kluge!'

Frau Kluge was unyielding: 'I don't have a husband any more, Frau Gesch. I told you, I don't want to hear any more.'

And she started to go back inside her flat. Frau Gesch said quickly, 'Now don't you be in so much of a hurry, Frau Kluge. After all, he's your husband. You had children together . . .'

'Now that's something I'm especially proud of, Frau Gesch!'

'There is such a thing as inhumanity, Frau Kluge, and what you're proposing to do is inhuman. You can't put him out in his condition.'

'And what about the way he treated me over all those years, was that human? He tormented me, he ruined my entire life, and in the end he took away my beloved son from me – and I'm supposed to be human to someone like that, just because the SS has given him a beating? I wouldn't dream of it! All the beatings in the world won't change that man!'

After these angry and vehement words, Frau Kluge slammed the door shut in Frau Gesch's face. She couldn't stand to hear any more. Perhaps to avoid more talk, she might have taken the man into her flat, and then have regretted it ever after!

She sat down in her kitchen chair, stared at the blue gas flame, and thought back over her day. Once she'd told the official that she wanted to leave the Party, effective immediately, there had been no end of talk. He'd begun by taking her off mail delivery duties. And then she had been questioned. At midday, a couple of civilians with briefcases had arrived and interrogated her. She was to tell them her whole life story, her parents, her siblings, her marriage . . .

At first she had been compliant, glad to change the subject after the endless questions about why she wanted to leave the Party. But then, when she was supposed to tell them about her marriage, she had become mulish. After the husband, it would be the turn of her children, and she wouldn't be able to talk about Karlemann without those wily foxes noticing there was something the matter.

No, she'd refused to discuss it. Her marriage and her children were no one's business.

But these men were tough. They had lots of methods. One of them had reached into his briefcase and started reading a file. She would have loved to know what file it was: surely the police wouldn't keep a file like that on her, because she had by now noticed that these civilians had the air of policemen about them.

Then they went back to asking questions. The files must have contained something about Enno, because now she was asked about his illnesses, his shirking, his passion for horses, and his women. It all began harmlessly enough, as before, and then suddenly she saw the danger, and shut her mouth and refused to answer. No, that, too, was something private. That didn't concern anyone. Her dealings with her husband were her affair. Incidentally, she lived alone.

And with that she was trapped again. How long had she been living alone? When was the last time she had seen him? Did her desire to leave the Party have anything to do with him?

She had merely shaken her head. But she shuddered to think that they would probably now question Enno and they would squeeze everything out of that weakling within half an hour. Then she, who had previously kept her shame to herself, would stand exposed for all to see.

'Private! All private!'

Lost in thought, staring at the flickering gas flame, she suddenly jumped. She had made a serious mistake. She should have given Enno money to tide him over for a couple of weeks and told him to go and hide at one of his girlfriends' places.

She rings Frau Gesch's bell. 'Listen, Frau Gesch, I've had another think, I'd like at least to talk to my husband briefly.'

Now that the other woman is doing what she asked of her, Frau Gesch gets upset. 'You should have thought about that earlier. Your husband's been gone for twenty minutes at least. You're too late!'

'Where has he gone, Frau Gesch?'

'How should I know? You're the one who threw him out. I expect to one of his women!'

'And you don't know which one? Please, if you know, Frau Gesch, tell me! It could be very important . . .'

'You have changed your tune!' Reluctantly, Frau Gesch adds, 'He said something about some woman called Tutti . . .'

'Tutti?' she says. 'That must be short for Trudel or Gertrude . . . You wouldn't know her surname, would you, Frau Gesch?'

'He didn't know it himself! He didn't even know where she lived, he just thought he could manage to find her. But in the state the man's in . . .'

'Maybe he will come back,' says Frau Kluge reflectively. 'If he does, send him to me. Anyway, thank you for your help, Frau Gesch, and good evening!'

Frau Gesch doesn't reply, just slams the door back in her face. She hasn't forgotten how she was treated earlier. She's not at all sure she would send the man round, in the event that he does show up again. A woman shouldn't hem and haw, because it can easily become too late.

Frau Kluge returns to her kitchen. It's a strange thing: even though the conversation with Frau Gesch didn't achieve anything, she feels relieved. Things will take their course. She's done what she could to stay clean. She has cut herself off from husband and son, and now she will cut them out of her heart. She has declared her desire to leave the Party. Now whatever happens will happen. She can't change it, and even the worst shouldn't terrify her after what she's already been through.

It didn't terrify her, either, when the two men in suits went from asking her pointless questions to making threats. She did realize, didn't she, that leaving the Party would cost her her job at the post office? And more: if she now left the Party without declaring the reason, that would make her politically unreliable, and for such people there were concentration camps! She must have heard of them? There, politically unreliable individuals could be made reliable in very quick time, reliable for the rest of their days. She surely understood?

Frau Kluge hadn't been afraid. She insisted on her privacy, and refused to discuss private matters. In the end, they let her go. No, her leaving the Party has not yet been accepted; she will hear a decision in due course. But she has been suspended from the postal service. She is required to remain available in her flat should further questioning . . .

As Eva Kluge finally remembers to move the forgotten soup

pot over the gas, she suddenly decides not to obey in this point either. She's not going to sit there helplessly in her flat and wait for her tormentors. No, she will take the early morning train to her sister in Ruppin. She can stay there for two or three weeks without registering. They can feed her somehow. They have a cow and pigs and acres of potatoes. She will work with the animals and in the fields. It will do her good, better than delivering letters day in, day out.

Now that she has decided to go to the country, she finds herself moving around more nimbly. She gets out a small suitcase and begins to pack. For a moment, she wonders whether to tell Frau Gesch that she's going away – she doesn't have to say where she's going. But then she decides it's best not to say anything. Whatever she does, she will do alone. She doesn't want to involve any other person in it. She won't tell her sister and brother-in-law anything either. She will live alone, as never before. So far there has always been someone for her to look after: parents, husband, children. Now she's alone. At this moment it strikes her as very likely that she will enjoy the condition. Perhaps when she's all alone she will amount to more: she'll have some time to herself, and won't need to put herself last, after all the others.

The night that Frau Rosenthal is so afraid to be alone, the postie Eva Kluge smiles in her sleep for the first time in a long time. In her dreams she sees herself standing in a vast field of potatoes with a hoe in her hands. As far as she can see, only potatoes and herself, all alone: she needs to hoe the potatoes. She smiles, picks up her hoe, there's the clink of a pebble, a weed falls, she hoes her own row.

12

Enno and Emil after the Shock

Little Enno Kluge had a much worse time of it than his 'chum' Emil Borkhausen, whose wife, whatever her other shortcomings might be, at least bundled him off to bed following the experiences of that night, even if she did then promptly rob him. The little gambler also got much more knocked about than that long, bony snitch. No, Enno had an especially bad time of it.

While Enno is trotting around the streets, timidly looking for his Tutti, Borkhausen has got up from his bed, gone to the kitchen, and savagely and broodingly eats his fill. Then Borkhausen finds a pack of cigarettes in the wardrobe, slips it in his pocket, and sits down at the table again, pondering gloomily, head in hand.

Which is how Otti finds him when she returns from the shops. Of course she sees right away that he's helped himself to some food, and she knows he didn't have any smokes on him and traces the theft to her wardrobe. Apprehensive as she is, she starts an argument right away. 'Yes, that's my darling, a man who eats my food and snitches my cigarettes! Give them back, I want them back right now. Or pay me for them. Give me some money, Emil!'

She waits to hear what he will say, but she's pretty sure of her ground. The forty-eight marks are almost all spent, and there's not much he can do about it.

And she can tell from his answer, nasty though it is, that he really doesn't know anything about the money. She feels far superior to this man: she's robbed him and the silly jerk hasn't even noticed.

'Shut your face!' grunts Borkhausen, not even lifting his head out of his hands. 'And get out of the room while you're about it, or I'll break every bone in your body!'

She calls back from the kitchen doorway, simply because she always has to have the last word, and because she feels so superior to him (although he does frighten her), 'You should try to keep the SS from breaking all the bones in yours, jackass!'

Then she goes into the kitchen and takes her banishment out on the kids.

The man meanwhile sits in the parlour and thinks. He doesn't remember much about what happened in the night, but the little he recalls will do for him. And he thinks that up there is the Rosenthal flat, which the Persickes have probably picked clean, and it was all there for him, for nights and nights. And it's his own stupid fault it was fouled up.

No, it was Enno's fault, Enno got started on the drink, Enno was drunk right from the off. If it hadn't been for Enno, he would have got a whole heap of stuff, clothes and linen; and dimly he remembers a radio. If he had Enno in front of him now, he would pulverize him, that wretched cowardly twerp who screwed up the whole thing!

A moment later, Borkhausen shrugs his shoulders again. Who is Enno, anyhow? A cowardly parasite who scrounges off women! No, the real one to blame is Baldur Persicke! That rat, that schoolkid of a Hitler Youth leader always intended to betray him. The job was rigged to produce a guilty party, so that they could help themselves to the booty at their leisure. That was a fine scheme on the part of that bespectacled cobra! How could he let himself be beaten by a snotnosed kid like that!

Borkhausen isn't quite sure why he's sitting in his room at home rather than in a detention cell in the Alex.* Something must have interfered with their plan. Dimly he remembers a couple of mysterious figures, but he was too stupefied then to register who they were and what their role was, and he has even less idea now.

But one thing he does know: he's never going to pardon Baldur

---

*Commonly used abbreviation for the Alexanderplatz, a square in central Berlin that was the site of one of the city's major train stations, as well as Berlin's imposing, seven-storey police headquarters.

Persicke for this. He can creep as high as he likes up the ladder of Party favour, but Borkhausen is going to stay alert. Borkhausen has time. Borkhausen won't forget. The louse – one day he'll catch up with him, and then it'll be his turn to grovel! And he'll be grovelling more abjectly than Borkhausen, and he'll never get up out of it either. Betray a partner? No, that will never be forgiven or forgotten! All those fine items in the Rosenthal place, the suitcases and boxes and radio, they could all have been his!

Borkhausen goes on bitterly ruminating, always along the same lines, and in between times he sneaks out Otti's silver hand mirror, a keepsake from a generous john, and examines and gingerly touches his face.

By this time little Enno Kluge, too, has discovered what his face looks like, in a mirror in the window of a dress shop. That has only served to frighten him even more, in fact it throws him into a blind panic. He doesn't dare look anyone in the face, but he has the feeling everyone is staring at him. He pounds the back streets, his search for Tutti is getting more and more hopeless – it's not just that he can't remember where she lives, he has lost his own bearings. Still, he turns in at every entryway and looks up at the windows in the back buildings. Tutti . . . Tutti . . .

Darkness is falling fast, and he has to have found somewhere by nightfall, otherwise the police will take him in, and when they see the state of him, they'll make mincemeat of him till he's confessed everything. And if he confesses the bit about the Persickes (and in his fear he's bound to), then the Persickes will simply beat him to death.

He runs around aimlessly, on and on . . .

Finally, he can't go any further. He comes to a bench and hunkers down there, unable to walk on. He goes through his pockets looking for something to smoke – a cigarette would settle him.

He doesn't find any cigarettes, but he does find something he certainly wasn't expecting, namely, money. Forty-six marks. Frau Gesch could have told him hours ago that he had money in his pockets, to make the timid little man a bit more confident of finding somewhere for the night. But of course Frau Gesch didn't want to admit to having gone through his pockets while he was asleep. She is a respectable woman, and as such – after a little inner struggle – she put the money back in his pocket. If it had been her Gustav, well, she would have confiscated it right away, but she draws the line at robbing a man off the street! Of course, she did take three out of the forty-nine marks she found, but that wasn't theft, that was just payment for the food she gave Kluge. She would have given him the food without the money, but feeding a man for free when he's got money in his pockets? She's not so prodigal as that either.

At any rate, the possession of forty-six marks cheers up the fearful Enno Kluge no end, now he knows he can always rent a room for the night. His memory starts to function better, too. He still can't remember where Tutti used to live, but he suddenly recalls the small café where they met and where she was often to be found. Perhaps they will have an address for her there.

He gets up and trots off again. He sees where he actually is, and when a tram goes by, heading his way, he actually dares get up on the back platform of the first car. It's so dark and crowded there that no one will pay much attention to his battered face. Then he walks into the café. He's not there to eat or drink. He walks right up to the bar and asks the girl there if she knows Tutti, and if Tutti still comes here.

In a shrill loud voice that can be heard all over the bar, the girl asks him what Tutti he means. There was a fair few Tuttis in Berlin!

The shy little man answers awkwardly, 'Oh, the Tutti that always used to come here. A dark-haired lady, a bit on the heavy side . . .'

Oh, that Tutti! No, and they didn't want to see any more of that Tutti, thank you very much. If she dared to show her face here again! In fact, they didn't care if they never heard from her again!

And with that the indignant girl turns away from Enno, who mumbles a few words of apology and scurries out of the café.

He is still standing on the pavement outside, not knowing what to do, when another man comes out of the café, an older man, down and out, as it seems to Enno. He goes up to Enno, pulls himself together, tips his hat to him and asks if he wasn't the gentleman who asked a moment ago after a certain Tutti.

'I might be,' replies Enno Kluge cautiously. 'What's it to you?'

'Oh, just this. I might be able to tell you where she lives. I could even walk you to her flat, but you'd have to do me a little favour!'

'What favour?' asks Enno, even more cautiously. 'I don't know of any favours I could do for you. I don't even know you.'

'Oh, let's just walk a bit!' exclaims the old gentleman. 'No, it's not out of your way if we walk down here. The thing is that Tutti still has in her possession a suitcase full of my belongings. Perhaps you could get the suitcase out to me tomorrow morning, while Tutti's asleep or gone out?'

The elderly gent seems to take it for granted that Enno will be spending the night with Tutti.

'No,' says Enno. 'I won't do that. I don't get involved in business like that. I'm sorry.'

'But I can tell you exactly what's in the suitcase. It really is my suitcase, you know!'

'Why don't you ask Tutti yourself, then?'

'Hah! To hear you talk,' says the man, a little offended, 'it seems you can't know her very well. She's some woman, I thought you knew. Not just hair on her chest, but, my God, hedgehog bristles! She bites and spits like a gorilla – that's why they call her the Gorilla!'

And while the elderly man is painting this glowing portrait of her, Enno Kluge remembers with a start that Tutti really is like that, and that the last time he left her, he left with her purse and her ration cards. She really does bite and spit like a gorilla when she's in a temper, and presumably she will vent her temper on Enno the moment she sees him. His whole idea of being able to spend the night with her was a fantasy, a mirage . . .

And suddenly, from one moment to the next, Enno Kluge

decides that from now on his life is going to be different: no more women, no more petty thieving, no more betting. He has forty-six marks in his pocket, enough to tide him over till next payday. Battered as he is, he's going to give himself tomorrow off, but the day after he'll start working again properly. They'll soon see his worth, and not send him away to the Front again. After all he's been through in the past twenty-four hours, a gorilla tantrum of Tutti's is the last thing he can risk.

'Yes,' says Enno Kluge pensively to the man. 'You're right: that's Tutti, all right. And because that's the way she is, I've decided not to go and see her after all. I'm going to spend the night in the little hotel over the way. Goodnight, sir . . . I'm sorry, but it can't be helped . . .'

And with that he hobbles across the road, and in spite of his battered appearance and lack of luggage, he manages to wheedle a bed out of the impoverished-looking clerk for three marks. In the tiny, stinking hole of a room he crawls into bed, whose sheets have already served many before him. He stretches out and says to himself, I'm going to turn over a new leaf. I've been a mean sonofabitch, especially to Eva, but from this minute I'm going to be a changed man. I deserved the beating I got, and now I'm going to be different . . .

He lies perfectly still in the narrow bed, his hands pressed against his trouser seams, at attention, as it were, staring at the ceiling. He is trembling with cold, with exhaustion, with pain. But he doesn't feel any of it. He thinks about what a respected and well-liked worker he used to be, and now he's just a nasty little creep, the sort that people spit in front of in the street. No, his beating has straightened him out: from now on, everything's going to be different. And as he pictures the difference to himself, he falls asleep.

At this time, all the Persickes are also asleep, Frau Gesch and Frau Kluge are asleep, the Borkhausens are asleep – Emil silently allowed Otti to slip in beside him.

Frau Rosenthal is asleep, frightened and breathing hard. Little Trudel Baumann is asleep. This afternoon, she was able to whisper to one of her co-conspirators that she had an urgent message for them, and they've all arranged to meet discreetly tomorrow at the Elysium. She is a little worried, because she will have to admit to her gabbiness, but for the moment she is asleep.

Frau Anna Quangel is lying in bed in the dark, and her husband, as always at this time of night, is standing in his workshop directing everyone's tasks. They hadn't called him up to the boardroom after all, to hear his suggestions for technical improvements. So much the better!

Anna Quangel, in bed but not yet asleep, still thinks of her husband as cold and heartless. The way he reacted to the news of Ottochen's death, the way he threw poor Trudel and Frau Rosenthal out: cold, heartless, only concerned for himself. She will never be able to love him as before, when she thought he at least had something to spare for her. Clearly, he hasn't. Only offended by her blurted 'You and your Führer', only offended. Well, she won't hurt his feelings again for a while, if only because she won't be speaking to him. Today they didn't exchange a single word, not even hello.

The retired Judge Fromm is still up, because he's always up at night. In his neat hand, he is writing a letter that begins, 'Dear Attorney . . .'

Open under the reading lamp, his Plutarch lies waiting for him.

13

Victory Dance at the Elysium

The floor of the Elysium, the great dance hall in the north of Berlin, that Friday night presented the kind of spectacle that must gladden the heart of any true German: it was jam-packed with uniforms.

While the Wehrmacht with its greys and greens supplied the background to this colourful composition, what made the scene so vibrant were the uniforms of the Party and its various bodies, going from tan, golden brown, brown, and dark brown to black. There, next to the brown shirts of the SA* you saw the much lighter brown of the Hitler Youth; the Organization Todt was as well represented as the Reichsarbeitsdienst; you saw the yellow uniforms of Sonderführer, dubbed golden pheasants; political leaders stood next to air-raid wardens. And it wasn't just the men who were so delightfully accoutred; there were also many girls in uniform; the Bund Deutscher Mädel, the Arbeitsdienst, the Organization Todt – all seemed to have sent their leaders and deputies and rank and file to this place.†

The few civilians present were lost in this swarm. They were insignificant and boring among so many uniforms, just as the civilian population out in the streets and factories never amounted

---

* SA is the 'Sturmabteilung' or 'storm troopers', a paramilitary group that helped bring Hitler to power and whose members were known because of their uniform colour as the 'brown shirts'.

† Organization Todt was a military construction and logistics unit run by Fritz Todt. The RAD, or Reichsarbeitsdienst ('Empire work service') was a six-month forced labour programme for all young Germans, with a component of military training. Sonderführer ('Special leader') was not a specific position in any hierarchy, but conferred as the need arose. A Politischer Leiter, or political leader, was any Nazi Party official. They wore golden brown uniforms. 'Golden pheasant' was a nickname for Hermann Göring, who was given to ostentatious uniforms. The BDM, or Bund Deutscher Mädel (The 'League of German Girls') was the girls' branch of the Hitler Youth, for girls of ten to twenty-one years old.

to anything compared to the Party. The Party was everything, and the people nothing.

Thus, the table at the edge of the dance floor occupied by a girl and three young men received very little attention. None of the four wore a uniform; there wasn't so much as a party badge on display.

A couple, the girl and a young man, had been the first to arrive. Then another young man had asked for permission to join them, and later on a fourth civilian had come forward with a similar request. The couple had made one attempt to dance in the seething mass. While they were away, the other two men had started a conversation in which the returning couple, looking hot and crushed, participated from time to time.

One of the men, a fellow in his early thirties with thin, receding hair, leaned way back in his chair and silently contemplated the crowd on the dance floor and at the other tables. Then, barely looking at his companions, he said, 'A poor choice of venue. We're almost the only civilian table in the whole place. We stick out a mile.'

The girl's partner smiled at her and said – but his words were meant for the balding man – 'Not at all, Grigoleit, we're practically invisible here, and if they do see us, at the most they despise us. The only thing on the minds of these people is that the so-called victory over France has secured them dancing rights for a couple of weeks.'

'No names! You know the rules!' the balding man said sharply.

For a while no one spoke. The girl doodled something on the table and didn't look up, though she could feel they were all looking at her.

'Anyway, Trudel,' said the third man, who had an innocent baby face, 'it's time for whatever you wanted to tell us. What's new? The next-door tables are almost all empty, everyone's dancing. Come on!'

The silence of the other two could only indicate agreement. Haltingly, not looking up, Trudel Baumann said: 'I think I've made a mistake. At any rate, I've broken my word. In my eyes, admittedly, it's not really a mistake . . .'

'Oh, come on!' exclaimed the balding man angrily. 'Are you going to start gabbling like a silly goose? Tell us what it is, straight out!'

The girl looked up. She looked at the three men one after the other, all of them, it seemed to her, eyeing her coldly. There were tears in her eyes. She wanted to speak, but couldn't. She looked for her handkerchief . . .

The man with the receding hairline leaned back. He let out a long, soft whistle. 'I tell her she's not supposed to blab. I'm afraid she already has. Look at her.'

The cavalier at Trudel's side retorted quickly, 'Not possible. Trudel is a good girl. Tell them you haven't blabbed, Trudel!' And he squeezed her hand encouragingly. The Babyface directed his round, very blue eyes expressionlessly at the girl. The tall man with the receding hairline smiled contemptuously. He put his cigarette in the ashtray and said mockingly, 'Well, Fräulein?'

Trudel had got herself under control, and bravely she whispered, 'He's right. I talked out of turn. My father-in-law brought me news of my Otto's death. That somehow knocked me off balance. I told him I was in a cell.'

'Did you name names?' No one would have guessed that the Babyface could ask questions so sharply.

'Of course not. That's all I said, too. And my father-in-law is an old workingman, he'll never say a word.'

'Your father-in-law's the next chapter, you're the first! You say you didn't give any names . . .'

'I'll thank you for believing me, Grigoleit! I'm not lying. I'm freely confessing.'

'You just used a name again, Fräulein Baumann!'

The Babyface said, 'Don't you see it's completely immaterial whether she named a name or not? She said she was involved in a cell, and that means she's blabbed, and will blab again. If the men in black lay hands on her, knock her about a bit, she'll talk, never mind how much or how little she's said so far.'

'I will never talk to them, even if I have to die!' cried Trudel with flaming cheeks.

'Pah!' said the balding man. 'Dying's the easy bit, Fräulein Baumann, sometimes they do rather unpleasant things to you before that!'

'You're unkind,' the girl said. 'Yes, I've done something wrong, but . . .'

'I agree,' said the fellow on the sofa next to her. 'We'll go and see her father-in-law, and if he's a reliable sort . . .'

'Under the torturer's hand there are no reliable sorts,' said Grigoleit.

'Trudel,' said the Babyface with a gentle smile, 'Trudel, you just told us you haven't told anyone any names?'

'And that's the truth, I haven't!'

'And you claimed you would rather die than give us away?'

'Yes, yes, yes!' she exclaimed passionately.

'Well then, Trudel' said the Babyface, and smiled charmingly, 'what if you were to die tonight, before you blabbed any more? That would give us a certain measure of security, and save us a lot of trouble . . .'

A deathly hush descended on the four of them. The girl went white. The boy next to her said 'No,' and laid his hand over hers. But then he took it away again.

The dancers returned to their various tables and for a while made it impossible to continue the conversation.

The balding man lit another cigarette, and the Babyface smiled subtly when he saw how the other's hands were shaking. Then he said to the dark-haired boy next to the pale, silent girl. 'You say no? But why do you say no? It's an almost entirely satisfactory solution to the problem, and as I understand it, was suggested by your neighbour herself.'

'It's not a satisfactory solution,' said the dark-haired boy slowly. 'You'll remember that sentence when the People's Court has you and me and her . . .'

'Quiet!' said the Babyface. 'Go away and dance for a few minutes. It seems like a nice tune. You can discuss things between yourselves there, and we will here.'

Reluctantly, the dark-haired boy got up and bowed lightly to the lady. Reluctantly, she laid her hand on his arm, and the two pale figures headed, with a whole stream of others, to the dance floor. They danced earnestly, in silence, and he had the sense he was dancing with a corpse. He shuddered. The uniforms on all sides of them, the dangling swastikas, the blood-red banners on the walls with the repulsive emblem, the portrait of the Führer tricked out in green: swingtime for Hitler. 'Don't do it, Trudel,' he said. 'He's crazy to ask for something like that. Promise me . . .'

They were almost dancing in place in the ever thickening mass of bodies. Perhaps because there were continual collisions with other couples, she didn't speak.

'Trudel!' he said again. 'Please promise me! You can go to a different company, work there, stay away from them. Promise . . .'

He tried to force her to look at him, but she kept her eyes obstinately directed at a point behind his shoulder.

'You're the best of us,' he said suddenly. 'You're humanity. He's just dogma. You must go on living, don't give in to him!'

She shook her head, whether it was yes or no was unclear. 'I want to go back,' she said. 'I don't feel like dancing any more.'

'Trudel,' said Karl Hergesell hastily as they made their way back through the dancing couples, 'your Otto died yesterday, or at least yesterday you got news of his death. It's too soon. But you know it anyway: I've always loved you. I've never expected anything from you, but now I expect at least that you stay alive. Not for my sake, nothing like that, but, please, just stay alive!'

Once again she moved her head slightly, and it was unclear what she thought of either his love or his wish that she at least remain alive. Then they were back at their table with the others. 'Well?' asked Grigoleit with the receding hair. 'What's the feeling on the dance floor? A bit packed, eh?'

The girl hadn't sat down. She said, 'I'm going now. All the best. I would have liked to work with you . . .'

She turned to leave.

But now the plump, innocent-looking Babyface got up and took her by the wrist, and said, 'One moment, please!' He said it with due politeness, but there was menace in his expression.

They returned to the table and sat down again. The Babyface asked, 'Do I understand correctly what you meant by your goodbye just now?'

'You understood me,' she said, looking back at him with unyielding eyes.

'Then I would like permission to accompany you for the rest of the evening.'

She made a motion of appalled resistance.

He said very politely, 'I don't want to force myself upon you, but I would like you to consider that further mistakes can be made in the execution of such a plan.' He whispered threateningly, 'I don't want to have some idiot fishing you out of a canal, or have you coming round from an attempted overdose in hospital tomorrow morning. I want to be there!'

'That's right!' said the balding one. 'I agree. That's our only insurance . . .'

The dark-haired boy said emphatically, 'I will remain at her side today and tomorrow and every following day. I will do everything I can to foil the execution of such a plan. I will even go to the police for help, if you force me to!'

The balding man whistled again, low, long, and maliciously.

The Babyface said, 'Aha, it seems we have a second blabber among us. In love, eh? I always suspected it. Come on, Grigoleit, this cell is wound up. There is no cell any more. And that's what you call discipline, you women!'

'No, no!' cried the girl. 'Don't listen to him. It's true, he does love me. But I don't love him. And I want to go with you tonight . . .'

'Forget it!' said the Babyface, now furious. 'Can't you see that we're in no position to do anything any more, now that you . . .'

He tipped his head in the direction of the dark-haired boy. 'Ach, who cares!' He then said. 'It's over. Come on, Grigoleit!'

The balding one was already on his feet. Together, they walked toward the exit. Suddenly a hand was laid on the Babyface's arm. He looked into a smooth, slightly puffy face in a brown uniform.

'One moment, please! What was that you just said about a cell being wound up? I would be very interested to know . . .'

The Babyface pulled his arm away. 'You leave me alone!' he said, very loudly. 'If you want to know what we were talking about, ask the young lady over there! Yesterday her fiancé fell, and today she's got the hots for someone else! Bloody women!'

He kept pushing toward the exit, which Grigoleit had already reached. Then he, too, left the premises. The fat man watched him go for a moment. Then he turned back to the table, where the girl and the dark-haired fellow were still sitting, both looking rather pale. That relieved him. *Perhaps I didn't make a mistake in letting him go. He took me by surprise. But . . .*

Politely he asked, 'Would you mind very much if I sat with you for a few minutes and asked you some questions?'

Trudel Baumann replied, 'I can't tell you any more than what the gentleman just said to you. I received news of the death of my fiancé yesterday, and today this gentleman here has asked me to become engaged to him.'

Her voice sounded firm and unwavering. Now that there was danger seated at the table, her fear and unrest were gone.

'Would you mind telling me the name and rank of your fallen fiancé? And his regiment?' She told him. 'And your own name? Address? Place of work? Do you have other documentation on you? Thank you! And now you, sir.'

'I work in the same factory. My name is Karl Hergesell. Here's my pay stub.'

'And the two other gentlemen?'

'Never met them before. They sat down at our table and got involved in our argument.'

'And what were you arguing about?'

'I don't love him.'

'Why was the other gentleman so indignant about you, then, if you don't love him?'

'How do I know? Maybe he didn't believe me. He was annoyed that I agreed to dance with him.'

'I see!' said the chubby face, snapping his notebook shut and looking from one to the other. They really did seem more like a quarrelsome pair of lovebirds than conspirators caught red-handed. Even the way they shyly avoided looking at each other . . . And yet their hands were almost touching on the tabletop. 'I see! Of course we'll have your answers checked, but it seems to me . . . anyway, I wish you a more congenial end to your evening . . .'

'I don't!' said the girl. 'I don't!' She got up simultaneously with the brownshirt. 'I'm going home.'

'I'll take you.'

'No, thanks, I'd rather go alone.'

'Trudel!' the boy begged. 'Just let me say two more words to you!'

The brownshirt smiled from one to the other. They clearly were lovers. A superficial check would do.

Suddenly she made up her mind: 'All right, but only two minutes!'

They walked out. At last they were away from this appalling hall and its atmosphere of concerted hatred. They looked about them.

'They've gone.'

'We will never see them again.'

'And you can live. No, Trudel, you must live! An unconsidered step on your part would plunge the others into danger, many others – always remember, Trudel!'

'Yes,' she said, 'now I must live.' And with a swift decision. 'Goodbye, Karl.'

For an instant she pressed herself against his chest and her lips brushed his. Before he knew what was happening, she was running across the carriageway to a waiting tram. The driver moved off.

He made as if to take off after her. Then he thought better of it.

I will see her in the factory from time to time, he told himself. A whole life lies ahead of us. And I know now that she loves me.

14

Saturday: Discord at the Quangels'

The Quangels didn't speak to each other all of Friday either – that meant three days of silence between them, not even giving each other the time of day. This had never happened in the entire course of their marriage. However laconic Quangel might be, he had managed a sentence from time to time, something about someone at work or at least the weather or that his dinner had tasted particularly good. But none of that now!

The longer it lasted, the more keenly Anna Quangel felt it. Her deep grief for her son was being sidetracked by disquiet about the change in her husband. She wanted to think only of her boy, but she couldn't when she saw Otto in front of her, her husband of so many years, to whom she had given the greater and better part of her life. What had got into the man? What was up with him? What had changed him so?

By midday on Friday Anna Quangel had lost all her rage and reproach against Otto. If she had thought it might accomplish anything, she would have asked him to forgive her for blurting out that sentence about 'You and your Führer'. But it was plain to see that Otto was no longer thinking about that reproach; he didn't even seem to be thinking about her. He seemed to look past her, if not right through her, standing by the window, his hands in the pockets of his work tunic, whistling slowly and reflectively, with long intervals between, which was something he'd never done before.

What was the man thinking about? What was going on inside him? She set down the soup on the table, and he started spooning it down. For a moment she observed him from the kitchen. His sharp bird face was bent low over the bowl, he lifted his spoon mechanically to his mouth, his dark eyes looked at something that wasn't there.

She went back into the kitchen, to heat up an end of cabbage. He liked reheated cabbage. She had decided she would say something to him when she returned with his cabbage. He could answer as sharply as he pleased: she had to break this unholy silence.

But when she came back into the dining room with the warmed-up cabbage, Otto was gone, and his half-eaten dinner was still on the table. Either Quangel had sensed her intention and crept away like a child intent on remaining stubborn, or he had simply forgotten to carry on eating because of whatever it was that was so consuming him. Anyway, he was gone, and she would have to wait till night-time for him to come back.

But on Friday night, Otto returned from work so late that for all her good intentions she was already asleep when he came to bed. It was only later that he woke her with his coughing. Softly, she asked, 'Otto, are you asleep?'

His coughing stopped; he lay there perfectly still. Again she asked, 'Otto, are you asleep already?'

Nothing, no reply. The two of them lay there in silence a very long time. Each knew that the other was not sleeping. They didn't dare move in bed, so as not to give themselves away. Finally, they both fell asleep.

Saturday got off to an even worse start. Otto Quangel had got up unusually early. Before she could put his watery coffee substitute out on the table, he had already set off on one of those rushed, mysterious errands that he had never undertaken before. He came back, and from the kitchen she could hear him pacing around the parlour. When she came in with the coffee, he carefully folded away a large white sheet of paper he had been reading by the window and put it in his pocket.

Anna was sure it wasn't a newspaper. There was too much white on the paper, and the writing was bigger than in a newspaper. What could her husband have been reading?

She got cross with him again, with his secrecy, with these changes that brought with them so much disturbance, and so many fresh anxieties in addition to all the old ones, which had surely been enough. All the same, she said, 'Coffee, Otto!'

At the sound of her voice, he turned and looked at her, as though surprised that he was not alone in the apartment, surprised that he had been spoken to by her. He looked at her, and yet he didn't: it wasn't his spouse, Anna Quangel, he was looking at, so much as someone he had once known and now had to struggle to remember. There was a smile on his face, in his eyes, spreading over the whole expanse of his face in a way she had never seen before. She was on the point of crying out: Otto, oh Otto, don't you leave me too!

But before she had made up her mind, he had walked past her and out of the flat. Once more no coffee, once again she had to take it back to the kitchen to warm it up. She sobbed gently. Oh, that man! Was she going to be left with no one? After the son, was she going to lose the father?

In the meantime, Quangel was walking briskly in the direction of Prenzlauer Allee. It had occurred to him that it was a good idea to look at a building like that properly, to see if his impression of it was at all accurate. Otherwise, he would have to think of something else entirely.

On Prenzlauer Allee, he slowed down; his eye scanned the nameplates on the housefronts as though looking for something specific. On a corner house he saw signs for two lawyers and a doctor, in addition to many other business plates.

He pushed against the door. It was open. Right: no porters in houses with so many visitors. Slowly, his hand on the banister, he climbed the steps, once a grand staircase with oak flooring, which through heavy use and years of war had lost all trace of grandeur. Now it looked merely dingy and worn, and the carpets were long since gone, probably taken in at the beginning of the war.

Otto Quangel passed a lawyer's sign on the first floor, nodded, and slowly walked on up. It wasn't as though he was all alone on the stairway, not at all. People kept passing him – either from behind, or coming down the other way. He kept hearing bells going off, doors slamming, phones ringing, typewriters clattering, people talking.

But in between there was a moment when Otto Quangel was

all alone on the stairs, or at least had his part of the stairs all to himself, when all of life seemed to have withdrawn into the offices. That was the moment to do it. In fact, everything was exactly the way he had imagined it. People in a hurry, not looking each other in the face, dirty windowpanes letting in only a murky grey light, no porter, no one anywhere to take an interest in anyone.

When Otto Quangel had seen the plate of the second lawyer on the first floor, and an arrow pointing visitors up another flight of steps to the doctor's office, he nodded in agreement. He turned around: he had just been to see a lawyer, and now he was leaving the building. No point in looking further: it was exactly the sort of building he needed, and there were thousands upon thousands of them in Berlin.

Foreman Otto Quangel is standing in the street again. A dark-haired young man with a very pale face walks up to him.

'You're Herr Quangel, aren't you?' he asks. 'Herr Otto Quangel, from Jablonski Strasse?'

Quangel utters a stalling 'Mhm?' – a sound that can indicate agreement as much as dissent.

The young man takes it for agreement. 'I am to ask you on behalf of Trudel Baumann,' he says, 'to forget her completely. Also tell your wife not to visit Trudel any more. Herr Quangel, there's no need for you to . . .'

'You tell her,' says Otto Quangel, 'that I don't know any Trudel Baumann and I don't like to be approached by strangers on the street . . .'

His fist catches the young man on the point of the chin, and he crumples like a wet rag. Quangel strides casually through the crowd of people gathering, straight past a policeman, toward a tram stop. The tram comes, he climbs in, and rides two stops. Then he rides back the other way, this time on the front platform of the second car. As he thought: most of the people have gone on their way; ten or a dozen onlookers are still standing in front of a café where the man was probably carried.

He is already conscious again. For the second time in the space of two hours, Karl Hergesell is called upon to identify himself to an official.

'It's really nothing, officer,' he assures him. 'I must have trodden on his toe, and he bopped me one. I've no idea who he was, I'd hardly started apologizing when he caught me.'

Once again, Karl Hergesell is allowed to leave unchallenged, with no suspicion against him. But he realizes that he shouldn't push his luck. The only reason he went to see Trudel's ex-father-in-law was to gauge her safety. Well, where Otto Quangel is concerned, he can set his mind at ease. A tough bird, and a wicked right. And certainly not a chatterbox, in spite of the big beak on him. The way he lit into him!

And for fear that such a man might blab, Trudel had almost been sent to her death. He would never blab – not even to them! And he wouldn't mind about Trudel either, he seemed not to want to know her any more. All the things a sock on the jaw can teach you!

Karl Hergesell now goes to work completely at ease, and when he learns there, by asking discreetly around, that Grigoleit and the Babyface have quit, he draws a deep breath. They're safe now. There is no more cell, but he's not even all that sorry. At least it means that Trudel can live!

In truth, he was never that interested in this political work, but all the more in Trudel!

Quangel takes the tram back in the direction of his home, but he goes past his own stop. Better safe than sorry, and if he still has someone tailing him, he wants to confront him alone and not drag him back home. Anna is in no condition to cope with a disagreeable surprise. He needs to talk to her first. Of course he will do that: Anna has a big part to play in the thing that he is planning. But he has other business to take care of first. Tomorrow is Sunday, and everything has to be ready.

He changes trams again and heads off into the city. No, the young man he silenced with a punch just now doesn't strike Quangel as a great threat. He's not convinced he has any further pursuers, and he's pretty sure the boy was sent by Trudel. She did suggest, after all, that she would have to confess to breaking a sort of vow. Thereupon they will have banned her from seeing him at all, and she sent the young fellow to him as a sort of envoy. All pretty harmless. Childish games for people who have let themselves in for something they don't understand. He, Otto Quangel, understands a little more. He at least knows what he's letting himself in for. And he won't approach this game like a child. He will think about each card before he plays it.

He sees Trudel in front of him again, pressed against the poster of the People's Court in that corridor – clueless. Once again, he has the disturbing feeling he had when the girl's head was crowned by the line, 'in the name of the German people': he can see their names up there instead of those of the strangers – no, no, this is a task for him alone. And for Anna, of course for Anna too. He'll show her who his 'Führer' is!

When he gets to the city centre, Quangel makes a few purchases. He spends only pennies at a time, a couple of postcards, a pen, a couple of engraving nibs, a small bottle of ink. And he distributes his custom among a department store, a Woolworths, and a stationery shop. Finally, after long thought, he buys a pair of thin, worsted gloves, which he gets without a receipt.

Then he sits in one of those big beer halls on the Alexander-platz, drinks a glass of beer, and has a bite to eat, without using his ration cards. It's 1940, the looting of the invaded nations has begun, the German people are suffering no very great hardship. You can still find most things in the shops, and they're not even all that expensive.

As far as the war itself is concerned, it's being fought in foreign countries a long way from Berlin. Yes, from time to time British planes appear over the city. They drop a few bombs, and the next day the populace treks out to view the damage. Most of them laugh at what they see, and say, 'Well, if that's the best they can do, they'll be busy for another hundred years, and meanwhile we'll have removed their cities from the face of the earth!'

That's the way people have been talking, and since France sued for peace, the number of people talking like that has grown considerably. Most people are impressed by success. A man like Otto Quangel, who during a prosperous period quits the ranks, is a rarity.

He sits there. He still has time, he doesn't have to go to the factory yet. But now the stress of the last few days falls away. Now that he's visited that corner building, now that he's made those few small purchases, everything is decided in his mind. He doesn't even need to think about what he still has to do. It'll do itself, the way is open before him. He only needs to follow it. The decisive first few steps have already been taken.

When it's time, he pays and heads out to the factory. Although it's a long way from the Alexanderplatz, he walks. He's spent enough money today, on transport, on little purchases, on food. Enough? Too much! Even though Quangel has decided on a whole new life, he won't change his old habits. He will remain frugal, and will keep people away from him.

And then he's back at work, alert and awake, laconic and unapproachable as ever. There's no visible sign of the change in him.

15

Enno Kluge Goes back to Work

When Otto Quangel turned up for work in the carpentry factory, Enno Kluge had already been standing at his lathe for six hours. Yes, the little man couldn't stay in bed any longer, and in spite of his pain and his weakness he travelled to work. His welcome there was admittedly not that friendly, but what else could he expect?

'Ah, this is a rare pleasure, Enno!' his supervisor exclaimed. 'How long are you planning on staying this time, one week or two?'

'I'm completely fit and healthy again, boss,' Enno Kluge eagerly assured him. 'I'm able to work, and I will work, as you'll see!'

'Well,' said his boss, unconvinced, and made as if to go. But he stopped a moment longer, looked Enno in the face appraisingly, and asked, 'What've you done to your face? You look like you've been put through a mangle . . .'

Enno keeps his face down over the piece he's working on and doesn't look up as he finally replies, 'Yes, that's right, boss, a mangle . . .'

The boss stands there thoughtfully and goes on studying him. Finally, he thinks he can make sense of the whole thing, and he says, 'Well, maybe it's done the trick, and helped you recover some enthusiasm for work!'

With that, the supervisor moved off, and Enno Kluge was happy that his beating had been taken in that way. Let him think he had been roughed up for shirking, so much the better! He didn't want to discuss it with anyone anyway. And if they all thought that, they wouldn't bother him too much with their questions. At the most, they would laugh about him behind his back, and he thought: Let them, I don't care. He wanted to work, and he wanted to astonish them!

With a modest smile, and yet not without pride, Enno Kluge put himself down for the voluntary extra shift on Sunday. A couple of older colleagues, who remembered him from before, made cynical remarks. He just laughed along, and was glad to see the boss grinning too.

The boss's erroneous assumption that he had been beaten up for shirking had certainly helped with the management as well. He was summoned up there straight after the lunch break. He stood as though in the dock, and the fact that one of his judges was in a Wehrmacht uniform, one in an SA uniform, and only one in a suit, admittedly also decorated with army insignia, only served to heighten his fear.

The Wehrmacht officer browsed in a file, and in a voice equally bored and disgusted proceeded to throw the book at him. On such and such a day released from the Wehrmacht to the armaments industry, first reported in the appropriate works on such and such, worked for eleven days, reported sick with stomach bleeding, used the services of three doctors and two hospitals. Such and such reported fit for work, worked for five days, took three days off, worked for one day, reported recurrence of stomach bleeding, etc., etc.

The Wehrmacht officer put away the file. He looked with disgust at Kluge, or rather he fixed his eyes on the top button of his jacket and said with raised voice, 'What do you think you're playing at, you rat?' Suddenly he was screaming, but you could tell he was a habitual screamer, without any inner excitement. 'Do you think you can fool a single one of us with your stomach bleeding? I'll send you off to a punishment company, and they'll pull your stinking guts out of your body, and then you'll learn what stomach bleeding is!'

The officer went on shouting in a similar vein for quite some time. Enno was used to that from the military; it didn't especially impress him. He listened to the lecture, hands correctly at his trouser seams, eye attentively on his scolder. When the officer stopped to draw breath, Enno said in the prescribed tone, clear and distinct, neither humble nor too cheeky, 'Yes, First Lieutenant! Whatever you say, First Lieutenant!' At one point he was even able to push in the sentence – admittedly without any visible effect – 'Beg permission to report, sir, volunteering for work. Ready and willing to work, sir!'

The officer stopped just as suddenly as he had begun. He shut his mouth, took his gaze off Kluge's top button and redirected it to his neighbour in brown. 'Anything else?' he asked, with disgust.

Yes, it seemed this gentleman also had something to say, or rather to scream – because all these commanding officers seemed only able to scream at their men. This one screamed about betrayal of the people and sabotage, of the Führer who wouldn't tolerate any traitors in the ranks, and concentration camps where he would get his comeuppance.

'And how have you come to us?' screamed the brownshirt suddenly. 'Look at the state of you, pig! Is this how you show up for work? Whoring around with girls! Come here sapped and drained, and we have the privilege of paying you! Where've you been, where did you get yourself those bruises, you miserable pimp!'

'They worked me over,' said Enno, shy under the other's gaze.

'Who, who was it who worked you over, that's what I want to know!' screamed the brownshirt. And he brandished his fist under Enno's nose and stamped his feet.

The moment had come when any kind of thought left Enno Kluge's skull. Threatened with fresh blows, he was deserted by caution and good intentions and whispered, trembling, 'Beg to report, sir, the SS worked me over.'

There was something so convincing in the man's fear that the tribunal immediately believed him. A comprehending, approving smile spread over their faces. The brownshirt screamed, 'You call that worked over? Punishment is the term for that, just punishment. What is it?'

'Beg to report, sir, just punishment!'

'Well, bear it in mind. Next time you won't get off so easily! Dismissed!'

For the next half hour Enno Kluge was shaking so hard that he couldn't work at his lathe. He hung around the lav, where the boss finally ran him to ground and chased him back to work with a tongue-lashing. He stood next to him, and watched as Enno wrecked one piece after another with his clumsiness. Everything was spinning round in the little fellow's head: the scolding from the boss, the mockery of his colleagues, the threat of concentration camp and punishment battalion; he could see nothing clearly. His normally deft hands let him down. He couldn't work, and yet he had to, otherwise he would be completely lost.

Finally the supervisor saw it himself, that this wasn't ill will and shirking. 'If you hadn't just been off sick, I would say go home to bed for a couple of days and get well.' With those words, the supervisor left him. And he added, 'Mind you, you know what would happen to you if you did that!'

Yes, he knew. He carried on, tried not to think of his pain, the unbearable pressure in his head. For a while, the shimmering, spinning iron drew him magically into its spell. All he need do was hold his fingers there and he would have peace, get put to bed, could lie there, rest, sleep, forget! But then he remembered that wilful self-mutilation was punishable by death, and his hand recoiled . . .

That was it: death in the punishment battalion, death in a concentration camp, death in a prison yard, those were the outcomes that daily threatened him, that he had to try and keep at bay. And he had so little strength . . .

Somehow the afternoon passed, and somehow, a little after five, he found himself in the stream of those going home. He had so longed for quiet and rest, but once he was standing in his cramped little hotel room again, he couldn't manage to put himself to bed. He trotted off again, and bought himself a few provisions.

And then the room again, the food on the table in front of him, the bed beside him – and it was more than he could do to stay there. He felt cursed, he just couldn't stand to be in that room. He needed to buy some toilet articles, and try to get hold of a blue work shirt at some second-hand stall.

Off he trotted again, and as he stood in a chemist's shop, he remembered that he had left a large, heavy suitcase full of things at Lotte's, when her husband returned on furlough and so roughly threw him out. He ran out of the chemist's, got on a streetcar, and chanced it: he went straight to Lotte's place. He couldn't abandon all his things there! He dreaded getting a beating, but he had to go, he had to go to Lotte's.

And he was in luck. Lotte was at home and her husband was away. 'Your stuff, Enno?' she said. 'I put it all down in the cellar, so that he wouldn't see it. Wait, I'll find the key!'

But he clutched at her, pressed his head against her thick bosom. The strains of the past few weeks had been too much for him, and he started crying.

'Oh, Lotte, Lotte, I can't stand it without you! I miss you so much!'

His whole body was convulsed with sobbing. She was taken aback. She was used to men of all shapes and sizes and types, including even a few weepers, but then they were drunk, whereas this one was sober . . . And all that talk of missing her and not managing without her, it was ages since anyone had said something to her like that! If they ever had!

She calmed him down as well as she could. 'He's only here for three weeks on his furlough, and then you can come back to me, Enno! Now pull yourself together, and get your things before he comes back. I don't need to remind you!'

No, he knew only too well what threatened him!

She took him to the tram, and carried his case.

Enno Kluge rode back to his hotel, feeling a little better. Only three weeks, four days of which were already up. Then the man would be back at the Front, and he would be able to sleep in his bed! Enno had imagined he could get by without women, but he couldn't, it was beyond him. He would visit Tutti in that time; he saw that if you put on a show and cried, then they weren't so bad. They even helped you right away! Maybe he could stay the three weeks at Tutti's. The lonely hotel room was too awful!

But even with the women, he would work, work, work! He wouldn't pull any stunts any more, not he! He was cured!

16

The Demise of Frau Rosenthal

On Sunday morning, Frau Rosenthal woke with a scream from deep sleep. Once again, she had had the horrible recurring nightmare: she was on the run with her Siegfried. They were hiding, and their pursuers walked right past them, even though the two were so badly hidden, she felt the men must be toying with them.

Suddenly Siegfried started running, and she set off after him. She couldn't run as fast as he could. She cried out, 'Not so fast, Siegfried! I can't keep up! Don't leave me behind!'

He lifted up off the ground, he flew. Flew at first just a few feet above the cobbles, but then higher and higher, until finally he disappeared over the rooftops. She was all alone on Greifs-walder Strasse. Tears ran down her face. A big, smelly hand snuck out and covered her face, and a voice hissed in her ear, 'Now I've got you at last, you Jewish bitch!'

She stared at the blackout screen in front of the window, at the daylight trickling in through the cracks. The terrors of the night faded before those of the day ahead. Another day! Once again, she had missed the judge, the only person in the world she could talk to! She had been determined to stay awake, but she had fallen asleep again. Another day alone, twelve hours, fifteen hours! Oh, she could stand no more of it! The walls of the room closing in on her, always the same face in the mirror, always counting the same bills – no, she couldn't go on like that any more. Even the very worst couldn't be as bad as being locked in alone, with nothing to do.

Quickly Frau Rosenthal gets dressed. Then she goes to the door. She draws the bolt, quietly opens the door, and peers out into the corridor. Everything is quiet in the apartment, and in the rest of the house. The children are not yet making their racket outside – it must be very early still. Perhaps the judge is still in his library? Then she can say good morning to him, exchange two or three sentences with him to gain the courage to withstand the unending day?

She risks it – in spite of his interdiction, she risks it. She crosses the corridor and goes into his room. She shrinks back from the brightness streaming in through the open windows, from the street, from the public life that seems to be here, along with the fresh air. But even more she shrinks back from a woman who is running a carpet sweeper back and forth over the Zwickau rug. She is a bony old woman; the kerchief tied round her head and the carpet sweeper confirm that this is his cleaning woman.

At Frau Rosenthal's entry, the woman stops her work. She first stares at the unexpected visitor, blinking rapidly, as though not quite believing her eyes. Then she props the carpet sweeper against the table and starts flapping her arms and hands at her, while going 'Shh! Shh!' to her as though shooing chickens.

Frau Rosenthal, already in retreat, says pitifully, 'Where is the judge? I must speak to him for a moment!'

The woman frowns and shakes her head violently. Then she embarks on a fresh round of hand flapping and 'Shh! Shh!' sounds, until Frau Rosenthal has gone back into her room. There, while the cleaning woman gently shuts the door, she collapses into the chair by the table and bursts into tears. All for nothing! Another day condemning her to lonely, senseless waiting! A lot of things are happening in the world – maybe Siegfried is dying right now or a German bomb is killing Eva – but she is condemned to sit in the dark and do nothing.

She shakes her head mutinously: she's not going to go on like this any more. She just won't! If she's going to be unhappy, and persecuted, and live in fear, then at least she'll do it in her own way. Let the door close behind her for ever; she can't do anything to prevent it. His hospitality was well-intentioned, but it's not for her.

When she's standing beside her door again, she reflects. She goes back to the table and picks up the heavy gold bracelet with the sapphires. Maybe . . .

But the cleaning woman is no longer in the study, and the windows have been closed again. Frau Rosenthal stands in the corridor, near the front door, and waits. Then she hears the sound of crockery, and she goes towards the sound till she finds the woman in the kitchen, washing up.

She holds out the bracelet to her and says haltingly, 'I really must speak to the judge. Take it, please take it!'

The servant has furrowed her brow at this latest disturbance. She casts a fleeting glance at the bracelet. Then she starts to shoo her away again, with those rowing motions of her arms and the 'Ssh! Ssh!' sounds. Put to flight, Frau Rosenthal goes back to her room. She sinks down beside the bedside table; out of the drawer she takes the sleeping pills the judge gave her.

She hasn't taken any of them yet. Now she shakes them all out, as many as there are, twelve or fourteen, into the hollow of her hand, goes over to the washstand, and washes them all down with a glass of water . . . Now she will be able to speak to the judge in the evening, and learn what she must do. She lies down on the bed, fully clothed, the blanket pulled up halfway. Still lying on her back, her eyes turned up to the ceiling, she waits for sleep to come to her.

And it seems to be coming. The tormenting thoughts, the recurring visions of terror born from the fear in her brain, fade. She shuts her eyes, her limbs relax, grow heavy, she has almost found safety in sleep . . .

But then, on the edge of sleep, it's as though a hand jolts her back into wakefulness. She starts, she feels such a powerful shock. Her body shudders as in a sudden cramp . . .

And again she's lying on her back, staring at the ceiling, the same mill churning out the same tormenting thoughts and images. Then – gradually – it slows, her eyes fall shut, sleep is at hand. Then once again, on the threshold, the jolt, the shock, the cramp that comes over her whole body. Once again, she is expelled from peace, quiet, oblivion . . .

After the third or fourth time, she no longer expects sleep to come. She gets up, walks slowly, a little unsteadily, to the table, and sits down. She stares into space. She knows that the white thing in front of her is the letter to Siegfried that she began three days ago; she has only written a few lines. She sees more: she sees the banknotes, the jewels. At the back of the table is the tray with her food for today. Normally, she would throw herself at it ravenously, but now she just eyes it indifferently. She doesn't feel like eating . . .

While she sits here like this, she has a dim sense that it's the sleeping pills that have wrought this change in her: they weren't able to put her to sleep, but they have at least taken away the desperate panic of the morning. She sits there like that, and sometimes she almost nods off in her chair, but then she jumps again. Time has passed, she doesn't know if it's a lot or a little, but some of this terrible day must have passed . . .

Then, later, she hears a footfall on the stairs. She collapses – in an instant of self-scrutiny, she tries to ascertain whether it's even possible for her to hear sounds on the stairs from this room. But the critical minute is already over, and she merely listens tensely to the sound of the person dragging himself slowly up the steps, continually stopping, coughing lightly, and then dragging himself further along by the banister.

Now she doesn't just hear Siegfried, she sees him, too. She sees him very clearly, as he makes his way up the still quiet staircase to their apartment. Of course they've abused him again, he has a couple of bandages carelessly thrown around his head, already bled through, and his face is bruised and splotchy from their blows. Siegfried is struggling to climb the stairs. His chest is whistling and wheezing, his chest hurt by their kicks. She sees Siegfried turn the corner of the staircase . . .

For a while she continues to sit. Most probably she has nothing on her mind, certainly not the judge and her agreement with him. She needs to get up to the apartment – what will Siegfried think if he finds it empty? – but she is so terribly tired, it's almost impossible to lever herself up out of the chair!

Finally she's on her feet. She takes the bunch of keys out of her handbag, reaches for the sapphire bracelet as if it were a talisman that could protect her – and slowly and uncertainly she makes her way out of the apartment. The door shuts behind her.

The judge, woken after long hesitation on the part of his cleaning woman, comes too late to keep his guest from this excursion into a too dangerous world.

He softly opens the outer door, stands for a while in the open doorway, listens above, listens below. Then, when he hears a sound, namely the swift energetic tramp of boots, he retreats into his apartment. But he doesn't leave the peephole. If there's a chance of saving the unhappy woman, he will open his door to her again, in spite of all the danger.

Frau Rosenthal isn't even aware of passing anyone on her way up the stairs. She is driven by one thought, and one thought only, which is to reach the apartment and Siegfried as quickly as possible. But the Hitler Youth commander Baldur Persicke, on his way to morning roll call, stands there open-mouthed with astonishment as the woman almost brushes past him. Frau Rosenthal, that Frau Rosenthal who has been missing so many days, up and about this Sunday morning, in a dark stitched blouse and *no star*, a bunch of keys and a bracelet in one hand, laboriously dragging herself up the banister with the other – that's how drunk she is! Early on Sunday morning, and already drunk out of her skull.

For an instant, Baldur stays where he is, completely dumbfounded. But when Frau Rosenthal turns the corner of the stairs, his mental powers return to him, and his mouth snaps shut. He has the feeling that the moment has come – he mustn't make a mistake now! No, this time he will take care of the thing himself, and no one, not his father or brothers or Borkhausen, is going to foul it up for him.

Baldur waits till he is sure Frau Rosenthal has reached the Quangels' floor, then creeps quietly back into his parents' flat. Everyone is still asleep, and the telephone is in the hallway. He picks up the receiver and dials, then asks for a particular number. He is in luck: even though it's Sunday, he gets put through, and to the right man. He quickly says his piece, then moves a chair over to the door, opens the door a crack, and prepares to sit and wait for half an hour or an hour, to be sure the quarry doesn't slip away again . . .

At the Quangels' only Anna is up and about, quietly pottering around the flat. In between she looks in on Otto, who is still fast asleep. He looks tired and tormented, even now, in sleep. As though something is leaving him no peace. She stands there and looks thoughtfully at the face of the man she has lived with day after day for almost thirty years. She has long since grown used to the face, the sharp birdlike profile, the thin, almost always shut mouth – it no longer frightens her, any of it. He's the man to whom she has given virtually her whole life. Looks aren't important . . .

But this morning she gets the impression that the face has become even sharper, the mouth even thinner, the furrows on either side of the nose even more deeply etched. He is worried, deeply worried, and she neglected to talk to him in time, to help him carry his load. This Sunday morning, four days after she received the news of the death of her son, Anna Quangel is once again firmly convinced not only that she has to stick it out with this man, but that her obstinacy was wrong in the first place. She ought to have known him better: he always preferred silence to speech. She always had to encourage him to speak – the man would never say anything of his own free will.

Well, today he will speak to her. He said he would, last night, on his return from work. Anna had had a bad day. When he ran off without any breakfast after she had spent hours waiting for him, and when he didn't come home for dinner, when she realized that his shift had begun and he certainly wouldn't come back until late, she had been in despair.

What had come over the man, ever since she let slip that unconsidered phrase? What drove him so remorselessly on? She knew him: ever since she'd said it, he'd been thinking only of how to prove to her that it was not 'his' Führer at all. As if she had ever seriously meant it! She should have told him she had only said it in the first rush of grief and rage. She could have said quite other things about those crooks who had senselessly robbed her of her son's life – but that happened to be the form of words that escaped her.

But now she had said it, and now he was here and there, running all sorts of risks to prove himself right and to show her, quite concretely if possible, how wrong she had been! Perhaps he wouldn't be back. Perhaps he had already said or done something that got the factory management or the Gestapo on his case – maybe he was already in prison! Restless as that calm man had been so early in the morning!

Anna Quangel can't stand it, she can't wait idly for him. She butters a couple of slices of bread, and sets off for the factory. She takes her wifely duties so seriously that even now, where every minute matters that will set her mind at rest, she doesn't take the tram. No, she walks – saving their pennies, as he does.

From the gatekeeper at the furniture factory she learns that Foreman Quangel had come in to work as punctually as ever. She has someone take him the bread and butter he 'forgot', and she waits for the person to return. 'Well, what did he say?'

'What do you mean, what did he say? He never says anything!'

Now she can go home with her mind at rest. Nothing has happened yet, despite all the chaos this morning. And tonight she will speak to him . . .

He comes home. She can see from his face how tired he is.

'Otto,' she beseeches him, 'I didn't mean it like that. It's just something that slipped out during my immediate reaction. Please don't be cross any more!'

'Me – cross with you? On account of something like that? Never!'

'But there's something you want to do, I can sense it! Otto, don't do it, don't plunge yourself into misfortune over something like that! I could never forgive myself.'

He looks at her for a moment, nearly smiling. Then he quickly lays both his hands on her shoulders. Quickly he takes them away again, as though ashamed of his spontaneous tenderness.

'What I want to do now is sleep! Tomorrow I'll tell you what *we* are going to do.'

And now it's tomorrow, and Quangel is still asleep. But another half hour or so doesn't matter so much now. He is here with her, he can't do anything that would get him into trouble, he is asleep.

She turns away from his bed and does a few little chores around the house.

By now Frau Rosenthal has reached her front door, in spite of her slow progress. She is not surprised to find the door locked – she unlocks it. She pays no attention to the wild disorder of the place, nor does she spend a lot of time in the flat looking for Siegfried, or calling to him; she has already forgotten that she came upstairs to follow her husband.

Her numbness is growing, growing all the time. You couldn't say she was asleep, but she's not awake either. Just as she can only move her heavy limbs slowly and clumsily, so, too, her mind feels heavy and numb. Pictures come up like snowflakes and dissolve before she can see what they are. She is sitting on the sofa, her feet resting on scattered linen, looking about her slowly and muzzily. In her hand she still has the keys and the sapphire bracelet Siegfried gave her at Eva's birth. The takings of an entire week . . . She smiles faintly to herself.

Then she hears the front door being carefully opened, and she knows: That's Siegfried. Here he is. That's why I came up here. I'll step out to meet him.

But she remains sitting where she is, a smile spread over the whole of her grey face. She will receive him here, sitting down, as though she had never been away, had always been sitting here to welcome him.

The door opens, but instead of the expected Siegfried, there are three men in the doorway. As soon as she sees a detested brown uniform among them, she knows: This isn't Siegfried. Siegfried won't be here. A slight fear stirs in her, but really only very slight. Now it's time!

Slowly the smile disappears from her face, which changes colour from grey to a greeny yellow.

The three men are directly in front of her. She hears a big, heavy man in a black cloak say, 'Not drunk, my boy. Probably an overdose of sleeping pills. Let's try to see what we can get out of her. Listen, are you Frau Rosenthal?'

She nods. 'That's right, gentlemen, Lore, or strictly speaking Sara Rosenthal. My husband's in prison in Moabit, I have two sons in the USA, a daughter in Denmark, and another in England . . .'

'And how much money have you sent them?' Detective Inspector Rusch asks quickly.

'Money? Why money? They all have plenty of money! Why would I send them money?'

She nods seriously. Her children are all comfortably off. They could quite easily take responsibility for their parents as well. Suddenly she remembers something she has to say to these gentlemen. 'It's my fault,' she says with a clumsy tongue that feels heavier and heavier in her mouth, and starts to babble, 'it's all my fault. Siegfried wanted to flee Germany long ago. But I said to him, 'Why leave all the lovely things behind, why sell the good business here for a pittance? We've done nothing to hurt anyone, they won't do anything to us.' I persuaded him, otherwise we would have been long gone!'

'And what have you done with the money?' the inspector asks, a little more impatiently.

'The money?' She tries to think. There was some left somewhere. Where did it get to? But concentrating is a strain for her, so she thinks of something else. She holds out the sapphire bracelet to the inspector. 'There!' she says simply. 'There!'

Inspector Rusch casts a swift look at it, then looks round at his two companions, the alert Hitler Youth leader and his own regular number two, that fat lump Friedrich. He sees the two of them are watching him tensely. So he knocks the hand with the bracelet impatiently aside, takes the heavy woman by the shoulders, and shakes her hard. 'Wake up, Frau Rosenthal!' he shouts. 'That's an order! I'm telling you to wake up!'

He lets her go, and her head lolls against the back of the sofa, her body sags – her tongue lisps something incomprehensible. This method of bringing her round seems not to have been the right one. For a while the three men look silently at the old

woman slumped on the sofa, not recovering her consciousness.

The inspector suddenly whispers very quietly, 'Why don't you
take her back to the kitchen with you, and wake her up!'

The assistant executioner Friedrich merely nods. He picks the
heavy woman up with one arm and carefully clambers with her
over the obstacles on the floor.

When he reaches the door, the inspector calls after him, 'And
keep it quiet, will you! I don't want any noise on Sunday morning
in a tenement. Otherwise we'll do it in Prinz Albrecht Strasse.*
I'll be taking her back there later anyway.'

The door shuts behind them, and the inspector and Hitler
Youth leader are alone.

Inspector Rusch stands by the window and looks down at the
street below. 'Quiet street, this,' he says. 'A real play street, eh?'

Baldur Persicke affirms that it is indeed a quiet street.

The inspector is a little nervous, but not because of the business involving Friedrich and the old Jewess in the kitchen. Pah,
worse things happen every day of the week. Rusch is a lawyer
manqué, who made his way into the police service. Later, he
graduated to the Gestapo. He likes his work. He would have
liked his work under any regime, but the brisk methods of the
present lot suit him down to the ground. 'Don't get sentimental,'
he sometimes tells newcomers. 'We have certain objectives. The
way we get there doesn't matter.'

No, the old Jewess doesn't bother the inspector at all – he
doesn't have any of that sentimentality in him.

But this boy here, Hitler Youth leader Persicke, is cramping
his style a bit. He doesn't like outsiders present at any action;
you never know how they'll react. This one, admittedly, seems
to be the right sort, but you really only know for sure when the
job's done.

'Did you notice, Inspector,' asks Baldur Persicke keenly – he
tries to ignore the sounds coming from the kitchen, that's their
affair! – 'did you notice she wasn't wearing her Jewish star?'

* Gestapo headquarters was located at number 8 Prinz Albrecht Strasse.

'I noticed more than that,' the inspector says. 'I noticed, for instance, that the woman's shoes are clean, and it's horrible weather outside.'

'Yes.' Baldur Persicke nods uncomprehendingly.

'So someone in the building must have been keeping her hidden since Wednesday, if she really hasn't been up to her flat for as long as you say.'

'I'm fairly certain,' says Baldur Persicke, a little confused by the thoughtful gaze still being levelled at him.

'Fairly certain means nothing, my boy,' says the inspector contemptuously. 'There's no such thing.'

'I'm completely sure, then,' says Baldur quickly. 'I am willing to testify on oath that Frau Rosenthal has not set foot in her flat since Wednesday.'

'All right, all right,' says the inspector, a little dismissively. 'You must know, of course, that by yourself you couldn't possibly have kept the flat under observation since Wednesday. No judge would take your word on that.'

'I have two brothers in the SS,' says Baldur Persicke eagerly.

'All right.' Inspector Rusch is content. 'It'll all take its course. But what I wanted to say to you is that I won't be able to have the apartment searched till tonight. Perhaps you would continue to keep the place under observation? I take it you have keys?'

Baldur Persicke assures him happily that he'll be delighted. His eyes shine with joy. Well, now – this was the other way, didn't he know it, all perfectly legal and above board.

'It would be nice,' the inspector drawls on, looking out of the window again, 'if everything was left lying around like it is now. Of course, you're not responsible for what's in wardrobes and boxes, but other than that . . .'

Before Baldur can get out a reply, there is a high, shrill scream of terror from inside the apartment.

'Damn!' says the inspector, but he makes no move.

Pale, Baldur stares at him. His knees feel like jelly.

The scream is stifled right away, and now all that can be heard is Friedrich cursing.

'What I wanted to say . . .' the inspector begins again.

But his voice trails off. Suddenly there's very loud cursing in the kitchen, footfalls, a running hither and thither. Now Friedrich is yelling at the top of his voice, 'Will you keep still! Will you!'

Then a loud scream. Worse cursing. A door is yanked open, boots thud across the hall, and Friedrich yells into the room, 'Well, what do you say to that, Inspector? I had just got her to the point of talking sensibly, and the bitch goes and jumps out the window on me!'

The inspector slaps him across the face. 'You goddamned fool, I'll have your guts for garters! Run, move!'

And he plunges out of the room, races down the stairs . . .

'In the yard!' Friedrich shouts after him. 'She fell in the yard, not on the street! There won't be no trouble, Inspector!'

He gets no answer. All three are running down the stairs, trying to make as little noise as possible on this quiet Sunday morning. The last of them, half a flight behind the others, is Baldur Persicke. He had the presence of mind to shut the Rosenthals' door after him. He is still in shock, but at least there is the consolation that he has all those beautiful things in his keeping. Nothing had better get lost!

The three go running past the Quangels' flat, past the Persickes', past retired judge Fromm's. Two more flights, and they're in the courtyard.

Otto Quangel had got up and washed, and was watching his wife make breakfast in the kitchen. After breakfast they would have their conversation so far they had only wished each other a good morning, but that was something.

Suddenly the two of them give a start. In the kitchen overhead, there's shouting and yelling, and they listen, each looking at the other with concern. Then their kitchen window is darkened for a second, something heavy plunges past – and they hear it land with a crash in the yard. Downstairs someone yells – a man. Then deathly silence.

Otto Quangel pulls the kitchen window open, but retreats when he hears the tramp of people coming down the stairs.

'Will you put your head out here, Anna!' he says. 'See if you

can see anything. A woman attracts less notice.' He takes her
by the shoulder, and presses her very hard. 'Don't scream!' he
commands. 'You mustn't scream. There, now shut the window
again!'

'God, Otto!' wheezes Frau Quangel, and stares at her
husband with a white face. 'Frau Rosenthal's fallen out of the
window. She's lying down in the yard. Borkhausen is standing
by her, and . . .'

'Enough!' he says. 'Quiet, now. We don't know anything. We
haven't seen or heard anything. Take the coffee into the parlour!'

And, once there, with emphasis, 'We don't know anything,
Anna. Hardly ever saw Frau Rosenthal. And now eat! Eat, I tell
you. And drink coffee! If anyone comes by, they're not to notice
anything out of ordinary!'

Judge Fromm had remained at his observation post. He had
seen two civilians going up the stairs, and now three men – the
Persicke boy was now with them – were charging down them.
Something had happened, and now his cleaning woman was
coming from the kitchen with the news that Frau Rosenthal had
just fallen into the courtyard. He looked at her in consternation.

For a moment he stood there perfectly still. Then he slowly
nodded his head.

'Yes, Liese,' he said. 'That's it. You can't just want to rescue
someone: they have to agree to be rescued.' And then quickly:
'Is the kitchen window shut?' Liese nodded. 'Hurry, Liese, and
tidy my daughter's room; no one must see that it's been used.
Plates out! Clothes out!'

Again, Liese nodded.

Then she asked, 'What about the money and the jewels on
the table, Judge?'

For a moment he stood there almost helplessly, looking
wretched, with a perplexed smile on his face. 'Well, Liese,' he
said. 'That'll be difficult. I don't suppose any heirs will come
forward. And for us it's just a burden . . .'

'Shall I put it in the bin,' suggested Liese.

He shook his head. 'No, they're too smart for that, Liese,' he

said. 'That's their speciality, rummaging around in dirt! I'll think
of something. But in the meantime, you get on with the room.
They could be here any minute!'

For now, though, they were still standing in the courtyard,
with Borkhausen.

Borkhausen had got the first and the worst of the shock. He
had been hanging around the courtyard from early morning,
racked by his hatred of the Persickes and his lust for the lost
things. He wanted to monitor events – and so he was keeping
the staircase under constant supervision, the windows at the
front . . .

Suddenly something fell very close to him, brushing past him
from a great height. He was so shocked that he collapsed against
the wall, and then he had to sit on the ground, because everything was going black in front of his eyes.

Then he jumped up again, because suddenly he was aware
that Frau Rosenthal was lying next to him in the courtyard. God,
so the old woman had thrown herself out of the window, and
he knew who was to blame for it, too.

Borkhausen could see right away that the woman was dead.
She had a little trickle of blood coming out of her mouth, but
that barely disfigured her. On her face was an expression of such
deep peace that the wretched little snoop had to look away. Then
his gaze lit on her hands, and he saw that she was holding something in one of them, a piece of jewellery, something with shining
stones.

Borkhausen cast a suspicious look around him. If he was to
do anything, he had to do it quickly. He stooped; then, turning
away from the dead woman so that he didn't have to look her
in the face, he pulled the sapphire bracelet from her grip and
dropped it into his pocket. Again, he looked around suspiciously.
He had a sense of the kitchen window at the Quangels' being
gently closed.

And already there they came, running across the courtyard,
three men, two of whom he recognized immediately. What was
important now was that he manage to behave correctly from
the start.

'Er, Inspector, Frau Rosenthal has just thrown herself out of the window,' he said, as though reporting a perfectly ordinary event. 'She almost landed on top of me.'

'How do you know me?' asked the inspector casually, while he and Friedrich bent down over the body.

'I don't know you at all, Inspector,' said Borkhausen. 'I just thought maybe that's what you were. Because I get to do little jobs for your colleague Inspector Escherich sometimes.'

'Is that right?' said the inspector. 'Well, then. Perhaps you'll stick around a bit. You, lad,' he turned to Persicke, 'will you keep an eye on this fellow, and make sure he doesn't disappear off somewhere. Friedrich, see to it that no one comes into the courtyard. Tell the driver to block the front entrance. I'll just go upstairs to your flat and make a phone call!'

By the time Inspector Rusch returned from telephoning, the situation in the courtyard had changed a little. In all the windows of the back building there were faces, there were even a couple of people up on the roof – but some way off. The corpse had been covered with a sheet, but the sheet was a little small, and Frau Rosenthal's legs were exposed to the knees.

Herr Borkhausen meanwhile was looking a bit yellow, and was wearing a pair of handcuffs. Watching him silently from the side of the courtyard were his wife and five children.

'Inspector, I protest!' Borkhausen called out plaintively. 'I never threw the bracelet down into the cellar. Young Herr Persicke has got something against me . . .'

What had happened was that Friedrich, having quickly performed his allotted tasks, had then begun looking for the bracelet. Up in the kitchen, Frau Rosenthal had had it in her hand – it was over the bracelet, which she had refused to relinquish, that Friedrich had got into a heated argument with her. Distracted by this argument, he hadn't paid as close attention as he would normally, and the woman had been able to jump out of the window. So the bracelet must still be lying in the courtyard somewhere.

When Friedrich began looking around, Borkhausen was standing by the wall. Baldur Persicke had caught sight of something flashing and heard a rattle in the coal cellar. He had gone down to look, and lo and behold, there was the bracelet!

'I certainly didn't throw the bracelet in there!' Borkhausen insisted timidly. 'It must have dropped from Frau Rosenthal into the cellar!'

'I see!' said Inspector Rusch. 'You're that sort, are you! That's the sort of bird who's working for my colleague. Escherich will be pleased when I enlighten him about the calibre of his occasional associates.'

But all the while the inspector was ruminating, his gaze moved back and forth, back and forth, between Borkhausen and Baldur Persicke. Then Rusch went on, 'Well, I'm sure you won't mind paying us a visit?'

'Not at all, sir!' said Borkhausen, trembling, as his face grew a few degrees paler. 'I'm happy to come along! It's in my interest to have this thing properly cleared up!'

'Very good,' said the inspector drily. And, following a swift look at Persicke, 'Friedrich, take the handcuffs off this man. You'll come with us without them, will you not?'

'Of course I'll come! Of course, gladly!' Borkhausen eagerly assured him. 'I'm not going to run off anywhere. And if I did – well, you'd find me easily enough, Herr Inspector!'

'That's right!' Rusch said, drily once more. 'A bird like you's never hard to find.' He broke off. 'Well, there's the ambulance, and the police. Let's see if we can't get the formalities over with quickly. I've got a lot on this morning.'

Later on, once the formalities were indeed 'over', Inspector Rusch and young Persicke once again climbed the stairs to the Rosenthals' apartment. 'Just to make sure the kitchen window's shut!' as the inspector said.

On the staircase young Persicke suddenly came to a stop. 'Did you notice something, Inspector?' he asked in a whisper.

'I noticed various things,' replied Inspector Rusch. 'But what did you think about the pencil, my lad?'

'Didn't you notice how quiet the building is? Did you notice that here in the front building no one leaned out of the window, and in the back building they were everywhere! That's suspicious, isn't it? They must have noticed something, the people who live here. They just want to claim not to have noticed anything. Shouldn't you now search those apartments, Inspector?'

'Well, and where better to start than with the Persickes,' replied the inspector, quietly walking on up the stairs. 'Because as I recall none of them were looking out the window, either.'

'They got really hammered yesterday . . .'

'Listen, Sunshine,' the inspector went on, as though he had heard nothing. 'What I do is my affair, and what you do is yours. I don't want any advice from you. You're too green for me.' He looked, quietly amused, over his shoulder at the wincing expression of the boy. 'Boy,' he said, 'if I don't conduct any house searches here, then it's purely because they've had time to get rid of any evidence. Anyway, why so much fuss about a dead Jewess? I've got enough on my plate with the living ones.'

By now they were outside the Rosenthals' apartment. Baldur unlocked the door. Rusch closed the kitchen window and picked up a fallen chair.

'There!' said Inspector Rusch, looking around. 'Everything hunky-dory!'

He went ahead into the parlour and sat down on the sofa, in exactly the spot where he had shaken old Frau Rosenthal into a complete collapse an hour before. He stretched out leisurely and said, 'Right now, Sunshine, and why don't you fetch us a bottle of cognac and a couple of glasses!'

Baldur went off, came back, poured. They clinked glasses.

'That's better, son,' said the inspector agreeably, and lit a cigarette. 'And now why don't you tell me what you and Borkhausen were doing in this apartment together?'

Seeing the indignant reaction on the face of young Persicke, he went on, a little more quickly, 'I would think about it carefully if I were you, son! It's not impossible I might take a young Hitler Youth leader back to Prinz Albrecht Strasse, if he got too fresh for my liking. Think about whether honesty wouldn't be the better policy. Maybe we can keep it under wraps, so let's hear your story.' And, seeing Baldur hesitating, 'I did – as you keep asking – notice a thing or two, you see. For instance, I've seen your bootmarks on the sheets in the corner. And *that's* not from today. And how come you know there's cognac, and exactly where to find it? What do you think Borkhausen told me in his panic? Do I need to sit here and have you tell me a string of porkies? No, as I say, you're too green for that!'

Baldur could see that, and he confessed everything.

'I see!' the inspector said finally. 'I see. Everyone does what he can. Stupid people do stupid things, and smart people often do much more stupid things. Well, son, at least you wised up in the end, and didn't try to lie to Papa Rusch. I have regard for that. What would you like out of this lot?'

Baldur's eyes lit up. A moment ago, he had been completely demoralized, but now things had suddenly brightened again.

'The radio and the phonograph with the record collection, Inspector!' he whispered greedily.

'Very well!' said the inspector graciously. 'I told you I won't be getting back here before six. Anything else?'

'Maybe one or two suitcases full of bed linen!' said Baldur. 'My mother doesn't have much.'

'Oh, I'm so touched!' the inspector said mockingly. 'What a devoted son! What a little mama's boy! Well, go on then. And no more. Everything else you're accountable to me for! And I have a damned good memory for what's stacked and lying around here, so don't think you'll pull one over on me! And as I said, in case of doubt, we just instigate a search of the Persicke place. Where I'm pretty sure we'll turn up a radiogram and two suitcases of sheets, if not more. But no worries, son – if you play straight with me, I'll play straight with you.'

He walked over to the door. In parting, he added, 'And by the way, in case Borkhausen turns up here, no argy-bargy with him. I don't like that kind of thing. Got it?'

'Yes, sir,' said Baldur Persicke, and with that the two parted company: it had been a most productive morning.

17

The First Card is Written

For the Quangels, Sunday was not quite so productive – at any rate there wasn't the clarifying conversation that Anna so fervently desired.

'No,' was Otto Quangel's response. 'No, Mother, not today. The day got off to a bad start, and on such a day I can't do what I really want to do. And if I can't do it, then I don't want to talk about it, either. Maybe next Sunday. Do you hear that? That'll be one of the Persickes sneaking up the stairs again – well, let them! So long as they leave us in peace!'

But Otto Quangel was uncommonly gentle that Sunday. Anna was allowed to talk about their dead son as much as she wanted; he didn't tell her to stop. He even looked with her through the few photos she had of him, and when she started crying, he laid his hand on her shoulder and said, 'Enough, Mother, enough. Perhaps it's for the best, when you think of everything he'll be spared.'

In short, the Sunday passed off well, even without the conversation. It had been a long time since Anna had seen her husband in such a gentle mood; it was like seeing the sun shining one last time over a landscape before winter came and buried everything under sheets of ice and snow. In the months to come, as Quangel became ever colder and more laconic, she would often think back to this Sunday, and it would be both a consolation and an encouragement to her.

Monday brought a new workweek, one of those workweeks that are all the same whether flowers are blooming or blizzards are blowing. Work is always work, and that week people remained as they had always been.

Only one unusual experience befell Otto Quangel that week. As he was going to the factory, he passed retired Judge Fromm in Jablonski Strasse. Quangel would have greeted him, but he was nervous about being seen by the Persickes. Nor did he want to be seen by Borkhausen, who Anna said had been taken away by the Gestapo. Because Borkhausen was back, if in fact he had ever been away, and had been hanging around the front of the building.

So Quangel walked straight past the judge as if he didn't see him. Judge Fromm apparently felt less need to be cautious – at any rate, he tipped his hat to his neighbour, smiled with his eyes, and went inside.

Very good! thought Quangel. Whoever saw that will have thought: Quangel, always the same rough clod, but that judge, what a gentleman. No one would think they were ever in cahoots!

The rest of the week passed off without any events of note, and then it was Sunday again, the Sunday that Anna Quangel hoped would finally bring the desperately desired and oft postponed discussion with Otto. He had got up late, but he was calm and in a good mood. She sneaked a sidelong look at him as he drank his coffee, a little to encourage him perhaps, but he seemed not to notice, and slowly chewed his bread and stirred his coffee.

Anna felt a certain reluctance to clear the table. But this time it really wasn't for her to speak the first word. He had promised her the conversation for this Sunday, and surely he would keep his word. Any coaxing on her part would seem like pressuring him.

With a barely audible sigh she got up and took the plates and cups into the kitchen. When she came back for the bread-basket and coffee pot, he was kneeling in front of a drawer in the sideboard, looking for something. Anna Quangel couldn't remember what they kept in the drawer. It could only be some old, long-forgotten rubbish. 'Are you looking for anything in particular, Otto?' she asked.

But he merely gave a grunt, so she retreated into the kitchen to do the dishes and get dinner ready. He didn't feel like it! Once again, he didn't feel like it. More than ever she felt the conviction that there was something going on inside him that she knew nothing about, and badly needed to know.

Later, when she came back into the parlour to sit near him as she peeled the potatoes, she found him at the table. The cloth had been pulled off, and the tabletop was now covered with little carving knives, and wood shavings littered the floor around him. 'What are you doing, Otto?' she asked, now thoroughly flummoxed.

'Wanted to see if I still knew how to work wood,' he retorted.

She was a little irked. Otto might not have the deepest insight into human character, but he must have some sense of what she felt like, as she waited with bated breath for his communication. And now he had got out his wood-carving tools from the early years of their marriage, and was whittling, just as he had done then, reducing her to despair with his endless silence. In those days, she wasn't as used to his taciturnity as she was now, but today, of all days, even though she was used to it, it seemed to her quite unbearable. Whittling, my God, if that was all it occurred to the man to do, in the wake of such events! If through hours of silent carving he planned to repeat now his jealously guarded silences of then – no, that would be a bad disappointment for her. She had often been badly disappointed in him, but this time she wasn't going to take it lying down.

While she was thinking all this anxiously, almost despairingly, she was looking half curiously at the longish, thick chunk of wood he was turning thoughtfully in his big hands, now and again chipping off a piece with one of his big knives. Well, it wasn't a washing-trough this time, that was for sure.

'What are you making there, Otto?' she asked, half unwillingly. She had had the odd idea that he was carving some tool or other, perhaps something for a bomb detonator. But even to think like that was absurd – what did Otto have to do with bombs? Anyway, wood probably wasn't the right material. 'What are you making, Otto?' she asked.

At first, he seemed to want to grunt by way of reply, but maybe he felt he had been too curt with her today already, or maybe he was just ready to give her some information. 'A bowl,' he said. 'Want to see if I can carve a bowl. Used to carve lots of pipe bowls, in my time.'

And he continued to turn the thing in his hands, and to whittle away at it.

Pipe bowls! Anna almost spat with indignation. Then, with great irritation, she said it: 'Pipe bowls! Otto, please! The world's falling apart, and you're thinking of pipe bowls! When I hear you talk like that . . . !'

He seemed to respond neither to her annoyance nor to her words. He said: 'Of course this isn't going to be a pipe bowl. I want to see if I can carve a likeness of our Ottochen, the way he used to look.'

Immediately, her mood swung. So he was thinking of Otto-chen, and if he was thinking of Ottochen and trying to carve a likeness of his head, then he was thinking also of her, and wanting to please her in some way. She got up from her chair, hurriedly setting down the dish of potatoes, and said, 'Wait, Otto, I'll bring the photographs, so you can remember what he looked like.'

He shook his head. 'I don't want to see any pictures,' he said. 'I want to carve Ottochen the way he is inside of me.' He tapped his brow. And after a while he added, 'If I can!'

She was moved again. So Ottochen was inside him, he had a firm sense of what the boy looked like. Now she was curious to see the finished head. 'I'm sure you can, Otto!' she said.

'Well,' he said, but it didn't sound doubtful – more like agreement.

With that, conversation between the two of them was at an end for the moment. Anna had to go back into the kitchen to see to dinner, and she left him at the table, turning the lump of linden wood between his fingers and, with a quiet, painstaking patience, trimming little curls and shavings off it.

She was very surprised, then, when she came in to lay the table for dinner, to find the table already cleared and the table-cloth replaced. Otto was standing by the window, looking down at Jablonski Strasse, where the children were playing noisily.

'Well, Otto?' she asked. 'Are you already done with your carving?'

'For today,' he replied, and at the same moment she knew that their conversation was now imminent, that he was planning something, this strangely persistent man who always waited for the right moment, who could never be induced to do something except in his own sweet time.

They ate their dinner in silence. Then she went back to the kitchen to tidy up, leaving him sitting on a corner of the sofa, staring into space.

When she emerged half an hour later, he was still sitting there. But now she felt she could no longer wait for him to decide: his patience, and her own impatience, made her restless. What if he were still sitting there like that at four o'clock, and after supper? She couldn't wait any longer! 'Well, Otto,' she asked, 'what's it to be? No after-dinner nap, like every other Sunday?'

'Today's not every other Sunday. "Every other Sunday" is gone for good.' He got up abruptly and left the room.

But today she wouldn't let him run off on one of his mysterious errands. She ran after him. 'No, Otto . . .' she began.

He was standing by the front door of the apartment, having just put the chain across. He raised his hand to call for silence, and listened to what was going on outside. Then he nodded and walked past her, back into the parlour. When she came in after him, he was sitting in his place on the sofa, and she sat down beside him.

'If anyone rings, Anna,' he said, 'don't open until I . . .'

'Now, come on, Otto, who's going to ring at such a time?' she said impatiently. 'Who's going to visit us? Tell me whatever it was you were going to tell me!'

'I will tell you, Anna,' he replied with uncharacteristic meekness. 'But if you pressure me, you'll only make it harder for me.'

She brushed his hand, the hand of a man who always found it hard to communicate what was going on inside him. 'I won't pressure you, Otto,' she said soothingly. 'Take your time.'

But right after that, he began to speak, and he spoke for almost five minutes, in slow, terse, carefully considered sentences, after each of which – as though it were the last – he closed his thin-lipped mouth tight. And while he spoke, he kept looking off to one side behind Anna.

Anna Quangel kept her eyes on him while he spoke, not taking them off his face, and she was almost grateful to him for not looking at her, so difficult was it for her to conceal the disappointment that came over her. My God, what had this man come up with! She had had great deeds in mind (and been afraid of them at the same time): an attempt to assassinate the Führer, or at the very least some active struggle against the Party and its officials.

And what was he proposing? Nothing at all, something so ridiculously small, something absolutely in his character, something discreet, out of the way, something that wouldn't interfere with his peace and quiet. Postcards with slogans against the Führer and the Party, against the war, for the information of his fellow men, that was all. And these cards he wasn't going to send to particular individuals, or stick on walls like placards, no, he wanted to leave them lying in the stairwells of widely visited buildings, leave them to their fate, without any control over who picked them up, where they might be trampled underfoot, torn up . . . Everything in her rebelled against this obscure and ignoble form of warfare. She wanted to be active, to do something with results she could see!

But Quangel, once he had finished talking, appeared not even to be expecting any form of demurral from his wife, and she sat there struggling with herself in silence in the corner of the sofa. Wasn't it her duty to say something to him, after all?

He got up and walked over to the door again to listen. When he came back, he took off the tablecloth again, folded it up, and hung it carefully over the back of a chair. Then he went to the old mahogany bureau, took the bunch of keys from his pocket, and unlocked it.

While he was rummaging in there, Anna made up her mind. Hesitantly she said, 'Isn't this thing that you're wanting to do, isn't it a bit small, Otto?'

He stopped his rummaging, and still standing there stooped, he turned his head to his wife. 'Whether it's big or small, Anna,' he said, 'if they get wind of it, it'll cost us our lives . . .'

There was something so terribly persuasive in those words, and in his dark, fathomless bird's eye, that she shuddered. For an instant she saw quite clearly the grey, stony prison yard and the guillotine standing ready, its steel dull in the early dawn light: a mute threat.

Anna Quangel felt herself trembling. Then she looked over at Otto again. He might be right: whether their act was big or small, no one could risk more than his life. Each according to his strength and abilities, but the main thing was, you fought back.

Still Quangel eyed her silently, as though witnessing the struggle she was having with herself. Then his eye brightened, he took his hands out of the bureau, straightened up, and said, almost with a smile, 'But they're not going to catch us that easily. If they're canny, we can be canny too! Canny and careful. Careful, Anna, always on guard – the longer we fight them, the longer we'll be effective. There's no use in dying early. We want to live, we want to be around when they fall. We want to be able to say, We were there, Anna!'

He said these words lightly, almost jocularly. Then he went back to rummaging, and Anna leaned back into the sofa, relieved. A load had been taken from her mind. Now she was convinced that Otto had some great plan.

He carried his little bottle of ink, his postcards in their envelope, and the large white gloves to the table. He uncorked the bottle, seared the pen nib with a match, and dipped it in the ink. There was a quiet hiss; he looked attentively at the pen and nodded. Then he awkwardly pulled on the gloves, took a card from the envelope, and laid it down in front of him. He nodded slowly at Anna. She was alertly following every one of these meticulous and long-considered preparations. Then he indicated his gloves and said, 'Fingerprints – see!'

Then he picked up the pen, and said softly but clearly, 'The first sentence of our first card will read: "Mother! The Führer has murdered my son."'

Once again, she shivered. There was something so bleak, so gloomy, so determined in the words Otto had just spoken. At that instant she grasped that this very first sentence was Otto's absolute and irrevocable declaration of war, and also what that meant: war between, on the one side, the two of them, poor, small, insignificant workers who could be extinguished for just a word or two, and on the other, the Führer, the Party, the whole apparatus in all its power and glory, with three-fourths or even four-fifths of the German people behind it. And the two of them in this little room in Jablonski Strasse!

She looks across at her husband. While she's been thinking all this, he has just got to the third word of the first sentence. With unbearable patience, he is drawing the capital *F* of the word *Führer*. 'Why don't you let me write, Otto!' she begs. 'I can do it much more quickly!'

At first he just growls back. But then he does give her an explanation. 'Your handwriting,' he says. 'They would catch us sooner or later by the handwriting. This here is a sign-writing style, block capitals, like type . . .'

He stops, and goes on drawing the letters. Yes, he's planned it all. He doesn't think he's forgotten anything. He knows this style from the plans of furniture designers; no one can tell from such a style who's doing it. Of course, with Otto Quangel's large hands unused to writing, it looks particularly crude and coarse. But that doesn't matter, that won't betray him. If anything, it's a further advantage: the postcard will have something poster-like about it that will catch the eye. He goes on drawing patiently.

And she, too, has become patient. She is beginning to adjust to the idea that this will be a long war. She is calm now; Otto has considered everything; Otto is dependable, come what may. The thought he has given to everything! The first postcard in the war that was started by the death of their son is rightly about him. Once, they had a son; the Führer murdered him; now they are writing postcards. A new chapter in their lives. On the outside, nothing has changed. All is quiet around the Quangels. But inside, everything is different, they are at war . . .

She gets her darning basket and starts darning socks. Now

and then, she looks across at Otto slowly drawing his letters, not ever changing his tempo. After almost every letter he holds the postcard out at arm's length and studies it with narrowed eyes. Then he nods.

Finally, he shows her his first completed sentence. It occupies one and a half very generous lines of the postcard.

She says, 'You won't get much on each postcard!'

He answers, 'Never mind! I'll just have to write a lot of postcards!'

'And each card takes a long time.'

'I'll write one card every Sunday, later on maybe two. The war is far from over, the killing will go on.'

He is unshakeable. He has made a decision, and will act on it. Nothing can reverse it, nothing can deflect Otto Quangel from his chosen path.

He says, 'The second sentence: "Mother! The Führer will murder your sons too, he will not stop till he has brought sorrow to every home in the world."'

She repeats it: 'Mother, the Führer will murder your sons too!'

She nods, she says, 'Write that!' She suggests, 'We should try to leave that card somewhere where a lot of women will see it!'

He reflects, then shakes his head. 'No. Women who get a shock, you never know what they will do. A man will stuff it in his pocket, on the staircase. Later on, he'll read it carefully. Anyway, all men are the sons of mothers.'

He stops talking, and goes back to his drawing. The afternoon goes by; they don't think about supper. It's evening, and the card is finished at last. He stands up. He takes one more look at it.

'There!' he says. 'That's that. Next Sunday the next one.'

She nods.

'When will you deliver it?' she whispers.

He looks at her. 'Tomorrow morning.'

'Let me come with you, the first time!'

He shakes his head. 'No,' he says. 'And especially not the first time. I have to see how things go.'

'Come on!' she begs him. 'It's my card! It's the card of the mother!'

'All right!' he determines. 'You can come. But only as far as the building. Inside, I want to be on my own.'

'All right.'

Then the card is carefully pushed inside a book, the writing things put away, the gloves slipped into his tunic.

They eat their supper, barely speaking. They hardly notice how quiet they both are – even Anna. They are both tired, as though they have done an immense labour or been on a long journey.

As he gets up from the table, he says, 'I'm going to go and lie down.'

And she, 'I'll just tidy up in the kitchen. Then I'll come, too. I feel so tired, and we haven't done anything!'

He looks at her with a glimmer of a smile on his face, and then he goes to the bedroom and starts to get undressed.

But later, when they are both lying in bed in the dark, they can't get to sleep. They toss and turn, each listens to the other's breathing, and in the end they start to talk. It's easier to talk in the dark.

'What do you think will happen to our cards?' asks Anna.

'People will feel alarmed when they see them lying there and read the first few words. Everyone's frightened nowadays.'

'That's true,' she says, 'Everybody is . . .'

But she exempts the two of them, the two Quangels. Almost everybody's frightened, but not us.

'The people who find them,' he says, saying aloud things he's thought through a hundred times, 'will be afraid of being seen on the stairs. They will quickly pocket the cards and run off. Or they may lay them down again and disappear, and then the next person will come along . . .'

'That's right,' says Anna, and she can see the staircase before her eyes, a typical Berlin staircase, badly lit, and anyone with a card in his hand will suddenly feel like a criminal. Because in fact everyone thinks the way the writer of the cards thinks, but they can't let it show, because it's a capital crime . . .

'Some,' Quangel resumes, 'will hand the card in right away, to the block warden or the police – anything to be rid of it!* But even that doesn't matter: whether it's shown to the Party or not, whether to an official or a policeman, they all will read the card, and it will have some effect on them. Even if the only effect is to remind them that there is still resistance out there, that not everyone thinks like the Führer . . .'

'No,' she says. 'Not everyone. Not us.'

'And there will be more of us, Anna. We will make more. We will inspire other people to write their own postcards. In the end, scores of people, hundreds, will be sitting down and writing cards like us. We will inundate Berlin with postcards, we will slow the machines, we will depose the Führer, end the war . . .'

He stops, alarmed by his own words, these dreams that so late in life have come to haunt his heart.

But Anna Quangel is fired by this vision: 'And we will have been the first! No one will know, but we will know.'

Suddenly sober, he says, 'Perhaps already there are many thinking as we do. Thousands of men must have fallen. Maybe there are already writers like us. But that doesn't matter, Anna! What do we care? It's we who must do it!'

'Yes,' she says.

And he, once again carried away by their prospects: 'And we will keep the police busy, the Gestapo, the SS, the SA. Everywhere people will be talking about the mysterious postcards, they will inquire, suspect, observe, conduct house-to-house searches – in vain! We will go on writing, on and on!'

And she: 'Maybe they'll even show the Führer himself cards like ours – he will read our accusations! He will go wild! It's said he always goes wild when something doesn't happen according to his will. He will order his men to find us, and they won't find us! He will have to go on reading our accusations!'

They are both silent, dazzled by their prospects. What were they, previously? Obscure characters, extras. And now to see

---

* A 'Blockwart' was a low-ranking Party official installed to be janitor of a building (or a block of buildings) and gather information about the tenants.

them alone, exalted, separate from the others, not to be confused with any of them. They feel a shiver; that's how alone they are.

Quangel can imagine himself at work, in front of the same machinery, driving and driven, alert, looking around from machine to machine. For them he will always be idiotic old Quangel, obsessed by work and his squalid avarice. But in his head he carries thoughts like none of them. They would die of fright if they carried such thoughts. But he, silly old Quangel, he has them. He stands there, fooling everyone.

Anna Quangel is thinking of their expedition tomorrow to deliver the first postcard. She is a little dissatisfied with herself for not insisting on going into the building with Quangel. She wonders whether to ask him to let her. Maybe. Generally, Otto Quangel doesn't allow his mind to be changed by appeals. But maybe tonight, given his unusually affable mood? Maybe right now?

But it's taken her too long to get there. Quangel is already asleep. So she closes her eyes, she will see if it's possible tomorrow. If it is, she will certainly ask.

And then she, too, is asleep.

18

The First Card is Dropped

She doesn't dare mention it until they are on the street, that's how taciturn Otto is this morning. 'Where are you going to drop the card, Otto?'

He answers gruffly, 'Don't talk about it now. Not on the street.'

And then he adds, in spite of himself, 'I've got a house on Greifswalder Strasse in mind.'

'No,' she says decisively. 'No, don't do that, Otto. That's a bad idea!'

'Come along!' he says angrily, because she has stopped, 'I tell you, not on the street!'

He walks on, she follows him, and insists on her right to debate. 'Not so close to where we live,' she stresses. 'If it winds up in their hands, they'll have an indication of the area right away. Let's go down to the Alex . . .'

He reflects. Perhaps she's right, no, she is right. One has to reckon on anything. And yet, this abrupt change of plan doesn't suit him at all. If they go all the way down to the Alexanderplatz, time will get short, and he has to go to work. Also, he doesn't know of any appropriate buildings around the Alex. There are bound to be loads of them, but you have to look for the right one first, and he'd rather do that on his own, not with his wife.

Then, quite suddenly, his mind is made up. 'OK, Anna,' he says. 'you're right. Let's go to the Alex.'

She looks at him gratefully. She is glad he has accepted some advice from her. And because he has just made her so happy, she decides she won't ask him for the other thing, his permission to enter the building with him. He can go alone. She will be a bit scared while she waits for him to come out – but why, really? Not for a moment does she doubt that he will come out. He is so calm and cold, he won't let himself be caught out. Even if he were in their hands, he wouldn't give himself away, and he would fight himself free.

As she walks along, thinking such things, at the side of her silent husband, they have turned off Greifswalder Strasse into Neue Königstrasse. She has been so preoccupied with her thoughts that she hasn't noticed the intensity with which Otto Quangel's eyes have been scanning the houses opposite them. Now he suddenly comes to a stop – it's quite a bit further to the Alexanderplatz – and says: 'There, have a look in that shop window, I'll be back in a jiffy.'

And already he's off across the road, walking toward a large, bright office building.

Her heart starts to pound. She feels like calling out: No, not there, we said the Alex! Let's stay together a bit longer! And: Won't you at least say goodbye to me first! But already the door is banging shut behind him.

With a deep sigh, she turns toward the shop window. But she sees nothing. She presses her brow against the cold glass, and everything flickers and runs before her eyes. Her heart is beating so hard she can hardly breathe; all the blood seems to have rushed to her head.

So I am afraid, she thinks. My God, he must never find out, otherwise he'll never take me with him again. But then, I'm not really afraid, she thinks. I'm not afraid for me, I'm afraid for him. What if he doesn't come out?

She can't stop herself, she has to look at the office building. The door is pushed open, people come, people go; why doesn't Quangel come? He must have been gone five minutes, no, ten. Why is there a man running out of the building? Is he calling the police? Don't say they've caught Quangel the very first time!

Oh, it's more than I can stand! What has he got himself into? And there I was, thinking this was something small! Once a week, and if he writes two cards, twice a week endangering his life! And he won't always want to take me with him. I noticed that right away – he doesn't really want me there. He will go by himself, he will drop the cards by himself, and then he will

go on to the factory (or he will never go to the factory again!),
and I will sit at home waiting, waiting in terror, and this terror
will never end, and I will never get used to it. Here's Otto! At
last! No, it's not him. Not him again. Now I'm going to go and
get him, I don't care how angry he is! Something's wrong, he
must have been gone for a quarter of an hour, it can't possibly
take that long! I'm going after him!

She takes three steps towards the building – and turns around.
Stops in front of the window, stares at it.

No, I won't go in after him, I won't go looking for him. I can't
let him down like that the very first time. I'm just imagining
something has happened to him; people are walking in and out
of the building, just as always. I'm sure Otto hasn't been gone
a quarter hour either. Now, let's see what's in this shop window.
Corsets, garter belts . . .

In the meantime, Quangel has indeed entered the office
building. He settled on it so quickly because of his wife. She
was making him nervous: any moment she might start talking
about 'it' again. He couldn't stand to prolong his search in her
company. She was sure to start talking again, be in favour of
this building or against that one. No, enough! He would rather
walk into the first building he came to, even if it wasn't ideal.

This one was a long way short of ideal: It was a bright modern
office building that no doubt housed many companies but that
still had a porter in a grey uniform. Quangel walks past him
with an indifferent expression. He is prepared for the question,
Where are you going; he has noted that a lawyer named Toll is
on the fourth floor. But the porter doesn't stop him; he's busy
talking to someone else. He casts a fleeting, indifferent regard
at Quangel as he walks in. Quangel turns left to take the stairs,
then hears the purr of an elevator. There's another thing he has
failed to allow for, that a modern building like this will have an
elevator and the stairs will hardly be used at all.

But Quangel continues up the stairs. The liftboy will think,
An old man, fearful of elevators. Or: Only going up to the first
floor. Or perhaps he won't think anything. Anyway, the stairs
are hardly in use. He's already on the second floor, and so far

he has met only an office boy in a tearing rush, plunging down-stairs with a bundle of letters in his hand, who didn't even look at Quangel. He could drop his postcard anywhere here, but he doesn't forget for a moment that there's that elevator, and he could be seen at any second through its glinting glass. He needs to climb higher, and the elevator needs to be on its way down, and then he can do it.

He stops in front of one of the tall windows between storeys, and stares down at the street. There, well hidden from view, he pulls a glove out of his pocket and puts it on his right hand. He then puts that hand in his pocket, slips it in past the waiting postcard, carefully, so as not to crease it. He takes it between two fingers . . .

While Otto Quangel is doing all this, he has noticed that Anna is not at her place in front of the shop window at all, but is standing by the side of the road, looking pale and conspicuous as she stares up at the office building. She doesn't raise her eyes as high as where he is – she's probably watching the entrance. He shakes his head crossly at her, firmly resolved never to take his wife on another errand like this. Of course she's worried for him. But why is she worried for him? She ought to be a little worried for herself, badly as she is behaving. It is she who is endangering them both!

He climbs further up the steps. As he passes the next window, he looks down at the street again, and this time Anna is standing in front of the shop window where she's supposed to be. Good for her, she's fought down her fear. Brave woman. He won't even mention it to her. And suddenly Quangel takes out the card, lays it cautiously on the windowsill, pulls the glove off his hand as he begins walking downstairs, and puts it in his pocket.

Climbing down the first few steps, he looks back. There it is in bright daylight, he can still see it from where he is now – the big, legible, bold writing on his first card! Anyone will be able to read it! And understand it, too! Quangel smiles grimly to himself.

At that moment, he hears a door opening on the floor above

him. The elevator has just left, heading downstairs. If whoever is upstairs can't be bothered to wait for the elevator, if he takes the stairs and finds the card . . . Quangel is only one flight ahead of him. If the man runs, he will be able to catch up with Quangel, perhaps only at the bottom of the building, but he can catch up with him, because Quangel is not allowed to run. An old man, running down the stairs like a schoolboy – that would attract attention. And he must not attract attention, no one must recall seeing a man of such and such an appearance anywhere in the building . . .

He walks fairly quickly down the stone stairs, and between the sound of his own footsteps, he listens to hear if the other man really has taken the stairs. If so, he will have seen the card; it's not possible to miss it. But Quangel isn't quite sure. Once, he thinks he hears steps, but then he doesn't hear anything more for some time. And by now he's too far down to hear much. The elevator rides up with a flash of lights.

Quangel sets foot in the lobby. A large group of people are just coming from the courtyard, workers from some factory or other, and Quangel mingles with them. This time, he's quite convinced, the porter hasn't even seen him.

He crosses the roadway and comes to stand beside Anna.

'Done!' he says.

And as he sees the gleam in her eyes, and the tremble on her lips, he adds, 'No one saw me!' And then: 'Let's go. I've just got time to make it to the factory on foot.'

They go. But both throw a look over their shoulder back to this office building, where the first of the Quangels' postcards has now embarked on its journey into the world. They nod goodbye to the building. It's a good building, and however many buildings they visit at weekly intervals in the course of the next months and years, they'll never forget this one.

Anna Quangel wishes she could stroke her husband's hand, but she doesn't dare. She just brushes it, as if by accident, and says, 'Oh, sorry, Otto!'

He looks at her in surprise, but doesn't say anything.

They walk on.

PART II

The Gestapo

19

The Postcards Make Their Way

The actor Max Harteisen had, as his friend and attorney Toll liked to remind him, plenty of butter on his head from pre-Nazi times.* He had acted in films made by Jewish directors, he had acted in pacifist films, and one of his principal theatre roles was that of the despicable weakling, the Prince of Homburg, whom every red-blooded National Socialist could only spit at. Max Harteisen therefore had every reason to be extremely cautious; for a while it was far from certain whether he would even be allowed to work under the Nazis.

But in the end it had all panned out. Of course he had had to exercise a little restraint, and first of all cede the limelight to actors of a browner hue, even if they were far less gifted than himself. But he had fallen down on this matter of restraint; he had acted so well, he had even drawn the attention of Minister Goebbels. Yes, the minister had fallen for Harteisen. And as far as these ministerial infatuations went, as every child knew, there was no more fickle and unpredictable man than Dr Joseph Goebbels.

At first it had all been sweetness and light, because when the minister wanted to honour someone, he made no distinctions of gender. Dr Goebbels treated Harteisen like a mistress: he telephoned him every morning to ask how he had slept, sent him chocolates and flowers as he would to a diva, and not a day passed without the minister spending at least a few minutes with his Harteisen. He even took him along him to the Party Congress at Nuremberg and explained National Socialism to him, and Harteisen duly understood everything he was supposed to understand.

* From the proverb 'He who has butter on his head should not go into the sun.'

The only thing he didn't understand was that under National Socialism a citizen does not go about contradicting a minister. Because a minister, by simple fact of being a minister, is bound to be ten times cleverer than anyone else. On some perfectly trivial film question, Harteisen contradicted his minister, and even declared that what Dr Goebbels had said was rubbish. It is unclear whether it was the trivial and utterly theoretical film question that had so engaged the actor's passion, or whether it was more that he was fed up with so much adoration and desired to bring it to an end. At any rate, he stood by his words in spite of various suggestions that he take them back – minister or no minister, the view was and remained rubbish.

Oh, how the world then suddenly changed for Max Harteisen! No more morning inquiries after the quality of his sleep, no chocolates, no flowers, no more visits to Dr Goebbels, and no more instructions in the true National Socialism either! All that might have been borne – perhaps it was even in some ways an improvement – but suddenly Harteisen found he had no more bookings either. Even signed film contracts were ripped up, provincial tours evaporated, and there was no more work for the actor Harteisen.

Since Harteisen was a man who not only looked to his profession for an income, but who was an actor to his finger-tips, one whose life found its purpose on the stage or in front of the camera, he was completely destroyed by this enforced idleness. He couldn't and wouldn't believe that the minister who for a year and a half had been his dearest friend had now turned into a deplorable and unscrupulous enemy, or that he was using the power of his position to rob Harteisen of all *joie de vivre* merely because Harteisen had contradicted him. (In the year 1940, he had not yet understood, our good Harteisen, that any Nazi at any time was prepared to take away not only the pleasure but also the life of any differently minded German.)

But as time passed and no possibilities of work appeared, the penny finally dropped for Max Harteisen. Friends reported to him that the minister had declared at a conference on films that the Führer never wanted to see that particular actor wearing the tunic of an officer on screen again. Not much later, he heard that the Führer did not want to see him again in any capacity. The actor Harteisen had become 'undesirable'. Over, chum, finished, blacklisted at thirty-six – for the whole of a Thousand-Year Reich!

Now, the actor Harteisen really did have butter on his head. But he didn't give up, he asked and inquired, he tried everything to find out whether this destructive judgement really was the Führer's or the little minister had merely made it up to finish off his enemy. And that Monday, Harteisen had run to his attorney Toll, completely confident of victory, and had declared, 'I've got it! Erwin, I've got it! The bastard was lying! The Führer never even saw the film where I played the Prussian officer, and he's never said a word against me, either!'

And he reported excitedly that the news was perfectly reliable, because it came from Göring himself. A friend of his wife's had an aunt, whose cousin had been invited to the Görings' at Karinhall. There she had raised the matter, and Göring had expressed himself as stated.

The attorney looked at his excited client a little mockingly. 'Well, Max, and how does that change things?'

The actor muttered in some bafflement, 'Well, Erwin, it means Goebbels was lying.'

'And so? Did you ever believe everything that club-foot said was true?'

'No, of course not. But if we take the case to the Führer . . . He's misused the name of the Führer!'

'Yes, and then the Führer will throw out his old Party veteran and propaganda minister, for stymieing Harteisen's career!'

The actor looked imploringly at his mocking, condescending attorney. 'But something's got to happen in my case, Erwin!' he said. 'I want to work! And Goebbels is wrongly and wilfully obstructing me!'

'Yes,' said the attorney. 'True!' And no more. But seeing Harteisen gazing at him so expectantly, he went on, 'You're a child, Max, such a child!'

The actor, who was used to hearing himself described as a man of the world, tossed his head back angrily.

'Listen, Max, we're among ourselves,' the attorney went on. 'The door is padded, we can speak openly together. You know, if only dimly, how much injustice there is in Germany today, how much screaming, bloody injustice – and no one lifts a finger. On the contrary, they're proud of their disgrace. But because the actor Harteisen has suffered a teensy-weensy hurt, he suddenly makes the discovery that there is injustice abroad in the world, and he screams for justice. Come on, Max!'

Depressed, Harteisen said: 'But what shall I do, Erwin? I've got to do something!'

'What should you do? Well, that's completely obvious! You and your wife move to some pretty spot in the country, and you stay nice and quiet. Above all you stop this dangerous talk about "your" minister, and you don't talk about what Göring said. Otherwise it's possible that the minister will go after you in a completely different way.'

'But how long am I supposed to sit idly in the country?'

'A minister's moods come and go, Max. And go they will, you can be sure of that. One day, your name will be back in lights.'

The actor shivered. 'Not that!' he said. 'Please, not that!' He stood up. 'Are you really saying that's the best you can do for me?'

'Absolutely!' said the attorney, and smiled. 'Unless you fancy a spell in a concentration camp as a martyr for your art.'

Three minutes later, the actor Max Harteisen was standing in some bewilderment in the staircase of the office building, holding a postcard in his hand: 'Mother! The Führer has murdered my son . . .'

My God! he thought. Who would write something like that? They must be crazy! It's their death-warrant, for sure. Unthinkingly, he turned the card over. But there was no address, either of sender or recipient, just these words: 'PASS THIS CARD ON, SO THAT MANY PEOPLE READ IT! –DON'T GIVE TO THE WINTER RELIEF FUND! – WORK AS SLOWLY

AS YOU CAN!– PUT SAND IN THE MACHINES! – EVERY
STROKE OF WORK NOT DONE WILL SHORTEN THE
WAR!'

The actor looked up. The elevator passed in a spill of illumi-
nation. He had the feeling of many eyes on him.

Hurriedly he slipped the postcard in his pocket, only to pull
it out again a moment later. He was about to return it to the
windowsill when doubt assailed him. Perhaps the people in
the elevator had seen him there, with the postcard in his hand
– and lots of people knew his face. The card would be found,
and surely someone would come forward, prepared to swear
they had seen him putting it down there. In a sense it would be
true: he had put it down there, though he hadn't been the first
to do it. But who would believe him, in light of his falling-out
with the minister? He was in the doghouse badly enough as it
was, and now this!

Sweat beaded on his brow, suddenly he understood that it
wasn't just the writer of the postcard, but also himself, who
was in danger of his life, and perhaps he even more than the
other! His hand itched: he wanted to put the card down, he
wanted to take it away with him, he wanted to tear it to pieces,
just where he was . . . But perhaps there was someone at the
top of the stairs, watching him? In the last couple of days,
he had had the sensation now and then of being watched; he
thought it was nerves on his part, Goebbels's petty vindictive-
ness getting to him . . .

Maybe the whole thing was a trap for him? To show the world
how correct the minister had been in his assessment of the actor
Harteisen? Oh, Christ, he was going mad, he was seeing ghosts!
A minister wouldn't carry on in that way! Or was that exactly
the way he would carry on?

But he couldn't stand there all day. He had to make a decision
– this wasn't the time to think about Goebbels, he had to think
of himself!

He races back up half a flight of stairs; there is no one standing
watching him. But already he is ringing the bell for attorney
Toll. He charges past the secretary and slams the card down on

the attorney's desk: 'Here, I found this on the staircase a moment ago!'

The attorney takes a cursory look at the postcard. Then he gets up and carefully shuts the double-door to his office, which Harteisen in his agitation has left open. He returns to his chair. He picks up the card and reads it through slowly and carefully, while Harteisen stalks back and forth, casting impatient glances at him.

Now Toll lets the card drop and asks, 'Where did you say you found this?'

'Outside in the stairwell, half a flight down.'

'On the stairwell! Do you mean on the steps?'

'Don't be so pedantic, Erwin! No, it wasn't on the steps, it was on the windowsill.'

'And may I ask what prompted you to bring this charming billet-doux to me in my office?'

The attorney's voice has an edge to it, and the actor says pleadingly: 'But what am I supposed to do? It was lying there, I absentmindedly picked it up.'

'And why didn't you put it straight back? That would have been the natural thing to do.'

'The elevator passed me while I was reading it. I had the feeling someone might have seen me. My face is so widely recognized.'

'That's good – I like that!' said the attorney bitterly. 'And so you turned back and came running to me waving the card in your hand?' The actor nodded, grim-faced. 'No, my friend,' said Toll decisively, and held out the postcard. 'Here, take it. I don't want anything to do with it. *Nota bene*, you may not refer to me in any way. I've never seen this card. Here, take it back!'

White-faced, Harteisen stared at his friend. 'I thought of you,' he said, 'not just as my friend but my attorney, the man who represents me at law.'

'Not on this, or, perhaps better, not any more. You're an accident waiting to happen, you have an incredible talent for blundering into the worst situations. You will plunge others into destruction with you. So here, take it back!'

He held it out to him again.

Harteisen stood there, white-faced, hands dug into his pockets.

After a long silence, he said, 'I daren't. In the last few days I've quite often had the sense I was being watched. Do me a favour and just tear it up, will you! Put it with the other rubbish in your wastepaper basket!'

'Much too dangerous, my dear fellow! It would just take the office boy or some nosy cleaning woman turning it up, and I'd be in it up to my neck!'

'Burn it, then!'

'You forget we have central heating here!'

'Take a match, and burn it over your ashtray. No one would ever know.'

'You would know.'

Pale-faced, they stared at each other. They were old friends, going back to school days, but now fear had come between them, and fear had brought mistrust with it. They eyed one another silently.

He's an actor, thought the attorney. Maybe he's putting on a show for me, to draw me into something. Comes here with instructions to test my reliability. I barely got away with it that other time, with that wretched defence before the People's Court. But ever since, they've wondered about me . . .

How much is Erwin actually doing in my interests? thought the actor grimly. He won't help me with the minister, and now he's even prepared to declare he's never set eyes on that postcard. How is that acting for me? He's acting against me. Who knows whether this postcard – you hear so much about traps being set for people. Come off it, that's all nonsense, he's always been a perfectly trustworthy friend . . .

And both looked at each other and thought better of it. They smiled.

'We're crazy to doubt each other!'

'We've been friends for twenty years!'

'School together!'

'Look at how far we've come!'

'What were we thinking? The son betrays his mother, the sister her brother, the boyfriend his girlfriend . . .'

'But not you and me!'

'Let's think about what to do with this postcard. It would really be dangerous for you to leave here with it in your pocket if you feel you're being watched.'

'Maybe it was just nerves. Give it to me, I'll get rid of it somewhere!'

'You and that dangerous thoughtlessness of yours – I don't think so. Leave the card here with me!'

'You've got a wife and two kids, Erwin. Maybe your office staff isn't completely reliable. Who is, anyway, nowadays? Give me the postcard. I'll phone you in fifteen minutes and tell you it's disappeared.'

'My God! That's you all over, Max! A phone call over something like that! Why don't you just ring Himmler, and get it over with?! At least that's quicker!'

And once again they look at each other, each a little comforted not to be quite alone, but to have a dependable friend.

Suddenly, the attorney pounds his fist down on the card. 'I wonder what was on the mind of the idiot who wrote this thing, and left it on the staircase! Dragging strangers to the gallows!'

'And for what? What is he actually saying? Nothing that each one of us doesn't know for himself. He must be a madman!'

'This whole nation has become a nation of madmen; I think it's a contagion!'

'If only they could nab the person who put others at such risk! Honestly, I think I would be pleased . . .'

'Ach, don't. I don't think you would be pleased if yet another person had to die. But how do we get out of this situation?'

The attorney looked thoughtfully down at the card. Then he reached for the telephone. 'We've got a political commissioner here in the building,' he said to his friend by way of explanation. 'I'm going to present the card to him, tell him what actually happened, and not put too much importance on any of it. Are you sure of your statement?'

'Completely.'

'And your nerves?'

'Of course, my dear fellow. I've never yet had stage fright. I was always nervous beforehand, mind you! What kind of person is this political commissioner?'

'No idea. I don't think I've ever seen him. Probably some little pen-pusher. Anyway, I'm going to call him.'

But the manikin who turned up didn't look much like some pen-pusher, more like a fox – and he felt very flattered to meet the renowned actor whom he had seen so many times in films. He reeled off six titles right away; the actor hadn't been in any of them. Max Harteisen praised the manikin for his memory, and then they passed on to the substantive part of the meeting.

The little fox read the card, and it wasn't possible to tell from his expression what he thought of it. He remained inscrutable. Then he listened to the account of the finding of the card, and of its delivery here to the office.

'Very good! Absolutely right!' the commissioner praised them. 'And what time was that, would you say?'

For a moment, the attorney faltered, and glanced at his friend. Best not to lie, he thought to himself. After all, people had seen him come in here with the card, in a highly excited state.

'About half an hour ago,' said the attorney.

The manikin raised his eyebrows. 'So long as that?' he asked with quiet surprise.

'We had other things to talk about,' explained the attorney. 'We didn't attach that much importance to it. Or do you think it could be important?'

'Everything is important. It would have been important to catch the fellow who left the card. But, of course, after half an hour it's too late for that.'

Each one of his words sounded like a faint reproach against that 'too late'.

'I'm sorry about the delay,' said the actor Harteisen smoothly. 'It was my fault. I thought my own affairs were more important than this – this trash here!'

'I should have known better myself,' the attorney chimed in.

The little fox smiled soothingly. 'Well, gentlemen, what's done is done. At any rate, I'm glad to have had the pleasure to meet Herr Harteisen in person. Heil Hitler!'

Loudly, jumping to their feet: 'Heil Hitler!'

And when the door had closed behind him, the two friends looked at each other.

'Thank God, we're rid of that bloody card!'

'And he didn't suspect us!'

'No, he didn't think it was our handiwork, but he did see that we hesitated between handing it over and not handing it over.'

'Do you think we'll hear any more of the matter?'

'No, I have to say I don't. At the worst, a harmless interrogation, where and when and how you found the card. And there you just have to tell them what happened.'

'You know, Erwin, I think I'll be quite relieved to be leaving the city for a while.'

'You see.'

'There's something corrosive about it!'

'Corrosive! I'd say we were pretty corroded already!'

In the meantime, the little fox had driven to his local group. Now a brownshirt was holding the card in his hands.

'This is a matter for the Gestapo,' said the brownshirt. 'Why don't you take it there yourself, Heinz. Wait, I'll write you a note to take with it. What about the two gentlemen themselves as culprits?'

'Out of the question! Of course, neither of them is exactly politically reliable. But I tell you, they were sweating blood and water when they started talking about the card.'

'You know, Harteisen's supposed to be in bad odour with Minister Goebbels,' the brownshirt mused.

'Even so!' said the little fox. 'He would never have dared anything like this. Much too frightened. I listed six films to his face that he never appeared in, and admired his performances in them. He was bowing and scraping like there was no tomorrow. He was beaming with gratitude. And all the time I could smell the sweat of fear on him!'

'Show me one that isn't afraid!' said the brownshirt contemptuously. 'And it's so unnecessary. They just need to do what we tell them.'

'It's because people have got in the habit of thinking. They have the idea that thinking will help them.'

'They need to do as they're told. The Führer can do their thinking for them.'

The brownshirt tapped the card. 'And this man here. What do you make of him, Heinz?'

'What can I say? I guess he probably really did lose a son . . .'

'Pah! The people that do these things are always rabble-rousers. Trying to follow their own ends. Sons – Germany – they don't care. I reckon it's some old Communist or Socialist . . .'

'I don't agree. I think you're wrong. They can never do without their phrases, you know, their "fascist reactionaries" and "solidarity" and "proletariat" – but there's none of that on this postcard. I don't think he's a Communist or Socialist; I'd smell that ten miles off, against the wind!'

'Ah well, I do. They've all learned to camouflage themselves . . .'

But the Gestapo gentlemen didn't agree with the brownshirt either. Incidentally, the report of the little fox was received there with great calm. They had plenty of other things to occupy them.

'Ah well,' they said. 'Okay. We'll see. If you'd like to take this up to Inspector Escherich, we can notify him by telephone, and he'll get on the case. Give him a detailed report on the behaviour of the two gentlemen. Of course no steps will be taken against them for the time being, but it's useful material to have on file, you understand?'

Inspector Escherich, a tall, gangling man with a drooping, sandy moustache, in a light grey suit – a man so dry, you could easily take him for a creation of office dust; well, then, Inspector Escherich – turned the card in his hands.

'A new record,' he said. 'I haven't got this one in my collection. A heavy hand, hasn't had occasion to do much writing in his life, a manual labourer, I should say.'

'Communist?' asked the little fox.

Inspector Escherich sniggered. 'Communist? You must be joking! If we had a police force worthy of the name and we prioritized the case, we'd have the guy locked up inside twenty-four hours.'

'How would you do that?'

'Very simple! I would get data for the whole of Berlin, and see who's lost a son in the previous two or three weeks – an only son, by the way, the writer only had one son!'

'How do you know that?'

'It says so in the first sentence, where he's talking about himself. It's in the second, when he's addressing others, that he says sons, plural. Well, and people in that position in Berlin – there won't be all that many of them – they would be my pool of suspects, and I'd have the writer put away in no time!'

'Then why don't you?'

'I told you already. We don't have the manpower for it and, second, the case isn't important enough. You see, there are two possibilities. He'll write another two or three postcards, and then he'll have had enough. You know, it's too much trouble, or the risk is too great. Then he won't have done much damage, and we won't have committed much in the way of resources.'

'Do you think all the postcards will be handed in to you?'

'Not all, but I would have thought most. On the whole the German people are pretty reliable . . .'

'Because they're afraid!'

'No, I didn't say that. For instance, I don't think this man, here,' he taps his knuckle against the card, 'is afraid. My hunch is for our second possibility: he will go on writing. Let him; the more he writes, the more he gives himself away. So far, he's only given away a tiny bit about himself, that he's lost a son. But with each card, he'll give away a little bit more of himself to me. I don't even need to do anything. I just need to sit here, stay alert, and one day – bingo – he's mine! In our department we just need to be patient. Sometimes it takes a year, sometimes even a bit more, but in the end we get our man. Almost always.'

'And what then?'

The dust-coloured man had pulled out a streetmap of Berlin and pinned it on the wall. Now he stuck in a red flag, exactly over the office block in the Neue Königstrasse. 'You see, this is all I can do for the moment. But over the next few weeks, more and more flags will go up, and where the density is greatest, that's where our hobgoblin will be found. Because over time he will wear out, and he won't want to go all that way to drop one of his postcards. You see, our hobgoblin isn't even thinking about this map. But it's so simple! And then bingo again, and I'll have caught him!'

'And what then?' the little fox asked again, impelled by a greedy curiosity.

Inspector Escherich looked at him a little sardonically. 'Do you really want to hear the details? All right, I'll tell you: People's Court, and then off with his head! What do I care? Why did the guy have to write an idiotic postcard that no one reads and no one wants to read! That's none of my concern. I draw my salary, and whether I sell postage stamps for it, or pin little flags on a map, I don't really care. But I'll think of you, I won't forget that it was you who brought me the first news of this guy, and when I've caught him and the time has come, I'll send you an invitation to his execution.'

'Oh, no thanks. I didn't really mean it like that!'

'Of course you meant it like that. Why be coy with me? No man needs to be coy with me, I know what people are like! If we, here, didn't know, then who on earth would? Not even God Almighty, I suspect. So that's a deal then: I'll send you an invitation to the execution. Heil Hitler!'

'Heil Hitler! And don't forget!'

20

Six Months Later: The Quangels

After six months, the writing of the postcards on Sunday afternoons had become a habit, a sacred habit, if you like, that was part of their everyday lives, just like the profound quiet they lived in, or their relentless economizing. For them, these were the best hours of the week, when they sat together on a Sunday, she on the sofa with some mending or darning, and he at the table, the pen in his big hand, slowly crafting one word after another.

Quangel had now indeed doubled his initial output of one card per week. On some good Sundays, he even managed to turn out three. No two cards ever said the same thing. Instead, the more the Quangels wrote, the more mistakes by the Führer and his Party they discovered. Things that when they first had happened had struck them as barely censurable, such as the suppression of all other political parties, or things that they had condemned as merely excessive in degree or too vigorously carried out, like the persecution of the Jews – such things, now that the Quangels had become enemies of the Führer, came to have a completely different weight and importance. They proved the mendacity of the Party and its Führer. And, like all converts, the Quangels had the desire to convert others, and so the tone of their postcards was never monotonous, and they were never short of material.

Anna Quangel had long since forsaken her quiet listening role. Now she sat on the sofa, speaking animatedly, suggesting topics, formulating sentences. They did their work in the most harmonious togetherness, and this deep, inner togetherness that they had only discovered now, after long years of marriage, became a great source of happiness to them, spreading its glow across their weeks. They saw each other, so to speak, with a single glance, they smiled, each knowing that the other had just thought about their next card, or the effect of their cards, of the steadily increasing number of their followers, and of the public that was already impatiently waiting.

Neither Quangel doubted for one moment that their cards were being passed from hand to hand in factories and offices, that Berlin was beginning to hum with talk about these oppositional spirits. They conceded that some of their cards probably wound up in the hands of the police, but they reckoned no more than one out of every five or six. They had so often thought and spoken about the great effectiveness of their work that the circulation of their cards and the attention that greeted them was, as far as they were concerned, no longer theoretical but factual.

And yet the Quangels didn't have the least actual evidence for this. Whether it was Anna Quangel standing in a food-queue, or the foreman with his sharp eyes taking up position among a group of chatterers – bringing their prattle to an end merely by standing there – not once did they hear a word about the new struggler against the Führer and the missives this unknown sent out into the world. But the silence that greeted their work could not shake them in their faith that it was being discussed and having an effect. Berlin was a very large city, and the scattering of the postcards took place over a very wide area, so it was clear that it would take time for knowledge of their activities to permeate everywhere. In other words, the Quangels were like most people: they believed what they hoped.

Of all the precautions that Quangel had deemed necessary at the outset only one had been dropped: the gloves. Careful consideration had led him to conclude that these awkward accoutrements that did so much to slow down his work were of no practical value. He presumed the cards would go through so many pairs of hands before one ever landed with the police that not even the most sophisticated detective would be able to work out which set of prints was that of the author. In other respects, Quangel continued to observe extreme caution. He always washed his hands before sitting down to write, held the cards gently and by the edge, and when he wrote he always kept a piece of blotting paper under his writing hand.

Meanwhile, the act of dropping the cards in large office buildings had long since lost the charm of novelty. The drops, which had once seemed so fraught with danger to him, had, over time, turned out to be the easiest part of his task. You walked into a busy building, you waited for the right moment, and then you were on your way back downstairs, a little relieved, a little easier in the gut, with the thought in your mind, 'Another one that passed off well,' but otherwise not particularly excited.

At first Quangel had dropped the cards on his own, and Anna's company had been particularly unwelcome to him. But then it came about quite of itself that here, too, Anna had become his active accomplice. It was a strict rule with Quangel that cards – whether one or two, or even three – always left the house the day after they were written. But there were days when he couldn't walk because of his rheumatism, and other days when caution demanded that the cards should be left in widely distant parts of the city. That implied time-consuming train rides, which a single person could hardly hope to accomplish in the course of a morning.

So Anna Quangel took over her share of the work in the deliveries as well. To her surprise she discovered that it was far more nerve-racking to stand in front of a building, waiting for her husband to emerge from it, than to go in and drop the cards herself. When doing it herself, she was always the embodiment of calm. As soon as she had entered a likely or designated building, she felt secure in the press of people going up and down stairs, she abided her opportunity patiently, and quickly set down her card. She was perfectly sure that no one had seen her making the drop, and that no one would remember her well enough to give a description of her person later. In truth, she was much less eye-catching than her husband with his sharp birdface. She really was every inch the little working-class woman, trotting off to the doctor.

There was only one occasion when the Quangels were disturbed during their Sunday writing. But even then, they hadn't shown the least agitation or confusion. As they had talked through many times, Anna Quangel had quietly crept out into the corridor at the sound of the ring and had looked at the visitors through the peephole. In the meantime, Otto Quangel had packed away the writing things and slipped the card, still in progress, inside a book. He had just written the words: 'Führer, lead – we follow! Yes, we follow, we're a herd of sheep for our Führer to drive to the abattoir. We have given up thinking . . .'

Otto Quangel slid the card inside a radio-kit manual of his dead son's, and when Anna Quangel came in with the two visitors, a short, hunchbacked man and a dark, tall, tired-looking woman, he was already sitting over his whittling, tinkering with the bust of their boy, which was now pretty well advanced, and, as Anna Quangel thought, becoming a better and better likeness. It turned out that the little hunchbacked man was Anna Quangel's brother; they hadn't seen each other for almost thirty years. The little hunchback had previously worked in an optical factory in Rathenow, and had recently been brought to Berlin to work as a specialist in a firm producing equipment for use on submarines. The dark, tired-looking woman was Anna's sister-in-law, whom she had never met before. Otto Quangel had not met these two relatives, either.

On that Sunday, there was no chance to do any more writing, and the half-finished card remained in Ottochen's radio-kit manual. However much the Quangels were opposed to visits, to friendship and family, for the sake of their peace and quiet, they couldn't find it in themselves to object to the unexpected appearance of this brother and sister-in-law. The Heffkes were quiet people themselves, members of some religious sect, that, to go by occasional hints they dropped, suffered persecution from the Nazis. But they hardly talked about such things, and politics formed little part of the conversation.

But Quangel listened in astonishment to hear Anna and her brother, Ulrich Heffke, swap childhood reminiscences. For the first time he heard what Anna had been like as a child, a girl full of glee, wickedness and tricks. He had met his wife when she was almost middle-aged; it had never occurred to him that she had once been completely different, before her arduous and joyless years as a domestic had robbed her of so much of her strength and optimism.

While the two siblings chatted together, he could picture the small, poor village in Brandenburg. He heard how she had had to keep geese, how she had tried to avoid the hated job of digging potatoes and had often been beaten for that reason. And he learned that she was well liked in the village, because, stubborn and brave as she was, she had rebelled against all forms of injustice. Once, she had even hit a tyrannical schoolteacher three times in a row with a snowball – and had never been betrayed as the guilty party. Only she and Ulrich had known it was her, and Ulrich never tattled.

No, this was no disagreeable visit, even though it meant their output was two cards fewer than usual. The Quangels were perfectly sincere when they promised to call on the Heffkes some time soon. They kept their word, too. Five or six weeks later, they looked them up in the little temporary accommodation they had been given in the west of the city, near Nollendorfplatz. The Quangels took advantage of this visit to finally drop a card out west. Even though it was a Sunday and offices had little traffic, it passed off safely.

From that time on, reciprocal visits took place every six weeks or so. They weren't overly stimulating, but for the Quangels it did at least mean a change of air. For the most part, Otto and his sister-in-law sat there silently and listened to the conversation between the two siblings, who never tired of talking about their childhood. It felt good to Quangel to get to know this other Anna too, even though he could never connect the woman who lived at his side and that girl who knew about farmwork, played tricks on people, and still had the reputation of being the best student in the little country school.

They learned that Anna's parents were still living in her birthplace, very old now – Ulrich mentioned that he was sending them ten marks a month. Anna Quangel was about to say that the Quangels would do the same, but she caught a warning look from her husband just in time, and stopped.

It wasn't till they were on their way home that he said, 'Nah, better not, Anna. Why spoil the old people? They have their pension, and if your brother sends them ten marks a month, that's plenty.'

'But we have so much money saved up!' Anna implored him. 'We'll never get through it. Earlier on, we thought it would do for Ottochen, but now . . . Let's do it, Otto! Even five marks a month!'

Unmoved, Otto Quangel replied, 'Now that we're involved in our undertaking, we have no idea what we might need money for at some stage. It's possible we'll need every last mark of it, Anna. And the old people have got by without us so far – why shouldn't they continue?'

She didn't reply – feeling a little offended – maybe not so much out of love for her parents, because she didn't often think about them, and only sent them a Christmas letter every year out of a sense of duty, but she did feel a little ashamed and mean in front of her brother. He wasn't to think they couldn't afford what he could afford.

Anna said obstinately, 'Ulrich will think we can't afford it, Otto. He won't think much of your job if it doesn't run to that.'

'What does it matter what other people think of me,' retorted Quangel. 'I'm not going to take money from the bank for something like that.'

Anna sensed this was his last word. She didn't say anything more, but knuckled under as she always did when she heard a sentence like that from Otto. Nevertheless she felt a bit hurt that her husband paid such scant regard to her feelings. But then, Anna Quangel soon forgot her injury when they resumed their work on the great project.

21

Six Months Later: Inspector Escherich

Six months after the receipt of the first postcard, Inspector Escherich stood stroking his sandy moustache in front of the map of Berlin, which he had marked with little red flags for the points where the Quangels' postcards had been found. There were now forty-four such flags on the map; of the forty-eight postcards that the Quangels had written and dropped in those six months, all but four were now in the hands of the Gestapo. And even those four hadn't been passed from hand to hand in factories and offices, as the Quangels believed; barely read, they had been immediately ripped up, flushed away, or consigned to the flames.

The door opens, and Escherich's superior, SS Obergruppenführer Prall walks in. 'Heil Hitler, Escherich! Why so thoughtful?'

'Heil Hitler, Obergruppenführer! It's the postcard phantom – the "Hobgoblin", as I like to call him.'

'Oh? Why's that?'

'No reason. Just thought of it. Maybe because he wants to make everyone afraid.'

'And how far along are we with the case, Escherich?'

Escherich gave a long, drawn-out 'Hmm!' He looked thoughtfully at the map. 'Well, according to the distribution, he ought to be somewhere north of Alexanderplatz; that's where we have the highest incidence. But the city centre and the east are fairly well covered, too. None at all in the south, and in the west, just two recorded drops south of Nollendorfplatz – I suppose he must have something that brings him there occasionally.'

'In other words, the map doesn't tell us anything! It's not a blind bit of use!'

'Wait! Patience! In another six months, unless my Hobgoblin

has already blundered in that time, the map will have far more to say.'

'Six months! You're priceless, Escherich! You want to leave that pig to wallow and grunt for six more months, and not do anything to harass him but stick in a few more of your dainty flags!'

'In our line of work we need to be patient, Obergruppenführer. In your terms, it would be like lying in wait for a stag. You can't shoot before he appears. But when he comes, I'll let him have it, don't you worry!'

'All I hear is patience, patience, Escherich! Do you think our bosses have that much patience? I'm afraid we'll get a dressing-down soon that we won't forget in a hurry. Think about it, forty-four cards, that's almost two a week delivered to us here. My superiors know that. And so they ask me: Well? Caught him yet? Why not? What is it you do? Stick flags in a map and twiddle our thumbs, I reply. And then I get my dressing-down, and the order to arrest the man within two weeks.'

Inspector Escherich was grinning behind his sandy moustache. 'And then you come along and you bawl me out, and give me the instruction to nab the man in one week!'

'Take that grin off your face, you loon! If something like this comes to Himmler's attention, all bets are off, and who knows if we won't meet one day in Sachsenhausen, reminiscing about the good old days when all we did was stick flags into maps!'

'Don't worry, Obergruppenführer! I'm an old hand at this, and I know we can't do anything better than what we're doing at the moment: wait. Let your superiors come up with some better way of capturing my Hobgoblin if they can. Of course, they can't.'

'Escherich, think about it, if we get forty-four of the things in here, well, that means at least as many, maybe over a hundred postcards, knocking around Berlin, sowing dissatisfaction, encouraging sabotage. We can't sit back and let it happen!'

'A hundred postcards in circulation!' Escherich said, and laughed. 'You just don't know the German people, Obergruppen-führer! Oh, I'm so sorry, please excuse me, Obergruppenführer,

I didn't mean it to sound like that, of course the Obergruppenführer has a very keen idea of the German people, certainly
better than I do, but the people are all so frightened now! They're
handing the things in like there's no tomorrow – I bet there's
no more than ten postcards in circulation that we haven't
accounted for.'

After a wrathful look on account of Escherich's offensive exclamation (these old policemen really were a bit dim, and acted
way too pally!) and a warning raising of his arm, the Obergruppenführer said: 'But even ten are too many! One is too many! I
don't want any circulating any more! Arrest the man, Escherich
– and fast!'

The inspector stood there in silence. He didn't lift his gaze
from his superior's gleaming bootcaps, but merely stroked his
moustache and remained silent.

'Well may you stand there in silence!' exclaimed Prall angrily.
'I know what you're thinking. You're thinking that I'm another
one of those clever dicks who can shout down your ideas, but
haven't any of their own.'

Inspector Escherich had long since lost the ability to blush.
But at that instant, when his secret thoughts were so exactly as
claimed by Prall, he was as near to doing it as he could be. He
felt more embarrassed than he had in a long time.

Obergruppenführer Prall was aware of this. Cheerily he said,
'Well, I don't want to embarrass you, Escherich! And I don't want
to dole out advice, either. I'm no detective, as you know, I've just
been delegated to head up this section. But now tell me something,
will you? In the next few days I will have to report on this case,
and I'd like to get my facts straight. The man has never been seen
in the act of dropping these cards, is that right?'

'Never.'

'And no suspicions exist in the buildings where the cards were
found?'

'Suspicions? Oodles of suspicions! There's suspicion everywhere nowadays. But there's nothing informing it beyond pettish-
ness against a neighbour, a bit of snooping, eagerness to come
forward with an accusation.'

'And the people bringing them in? All beyond suspicion themselves?'

'Beyond suspicion?' Escherich twisted his mouth. 'Good God, Obergruppenführer, no one is beyond suspicion these days.' And, with a hurried glance at the face of his superior, 'Or everyone is. But we've gone through all the finders twice through. None of them has anything to do with the writer of the cards.'

The Obergruppenführer sighed. 'You should have been a minister. You're so comforting, Escherich!' he said. 'Well, so we're left with the cards themselves. What sort of clues do they offer?'

'Few. Precious few!' said Escherich. 'And I wouldn't want to be a minister, I'm telling you the truth, Obergruppenführer! After the first mistake he made by mentioning his son, I thought he would betray himself. But he's turned out to be a cunning so-and-so.'

'Tell me, Escherich!' Prall suddenly exclaimed, 'did you ever think it might be a woman? It just occurred to me, hearing you speak of the only son.'

The inspector looked at his superior in surprise for a moment. He reflected. Then he said, sadly shaking his head, 'No, it's not that either, Obergruppenführer. That's one of the points I'm absolutely certain of. My Hobgoblin is a widower, or a man who lives by himself. If there was a woman anywhere involved, there'd have been some loose talk, I'm sure of that. Six months – no woman can keep a secret for that length of time!'

'Maybe a mother who's lost her only son?'

'Not possible. That least of all!' determined Escherich. 'Whoever has a sorrow will seek comfort, and to obtain comfort, you have to talk. I'm sure there's no woman in the picture. There's only one person who knows the story, and he's not telling anyone!'

'As I said: a minister! What other leads?'

'Few, Obergruppenführer, very few. I'm pretty sure the man is a miser, or has at some time had a run-in with the Winter Relief Fund. Because whatever else he writes on the cards, he never fails to say: DON'T GIVE TO THE WINTER RELIEF FUND!'

'Well, Escherich, if it's a matter of looking for people in Berlin who are loath to give to the Winter Relief Fund . . .'

'As I say, Obergruppenführer. It's not much.'

'What else?'

The inspector shrugged his shoulders. 'Nothing, really,' he said. 'We can fairly safely assume the card dropper doesn't have a regular job, because the cards have been found at all times of day, from eight in the morning to nine at night. And as the staircases that my Hobgoblin likes to use are much frequented, we can probably assume that there's only a short time between a card being dropped and its being handed in to us. And other than that? Perhaps a manual worker who hasn't had occasion to do much writing in his life, but not badly educated, hardly ever misspells a word, expresses himself fairly skilfully . . .'

Escherich stopped, and both men said nothing for quite a long time, as they stared blankly at the map with its red flags.

Then Obergruppenführer Prall said, 'A hard nut to crack, Escherich. A hard nut for both of us.'

The inspector said comfortingly, 'There's no nut that's too hard to crack – a nutcracker will do the job!'

'Sometimes you get your fingers jammed, though, Escherich!'

'Patience, Obergruppenfhürer, a little patience!'

'Well, as long as the people upstairs are patient; it's not my call. Go and rack your brain some more, maybe you'll find a better strategy than just waiting around. Heil Hitler, Escherich!'

'Heil Hitler, Obergruppenführer!'

On his own again, Inspector Escherich stood a while in front of the map, stroking his moustache. The case wasn't entirely the way he had presented it. Here, he wasn't the hard-boiled detective whom nothing could shock or surprise. He had become interested in this quiet and, alas, still unknown cardwriter, who had thrown himself so fearlessly and so deliberately into an almost hopeless struggle. The Hobgoblin case, to begin with, had been one among many. But now he was interested. He had to find the man who was out there under one of the ten thousand roofs of Berlin; he wanted to see him face to face, this man who, with the regularity of a machine, turned out two or three postcards every week, which arrived at his desk on Monday evening, or Tuesday morning at the very latest.

Escherich had long run out of the patience he had prescribed to the Obergruppenführer. Escherich was a huntsman – the old detective was a lover of the chase. It was in his blood. Others hunted wild boar; he hunted humans. The fact that the boar or the human had to die at the end of the chase – that didn't move him at all. It was preordained for the boar to die like this, as it was for humans if they wrote such postcards. He had been racking his brain for some time on how to find the Hobgoblin sooner – he didn't need Obergruppenführer Prall to prod him. But patience remained the only method. In such a minor matter, you couldn't unleash the resources of an entire police force, search every apartment in Berlin – quite apart from the fact that he wasn't supposed to provoke agitation in the city. He needed to have patience.

And then, if you were sufficiently patient, something might happen quite suddenly: almost always, something happened. The criminal would make a mistake, or luck would desert him. It was those two things you had to wait for, the mistake or the change of luck. One or the other almost always happened. Escherich hoped that in this case, though, there wouldn't be any 'almost'. He was interested, all right, powerfully interested. Basically, he didn't care now whether he settled some criminal's hash or not. Escherich, as noted, was a hunter. Not because he loved the taste of roast meat, but for the pleasure of the chase. He knew that at the moment the quarry was killed, or the criminal was caught and confronted with the evidence – at that moment his interest in a case would die. The quarry was killed, the man was in a detention cell, the hunt was over. Till the next one.

Escherich turns his colourless gaze away from the map. Now he sits at his desk and slowly and thoughtfully eats his lunch. When the telephone rings, he hesitates briefly, then picks up. Fairly indifferently, he listens to the voice at the other end: 'This is the Police Department at Frankfurter Allee. Inspector Escherich?'

'Speaking.'

'Are you working on the case of the anonymous postcards?'

'Yes, I am. Any developments? Come on, make it quick!'

'We're pretty sure we've caught the card dropper.'

'In the act?'

'All but. He denies it, of course.'

'Where are you holding him?'

'Here at the station.'

'Keep him, I'll be with you in ten minutes. And don't question him further! Leave the fellow in peace! I want to talk to him myself. Understood?'

'Perfectly, Inspector!'

'I'm on my way!'

For a moment, Inspector Escherich stood nearly motionless by the telephone. The lucky chance – Lady Luck! He knew it, it was a matter of patience!

He hurried off to the first interrogation of the cardwriter.

22

Six Months Later: Enno Kluge

The precision machinist Enno Kluge sat impatiently in the waiting room. He was sitting with some thirty or forty others. A tetchy assistant had just called out number 18. Enno was number 29. He would be another hour, and they were already waiting for him at the Also Ran.

Enno Kluge was fed up with sitting. He knew he couldn't go till the doctor had signed his certificate, otherwise there'd be trouble at the factory. But he couldn't wait any longer, or he'd miss making his bets.

Enno wants to pace back and forth. But the room's too full for that, the other people will complain. So he goes out to the corridor, and when the assistant sees him and tells him irritably to get back in the waiting room right away, he asks for the toilet.

She shows him unwillingly, and even thinks of waiting outside the door for him. But then the corridor bell sounds several times in succession, and she has to receive patients 43, 44 and 45, take down their details, fill in the card index entries, stamp their medical cards.

That's how it is from early morning till late at night. She's dead on her feet, the doctor's dead on his feet, and she never seems to get out of this state of irritation that she's been in for weeks and weeks now. In this state, she's capable of venting real hatred on the never-ending stream of patients who never leave her any peace, who are standing patiently at the door when she arrives at eight in the morning and are still hanging around at ten at night, filling the waiting room with their miasma: all of them shirkers, shirkers from work or from the Front, people hoping for a medical certificate to help them procure more rations or better rations. All of them are people dodging their duty, which she can't do. She has to stick it out here, she mustn't get sick. (What would the doctor do without her?) She even has to be friendly to all those liars that soil everything, piss on everything, puke over everything. The toilet's always full of cigarette ash.

That reminds her of the little creep she had to conduct to the toilet just a while ago. He's sure to be there still, puffing away. She leaps up, runs out, and rattles the door.

'Occupied!' comes the call from inside.

'Will you hurry up and get out of there!' she begins to scold. 'What makes you think you can monopolize the toilet! There's other people want to use it as well as you!'

As Kluge slinks past her she shouts after him, 'Of course it's all fugged up with smoke! I'll tell the doctor how ill you are! You've got it coming to you!'

Discouraged, Enno Kluge leans against the wall of the waiting room – his chair has been taken in the meantime. The doctor has got to patient 22. Probably completely pointless to go on waiting here. The bitch outside is perfectly capable of telling the doctor to refuse him a certificate. And then what? Then there's trouble in the factory! It's the fourth day he's been off; they're perfectly capable of sending him to a punishment battalion or a concentration camp – it's just the kind of thing they do! He needs a certificate today, and it's best he stays here, given that he's been waiting so long anyway. If he goes to a different doctor, the other waiting room will be just as full, and he'd have to sit there till night, and at least he's heard this guy is pretty free with his certificates. So he'll just have to give the gee-gees a miss today, his pals will have to get by without Enno, it can't be helped . . .

He leans against the wall and coughs, a feeble so-and-so. Better be nothing at all. He's never really got over his beating up by that SS man Persicke. True, work got a bit better after a couple of days, even though his hands never recovered their old dexterity. He was just about as good as a run-of-the-mill worker now. He would never recover his old finesse, or become a respected man in his field.

Perhaps that was why he felt so indifferent about work, but

it could equally well be that in the long run he didn't really enjoy it. He didn't see the point. Why strain yourself if you could live passably well without it! Was it the war? Let them fight their shitty war by themselves, he didn't care for it. If they sent the bigwigs to the front, then the war would be over just like that!

No, it wasn't the meaninglessness of his work that made it repugnant to him. It was the fact that Enno was able to get by without working. Yes, he had been weak, he would admit it now: he had gone back to his women, first to Tutti, then to Lotte, and they were both quite prepared to keep this small, adhesive man afloat for a while. And as soon as you got involved with women, any form of ordered existence went out the window. In the morning they started scolding him when he called for his coffee and breakfast at six. What was he thinking of? At such a time, normal people were asleep! He should just crawl back to his warm bed!

Well, once or twice you might come through a battle like that, but the third time, if you were Enno Kluge, you didn't. You gave in, you went back to the women in their beds, and you slept for another hour, or two, or even three hours.

If it was as late as that, then he didn't bother turning up at the factory, but took the day off. If it was any earlier, he came in late, with some lame excuse, got yelled at (but he was used to that, he'd stopped listening), put in a couple of hours, and went home, to be greeted with more yelling: What was the point of keeping a man in the house if he was gone all day? For the few marks he brought home! There were easier ways of earning money than that! No, if it had to be work, it would have been better to stay in his tight little hotel room – women and work were not compatible. There was one exception, and that was Eva – and of course Enno Kluge had tried to crawl back to her, the postie. But then he learned from Frau Gesch that Eva had gone away. Frau Gesch had got a letter from her, she was somewhere up in Ruppin, with relatives. Frau Gesch had the keys to the flat now, but she wouldn't dream of giving them to Enno Kluge. Who was it who paid the rent, him or his wife? So then, the flat was hers, not his! Frau Gesch had put herself to enough trouble on his account, she was damned if she was going to let him into the flat.

But if he wanted to do something for his wife, he ought to go round to the post office some time. They had tried to get in touch with Frau Kluge a couple of times, and once a summons to some Party tribunal had come; Frau Gesch had simply sent it back with 'Recipient no longer known at this address'. But why didn't he go to the post office and get it sorted out? His wife probably had some sort of outstanding claim there.

The part about the claim had tempted him; he could, after all, document himself as the lawful husband. But going there turned out to be a big mistake; they gave him a real going-over at the post office. Eva must have got in some trouble with the Party, they were furious with her! In the end he was in no hurry to document himself as her lawful husband – quite the opposite, he tried as hard as he could to prove that he had been separated from Eva for a long time, and knew nothing, and wished to know nothing about what she was doing.

In the end, they let him go. What was there they could do with a little man like that, who was all set to wail at a moment's notice and trembled each time they barked at him? So, let him go then, let him get the hell out, and if he did see his wife again, he should send her along to the office. Or better yet, he should tip them a wink where she was staying, and they could take care of the rest themselves.

On his way home to Lotte, Enno Kluge was grinning again. So, solid, hard-working Eva was in a jam herself, and had taken off to Ruppin to her relatives, and no longer dared show her face in Berlin! Of course, Enno hadn't been stupid enough to let the postal officials know where Eva had gone to; he was as smart as Frau Gesch any day of the week. It would be one last way out: if things ever came to a head in Berlin, he could always turn up at Eva's, maybe she would take him in. She might feel constrained in front of her relatives not to treat him too coldly. Eva still set store by appearances and a good reputation. Plus he had her over a barrel with Karlemann's heroic deeds; she wouldn't be able to stand it if he started telling her relatives about that. She'd sooner have him back.

One last way out, if everything went pear-shaped. For the time being, he still had his Lotte. She was really pretty okay, except for her gabbiness and her damned habit of bringing men back to the flat. He had to spend half the night, sometimes the whole of it, hunkered in the kitchen – and that meant no work again the following morning.

Work would never come right again, and he knew it really. But maybe the war would end sooner than people thought and he would succeed in keeping them off his back. And so he had very gradually fallen into his old habits of idling and staying away. When the boss saw him he would flush purple. Then there was a second telling-off from the management, but this time it hadn't had much effect on him. Enno Kluge knew the game: they needed workers, they couldn't afford to just throw him out!

Then there had been a run of three days off in quick succession. He had met this delightful widow, no longer in her first flush of youth, a bit of spare flesh on her, but still decidedly a cut above his other women of the moment. My God, she even had a flourishing pet shop business near the Königstor! She traded in birds and fish and dogs, she sold feed and collars and sand and dog biscuits and mealworms. You could buy tortoises there, frogs, salamanders and cats . . . A business that was really thriving, and she was a good, hard-working businesswoman.

He had identified himself to her as a widower, and he had made her believe Enno was his surname; she called him Hänschen. Definitely, he was in with a chance with this woman – he had seen that pretty clearly on his days off, when he helped her out in her shop. A man like him, in need of a little tenderness, that was just what she needed, really. She was at that point where a woman gets to wondering if she'll ever find a man again for her old age. Of course she would want to marry him, but he would be able to sort something out there. After all, there were now such things as war marriages, where they weren't that fussy about paperwork, and he certainly wouldn't have to worry about Eva making a nuisance of herself. She would be pleased to be rid of him for good, she wouldn't suddenly kick up!

With that, he suddenly felt a burning desire to be done with the factory for good. He had to play the invalid anyway, as he had been away for three days without permission, so why not go the whole way! And during his medical leave he could work on charming this widow, Hetty Haberle. He felt disgusted by Lotte now. He couldn't stand that situation any more, not the backchat, not the other men, and least of all, not her advances to him when she was juiced up. No, in three or four weeks he wanted to be a married man and living in a well-regulated home! And for that he needed a doctor.

Number 24. It'll be another half hour yet till it's Enno's turn. Mechanically, he climbs over everyone's feet and goes out in the hallway again. In spite of the dragon of an assistant, he wants another cigarette in the bog. He's in luck and gets there unnoticed, but no sooner has he taken the first couple of drags than the cunt is banging on the door again.

'You're on the toilet again! You're smoking again!' she yells. 'I know it's you! Get out of there at once, before I call the doctor!'

That awful shrill voice! He gives in right away, preferring, as he generally does, surrender to resistance. He lets her chase him back into the waiting room, without offering a word of apology or defence. And there he is leaning against the wall again, waiting for his number to come up. And her about to snitch on him to the doctor, the bloody bitch!

The receptionist, having chased little Enno Kluge back to his place, is walking back down the corridor. She's shown him who's boss, all right!

Then she sees a card on the floor, a little way away from the letterbox. It wasn't there five minutes ago, when she let in the last patient, she's sure of that. She never heard the bell go, and it's not the regular time for the mail, either.

All this has gone through the receptionist's mind as she stoops to pick up the postcard, and later she is sure that even before she held it in her hands, before she knew what sort of card it was, she had the feeling that it was something to do with that sneaky little man.

She casts an eye on the card, reads a few words, and runs into the doctor's office: 'Doctor! Doctor! See what I just found in the corridor!'

She interrupts the consultation, she has the half-naked patient dispatched into the other room, and then she gives the doctor the card to read. She can hardly wait for him to get to the end, and already she's voicing her suspicion: 'It really can't have been anyone but that little shit! I took against him right away, with his shifty eyes! He had such a guilty conscience, he couldn't sit still a minute, he was forever going out into the corridor, twice I had to chase him out of the toilet! And as I'm doing it the second time, I see the card lying on the floor. It can't have been dropped in from outside, it's too far from the letterbox! Doctor, call the police before the man slinks off! Perhaps he's run off already, I'd better look and see . . .'

With that she runs out of the doctor's office, leaving the door wide open behind her.

The doctor stands there with the postcard in his hand. He is terribly embarrassed that something like this had to happen during his office hours! Thank God it was his receptionist who found the card and he can prove that he hasn't been out of the office for the past two hours, not even to go to the toilet. The girl's right, the best thing is to call the police right away. He starts looking up the number of the local police station in the phone book.

The girl peeks through the open doorway. 'He's still here, doctor!' she whispers. 'Of course he thinks he can deflect suspicion from himself. But I'm completely certain . . .'

'All right,' the doctor interrupts his agitated assistant. 'Shut the door now. I'm talking to the police.'

He makes his report and is instructed to keep the man there till someone from the station arrives. He passes the instruction to his assistant, tells her to call him the moment the man gets ready to leave, and sits down at his desk. No, he can't see any more patients, he is too agitated. How could something like this happen, and why did it have to be to him? What a selfish and unscrupulous fellow, this postcard writer, plunging people into such difficulties! Didn't he think of the trouble he would cause with those confounded cards!

Really, this card was the final straw. Now the police were on their way, perhaps he would find himself under suspicion, they would search the premises, and even if it turned out that their suspicion was wrong, they would still find, in the servant's room at the back . . .

The doctor stood up, he at least had to warn her . . .

And sat down again. How could he come under suspicion? And even if they found her, she was his housekeeper, which was what it said on her papers. It had all been thought about and talked through a hundred times, ever since that time over a year ago when he had had to divorce his wife, a Jewess – under pressure from the Nazis. He had done it principally in response to her pleas, to keep the children safe. Later on, after changing his address, he had installed her as his 'housekeeper', with false papers. Really, nothing could happen, she didn't even look especially Jewish . . .

That damned card! Why it had to involve him, of all people! But probably that was how it was: whoever it came to, it would create panic and fear. In these times everyone had something to hide!

Perhaps that was precisely the purpose of the card, to provoke panic and fear? Perhaps such cards were a fiendish device, to be distributed among suspicious individuals, to see how they reacted? Perhaps he had been under surveillance for a long time already, and this was just a further means to monitor his response?

At any rate, he had behaved correctly. Five minutes after the card was found, he had got in touch with the police. And he was even able to come up with a suspect, perhaps some poor devil who had nothing to do with the affair. Well, it wasn't his problem, he had to get himself clear if he could! The main thing was that the doctor was spared.

And even though these thoughts have made the doctor a little calmer, he gets up and quickly and deftly fills a little morphine syringe. That will allow him to face the gentlemen who are on their way to him with serenity, even boredom. The little syringe is the aid to which the doctor has increasingly resorted ever since the humiliation, as he still considers it, of his divorce. He's not an addict, far from it, he sometimes goes five or six days without morphine, but when he encounters difficulties in his life, and that seems to be more and more frequently, then he takes it. It's the only thing that helps; without it he would lose his nerve. Oh, if only the war were over and he could leave this wretched country! He would be happy with the meanest little junior post abroad.

Some minutes later, a pale, slightly tired-looking doctor receives the two gentlemen from the police station. One of them is a uniformed sergeant, brought here to watch the door to the corridor. He immediately sits down in the receptionist's place.

The other, Deputy Inspector Schröder, is in civilian clothes – and the doctor hands him the postcard. Did he have a statement to make? Well, there's not much he can say, he's been treating patients for the past two hours without interruption, perhaps twenty or twenty-five patients. But he will ask Fräulein Kiesow.

The receptionist comes in, and she has plenty to say. She describes the creep – her term – with a venom that seems out of proportion to the crime of two harmless smoking episodes in the toilet. The doctor observes her closely, how aroused she is, her voice often cracking as she answers the questions. He thinks, I really must get her to do something about her hyper-thyroidism. It's getting worse and worse. She's so excited that she's basically no longer rational.

The deputy inspector seems to be thinking along the same lines. With a peremptory 'Thank you! I think we've heard enough for the moment!' he brings her account to an end. 'One more thing, Fräulein! Would you show me where you saw the card on the corridor? As precisely as you can!'

The receptionist puts the card down on a spot where it seems impossible it could have got to from the letterbox. But the deputy inspector, aided by his sergeant, repeatedly pushes the card through the slot till it lands close to the designated point. Perhaps just three or four inches away . . .

'Couldn't it have been lying here, Fräulein?' asks the deputy inspector.

The receptionist is visibly shocked at the success of the deputy inspector's experiment. She declares quite categorically, 'No, the card can't have been so close to the door! If anything, it was a bit further along the corridor than I first thought. I think it was just behind the chair here.' And she points to a spot a foot and a half further away. 'I'm almost sure I bumped against this chair when I picked up the card.'

'I see,' says the deputy inspector, and calmly studies the hate-filled woman. Privately, he strikes out all her evidence. She's a hysteric, he thinks. Short of a man. Well, they're all in the field, and she's not the best-looking girl I've seen, either.

He turns to the doctor: 'I would like to spend three minutes in your waiting room as a newly arrived patient, and observe the accused man without him knowing who I am. Would that be possible?'

'Of course. Fräulein Kiesow will tell you where he's sitting.'

'Standing!' says the receptionist angrily. 'A man like that won't sit! He'd rather trample around on everyone else's feet! His guilty conscience won't leave him in peace. That creep . . .'

'Where is he now?' the deputy inspector interrupts her again, rather impolitely.

'Before, he was standing next to the mirror by the window,' she replies, offended. 'Of course I can't tell you where he is now, he's so restless!'

'I'll find him,' says Deputy Inspector Schröder. 'I have your description to go on, after all.'

And he goes into the waiting room.

There is some unrest in the waiting room. It's twenty minutes since the last patient was called – how long are they meant to have to wait? God knows they have enough other things to do! Probably the doctor is attending to wealthy private patients, and leaving the others to rot! But that's what all doctors do, you can go to anyone you like, it's always the same story! Money talks, and to hell with everything else!

While the patients trade increasingly lurid anecdotes on the venality of doctors, the deputy inspector silently scrutinizes his man. He identified him right away. The man is neither as restless nor as creepy as the receptionist described him. He is standing quite calmly beside the mirror, taking no part in the general conversation. He looks dull-witted and a little timid. Labourer, reckons the deputy inspector. No, a little better than that, his hands look deft, traces of work, but not hard work, suit and coat kept up with great care, though not enough to prevent their age and wear from becoming apparent. Nothing resembling the profile of the man you would expect from the tone of the card. The card writer had a forceful style, after all, and this scaredy-cat . . .

But the deputy inspector knows there's only so much point in going by appearances. And this man is sufficiently implicated by the witness's statement that they will have to look him over. The postcard writer seems to have flustered a few feathers upstairs – not long ago, there was another 'Highly Confidential' order to give top priority to the case.

It would be nice to book a little success, thinks the deputy inspector. It's time for a promotion.

Amid the general unrest he walks almost unnoticed to the little man by the mirror, taps him on the shoulder, and says, 'Would you mind coming out into the corridor for a moment or two. I've got some questions for you.'

Enno Kluge follows him out, obedient as he always is when faced with an order. But as he follows this unknown gentleman, he feels a surge of fear: What's this about? What does he want? He looks like a policeman, talks like a policeman, too. What do the police want with me – I've not done anything!

At the same moment, he remembers the break-in at the Rosenthals'. There's no doubt about it, Borkhausen's gone and stitched him up. And his fear grows. He's been sworn to silence and if he does say something, that SS man will beat him up again, only much worse! He daren't say anything, but then this cop will have a go at him, and then he will end up talking after all. He's between a rock and hard place . . . Oh the fear!

As he steps out into the corridor, four faces look expectantly at him – but he doesn't see them, he just sees the policeman's uniform, and he knows he was right to be afraid, and that he really is between a rock and a hard place.

His fear lends Enno Kluge qualities he doesn't ordinarily possess, namely decisiveness, strength and speed. He shoves the surprised deputy inspector, who never expected it from the little weakling, into the arms of the sergeant, runs past the doctor and receptionist, tears open the door, and is already running down the stairs . . .

But behind him the sergeant is blowing a whistle, and Enno isn't fast enough to get away from the long-legged young man. He catches up with Enno on the bottom step, gives him a clout that knocks him down on to the steps, and when Enno can see again past the spinning suns and stars, the sergeant says with a friendly smile, 'All right, then, give us your mitts! Gonna have to cuff you. Next time you go anywhere, I'm coming, too, okay?'

And already the steel is jingling around his wrists and he's headed back upstairs, between the silent, angry-looking detective and this contentedly smiling sergeant, for whom this attempt at flight was just a little escapade.

Upstairs, where the patients are now thronging the corridor and aren't at all annoyed any more at having to wait so long to be examined by their doctor, because an arrest is always an interesting development – and to go by what the receptionist said, this arrest is of a political nature, a Commie apparently, and Commies deserve whatever is coming to them – upstairs, then, they file past all these faces into the doctor's office. Fräulein Kiesow is immediately sent outside by the deputy inspector, but the doctor is permitted to be present during the questioning, and he hears the deputy inspector say: 'All right, my son, sit down, take a breather after your recent exertions! You look pretty shattered, I must say! Sergeant, why don't you take the cuffs off this gentleman. He won't run off again – will you?'

'No, no!' promises Enno Kluge in despair; already the tears are pouring down his face.

'I wouldn't advise it either! The next time, we'll draw pistols, and I'm a decent shot, son.' The deputy inspector continues to address Kluge, who is twenty years his senior, as 'son'. 'Now, don't cry like that! You won't have done anything too terrible. Or . . .'

'I've done nothing!' Enno Kluge blurts out between tears. 'Nothing whatever!'

'Of course not, son!' the deputy inspector agrees. 'That's why you take off like a startled bunny when you see the sergeant's uniform! Doctor, haven't you got anything that would help this poor wretch feel a little better?'

Now that the doctor feels all danger to himself is averted, he looks at the unhappy little man with a good deal of sympathy: he's one of those natural victims who are invariably knocked for a loop by any setback. The doctor is tempted to give the man a jab of morphine, in the lowest concentration. But in the presence of the detective, of course, he doesn't dare. A little bromide . . .

But while the bromide is dissolving in a glass of water, Enno Kluge says: 'I don't need anything. I don't want to take anything. I'm not letting you poison me. I'd rather speak . . .'

'Well, then!' says the detective. 'Didn't I know you'd see sense, my son! Then tell us . . .'

And Enno Kluge wipes the tears off his cheeks, and starts to talk . . .

When he began to cry, the tears were real enough, because his nerves were shot. But even then, as Enno has learned from his dealings with women, it's possible to think quite well while crying. And in the course of his thinking, it came to him that it was most unlikely that they were picking him up in a doctor's waiting room over the break-in. If they really were shadowing him, then they could perfectly well have arrested him on the landing outside, or in the street; they didn't have to let him stew in a waiting room for two hours . . .

No, this present business is probably nothing to do with the break-in at Frau Rosenthal's. Probably it's down to a mistake, and Enno Kluge has a dim idea that the receptionist, that nasty piece of work, has something to do with it.

But now he's tried to make a break for it, and he'll never be able to persuade a policeman that he did so merely out of nerves, because he loses his head at the sight of a uniform. A policeman would never believe that. So he has to admit something credible and checkable, and he has an idea what that should be, too. It's bad to talk about it, and the consequences are unpredictable, but of two evils such a confession is certainly the lesser.

So when he's invited to speak, he mops his face and starts talking in a reasonably steady voice about his work as a machinist, and how he's been ill such a lot of late that they lost patience with him and want to stick him in a concentration camp, or else in a punishment battalion. Of course Enno Kluge doesn't say anything about his habitual shirking, but he thinks the detective will get the picture anyway.

And he's pretty much right about that: the detective sees what a specimen this Enno Kluge is. 'Yes, Inspector, and when I saw you and the sergeant's uniform, and I was just waiting to see the doctor, to get myself on disability, then I thought, My time's up, and they're picking me up to take me to a concentration camp, and so I scarpered . . .'

'I see,' the deputy inspector says. 'I see!' He thinks for a while, and then he says: 'But it seems to me, son, that in your heart of hearts you don't really believe that that's what we've come about.'

'No, not really,' Kluge admits.

'And why don't you really believe that, son?'

'Well, because it would have been much easier for you to come for me in the factory, or at home.'

'So you've got a home to go to, have you, son?'

'Of course, I do, Inspector. My wife works at the post office, I'm a married man. My two sons are in the field, one of them's with the SS in Poland. I've got papers with me to prove it all, the flat and the place of work.'

And Enno Kluge pulls out his tatty, beaten-up looking wallet, and starts pulling out papers.

'Never mind your papers for now, son,' says the deputy inspector, waving his hand. 'There's plenty of time for that later . . .'

He lapses into thought, and no one speaks.

Now at his desk the doctor hurriedly begins writing. Perhaps he will get a chance to furnish the little man, who is being chased from one fear into another, with a disability certificate. Problem with his gall bladder, he said, well then. In these times people need to help each other whenever possible!

'What's that you're writing, Doctor?' asks the deputy inspector, suddenly emerging from his ponderings.

'Medical notes,' the doctor explains. 'I'm trying to spend the time usefully; I've still got a roomful of patients waiting to see me.'

'You're quite right, doctor,' says the deputy inspector, getting to his feet. He has come to a decision: 'I won't detain you any longer.'

Enno Kluge's story may be true, it most probably is true, but the deputy inspector can't shake the feeling that there's something else involved as well and that he hasn't yet heard the whole truth. 'Well, come on, my son! You'll accompany me a little further, won't you? Oh, no, not to the Alex, only to our local station. I'd like to chat with you a little longer, my son, alert fellow that you are, and we mustn't get under the doctor's feet any more than we have already.' He says to the sergeant, 'No, no need for handcuffs. He'll come along willingly, bright boy that he is. Heil Hitler, Doctor, and many thanks!'

They're already in the doorway, and everything looks as though they really are leaving. But then the deputy inspector suddenly pulls the postcard, Quangel's postcard, out of his pocket, holds it under Enno Kluge's nose, and hisses at the bemused man: 'There, son, read that back to me, would you! But quickly, no um-ing and er-ing, and no stumbling!'

He sounds very like a policeman.

But the deputy inspector knows, even from the way Kluge holds the card, the way his goggling eyes become ever less comprehending, and then the way he stumblingly begins to read

– 'GERMAN, DON'T FORGET! IT BEGAN WITH THE ANSCHLUSS OF AUSTRIA. THERE FOLLOWED THE SUDETENLAND AND CZECHOSLOVAKIA. POLAND WAS ATTACKED, BELGIUM, HOLLAND' – the deputy inspector is pretty sure: the man has never held the card in his hands in his life, has never read its contents, never mind being in a position to have written them. He's far too stupid!

Angrily he tears the card away from Enno Kluge, says quickly, 'Heil Hitler!' and leaves the office with his sergeant and his captive.

Slowly the doctor rips up the treatment form he filled in for Enno Kluge. There was no chance to slip it to him. A pity! But probably it wouldn't have helped in any case, probably the man was so unequal to the complexities of these times he was already doomed. No help could reach him from the outside world, because there was no stability within him.

A pity . . .

23

The Interrogation

When the deputy inspector – in spite of his firm conviction that Enno Kluge was not the author nor the distributor of the postcards – when, even so, he intimated to Inspector Escherich that Kluge was probably the distributor of these writings, he did so because a wise inferior should never try to second-guess his superior. Against Kluge, there was a firm charge from the doctor's receptionist, Fräulein Kiesow, and whether this had substance or not, that was something the inspector could determine for himself.

If it had substance, then the deputy was a capable man, assured of the future benevolence of the inspector. If it remained unsubstantiated, then it merely showed that the inspector was wiser than the deputy, and the determination of this margin of wisdom on the part of the superior can be more useful to the inferior than any bravura of his own.

'Well?' asked the long, grey Escherich, striding into the station. 'Well, Schröder? Where have you put your captive?'

'In the left-hand corner cell at the back, Inspector.'

'Has the Hobgoblin confessed?'

'Who? Hobgoblin? Oh, I see, I get it! No, Inspector, but of course immediately after our conversation I had him booked.'

'Good!' Escherich praised him. 'And what does he know about the cards?'

'I did,' the deputy inspector said cautiously, 'I did ask him to read the card aloud. Just the beginning of it, really.'

'Impression?'

'I don't want to presume, Inspector,' said the deputy.

'Don't be shy, Schröder! Impression?'

'Well, to put it no higher, I don't think it's very likely that he's the author of the card.'

'Why not?'

'Isn't the brightest. Also, incredibly timid.'

Inspector Escherich stroked his sandy moustache unhappily. 'Not the brightest – incredibly timid,' he repeated to himself. 'Well, my Hobgoblin is pretty bright, and certainly not timid. Then what makes you think he *is* the right man? Report!'

Assistant Schröder did so. He emphasized the evidence of the receptionist, and Enno's attempted flight. 'I had no choice, Inspector. Following the recent orders, I had to detain him.'

'Right, Schröder. Absolutely right. Wouldn't have done it differently myself.'

Escherich felt somewhat re-encouraged by this report. It sounded a little better than 'not the brightest' and 'incredibly timid'. Perhaps a distributor of the cards, even though the inspector thus far had worked on the assumption that the Hobgoblin acted alone.

'Did you go through his papers?'

'They're here. In general they confirm what he told us. I got the impression, Inspector, that he's a bit of shirker, afraid of being packed off to the front, doesn't feel like working, likes the horses, too – I found a whole sheaf of racing papers and calculations on him. And then some pretty plainspoken letters by shared women. One of those types, Inspector. But pushing fifty.'

'Very good, very good,' said the inspector, but really it was pretty lousy. Neither the author nor any possible distributor of the cards would have much to do with women. He was pretty certain of that. His hopes began to fade again. But then Escherich thought of his superior, Obergruppenführer Prall, and his senior superiors all the way up to Himmler. They would make life pretty hellish for him if he didn't have some sort of lead. Here was a lead, or at least a strong accusation and suspicious conduct. You could follow such a lead, even if in your heart of hearts you didn't think it was the right one. No one suffered. What did a good-for-nothing like that matter anyway!

Escherich stood up. 'I'm going down to the cells, Schröder. Give me the postcard, and wait for me here.'

The inspector walked on tiptoe, and gripped the keys in his

hand so that they wouldn't rattle. Very gently he slid open the spyhole and looked into the cell.

The arrested man was sitting on a stool. He had his head propped in his hands, and his eyes directed at the door. It looked for all the world as though the man was staring into the lurking eye of the inspector. But Kluge's facial expression indicated that he saw nothing. The man did not flinch when the cover was pushed aside, and his face had nothing taut about it, as was usually the case with someone who feels he is being observed.

He was just staring into space, not thinking, merely drifting, and full of gloomy presentiments.

The inspector at his peephole now knew for a certainty: this was neither the Hobgoblin himself nor any sort of accomplice. He was just a plain and simple mistake – whatever the evidence against him, however suspicious his behaviour.

But then Escherich remembered his superiors. He chewed his moustache, and thought about how long he could drag out this thing, till it was established that he had the wrong man. He mustn't make a fool of himself.

Abruptly he unlocked the cell and strode in. The prisoner had jumped at the sound of the key turning in the lock, first staring in confusion at the visitor, then making an attempt to get up.

But Escherich pressed him down on the stool.

'Don't get up, Herr Kluge, don't get up. It takes a lot of effort, and at our age we have to be sensible.'

He laughed, and Kluge made an effort to look amused too, out of pure politeness, and he achieved a miserable-looking smile.

The inspector folded down the bed from the wall and sat down. 'Well, Herr Kluge,' he said, and looked alertly at the pale face with the weak chin, the strangely thick-lipped mouth, and the pale eyes that were continually blinking. 'Well, Herr Kluge, and now tell me what's on your chest. I'm Inspector Escherich of the Gestapo.' He carried on talking gently, even as he saw Kluge shrink back in terror at the word. 'There's no need to be afraid. We don't eat babies. And you're just a baby yourself, I can see that . . .'

At the ghost of sympathy conveyed by those words, Kluge's

eyes immediately filled with tears, his face quivered, and his jaw muscles worked.

'Come, come!' said Escherich, patting the little man's hand. 'It won't be so bad as all that. Or – is it?'

'I'm lost!' cried Enno Kluge in despair. 'I've had it! I don't have a medical note, and I have to go to work. And now I'm sitting here, and they'll put me in a concentration camp, and I'll go to the wall, I won't last a fortnight!'

'Come, come!' said the inspector again, soothingly. 'The thing with your factory, that can be sorted out. If we arrest someone, and it turns out that he's a law-abiding individual, then we take the trouble to see he doesn't suffer any adverse consequences. You're a law-abiding individual, aren't you – Herr Kluge?'

Once again, Kluge's jaw worked, and then he decided to make a partial confession to this sympathetic gentleman. 'They say I don't work hard enough.'

'Well, and what's your view, Herr Kluge? Do you work hard enough?'

Once again, Kluge thought. 'I get ill such a lot,' he said pathetically. 'But they just say this is no time for being ill.'

'You're not always ill, are you? Well, and when you're not ill and you work – do you work enough then? What's your view of that, Herr Kluge?'

Again Kluge made a decision. 'Oh God, Inspector,' he wailed, 'so many women want a piece of me!'

It sounded equally miserable and vain.

The inspector tutted amiably and shook his head, as though this were really quite a problem.

'That's not good, Herr Kluge,' he finally said. 'At our time of life we don't like to say no, do we?'

Kluge merely looked at him with a watery smile, happy to have met with a little understanding from this gentleman.

'Well now,' said the Inspector, 'and how are you off for money?'

'I have a flutter now and again,' Kluge admitted. 'Not often and never very much. Five marks tops, and then only if I've got a certainty, I swear, Inspector!'

'And how do you pay for those avocations of yours, Herr Kluge, the women and the horses? If you don't work much?'

'But the women pay me, Inspector!' said Kluge, almost a little offended at so much incomprehension. He smiled conceitedly. 'Because I'm so dependable!' he added.

It was at that moment that Inspector Escherich finally laid to rest the notion that Enno Kluge had anything to do with the composition or distribution of the postcards. This Kluge was just not up to something like that; he didn't have any of the qualifications. But Escherich still had to interrogate him, because he had to work up a statement about this interrogation, a statement for his superiors, to keep them quiet, a statement that kept Kluge under continued suspicion and justify further steps against him . . .

So he pulled the card from his pocket, laid it in front of Kluge, and said casually, 'Do you know this postcard, Herr Kluge?'

'Yes,' said Enno Kluge right away, before abruptly correcting himself: 'I mean, no. I was given it to read aloud earlier, just the beginning. That's all I know of the card. God's holy truth, Inspector!'

'Well,' Escherich said, a little doubtfully, 'Herr Kluge, if we understand each other on such a major question as your work and the concentration camp, and since I will go personally to your bosses and straighten things out for you, surely we'll be able to come to terms on such a trifle as your card!'

'I've got nothing to do with it, nothing at all, Inspector!'

'I don't, Herr Kluge,' said the inspector, unmoved by these protestations, 'I don't go as far as my colleague, who takes you for the author of the card and is inclined to drag you in front of the People's Court and you know what then: Off with your head, Herr Kluge!'

The little man shuddered convulsively, and his face turned ashen.

'No,' said the inspector soothingly, and once again laid his hand on the other man's. 'No, I don't take you for the author of the card. But it's a fact that the card was lying in the corridor, and you did go out there suspiciously often, and then there's your panic, and your attempt to run away. And there are good witnesses for all of this – no, Herr Kluge, it's better you tell me the truth. I don't want you to plunge yourself into destruction!'

'The card must have been posted from outside, Herr Inspector. I've got nothing to do with it, God's holy truth, Herr Inspector!'

'From where it was lying, it can't have been posted from outside. And five minutes earlier there was nothing there, the doctor's receptionist will testify. During that time, you went to the toilet. Or do you want to claim there was someone else in the toilet, or outside the waiting room?'

'No, I don't think so, Inspector. No, I'm sure there wasn't. If it's a matter of five minutes, there can't have been. I wanted to go out for a whole while, and that's why I kept an eye open to see if there was anyone in the toilet.'

'Well, then!' said the inspector, apparently highly satisfied, 'you said it yourself: only you could possibly have laid the card on the floor!'

Kluge stared at him again with terrified-looking eyes.

'So since you've admitted that . . .'

'I haven't admitted anything, nothing! All I said was that no one went to the toilet during the five minutes before I did!'

Kluge was almost shouting.

'Now come, come!' said the inspector, shaking his head disapprovingly. 'You don't want to retract a confession you've only just made – you're far too sensible a man for that sort of behaviour. I would have to note the retraction in my report as well, Herr Kluge, and that sort of thing doesn't make a good impression.'

Kluge stared at him in despair. 'I didn't confess to anything . . .' he whispered in a dead voice.

'We'll come to an agreement about that as well,' said Escherich calmly. 'Now why don't you begin by telling me who gave you the card to drop? Was it a good friend, or an acquaintance, or someone who approached you on the street and offered you a few marks?'

'None of it! None of it!' screamed Kluge. 'I never touched the card, I never set eyes on it before your colleague gave it to me!'

'But Herr Kluge! You just admitted you dropped the card on the floor . . .'

'I didn't! I never said anything like that!'

'No,' said Escherich, stroking his moustache and wiping away his smile. He was already enjoying the experience of getting this cowardly, whimpering dog to dance. It would turn out to be quite a nice statement with strong suspicion – for his superiors. 'No,' he said. 'You didn't say it in so many words. What you said was that you were the only one who could have put the card down in that place, and that no one but you was there – which seems to me to come to the same thing.'

Enno stared at him with huge eyes. Then, suddenly mutinous, he said: 'I didn't say that either. Other people could have gone to that toilet too, only not from the waiting room.'

He sat down; in his excitement at the false accusations he had jumped to his feet.

'But I'm not saying any more now. I want a lawyer. And I'm not signing any statement.'

'Come, come,' said Escherich. 'Did I ask you to sign a statement, Herr Kluge? Did I even take a note of anything you've said? We're just sitting here like a couple of old friends, and the things we chat about needn't concern anyone.'

He stood up, and threw the cell door wide open.

'You see, no one's listening in the corridor, either. And there you are making such a fuss about a ridiculous postcard. Do you think I care about the postcard? The man who wrote it is obviously a complete imbecile. But with the doctor's receptionist and my colleague making such a fuss, it's no more than my duty to look a little deeper! Don't be a fool, Herr Kluge, just tell me: A gentleman gave it to me on the Frankfurter Allee, he wanted to make trouble for the doctor, he said. And he paid me ten marks. You had a new ten-mark note in your pocket when we took you in; I've seen it. You see, if you tell me that now, then you're my man. Then you don't make any trouble for me, and I can knock off and go home.'

'And me? Where do I go? Chokey! And then off to be beheaded! No, thank you, Inspector, I'm never ever going to confess to that for you!'

'You ask me where you go, Herr Kluge, when I go home? You go home too, haven't you understood? You're free either way, I'm letting you go . . .'

'Is that the truth, Inspector? I'm free to go now, without a confession, without a statement?'

'But of course you are, Herr Kluge, you can leave right now if you like. There's just one thing I'd like you to think about before you go . . .'

And with one finger, he tapped Kluge – who had leaped to his feet again and had turned toward the door – on his shoulder.

'Listen. I'm going to sort out the thing in the factory for you, out of the kindness of my heart. I've promised you that, and I like to keep my promises. But now think about me for a minute, please, Herr Kluge. Think of all the trouble I stand to get from my colleague if I let you go. He'll go on about me to my bosses, and I can get into hot water over you. I think it would be decent of you, Herr Kluge, if you would put your name to the story of the man on the Frankfurter Allee. Where's the risk in it for you? It's not as though we can find the man anyway, so how about it, Herr Kluge?'

Enno Kluge had never been a great one for resisting temptation. He stood there doubtfully. Freedom beckoned, and the factory would be sorted too, if he managed not to antagonize this man. He was terrified of antagonizing this nice inspector. Then that policeman would take over the case again, and he might pursue the matter to the point where one day he would force Enno to confess to the break-in at the Rosenthals'. And then Enno Kluge would be lost, because the SS man Persicke . . .

He really could do the inspector such a favour – what would it cost him? It was a stupid card, something political, and he'd never got involved in any of that, didn't know the first thing about it. And the man on the Frankfurter Allee would never be caught, simply because he didn't exist. Yes, he would help the inspector out, and sign his name.

But then his timidity, his inborn caution, warned him again. 'Yes,' he said, 'and then when I've signed, you won't let me go after all.'

'Oh, come, come!' said Inspector Escherich, and saw his game as good as won. 'Because of a stupid card like that, and when you're doing me a good turn? Herr Kluge, I give you my word of honour both as detective inspector and as a human being: As soon as you've signed the statement, you're free.'

'And if I don't sign?'

'Why, then, you're free too!'

Enno Kluge decided. 'All right, Herr Inspector, I'll sign, just so that you don't have any unpleasantnesses, and to do you a favour. But you won't forget the bit with my factory?'

'I'll see to it today, Herr Kluge. This very day! I suggest you check in there tomorrow – and go easy on the disability! If you take the occasional day off, say one a week, none of the people I'm going to speak to will bat an eyelid over it. Will that suit you, Herr Kluge?'

'Down to the ground! I'm very grateful to you, Inspector!'

This exchange had seen them down the corridor of the cell block, back to the room where Deputy Inspector Schröder was sitting, curious to learn how the questioning had gone, but on the whole already somewhat reconciled to the probable outcome. He jumped to his feet as the two men walked in.

'Well, Schröder,' said the Inspector, smiling, and inclining his head at Kluge, who stood beside him small and timid, because the policeman looked so terrifying. 'Here's our friend back again. He's just admitted to me that he left the card in the doctor's corridor, having been given it by a gentleman on the Frankfurter Allee . . .'

A sound like a groan broke from the chest of the deputy inspector. 'My God!' he finally said. 'But he couldn't . . .'

'And now,' the inspector continued serenely, 'and now we're going to draw up a little statement together, and after that Herr Kluge will go home. Is that right, Herr Kluge, or is that right?'

'Yes,' replied Kluge, but very softly, because the presence of the policeman filled him with fresh fears and anxieties.

The deputy inspector meanwhile stood there feeling dumb-founded. Kluge hadn't left the card, never, not possibly, that was beyond a doubt for him. And yet here he was prepared to put his name to it.

What a fox Escherich was! How on earth did he do it? Schröder admitted – not without a twinge of envy – that Escherich was streets ahead of him. And then, following the confession, to let the fellow go! It passed comprehension, he couldn't understand the game. Well, however clever you thought you were, there were always some people who were cleverer.

'Listen, Schröder,' said Escherich, having sufficiently enjoyed the bafflement of his colleague. 'Do you feel like going on an errand for me to headquarters?'

'At your orders, Inspector!'

'You remember I've got this case going on there – what was it called again – oh yes, the Hobgoblin case. You do remember?'

Their eyes met and understood each other.

'Well, I'd like you to go to headquarters for me, and tell a Herr Linke – oh, do sit down, Herr Kluge, I just have something to arrange with my colleague here.'

He walked with the deputy inspector to the door. He whispered: 'I want you to pick up a couple of men there. They're to come here right away, good, experienced shadowers. I want Kluge followed from the moment he leaves the station. Reports on all his movements at two- or three-hour intervals, phoned through to me at the Gestapo. Code word: Hobgoblin. Give both men a sight of Kluge; I want them to take it in turns. And you come back in here when you've got the men ready. Then I'll let him go.'

'Understood, Inspector. Heil Hitler!'

The door banged, the deputy was gone. The inspector now sat next to Enno Kluge and said: 'Well, that's got rid of him! I take it you're not overly fond of him, Herr Kluge?'

'Not as much as you are, Inspector!'

'Did you see the face he made when I told him I was letting you go? He was pretty hacked off! That's why I sent him away, I didn't want him to be here for our little statement. He would have kept butting in. I won't even have a secretary come in – I'd rather write it out myself. It's just something between the two of us, so that I'm slightly covered with my bosses for letting you go.'

And after he'd quieted down the frightened little so-and-so, he picked up a pen and began to write. Sometimes he repeated what he was writing loudly and clearly (if indeed he was writing what he was saying, which was by no means a given with such a wily detective as Escherich), and sometimes he just muttered under his breath. Kluge couldn't make out what he was saying then.

All he saw was that it wasn't just a couple of lines: this statement took up almost four full pages of foolscap. But that didn't interest him all that much just then – all he was interested in was whether they would indeed spring him right away. He looked toward the door. On a sudden impulse, he got up, walked over, and opened it slightly . . .

'Kluge!' came a call behind him, though not a peremptory one. 'Oh please, Herr Kluge!'

'Yes?' he asked, and looked back. 'May I not go then?' He smiled fearfully.

The inspector, pen in hand, smiled at him. 'Are you having second thoughts about our little deal, Herr Kluge? Your firm promise? All right then, I've wasted my time.' He slammed down the pen. 'Then get lost, Kluge – I see you're no man of your word. Go along, I see you won't sign! I'll get by . . .'

And in this way, the inspector ensured that Enno Kluge really did sign the statement. Yes, Kluge didn't even ask to have it read back to him. He signed it in complete ignorance of its contents.

'Now may I go, Inspector?'

'Of course. Thank you for your help, Herr Kluge, you did very well. Goodbye. Or perhaps better not, given the circumstances. Ach, one more moment, if you please, Herr Kluge . . .'

'Can I not go yet?'

Kluge's face was starting to tremble again.

'But of course you can! Are you back to not trusting me again?

You are a suspicious character! I just thought, wouldn't you like to take your papers and your money away with you? There, you see! Let's make sure there's nothing missing, Herr Kluge . . .'

And they started to compare: employment book, army conduct book, birth certificate, marriage licence . . .

'Why do you carry all those papers everywhere with you, if I might ask, Herr Kluge? Imagine if you mislaid them somewhere!'

. . . Police registration, four wage-slips . . .

'You don't make very much, do you, Herr Kluge! Oh, I remember, you've only been working three or four days a week, you little shirker, you!'

. . . Three letters . . .

'No, don't worry, I'm not interested in them!'

. . . Thirty-seven Reichsmarks in notes, and sixty-five Reichspfennigs in coins . . .

'Ah, there's the new ten-mark note you got from the gentleman. I'd better keep that back for the files. But, hang on, I don't want you to lose out, so here's ten marks out of my own pocket to replace them . . .'

The inspector kept this up until Deputy Inspector Schröder came in again. 'I've carried out your instructions, Inspector. And Inspector Linke says he'd like a word with you on the Hobgoblin case.'

'Fine. Fine. Thanks again. Well, we're all done here. Goodbye then, Herr Kluge. Schröder, please show Herr Kluge out. Herr Schröder will accompany you out. Goodbye now, Herr Kluge. I won't forget about the factory. Don't worry about anything! Heil Hitler!'

'Well then, Herr Kluge, no hard feelings,' Schröder said on Frankfurter Allee, and they shook hands. 'You know, a job's a job, and sometimes things can get a bit rough. But remember I asked them to remove the handcuffs from you right away. And no ill-effects from where the sergeant hit you, eh?'

'No, none at all. I understand . . . I'm sorry to have put you to so much trouble, Inspector.'

'That's all right. Heil Hitler, Herr Kluge!'

'Heil Hitler, Inspector!'

And weedy little Enno Kluge trotted off. He jogged at a fast clip through the crowds on Frankfurter Allee, and Deputy Inspector Schröder watched him go. He checked to see that both of the men he had set on his tail were there, and then he nodded and walked back into the station.

24

Inspector Escherich Gets to
Work on the Hobgoblin Case

'There, read that!' said Inspector Escherich to Deputy Inspector Schröder, and passed him the statement.

'Hmm,' replied Schröder, handing it back. 'So he's confessed and is going to face the People's Court and the executioner. I'm surprised.' He added thoughtfully, 'And to think that someone like that is at liberty!'

'That's right!' said the inspector, as he laid the statement in a file and dropped the file into his leather briefcase. 'That's right, someone like that is now at liberty – but, I trust, properly tailed by our people!'

'Certainly!' Schröder hastened to assure him. 'I checked. They were both solidly on his tail.'

'So there he is, running around,' mused Inspector Escherich, stroking his moustache, 'and our people are running after him! Then one day – maybe today, or in a week, or six months – and our enigmatic little Herr Kluge will run to his cardwriter, the man who gave him the instruction. Drop it at such and such a place. It's as certain as the amen in church. And then I snap the trap shut, and only then will the two of them be properly ripe for prison and so on and so forth.'

'Inspector,' said Deputy Inspector Schröder, 'I still can't quite believe that Kluge dropped the card. I watched him when I put the thing in his hand, and it was certainly the first time he'd ever seen it. It was all made up by that hysterical bitch, the doctor's receptionist.'

'But he says in his statement that he dropped it,' objected the inspector, albeit rather mildly. 'Incidentally, if I were you, I would avoid terms like hysterical bitch. No personal prejudices, just objective facts. If you wanted to, though, you could question the doctor on the trustworthiness of his receptionist. Ach, no, I wouldn't bother with that either. That would just turn out to be another personal opinion, and we can leave it to the examining magistrate to assess the various witnesses. We work completely objectively here, isn't that right, Schröder, without any prejudice?'

'Of course, Inspector.'

'A witness statement is a statement, and we stick to it. How and why it came about, that doesn't interest us. We're not psychologists, we're detectives. The only thing we're interested in is crime. And if someone confesses to a crime, that's enough for us. At least that'd be my way of looking at it, but I don't know, perhaps you have another, Schröder?'

'Of course not, Inspector!' exclaimed Deputy Inspector Schröder. He sounded quite shocked at the idea that his view might differ from his superiors. 'My thoughts exactly! Always opposed to crime in all its forms!'

'I knew it,' said Inspector Escherich drily, and stroked his moustache. 'We old-school detectives are always of one mind. You know, Schröder, there are a lot of newcomers working in our profession nowadays, so it's important that we stick together. There's some benefit in that. All right, Schröder,' now he sounded strictly professional, 'I'd like your report today on the Kluge arrest and the protocol of the witness statements of the receptionist and the doctor. Ah, yes, you had a sergeant with you as well, I believe, Schröder . . .'

'Sergeant Dubberke, based at the station here . . .'

'Don't know the man. But I'd like a report from him too, on Kluge's attempted escape. Short and to the point, no verbiage, no subjective personal opinions, got that, Schröder?'

'Whatever you say, Inspector!'

'All right then, Schröder! When you've handed in these reports, you won't have anything more to do with this case, unless there's some further statement needed, to a judge, or to us at the Gestapo . . .' He looked thoughtfully at his junior. 'How long have you been deputy now, Schröder?'

'Three and a half years already, Inspector.'

The eye of the 'policeman' as it rested on the inspector had something rather wistful about it.

But the inspector merely said, 'Well, it's about time, then,' and he left the station.

Back at Prinz Albrecht Strasse, he had himself announced immediately to his direct superior, SS Obergruppenführer Prall. He had to wait almost an hour; not that Herr Prall was very busy, or rather, because he was particularly busy in a particular way. Escherich heard the tinkle of glasses, and the popping of corks, he heard laughter and shouting: one of the regular meetings of the higher echelons, then. Conviviality, booze, cheerful relaxation after the heavy effort of torturing and putting to death their fellow men.

The inspector waited without impatience, even though he still had a lot he hoped to do today. He knew what superiors were like, in general, and he knew this one superior in particular. Pestering him was no use. If Berlin was ablaze, and he wanted a drink, well, then he had his drink first. That was just the way he was!

After an hour or so, Escherich was finally admitted. The room looked the worse for wear, with clear evidence of a booze-up, and Prall, purple with Armagnac, looked rather the worse for wear himself. But he said cheerily: 'Hey, Escherich! Pour yourself a glass! The fruits of our victory over France: real Armagnac, ten times better than cognac! Ten? Hundred times! Why aren't you drinking?'

'I've still got quite a bit to do today, Obergruppenführer, and I want to keep a clear head. Anyway, I'm not used to drinking any more.'

'Bah, not used to it! Clear head, pish! What do you want a clear head for? Let someone else do your work for you, and sleep late. Cheers, Escherich – the Führer!'

There was no getting out of this. Escherich raised his glass, and a second time, and a third, and he thought how the combination of alcohol and the company of his comrades had altered this man. Normally, Prall was pretty bearable, not half as bad as a hundred other fellows running around the building in their black uniforms. If anything, he was a bit skeptical, just 'here to learn', as he sometimes said, and by no means convinced of everything.

But under the influence of alcohol and his comrades, he became like them: unpredictable, brutal, impulsive and always ready to rule out any other view, even if it was nothing but a different view on drinking and schnapps. If Escherich had refused to touch glasses with him, he would have been as lost as if he had allowed the worst offender to run free. If anything, it would have been slightly worse, because there was an element of personal insult if the junior did not raise a full glass with his superior as often as he was required to do.

Escherich, then, clinked glasses with Prall – clinked glasses several times – and drank.

'Well now, Escherich, what's up?' Prall said at last, gripping his desk to steady himself. 'What's that you've got with you?'

'A statement,' said Escherich. 'One that I've drawn up on that Hobgoblin case I'm working on. There are a couple more reports and statements to come, but this is the main part of it. If you please, Obergruppenführer.'

'Hobgoblin? Hobgoblin?' said Prall, thinking as hard as he could. 'Oh, you mean the fellow with the postcards? Ah, did you manage to come up with some plan, as I ordered?'

'At your orders, Obergruppenführer. Would you care to read the statement?'

'Read? Nah, not now. Maybe later. Tell you what, why don't you just read it to me, Escherich?'

He interrupted the reading after only three sentences. 'Let's have another one first. Cheers, Escherich! Heil Hitler!'

'Heil Hitler, Obergruppenführer!'

After he had emptied his glass, Escherich went back to his statement.

But now the drunken Prall had thought of an amusing game. Each time Escherich had read three or four sentences, he interrupted him with a call of 'Cheers!' and Escherich, after he had clinked glasses again, would have to begin again at the beginning.

Prall wouldn't let him get past the first page, he kept calling out another 'Cheers!' He could see – despite his drunkenness – the man struggling, how reluctant he was to drink, how ten times at least he thought of throwing down his statement and walking out, and how he didn't dare, because the other was his superior and he had to kowtow, suppress all signs of his rage . . .

'Cheers, Escherich!'

'Thank you, Obergruppenführer, sir! Cheers!'

'Now read on, Escherich! No, start at the top. That part I didn't quite get. Always been slow on the uptake . . .'

And Escherich read. Yes, now he was being tormented just as a couple of hours ago he himself had tormented the skinny Kluge. Just like Kluge he was tormented by the desire to get out the door. But he was forced to read, to read and to drink, as long as the other man wanted. Already he could feel his head fogging up – the good work he had done, for nothing! Too bloody well behaved!

'Cheers, Escherich!'

'Cheers, Obergruppenführer!'

'Okay, start again!'

Until Prall got bored with his game, and said, 'Ach, stop with all this stupid reading! You can see I'm drunk, can't you? How am I going to understand that stuff? Showing off to me with your smarty-pants report! Other reports will follow – not so important as that by the great detective Escherich! How dare you! Cut to the chase: Have you caught the postcard writer, or not?'

'At your orders, Obergruppenführer, no. But . . .'

'Then what are you doing here? Stealing my valuable time, and swilling my lovely Armagnac?' This, already, in a yell. 'Have you completely lost your mind? But from now on I'm going to speak to you in a different tone! I've been far too kind to you, I've stood for your cheek. Do you understand me?'

'At your orders, Obergruppenführer!' And quickly, before the yelling could begin again, Escherich blurted out, 'But I've at least caught someone who dropped the postcards. Or I think he has.'

This news calmed Prall a little. He glowered at the Inspector and said, 'Bring him in! I want him to tell me who supplied him with the cards. I'm going to twist it out of him – I feel in the mood now.'

For a moment, Escherich reeled. He could say that the man wasn't in the building and that he would go and pick him up – and then he would do just exactly that, from the street, or from his flat, with the help of those trailing him. Or he could carefully stay away, wait for the Obergruppenführer to sleep off his drink. By then he would probably have forgotten everything.

But then, Escherich being Escherich, which is to say a detective set in his ways, and not a coward but rather a man of courage, he said: 'I let the man go, Obergruppenführer!'

The roar – Jesus Christ, the animal roar! The normally – by the standards of Nazi top brass – rather sedate Prall forgot himself to the degree that he grabbed his inspector by the scruff of his neck, and shook him about, as he yelled, 'Let him go? You let him go? Do you know what I'm going to do to you, you son of a bitch? I'm going to lock you up, give you a taste of chokey! You'll have a thousand-watt lamp dangling off your moustache, and if you drop off, I'll get them to beat you awake . . .'

It went on like that for quite a while. Escherich kept quite still and allowed himself to be shaken about and scolded. Now it was a good thing that he had had a few. Slightly numbed by the Armagnac, he had only a vague sense of what was going on; it felt a little like a dream.

Oh, shout all you like! he thought. The longer you shout, the sooner you'll lose your voice. Go ahead, give old Escherich an earful!

And indeed, after shouting himself hoarse, Prall let go. He poured himself another glass of Armagnac, glared at Escherich, and wheezed, 'Now, tell me what possessed you to commit an act of such colossal stupidity!'

'First, I want to report,' Escherich said quietly, 'that the man is under the constant surveillance of two of our best men from

HQ. I think that sooner or later he will lead us to his taskmaster, the writer of the postcards. At present, he denies knowing him. The well-known great unknown.'

'I would have squeezed the name out of him all right! Putting a tail on him – they'll end up losing the fellow altogether!'

'Not these people! They're the best at the Alex!'

'Well, I don't know!' But it was clear that Prall was feeling a little sunnier. 'You know I don't like these independently made decisions. I want the man in my own grasp, where I can get at him!'

You're damned right you do, thought Escherich. And in half an hour you'll have realized that he's got nothing to do with the postcards, and you'll be on my case again . . .

But aloud he said: 'He's such a timid little creature, Obergruppenführer! If you rough him up, he'll tell you whatever you want to hear, and we'll be chasing a hundred false trails. This way he'll lead us straight to the writer.'

The Obergruppenführer laughed: 'Ha, you old fox! Well, let's have another anyway!'

And they did.

The Obergruppenführer looked appraisingly at the inspector. His outburst had done him a lot of good, had even sobered him up a little.

He thought for a moment, and then he said, 'That statement of yours, you know . . .'

'Yes, sir!'

'. . . I want you to give me a few copies of it. For now you can put it away.' Both men grinned. 'You never know, it just might get a few Armagnac stains in here . . .'

Escherich put the statement back in the file, and the file back in his briefcase.

In the meantime, his superior was rummaging around in a drawer of his desk, and now he came round the side of it, a hand behind his back. 'As a matter of interest, Escherich, do you have the Iron Cross?'

'No, Obergruppenführer!'

'That's where you're wrong, Escherich! Now you do!' And he held out his hand. And in the flat palm of it was a cross.

The inspector was so overwhelmed that he was only able to mumble, 'But, Obergruppenführer! I don't deserve this . . . I have no words . . .'

He was ready for everything, he thought, during his dressing-down five minutes ago, even a couple of days and nights in the basement, but being awarded the Iron Cross at the end of it, that . . .

'. . . Sir, my humble thanks . . .'

Obergruppenführer Prall enjoyed the bewilderment of the newly decorated man.

'Well now, Escherich,' he said after a time. 'You know I'm not really like that. And at the end of the day, you're a hardworking official. You just need a little prodding from time to time, to keep you from going to sleep. Let's have one more. Cheers, then, Escherich, here's to you! Here's to your cross!'

'Cheers, Obergruppenführer! And once again, my very humble thanks!'

The Obergruppenführer started to babble: 'Actually, the cross wasn't being kept for you at all, Escherich. Your colleague Rusch was supposed to get it for a smart operation he conducted involving an old Jewess. But then you turned up.'

He went on babbling for a while, then he turned on the red light over his door, which signified: 'Important meeting in progress! Do not disturb!' and settled down to sleep on the sofa.

When Escherich, still clutching his medal, walked into his own office, his deputy was sitting there on the telephone, calling out, 'What? Hobgoblin case? Never heard of it! Are you sure?'

'Give it to me!' said Escherich, and took the receiver. 'And get lost!'

He shouted into the mouthpiece: 'Inspector Escherich speaking! What's that about the Hobgoblin? Do you have something to report?'

'Beg to report, Inspector Escherich, unfortunately we lost the man . . .'

'You what?'

Escherich was close to exploding with rage, as his superior

had done just a quarter of an hour before. He mastered himself and said, 'What can possibly have happened? I was told you were a good man, and the fellow you were observing was just a little whippet!'

'Well, that's one way of putting it, Inspector. He can certainly run like one, and he suddenly got away in the crush on the subway platform at the Alex. He must have noticed we were shadowing him.'

'Oh no, not that too!' Escherich groaned. 'You bloody fools have completely messed up my plan. Well, I can't send you any more, because he knows you. And other men wouldn't know him!' He reflected. 'All right, get back to headquarters, quick as you can! Each of you is to get a stand-in. And one of you is to position himself round the corner from his flat, but keep hidden, all right? I don't want him running away a second time. It's your job to show your stand-in which one Kluge is, and then you buzz off. And I want the other man to go to the factory where he works, and report to the management. Hang on, you buffoon, I haven't given you the address yet.' He looked it up, and read it over the line. 'Right, and now get to your places, quick as you can! The second stand-in doesn't have to go to the factory till tomorrow morning, and he can go alone! They'll point him out all right! I'll talk to the management. And in an hour I'll be at the flat . . .'

But he had so much dictating and telephoning to do that he didn't get to Eva Kluge's flat until very much later. He didn't see his men, and he rang the bell in vain. The only person he could turn to was the neighbour, Frau Gesch.

'Kluge? Herr Kluge? No, he doesn't live here. It's just his wife who lives here, sir, and she won't let him into the house. She's away. An address for him? How should I know? He's always hanging around with some woman or other. Or so I've heard, but I'm not saying anything. The wife was furious with me once because I helped her husband get into the flat.'

'Listen, Frau Gesch,' said Escherich, having slipped into the flat as she threatened to shut the door on him. 'Why don't you just tell me everything you know about the Kluges!'

'Why should I? Anyway, who are you to walk into my flat just like that . . .'

'Inspector Escherich of the Gestapo. If you'd like to see my ID . . .'

'No, no!' cried Frau Gesch, shrinking back against the kitchen wall. 'I don't want to see nor hear nothing! And as for the Kluges, I've just told you everything I know!'

'Oh, I don't know, it seems to me you might think it over, Frau Gesch, because if you don't want to talk to me here, I'd have to invite you back to Prinz Albrecht Strasse and conduct a proper interrogation. I'm sure you wouldn't like that. This is just a cosy chat we're having here, you see I'm not taking any notes . . .'

'Honest, Inspector. I really don't have any more to say. I don't know anything about those two.'

'Please yourself, Frau Gesch. Get your coat, I've got a couple of men downstairs waiting, we can take you with us right away. And I suggest you leave your husband – you do have a husband? Of course you have a husband! – just leave him a note: "I've popped out to the Gestapo. Don't know when I'll be back." All right, Frau Gesch! Get writing!'

Frau Gesch had turned pale, her limbs shook, her teeth were rattling away.

'You wouldn't do such a thing to a poor woman, sir!' she begged.

He replied with a show of coarseness: 'That's exactly what I'll do, Frau Gesch, if you continue to refuse to answer a few simple questions. So now, see sense, sit down and tell me everything you know about the Kluges. What is the wife like?'

Frau Gesch saw sense. Basically, the gentleman from the Gestapo was a very kind gentleman, not at all the way she expected. And, of course, Inspector Escherich learned all there was to be learned from Frau Gesch. He even learned about the SS man Karlemann, because what the corner pub knew, Frau Gesch also knew. It would have wrung the heart of the ex-postie Eva Kluge if she had learned how much she and her former darling son Karlemann were the subject of gossip.

When Inspector Escherich said goodbye to Frau Gesch, he left behind not only a couple of cigars for her husband, but also an eager, unpaid and invaluable spy for the Gestapo. She would keep a vigilant eye on the Kluges' apartment, but more than that, she would listen to everything that went on in the house and in the shops, and she would call the kindly inspector the moment she heard anything she felt would be useful to him.

Following this conversation, Inspector Escherich called off his two men. The chances of finding Kluge anywhere near his wife's flat were pretty slender and, anyway, he now had Frau Gesch there. Then Inspector Escherich went to the post office and the Party branch, to collect further data on Frau Kluge. You never knew when such things might come in handy.

Escherich could quite easily have told the people at the post office and at the Party HQ of the probable connection between Frau Kluge's leaving the Party and the atrocities perpetrated by her son in Poland. He could have given away her address in Ruppin, having jotted it down when Frau Gesch showed him her letter enclosing the keys to the flat. But Escherich didn't do so. He asked plenty of questions, but he didn't supply any information. They might be the Party and the post office, both official institutions, but the Gestapo wasn't there to help others run their affairs. It regarded itself a little too highly for that – and in that respect, Inspector Escherich shared the general overweening ethos of the Gestapo.

The gentlemen at the factory then got the same treatment. They were in uniform, and as far as salary and rank went they were far superior to the colourless inspector. But he was adamant: 'No, gentlemen, the case against Kluge is purely a Gestapo matter. I can't say any more about it. I will only tell you to allow Herr Kluge to come and go at work as and when he pleases. I don't want him shouted at or bullied, and you're to admit my officers into your factory without let or hindrance, and support them in their work to the utmost of your ability. Have I made myself clear?'

'I want written confirmation of those instructions!' shouted the officer. 'And I want it today!'

'It's a bit late for today. But maybe tomorrow. Kluge won't be coming in before tomorrow anyway. If he comes in again at all! All right then, gentlemen, Heil Hitler!'

'Goddamnit!' growled the officer. 'Those guys get more and more arrogant! I wish the whole Gestapo would go to hell! Just because they have the power to arrest anyone in the country, they think they can do as they please. I'm an officer, a professional officer . . .'

'Oh, one more thing . . .' Escherich's head appeared again in the doorway. 'Does the man keep papers, letters, personal effects here?'

'You'd better ask his supervisor about that! He's got a key to the lockers . . .'

'Very good,' said Escherich. He sat down. 'Will you ask him then, First Lieutenant. And if it's not too much trouble for you, make it snappy?'

For a moment, the two eyed each other. The eyes of the mocking, colourless Escherich and those of the first lieutenant, dark with rage, fought it out. Then the officer clicked his heels together and rushed out of the room to obtain the desired information.

'There's a queer fish!' said Escherich to a Party official suddenly scrabbling about with papers at his desk. 'Wishes the Gestapo would go to hell. I'd like to know how long you'd be sitting securely in your places, if it weren't for us. Ultimately, the Gestapo is the state. Without us, everything would collapse – and it'd be you going to hell in a handcart!'

25

Frau Hetty Makes up Her Mind

Both Inspector Escherich and his two spies from the Alex would have been surprised to learn that little Enno Kluge had had no sense of being followed after all. But from the moment that Deputy Inspector Schröder let him go, he'd had only one thought: I want to get out of here, and back to Hetty!

He ran through the streets without seeing a soul – he noticed no one behind him or beside him. He didn't look up, he just kept thinking *Hetty!*

The underground entrance swallowed him up. He got on to a train and so for the time being gave Inspector Escherich, the gentlemen of the Alex, and the entire Gestapo the slip.

His shadows lost him in the crowds and the dim lights of the underground. He was no more than a shadow himself, little Enno! If he had gone straight to Hetty's, well, the Königstor was just a little way on foot from the Alex, and he wouldn't have needed to take the underground, and then they wouldn't have lost him, and would have had the little pet shop as a focus for their inquiries.

But Enno Kluge had decided he would go to Lotte first and pick up his things. He would show up at Hetty's with a suitcase: that way he would see whether she really loved him, and he would prove to her that he wanted to be done with his old life.

He was lucky with Lotte. She wasn't at home, and he hurriedly packed a few belongings in his case. He even resisted the temptation to go through her things – no, this time everything would be different. It wasn't going to be provisional, like last time, when he moved into the tiny hotel room. No, this time it was going to be the beginning of a new life – so long as Hetty took him in.

As he approached the shop, he walked more and more slowly. He kept putting down his suitcase, though it wasn't that heavy. He kept wiping his brow, though it wasn't that hot.

Then he was standing in front of the shop and peering in through the shiny silver bars of the birdcages – yes, there was Hetty. She was waiting on customers; four or five people were in the shop. He joined them and watched with pride and a trembling heart how skilfully she served them, how polite she was with them.

'We no longer carry Indian millet, madam. India is part of the British Empire. But I have Bulgarian millet, which is much better.'

And in the middle of helping customers, she said, 'Oh, Herr Enno, it is nice of you to have come to help out. Leave your suitcase in the parlour. And then will you fetch me some bird litter from the basement. And I need cat litter as well. And ants' eggs . . .'

And while he was chasing up and down the stairs with these and other orders, he thought, She saw me right away, and she saw that I had a suitcase with me as well. The fact that I was told to put it in the parlour was a good sign. But I'm sure she'll ask me a lot of questions first; she's very pernickety about everything. I'll have to tell her some story or other.

And this man of fifty or so, this habitual drifter, idler, and womanizer began to pray like a schoolboy: Please, God, let me be lucky once more in this life, just this once more! I promise to turn over a new leaf, only please let Hetty take me in!

So he prayed. And he wished also that the hours till closing time might stretch and stretch, to postpone their comprehensive discussion and his confession, because he would have to confess something to Hetty, that was clear. How else was he going to explain to her why he had come to her with everything he had in the world – though that was little enough! He had always tried to play the big man to her in the past.

And then, quite suddenly, it was time. The shop had been closed for an hour and a half – that was how long it took to feed and water all its denizens and to tidy up at the end of the day. Now the two of them were sitting facing each other across the round coffee table, having eaten and chatted a little, always timidly avoiding the main subject between them, when suddenly the shapeless, blowsy woman had raised her head and said: 'Well, Hänschen? What is it? What's happened?'

No sooner had she spoken the words in a concerned, almost maternal tone, than Enno's tears began to flow. First slowly, then more and more copiously they streamed down his bony, colourless face, making his nose appear more and more pinched.

He moaned, 'Oh, Hetty! I can't go on! It's too awful! The Gestapo pulled me in . . .'

And, sobbing loudly, he buried his head in her large motherly bosom.

At those words, Frau Hetty Haberle raised her head. Her eyes acquired a hard gleam, her neck stiffened, and she almost gabbled back: 'What did they want with you?'

Little Enno Kluge had – by luck or inspiration – hit upon exactly the right word. None of the other stories with which he could have come to her for love or sympathy would have benefited him as much as the single word *Gestapo*. Because the widow Hetty Haberle hated disorder, and she would never have taken a dissolute drifter and time waster into her house or her motherly embrace. But the one word *Gestapo* opened all the doors of her soft heart: anyone pursued by the Gestapo could depend on her sympathy and her help.

Her first husband, a minor Communist Party official, had been put in a camp by the Gestapo as early as 1934, and that was the last she had seen or heard of him, aside from a parcel containing his torn and dirty effects. On top of it was a death certificate, issued by the Registry Office in Oranienburg, stating cause of death: pneumonia. Later on, she had heard from other inmates who had been released what 'pneumonia' was used to mean in Oranienburg and the nearby concentration camp of Sachsenhausen.

And now she had in her arms another man, a man she had thus far taken for a shy, affectionate, love-starved creature, all of which commended him to her, and it turned out that he too was being followed by the Gestapo.

'There now, Hänschen!' she said soothingly. 'You can tell me all about it. If someone is wanted by the Gestapo, there's nothing I won't do for him!'

Those words were music to his ears, and he didn't even have to be Enno Kluge, with all his experience of women, to make the most of his chance. What he now brought out, amidst sobs and tears, was a curious mixture of fact and fiction: he even managed to work in his maltreatment at the hands of the SS man Persicke as part of his latest tribulations.

Whatever implausibility the story might have was glossed over by Hetty Haberle in her hatred of the Gestapo. Already her love was weaving a splendid aura round the ne'er-do-well at her breast, and she said: 'So you signed the statement and thus concealed the identity of the culprit, Hänschen. That was very brave of you. I don't think one man in ten would have it in him to do that. But you know, if they do catch you, you'll be in for it, because with that statement hanging over you, you'll always be in danger.'

Already half comforted, he said, 'Oh, if you stand by me, they'll never find me!'

But she shook her head quietly and worried. 'I don't really understand why they let you go at all.' Suddenly the horrifying thought came to her: 'Oh my God, what if they shadowed you, so that you would lead them to someone else?'

He shook his head. 'I don't think so, Hetty. I first had to go to – somewhere else, to pick up my things. I would have noticed if someone had been following me. Anyway, why did they let me go at all? They could just as easily have kept me locked up.'

But she had already thought of this. 'They think you know the author of the postcards and will lead them to him. Maybe you really do know him, too, and you did drop the card, as they say you did. I don't want to know, I don't want you ever to tell me!' She leaned down over him and whispered: 'I'm going to go out now for half an hour, Hänschen, and take a peek outside, to see if there isn't a spy hiding somewhere. And you, you'll stay here quietly by yourself?'

He told her there was no point in going out looking: he was positive that no one had followed him.

But she was haunted by the terrible memory of the time they had once before dragged a man out of her flat, and out of her life. Her anxiety wouldn't permit it, she had to go out and check.

And while she walks slowly round the block – for company she has taken the adorable Scotch terrier Blackie out of her shop, with him her evening walk looks completely innocent – while she strolls up and down, apparently intent on the dog, but aiming her alert eyes and ears everywhere – in that time Enno undertakes a cautious first inventory of her parlour. It can only be fleeting, and anyway most of her drawers are locked. But even this first inspection is enough to tell him that never in his life has he been with a woman like this, a woman with a bank account and even a chequebook, with all the cheques printed with her name!

And again Enno Kluge resolves to turn over a new leaf, and always behave properly in this flat, and never take anything that she doesn't freely give him of her own accord.

She comes back and says, 'No, I didn't see anything out of the ordinary. But it's possible they did see you come in here, and they will be back tomorrow morning. I'll set the alarm for six and have another look around then.'

'You don't have to do that, Hetty,' he says. 'I'm sure no one followed me.'

She makes up a bed for him on the sofa, then goes to bed herself. But she leaves the door open between the two rooms, and so she hears him tossing and turning, hears his groans and cries and how restless he is when he finally does sleep. Then, just after she's dropped off herself, she's wakened up again by the sound of him crying. He's crying again, asleep or awake. Hetty can see his face clearly before her in the dark, his face that for all his fifty years still has something childlike about it – perhaps it's the weak chin, or the full, crimson mouth.

For a while she listens to him crying and crying in the quiet of the night, as though it was the night itself, mourning the sorrow of the world.

Then Frau Heberle makes up her mind, and gets up and gropes her way to the sofa in the dark.

'Don't cry, Hänschen! You're safe with me. Hetty will help you . . .'

She comforts him, and when he still won't stop crying, she leans down over him, pushes her arm under his, and leads the crying man to her bed, where she takes him in her arms and holds him to her bosom . . .

An ageing woman, an older man needy as a child, a little comfort, a little passion, a small aura round her beloved's head – and it never occurs to Frau Hetty to wonder how this weepy, feeble creature could possibly be the fighter and hero of her imaginings.

'But now everything's all right, isn't it, Hänschen?'

But no, the question causes the briefly stanched stream of tears to flow again, and he shakes in her embrace.

'What's the matter, Hänschen? Is there anything else worrying you that you haven't told me about yet?'

This, now, is the moment the old ladykiller has been working toward for the past several hours, because he has concluded that in the long run it is too dangerous and perhaps even impossible to leave her in the dark about his marriage and his real name. He is in confessional mode, all right. He will confess this as well, she will take it, and not love him any the less. She'll hardly throw him out on the street now, moments after she's taken him in her arms for the first time!

She has asked Hänschen whether there is was anything else worrying him that he hasn't told her about. Now, racked, crying, he admits that his name isn't Hans Enno at all, but Enno Kluge, and that he is a married man with two grown-up sons. Yes, he is a wretch who wanted to lie to her and deceive her, but now that she's been so good to him, he can't bring himself to do that.

As always, his confession is only a partial confession, a little truth mixed with plenty of fiction. He sketches the portrait of his wife, a tough, evil Nazi working in the post office, who won't keep her husband because he refuses to join the Party. This woman forced her older son to join the SS – and he tells her about Karlemann's atrocities. He paints the picture of an unequal and bad marriage, the quiet, patient, long-suffering husband and the wicked, ambitious Nazi wife. They can't live together, they are bound to hate one another. And now she has thrown him out of their joint apartment! He lied to his beloved Hetty, because he loves her so much, and because he didn't want to cause her any pain!

But now he has confessed everything. No, he won't cry any more. He will get up and pack his things and leave her – go out into the cruel, cruel world. He will find somewhere to hide away from the Gestapo, and if they catch up with him, well, that won't really matter, either, now that he has lost the love of Hetty, the only woman he has ever really loved in his life!

Yes, he's quite a wily seducer, is Enno Kluge. He knows what buttons to press with women: loving and lying are all one. There just needs to be a little grain of truth, she needs to be able to credit a bit of the stuff he tells her, and above all, tears need to be at the ready, and helplessness . . .

On this occasion, Hetty listens to his confession with absolute horror. Why did he lie to her in the first place? When they met, he had no reason to tell such lies! Did he already have such designs on her then? They can only have been wicked designs, if they necessitated such lies as that.

Her instinct tells her to send him packing, a man who is capable of deceiving a woman from the very start will always be ready to lie to her later on. And she cannot share her life with a liar. She led a clean and honest life with her first husband, and the few stories she heard about him after his death, well, an experienced woman can only laugh at such things.

No, she would send him packing from her very arms – if that weren't tantamount to sending him into the arms of the enemy, the hated Gestapo. Because she is firmly convinced that this is what would happen if she did indeed send him away. The story of his persecution by the Gestapo she believes implicitly. It doesn't even occur to her to question its veracity, even though she has just learned that the man is a liar.

And then the matter of the wife . . . It's not possible that everything he said about the woman is untrue. No one can imagine something like that, there must be some truth in it. She thinks she knows the man lying at her side, a weak creature, a child, someone with good in him: it would only take a few friendly words to lead him. But that woman, tough, ambitious, a Nazi trying to make her way up through the Party ranks – of course a man like him wouldn't suit her, a man who refused even to join her beloved Party, a man who hated the Party, perhaps secretly was even trying to work against it!

Could she send him back to such a wife? Into the arms of the Gestapo?

She couldn't, and she won't.

The light clicks on. He is standing at her bedside, wearing a too short blue undershirt, tears silently pouring down his pale cheeks. He bends down to her and whispers, 'Farewell, Hetty! You were too kind to me. I don't deserve it, I am a bad person. Farewell! I am going now . . .'

She holds him back. She whispers, 'No, you're staying with me. I gave you my promise, and I keep my promises. Don't say anything. Go back to the sofa now, and try to get some sleep. I will think about what's best to do.'

Slowly, sadly, he shakes his head. 'Hetty, you're too good for me. I will do everything you tell me, but in all truth, Hetty, it's better that you let me go.'

But of course he doesn't go. Of course he allows himself to be persuaded to stay. She will think about everything, sort it all out. And his banishment to the sofa, of course he gets that commuted too. He is allowed to return to her bed. Enwrapped in her motherly warmth, he soon falls asleep, this time without any more crying.

She, however, remains awake a long time. Actually, she stays awake all night. She listens to his breathing, it is lovely to listen to a man's breathing again, to have him close in bed. She was alone for such a long time. Now she once again has someone she can look after. Her life is no longer void of content and purpose. Oh, yes, it's quite possible that she'll have more trouble from him than is good for her. But trouble like that, trouble from a man one cherishes, that is good trouble.

Hetty resolves to be strong enough for two. Hetty resolves to keep him safe from the threat of the Gestapo. Hetty resolves to educate him, to make a real human being out of him. Hetty resolves to free her Hänschen – but no, that's not his name, his name is Enno – anyway Hetty resolves to free her Enno from the shackles of that other woman, the Nazi. Hetty resolves to bring order and cleanliness to this life now lying at her side.

And Hetty has no idea that this feeble man at her side will be strong enough to plunge her life into disorder, grief, self-reproach, tears, and danger. Hetty has no idea that all her strength was nullified the moment she decided to keep Enno Kluge in her house and to protect him against all the world. Hetty has no idea that she has put herself, and the whole little world she has built up, into terrible danger.

26

Fear and Terror

Two weeks have passed since that night. Hetty and Enno Kluge have each learned much about the other, living together in close proximity. As the man couldn't leave the house for fear of the Gestapo, they lived as if on an island, the two of them alone. They couldn't avoid each other, or refresh themselves by seeing other people. They were strictly dependent on one another.

During the first few days, she hadn't even allowed Enno to help out in the shop – those first few days, she was never completely sure there wasn't some Gestapo agent crawling outside. She had told him to stay in the house. He mustn't let anyone see him. She was a little surprised at how calmly he accepted this instruction; to her it would have been ghastly to find herself condemned to such inactivity. But Enno had simply said: 'That's fine, I can occupy myself!'

'But what will you do, Enno?' she had asked. 'It's a long day, and I won't be able to see to you much, and mooching around won't make you rich.'

'Do?' he had asked in surprise. 'How do you mean? Oh, you mean work?' He had it on the tip of his tongue to say he thought he had done enough work to last him a lifetime, but he was still a little wary of her, and so he said instead, 'Of course I wish I could work. But what can I do in the parlour? Now, if you had a lathe here!' And he laughed.

'I know what you can do! Look at this, Enno!'

She carried in a big box, full of all different types of seeds. Then she put a board down in front of him, the kind of wooden counting board with a milled edge that used to be found on many shop counters. And she picked up a fountain pen with a nib stuck upside down. Using it as a shovel, she started to separate a handful of seeds she had spilled on the counter into their different varieties. Quickly and deftly, the pen went here and there, separated some out, pushed them into a corner, sorted others, and she explained, 'These are all leftover feed grains, swept out of various corners and from burst sacks. I've collected them for years. Now that feed is getting so scarce, I'm glad I did. I'm sorting it . . .'

'What are you doing that for? It's incredibly laborious! Why not give it to the birds straight, and let them sort it!'

'And spoil three-quarters of it! Or else have them eat feed that doesn't agree with them, and die on me! No, it's just a little job that needs doing. I did it myself in the evenings, and on Sundays, whenever I had a bit of spare time. Once on a Sunday, I sorted through five pounds, as well as doing my housework! That's still my record. Now we'll see if you can beat it or not! You've got a lot of time on your hands, and it's good meditative work. I'm sure you have a lot of things you want to meditate about. Give it a go, Enno!'

She gave him the little shovel, and watched as he began to work.

'Why, you're quite dexterous!' she praised him. 'You have clever hands!'

And then, a moment later: 'But you need to pay closer attention, Hänschen – I mean Enno! I can't quite get used to it. You see, this pointy, shiny seed is millet, and this dull, black, round one is rapeseed. You mustn't get them mixed up. It's best to pick the sunflower seeds out with your fingers beforehand, it's quicker than with the pen. Wait, I'll bring you some bowls that you can put the grains in when you've sorted them!'

She was full of eagerness to find him work for his boring days. Then the shop bell rang for the first time, and from that moment there was an unbroken stream of customers, and she was only able to look in on him for moments at a time. Then she would find him dreaming over his counting board full of seeds. Or else, and worse, she would find him creeping back to his workplace, alerted by the sound of the door, like a guilty child caught truanting.

She soon saw that he would never break her record of five

pounds – he couldn't even manage two pounds. And even those she would have to go through afterward herself, so messy had been his work.

She was a little disappointed, but she agreed when he said: 'Not quite satisfied, Hetty, are you?' He laughed sheepishly. 'But you know, it's not real man's work. Give me some proper man's work, and just watch me light into it!'

Of course he was right, and the next day she didn't put the board with the seeds in front of him. 'You poor man, you'll just have to get through the day by yourself!' she said comfortingly. 'It must be awful for you. But maybe you'd like to read? I've got a lot of books of my late husband's in the bookcase over there. Wait, I'll open it for you.'

He stood behind her as she scanned the shelves. 'He was an official in the Communist Party. That copy of Marx I just managed to save during a search. I had hidden it in the stove, and an SA man was about to look there when I offered him a cigarette, and he forgot.' She looked him straight in the eye. 'But maybe this isn't your sort of reading matter, darling? I must admit, I've barely looked at them since my husband's death. Perhaps that was mistaken of me – everyone ought to be interested in politics. If we all had been, then maybe the Nazis wouldn't have got their hands on power; that's what my Walter always said. But I'm just a woman . . .'

She broke off, realizing he wasn't listening.

'Down at the bottom there are a couple of novels that I like.'

'What I like is a proper thriller, you know, with criminals and murder, that sort of thing,' proclaimed Enno.

'I don't think I have anything like that. But this is a lovely book, I've read it many times. Wilhelm Raabe's *Sparrow Street*. Why don't you try that, I'm sure it'll cheer you up . . .'

But when she came into the parlour by and by, she didn't see him reading it. It lay open on the table, and later she found it pushed to the side.

'Aren't you enjoying it?'

'Ach, you know, not really . . . They're all such terribly good people, and I get bored. It's too much like a proper book. Not a book that a man can sink his teeth into. I'm looking for something with a bit more excitement, you know.'

'Too bad,' she said. 'Too bad.' And she put the book back on the shelf.

It bothered her when she walked into the parlour now, to see the man sitting there, always in the same slumped posture and staring into space. Or else he would be asleep, with his head on the table. Or standing by the window, looking into the courtyard, always whistling the same tune. It bothered her. She had always been an active woman, and she still was. A life without work would have struck her as pointless. What made her happiest was having the whole shop full of customers – she would have liked to divide herself up into ten little Hetties to serve them all.

And now this man here, standing, sitting, squatting, lying, for ten, twelve, fourteen hours a day, doing nothing, absolutely nothing! He was stealing God's sweet time! What was the matter with him? He slept well, he ate with a healthy appetite, he wanted for nothing, but he refused to work! Once her patience snapped, and she said irritably: 'If only you wouldn't always whistle that same tune, Enno! It's six or eight hours now you've been whistling: *Bedtime now for little girls . . .*'

He laughed sheepishly. 'Does my whistling bother you? Well, I know some other tunes. Shall I whistle the Horst Wessel song instead?'* And he began: *Raise high the flag! The ranks in strict formation . . .*

Without a word she went back to the shop. This time she wasn't just annoyed with him, she was seriously offended.

It passed. She didn't bear grudges, and besides, he too had noticed that he had overstepped the mark, and so he surprised her by fixing the lamp over the bed. Yes, he could do things like that too; if it suited him, he was deft enough, but usually it didn't suit him.

---

* Horst Wessel was a minor Nazi activist murdered in 1930 in a dispute over back rent or politics – it was never determined. Nevertheless the Nazis made him a martyr, and a song he wrote – 'Die Fahne hoch' or 'Raise high the flag' – was renamed the Horst Wessel Song and made into the official song of the Nazi Party.

The period of his banishment to the parlour soon came to an end. Hetty convinced herself that there were no spies prowling around outside, and Enno was permitted to help out in the shop again. He still wasn't allowed out on the street, as there was always a chance he might run into someone who knew him. But helping out in the shop was all right, and he turned out to be useful and deft. She noticed that working for long periods at some repetitive task tired him out, so she took care to offer him plenty of variety.

Before long she allowed him to help with the customers. He was good with them: polite, confident, even witty in his slightly sleepy way.

'That gentleman is an asset to your business, Frau Haberle,' old customers would say. 'Must be a relation?'

'Yes, he's a cousin of mine,' lied Hetty, happy about the praise for Enno.

One day she said to him, 'Enno, I want to go out to Dahlem today. You remember, Herr Lobe is having to close his pet shop there because he's been called up. I have an opportunity to buy some of his stock. He has a lot, and it would be a big help to us, because things are in shorter and shorter supply. Do you think you can manage the shop on your own?'

'Of course I can, Hetty, of course I can! Easy. How long are you going to be gone for?'

'Well, I'll set off right after lunch, but I don't think I'll be back before the end of the day. I'd like to see my dressmaker at the same time . . .'

'Why not, Hetty? As far as I'm concerned, you can be away till midnight. Don't worry about the shop, I can handle everything here.'

He walked her to the underground. It was during the lunch break, and the shop was closed.

She smiled to herself as the train moved off. Living with someone else was such a completely different proposition! It was fun working together. Only then did you really have a feeling of achievement at the end of the day. And he was trying as hard as he could to please her. He did his best. No, he wasn't an energetic or even a hard-working man, she had to admit that. When he had been made to run around too much for his liking, he often withdrew to the parlour, regardless of how full the shop was, and she had to serve the customers by herself. Once, after calling him many times, she found him in the cellar, perched on the rim of the sandbox, half asleep, the little sand pail half filled in front of him – and she waiting for it for the past ten minutes!

He'd jumped when she called out: 'Enno! What's keeping you? I'm waiting and waiting!'

Like a frightened schoolboy he'd got to his feet. 'Just dropped off a bit,' he murmured sheepishly, and started scooping up sand. 'Just coming, boss, won't happen again.'

Little jokes like that were his way of appeasing her.

No, not a mighty worker before the Lord, our Enno, that was certainly clear to her, but he did what he could. And then he was likeable, polite, decent, affectionate, without obvious vices. She forgave him his excessive consumption of cigarettes. She wasn't averse to smoking the odd one herself, when she was tired . . .

But that day Hetty was unlucky with her errands. Lobe's store in Dahlem was closed when she got there, and no one was able to tell her when he might be back. No, he hadn't yet been called up, but he probably had things to do in connection with the army. Normally, the shop opened at ten in the morning – perhaps she might try tomorrow?

She said thank you, and went to see her dressmaker. But when she reached the premises, she stopped in bewilderment. The house had been bombed overnight; there was nothing but rubble. People hurried past it, some purposely averting their eyes, unwilling to see the devastation or afraid of being unable to conceal their anger. Others went by especially slowly (the police saw to it that no one stopped), either with expressions of curiosity or else frowning at the destruction.

Yes, Berlin was being sent down to bomb cellars more and more often, and more and more bombs were falling on it, among them the feared phosphorous canister bombs. More and more people now quoted Göring's saying that his name would be Meier if an enemy plane showed its face over Berlin. The night before, Hetty had sat in her bomb shelter – alone, because she didn't want Enno to be seen as her official boyfriend and housemate. She had heard the nerve-racking sound of planes, like mosquitoes droning and whining. She hadn't heard any bombs falling: thus far her part of the city had been spared. People told each other the British didn't want to hurt working people, they just wanted to bomb the rich people out west . . .

Her dressmaker hadn't been rich, but she had been bombed just the same. Hetty Haberle tried to find out from a policeman what had happened to her. The policeman regretted that he was unable to help her. Perhaps she could ask at the local police station, or the nearest air-raid protection office?

But Hetty lacked the peace of mind to do that. However sorry she felt for her dressmaker, and however much she wanted to learn about her fate, she now felt she had to go home. Whenever she saw something like this, she felt the need to go home. She had to check whether things were still all right there. It was foolish, she knew, but she couldn't help it. She first needed to see with her own eyes that nothing had happened there.

Unfortunately something had happened to the little pet shop at the Königstor. Nothing tragic by any means, but still it shook Frau Haberle, and more profoundly than other things she had experienced of late. Frau Haberle found the grating down and a note with the silly legend that never failed to annoy her: 'Back soon'. And underneath that: 'Frau Hedwig Haberle'.

To have her name on that note, to have her own good name associated with such sloppiness and laziness, offended her almost as much as the breach of trust of which Enno was guilty. He had crept off behind her back, and he would have reopened the shop behind her back, and not have breathed a word to her of his deception. On top of everything it was so stupid of him, because it was almost inevitable that one of her regulars would ask her, 'How come you were shut yesterday afternoon? Did you have to go out, Frau Haberle?'

She enters her flat through the back. Then she pulls up the

grating and unlocks the door. She waits for the first customers to arrive, but no, she doesn't really want even one to come now. To be so betrayed behind her back – never once in the years of her marriage with Walter was there ever anything like this. They always trusted each other, never let each other down. And now this! She hadn't given him the least cause to behave so.

The first customer comes and is served by her, but when Hetty opens the till to make change for a twenty-mark note, she finds it empty. There was plenty of change there when she left, around a hundred marks. She masters herself, gets some money out of her purse, gives the lady her change, there, done. The bell over the door rings.

Now she wants to shut up shop and be all alone. It occurs to her – all the while she continues to serve customers – that in the past few days she has occasionally had the sense that there was something wrong, that the daily takings ought to have been higher than it seemed they were. At the time she had quickly dismissed such thoughts from her mind. What would Enno do with the money in any case? He never left the house, and he was always under her watchful eye!

But now she remembers the bathroom out on the landing, and that he has smoked more cigarettes than he can have brought with him in his little case. He must have found someone in the house who had agreed to get him cigarettes on the black market, for cash, without coupons, behind her back! How low and how mean! She would have loved to provide him with cigarettes – he only had to open his mouth and ask!

In the ninety minutes or so till Enno's return, Frau Haberle struggles with herself. Over the past few days, she has reaccustomed herself to the presence of a man about the house, to not being alone any more, to having someone to look after, someone she is fond of. But if the man is as he appears to be, she must surely root the love out of her heart! Better to be alone than live with permanent suspicion and fear. She can hardly pop out to the greengrocer's any more without being afraid of being cheated by him in some way.

And then it occurs to Hetty that she has also had the impression of things not being the way she left them in her linen closet. No, she must, she must send him packing – today, however difficult it feels. Later on, it will only be more difficult.

But then she remembers that she is a woman past her best, and that this might be her last chance of escaping a solitary old age. After this experience with Enno Kluge, she will hardly feel able to try again with some other man. After this terrifying, catastrophic experience with Enno!

'Yes, we've got mealworms in again. How many would you like, Madam?'

Half an hour before closing, Enno walks in. It's indicative of the state of her mind that only now does it occur to her that it's not safe for him to go out on the street, with the Gestapo looking for him! Up till this moment she hasn't been able to think like that, so preoccupied has she been with his betrayal of her. But what use are all the precautions in the world if he just runs off whenever she goes out? Maybe all that business with the Gestapo was just deception anyway? Who knows, with such a man!

He has noticed, of course, from the raised shutters, that she's back in the shop earlier than expected. He walks in off the street, carefully makes his way through the line of customers, smiles at her as if nothing has happened, and says, as he disappears into the parlour, 'I'll be back in a jiffy to help out, boss!'

And he is back, and very quickly too, and then, to keep her dignity in front of the customers, she has to speak to him, give him instructions, act as if nothing were amiss   and all this when her entire world has collapsed! But she doesn't let on; she even responds to his feeble little jokes, which he makes in unusual quantity today, and only when he starts to go to the cash register does she say, sharply, 'If you don't mind, I'll look after that myself!'

He jumps slightly at that and looks at her with a shy sidelong glance – like a dog, yes, just like a beaten dog, she thinks. Then his hand feels its way into his pocket, a smile appears on his face, and yes, he's already over the shock.

'At your orders, boss!' he barks, and scrapes his heels together.

The customers laugh at him, the funny little fellow playing soldiers, but she doesn't feel like laughing just now.

Then the shop shuts. For another hour and a quarter they continue to work together, busy with feeding and watering and tidying up, both of them in near silence after she has failed to respond to his latest series of jests.

Hetty is in the kitchen, making supper. She is making fried potatoes, real lovely fried potatoes, with bacon. She got the bacon from a customer in exchange for some old cheese. She had been looking forward to surprising Enno with something good for supper, because he likes good things. The potatoes are turning a fine golden yellow.

But then all at once she turns off the gas under the pan. All at once, she is impatient to clear the air. She goes into the parlour, leans against the Dutch stove, sombre and grim, and asks, almost menacingly, 'Well?'

He is sitting at the table, at their supper table, which he has laid for both of them, humming away to himself as he always does.

At that menacing 'Well?' he jumps, and then he stands up and looks across at her dark form.

'Yes, Hetty?' he says. 'Is supper ready soon? I'm really famished.'

She feels like hitting him, this man who supposes she will pass over such a betrayal in silence! He must feel mighty sure of himself, this fellow, merely no doubt because he has spent the nights in her bed! She is furious: she feels like giving him a good shaking and beating and then repeating the dose.

But she gets a grip on herself and says 'Well?' again, but this time more menacingly still.

'Ah, I get it, Hetty!' he says. 'You mean about the money.' He reaches into his pocket, and pulls out a bundle of notes. 'Here, Hetty, here are 210 marks – I took 92 out of the till.' He laughs a little sheepishly. 'My contribution to the household, if you like.'

'How did you come by so much money?'

'This afternoon there was the big race in Karlsbad. I got there just in the nick of time to place a bet on Adebar. Adebar to win. I like betting on horses. I know quite a bit about racing, Hetty.' He says it with a rare touch of pride. 'I didn't place all 92, just 50. The odds were . . .'

'And what would you have done if your horse hadn't won?'

'Adebar was a cert to win – it's a meaningless question.'

'But what if he hadn't won?'

Now it's his turn to feel superior to the woman. He smiles as he says, 'Listen, Hetty, it's clear you don't know much about racing, and I know all there is to know. And if I say Adebar to win, and put 50 marks on him . . .'

She interrupts him. She says angrily, 'You gambled with my money! I won't have that! If you want money, tell me – I don't want you working for me just for bed and board. But you don't help yourself out of the till without my permission! Understand?'

The unwontedly sharp tone completely unhinges him. In a plaintive tone – she knows he is about to burst into tears, and she is already dreading the tears – in a plaintive tone he says, 'How can you talk to me like that, Hetty? As if I were just your employee! Of course I'll never take money out of the till again. I just thought it would make you happy if I made some money so easily. I was sure he would win!'

She doesn't even respond to such nonsense. The money is secondary to her; what matters is the breach of trust. If he thinks she's upset about the money, more fool him! She says: 'And you simply shut up shop here, so that you could go and bet on the race?'

'Yes,' he says. 'You would have had to shut it, if I hadn't been there!'

'And you knew you were going to shut it when I went away this morning?'

'Yes,' he says, stupidly. Only quickly to correct himself, 'No, I mean no, otherwise I would have asked you for permission. It only occurred to me when I passed the little bookie's shop on the Neue Königstrasse, you know. I read the odds as I was passing, and when I saw Adebar at such long odds, that decided me.'

'I see!' she says. She doesn't believe him. He already had it in mind before he walked her to the underground. She recalls him sitting over the paper for a long time this morning, and doing some calculations on a scrap of paper even when the first of the day's customers were in the shop. 'I see!' she says again. 'So you just go for a stroll in the city, when we've agreed that because of the Gestapo, it's best that you don't go outside at all?'

'You let me take you to the underground, though!'

'We were together. And I told you then it was strictly an experiment! It's not the same as running around half the day in the city. Where did you go?'

'Oh, this little bar I used to frequent earlier. No one from the Gestapo ever goes in there, just bookies and bettors.'

'Who all know you! Who can tell anyone who asks, We saw Enno Kluge at such and such a time!'

'But the Gestapo know I have to be somewhere. Only they don't know where. The bar is a long way away – it's over in Wedding. And there wasn't anyone I knew there who would give me away!'

He talks enthusiastically and good-heartedly; if you listen to him, he's completely within his rights. He doesn't even understand how deeply he's shaken her faith in him or what a struggle she's having with herself. Taken money – to please her. Shut the shop – she would have done the same. Gone to a bar – but a long way away, in Wedding. The fact that she had feared for her love he failed completely to understand. It never even crossed his mind!

'Well now, Enno,' she asks, 'is that all you have to say? Or is there anything else?'

'What else could I say, Hetty? I can see you're cross with me, but it doesn't seem to me like I've done a whole lot wrong!' And there they were, the dreaded tears. 'Oh, Hetty, I just want you to be nice to me, like you were before! I promise to ask your permission before I do anything in future! Just be nice to me! I can't stand it when you're like this . . .'

But this time neither tears nor pleas could move her. There was something wrong about them. She was almost disgusted by the weeping man in front of her.

'I need to think about all this, Enno,' she said toughly. 'You don't seem to understand how much you've shaken my trust in you.'

And she walked past him to the kitchen, to see to the potatoes again. So, she had had her showdown with him. And what had been the upshot? Had she clarified the situation, or made a decision any easier?

Not a bit! All it had done was show her that this man had no sense of guilt, that he lied wildly when the situation seemed to him to demand it, and that he cared not a whit about who he lied to.

No, a man like that wasn't the man for her. She had to finish with him. Of course she couldn't put him out on the street tonight. He seemed not even to know what he was guilty of. He was like a puppy who has chewed up a pair of slippers and has no idea why his master is beating him.

No, she had to give him a day or two's grace, so that he could find himself new lodgings. And if he fell into the hands of the Gestapo – well, it wouldn't be her concern. He took his own chances – and over a bet! No, she must free herself of him, she would never be able to trust him again. She must live alone, from now on till her death! And at that thought, she felt a chill.

In spite of the chill, she says to him, when supper is over, 'I've thought it all over, Enno, and we must break up. You're a nice man, and a dear man, but your view of the world is very different from mine, and in the long run we're not compatible.'

He looks blankly at her, as she makes up a bed for him on the sofa, to lend credence to her words. At first he cannot believe his ears, and then he starts whimpering: 'Oh, God, Hetty, you can't mean it! When we love each other the way we do! You surely can't want to drive me out on to the street, and into the arms of the Gestapo!'

'Ach!' she says, trying to calm herself with words of her own. 'The business with the Gestapo can't be so bad as all that, otherwise you would hardly have spent half the day running around the city!'

He falls to his knees. He really does, he drops to his knees in front of her. Fear has made him mindless. 'Hetty! Hetty!' he wails and cries. 'Do you want to kill me? You have to keep me here! Where am I supposed to go? Ach, Hetty, won't you love me just a little bit, I'm so unhappy . . .'

Wailing and crying, a little puppy whimpering with fear!

He tries to clasp her legs, he reaches for her hands. She breaks away, runs to the bedroom, and bolts the door. But all night she has to listen to him banging against the door, trying the handle, whimpering and imploring . . .

She lies there perfectly quietly. She summons all her strength so as not to give in, not to weaken in the face of her own heart and all the begging outside! She remains true to her resolve no longer to live with him.

At breakfast, the two sit facing one another with pale, weary faces. They barely speak. They don't refer to their dispute.

But he understands now, she thinks, and even if he doesn't go looking for a room today, he'll have to leave my house tomorrow at the latest. I'll tell him one more time, tomorrow at lunchtime: We must separate!

It's true, Hetty Haberle is a courageous and decent woman. And the fact that she doesn't put her resolution into effect, doesn't put out her Enno, is no fault of hers, but the fault of other people, people she has yet to meet. Inspector Escherich, for example, and Emil Borkhausen.

27

Emil Borkhausen Makes Himself Useful

While Enno Kluge and Frau Haberle were linking their destinies, however temporarily, Inspector Escherich had been through some rough times. He had declined to keep it secret from his superior Prall that Enno Kluge had promptly shaken off his shadows and disappeared without trace in the sea of the metropolis.

Inspector Escherich had meekly allowed all the abuse to rain down on him: he was an idiot, he was an incompetent, he should be locked up, the dunderhead who in almost a year hadn't even managed to catch a stupid anonymous postcard writer!

And then, once he had a lead, he let the fellow go, imbecile that he was! Truly, Inspector Escherich had aided and abetted treason, and that was the basis on which they would proceed against him if he failed to produce Enno Kluge to Obergruppenführer Prall within the week.

Inspector Escherich listened meekly to these attacks. But they had a strange effect on him nevertheless: even though he knew perfectly well that Enno Kluge didn't have anything to do with the postcards and was unable to help him take a single step toward the apprehension of the real culprit, in spite of that the inspector's interests were suddenly almost exclusively concentrated on the insignificant little Enno Kluge. It was too annoying that this insect he had meant to hold up to his superiors as a distraction had now slipped through his fingers. During these weeks the Hobgoblin had been especially busy: three of his postcards had wound up on the inspector's desk. But for the first time since he had joined the case, Escherich took not the least interest in the postcards or their author. He even forgot to flag the sites where they were found on his map of Berlin.

No, as a matter of urgency he had to lay hands on Enno Kluge again, and Inspector Escherich went to unusual lengths to get his man. He even travelled out to Ruppin, to Eva Kluge, prepared for all eventualities with a warrant for her arrest and his. But he saw pretty quickly that the woman had nothing to do with the man and knew very little of the life he'd led over the past few years.

What she did know she told the inspector, neither especially willingly nor exactly reluctantly, more with utter indifference. The woman didn't care one way or another what had happened to her husband, what he had done or not done. The inspector learned the names of two or three bars where Enno Kluge had once been a regular, he heard of his love of betting and got the address of one Tutti Hebekreuz, who had sent a letter to the flat once. The letter had accused Enno Kluge of having stolen money and ration cards from her. No, on the last occasion she had seen him, Frau Kluge had neither given him the letter nor mentioned it to him. Only the address had stuck in her head; as a postwoman, or former postwoman, she had a keen eye for addresses.

Armed with this new knowledge, Inspector Escherich returned to Berlin. True to his principle of asking questions but not answering any, of never passing on information, he had not told Eva Kluge of the process against her in Berlin. So he didn't come back with much, but it was a start, a sniff of a lead – and he was able to show Prall that he was doing something, not just sitting on his hands. That was all his superiors really cared about: something had to be done, even if it was the wrong thing, as the whole pursuit of Kluge was wrong. It was the waiting around that the gentlemen couldn't endure.

Inquiries at Tutti Hebekreuz's were unsuccessful. She had met Kluge in a café, and she knew where he worked as well. Once he had stayed in her flat for two weeks, yes, that was the case, and she had written to complain to him about the missing money and ration cards. But he had managed to clear that up on a later visit; it was another subtenant who had done that.

Then he had disappeared again without a word to her: some other woman, doubtless, that was Enno's way. No, of course *she* had never been linked to him romantically in any way. No, she had no idea where he had moved to. But it wouldn't be anywhere in the area, otherwise she would surely have heard about it.

In the two bars, he was known under the name Enno, yes indeed. He hadn't been seen for a long time, no, but he did drop in from time to time. Yes, Inspector, we'll not tell him you asked after him. We are law-abiding publicans who only serve respectable people who are interested in the sport of kings. We'll let you know the moment he comes in. Heil Hitler to you too, Inspector!

Inspector Escherich assigned ten men to go around all the pubs and bookies' premises in the north and east of Berlin, to keep asking about Enno Kluge. And while Escherich waited for their inquiries to bear fruit, the second bizarre thing happened: it no longer seemed to him out of the question that Enno Kluge might have something to do with the postcards after all. Too many curious coincidences clustered round the fellow: the postcard found at the doctor's, for a start, and then the wife being first a Nazi, and then requesting to leave the Party, presumably because the son in the SS had done something she didn't approve of. Perhaps Enno Kluge was much more cunning than the inspector had thought, perhaps he was involved in other affairs than simply these postcards. There was something he was trying to live down, that seemed almost certain.

This was confirmed by Deputy Inspector Schröder, with whom the inspector talked the whole case through in detail in order to refresh his own memory. Deputy Inspector Schröder also had the feeling there was something not quite right about Kluge, that he was sitting on something. Well, they would see, something was bound to come up soon. The inspector had a feeling, and his feelings rarely deceived him in matters like this.

And this time they really didn't deceive him. During those days of anxiety and irritation, it happened that the inspector was told one Borkhausen desired to speak to him.

Borkhausen? Inspector Escherich wondered to himself. Borkhausen? Who the hell is Borkhausen again? Ah, I remember, that little snitch that would sell his mother for eight pfennings.

Then, aloud, 'Show him in!' But as soon as Borkhausen came

in, he greeted him with the words 'If this is about the Persickes again, I don't want you here!'

Borkhausen eyed the inspector truculently and said nothing. He gave every impression of wanting to speak about just that.

'Well, then!' said the inspector. 'Why are you still here, Borkhausen?'

'Persicke's took the radio off that Rosenthal woman, Inspector,' he said reproachfully. 'I know it for a fact, I've been . . .'

'Rosenthal?' asked Escherich. 'The old Jewish woman who jumped out of the window in Jablonski Strasse?'

'That's exactly right!' confirmed Borkhausen. 'And he stole her radio – that is, she was already dead, but he went in her flat . . .'

'Let me tell you something, Borkhausen,' said Escherich. 'I've discussed this case with Inspector Rusch. If you don't stop agitating against the Persickes, we're going to haul you over the coals. We don't want to hear one more word about that business, and least of all from you! You are the very last person who ought to be poking around in that business, Borkhausen!'

'But he stole her radio . . .' Borkhausen began again with that stubborn persistence that comes of blind hatred. 'I can prove it . . .'

'Get out, Borkhausen, or I'll have you arrested and carted down to the basement!'

'Then I'll go to the police headquarters on the Alex!' said Borkhausen, offended. 'The law's the law, and theft is breaking it . . .'

But Escherich had moved on to something else, namely his Hobgoblin case, which these days preoccupied him. He had stopped listening to this idiot. 'Tell me, Borkhausen,' he said, 'you know a lot of people and you go to pubs a lot. Have you ever come across a certain Enno Kluge?'

Borkhausen, sensing business, said a little gruffly: 'I know someone called Enno. I don't know if his other name's Kluge or not. I always thought Enno was his last name.'

'Small man, slight build, pale, quiet, shy?'

'Could be the same man, Inspector.'

'Light-coloured coat, checked brown cap?'

'That's my man.'

'Always sniffing around women?'

'I wouldn't know about women. Where I saw him, you don't get many women.'

'Likes to play the gee-gees –'

'That's right, Inspector.'

'Favourite bars: the Also Ran and Starter's Orders?'

'The self-same man, Inspector! Your Enno Kluge must be my Enno!'

'I want you to find him for me, Borkhausen! Drop that stupid Persicke stuff; that'll only land you in concentration camp if you pursue it! Find me Enno Kluge instead!'

'But what would you want with him, Inspector!' exclaimed Borkhausen. 'He's a real tiddler. Pathetic little squirt! What would you trouble yourself over such an eejit for, Inspector?'

'Never you mind, Borkhausen! If you help me land Enno Kluge, there's five hundred marks in it for you!'

'Five hundred marks, Inspector! Ten Ennos ain't worth that! You must be making a mistake!'

'Well, maybe I am and maybe I'm not, but that needn't concern you either way, Borkhausen. You'll get your five hundred.'

'Well, if you say so, Inspector, then I'll see if I can't get hold of Enno for you. But is it okay if I just point him out to you? I don't have to bring him in, do I? I don't like to talk to people like that . . .'

'I wonder what you two got up to together! You're not usually so sensitive as that, Borkhausen! I'd guess you got into some mischief together in the past, and you're trying to forget it. Well, I won't meddle with painful memories. Off you go, Borkhausen, and find me Kluge!'

'Might I ask the inspector for a little advance first? No, not so much an advance,' Borkhausen corrected himself, 'as some cash toward my expenses.'

'What expenses, Borkhausen? That sounds like a challenging proposition to me.'

'Well, I'll need to ride around on the underground, and spend time in various establishments, and stand a short here and a pint there, you know, and it all costs money, Inspector! But I think fifty marks ought to cover it!'

'Of course, any time the great Borkhausen goes out, everyone's just waiting to see the colour of his money! I'll give you ten, and now scram! Do you think I've got nothing better to do than talk to you all day?'

In fact, Borkhausen did think precisely that: that an inspector had nothing better to do than pump people for information and get them to do his work for him. But he carefully declined to say so. Indeed, as he made his way to the door, he said, 'But if I find Kluge for you, then you've got to help me with the Persickes. Those blokes made me angry . . .'

With a single bound, Escherich was after him, seized him by the shoulder, and held his fist under his nose.

'Do you see this?' he screamed at him furiously. 'Sniff on that, you fuckwit! One more peep out of you about the Persickes and you'll be on your way down to the basement, and I don't care if all the Enno Kluges in the world are still at large!'

And he drove his knee into the other man's rump, sending him careering down the hallway like a cannonball. And as Borkhausen happened to have been discharged in the direction of an SS adjutant, he received a second powerful kick . . .

The noise of these successive detonations had alerted two more SS sentries by the stairs. They caught hold of the still staggering Borkhausen and slung him down the stairs like a sack of potatoes, tumbling over and over.

And when Borkhausen got to the bottom and lay there stunned and bleeding, the next sentry grabbed him by the scruff of his neck, and screamed, 'You think you can dirty our nice floor here, you pig!' dragged him to the exit, and heaved him out into the street.

Inspector Escherich witnessed Borkhausen's progress with satisfaction, until the stairs blocked his view.

The passersby on Prinz Albrecht Strasse studiously avoided looking at the man sprawling in the dirt, because they knew perfectly well the dangerous nature of the premises he had been thrown out of. It might already be accounted a crime to gaze at someone like that sympathetically, and you certainly couldn't think of helping them. The sentry, though, emerging from the exit with a heavy tread, said, 'Listen, pig, if you're still disfiguring our entrance in three minutes, then I'll give you a personal escort you won't forget in a hurry!'

That did the trick. Borkhausen pulled himself to his feet and staggered off home with sore, bruised limbs. Inside he was burning with helpless rage and fury, and this hatred was stronger in him than his physical pain. He firmly resolved not to lift a finger for that bastard inspector: let him find his dratted Enno Kluge by himself!

But the next day, when his rage had lessened somewhat and the voice of his common sense began to make itself heard once more, he told himself that, first, he had taken ten marks from Inspector Escherich and would have to earn them, otherwise he would be had up for dishonesty. And, second, it wasn't a good idea to be on the outs with such a powerful figure. He had the power, and if you were small fry, you had to knuckle under. Being thrown out yesterday, that had just been a chapter of accidents really. If he hadn't collided with the adjutant, it would have been pretty harmless. To them it was just a joke, and if it had been Borkhausen watching it happening to someone else, he would have laughed – for instance if it had happened to Enno Kluge.

Yes, and that was the third reason why Borkhausen decided to accept his assignment: he could get one back on stupid Enno Kluge, whose wretched boozing had messed up the original break-in.

So Borkhausen, with aching limbs but with goodwill, betook himself to the two bars that Inspector Escherich had previously visited, and some others besides. He didn't ask the publicans if they had seen Enno, he just hung around, nursing a beer for an hour or more, shooting the breeze about horses – he had picked up a fair bit from hearing others talking, though betting had never been his thing – and then went on to the next place and did much the same thing there. Borkhausen was a patient sort; it didn't bother him spending whole days like this.

He didn't even need to have all that much patience, because on his second day he saw Enno in the Also Ran. He witnessed the little fellow's triumph with Adebar and felt violent envy of the fool's good fortune. He was also struck by seeing the fifty-mark note that Kluge passed to the bookmaker. That wasn't earned money – Borkhausen could smell that a mile off. The little creep must be living the high life somewhere!

It's in no way surprising that Herrs Borkhausen and Kluge failed to acknowledge each other – yes, you might say they didn't even see each other.

What is a little more surprising, perhaps, is the fact that the bartender never gave Inspector Escherich a call, in spite of his promise to do so. But that was simply the way things were; on the one hand you were afraid of the Gestapo and lived in constant fear of them, but it was something else to do their dirty work for them. Things weren't taken to that degree, and if no one tipped Enno Kluge off about them, no one ratted on him either.

(Incidentally, Inspector Escherich would not forget this lack of communication. He would inform a certain department about it, whereupon a file would be opened on the the bartender, in which the word 'unreliable' appeared prominently. One day, perhaps sooner rather than later, the bartender would get to know what it meant to be thought of as 'unreliable' by the Gestapo.)

Of the two gentlemen, it was Borkhausen who was the first to leave the bar. He didn't go far, though, but stood behind a poster pillar, and waited for his man to emerge. Borkhausen was a shadow who wouldn't easily let his prey out of his sight, and especially not this prey. He even managed to squeeze into the same underground carriage as the other, and even though there was plenty of Borkhausen to see, little Enno Kluge didn't see him.

Enno Kluge was completely preoccupied with his triumph with Adebar and the money that crackled in his trouser pocket again for the first time in ages, and then he thought about Hetty, who was so good to him. With fond emotion he thought of the kind, elderly, shapeless woman, without remembering that a few hours ago he had robbed and lied to her.

True enough, when he reached the shop and saw that the grating was up and she was there working again, and must certainly have taken his disappearance badly, his good mood left him again. Even so, supported by the fatalism with which people of his stamp respond to adversity, he walked into the shop to face the music. The fact that preoccupied as he was he failed to notice who was on his tail is something that can't really surprise anyone.

Borkhausen saw Kluge disappear into the shop. He stood in a gateway a little way off, because he assumed that Kluge had gone in to buy something, and would shortly be out again. But as other customers came and went, Borkhausen began to feel anxious. He had thought the five hundred were practically in his pocket, but if he had missed Kluge's leaving the shop . . .

The steel grates came down with a crash, and now he felt sure: Enno had somehow given him the slip. Perhaps he had got some sense that he was being shadowed, had gone through the shop on some pretext or other and on into the house, and disappeared through the main entrance. Borkhausen cursed his own stupidity for not having kept half an eye on the house entrance. Idiot that he was, he had focused entirely on the door to the shop!

Well, there was always the chance of running into Enno again tomorrow or the next day in the bar. Now that he had made a killing on Adebar, his betting mania would leave him no peace. He would go in every day and bet until he had gone through his winnings. It wasn't every week that there was an outsider like Adebar running, and when there was, chances were you hadn't put anything on him. Enno would be in a hurry to give his money back to the bookies.

Borkhausen headed home past the little pet shop. Then he suddenly saw through the window (it was only the front door that was shuttered off) that there was a light on inside, and as he pressed his nose against the glass, peeping over the fishbowls and through the birdcages, he saw there were two people still at work in there: a dumpy pudding of a woman at a critical age, as he immediately sensed, and with her his friend Enno: Enno in shirtsleeves and a blue apron, Enno doughtily filling bowls with seed, pouring water, brushing down a Scotch terrier.

What incredible luck that moron Enno had! What was it that women continued to see in him? He, Borkhausen, was stuck with Otti and her (if not his) five kids, and an old laggard like that could just walk into a bijou pet shop, complete with woman, birds, and fishes.

Borkhausen spat. What a rotten world it was, that kept good things away from Borkhausen only to drop them in the lap of a fool like that!

But the longer Borkhausen watched, the more apparent it became that the couple inside were not full of the joys of spring. They were hardly talking to each other, hardly looking at each other, and it appeared likely that little Enno Kluge was nothing but an employee, who was helping the woman in there tidy up her shop. In which case, he would be out in a while.

Borkhausen retreated back to his observation post in the doorway opposite. As the shutters were down, Kluge would come out of the house entrance, and so Borkhausen kept an eye on that. But the light in the shop went out, and there was still no sign of Kluge. Then Borkhausen decided to take a chance. At the risk of bumping into Enno on the stairway, he sneaked into the house.

First Borkhausen made a mental note of the nameplate, H. Haberle, and then he crept through the outer door into the courtyard. He was in luck: they already had the lights on, even though it was only just beginning to get dark outside, and, looking through a crooked blind, Borkhausen had a good view of the whole parlour. What he saw surprised him so much, he was almost shocked.

Because there was his friend Enno on his knees on the floor, slithering about after the fat woman, who was nervously holding her skirts down and retreating from him. Little Enno had his arms upraised, and seemed to be weeping and lamenting.

People! thought Borkhausen, and in delight he shifted about from foot to foot, People, if that's your way of getting in the mood, I'm sorry for you! But I'll happily stand here half the night and watch you.

But then the door slammed behind the old woman, and there Enno stood on the other side of it, turning the knob, apparently still wailing and appealing to her.

Perhaps it wasn't some romantic ritual here, thought Borkhausen. Perhaps they've just had a quarrel, or Enno asked her for something she didn't want to give him, or she wants nothing to do with the infatuated jerk any more . . . What's it to do with me? At any rate, he'll be spending the night here, why else would she have made him a nice white bed on the sofa?

Enno Kluge stood just in front of the aforementioned bed. Borkhausen could see the face of his erstwhile companion in crime quite clearly. There was an astonishing transformation in it: a moment ago, he had been crying and wailing, now he had a big grin all over his face, and as he looked over to the door, and grinned again . . .

So he's just been putting on a show for the old lady. Well, good luck, son, is all I can say. I'm afraid Escherich will be spitting in your soup!

Kluge had lit himself a cigarette. He made straight for the window where Borkhausen stood, forcing Borkhausen to duck. The black-out came abruptly down, and now he could give up his observation post for the night. There were no more great excitements to be expected, or at least he wouldn't be privy to them. But he had Enno in his clutches, for tonight at least . . .

The deal he had made with Inspector Escherich was that he would call him the moment he spotted Enno Kluge, at any time of the day or night. But as Borkhausen walked away from the Königstor in the gathering gloom, he began to wonder whether an immediate call was in his own best interests. It occurred to him that there were two sides involved, and that he could try and exploit them both.

He had Escherich's money in the bag, so why not try to make a bit out of Enno too? The little fellow had had a fifty in his hand, which he had made into two hundreds, with a little help from Adebar – well, why shouldn't he, Borkhausen, have that money? Escherich wouldn't be affected, he would still get his man, and Enno wouldn't really suffer, either, because the Gestapo would have take his money off him anyway. What was he waiting for?

And then there was that fat woman that Enno had gone slithering after on his knees. She was bound to have money, perhaps quite a bit of money. The shop looked prosperous: there was still plenty of stuff on sale, and she didn't seem to want for customers either. True, all that wailing and pleading of Kluge's didn't exactly create the impression that the two of them were soulmates, but who would hand a lover, even an ex-lover, over to the Gestapo? The fact that the old baggage still tolerated Enno in her flat, even after rejecting him, that she had set up a bed on her sofa for him, surely that proved that she still cared something for him? And if she cared about the old geezer, then she would pay something, maybe not a lot, but something. And why should Borkhausen stand in her way?

When Borkhausen reached this point in his thoughts – and on his way home and later that night, lying beside his Otti, he reached it several more times – he was seized by a little frisson of fear, because he realized this was a pretty dangerous game he was proposing to play. Escherich was certainly not a man to tolerate such private initiatives. These Gestapo types were all like that, and it was the easiest thing in the world for the inspector to send a man to a concentration camp. And concentration camp was something that Borkhausen had a healthy respect for.

But he was sufficiently infected by the thinking and ethos of a criminal that he persisted in telling himself that a job that could be done was a job that needed doing. And this Enno thing was certainly that. For now, Borkhausen would sleep on it, and in the morning he could decide whether to report back to Escherich right away or look in on Kluge first. Now he was going to sleep . . .

But he didn't sleep; he kept thinking that one person wasn't enough to handle this. He, Borkhausen, needed to have some freedom of movement. For instance, he had to be able to go to

Escherich, and in that time Enno Kluge would be unsupervised. Or when he put the squeeze on the fat lady, Enno might pick that time to run off. But he had no one he could trust, and anyway a partner would demand his share of the business. And Borkhausen didn't like sharing.

Finally, Borkhausen remembered that among the five kids there was one boy of thirteen or so who might even be his son. He had always had the feeling that this squirt, who bore the absurdly fancy moniker of Kuno-Dieter, might perhaps be his own, even though Otti had always insisted she had him with a count, some Pomeranian landowner, by god. But Otti had always been one to show off, as the choice of name – after that of the alleged father – demonstrated.

With a heavy sigh, Borkhausen decided to take the boy with him as a reserve lookout. That wouldn't cost more than a bit of a run-in with Otti, and a few marks for the kid. Then Borkhausen's thoughts began revolving around the whole under-taking from the beginning, until they grew indistinct, and he finally fell asleep.

28

A Pretty Little Job of Blackmail

It has already been reported how Hetty Haberle and Enno Kluge breakfasted together that morning in near silence, then worked side by side in the shop, both pale from their almost sleepless night and preoccupied with their own thoughts. Frau Haberle was thinking that Enno needed to be sent packing tomorrow, come what may, and Enno that he absolutely didn't want to go.

Into this silence walked the first customer of the day, a long tall man, who said to Frau Haberle, 'Morning, lady. I see you have a pair of canaries in the window, and I was wondering how much they were. They have to be a mating pair, though, I've always been one for mating pairs . . .' And Borkhausen spun round, in a show of surprise – a deliberately badly acted show of surprise – and called out to Kluge, who was just slipping off into the back room of the shop, 'Well, I'm damned if it isn't you, Enno! Here I am, I'm talking, I'm looking, I'm thinking that's not my Enno, what would my Enno be doing in a little pocket zoo like this? And it's you all along. Whatcher doing, pal?'

Enno, the doorknob already in his hand, stood frozen, unable either to run off or to make some reply.

But Hetty stared at the tall man, who had addressed her Enno with such intimate friendliness. Her lips began to tremble, and her knees shook. So there it was, the danger; it wasn't a lie that Enno had told her about being threatened by the Gestapo. Because she didn't question for a moment that this man – half-thug, half-coward – was from the Gestapo.

But now that the danger was physically at hand, it was only physically that Hetty shook. Her mind was calm, and what her mind said was, Whatever you think of Enno, you can't possibly abandon him now.

And Hetty said to the man with the piercing regard that kept sliding away, she said to the man who looked like a real hoodlum, 'Perhaps you'll have a cup of coffee with us, Herr – what did you say your name was?'

'Borkhausen. Emil Borkhausen,' the spy introduced himself. 'I'm an old friend of Enno's, a fellow sportsman. What do you say, Frau Haberle, to that grand win he landed on Adebar yesterday? We met at the sports bar – didn't he say?'

Hetty threw a quick glance in Enno's direction. He was still standing there, with his hand on the doorknob, exactly as he had been when first surprised by Borkhausen's greeting. No, he hadn't mentioned this meeting with an old acquaintance; he had even claimed he hadn't seen anyone he knew. So he had lied to her again – and very much to his own detriment, because now it was quite clear how this spy had traced him to his refuge with her. If he had said anything about the encounter yesterday, it might have been possible to hide him somewhere else . . .

But this wasn't the moment to take issue with Enno Kluge or to upbraid him for lying. This was the time to act. And so she said again, 'Well then, Herr Borkhausen, let's have a cup of coffee, shall we? I don't have many customers so early in the morning. Enno, will you mind the shop? I'm just going to have a chat with your friend . . .'

By now, Hetty had completely stopped trembling. All she thought about was how it had been that other time, with her Walter, and those memories gave her strength. She knew that no amount of trembling, protesting, or appeals for help cut any ice with these people. They had no hearts: they were the paid helpers of Hitler and Himmler. If anything did help, then it was courage, not being cowardly, not showing fear. They worked on the assumption that all Germans were cowards, like Enno, now, but she, Hetty, the widow Haberle, she wasn't.

Her calm demeanour gave her authority over both men. As she went into the parlour, she said to Enno: 'Don't play any silly tricks, now! Don't try and run off or anything! Remember, you've left your coat hanging in the parlour, and you won't have much in the way of money on you either!'

'You're a clever woman,' said Borkhausen, as he sat down at

the table and accepted a cup of coffee. 'And you're tough with it. I wouldn't have thought that of you the first time I laid eyes on you, last night.'

Their eyes met.

'Well,' Borkhausen added, 'actually you were pretty tough yesterday too, shutting the door in his face as he was slithering about on his knees. I don't supposed you let him in later either, or did you?'

A little blush shot into Hetty's cheeks at the pert suggestion. To think that yesterday's horrid scene had had a witness, and such a repulsive one at that! But she quickly got a grip on herself, and said: 'I expect you're a clever man yourself, Herr Borkhausen, but let's not beat about the bush. You're here on business, I take it?'

'Maybe, maybe, who knows . . .' Borkhausen hemmed and hawed, a little intimidated by the speed with which the woman was moving forward.

'So,' Hetty resumed, 'you want to buy a pair of canaries. I expect you'd then let them go. Because if they stay in their cage, it's not much use to them . . .'

Borkhausen scratched his head. 'Frau Haberle,' he said, 'this thing with the canaries is over my head. I'm a simple man; you're probably much more sophisticated than I am. I only hope you don't trick me.'

'Nor you me!'

'How would I do that! Let me be perfectly open with you, with no more talk about canaries and such. I'll give it you straight, the whole truth. I've got instructions from the Gestapo, from Inspector Escherich, if that's a name you're conversant with?' Hetty shook her head. 'My instructions are to track down Enno. That's all. Why and what for, I've no idea. I want to say this to you, Frau Haberle, I'm a perfectly straightforward, honest human being . . .'

He leaned across to her; she looked piercingly into his eyes. Then his look, the look of the straightforward, honest human being, wandered off.

'I was surprised by my instruction, too, let me tell you, Frau

Haberle. Because we both of us know what sort of man Enno is, namely a dud, with nothing in his head except a bit to do with racing and a bit to do with women. And it's this Enno that the Gestapo want, the political department and all, where it's all high treason and off-with-his-head. I don't understand it – do you understand it?' He looked at her expectantly. Again their eyes met, and the same thing happened: he couldn't hold her look.

'Go on, Herr Borkhausen,' she said, 'I'm listening . . .'

'Clever woman!' nodded Borkhausen. 'Damned clever woman, and tough with it. That episode yesterday with the man on his knees . . .'

'I thought this was about business, Herr Borkhausen!'

'I'm a good, upright German citizen, which you may be surprised to hear, given that I'm with the Gestapo. As you might think. That's where you're wrong, Frau Haberle. I'm not with the Gestapo, I just sometimes do odd jobs for them, that's all. A man wants to live, isn't that right? and I've got five kids at home, the oldest of them just barely thirteen. And I've got to keep them all fed . . .'

'Stick to business, if you please, Herr Borkhausen!'

'No, Frau Haberle, I'm not with the Gestapo, I'm an honest man. And when I hear that they're looking for my pal Enno, and offering a sizeable reward for finding him, and I know Enno from old times, and I'm his true friend – then, Frau Haberle, then I thought, Well, isn't that something, they're looking for Enno! The little worm. If I happened to find him, I thought, then I could tip him the wink, you know, Frau Haberle, and he can scarper while there's still time. And I said to Inspector Escherich, "Don't you worry about Enno, I'll catch him for you, because he's an old friend of mine." And then I got the instruction and my expenses, and here I am with you, Frau Haberle, and Enno's working in the shop, and everything's coming up roses . . .'

For a moment they were both silent, Borkhausen expectantly, Frau Haberle reflectively.

Then she said, 'You haven't told the Gestapo anything yet?'

'Ooh, no, I'm in no hurry with them, they'll only mess up my game!' He corrected this to, 'Of course I wanted to tip my old friend Enno the wink . . .'

Once again they were silent. Finally Hetty asked: 'And what sort of reward did the Gestapo offer you?'

'A thousand marks! It's a load of money for such a worm as Enno, I admit that, Frau Haberle, I was startled myself. But Inspector Escherich said to me: "If you bring in that Kluge, I'll pay you a thousand marks." That's what Escherich said to me. And he approved expenses for me of another hundred marks, which I've got already. That's on top of the thousand marks.'

They sat there pensively for a long time.

Then Hetty began, 'I meant what I said about the canaries before, Herr Borkhausen. Because if I was to pay you a thousand marks . . .'

'Two thousand marks, Frau Haberle, among friends it's always two thousand marks. And then the hundred expenses on top of that . . .'

'Well, if I was to pay you that, and you know Herr Kluge hasn't got any money, and nothing ties me to him . . .'

'Frau Haberle, Frau Haberle, please! You're a highly respectable woman. You won't want to hand over your friend who was on his knees before you, to the Gestapo, and all for a little bit of money! Where I've told you that anything's possible, with the high treason and the off-with-his-head? You wouldn't do that, Frau Haberle, I know you better than that!'

She could have told him that he, the simple, decent German man, was in the process of doing exactly what she, the highly respectable woman, was not allowed to do, namely sell his friend down the river. But she knew that remarks like that were pointless, and didn't impress such gentlemen.

And so in the end she said, 'All right, but if I were to pay you two thousand one hundred, what guarantee is there that the canaries will be released from their cage?' When she saw him scratch his head again, she decided to be completely brazen. 'Put it another way: What's my guarantee that you won't take my money and then go to Escherich and take his as well?'

'But I'm your guarantee, Frau Haberle! I give you my word: I am a simple straightforward human being, and if I make a promise, I keep it. You saw the way I went straight to Enno to warn him, at the risk of him doing a runner out of the shop. And if he had, my whole plan would be up the spout.'

Frau Haberle looked at him with a thin smile. 'That's all well and good, Herr Borkhausen,' she said. 'But just because you're such a good friend of Enno's, you'll understand why I have to have every reassurance of his safety. If I can even raise so much money.'

Borkhausen made a pooh-poohing gesture, as though suggesting that a woman like herself would never be short.

'No, no, Herr Borkhausen,' Hetty went on, because she could see he had no sense of irony, and that she had to be completely plain with him, 'who is to guarantee to me that you don't take my money now . . .'

Borkhausen got very excited at the prospect of receiving the dizzying sum of two thousand marks, more money than he had ever seen in his life . . .

'. . . and there's a Gestapo agent standing outside the door, who will simply arrest Enno? I require other guarantees from you!'

'But there isn't anyone standing outside the door, Frau Haberle, I swear! I'm an honest man, why should I lie to you? I've come straight from home, you can ask my Otti, if you like!'

She interrupted him in his excitement: 'Well, what other forms of guarantee can you give me – other than your word?'

'There aren't any! It's a business, it's based on trust. And surely you'll trust me, Frau Haberle, when I've spoken to you so frankly!'

'Yes, trust . . .' began Frau Haberle vaguely, and then they both lapsed into another long silence, he simply waiting for her to decide, she racking her brain as to how to obtain at least a modicum of security.

In the meantime, there was Enno Kluge, minding the shop. He served the now more numerous clientele promptly and not unskilfully, even managing a joke every now and again. The

first shock he had felt at the sight of Borkhausen had now dissi-
pated. Hetty was in the parlour, talking to Borkhausen, and she
would surely be able to sort it out. Meanwhile, the fact that she
was sorting it out, that was proof, if proof were needed, that
she was never in earnest about her threat to send Enno away.
So he felt relieved, and in his relief he was able to crack jokes
again.

In the parlour, Frau Haberle at long last broke the silence. Resolutely, she said, 'All right, Herr Borkhausen, I've had a think. I want
to make a deal with you on the following conditions . . .'

'All right . . . Go on, tell me!' said Borkhausen, avidly. He felt
he was very close to getting his money.

'I will give you two thousand marks, but I won't give them
to you here. I'll give them to you in Munich!'

'In Munich?' He goggled stupidly. 'I'm not going to Munich!
What on earth would I do in Munich?'

'We're going to go to the post office now, you and I,' she
continued, 'and I will draw a postal order for two thousand
marks, payable to you in the main post office in Munich. And
then I will see you to the station, and you will board the next
train to Munich, where you will pick up your money. At the
Anhalter Bahnhof, I will give you another two hundred marks
for the journey, in addition to your ticket . . .'

'No!' Borkhausen exclaimed angrily. 'I'm not doing that. I'm
not agreeing to something like that. I'll get down to Munich
only to find out you've cancelled the order at the post office!'

'When we go, I will give you my payment receipt, and then
it won't be possible for me to cancel it.'

'And Munich!' he cried. 'What's the point of Munich! We're
honest people here! Why not here and now, in the shop, and
have done with it? Munich and back will take me at least two
days and a night, and by then Enno will have gone God knows
where!'

'But Herr Borkhausen, that was what we had agreed, and
that's what I'm giving you the money for! The canary isn't to
stay in his cage. Enno's supposed to get a chance to hide somewhere. That's what the two thousand marks are for!'

Borkhausen didn't really have an answer to that, but sullenly he said anyway: 'And I get a hundred in expenses as well!'

'You'll get them as well. In cash. All at the station.'

But not even that could sweeten Borkhausen's mood. He remained sullen: 'Munich! I've never heard such nonsense in my life! It was all so simple – and now Munich! Why Munich, for Christ's sake? Why not just say London and have done with it, so I can go there when the war's over! It's all messed up! It could have been so simple, but no, you wanted to go and complicate it! And why? Because you have no trust in your fellow men, because you've got a suspicious mind, Frau Haberle! I was so straight with you . . .'

'And I'm being straight with you! Those are my terms, and nothing else!'

'Well!' he said. 'Then I can go.' He got up and picked up his cap. But he didn't go. 'I'm absolutely not going to Munich . . .'

'It'll be an interesting trip for you,' Frau Haberle urged. 'It's a pretty route, and there are supposed to be good things to eat and drink still available in Munich. The beer is much stronger than ours here, Herr Borkhausen!'

'I don't drink,' he said, less sullen now than pensive.

Hetty could see that he was struggling to find some way of taking the money and still handing Enno over. She went over her plan again in her head. It seemed good to her. It would get Borkhausen out of the way for at least two days, and if the house really wasn't being watched (which she would check as soon as possible), then that was enough time to move Enno somewhere.

'Ah, well,' said Borkhausen at long last, and looked at her. 'And you'll do it no other way?'

'No,' said Hetty, 'those are my terms, take it or leave it.'

'Then I guess I'll have to accept,' said Borkhausen. 'I can't just kiss two thousand smackers goodbye.'

He said it mostly to himself, for his own justification.

'Then I'll go to Munich, I suppose. And you'll take me to the post office now.'

'In a minute,' said Frau Haberle thoughtfully. Now that he

had agreed, she was still a little dissatisfied. She was certain he had some new scheme. She needed to find out what it was.

'Yes, we'll go in a minute,' she repeated. 'Just as soon as I've got myself ready, and closed the shop.'

He objected immediately: 'Why would you close the shop, Frau Haberle? You've got Enno here to mind it!'

'Enno's coming with us,' she said.

'Whatever for? Enno's got nothing to do with our arrangement!'

'Because I want him there. Otherwise it could be,' she added, 'that at the very moment I'm handing my money over to you, Enno will find himself being arrested. Misunderstandings like that do occur, Herr Borkhausen.'

'But who's going to arrest him?'

'Well, the spy outside the door, for example . . .'

'There isn't a spy outside the door!' She smiled. 'You can check, Frau Haberle, look at all the people. I haven't got a spy outside the door. I'm an honest man . . .'

'I want to keep Enno with me,' she insisted. 'That'll make me feel safer.'

'You're so stubborn!' he cried furiously. 'All right, Enno's coming with us. Now get a move on!'

'We're in no great hurry,' she said. 'The Munich train doesn't leave till noon. We've got a lot of time. And now will you excuse me for fifteen minutes, I have to get myself ready.' She looked at him, sitting at the table, his eye on the window through to the shop. 'And one more request, Herr Borkhausen. Don't talk to Enno now, he's got plenty of things to do in the shop, and anyway . . .'

'I've got nothing to say to that idiot!' Borkhausen said irritably. 'I don't talk to fools like that!'

But to please her, he got up and sat down facing the parlour door and the window on to the courtyard.

29

Enno's Eviction

Two hours later, it was all over. The Munich express had rolled out of the departure hall of the Anhalter Bahnhof, with Borkhausen on board in a second-class compartment – an absurdly puffed-up, swaggering Borkhausen, who was travelling second class for the first time in his life. Yes, Frau Haberle had generously bought the spy an upgrade to second class on his request, either to keep him sweet or else because she was so relieved to be rid of him for at least two days.

Now, as the other people who had seen off passengers slowly made their way out past the barriers, she said quietly to Enno, 'Hold on, Enno, let's sit down in the waiting room for a minute, and consider what to do next.'

They sat down with the door in view. The waiting room was half empty, and for a long time no one came in after them.

Hetty asked, 'Did you pay attention to what I said to you? Do you think we were followed?'

And Enno Kluge, with his familiar irresponsibility returning as soon as the greatest danger was over said, 'Bah! Followed? Do you think anyone would take instructions from an idiot like Borkhausen? No one would be that stupid!'

She had it on the tip of her tongue to say that in her view Borkhausen with his wiliness and suspicion was considerably more intelligent than the feckless little coward seated beside her, but she didn't. She had sworn to herself while getting dressed this morning that the time for reproaches and criticism was past. All that remained to be done was to get Enno Kluge to safety. Once that was accomplished, she never wanted to see him again.

Full of the envy that had been gnawing at him for the past hour, he said, 'If I was you, I would never have paid that guy two thousand one hundred marks. And two hundred and fifty in expenses on top of that. And a rail ticket and upgrade. You gave that bastard son of a bitch two and a half thousand marks! I'd never have done that!'

She asked, 'What would have happened to you if I hadn't?'

'If you'd given *me* the two and a half thousand instead, you should have seen how I handled it! I tell you, Borkhausen would have been happy with five hundred!'

'But the Gestapo had offered him a thousand!'

'A thousand – don't make me laugh! As if the Gestapo tossed around money like that! At a little stoolie like Borkhausen. All they had to do was give him an order, and he'd have had to do just what they wanted, at five marks a day! A thousand here, two and a half there – he really has plucked you, Hetty!'

He laughed mockingly.

His ingratitude upset her, but she didn't feel like arguing with him. Instead, she said curtly, 'I don't want to talk about it any more! Do you understand, I'm done!' She looked at him until he lowered his pale eyes. 'Let's think about what to do with you now.'

'Ach, there's plenty of time for that,' he said. 'He won't be back before the day after tomorrow. We can go back to the shop. We'll think of something before he gets back.'

'I'm not so sure. I don't want to take you back to the shop, or if I do, then just to get your things packed. I feel uneasy – do you think we were followed after all?'

'I tell you we weren't! I know more about these kind of things than you do! Borkhausen couldn't afford to pay anyone, he doesn't have any money!'

'But the Gestapo could have set someone on him!'

'And so the Gestapo spy stands and watches while I put Borkhausen on the train to Munich! Don't be silly, Hetty!'

She had to agree that his objection made sense. But she remained uneasy. She asked, 'What happened with the cigarettes?'

He couldn't remember. She had to remind him how as soon as they left the house, Borkhausen had looked around everywhere for cigarettes – he absolutely had to have some. He had asked Hetty and Enno for some, but they were out, Enno having smoked the last of his during the night. Borkhausen had insisted on having some, he couldn't stand not to, he depended on his early morning puff. He had hurriedly 'borrowed' twenty marks from Hetty and called out to a youth who was playing around on the street, making a lot of noise.

'Hey there, Johnny, would you know somewhere I can get hold of some cigarettes? But I got no tobacco coupons.'

'I might do. You got 'ny money?'

The boy that Borkhausen had addressed was very blond and blue-eyed, wearing a Hitler Youth uniform, an authentic, alert Berlin face.

'Well, give us yer twenty then, and I'll go and get some for you . . .'

'And forget to come back! Not likely, I'm coming with you. I won't be a minute, Frau Haberle!'

With that, the two of them had disappeared inside a nearby building. After a while, Borkhausen had emerged from it alone, and without being asked had returned Hetty's twenty.

'They were out. The lout just wanted to cheat me of twenty marks! I clouted him one, and he's still lying there in the court-yard!'

And they had gone on, first to the post office, and then the travel agent.

'Well, and what strikes you as odd about that, Hetty? Borkhausen's just like me. if he wants a smoke he'll stop a general on the street – and cadge the end of his cigarette off him!'

'But then he didn't say another word about cigarettes, even though he didn't get any! I think that's strange. Was the boy in on the plan?'

'What do you mean, was the boy in on the plan? He will have cuffed him, just like he said.'

'You don't think the kid was there to watch us?'

For a moment, even Enno Kluge paused. But then he went on, with his customary ease, 'You have a vivid imagination! I only wish I had your worries!'

She said nothing. But her unease remained with her, and so she insisted that they go into the shop very quickly to fetch his things. Then, using every conceivable care, she would take him to a friend's.

He wasn't at all happy with the plan. He could sense she wanted to shake him off, and he didn't want to go. She offered him security and good food and no more work than he could handle. And love and warmth and comfort. And then, on top of that: there was abundant wool waiting to be fleeced: Borkhausen had just taken her for two and a half thou, and now it was his turn!

'Your friend!' he said unhappily. 'What friend? A man or a woman? I don't like going to strangers.'

Hetty could have told him that the lady in question was an old comrade of her husband's who was still discreetly working for the cause and would take in any refugee. But now she was suspicious of Enno. She had witnessed his cowardice a couple of times now, and it was better for him not to know too much.

'My friend?' she said. 'A woman like me. Similar sort of age. Maybe a year or two younger.'

'And what does she do? What does she live off?' he asked.

'I'm not exactly sure. I expect she works as a secretary some-where. She's unmarried, by the way.'

'Well, if she's your sort of age, she's leaving it a bit late,' he said sarcastically.

She winced, but made no reply.

'Nah, Hetty,' he said, giving his voice a more tender inflection. 'What will I do at your friend's? The two of us, alone together, that's the best. Let me stay at yours – Borkhausen'll be back the day after tomorrow – at least until then!'

'No, Enno!' she said. 'I want you to do what I say now. I'll go into the flat myself and pack. You can wait for me in a bar. Then we'll go to my friend's together.'

He still had many objections, but in the end he gave in. He gave in when – not without some calculation on her side – she said: 'You'll be needing money. I'll put some money in your suitcase, enough to see you through the beginning, at least.'

The prospect of finding money in his suitcase – and she couldn't possibly give him less than she had given Borkhausen! – that prospect tempted him, and finally convinced him. If he stayed with her till the day after tomorrow, then there wouldn't be money till the day after tomorrow. But he wanted to know right away how much she was giving him.

She noticed with sadness what had caused him to relent. He himself was responsible for destroying the last elements of love and respect in her. But she adjusted silently. She had known for a long time that you had to pay for everything in life, and usually more than it was worth. The most important thing now was that he did what she told him.

When Frau Hetty Haberle approached her flat, she noticed the blond, blue-eyed boy that she had seen before. He was playing on the street with a crowd of other boys. She flinched. Then she waved him over: 'What are you still doing here?' she asked. 'Do you have to do your running around here on my doorstep?'

'I live here!' he said. 'Where else am I going to run around?'

She scanned his face for the red mark of a slap, but didn't see one. Clearly, the brat hadn't recognized her. He probably hadn't paid any attention before; he'd been too busy talking with Borkhausen. That would argue against his being a spy.

'You live here, do you?' she asked. 'Funny, I've never seen you before.'

'It's not my fault if you're short-sighted!' he retorted cheekily. He whistled piercingly on two fingers, and yelled up the house-front: 'Ma, ma, look out the window! There's a woman here who doesn't believe you've got a squint! Ma, show her your squint, will you!'

Laughing, Hetty went into her shop, now quite convinced that as far as this boy was concerned, she was imagining things.

But while packing she grew serious again. She wondered if it was right for her to take Enno to her friend Anna Schönlein. Of course, Anna was forever risking her life by taking in unknowns and giving them shelter. But Hetty felt that by leaving Enno Kluge with her, she was taking her a cuckoo's egg. To be sure, Enno was a bona fide political rather than a common criminal – Borkhausen had corroborated that, but all the same . . .

He wasn't so much thoughtless as utterly indifferent as to what happened to his fellow humans. He simply didn't care. All he thought about was himself, and he was perfectly capable of running to her, Hetty, twice a day, claiming that he was missing her, and so plunging Anna into danger. But she, Hetty, had some control over him that Anna didn't have.

With a heavy sigh, Hetty Haberle puts three hundred marks in an envelope and lays it on top of his things in the suitcase. On this one day she has got through more money than she has put aside in two years. But she is prepared for further sacrifice: she's prepared to offer Enno a hundred marks for every day he stays in Anna's apartment. Unfortunately, he's the type of man who is receptive to such a proposition. He won't be offended; at most, he will put on a show of being offended to begin with. But at least it should keep him there, since he is so greedy for money.

Hetty leaves her house with the suitcase in her hand. The fair-haired boy is no longer playing on the street – perhaps he's gone in to his squinting mother. She makes for the pub on the Alex where she's arranged to meet Enno.

30

Emil Borkhausen and His Son

Yes, Borkhausen felt exceedingly comfortable in that nice express train in the fine second-class compartment in the company of officers and generals and exquisitely perfumed ladies. It disturbed him not at all that he was neither elegant nor exquisitely perfumed, and that his fellow travellers cast no kindly looks his way. Borkhausen was used to being looked at unkindly. Hardly ever in the course of his wretched life had a fellow being favoured him with a kindly look.

Borkhausen took care to enjoy his good fortune, because he knew it would be brief. It didn't last till Munich, not even as far as Leipzig, which had been his first thought, but only as far as Lichterfelde, because the train happened to make its first stop at Lichterfelde. That had been the mistake in Hetty's calculations. If one had money to collect in Munich, one didn't have to go there right away. One might do it later, once one had seen to more urgent business here in Berlin. And the most urgent business he had was to report Enno's whereabouts to Escherich and collect his 500-marks reward. Anyway, perhaps he didn't have to travel to Munich at all, perhaps it was enough to ask the post office to wire the money to Berlin for collection there. He didn't feel up to a journey to Munich just at the moment.

So – not without a subtle regret – Borkhausen got off at Lichterfelde. He had a short, spirited debate with the stationmaster about the plausibility of his having reconsidered a journey to Munich between Anhalter Bahnhof and Lichterfelde. Borkhausen struck the stationmaster as a most suspicious individual in any case.

Borkhausen remained adamant: 'Just call the Gestapo if you like, ask for Inspector Escherich, and you'll soon see whether I'm spinning a line or not, Stationmaster! But you'll get in plenty of hot water, I'm telling you! I'm here on official Gestapo business!'

Finally, the official shrugged his shoulders, and allowed him to claim reimbursement for the ticket – it was no skin off his nose. Anything was possible nowadays, and that such dubious characters were running around on Gestapo business was well within the bounds of possibility. So much the worse for everyone!

Emil Borkhausen then started looking for his son.

He couldn't see him outside Hetty Haberle's pet shop, though the shop was open and customers were coming and going. Hidden behind a poster pillar, his eyes fixed on the door of the shop, Borkhausen wondered what could have happened. Had Kuno-Dieter got bored and simply left his post? Or had Enno gone away – maybe back to the Also Ran? Or had the little fellow moved on and left the woman all alone in the shop?

Emil Borkhausen was just wondering whether to appear brazenly in front of the outwitted Frau Haberle and demand information from her when a little squirt of nine or so addressed him: 'Hey, mister! Are you Kuno's dad?'

'I am! What is it?'

'You're s'posed to give me a mark!'

'What would I give you a mark for?'

'For me to tell you my information what I know!'

Borkhausen made a swift grab at the boy. 'First the goods, then the money!' he said.

But the boy was quicker, and slipped through the man's arm and shouted: 'Forget it! Keep your mouldy mark!' And he rejoined his playmates outside the petshop.

Borkhausen couldn't follow him there: he preferred not to show himself after all. He shouted and whistled for the boy, cursing him – and himself too, for his own inappropriate economies. But the boy proved not so easy to lure; it was another fifteen minutes before he turned up beside Borkhausen again, standing carefully some yards away from the irascible fellow and announcing cheekily, 'Price's gone up! Two marks now!'

Borkhausen felt a keen desire to grab him and give him a

good hiding, but what was he to do? He had to do what the boy said, because he couldn't chase him down. 'I'll give you a mark,' he said grimly.

'No! I want two!'

'All right, you'll get two!'

Borkhausen took a bundle of money out of his pocket, peeled off a two-mark note, stuffed the rest back in his pocket, and waved the bill in the direction of the boy.

The kid shook his head. 'I know you!' he said. 'If I take yer money, you'll make a grab at me. No, lay it down on the ground!'

Grimly, without a word, Borkhausen did as the boy said. 'Well?' he said, straightening up and taking a step back.

The kid slowly inched toward the note, keeping a watchful eye on the man. When he stooped to pick up the money, Borkhausen was barely able to restrain himself, he so badly wanted to grab the little squirt and teach him a lesson. He could have got him, too, but he withstood the temptation – maybe he would have got no information then, and the brat would scream the whole place down.

'Well?' he asked once more, menacingly this time.

The boy answered: 'I could play silly buggers and ask for more money, and keep doing it again and again. I could. But I'm not like that. I know you wanted to make a grab at me again this time, but me, I'm not such a silly bugger!' Then, after thus clearly establishing his moral superiority over Borkhausen, he quickly said, 'You're to go home and wait for a message from Kuno!' And with that the boy was gone.

The two solid hours that Borkhausen had to wait in his basement flat for Kuno's message did nothing to diminish his rage; if anything they exacerbated it. The kids were howling, and Otti was on the warpath, not sparing him her usual remarks about lazy sons of bitches that sit around all day, not doing anything except smoke cigarettes, and leave all the work to their wives.

He could have pulled out a fifty, or even a ten, and changed Otti's foul weather into the sweetest sunshine, but he didn't feel like it. He didn't want to be spending yet more money, having just wasted two marks on a useless piece of information he could have got by himself. He was enraged with Kuno-Dieter for having planted a little shit like that in his way. He must have fouled up himself in some way. Kuno-Dieter, Borkhausen decided, was going to get the punishment that other little rat had oiled out of.

Then there was a knock on the door, and instead of a messenger from Kuno-Dieter, it was a man in civilian clothes who had all too obviously been a corporal in another life.

'Are you Borkhausen?'

'Yes, what is it?'

'Inspector Escherich wants to see you. Get ready, I'll take you there.'

'I can't now,' said Borkhausen, 'I'm waiting for a messenger. You can tell the inspector I've caught his fish.'

'I'm to take you to him,' said the ex-corporal stubbornly.

'Not now! I'm not letting you mess this up. Not the likes of you!' Borkhausen was angry, but mastered himself. 'You can tell the inspector I've got the bird, and I'm coming to see him later.'

'Will you not make a fuss, and come along now!' the other repeated stubbornly.

'I suppose you've learned that by heart and they're the only words you know: "Come along now!" Don't you understand what I'm telling you?' Borkhausen yelled. 'I'm waiting here for instructions, I have to sit here, otherwise our quarry will slip the noose! Is that too hard for you to grasp?' He looked slightly breathlessly at the man facing him, and added grouchily, 'It's the inspector's rabbit I'm catching, you understand?'

The ex-corporal said implacably, 'I don't know anything about any of that. The inspector said to me, "Fritsche, get me Borkhausen!" So come along, will you!'

'I don't believe it!' said Borkhausen. 'You're too stupid for words. I'm staying here – or are you going to arrest me?' He could see by the other's expression that that was an impossibility. 'Well, get lost then!' he shouted and slammed the door in the corporal's face.

Three minutes later he saw the old corporal shuffle across the courtyard, having reconsidered his 'Come along with me!'

As soon as the man had disappeared through the entryway of the front house, Borkhausen started to worry about the consequences that his cheeking the representative of the all-powerful inspector might have. It was purely his rage with Kuno-Dieter that was to blame. It was shameless to leave his father sitting there for hours on end, possibly far into the night. Everywhere you looked, on every street corner, there were boys you could send with a message! But he would show Kuno what a view he took of such behaviour. He wasn't to think he could get away with it!

Borkhausen luxuriated in fantasies of chastisement. He saw himself thrashing the childish body, doing it with a smile on his face, but not a smile of diminishing fury . . . He heard him cry out, and he placed one hand over the kid's mouth while continuing to thrash him with the other, thrash him and thrash him until he was shaking from top to toe, whimpering . . .

Borkhausen never tired of rehearsing such scenes to himself. As he did so, he stretched out on the sofa and groaned lustfully.

He was almost disappointed by the knock of Kuno's messenger, when it finally came. 'What is it?' he asked.

'I'm to take you to Kuno.'

This time it was an older boy, of fourteen or fifteen, in a Hitler Youth tunic.

'But you're to give me five marks first.'

'Five marks!' spat Borkhausen, not daring to openly refuse this big lout in the brown shirt. 'Five marks! You're dab hands at chucking my money around!' He rummaged through his bills, looking for a fiver.

The big Hitler Youth boy looked tensely at the bundle of money in the man's hands. 'I had to buy a ticket,' he said. 'And what sort of time do you think it takes, getting here from the west end?'

'And your time is precious, eh?' Borkhausen still hadn't found the note he was looking for. 'And the west end, whatever that means! That can't be. You probably mean Mitte, anyway!'

'Well, if Ansbacher Strasse isn't out west, I don't know . . .'

The boy understood too late that he had blabbed. Borkhausen's money went back in his pocket. 'Thanks!' he said with a mocking laugh. 'No need to waste any more of your precious time. I'll find my own way there. The best way is probably the under-ground to Viktoria-Luise Platz, wouldn't you say?'

'You can't treat me that way! You can't treat me that way!' said the Hitler Youth, and walked up to the man with fists clenched. His dark eyes glowed with fury. 'I spent ticket money, I've . . .'

'You've wasted your precious time, I know, you've told me!' laughed Borkhausen. 'Get lost, sonny. Stupidity always costs!' Suddenly his rage boiled over again. 'What are you doing, still standing around in my flat? Are you hoping to beat me up in my own parlour? Get out of here, unless you like the sound of your own wailing!'

He shoved the furious boy out of the room and slammed the door shut behind the two of them. And all the way there, till they emerged from the underground at Viktoria-Luise Platz, he had a stream of scathing comments for the boy, who never left his side, but who – while still pale with anger – made no more references to money.

Once on Viktoria-Luise Platz, the boy suddenly broke into a trot and was soon far ahead of the man. Borkhausen had to follow him as fast as he could: he didn't want to leave the two boys talking alone together for any longer than he had to. He wasn't quite sure who Kuno-Dieter would side with: his father, or this pup.

There they were, in front of a house on Ansbacher Strasse. The Hitler Youth kid was talking nineteen to the dozen to Kuno-Dieter, who was listening to him with his head down. When Borkhausen walked up, the messenger withdrew a dozen paces and let them confer.

'What's going on, Kuno-Dieter,' Borkhausen began angrily. 'How can you send me this stream of cheeky brats, who ask for money before they open their mouths?'

'No one does anything without money, Dad,' replied Kuno-Dieter equably. 'As you well know. And I'm waiting to hear what I'm going to make out of this business – I've spent travel money . . .'

'Christ, it's the same broken record with all of you! No, Kuno-Dieter, first you tell your father what's going on here at Ansbacher Strasse, and then you'll see what your father's prepared to do for you. It's not my style. This hustling doesn't agree with me!'

'No, Father,' replied Kuno-Dieter. 'I'm afraid you'll forget to pay me later – money that is. I expect you'll remember the slaps. You've already made loads of money from this business, and you probably stand to make even more, I'm thinking. Now I've been standing around all day for you, I want to see some money myself. I thought, fifty marks . . .'

'Fifty marks!' This impertinence took Borkhausen's breath away. 'I'll tell you what you'll get. I'll give you five marks, the five marks that beanpole over there asked me for, and you'll be grateful for them! I'm not like that, but . . .'

'No, Dad,' said Kuno-Dieter, and fixed his blue eyes defiantly on his father. 'You stand to earn a packet with this deal, and I'm not doing all the work for nothing, so in that case I'll just refuse to tell you!'

'What have you got to tell me anyway!' sneered Borkhausen. 'I don't need you to tell me the little fellow's holed up in that building. I can work out the rest by myself. Why don't you go home and ask your mother to give you something to eat! You can't make a monkey of your father, not yet! You pair of heroes!'

'In that case,' Kuno-Dieter said decisively, 'I'll go upstairs and tell him you're watching him. I'll give you away, Father!'

'You damned snotnosed kid!' screamed Borkhausen, and swung at his son.

But Kuno-Dieter was already running, running into the side entrance of the house. Borkhausen chased him across the court-yard and caught up with him on the bottom step of the back house. He knocked him to the ground and began kicking him as he lay there. It was almost the way he had imagined it earlier on the sofa, only Kuno-Dieter wasn't whimpering, he was furiously defending himself. That only heightened Borkhausen's own rage. Quite deliberately he smashed his fist in the boy's face, and kicked him in the stomach. 'I'll teach you!' he snorted, and a red mist swam before his eyes.

Suddenly he felt himself gripped from behind, someone was pulling his arm back. Something grabbed first one, then both of his legs. He looked round: it was that Hitler Youth punk, with a whole gang of youths, four or five of them, that had latched on to him. He had to lay off Kuno-Dieter, to defend himself against these louts, any one of whom he could have polished off with one hand tied behind his back, but who together might prove dangerous indeed.

'You cowards!' he roared, and tried backing against the wall to dislodge the boy who was clinging to him. But the others took away his legs, and he was down.

'Kuno!' he wheezed. 'Help your father! Those cowards . . .'

But Kuno didn't help his father. He had got to his feet, and it was he who first drove his fist into Borkhausen's face.

A low rumbling moan broke from the man's chest. Then he was rolling about on the floor with the boys, trying to press them against walls and steps, to crush them and get back on his feet again.

Now the only sound to be heard was the panting and groaning of the combatants, the smack of punches, the scraping of feet . . . they fought savagely and wordlessly.

An old lady coming down the stairs stopped in horror as she saw the wild scenes below. She clutched the banister, and called out helplessly, 'No! Not here! Not in this house!'

Her purple cloak billowed out. Then she made up her mind, and launched a scream of horror.

The boys left off Borkhausen and disappeared. The man sat up and stared wild-eyed at the old lady.

'A whole gang of them!' he panted. 'Setting upon a helpless old man, and my own son among them!'

When the old lady screamed, a couple of doors had opened, and a few neighbours peered out and conferred in whispers while looking at the man sitting on the steps.

'They were fighting!' squeaked the purple lady indignantly. 'They were fighting in our respectable house!'

Borkhausen thought for a moment. If Enno Kluge was living here now, then it was high time he, Borkhausen, wasn't here. Enno might appear at any moment, curious to learn what the commotion had been about.

'I just gave my boy a bit of a pasting,' he explained with a grin to the silent, staring tenants. 'It's all over. Nothing more to say. Everything's okay.'

He stood up and crossed the courtyard back out on to the street, where he brushed himself off and retied his tie. Not a sign of the gang, of course. Well, Kuno-Dieter had it coming to him, that was for sure! Raising his hand against his own father, socking him on the jaw! Not all the Ottis in the world would be able to keep him off that boy now! No, and she would get hers too, for that bloody serpent egg she had planted in his nest!

While Borkhausen watches the house, his rage against Kuno-Dieter grows. It becomes almost insensate when he discovers that during the fight the louts have stolen the entire roll of banknotes from his pocket. All he has left is a few marks in his waistcoat. Those little shits! He feels like setting off after them right now and making mincemeat of them, getting his money back!

And he charges off.

Then he remembers: He can't go anywhere! He has to stay right where he is, otherwise he'll lose out on the five hundred as well! It's clear to him that he'll never get his money back off the boys, the most he can do is try to rescue the five hundred!

Consumed with rage, he goes into a little café, and calls Inspector Escherich. Then he goes back to his observation post and waits impatiently for him to show. Oh, how wretched he feels! All the trouble he's been to – and everything goes wrong. Other people, anything they touch turns to gold; a little squirt like Enno gets a woman with bags of money and a nice shop, a zero like that only has to put his money on a horse, and it comes in first, but not Borkhausen! He can try what he likes: it all goes skew-whiff. The trouble he had with the Haberle woman, and then he was so happy to have a bit of money in his pocket for once – and now it's gone again! The Rosenthal woman's bracelet – gone! That nice break-in, a whole shop full of linen – all gone! Whatever he lays his hands on turns to shit.

I'm a loser, that's what I am, he says bitterly to himself! Well, as long as the inspector comes across with the five hundred! And I'll murder Kuno! I'll torture him, I'll starve him to death. I'll not let him forget this!

On the telephone Borkhausen asked the inspector to bring the money with him.

'We'll see about that!' the inspector replied.

Wonder what that's supposed to mean? Is he going to swindle me as well . . . ? It's not possible!

No, the only thing of interest to him in all this is the money. As soon as he's got the money, he's going to scarper, he doesn't care what happens to Enno! Not interested! Maybe he will go to Munich after all. He's so fed up with things here! He just can't hack it any more. Kuno – his own son – punching him in the mouth and stealing his money, unbelievable!

No, the Haberle woman was right: he has to go to Munich. As soon as Escherich brings the money; otherwise he can't afford the ticket. Just as well there's no such thing as an inspector who doesn't keep his word! Or is there?

31

A Visit to Fräulein Anna Schönlein

Borkhausen's announcement that he had run Enno Kluge to ground in the west of Berlin had plunged Inspector Escherich into a quandary. He had answered reflexively: 'I'm coming right over!' Then, once he was ready to go, he had second thoughts.

So there was the wanted man, the man he had spent the last several days hunting for. He just needed to lay his hands on him. Throughout the tense and impatient search, he had looked forward to the moment when he would get him in his grip; any thoughts of what he would do with him once he had him he had angrily put from his mind.

But that time was now at hand, and the question arose: what was he going to do with Enno? He knew it, he knew it with the utmost certainty: Enno Kluge was not the author of the post-cards. During the search for him, he had been able to obscure that knowledge, he had even, in his chat with Deputy Inspector Schröder, discussed the possibility that Kluge was guilty of other things besides.

Yes, precisely – other things, not this. He hadn't written the postcards! Not in a million years! If he arrested him and brought him back here to Prinz Albrecht Strasse, then nothing would keep his boss from interrogating Kluge personally, and then everything would come out, nothing about any postcards, but plenty about a deceitfully procured signature on a statement, that was for sure! No, it wasn't possible to bring Kluge back here!

But it was equally impossible to allow Kluge to continue to roam, even under constant supervision; Prall would never concede that. Nor would he allow himself to be jollied along much longer, if Escherich suppressed the news that Kluge had been found. He had dropped a couple of pretty broad hints that he was ready to put someone else in charge of the whole

Hobgoblin case – someone more diligent, more proactive. The inspector couldn't take the humiliation – and anyway, the case had become important to him personally.

Escherich sits at his desk, staring into space, gnawing at his beloved sand-coloured moustache. I'm in a trap, he says to himself. A bloody trap I've gone and made for myself. Whatever I do is wrong, and if I don't do anything that's the worst of the lot. I'm bloody stuck.

He sits there, thinking. Time goes by, and Inspector Escherich is still thinking. Borkhausen – bloody Borkhausen! Let him stay there and watch the house! He's got all the time in the world! And if he lets Enno slip through his fingers, then I'll rip his guts out, inch by inch! Five hundred marks, and can I bring them with me, please! A hundred Ennos aren't worth five hundred marks! I'll smash his face in, bloody fucking Borkhausen! What do I care about Kluge, I need the author of the postcards!

But then, while he continues to sit and brood, Inspector Escherich comes to a slightly different view of what to do with Borkhausen. At any rate he gets up, and goes to Accounts. There he takes receipt of five hundred marks ('paperwork later'), and returns to his office. He had thought of driving to Ansbacher Strasse in his official car and taking a couple of men with him, but he cancels the request – he doesn't need a car or manpower.

It's possible that not only has Escherich come to a different view of what to do with Borkhausen, perhaps he's thought of what to do with Enno Kluge as well. Anyway, he takes his big service revolver out of his pocket, and instead pockets a light pistol, recently picked up in the course of a confiscation. He's already tried it out, the little thing fits nicely in his hand, and it shoots straight.

All right, let's go. The inspector stops in the doorway, takes a last look around. Something odd happens: without meaning to, he makes a sort of salute to the room, he bids goodbye to his office. So long . . . A dark presentiment, a feeling he's almost ashamed of, that he won't see the office in quite the same way again. Till now, he was an official, someone who hunted human beings in the same way you might sell stamps: diligent, methodical, by the book.

But when he gets back to this room later tonight, or maybe even early tomorrow morning, he might not be the same official. He will have something on his conscience, something he won't be able to forget. Something he alone knows, but all the worse for that: he will know it, and he will never be able to exonerate himself.

Escherich leaves his office, half-ashamed of his little histrionics. We'll see, he says, to calm himself. It could all pan out differently. But first I'm going to have to talk to Kluge . . . He takes the underground, and it's dark by the time he gets to Ansbacher Strasse.

'You do like to leave a man hanging around!' growls Borkhausen furiously when he sees him. 'I've not eaten anything all day! Did you remember my money, Inspector?'

'Shut up!' snaps the inspector, which Borkhausen correctly interprets as an affirmative. His heart begins to beat a little more easily: money in prospect!

'Where is he then, Kluge?' the inspector asks him.

'I don't know!' replies an offended-sounding Borkhausen, to anticipate possible remonstrations. 'I can't go inside and ask after him, when he knows me from before! My guess is he's probably in the garden house at the back, but you'll have to find that out for yourself, Inspector. Anyway, I've done my job, now I want my money.'

Disregarding this, Escherich asks Borkhausen what Enno's doing this far west, and how he managed to find him.

Borkhausen is obliged to give him a detailed report, and the inspector takes notes on Hetty Haberle, the pet shop, the evening scene on his knees: this time the inspector writes everything down. Of course, Borkhausen's report is not complete in every detail, but that's not to be expected. No one can demand that a man admit his own humiliation. Because when Borkhausen reports on how he came to take money from Frau Haberle, he ought also to report on how it went missing again. He ought also to have reported on the two thousand marks that are now sitting in Munich waiting to be collected. No, no one can expect that of him!

If Escherich had been on slightly better form, he might have noticed a few inconsistencies in the snoop's report. But Escherich is still preoccupied with other things. Ideally he would send Borkhausen away, but he needs him a while longer, and so he says: 'Wait here!' and goes into the house.

He doesn't go straight through to the back but first to the concierge's flat in the front house, and makes some inquiries there. Only then, accompanied by the concierge, does he enter the garden house, and slowly climbs the stairs to the fourth floor.

The concierge was unable to confirm to him that Enno Kluge was living in the building. The concierge is only responsible for tenants in the front house, not the people in the garden building. But of course he knows everyone who lives there too, not least because he allocates the ration cards to all. Some of them he knows well, some less well. For example, there is Anna Schönlein, who lives on the fourth floor, and in his view, she's well capable of taking in a man like that. The concierge has his eye on her anyway, because all sorts of rabble are forever spending the night at her flat, and the post secretary on the floor below is adamant that she had the radio tuned to foreign stations at night. The secretary wouldn't quite swear to the fact, but he did promise to keep his ear cocked in that direction. Yes, the concierge had been meaning to talk to the block warden about Schönlein, but why not to the inspector now. He urged him to start his inquiries at Schönlein's, and only if it turned out that the man really wasn't there, to ask on the other storeys. All in all, the people living in the garden house were decent enough.

'This is the one!' whispers the concierge.

'You stand here, so that she can see you through the peephole,' the inspector whispers back. 'Now give a reason why you've come up, pigfood for the NSV or the Winter Relief Fund.'*

---

* NSV: 'Nationalsozialistische Volkswohlfahrt', literally, Nazi Public Welfare, an organization partly funded by the Winter Relief Fund.

'Done!' says the concierge, and he rings the bell.

Nothing happens, and the concierge rings again, and a third time. All is quiet within.

'Not at home?' whispers the inspector.

'I doubt it!' says the concierge. 'I haven't seen her go out all day.'

And he rings a fourth time.

Suddenly, without the two men hearing a sound within, the door opens. A tall, bony woman stands in front of them. She is wearing baggy, faded tracksuit trousers, and a canary yellow jersey with red buttons. She has a thin, sharp face, splotched with red, as the faces of consumptives often are. Also, she has that feverish gleam in her eyes.

'What is it?' she asks curtly, and betrays no shock when the inspector plants himself in the doorway, so that the door can't be closed.

'I'd like a few words with you if I may, Fräulein Schönlein. I'm from the Gestapo. Escherich is my name.'

Again, no sign of shock; the woman continues to look at him with her fevered eyes. Then quickly she says: 'Come in!' and leads the way into her flat.

'You stay by the door!' the inspector whispers to the concierge. 'If anyone tries to get in or out, shout!'

The room in which the inspector now finds himself is a little messy and dusty. Ancient velvet upholstery with carved pilasters and ball and claw feet from the last century. Velvet curtains. An easel with the picture of a bearded man on it, a blown-up colour photograph. There's cigarette smoke in the air, a few butts in an ashtray.

'What is it?' repeats Fräulein Schönlein.

She's standing by the table, hasn't offered the inspector a seat.

The inspector sits down anyway, takes a pack of cigarettes out of his pocket, and gestures at the picture. 'Who's that of?' he asks.

'My father,' says the woman. And again she asks: 'What is it?'

'I had some questions I wanted to ask you, Fräulein Schönlein,' says the inspector, and offers her a cigarette. 'Sit down, have a cigarette!'

The woman says quickly: 'I never smoke!'

'One, two, three, four,' Escherich counts the stubs in the ashtray. 'And the room smells smoky. Have you got visitors, Fräulein Schönlein?'

She looked at him calmly, without panic. 'I never admit to smoking,' she said, 'my doctor has forbidden me to smoke on account of my lung.'

'So you don't have any visitors?'

'I don't have any visitors.'

'I'll just take a quick look around your flat,' says the inspector, and gets up. 'No, please don't trouble yourself. I'll find my own way around.'

He walked quickly through the other two rooms packed with sofas, cabinets, wardrobes, armchairs and gilt. Once, he stopped to listen, his face up to a wardrobe, smiling. Then he returned to Fräulein Schönlein. She was still standing as he had left her, by the table.

'It has been reported to me,' he said, sitting down again, 'that you receive plenty of visitors, visitors who tend to stay with you for two or three nights, but are never registered. Are you aware of your obligation to register visitors?'

'Almost all my visitors are nephews and nieces, who never stay with me for more than two nights. So far as I know, I'm not obliged to register visitors for under four nights.'

'You must have a very large family, Fräulein Schönlein,' said the inspector gravely. 'Almost every night you have one, two, even three people camping here with you.'

'That's a gross exaggeration. In point of fact, I do have a very large family. Six siblings, all of them married with children.'

'And some dignified old ladies and gentlemen among your nephews and nieces!'

'Naturally, their parents call on me once in a while as well.'

'A very large family, and very fond of travelling . . . By the way, something else I'd been meaning to ask you: Where do you keep your radio, Fräulein Schönlein? I didn't see one on my rounds just now.'

She pressed her lips together: 'I don't own a radio.'

'Of course not!' said the inspector. 'Of course not. Just as you'll never admit that you smoke cigarettes. At least radio music does no harm to the lungs.'

'No, just the political orientation,' she said ironically. 'No, I don't own a radio. If music has been heard playing in my apartment, it's from the portable gramophone on the shelf behind you.'

'Which has been heard to speak in foreign languages,' added the inspector. ·

'I own many foreign dance records. I don't think it's a crime to play them on occasion to my visitors, even in wartime.'

'You mean, to your nephews and nieces? No, surely that's not a crime.'

He stood up, thrust his hands in his pockets. Suddenly he wasn't speaking teasingly, he said brutally: 'What do you think will happen, Fräulein Schönlein, if I arrest you, and leave an agent in your place? He would welcome your visitors, and scrutinize the papers of those nephews and nieces of yours. It could be one of your visitors could even come bearing gifts – say, a radio! What do you say?'

'I say,' replied Fräulein Schönlein coolly, 'that you came here with the intention of arresting me, so it doesn't really matter what I say. Let's go! I suppose you'll allow me to slip on a dress for these tracksuit bottoms?'

'Not so fast! Of course, it's to your credit that your first thought should be to free the gentleman hiding in your closet before we leave. Even a moment ago, when I was walking around your bedroom, he seemed to be suffering from shortage of breath. I daresay the mothballs in the closet . . .'

The red splotches were gone from her face. She was white as a sheet as she stared at him.

He shook his head. 'Dear, oh dear!' he said with mock disapproval. 'You do make it so terribly easy for us! And you'd like to be conspirators? You're trying to bring down the state with your childish games? The only people you'll bring down are yourselves!'

Still she stared at him. Her mouth was tight shut, her eyes had a feverish gleam, her hand was still on the doorknob.

'Well, you're in luck, Fräulein Schönlein,' the inspector continued, in a tone of easy, contemptuous superiority, 'inasmuch as you're of no interest to me, not tonight anyway. All I'm interested in is the man in your closet. It could be that, once I consider your case more narrowly back in my office, I may feel obliged to pass on a report about you to the appropriate authorities. As I say, it could be, I'm not sure yet. Perhaps at the given time, your case will seem too trivial – not least in view of your state of health . . .'

Suddenly it burst from her: 'I don't want your mercy! I hate your pity! My case is not trivial! Yes, I regularly put up political victims here in my flat! I have listened to foreign radio stations! There, now you know! Now you can't spare me any more – regardless of my lungs!'

'Now now, old girl!' he said mockingly, looking almost pityingly at the strangely old maidish figure in her tracksuit bottoms and yellow jersey with the red buttons. 'It's not just your lungs, it's your nerves that are shot! Half an hour's interrogation from us, and you'd be surprised what a whimpering wreck we'll have reduced you to! It's a very unpleasant thing to experience. Some people never get over it, they just string themselves up.'

He looked at her once more, nodded gravely. Contemptuously he said: 'And those are the kind of people who like to call themselves conspirators!'

She flinched, as though struck by a whip, but said nothing in reply.

'But in the course of our nice conversation we're forgetting all about the visitor in the closet,' he carried on. 'You'd better come along, Fräulein Schönlein! Unless we spring him soon, it'll be all up with him!'

Enno Kluge really was close to suffocation when Escherich dragged him out of the closet. The inspector laid the little fellow on the chaise longue, and moved his arms up and down a few times, to help start him breathing again.

'And now,' he said, and looked at the woman, who was standing silently in the middle of the room, 'and now, Fräulein Schönlein, I suggest you leave me and Herr Kluge alone for a quarter hour or so. It's probably best you sit in the kitchen, where you won't be able to snoop!'

'I'm not a snoop!'

'No no, just as you never smoke cigarettes, and only play dance records to the edification of your nieces and nephews! Come on, go and sit in the kitchen. I'll call you when I need you!'

He nodded to her once more, and saw that she really did go into the kitchen. Then he turned his attention to Herr Kluge, who was now sitting up on the sofa, training his colourless eyes fearfully on the inspector. Already, the tears were beginning to trickle down his cheeks.

'Well now, Herr Kluge,' said the inspector soothingly. 'Are those tears of joy at this unexpected reunion with your old friend Escherich? Did you miss me very much? To tell the truth, I've missed you too, and I'm very glad I've run into you again. But I don't think anything will come between us now, Herr Kluge!'

Enno's tears poured down his cheeks. He gulped back a sob: 'Oh, inspector, you promised to let me go!'

'And didn't I do just that?' asked the inspector in surprise. 'But that doesn't mean I can't take you back if I find I can't do without you. What if I have a new statement for you to sign, Herr Kluge? As my good friend, you surely wouldn't refuse me such a small favour, would you?'

Enno trembled under the level stare of those mocking eyes. He knew the eyes would draw everything out of him, he would blab, and then one way or another he was lost for ever more . . .

32

Escherich and Kluge Take a Walk

It was already completely dark when Inspector Escherich left the garden house on Ansbacher Strasse in the company of Enno Kluge. No, in spite of her pulmonary condition, the Inspector had not been able to view the case of Fräulein Anna Schönlein as venial. That old maid really seemed in the habit of putting up criminals quite indiscriminately – or even purposely – without even knowing their story. With Enno Kluge, for instance, she hadn't even asked his name; she had agreed to hide him merely because a friend of hers had brought him along.

He would also have to take a closer look at Frau Haberle. These Germans were a disgrace! With the greatest war in history being waged to assure them of a happy future, they persisted in their ingratitude. There was a bad smell wherever you stuck your nose. Inspector Escherich was firmly convinced that he would find a knot of secrecy and deceit in well-nigh every German home. Almost no one had a clean conscience – of course with the exception of Party members. And he knew better than to institute the sort of search he had conducted at Fräulein Schönlein's at any Party member's home.

Well, at least he had put the concierge in charge of the flat. He seemed a reliable fellow, Party member by the way; he should remember to get him some small well-paid job. That kept people like him on their toes, and sharpened their eyesight and hearing. Stick and carrot, that was the way to go.

The inspector, arm in arm with Enno Kluge, makes for the poster pillar behind which Borkhausen is waiting. Borkhausen isn't at all keen to see his erstwhile partner; to avoid meeting him, he sidles round the pillar. But the inspector changes direction and catches him, and Emil and Enno confront one another.

'Evening, Enno!' says Borkhausen, and puts out a hand.

Kluge won't shake. A bit of indignation stirs even in this pathetic creature. He hates Borkhausen, who talked him into that break-in that earned them nothing but blows, who made thousands from blackmail this morning, and who has still betrayed him now.

'Inspector,' says Kluge excitedly, 'did Borkhausen not tell you that he blackmailed my friend Frau Haberle for two thousand five hundred marks this morning? He promised to let me go in return, but now . . .'

The inspector was only going to Borkhausen to give him his money and pack him off home. But now he leaves the little wad of notes in his pocket, and listens in amusement as Borkhausen replies coarsely: 'And didn't I let you go, Enno? If you go and get yourself caught again right away like the bloody fool you are, that's no fault of mine. I kept my promise.'

The inspector says: 'Well, we can talk about that some other time, Borkhausen. But for now, you should go home.'

'First I want my money, Inspector,' demands Borkhausen. 'You promised me five hundred smackers if I hand Enno over to you. You've got him, let's see your money!'

'You don't get paid twice for the same work, Borkhausen!' says the inspector. 'You've already had two thousand five hundred!'

'But I haven't got it!' Borkhausen almost screams back. 'She transferred it to the post office in Munich, to try and get me out of the way!'

'Clever woman!' says the inspector admiringly. 'Or was that your idea, Herr Kluge?'

'He's lying again!' Enno shouts bitterly. 'Only two thousand were sent to Munich. Five hundred, more than five hundred, were paid out to him in cash. Look in his pockets, Inspector!'

'They've been stolen off me! A gang of youths attacked me and stole all my money! You can pat me down from top to toe, Inspector, I'm only carrying a few marks that I happened to keep in my waistcoat!'

'One obviously can't entrust money to you, Borkhausen,' says the inspector sorrowfully. 'You don't look after it properly. How can a great big man like you get mugged by a gang of youths!'

Borkhausen starts begging again, demanding, wheedling, but the inspector – they are back at Viktoria-Luise Platz by now – commands: 'All right, Borkhausen, that's enough. Go home now!'

'But Inspector, you promised me . . .'

'And if you don't go down into the underground right now, I'll hand you over to that constable! He can take you in for blackmail.'

With those words, the inspector makes for the policeman, and Borkhausen, angry Borkhausen, the would-be criminal, who always manages to get separated from the loot moments after finishing the job, Borkhausen quits the scene. (Just you watch out, Kuno-Dieter, when I get home!)

The inspector has a word with the policeman, he identifies himself and instructs him to arrest Anna Schönlein, and hold her at the station, for: 'Well, let's just say for listening to enemy radio stations. I don't want her questioned. Someone from the Gestapo will be along for her in the morning. Evening, Constable!'

'Heil Hitler, Inspector!'

'Well now,' says the inspector, heading down Motzstrasse in the direction of Nollendorfplatz. 'What shall we do now? I'm hungry. Normally I have something to eat round about now. You know what, why don't I treat you to dinner? I take it you won't be in any great rush to get back to Gestapo headquarters. I'm afraid our catering isn't of the best, and the worst thing is people are so forgetful, they sometimes don't bring you anything for two or three days. Not even water. Poor organization. What do you say, Herr Kluge?'

Amidst such quips, the inspector brings the now totally bewildered Kluge to a small wine bar, where he seems to be a regular. The inspector has a good meal, the food is excellent, with wine and brandy, and there is real coffee, cake, and cigarettes. Over dinner Escherich explains shamelessly: 'Don't imagine I'm footing the bill for all this, Kluge! No, this is on Borkhausen. I'm paying with the money that would have gone to him. Isn't it nice to fill up on the reward that was posted for you. A sort of poetic justice about that . . .'

The inspector talks and talks, but perhaps he's not quite as controlled as he appears. He hasn't had much to eat, but he's drunk quite a lot in a short time. He appears nervous, unusually fidgety. Sometimes he plays with the bread, and then he reaches for his back pocket, where he's stowed the little pistol, darting a quick look at Kluge as he does so.

Enno sits there looking rather apathetic. He has had plenty to eat, but barely anything to drink. He is still completely bewildered, and has no idea what to make of the inspector. Is he under arrest now, or not? Enno doesn't get it.

Just then Escherich fills him in. 'So here you are, Herr Kluge,' he says, 'and I'm sure you're wondering what to make of me. Of course I wasn't telling the truth, I wasn't hungry at all. I just want to kill time until ten o'clock. Because we're going to take a little walk, and in the course of it we'll find out what I'm going to do with you. Yes, one way or another, that's what we'll find out . . .'

The inspector's speech gets ever quieter, slower, more thoughtful, and Enno Kluge looks at him doubtfully. Some new devilment, he's sure, in this planned walk at ten o'clock at night. But what? And how can he avoid it? Escherich is vigilant as hell, he doesn't so much as let Kluge go to the toilet by himself.

The inspector continues: 'The thing is, I can only contact my man after ten p.m. He lives out in Schlachtensee, you know, Herr Kluge. That's what I mean by our little walk together.'

'What have I got to do with it? Do I know the man? I don't know anyone in Schlachtensee! I've lived around Friedrichshain all my life . . .'

'I think you might know him after all, but I'd like you at least to take a look at him.'

'And if I see him, and it turns out I don't know him, what then? What happens to me then?'

The inspector shrugs: 'We'll see about that. I think you'll know the man.'

Both are silent. Then Enno Kluge asks: 'Is all this to do with that damned postcard story? I wish I'd never signed the statement. I shouldn't have done you that favour, Inspector.'

'Is that so? I almost think you're right, it would have been better for both of us if you hadn't signed, Herr Kluge!' He looks so grimly at the other that Enno Kluge gets a fresh shock. The inspector notices. 'Now now,' he says soothingly, 'we'll see. I think we'll have one more for the road, and then head off. I'd like to catch the last train back to town.'

Kluge stares at him in dismay. 'And me?' he asks, with trembling lips. 'Am I to – stay – out there?'

'You?' The inspector laughed. 'Of course you'll be with me, Herr Kluge! What are you staring at me for with that horrified expression? I haven't said anything that should horrify you. Of course we'll ride back into town together. Here's the waiter with our schnapps. Waiter, one moment, we'll give you our glasses to refill.'

Shortly afterwards, they were on their way to Bahnhof Zoo, to the S-Bahn. It was so dark when they got off in Schlachtensee, that they spent a few moments standing stunned outside the station. Because of the blackout, there were no lights anywhere.

'We'll never find our way in the dark,' said Kluge timidly. 'Please, Inspector, can we go back! I'd rather spend the night at the Gestapo, than . . .'

'Don't talk nonsense, Kluge!' the inspector interrupted him brusquely, and pulled the little man's arm through his. 'Do you imagine I'd ride around half the night with you, only to turn back a quarter of an hour before my destination?' A little more mildly, he continued: 'I can see quite well now. We need to take the side road, that'll take us to the lake fastest . . .'

In silence they headed off, both feeling for obstacles with every step.

After they'd walked a little way, the air in front of them appeared to brighten.

'You see, Kluge,' said the inspector, 'I knew I could rely on my sense of direction. There's the lake ahead of us!'

Kluge said nothing, and the two went on in silence.

It was a calm night. Everything was quiet; they passed no one. The unruffled water on the lake, which they sensed rather than saw, seemed to breathe out a dim grey light that looked as though it was returning part of the light of the day.

The inspector cleared his throat, as though to speak, but didn't.

Suddenly Enno Kluge stopped. With a jerk he freed his arm from his companion's. In an almost hysterical voice he cried: 'I'm not going to take another step! Whatever you want to do to me, you can do it here as much as in fifteen minutes. No one will come to assist me! It must be midnight!'

As if to bear out his words, a clock began to strike. The clang was surprisingly close and loud in the darkness and mist. Involuntarily, the men counted the strokes.

'Eleven!' said the inspector. 'Eleven o'clock. Fully an hour till midnight. Come along, Kluge, we've got five more minutes ahead of us.'

And he took the other man's arm.

Kluge broke away with surprising force: 'I said I'm not going to take another step, and I'm not going to!'

His voice cracked with dread, so loudly did he shout. A startled water-fowl flew up from the reeds and laboured away.

'Don't shout like that!' said the inspector angrily. 'You'll awaken the whole lake!'

Then he stopped to think: 'All right, you can rest here a minute. You'll see sense. Shall we sit down here?'

He reached for Kluge's arm again.

Enno Kluge struck out at his hand. 'I'm not letting you touch me again! You can do what you want, but don't touch me!'

The inspector replied harshly: 'You don't talk to me in that tone, Kluge! Who in hell do you think you are? A nasty, cowardly little bastard!'

'And you?' Kluge shouted back, 'who do you think you are? You're a killer, a low-down killer!'

What he said seemed to frighten him. He muttered: 'Ach, I'm sorry, Inspector, I didn't mean it like that . . .'

'It's nerves,' said the inspector. 'You're in the wrong life, my friend. Your nerves aren't up to it. Well, let's sit down on the pier. Don't be afraid, I won't touch you, if you're that frightened of me.'

They approached the pier. The wood creaked when they set foot on it. 'A few steps more,' said Escherich encouragingly. 'It's best we sit down at the far end. I like places like this, all surrounded by water . . .'

Again, Kluge stopped short. After his show of courage and resolution, he suddenly started whimpering: 'I'm not going any further! Oh, have pity on me, Inspector! Don't throw me in! I can't swim, I'll tell you right now! I've always been terrified of water! I'll sign any paper you want! Help! Help! Hel . . .'

The inspector had seized the little fellow, and carried him, wriggling, to the end of the pier. He pressed Enno's face to his own chest so hard that he could no longer yell. He carried him down to the end of the pier, and dangled him over the water.

'If you yell once more, you bastard, I'll throw you in!'

A deep sob escaped Enno's throat. 'I won't yell,' he whispered. 'Ach, I'm done for, just throw me in! I can't stand it any more . . .'

The inspector sat him down on the pier, and sat down beside him.

'There,' he said. 'And now that you've seen that I could have thrown you in the lake and didn't, you'll agree that I'm no murderer, isn't that right, Kluge?'

Kluge muttered inaudibly. His teeth were chattering too hard.

'Right, now listen to me. I have something to say to you. The thing about meeting someone here in Schlachtensee for you to identify, that was hokum.'

'But why?'

'Hang on. And I know that you're nothing to do with the author of those anonymous postcards; I thought our statement might do to buy time with my superiors, to show some semblance of a line of inquiry until I'd arrested the true culprit. I'm afraid it didn't turn out that way. It's you they want now, Kluge, the gentlemen of the

SS, and they're keen to question you in their own inimitable fashion. They believe the statement, and they believe you're the author, or at the very least, the distributor of the cards. And they'll wring that from you, they'll wring everything they want from you with their techniques, they'll squeeze you like an orange, and then they'll beat your brains out, or they'll put you on trial before the People's Court, which comes to pretty much the same thing, only your agonies will be more drawn out.'

The inspector paused, and the wholly terrified Kluge pressed himself trembling against him – the man he had just called a murderer – as though seeking help from him.

'But you know it wasn't me!' he stammered. 'God's own truth! You can't deliver me to them, I can't stand it, I'll scream . . .'

'Of course you'll scream,' affirmed the inspector equably. 'Of course you will. But that won't bother them, they'll enjoy it. You know what, Kluge, they'll sit you down on a stool and they'll hang a strong light in your face, and you'll keep staring into the light, and the heat and the brightness will be like nothing you've ever experienced. And at the same time they will ask you questions, one man will take over from another, but no one will take over from you, however exhausted you get. Then when you fall over from exhaustion, they'll rouse you with kicks and blows, and they'll give you salt water to drink, and when none of that does any good, they will dislocate every bone in your hand one by one. They will pour acid on the soles of your feet . . .'

'Please stop, sir, oh, please stop, I can't hear any more . . .'

'Not only will you hear it, you will have to suffer it, Kluge, for a day, for two, three, five days – and all the time, day and night they will give you nothing to eat, your belly will shrivel up to the size of a string bean, and you will think you can die from sheer pain. But you won't die; once they have someone in their hands, they don't let them go that easily. No, they will . . .'

'No, no, no,' screamed little Enno, holding his hands over his ears. 'I don't want to hear any more. Not one more word. I'd rather be dead!'

'Yes, I think you're right there,' confirmed the inspector, 'you'd be better off.'

For a while, there was a profound silence between them and around them.

Then, with a shudder, little Enno said: 'But I'm not going in the water . . .'

'No, no,' said the inspector, speaking kindly. 'Nor shall you, Kluge. You see, I've brought you something, this cute little pistol here. You just need to press that against your forehead – don't be afraid, I'll hold your hand to keep it from shaking, and then you just crook your finger ever so slightly . . . You won't feel any pain, and suddenly you'll be free from all these torments and persecutions, and you'll have peace and quiet . . .'

'And liberty too,' said little Enno Kluge pensively. 'That's exactly the way you talked me into signing your statement, Inspector, you promised me liberty then too. Wonder if it'll be true this time? What do you think?'

'But of course, Kluge. It's the only real freedom that's open to us mortals. Then I won't be able to arrest you all over again, and intimidate you and torment you. No one can. You'll be laughing . . .'

'And what'll happen then, after the peace and the liberty? What do you think'll happen then? Eh?'

'I don't think there's anything after that, no trial, no hell. Only peace and liberty.'

'Then what have I been alive for? Why have I had to take so much? I haven't done anything, my life hasn't made anyone happy, I've never really loved anyone.'

'Hmm,' said the inspector, 'it's true, you haven't been a heroic figure exactly, Kluge. And you've never been exactly useful either. But why think about all that now? Whatever you do now, it's too late, whether you follow my suggestion, or whether you go back with me to the Gestapo. I tell you, Kluge, half an hour there, and you'll be on your knees begging for someone to give you a bullet. But it will take many, many hours before they've tortured you out of your life . . .'

'No, no,' said Enno Kluge. 'I'm not going to them. Give me the pistol to hold – is that the right way?'

'Yes . . .'

'And where should I hold it? There against my temple?'

'Yes . . .'

'And then the finger on the trigger. I'll be careful, I don't want to do it right now . . . I want to talk to you a bit more first . . .'

'You don't need to worry, the safety catch is still on . . .'

'Escherich, you know that you'll be the last person I'll speak to in my life? After you, there'll just be peace, and I'll never be able to talk to anyone again.'

He collapsed with a shudder.

'When I held the pistol against my temple just now, I felt a kind of chill from it. That's how icy cold the peace must be, and the liberty, that are awaiting me.'

He leaned across to the inspector and whispered: 'Will you promise me one thing, Escherich?'

'Yes. What?'

'But you must keep your promise!'

'I will, if I can.'

'Don't let me slide into the water once I'm dead, will you promise me that? I'm scared of water. Leave me lying up here, on the pier, where it's dry.'

'Of course. I promise.'

'Okay. Shake on it, Escherich.'

'There!'

'And you won't trick me, Escherich? You see, I'm just a wretched little fuck, it doesn't much matter if you trick me or not. But you won't trick me?'

'I promise I won't, Kluge!'

'Give me the pistol again, Escherich – is the safety on still?'

'Yes, yes, I won't take it off till you say.'

'Is this the right way to point it, here? Now I can feel the cold from the muzzle, I'm just as cold as the pistol. Do you know that I have a wife and children?'

'I've even spoken to your wife, Kluge.'

'Oh!' The little man was so interested that he quickly set down the pistol. 'Is she here in Berlin? I wouldn't mind talking to her again.'

'No, she's not in Berlin,' said the inspector, and cursed himself for violating his principle of not sharing information. Idiot! 'She's still in Ruppin with her relations. It's better you don't talk to her again, Kluge.'

'She doesn't have a good word to say for me.'

'No, not at all, she just has bad words to say for you.'

'That's a shame,' said the little fellow. 'That's a shame. Actually it's funny, Escherich. I'm just a zero, no one could love me. But apparently a lot of people hate me.'

'I don't know that your wife hates you exactly. I think she just wants to be left alone by you. You bother her . . .'

'Has the pistol still got the catch on, Inspector?'

'Yes,' said the inspector, surprised that Kluge, who had become calm in the last quarter an hour, still asked the question so excitedly. 'Yes, it's still on . . . What the hell?'

The pistol's muzzle fire flashed so close to his eyes that he fell back on the pier with a groan; still with the feeling of being blinded, he pressed his hands to his eyes.

Kluge whispered in his ear: 'I knew it was off! You wanted to cheat me once more! And now you're in my hands, now I can give you peace and liberty . . .' He held the muzzle against the brow of the groaning man, and giggled: 'Can you feel how cold that is? That's peace and freedom, that's the ice we'll be buried in, for ever and ever . . .'

The inspector dragged himself upright with a groan. 'Did you do that on purpose, Kluge?' he asked severely, and cracked open his scorched lids from his stinging eyes. The other man looked to him like a slightly blacker clump in all that darkness.

'Yes, on purpose,' giggled the little man.

'You tried to kill me!' said the inspector.

'But you said the catch was on!'

Now the inspector was certain that nothing had happened to his eyes.

'I'll throw you in the water, son of a bitch! And it'll be self-defence.' He grabbed the little man by the shoulder.

'No, no, please not! Please not that! I'll do the other thing! But not in the water! You promised me . . .'

The inspector had seized him by the shoulder.

'Bah, stop it! No more of your whimperings! You've not got the courage! Into the water . . .'

Two shots rang out in quick succession. The inspector felt the man crumple between his fists, and topple over. Reflexively, Escherich made a move as he saw the dead man slip off the edge of the pier into the water. His hands wanted to grab hold of him.

Then with a shrug the inspector watched as the heavy body smacked into the water and straightaway disappeared.

Better that way! He said to himself, as he moistened his dry lips. Less evidence.

For an instant he stood there, wondering whether to kick the pistol into the water or not. He let it lie. He walked slowly back down the pier, up the bank of the lake, towards the station.

The station was locked, the last train was gone. Indifferently, the inspector set off on the long walk back to Berlin.

The clock struck.

Midnight, thought the inspector. He made it to midnight. I'm curious how he'll like his peace, really curious. Wonder if he'll feel cheated again? The piece of shit, the little whimpering piece of shit!

PART III

*Things Begin to Go Against
the Quangels*

33

Trudel Hergesell

The Hergesells were on the train from Erkner to Berlin. Yes, that's right, there was no Trudel Baumann any more. Karl's stubborn passion had prevailed, they were married, and now, in the year of disgrace 1942, Trudel was five months pregnant.

After their marriage, they had given up their jobs in the uniform factory – following the run-in with Grigoleit and the Babyface, neither of them had felt easy there. Karl was now working in a chemical factory in Erkner, and Trudel earned a few marks by taking in sewing. With quiet embarrassment, they thought back to the time of their illegal activity. Both knew that they had failed, but both knew too that they were not suitable for such work, which demands that one put oneself second. Now they lived only for the happiness of their home life and looked forward to the arrival of their baby.

When they left Berlin and moved out to Erkner, they thought they would be able to live in complete seclusion. Like many city dwellers, they'd had the mistaken belief that spying was only really bad in Berlin and that decency still prevailed in small towns. And like many city dwellers, they had made the painful discovery that recrimination, eavesdropping, and informing were ten times worse in the small towns than in the big city. In a small town, everyone was fully exposed; you couldn't ever disappear in the crowd. Personal circumstances were quickly ascertained, conversations with neighbours were practically unavoidable, and the way such conversations could be twisted was something they had already experienced in their own lives, to their chagrin.

Because neither of them belonged to the NSDAP, because they both contributed the bare minimum to any collection, because they both had the inclination to live in quiet privacy, because they both preferred reading to attending meetings, because Hergesell with his long, tangled hair and dark burning eyes looked the embodiment of a Socialist and pacifist (in the view of the Party), because Trudel had once been heard to say that you had to feel sorry for the Jews – for all of these reasons they very soon acquired the reputation of being politically unreliable, and every step they took was watched, every word they said passed on.*

The Hergesells suffered under the atmosphere they were obliged to live in at Erkner. But they told themselves and each other that it didn't concern them and that nothing could happen to them, as they were doing nothing against the State. 'Thoughts are free,' they said – but they ought to have known that in this State not even thoughts were free.

So, increasingly, they took refuge in their happiness as husband and wife. They were like a pair of lovers clasped together in a flood, with waves and currents, collapsing houses and the bloated corpses of cattle all around them, still believing they would escape the general devastation if they only stuck together. They had failed to understand that there was no such thing as private life in wartime Germany. No amount of reticence could change the fact that every individual German belonged to the generality of Germans and must share in the general destiny of Germany, even as more and more bombs were falling on the just and unjust alike.

The Hergesells parted on Alexanderplatz. She had some sewing to deliver in Kleine Alexanderstrasse, and he wanted to inspect a second-hand baby carriage he'd seen advertised in the paper. They arranged to meet up again at the station around noon, and went their separate ways. Trudel Hergesell, who after initial difficulties had gained a wholly new feeling of confidence and happiness from her now advancing pregnancy, soon reached her destination on Kleine Alexanderstrasse and started up the staircase.

There was a man going up the stairs ahead of her. She saw him only from behind, but she knew him right away from the characteristic way of holding his head, his stiff neck, his lanky

---

* The National Socialist German Workers' Party (NSDAP) – the full title of the Nazi Party, the only legally permitted political party in Germany for the duration of the Reich.

form, his hunched shoulders: it was Otto Quangel, the father of her onetime fiancé, the man to whom she had once betrayed the existence of her illegal organization.

Instinctively, she hung back. It was evident that Quangel was unaware of her presence. He climbed the stairs at an even speed, without haste. She followed half a flight behind, always ready to stop the moment Quangel rang at one of the many bells in the office building.

But he didn't ring. Instead she watched as he stopped at a window, took a postcard from his pocket, and laid it on the sill. As he did so, he turned and his eyes met hers. It wasn't clear whether he recognized her or not. He walked past her down the stairs, not looking at her.

When he was a little way below her, she hurried up to the window and picked up the card. She read only the first few words: 'HAVE YOU STILL NOT UNDERSTOOD THAT THE FÜHRER WAS LYING TO YOU WHEN HE CLAIMED RUSSIA WAS ARMING FOR A SURPRISE ATTACK ON GERMANY?'

Then she ran down after Quangel.

She caught up with him as he was leaving the building, pressed against his side, and said, 'Did you not recognize me a moment ago, Dad? It's me, Trudel, Ottochen's Trudel!'

He turned his head toward her, and never had it looked so tough and birdlike to her as it did then. For a moment she thought he didn't recognize her, but then he nodded curtly and said, 'You're looking well, girl!'

'Yes,' she said, and her eyes shone. 'I feel stronger and happier than I've ever felt in my life. I'm having a baby. I'm married. You're not angry with me, are you, Dad?'

'Why would I be angry? Because you've got married? Don't be silly, Trudel, you're young, and Ottochen's been dead for two years. No, not even Anna would hold your marrying against you, and she still thinks of her Ottochen every day.'

'How is Mother?'

'As ever, Trudel, as ever. Nothing much changes with us old people.'

'But it does!' she said, and she came to a stop. Her expression now was very serious. 'It does, lots of things have changed with you. Do you remember the time we stood in the corridor in the uniform factory, under the posters with the executions? Back then, you warned me . . .'

'I don't know what you're talking about, Trudel. An old man forgets.'

'Today it's me warning you, Dad,' she went on quietly, but all the more penetratingly. 'I saw you put the card down in the stairwell, that terrible card that I've now got in my purse.'

He stared at her with his cold eyes, which now took on an angry gleam.

She whispered, 'Dad, you're risking your life. Other people could see you like I saw you. Does Mum know you're doing this? Do you do it often?'

He was silent for such a long time that she thought she wasn't going to get an answer. Then he said, 'You know I don't do anything without Mother.'

'Oh!' she exclaimed, and tears sprang to her eyes. 'That's what I was afraid of. You're dragging her into it too.'

'Mother's lost her son. She's not over it yet – don't forget that, Trudel!'

Her cheeks coloured, as if he had reproached her. She murmured, 'I don't think Ottochen would have approved of his mother getting involved in something like this.'

'We all make our own way in life, Trudel,' replied Otto Quangel coldly. 'You go your way, we go ours. That's right, we go ours.' His head jerked backward, then forward again – like a pecking bird's. 'And now we'd better say goodbye. I wish you well, Trudel, you and your baby. I'll pass on your regards to Mother – maybe.'

He was gone.

Then he came back. 'That card,' he said, 'don't keep it in your purse, you understand? Put it down somewhere, like I did. And don't breathe a word of it to your husband – will you promise me that, Trudel?'

She nodded, and looked fearfully at him.

'And then forget all about us. Forget you ever knew the Quangels; if you ever see me again, you don't know me, understand?'

Again, she could only nod.

'All right, then, be good,' he said once more, and he was gone, when she had so many things still to say to him.

When Trudel dropped Otto Quangel's card, she felt all the fear of the criminal, the fear of being caught in the act. She hadn't read any more of it. Tragic fate, even for this card of Quangel's: found by a friendly person and even then not having its desired effect. It, too, had been written in vain, for the friendly person who had taken it in her hands felt nothing but the desire to be rid of it as soon as possible.

Once Trudel had put the card down on exactly the same windowsill where Otto Quangel had originally left it (it would never have occurred to her that it could have gone anywhere else), she darted up the last few steps and rang the bell at the office of a lawyer for whose secretary she had sewn a dress – made of fabric looted from France and sent to the secretary by a friend in the SS.

During the fitting, Trudel felt hot and cold flushes, and then suddenly she blacked out. She had to lie down in the lawyer's office – he was away in court – and later drink a coffee, a good, strong coffee (procured from Holland, by one of the secretary's other SS friends).

While all the office personnel were being touchingly solicitous – her condition was quite apparent because she carried her bump at the front – all this time Trudel Hergesell was thinking, He's right, I must never tell Karl about this. Please God it doesn't hurt the baby that I got so upset. Ach, I wish Dad didn't do such stuff! Doesn't he even think about the trouble and fear he inflicts on people? Life is difficult enough as it is!

By the time she finally went back down the stairs, the card was gone. She sighed with relief, but her relief didn't last. She couldn't help wondering who had found the card next, and whether he would feel as great a shock as she had, and what he would do with it. Her thoughts kept circling round that question.

She returned to Alexanderplatz rather less carefree than when she had left it. She had meant to go on some more errands, but she didn't feel up to it. She sat down quietly in the waiting room and hoped Karl would come soon. Once he was there, the fear she still felt would disappear – even if she didn't say anything to him. His mere being there had that effect . . .

She smiled and shut her eyes.

Dear Karl! she thought. My own darling . . . !

She fell asleep.

34

Karl Hergesell and Grigoleit

Karl Hergesell hadn't done the swap for the baby carriage after all, no, in fact he had got rather angry about it. The pram was twenty or twenty-five years old, a real antediluvian model; presumably Noah had used it to push his youngest on board the Ark. And the old woman had wanted a pound of butter and a pound of bacon in exchange for it. With baffling stubbornness she had insisted that 'you people out there, you've got the best of everything. You're all living off the fat of the land!'

People's notions were absurd. In vain, Hergesell assured her that Erkner was anything but the countryside and that they didn't get one gram of fat more in their rations than people did in Berlin. Plus he was a simple worker and not in any position to pay extortionate prices to black marketeers.

'Well,' the woman had said, 'do you imagine I'd part with the piece I carried both my babies in, if I didn't get something decent back for it? Offering to pay me a lousy couple of marks is an insult! No, sir, you'd better find yourself someone stupider than me!'

Hergesell, who wouldn't have paid fifty marks for this high-wheeled, wobbly-suspensioned monster of a baby carriage, was adamant that her price was an outrage. Moreover she was committing an offence – it was illegal to demand fat in exchange for goods.

'Offence!' The old woman snorted contemptuously. 'Offence! Why don't you try placing a small ad in the press, young man! My husband's a sergeant with the police, there's nothing that's an offence for us. And now I suggest you get out of my flat. I won't be yelled at within my own four walls! I'm going to count up to three, and if you're not gone by then, it's a breach of the peace, and I'll charge you!'

Well, Karl Hergesell had told her what he thought of her, in great detail, before he left. He told her just exactly what his views were of exploiters like her, who were trying to grow fat on the neediness of many Germans. And then he had walked out, but he was still angry.

It was in this state of undiminshed anger that he had walked into Grigoleit, that man from the time when he and Trudel were still fighting side by side for a better future.

'Well, Grigoleit,' Hergesell said as he crossed paths with the lanky man with the lofty, balding brow, who was laden down with two cases and a briefcase, 'are you back in Berlin now?' He picked up one of the cases. 'Wow, what have you got in there! Are you going to Alexanderplatz as well? I'll carry this for you, then.'

Grigoleit smiled thinly. 'Very good, Hergesell, that's nice of you. I can see you're still the same old, helpful comrade you always were. What are you up to these days? And that pretty little girl back then – what was she called?'

'Trudel – Trudel Baumann. Since you ask, I married that pretty little girl, and we're expecting our first child.'

'That was probably always on the cards. Congratulations.' The changed circumstances of the Hergesells appeared not to interest Grigoleit overly – and yet for Karl they were a continually bubbling source of fresh happiness.

'And what about yourself, Hergesell?' Grigoleit went on to ask.

'You mean work? I'm an electrical engineer in a chemical plant in Erkner.'

'No, I mean what are you really doing, Hergesell – toward our future?'

'Nothing, Grigoleit,' replied Hergesell, and suddenly felt a pang of something akin to guilt. He said by way of justification, 'Look, Grigoleit, we're a couple of young newlyweds and we live for ourselves. What is the world out there to do with us, them and their shitty war? We're happy we're having a child. You see, that's something too, isn't it, Grigoleit? If we try to remain decent, and try to make a decent human being out of our kid . . .'

'You've set yourself a hell of a task in this Nazi-ruled world! Well, never mind, Hergesell, we never thought anything more of you anyway. You were always more concerned with your balls than your brains!'

Hergesell went red with fury. Grigoleit's contempt was scathing. He didn't even seem to be going out of his way to give offence, because he continued perfectly calmly, oblivious to the reaction of the other, 'I'm carrying on, and Babyface is, too. No, not here in Berlin. We've relocated west of here, although *located* is the wrong word really, because I'm always on the go; I'm working as a kind of courier . . .'

'And you really think it'll bring results? Your little bunch and this bloody great machine . . .'

'First of all, we're not a little bunch, as you put it. Every decent German, and there are still two or three million of them, will make common cause with us. They just need to overcome their fear. At the moment, their fear of the future the Nazis are creating is still less than their fear of the present. But that will change before too long. Hitler may continue to triumph a little longer, but then the reversals will come, and the triumphs will stop, and the bombing raids will get heavier . . .'

'And second?' asked Hergesell, who was mightily bored by Grigoleit's predictions regarding the war. 'Second . . .'

'Second, my dear chap, you ought to know that it doesn't matter if there's a handful of you against many of them. Once you've seen that a cause is right, you're obliged to fight for it. Whether you ever live to see success, or the person who steps into your shoes does, it doesn't matter. I can't very well sit on my hands and say, Well, they may be a bad lot, but what business is it of mine?'

'Yes,' said Hergesell. 'But you're not married; you don't have to look after your wife and child . . .'

'Oh, you go to hell!' shouted Grigoleit, manifestly disgusted. 'Enough of that sentimental twaddle of yours! You don't believe a word of it anyway! Wife and child! You idiot, it doesn't seem to have occurred to you that I could have got married twenty times over, if starting a family had been my intention in life! But it's not, see! I say what right do I have to any personal happiness while there's room for such unhappiness on this earth!'

'We have drifted apart!' murmured Karl Hergesell, half sadly. 'My happiness doesn't cost anyone else a thing.'

'But it does! You're stealing it! You're robbing mothers of their sons, wives of their husbands, girlfriends of their boyfriends, as long as you tolerate thousands being shot every day and don't lift a finger to stop the killing. You know all that perfectly well, and it strikes me that you're almost worse than real dyed-in-the-wool Nazis. They're too stupid to know what crimes they're committing. But you do, and you don't do anything against it! Aren't you worse than the Nazis? Of course you are!'

'Here's the station, not a minute too soon,' said Hergesell as he set down the heavy case. 'I don't have to listen to your abuse any more. If we'd spent any more time together, you would have told me it wasn't Hitler but Hergesell who was responsible for the war!'

'And so you are! In an extended sense, of course. In a _broader_ sense, your apathy made it possible . . .'

Now Hergesell could contain himself no longer: he started to laugh, and even the grim Grigoleit broke into a grin when he looked into that laughing face.

'Well, enough, anyway!' said Grigoleit. 'We'll never understand one another.' He passed his hand over his high brow. 'But tell you what, there's a little favour you could do me, Hergesell.'

'Happy to, Grigoleit.'

'I've got this heavy old case, which you've just been lugging. In an hour I'm travelling to Königsberg, and I don't need it there. Couldn't you keep it in your house while I'm away?'

'Ha, Grigoleit,' Hergesell said, and looked disapprovingly at the suitcase. 'I already told you I'm living out in Erkner. That'd mean I'll have a fair bit more lugging to do myself. Why don't you just put it in left luggage here?'

'Why not? Why is a banana crooked? Because I don't trust the people here. I've got all my linen and shoes and my best suits in it. I don't think they're honest. Plus given the bombs that the Tommies are dropping these days – and stations are some of their preferred targets – I could lose all I have in the world.'

He pressed: 'Go on, Hergesell, say yes.'

'Well, if you insist. My wife won't be at all happy. But because it's you. Although you know, Grigoleit, it's probably better that I not tell my wife I ran into you. She'll get excited, and in her condition that won't be good for her or the baby, you know?'

'All right, all right. Whatever you like. Main thing is you keep the damn thing safe for me. In a week I'll be back and will pick it up. What's your address? Okay! Well, see you, Hergesell!'

'So long, Grigoleit!'

Karl Hergesell went to the waiting room to look for Trudel. He found her pressed into a dark corner, head thrown back, fast asleep. For a moment he stopped to look at her. She was breathing gently. Her bosom rose and fell. Her mouth was slightly agape, but her face was very pale. She looked worried, and there were little beads of sweat on her brow, as though she had been through something strenuous.

He gazed down at his beloved. Then, on a sudden impulse, he picked up Grigoleit's suitcase and took it to the left luggage office. The most important thing in the world for Karl Hergesell now was that Trudel didn't think upsetting thoughts and get excited. If he took the suitcase with him to Erkner, then he would have to tell her about Grigoleit, and he knew that everything that reminded her of her 'death sentence' upset her terribly.

When Hergesell returns from the left luggage office with the ticket in his wallet, Trudel has woken up and is just putting on her lipstick. She smiles at him, still a little peaky, and asks, 'What were you just doing with that huge suitcase? Was there a baby carriage in there, Karli?'

'Huge suitcase!' he acts surprised. 'I haven't got any huge suitcase! I've just this moment arrived, and I'm afraid the carriage was no good, Trudel.'

She looks at him in astonishment. Is her husband lying to her? But why? What secrets is he keeping from her? She saw him very clearly just a moment ago, standing by the table with the suitcase and then turning and lugging it out of the waiting room.

'But Karli!' she says, a little offended. 'I just saw you standing there with it a moment ago!'

'How would I come by a suitcase?' he asks, a little irritably. 'You were dreaming, Trudel!'

'I don't understand why you would lie to me about that. We never lie to each other!'

'I'm not lying to you; please don't accuse me of such a thing!' He is rather agitated by now, because of his guilty conscience. He stops for a moment, then goes on in a calmer tone of voice, 'I told you, I just got here. There's no suitcase, Trudel, you must have been dreaming.'

'All right,' she says, and looks at him blankly. 'All right. Then I was dreaming, Karli. Let's change the subject.'

She lowers her gaze. She is deeply hurt that he is keeping secrets from her, and what makes it worse is that she is keeping secrets from him, too. She promised Otto Quangel not to tell her husband anything about their meeting, much less about the postcard. But it still doesn't feel right. Married people shouldn't keep secrets from each other. And now he's keeping something from her as well.

Karl Hergesell feels ashamed, too. It's awful how brazenly he lied to her, even shouted at her when she was telling the truth. He wrestles with himself about whether it wouldn't be better to tell her about the meeting with Grigoleit. But he decides no, it would only upset her more.

'I'm sorry, Trudel,' he says, and squeezes her hand. 'Sorry I yelled at you. But the woman with the baby carriage made me so angry. Here's what happened . . .'

35

The First Warning

Hitler's surprise attack on Russia had given Quangel's rage against the tyrant new fuel. This time Quangel had been able to follow a policy from its very inception. None of it had surprised him, from the first 'defensive' concentrations of troops on the border to the actual invasion. He had known all along that they were lying – Hitler, Goebbels, Fritzsche, whatever their names were, their every word was a lie. They were incapable of leaving anyone in peace, and in angry dismay he had written on one of his postcards, 'What were the Russian soldiers doing when Hitler attacked? Why, they were playing cards – no one in Russia was thinking of war!'

Nowadays, when he walked up to groups of people in the factory talking about politics, he sometimes wished they wouldn't scatter quite so quickly. He wanted to know what other people had to say about the war.

But they lapsed into sullen silence; loose talk had become very dangerous. The relatively harmless carpenter Dollfuss had long since been replaced and Quangel could only guess at the identity of his successor. Eleven of his workforce, including two men who had been at the furniture factory for twenty years, had disappeared without trace: either in the middle of the shift or they hadn't come to work one morning. He was never told what had become of them, and that was further evidence that they had spoken a word out of turn somewhere and been packed off to a concentration camp.

In place of these eleven men there were now new faces, and often the old foreman asked himself whether all eleven weren't spies, whether half his workforce wasn't set to eavesdrop on the other, or vice versa. The air was thick with betrayal. No one could trust anyone else, and in that dismal atmosphere the men

seemed to grow ever duller, devolving into mechanical exten-
sions of the machines they serviced.

But sometimes out of that dullness a terrifying rage would
explode, like the time a worker had fed his arm into the saw
and screamed, 'I wish Hitler would drop dead! And he will! Just
as I am sawing off my arm!'

They had had a job pulling that lunatic out of the machinery,
and of course nothing had been heard of him since. He was
probably long dead now, or so you had to hope! Yes, you had
to be damned careful, not everyone was as far beyond suspicion
as that ancient, work-dulled workhound Otto Quangel, who
seemed to have no interest in anything beyond completing the
daily quota of coffins. Yes, coffins! From bomb crates they had
descended to coffins, wretched things made out of the cheapest,
thinnest pasteboard and stained brown-black. They knocked out
tens of thousands of these coffins, filling freight trains, entire
train stations, many stations, all full of them!

Quangel, his head alertly jerking toward all the machines in
turn, often thought of the many lives that were put in the ground
in these coffins, lives cut short, futilely cut short, and wondered
whether they were the victims of bombing raids, and thus mainly
old people, mothers, and children, or whether they had been
bundled off to concentration camps – a couple of thousand
coffins every week for men who hadn't been able to mask their
convictions, or didn't want to – every week a couple of thousand
coffins to one single concentration camp. Or perhaps these freight
trains full of coffins really did travel the long distance to the
Front – though Otto Quangel didn't really want to believe that,
because what did they care about dead soldiers! A dead soldier
was no more to them than a dead field vole.

The cold, birdlike eye blinks angry and tough in the electric
light, the head moves jerkily, the thin-lipped mouth is pressed
tight. Of the turbulence, the revulsion that live in this man's
breast no one has the least inkling, but he knows there is still
much to do. He knows he has been summoned to a great task,
and now he no longer writes only on Sundays. He also writes
on weekdays before going to work. Since the attack on Russia,

he has also written letters; these take him two days to write, but he needs an outlet for his rage.

Quangel admits to himself that he is no longer working with his old caution. He has happily escaped detection now for two years; never has the least suspicion fallen on him, and he feels quite secure.

A first warning to him was the meeting with Trudel Hergesell. If instead of her it had been someone else standing on the steps watching, then it would have been all up with him and Anna. Not that it mattered about the two of them; no, the only thing that mattered was that the work got done, today and every day to come. But the fact that Trudel had seen him drop the card had been the grossest carelessness on his part.

What Otto Quangel had no way of knowing was that at this point Inspector Escherich already had two descriptions of his person. Otto Quangel had been seen on two other occasions dropping the cards, each time by women who had then curiously come up and looked at the cards but hadn't raised the alarm in time to trap the culprit in the building.

Yes, Inspector Escherich had two descriptions. The only regrettable thing was that they departed from each other in almost every detail. There was only one point that they agreed on, which was that the culprit's face had been very striking, not at all like an ordinary face. But when Escherich asked for a closer description of this striking face, it turned out that the two women either had no gift of observation or else were unable to find words for what had struck them. Neither of them was able to say more than that the culprit had looked like a real criminal. Asked what a real criminal looked like, they shrugged their shoulders and said that was something that he and his men ought to know better.

Quangel had long hesitated over whether to tell Anna about his encounter with Trudel or not. In the end he decided to do so: he didn't want to keep anything secret from her.

She had a right to learn the truth: the danger of Trudel giving them away was very small, but if there was any danger at all Anna had a right to know it. So he told her about it exactly as it had happened, not glossing over his carelessness.

Anna's reaction was absolutely characteristic. Trudel getting married and expecting a baby did not interest her in the least, but she whispered in consternation, 'But think what would have happened, Otto, if it had been someone else standing there, someone in the SA!'

He smiled contemptuously, 'But it wasn't anyone else! And from now on I'm going to be more careful!'

But she was not at all assured. 'No, no,' she said vehemently. 'From now on, I'll do all the drops. No one notices an old woman. You're too striking; everyone notices you, Otto!'

'No one's noticed me in two years, Mother. There's no chance of me letting you do the most dangerous job of all on your own! I would feel I was hiding behind your apron skirts!'

'Yes,' she said irritably, 'now you trot out all your stupid masculine clichés! What nonsense: hiding behind my apron skirts! I know you're brave, you don't have to prove it to me. But I've also learned that you're incautious, and that's what's changed my mind. I don't care what you say!'

'Anna,' he said, and he took her hand, 'you mustn't do what other women do, and claim that a mistake is a habitual mistake! I've said I will be more careful in future, and you must believe me. For two years I've done it pretty well – why should it go any worse in future?'

'I don't see why I shouldn't drop the cards,' she replied stubbornly. 'I have had some experience of it.'

'And so you will continue to do, in future. If there are too many for me, or if my rheumatism plays up.'

'I've got more free time than you. And I really don't attract notice. Plus my legs are in better shape. And I don't want to be shaking with fear all the days I know you're going out with the cards.'

'What about me? Do you think I can sit here happily at home while I know you're running around outside? Don't you understand I'd be ashamed if you bore the bulk of the danger? No, Anna, you can't demand that of me.'

'Well, let's go together. Four eyes see more than two, Otto.'

'If there are two of us, we're more conspicuous. It's easier for a single person to disappear in the crowd. And I don't believe that four eyes see more than two in something like this. Plus, don't be angry with me, Anna, but it would make me nervous to have you walking at my side, and I think it would be the same for you.'

'Oh, Otto,' she said. 'I know that when you want something, you get your way. I can never talk you out of anything. But I'll be sick with worry now that I know you're in so much danger.'

'The danger is no greater than it ever was, no greater than when I dropped the very first card in Neue Königstrasse. There is always danger, Anna, for anyone who does what we do. Or do you want us to stop?'

'No!' she exclaimed. 'No, I couldn't go two weeks without our postcards! What are we living for? Those cards are our life!'

He smiled grimly, and looked at her with a grim pride.

'You see, Anna,' he said then. 'That's the way I like you. We aren't afraid. We know what the risks are, and we're ready, ready anytime – but with luck it'll happen a long way down the road.'

'No,' she said. 'I always think it will never happen. We will survive the war, survive the Nazis, and then . . .'

'Then?' he asked now, because suddenly – after their eventual victory – there was a vista of a completely empty life ahead of them.

'Well,' she said, 'I think even then we'll find something that's worth fighting for. Maybe quite openly, and without so much danger.'

'Danger,' he said. 'There's always danger, Anna; otherwise, it's not fighting. Sometimes I feel sure they won't get me, and at other times I lie awake for hours and hours, thinking about some lurking danger that hasn't occurred to me. I think and think, and nothing comes up. But there is danger threatening from somewhere, I can sense it. What could we have forgotten, Anna?'

'Nothing,' she said. 'Nothing. So long as you're careful with the drops . . .'

He shook his head impatiently. 'No, Anna,' he said, 'that's not the way I meant. Danger's not on the doorstep, and not in the writing part. Danger is somewhere else, but I can't think where. We'll wake up one day and know it was always there, but we never saw it. And then it'll be too late.'

She still didn't understand. 'I don't know why you're suddenly worrying, Otto,' she said. 'We've thought and tested everything a hundred times. As long as we're careful . . .'

'Careful!' he exclaimed, annoyed because she didn't understand him. 'How can you guard against something when you don't know what it is! You don't understand me, Anna! It's not possible to calculate everything in life!'

'No, I suppose I'm not understanding you,' she said, shaking her head. 'But I do think you're worrying about nothing, Father. I wish you would sleep more at night, Otto. You're not getting enough sleep.'

He didn't say anything.

After a while she asked, 'Do you know Trudel Baumann's new name, and where she lives?'

He shook his head. He said: 'I don't know, and I don't want to know.'

'But I want to know,' she said obdurately. 'I want to hear it with my own ears that there was no problem with dropping the card. You shouldn't have left it to her, Otto! A girl like that, how does she know what to do? Perhaps she put the card down where people could see her. And once they have a young woman like that in their power, it won't be long before they know the name Quangel!'

He shook his head, 'No, I'm sure there's no threat to us from Trudel.'

'But I want to be sure!' cried Frau Quangel. 'I'm going to go to her factory and ask after her.'

'You'll do no such thing, Mother! Trudel no longer exists for us. No, don't say anything, you're staying here. I don't want to hear one more word about it.' Then, seeing her still looking stubbornly at him, 'Trust me, Anna, I'm right. We don't need to talk about Trudel any more – that's over. But,' he went on more quietly, 'but when I lie awake at night, I often think we're not going to make it, Anna.'

She looked at him with big, staring eyes.

'And then I picture to myself how it will be. It's good to think about such things in advance, that way nothing will surprise you. Do you think about it sometimes?'

'I know what you're talking about, Otto,' Anna Quangel replied evasively.

He stood with his back against Ottochen's bookcase, his shoulder brushing against the boy's radio assembly guide. He looked piercingly at her.

'As soon as they've arrested us, we'll be separated, Anna. We might see each other two or three times more, at the interrogation, at the trial, maybe for the last time half an hour before the execution . . .'

'No! No! No!' she screamed. 'I don't want you to talk about it. We'll get through, Otto, we have to!'

He laid his big, rough worker's hand calmingly on her small, warm, trembling one.

'And what if we don't make it? Would you regret anything? Would you like any of what we've done to have remained undone?'

'No, nothing! But we'll get through undiscovered, Otto, I feel it!'

'You see, Anna,' he said, without responding to her latest assertion. 'That's what I wanted to hear. We will never regret anything. We will stand by what we've done, no matter how they torture us.'

She looked at him, and tried to suppress a shudder. In vain. 'Oh, Otto!' she sobbed. 'Why do you have to talk like that? You'll only draw the calamity upon us. You never used to talk like that!'

'I don't know what's making me talk to you like this today,' he said, stepping away from the bookcase. 'I have to, at least once. Probably I'll never talk about it to you again. But I had to do it once. Because you must know, we'll be very much alone in our cells, without a word to each other, we who haven't been apart for one single day in twenty years and more. It will be very difficult. But we can be sure the other won't weaken, that we can depend on each other, in death as in life. We will have to die alone too, Anna.'

'Otto, to hear you talk, it's as though it was imminent! And yet we're free, and no one suspects us. We could stop any day, if we wanted . . .'

'But do we want to? Is it even possible for us to want to?'

'No, and I'm not saying we want to, either. I don't, you know that! But I don't want you to talk as though they'd caught us and there was only death ahead of us. I'm not ready to die yet, Otto, I want to live with you!'

'Who wants to die?' he asked. 'Everyone wants to live, everyone – even the most miserable worm is screaming for life! I want to live, too. But maybe it's a good thing, Anna, even in the midst of life to think of a wretched death, and to get ready for it. So that you know you'll be able to die properly, without moaning and whimpering. That would be disgusting to me . . .'

For a while there was silence.

Then Anna Quangel said quietly, 'You can rely on me, Otto. I won't let you down.'

36

The Fall of Inspector Escherich

In the twelve months after the 'suicide' of little Enno Kluge, Inspector Escherich had been able to lead a fairly tranquil existence, not too burdened by the impatience of his superiors. When the suicide was reported and it was clear that the scrawny little man had put himself beyond interrogation by the Gestapo and the SS, Obergruppenführer Prall had of course thrown one fit after another. But in time he had calmed down: that trail had gone cold, and now they were forced to wait for another.

And besides, the Hobgoblin didn't seem so important any more. The sheer unvarying monotony with which he wrote his postcards that no one read, that no one wanted to read, that plunged everyone who found them into embarrassment or dread, made him a ridiculous, stupid figure. Of course, Escherich continued to stick his little flags into the map of Berlin. With some satisfaction he saw that they were concentrating more and more in the area north of Alexanderplatz – that was where the bird must have his nest! And that striking group of almost a dozen flags south of Nollendorfplatz – that must be somewhere that the Hobgoblin had some regular, if occasional, business. All that would come out in the wash, one day . . .

You're coming along! You're coming along nicely, all in your own time! chuckled the inspector to himself, and rubbed his hands.

But then his attention was claimed by other work. There were more urgent and important cases. A madman – a devout Nazi, as he called himself – was just then very current: he did nothing but send Minister Goebbels daily letters that were crude, and often pornographic in nature. At first the letters had amused the minister, then they'd bothered him, and finally he had thrown a fit and demanded the man's head. His vanity was mortally offended.

Well, Inspector Escherich was in luck, he had managed to solve the 'Filth' case within three months. The letter writer, who really was in the Party, and had a low joining number, had been taken to Minister Goebbels, and with that Escherich could wash his hands of the case. He knew he would never hear anything about 'Filth' again. The Minister never forgave anyone who had offended him.

Then there were other cases – above all, the case of the man who sent papal encyclicals and radio addresses from Thomas Mann, both real and fake, to prominent persons. A wily fellow – nabbing him wasn't easy. But in the end, Escherich booked him into his death cell in the Plötze.

And then there was the middle manager who had suddenly turned into a megalomaniac and announced that he was the director of a non-existent steelworks. He addressed confidential letters not merely to other directors but also to the Führer himself, with details of the parlous state of the German weapons industry, details that were in many cases true. Well, that bird was relatively easy to catch; the number of people privy to such information was relatively small.

So Inspector Escherich had enjoyed some important successes, and his colleagues were muttering he might be due an exceptional promotion. It had been a pleasing year, since the suicide of little Kluge; Inspector Escherich was quite happy.

But then a time came that saw Escherich's superiors once again grouped in front of the map with the Hobgoblin's pins. They listened to explanations of the flags, they nodded thoughtfully when the clustering north of Alexanderplatz was explained to them, they nodded thoughtfully again when Escherich drew their attention to the second, smaller cluster south of Nollendorfplatz, and then they said, 'Do you have any other leads, Herr Escherich? What plans have you made for the apprehension of this Hobgoblin? The invasion of Russia seems to have inspired the man to new spasms of literary activity. The past week alone has seen five postcards and letters from him!'

'True,' said the inspector. 'And there are three already this week!'

'So what's the state of play, Escherich? Think of how long the man's been writing now. We can't let him go on like this! This isn't a statistical office for the analysis of treasonable postcards – you're a detective! So, what leads are you following?'

Thus pressed, the inspector complained bitterly about the idiocy of the two women who had seen the man and not stopped him, who had seen him and couldn't even come up with a description of what he looked like.

'That's all very well, my dear fellow. But we're not talking about brainless witnesses, we're talking about clues uncovered by your shrewd brain!'

Whereupon the inspector led the gentlemen back to the map, and, speaking in a whisper, showed them how although there were flags evenly sowed all over the area north of the Alex, one little area had none at all.

'And that's where my Hobgoblin lives. He doesn't drop any cards there, because he is too well known; he would have to worry that a neighbour might see and identify him. It's a little working-class enclave, just a couple of streets. That's where he lives.'

'And why do you let him live there? Why haven't you called for a house-to-house search in those few streets? You've got to catch him, Escherich! We don't understand you – you have an impressive record otherwise, but in this case it's one blunder after another. We've seen the files. There was the run-in with Kluge, whom you let go, even after he confessed! And then you let him drop out of sight, and you even allowed him to do himself in, and that at a time when we really needed to talk to him! One blunder after another, Escherich!'

Inspector Escherich, nervously tugging at his moustache, permits himself to point out that Kluge manifestly had nothing to do with the author of the postcards. The postcards had continued to come in after his death.

'In my opinion, his confession that an unknown man gave him the card to drop is absolutely credible!'

'Well, as long as you think so! We think it's absolutely necessary that you do something! We don't care what it is, but we want to see movement! Conduct house-to-house searches in those streets. Let's see what that throws up. It's bound to be something, the infestation is everywhere!'

In turn, Inspector Escherich humbly begs to remind his visitors that even searching those few streets will mean knocking on close to a thousand doors.

'It will cause great disquiet among the residents. People are getting more nervous as it is, on account of the intensified bombing raids, and now if we give them further grounds to complain! And ask yourselves, What will a search accomplish? What are we looking for? All the man requires for his criminal activities is a pen, and every household has one, and a bottle of ink, ditto, and a couple of postcards, ditto, ditto. I wouldn't know what to tell my men to look for. At the most, a negative indication: the author has no radio. Never in all the cards have I seen any suggestion that he may have got his news from the radio. Often, too, he is badly informed. No, I wouldn't know how to instruct a search.'

'But, my dear Escherich, we simply don't understand you any more! You are full of doubts and hesitations, but you don't come to us with a single positive suggestion! We must capture the man, and soon!'

'And we will capture him,' said the inspector, smiling, 'but I don't know how soon. I can't guarantee it. But I don't think he'll still be writing his postcards in two years' time.'

They groaned.

'And why not? Because time is working against him. Look at the little flags – another hundred of them, and we'll be much further along. He is an incredibly tough, cold-blooded guy, my Hobgoblin, but he's also been incredibly lucky. Cold-bloodedness on its own isn't enough – you need a bit of luck as well, and he's had that to the most baffling degree. But it's just like playing cards, gentlemen: for a while the cards will favour you, but then your run comes to an end. And suddenly the deck will be stacked against the Hobgoblin, and we'll have all the trumps!'

'That's all very well, Escherich! Detection theory, I'm sure – we understand. But we are not so interested in theoretical questions, and all we take from your words is that we may be kept waiting for two more years before you decide to take any action. Well, we haven't got the patience. We suggest you think through the whole case again and come to us with fresh proposals, in, say, a week. Then we'll see if you're a suitable man to take care of this or not. Heil Hitler, Escherich!'

After they had all gone, Obergruppenführer Prall, who had kept quiet because of the presence of higher-ranking officers and officials, came storming back in: 'You moron! You imbecile! Do you think I'll allow my department to be further damaged by a fool like you! You've got one week!' He waved his fists furiously at Escherich. 'Heaven help you if you don't come up with anything this time! I'll haul you over the coals!' And so on and so forth. Inspector Escherich no longer listened to such talk.

Over the next week Inspector Escherich busied himself with the Hobgoblin case by doing nothing at all. Once before, he had allowed himself to be pressured by his superiors out of his patient waiting game, and as a result, everything had gone wrong, and that was what had ultimately made necessary the sacrifice of Enno Kluge.

Not that Kluge weighed heavily on his conscience. A useless, pathetic moaner – what did it matter whether such a creature lived or died. But Inspector Escherich had had a lot of trouble over that little wretch. Once that mouth had been opened it had cost him quite a bit to close it. Yes, on a certain night that the inspector didn't like to recall, the inspector had been rather agitated, and if there was anything the gaunt, colourless, grey man disliked, it was being agitated.

No, he wasn't going to be tempted out of his patient insistence, not even by his high-and-mighty superiors. What could they do to him? They needed their Escherich; he was in many ways irreplaceable. They might rant and rave at him, but in the end they would do the one thing that was right: wait. No, Escherich had no proposals to make . . .

It was a remarkable meeting. This time, it wasn't held in Escherich's office, but in the conference room, under the chairmanship of one of the top officials. Of course the Hobgoblin case wasn't the only one on the agenda – many other cases from other departments were also discussed. There were reprimands, yelling, and mockery. And then it was Next, please!

'Inspector Escherich, would you now tell us what you have to say in the case of the anonymous postcard author?'

The inspector told them. He gave a little report on what had been done thus far and what had been learned. He did it extremely well: short, to the point, not without wit, all the while thoughtfully stroking his moustache.

Then came the chairman's question: 'And what proposals do you have to make for wrapping up this case, which has now gone unsolved for more than two years? Two years, Inspector Escherich!'

'I can only recommend further waiting; there is no other solution. But perhaps one might hand the case over to Inspector Zott for a second opinion?'

For a moment, there was deathly silence.

Mocking laughter broke out in various parts of the hall. A voice called out: 'Slacker!'

And another: 'First you make a mess of it, then you try to make a present of it to someone else!'

Obergruppenführer Prall slammed his fist down on the table. 'I'll haul you over the coals, you son of a bitch!'

'Silence, please!'

The voice of the chairman carried an undertone of disgust. The room fell silent.

'Gentlemen, the response we have just heard reminds me of – desertion in the face of the enemy. Cowardly running away from difficulties that are an inevitable part and parcel of any struggle. I deplore your conduct, Escherich, and relieve you immediately of your participation in this meeting. Go back to your office to await further instructions!'

The inspector, ashen-faced (he had not been expecting this), bowed. Then he walked over to the door, clacked his heels together, and, with extended arm, roared, 'Heil Hitler!'

No one paid him any attention. The inspector went to his office.

The instructions he had been told to await came in the guise of two glowering SS men, of whom one said, 'You're not to touch anything here, understand!'

Escherich turned his head toward the man. This was a new tone. Not that Escherich was wholly unacquainted with it, but it had never been used on him before. A simple SS man – things must be in a bad way with Escherich if they talked like that to an inspector.

A brutal face: broad nose, prognathous jaw, inclination to violence, low intelligence, dangerous when drunk, summarized Escherich. What was it the commander had said upstairs? Desertion? Ridiculous! Inspector Escherich and desertion! But that was their style, always big words, and afterward nothing happened!

Obergrüppenfuhrer Prall and Inspector Zott walk in.

Well then, so they took my suggestion! The most sensible thing they could have done, even though I don't myself believe that even that wily mind can make anything different out of the available material.

Escherich is on the point of giving Inspector Zott a friendly greeting, not least to show that he isn't at all miffed about the handing on of his case, when he feels himself pulled aside roughly by the two SS men. The one with the thuggish face shouts, 'At your service, SS men Dobat and Jacoby with prisoner!'

Prisoner, Escherich thinks in bewilderment – are they referring to me?

And aloud he says, 'Obergruppenführer, might I add that . . .'

'See that that pig keeps its muzzle shut!' roars Prall, who has probably gotten his knuckles rapped, too.

SS man Dobat hits Escherich flush on the mouth with his fist. The inspector feels a vivid pain and the disgusting warm taste of blood in his mouth. Then he leans over and spits a couple of teeth out on the carpet.

While he does all this – does it perfectly mechanically; not even the pain really hurts – he thinks, I must make my position clear. Of course I'm ready to do anything. Door-to-door searches the length and breadth of Berlin. Spies in every building that has more than one doctor's or lawyer's office. I'll do whatever you want, but you can't just tell your stooges to punch me in the face, me, a long-serving detective and holder of the Iron Cross!

While he is feverishly thinking such thoughts, and trying mechanically to get out of the clutches of the two SS men, and trying to speak – but how can he speak through his ripped upper lip and bleeding mouth? – while he is struggling, Obergruppen-führer Prall has launched himself at him, grabbed him by the lapels with both hands, and began screaming, 'Now at last we've got you where we wanted you, you arrogant fuck! You always thought you were so smart, giving me the benefit of your bullshit lectures, eh? Do you think I didn't notice how stupid you thought I was, while you were so smart? Well, now we've got you, and we'll haul you over the coals like you won't believe!'

For an instant, Prall, almost insensate with fury, stared at the bleeding detective.

Then he screamed again: 'What are you doing spewing your vile blood all over my carpet? Gulp it down, you miserable hound, or I'll give you one in the chops myself!'

And Inspector Escherich – no, miserable, terrified little manikin Escherich, who only an hour before had been a mighty Gestapo inspector – strove, death-sweat beading on his brow, to gulp down the disgusting warm stream of blood and not to foul the carpet, which was his own carpet, no, now it was Inspector Zott's . . .

The Obergruppenführer watched the wretched inspector with sadistic pleasure. Then he turned away from Escherich with an angry, 'Bah, scum!' and asked Zott, 'Do you require this man for briefing purposes, Herr Zott?'

It was an unwritten rule that all long-serving detectives trans-ferred to the Gestapo stayed together through thick and thin, just as the SS itself also stuck together – often against the detec-tives themselves. It would never have occurred to Escherich to betray a colleague to the SS, whatever his faults; rather, he would have been at pains to hide his shortcomings from them. And now he had to look on as Zott, with a cursory glance in Escherich's direction, coldly said, 'This man? For a briefing? No thanks, Obergruppenführer. I'd do better briefing myself!'

'Take him away!' screamed the Obergruppenführer, 'and give him a bit of a gee-up, boys!'

And Escherich was whisked down the corridor between the two SS men, the same corridor, incidentally, down which he had dispatched Borkhausen with a kick in the pants, laughing at the humour of it. And they threw him down the same stone steps, to lie bleeding on the same spot where Borkhausen had lain bleeding. Then he was booted upright, and tossed down more stairs to the basement cells . . .

Every joint hurt him, and then it was out of his clothes and into the striped zebra suit, and the shameless redistribution of his possessions among the SS guards. All amid continual kicks and punches, and threats . . .

Oh yes, Inspector Escherich had seen it all many times in the past few years, and seen nothing surprising or reprehensible in any of it, because that was how you dealt with criminals. Naturally. But the fact that he, Detective Inspector Escherich, was now ranked among these criminals and stripped of all rights, that was something he couldn't get into his head. He hadn't broken the law. All he had done was make the suggestion that a case be passed along, a case on which his superiors had had not one useful idea between them. It would all be cleared up – they would have to get him out. They couldn't do without him! And until that time, he had to maintain his dignity, show no fear, not even show pain.

They were just bringing someone else down into the basement. A petty thief, he managed to overhear, who had been unfortunate enough to try to rob a woman who kept company with a high SA official, and had been caught in the act.

Now they brought him down here, after probably already softening him up: a whimpering creature, stinking of his own excrement, repeatedly going down on his hands and knees, hugging the SS men round their legs: please for the love of Mary not to hurt him! Have mercy – Jesus would repay them!

The SS men made a joke of letting the little fellow tug at their legs and beg and then smashing their knees in his face. Then the pickpocket would roll around on the floor, wailing – till

the next time he looked in their hard faces, thought he saw a
trace of clemency in one of them, and launched into a new
round of appeals . . .

And it was with this worm, this excrement-stinking coward,
that the all-powerful Inspector Escherich was made to share a
cell.

37

The Second Warning

One Sunday morning, Anna said a little nervously to her Otto, 'I think it's time we visited my brother Ulrich again. You remember, it's our turn. We haven't been to see the Heffkes for eight weeks now.'

Otto Quangel looked up from his writing. 'All right, Anna,' he said. 'What about next Sunday? Is that all right?'

'This Sunday would be better for me, Otto. I think they're expecting us.'

'But one Sunday's the same as any other to them. It's not as though they have any extra work, the pussyfooters!'

And he laughed sardonically.

'It was Ulrich's birthday on Friday,' Anna put in. 'I baked a little cake for him that I'd like to take. I'm sure they're expecting us today.'

'I wanted to write a letter as well as this card,' said Quangel grumpily. 'That was my plan. I don't like to make changes.'

'Please, Otto!'

'Couldn't you go on your own, Anna, and tell them I've got my rheumatism? You've done it once before.'

'And just because I've done it before, I don't want to do it again,' Anna begged. 'It's his birthday . . .'

Quangel looked at his wife's beseeching expression. He wanted to oblige her, but the prospect of leaving his parlour today made him unhappy.

'But Anna, I wanted to write the letter today! The letter's important. I've thought about it long and hard . . . I'm sure it will have a great effect. And then I know all your childhood stories, Anna, I know them all by heart. It's so boring at the Heffkes'. I've got nothing to say to him, and your sister-in-law sits there in silence, too. We should never have got involved with relatives, family is a nightmare. You and I are enough for each other!'

'All right, Otto,' she half conceded, 'then let's make today our last visit. I promise you I won't ask to go again. But today, when I've baked my cake and it's Ulrich's birthday! Just this once! Please, Otto!'

'Today is especially inconvenient,' he said. But finally, overcome by her imploring eyes, he growled, 'All right, Anna, I'll think about it. If I can finish two cards by lunchtime . . .'

He finished his two cards, and so at around three o'clock the Quangels left their apartment. They had intended to take the U-Bahn as far as Nollendorfplatz, but just before Bülowstrasse, Quangel suggested they get off there – maybe they could do something.

She knew he had the two postcards in his pocket, understood what he meant right away, and nodded.

They walked down Potsdamer Strasse a ways, without seeing a suitable building. Then they had to turn right into Winterfeldtstrasse, otherwise they would end up too far away from Heffkes' place. They carried on looking there.

'It's not such a good area as round ours,' Quangel said unhappily.

'And remember, it's a Sunday as well,' she added. 'Be careful!'

'I am careful,' he replied. And then: 'I'm going in there!'

Already, before she had time to say anything, he had vanished into a building.

For Anna the minutes of waiting now began, those painful minutes in which she was terrified for Otto but could do nothing but wait.

Oh God, she thought, looking at the building, this building doesn't look good at all! I hope to God it goes smoothly! Perhaps I shouldn't have talked him into coming here today. He really didn't want to, I could tell. And it wasn't just on account of the letter he wanted to write. If something happens to him today, I will never forgive myself! Here he comes now . . .

But it wasn't Otto leaving the building, it was a lady who fixed Anna with a sharp look before going on her way.

Did she just give me a suspicious look? I could have sworn she did. Has something happened in the building? Otto's been in there such a long time already, it must be all of ten minutes! Ach, I ought to know better, I've done it often enough: if you stand and wait outside a building, time always seems to crawl past. Thanks be to God, here he is at last!

She started to walk up and greet him – then stopped dead.

Because Otto hadn't come out alone. He was in the company of a very tall gentleman in a black coat with a velvet collar, half whose face was disfigured by a bright red birthmark. In his hand the gentleman carried a large black attaché case. Without exchanging a word, the two men passed Anna, whose heart turned over with fear, in the direction of Winterfeldtplatz. She set off after them with almost fainting feet.

What's happened now? she asked herself fearfully. Who is the gentleman walking alongside Otto? Is he from the Gestapo? He looks awful with that birthmark! They're not saying a word to each other – Oh my God, if only I hadn't approached Otto. He acted as though he didn't know me, so he must be in danger! That dratted card!

Suddenly Anna could stand it no longer. She could take no more of the painful uncertainty. With a sudden access of determination, she overtook the two gentlemen and stopped in front of them. 'Herr Berndt!' she called out, and gave Otto her hand. 'I'm lucky to run into you! You must come to us right away. I have a burst pipe and the whole kitchen is under water ... .' She broke off, with the sensation that the man with the birthmark was looking at her very strangely, condescendingly, almost contemptuously.

But Otto said, 'I'll come by as soon as I can. I'm just escorting the doctor to my wife.'

'I can go on ahead, if you want,' said the man with the birthmark. 'Seventeen Von Einem Strasse, did you say? All right. I'll see you very shortly.'

'In a quarter of an hour, doctor, I'll be there in a quarter hour at the latest. I'll just go and turn off the main tap.'

Ten steps further on, he pressed Anna's arm to his chest with unusual fervour. 'You were terrific, Anna! I didn't know how to get rid of the guy! What inspired you to do that?'

'Who was he? A doctor? I thought he must be in the Gestapo, and I couldn't stand the uncertainty any longer. Otto, slow down, my legs are shaking. What happened? Does he know anything?'

'Nothing at all. Be calm. He doesn't know a thing. Nothing happened, Anna. But ever since this morning, when you said you wanted to go to your brother's, I haven't been able to shake off a bad feeling. I thought it was because of the letter I was planning to write. And then it was the boredom at the Heffkes'. But now I know it was because I had the feeling something was going to happen today. I should never have left home . . .'

'So something did happen, Otto?'

'No, not at all. I told you nothing happened, Anna. I'm going up the stairs and am about to put down the postcard, I've got it in my hand, then this man comes running out of his apart-ment. I tell you, Anna, he was in such a hurry he almost bowled me over. I had no time to put the card back in my pocket. "What are you doing here?" he shouts. Well, you know I always make a habit of remembering one of the names on the signs on the door. "I'm looking for Dr Boll," I say. "That's me!" he says. "What's the matter? Is someone sick at home?" Well, what can I do but play along? I tell him you're sick, and could he visit. Thank God I think of the name Von Einem Strasse. I thought he would say he would come in the evening, or tomorrow morning, but he shouts, "Great! It's on my way! Come with me, Herr Schmidt!" – I said I was called Schmidt, you know, lots of people are.'

'Yes, and I called you Herr Berndt in his hearing,' Anna cried out in alarm. 'He must have noticed that.'

Quangel stopped in consternation. 'You're right!' he said, 'I didn't even think of that! But it didn't really seem to bother him. The street's deserted. There's no one coming after us. Of course he'll look in vain in Von Einem Strasse, because we'll be sitting with the Heffkes.'

Anna stopped. 'You know, Otto,' she said, 'now it's my turn

to say let's not go to Ulrich's today. Now I have the feeling today's an unlucky day. Let's go home. I'll drop the cards tomorrow.'

But he shook his head and smiled. 'No, no, Anna, now we've come this far, let's fulfil our obligation. We agreed it was going to be our last visit. And anyway I don't want to go to Nollendorfplatz right now either. We might run into the doctor.'

'Then give me the postcards, at least! I don't want you running around with the cards still in your pocket!'

After some initial resistance, he gave her the two postcards.

'It really isn't a good day, Otto . . .'

38

The Third Warning

But then, when they got to the Heffkes' they forgot all about their grim forebodings. It turned out they really were expected. The dark, taciturn sister-in-law had baked a cake, and after coffee and cake, Ulrich Heffke produced a bottle of schnapps that his colleagues at work had given him.

Unaccustomed to alcohol, they all drank slowly, but with enjoyment, from small glasses, and it made them livelier and more talkative than usual. Finally – the bottle already empty – the little hunchback with the gentle eyes started singing. He sang hymns and psalms: *'Es kostet viel, ein Christ zu sein'* and *'Zeuch ein zu deinen Toren, sei meines Herzen Gast'* – all thirteen verses.

He sang in a very high falsetto that sounded clear and devout, and even Otto Quangel felt himself taken back to his childhood, when such singing had meant something to him, as he had been a believer then. Back then, life had been simple: he had believed not only in God but also in man. He had believed in Love thine enemy and Blessed are the peacemakers. Sayings like that had some validity in that world. Things had changed since, and not for the better. No one could believe in God any more; it was impossible to credit that a benevolent God would tolerate such widespread wickedness on earth, and as far as men were concerned, those swine . . .

The hunchbacked Ulrich Heffke was still singing in his high, pure voice, *'Du bist ein Mensch, das weisst du wohl, was strebst du denn nach Dingen . . .'*

The Quangels declined all urgings to stay for supper. Yes, it had been very nice, but they had to be getting along home. Otto still had some work to do. It wasn't possible anyway, each household's food was rationed, they all understood that. In spite of the Heffkes' assurances that they could manage it this once, it wasn't Ulrich's birthday every week, and everything was ready, they could look in the kitchen themselves – in spite of all those assurances, the Quangels insisted they had to be going.

And go they did, even though the Heffkes seemed rather offended.

Once outside, Anna said, 'Did you see, Ulrich made a face, and his wife, too . . .'

'Let them make faces if they want to! That was our last visit anyway!'

'But it was especially nice this time, didn't you think so, Otto?'

'Sure. Yes. The schnapps did its bit . . .'

'And Ulrich sang so beautifully – didn't you think so?'

'Yes, very nicely. Queer fish. I bet he still says his bedtime prayers like a good boy.'

'Oh, leave him alone, Otto! People with a faith have an easier time of it nowadays, I'm sure. They have someone they can turn to with their worries. They think all this killing is for a reason.'

'Thanks!' said Quangel, suddenly vicious. 'A reason! It's all senseless! Because they believe in heaven, they don't want to fix anything on earth. Always crawl and keep a low profile. Heaven will fix everything. God knows why it's happening. On the Day of Judgement we'll find out. No, thanks!'

Quangel had spoken quickly and viciously. Not used to alcohol, it was having its effect on him too. 'There's a building!' he said suddenly. 'I'm going in there! Give me a postcard, Anna!'

'No, Otto, don't do it! We agreed we wouldn't do anything more today. It's a bad day for us!'

'Not any more, not now. Give me the card!'

Reluctantly she gave it to him. 'Please God it doesn't go wrong, Otto. I feel so scared . . .'

But he didn't pay any attention to her, and was already on his way.

She waited. This time she didn't have long to worry; Otto came right back out again.

'There,' he said, taking her arm. 'That's done. You see how simple it was? These presentiments are just superstition.'

'Thank God!' said Anna.

But hardly had they taken a few steps in the direction of Nollendorfplatz than a man came charging after them. In his hand he was waving Quangel's postcard.

'Hey! Hey you!' he shouted. 'You dropped this card on my floor! I saw you do it! Police! Hey! Constable!'

And he kept shouting, louder and louder. People gathered around them, and a policeman walked quickly toward the scene.

No question: suddenly the odds were stacked against the Quangels. After the foreman had worked successfully for over two years, his luck had turned. One failure after the other. Ex-inspector Escherich was absolutely right: you can't always trust that luck will favour you; you also need to factor in bad luck. Otto Quangel had forgotten to do that. He had failed to think of the little bits of adversity that life keeps at the ready, things that can't be predicted and that make a mockery of any calculation.

In this instance, chance had taken the form of a vengeful little official who had used his Sunday off to spy on the tenant living upstairs from him. He resented her because she liked to sleep in in the morning, ran around in men's clothes, and kept the radio on long past midnight. He suspected her of inviting 'fellows' back to her flat. If it was true, he would get her driven out of the house. He would go to the landlord and tell him he had no business tolerating a whore in his respectable house.

He had already spent three hours at the peephole in his apartment when, instead of his neighbour, Otto Quangel had walked up the stairs. With his own eyes he had clearly seen Quangel put the card down on a step – as he sometimes did when the windows had no sills.

'I saw him, I saw him with my own eyes!' the fellow called excitedly to the policeman, brandishing the postcard. 'Read this, constable! It's high treason if you ask me! The fellow wants stringing up!'

'Stop shouting, will you!' said the policeman. 'The man's perfectly calm, can't you see? He's not about to run off anywhere. Well, is there anything in what the gentleman's saying?'

'A load of nonsense!' replied Otto Quangel bitterly. 'It's a case of mistaken identity. I've just been to my brother-in-law's birthday party in Goltzstrasse. I haven't been inside any building on Maassenstrasse – ask my wife . . .'

He looked around for her. Anna was making her way forward through the dense crowd of onlookers. She had thought immediately of the second postcard, which she was still carrying in her handbag. She had to get rid of it right away – that was the highest priority. She had pushed her way through the crowd, seen a post box, and perfectly unobtrusively – all eyes were on the noisy denouncer – dropped the card in the box.

Now she was standing beside her husband again, smiling encouragingly.

In the meantime, the policeman had read the card. With a very serious expression, he tucked it inside his cuff. He had heard of these cards; every station had been briefed about them, not once but ten times. They were under orders to follow the merest trace of evidence.

'You're both coming back to the station!' he decreed.

'What about me?' cried an indignant Anna Quangel, linking arms with her husband. 'I'm going along, too! I'm not letting my husband go on his own!'

'You're right there, ma'am!' said a low voice from the ring of onlookers. 'You never know with those guys – better look after your old man!'

'Quiet!' cried the policeman. 'Quiet! Step back! Move along! There's nothing going on here that any of you needs to see!'

But the public was of another view, and the policeman, seeing that he couldn't possibly keep an eye on three individuals and disperse a crowd of some fifty strong, gave up the idea of dispersing the crowd.

'Are you sure you're not mistaken?' he asked the excitable show-off. 'Was the woman with him on the staircase?'

'No, she wasn't there. Yes, I'm sure I'm not making a mistake, officer!' He started yelling again. 'I saw him with my own eyes, I'd been sitting in front of the peephole in my door for three hours . . .'

A shrill voice called out, 'Another one of those damned snoopers!'

'All right, the three of you come along, please!' decided the policeman. 'The rest of you, break it up! Can't you see, we need to go that way. Damned busybodies! This way, please, Madam, gentlemen!'

At the station, they were made to wait five minutes before being called into the office of the supervisor, a tall man with a tanned, open face. Quangel's postcard lay on his desk.

The accuser repeated his charge.

Otto Quangel denied it. He had only been visiting his brother-in-law on Goltzstrasse and had never set foot in any house on Maassenstrasse. He spoke calmly, this old foreman, as he identified himself. The supervisor found him to be a pleasant contrast to the noisy, excitable, frothing accuser.

'Now tell me,' said the supervisor slowly to the man, 'how did you come to be standing at your peephole for over three hours? You couldn't have known someone would be along at some stage with a postcard? Or could you?'

'Ach, there's a whore living in the flat above, Herr Supervisor! Always running around in men's clothes, keeps the radio on half the night – and I just wanted to see what kind of men she was bringing back to the house. And then this gentleman here comes along . . .'

'I've never set foot in the house,' Quangel repeated obstinately.

'Why on earth would my husband get involved in something like that? Do you think I would allow it?' Anna cut in. 'We've been married for twenty-five years, and my husband has never been in any form of trouble!'

The supervisor casts a fleeting look at the rigid birdlike face of the man. Hard to know, with such a face! he thought. But writing postcards like that?

He turned toward the accuser again. 'What's your name? Millek? You're something at the post office, isn't that right?'

'Senior clerk, that's right, Supervisor!'

'So you're that Millek who comes to us about twice a week

with denunciations of various sorts, whether it's traders giving short weight, or carpets being beaten on a Thursday, or people defecating on your doorstep, and so on and so forth. That's all you, isn't it?'

'People are so bad, sir! They try to harm me in so many ways! Believe me, Herr Supervisor . . .'

'And this afternoon, you were on the lookout for a woman whom you describe as a whore, and now you come in and accuse this gentleman . . .'

The senior clerk assured him he was only doing his duty as a citizen. He had seen this man drop his postcard, and seeing at a glance that this was a case of high treason, he had immediately come after him.

'I see!' said the supervisor. 'One moment, please . . .'

He sat down at his desk and made as if to read the postcard again, though he had read it three times already. He reflected. He was convinced that this Quangel was just an old worker, whose answers were truthful, while Millek was a troublemaker, whose denunciations had never yet turned out to be accurate. Ideally, he would have sent all three of them packing.

But there it was, the postcard had been found, there was no getting around that, and he had strictest orders to follow up every lead. The supervisor didn't want to leave himself open for trouble. His standing with his bosses wasn't so hot at the moment. He was suspected of having a soft streak, of sympathizing with antisocial elements and Jews. He had to be on his guard. And when it came down to it, what could happen to this husband and wife if he handed them over to the Gestapo? If they were innocent, they would be allowed to go in an hour or two, and the bearer of false witness would get a ticking-off for wasting official time.

He was about to give Inspector Escherich a call when he remembered something. He rang the bell, and told the policeman who came in, 'Take these two gentlemen up front and search them both thoroughly. Be sure you don't get their possessions mixed up. And then send me someone else, while I search the woman!'

But the searches proved futile, nothing incriminating was found on Quangel. Anna Quangel was relieved that she had thought to drop the other postcard in the post box. Otto Quangel, who was still unaware of his wife's prompt and clever act, thought, Anna is sharp! Wonder what she did with the card? I never left her side. Meanwhile, Quangel's papers bore out his various answers.

On Millek, on the other hand, they had found a complete denunciation addressed to the station against one Frau Von Tressow, Maassenstrasse 17, who had allowed her dangerous dog to walk around without a leash. Twice already this animal had growled at the senior clerk. He feared for his trousers, which in wartime were irreplaceable.

'Those are worries, man!' said the supervisor. 'Now, in the third year of war! Do you think we've got nothing else on our minds! Why don't you ask the lady yourself if she wouldn't mind putting her dog on a leash!'

'I won't do that sort of thing, Supervisor! To address a lady of ill repute on the public street – not me! Afterward I'll only have her accusing me of making improper advances!'

'All right, sergeant, will you take these three up front. I'd like to make a phone call.'

'What? I'm being arrested?' exclaimed senior clerk Millek furiously. 'I bring substantive charges against someone, and you arrest me! I'll charge you!'

'Who said anything about arrest? Sergeant, take these three up front!'

'You've had me searched as if I was a common criminal!' screamed the clerk. The door slammed shut behind him.

The supervisor picked up the telephone, dialled, and said, 'I want to speak to Inspector Escherich. It's about the anonymous postcards.'

'Inspector Escherich is off, out, gone!' a pert voice shouted down the line. 'Inspector Zott is now in charge of the case!'

'Then give me Inspector Zott – if you can raise him on a Sunday afternoon!'

'Oh, he's always in! I'll put you through!'

'Zott speaking!'

'This is Station Supervisor Kraus. Inspector, we've just had a man brought in who may have something to do with the post-card case – you're in the picture?'

'Yes, yes! Hobgoblin case, so-called. What's the man's profession?'

'He's a carpenter. Foreman in a furniture factory!'

'Then you've got the wrong man! The real culprit works for the trams. Let him go, Supervisor! Bye!'

And so the Quangels came to be released, much to their own surprise, for they had expected that at the very least, they would be in for a thorough questioning, and a search of their flat.

39

Inspector Zott

Inspector Zott, a little man with a goatee beard and beer belly, might have sprung from an E. T. A. Hoffmann story. He was a creature compounded of small print, dust and a lot of shrewdness. He had once been a figure of ridicule among the Berlin detectives because he scorned the usual methods – he hardly ever interrogated a suspect or witness, and he went green at the sight of a corpse.

His preferred procedure was sitting over his colleagues' files, checking, comparing, writing out page-long summaries – but his particular hobbyhorse was the drawing up of charts. He tabulated anything and everything, drawing up endless, minutely considered charts from which he drew his shrewd conclusions. And since Inspector Zott, with his method of doing everything by pure logical deduction, had come up with some surprising successes in cases that had appeared intractable, his colleagues had become used to handing over all such cases to him – if Zott couldn't solve them, no one could.

In and of itself, Inspector Escherich's suggestion that the Hobgoblin case be passed to Inspector Zott was not exceptional. Only, Escherich should have allowed it to come from his superiors; put forward by himself it was simply an impertinence, no, it was fear of the enemy and desertion . . .

Inspector Zott closeted himself with the Hobgoblin files for three days, and only then asked the Obergruppenführer for a meeting. The Obergruppenführer, eager to see the case brought to a conclusion, had gone straight in to see him.

'Well, you old fox, what have you managed to sniff out for yourself? I'm sure you've got the man all taped up. That moron Escherich . . .'

There followed a long tirade against Escherich, who had made an almighty bollocks of everything. Inspector Zott listened without pulling a face, not even nodding or shaking his head to indicate agreement or otherwise.

Once the fire was extinguished, Zott said, 'Obergruppenführer, behold the author of the postcards; a simple man, not that well educated, hasn't had occasion to write that much in the course of his life, and who now finds it difficult to express himself in writing. He must be a bachelor or a widower and live all alone in his apartment; otherwise, his wife or landlady would surely have caught him in the act of writing at some time in the last two years. The fact that we have never heard anything about his appearance, even though we must assume that in the area north of the Alex there is a lot of gossip about these postcards, proves that no one can ever have seen him writing. He must lead an absolutely solitary life. He must be an older man – a younger one would have had enough of such an ineffectual campaign and would have gone on to some other activity. Also, he doesn't own a radio . . .'

'All right, all right, Inspector!' Obergruppenführer Prall interrupted him impatiently. 'I've heard all that long ago almost word for word from that idiot Escherich. What I need are conclusions, evaluations, results that help me lay hands on the fellow. I see you have a chart there. Tell me about it!'

'There in that chart,' replied Inspector Zott, not showing how hurt he was by Prall's interruption, and hearing all of his sharp deductions described as having been reached by Escherich previously, 'I have tabulated all the times when the cards were found. We are talking about two hundred and thirty-three cards and eight letters. If we analyse the times these were reported, we come to the following conclusions: no cards were left after eight p.m. or before nine a.m. . . .'

'But that's all blindingly obvious!' exclaimed the Obergruppenführer impatiently. 'The buildings are locked at those times. I don't need your charts to tell me that!'

'One moment, if you don't mind!' said Zott, now sounding a little irritated. 'I hadn't got to the end of my conclusions. And by the way, the buildings are not unlocked at nine, as you say, but at seven, and in some cases as early as six. To proceed. Eighty per cent of the postcards were reported between nine in the morning and midday. No cards were reported between midday and two p.m. Twenty per cent of the cards between two and eight p.m. It follows therefore that the author – who is certainly the same person as the distributor – eats lunch very regularly from twelve to two, that he works at night, or at any rate never in the morning, and rarely in the afternoon. If I take one site, let's say on the Alex, I see that the card was dropped at 11.15, and if I take the distance a man can cover in forty-five minutes, that is, by twelve noon, and I draw a circle with such a radius from the point, then to the north I intersect the area that is free of flags. That holds true for all the sites, with a few exceptions, which can be explained by the fact that the moment the cards were dropped is not always identical with the moment they were reported to us. From this I deduce, firstly, that the man is exceedingly punctual. Secondly, he doesn't like to take public transport. He lives in the triangle bordered by Greifswalder Strasse, Danziger Strasse, and Prenzlauer Strasse, and at the northern end of such a triangle, presumably in Chodowiecki, Jablonski, or Christburger Strasse.'

'Brilliant, Inspector!' said the Obergruppenführer, growing more and more disappointed. 'I seem to remember Escherich naming those particular streets as well. But he said there was no sense in mounting a house-to-house search. What's your view?'

'One moment, please,' said Zott, raising his small hand, which seemed to have been yellowed from all the files on which it had been resting. He was deeply offended by now. 'I want to communicate my conclusions to you quite precisely, so that you can see for yourself whether the measures I suggest are appropriate . . .'

He's trying to cover for himself, the cunning bastard! thought Prall to himself. Just you wait, there's no cover from me, and if I want to string you up by the thumbs, then I bloody well will!

'If you go back to my chart,' the inspector went on in his lecturing tone, 'then you'll see that all the cards were dropped on weekdays. From that we deduce that the man doesn't leave home on Sundays. Sunday is his writing day, which is borne out by the fact that most of the cards were reported on Mondays and Tuesdays. The man is always in a hurry to get the incriminating material out of his house.'

The little pot-belly raised a finger. 'The only exceptions are the nine cards that were found south of Nollendorfplatz. They were all dropped on Sundays, at almost exact three-monthly intervals, generally in the late afternoon or early evening. From which we draw the conclusion that the writer has a relative, perhaps an ageing mother, to whom he is obliged to pay regular visits.'

Inspector Zott paused and looked at the Obergruppenführer through his gold-rimmed spectacles, as if in expectation of some word of praise or recognition.

But all Prall said was, 'That's all well and good. Very shrewd, I'm sure. But I can't see where it gets us . . .'

'It gets us a little further!' the inspector ventured to contradict him. 'Of course I will arrange to have my men make discreet inquiries on the streets in question, to see if there is anyone living there who fits the bill.'

'Well, that's a start!' the Obergruppenführer exclaimed, relieved. 'Anything else?'

'Also,' said the inspector with an air of quiet triumph, producing a second chart, 'I have made up a second map, on which I have drawn red circles of one kilometre in diameter around the main sites where the cards have been found. I have left out Nollendorfplatz and the presumptive residence. If I look at the eleven principal sites – there are eleven, Obergruppenführer – then I make the surprising discovery that all of them, all without exception, are on or near the location of tram stations. See for yourself, Obergruppenführer! Here! And here! Here! Here the station is a little to the right, but still well within the radius. And here – bang in the middle again . . .'

Zott looked at the Obergruppenführer almost beseechingly. 'That can't be coincidence!' he said. 'There are no coincidences like that in detective work! Obergruppenführer, the man must have something to do with the electrical tram network. There's no other possibility. He must work night shifts there, occasionally afternoons. He won't do his work in uniform, we know that from the two witnesses who saw him drop his cards. Now, Obergruppenführer, I want your permission to put a very good man on each of these eleven stations. That strikes me as a more promising tactic than house-to-house inquiries. But if we do both, and both thoroughly, I'm sure we'll be crowned with success.'

'You cunning old fox, you!' shouted the Obergruppenführer, now very bullish, and he gave the inspector a whack on the shoulders that almost knocked him off his feet. 'You wily old crook! That plan with the tram stations is excellent. Escherich is a moron! How did he miss that? Of course you have my permission! Get a move on, and in two or three days tell me you've caught the fellow! I want to break it to that incredible fool of an Escherich what an ass he is!'

The Obergruppenführer left the office with a satisfied smile on his face.

Alone again, Inspector Zott coughed nervously. He sat down at his desk with his charts, squinted over at the door, coughed again. He hated all those loud-mouthed, brainless, bullying types. And this one in particular, who had just left him, he hated worst of all, that ape who kept holding Escherich up to him: 'Escherich said that, too,' and 'That's what that idiot Escherich always used to say.'

And then he had slapped him on the back, and the inspector detested any form of physical contact. No, that man – well, he could only wait and hope. Those fellows weren't as secure as they liked to make out; their yelling only masked their insecurity, the fear that they would one day be toppled. However confident and soldierly their bearing, they knew perfectly well that they knew nothing and were nothing. To have to explain to such a dunderhead his great discovery with the tram stations – a man who couldn't even follow such reasoning when it was demonstrated to him! Well, it was pearls before swine, the old story!

The inspector returns to his files, his charts, his plans. He has a tidy mind; he shuts a desk drawer and instantly forgets its contents. He opens the drawer marked TRAM STATIONS, and starts thinking about what sort of work the author of the postcards might do. He calls the personnel department of the public transport service and asks for a list of all the types of jobs there. He takes notes.

He is obsessed with the idea that the wanted man has something to do with trams. He is so proud of his discovery. He would be immeasurably disappointed if they brought him Quangel as the guilty man – a foreman in a furniture works. It would mean nothing to him that the culprit had been arrested – it would only pain him that his beautiful theory was wrong.

And for this reason, when a day or two later inquiries are in full swing both in the tram stations and the houses, and the supervisor tells him they might have caught the man, he merely asks what the man's job is. Carpenter, he is told, and the man has no more interest for him. He is looking for a tram employee!

He hangs up, end of story. So much so that the inspector doesn't even notice that the station is on Nollendorfplatz, that it's late afternoon on a Sunday, and that a card is due near Nollendorfplatz round about now. The inspector doesn't even make a note of the station number. Those fools, they do nothing but blunder around – end of story!

My people will inform me tomorrow, the day after at the latest. The uniformed police are all blunderers – after all, they aren't detectives.

And so it comes about that the Quangels are released . . .

40

Otto Quangel Grows Uncertain

That Sunday evening, both Quangels rode home without a word, and without a word they ate their supper. Anna, who at the critical moment was so brave and resolute, shed a few tears quietly in the kitchen, unbeknownst to Otto. After the event, when everything has passed off safely, she is in the grip of fear and alarm. It could so easily have gone wrong, and it would have been the end for both of them. If Millek hadn't been such a notorious querulant. If she hadn't been able to get rid of the postcard in time. If the station supervisor had been someone else – just from looking at him, you could tell that he couldn't bear that Millek! Well, it might have passed off safely this once, but never again must Otto put himself in such danger.

She walks into the parlour, where her husband is pacing back and forth. They don't have a light on, but the blackout screen is up, and it's a moonlit night.

Otto continues to pace back and forth, still without a word.

'Otto!'

'Yes?'

He comes to a sudden stop and looks across at his wife, who is sitting on the sofa, barely visible in the pallid wash of moonlight.

'Otto, I think we'd better have a break. I think our luck's changing.'

'Can't do that,' he replies. 'Can't do that, Anna. They would notice if the cards suddenly stopped. Now, after they almost caught us, they would notice all the more. They're not stupid – they would know there was a connection between us and the fact that the cards suddenly stopped. We've got to go on, whether we want to or not.'

And he added uncompromisingly, 'And I want to go on too!'

She sighed. She didn't have the courage to agree with him aloud, even though she could see he was right. This wasn't a path on which you could stop when you wanted to. There was no going back, and they weren't going to be left in peace. They had to go on . . . and on.

After thinking for a while, she said, 'Then let me take the cards from now on, Otto. I think your luck's out.'

Grumpily he said, 'I can't help it if some eager-beaver spends three hours sitting at his peephole. I looked around everywhere, I was careful!'

'I didn't say you weren't, Otto. I said you were out of luck. It's not your fault.'

He changes the subject. 'What did you do with the second card? Did you slip it under your clothes?'

'I couldn't do that, because there were people all round. No, Otto, I dropped it in a post box on Nollendorfplatz, during the first commotion.'

'In a post box? Very good. You did well, Anna. I think in the coming weeks we should drop cards in the post wherever we happen to be, so that this one doesn't stick out so. The post's not such a bad idea; they won't be all Nazis there either. And the risk is smaller.'

'Please, Otto, let me take the cards from now on,' she begged him once more.

'You mustn't think I made a mistake that you wouldn't have made, Mother. These are the chance things that I've always worried about, because you can't predict them. What can I do about a snoop sitting at his peephole for three hours? You could suddenly fall ill, or you trip over something and break your leg – they'll go through your pockets and find one of those postcards! No, Anna, there's no guarding against those flukes!'

'It would take such a load off my mind if you would let me take on the distribution!' she came back.

'Listen, Anna, I'm not saying no. I want to be truthful with you. All of a sudden I do feel unsure. It's like I can only stare at one point, which doesn't have any enemies there. But all around me there are enemies, and I can't see them.'

'You've got nervous, Otto. It's been like this for too long. If only we could take a break from it for a couple of weeks! You're right, though, we can't. But from now on I'll take the cards.'

'I'm not saying no. Do it! I'm not afraid, but you're right, I'm nervous. It's these unpredictable chances. I thought it would be enough, just going about our job properly. But it's not: we need to have luck on our side as well, Anna. We did have luck, for a long time, and now things look as though they're beginning to turn . . .'

'We got through,' she said calmingly. 'Nothing's happened.'

'But they've got our address; they can come back for us any time! Those bloody relations, I always said they were bad news.'

'You're being unfair now, Otto. You can't blame Ulrich for what happened!'

'Of course not! Who said I did? But if it wasn't for him, we never would have gone to that part of town. It's no good depending on other people, Anna. It just drags us all down together. Well, now we're under suspicion.'

'If we really were under suspicion, they wouldn't have let us go, though, Otto!'

'The ink!' he suddenly exclaimed and stopped. 'The ink's still here. The ink I wrote the card with, the same ink's here in the bottle!'

He ran over, and poured the ink down the drain. Then he put on his coat to go out.

'Where are you going, Otto?'

'I've got to get rid of the bottle! We'll buy a different sort tomorrow. Burn the pen in the meantime, and above all burn all the old cards and old writing paper we still have. Burn everything! Check in every drawer. None of that stuff can be allowed to remain here!'

'But Otto, we're not under suspicion! We've got plenty of time still!'

'We've got no time! Do as I tell you! Check everywhere, and burn the lot!'

He went out.

When he returned, he was calmer. 'I threw the bottle in the Friedrichshain park. Did you burn everything?'

'Yes!'

'Are you sure? Did you check through everything and burn it?'

'I just told you I did, Otto!'

'All right, Anna, that's good. But I still have that funny feeling, as though the one place I can't see is the one place where the enemy is lurking. As though I'd forgotten something!'

He pressed his hand against his forehead and looked at her thoughtfully.

'Calm yourself, Otto, I'm sure you haven't forgotten anything. There's nothing left in the flat.'

'Have I got any ink on my fingers? Do you understand, I can't have the least ink stain anywhere on me, not now that there's no ink in the house.'

They looked closely and found a stain on his right forefinger. She rubbed it away with her hand.

'You see, didn't I tell you, there's always something! Those are the enemies I can't see. Well, maybe it was just that ink stain that was still tormenting me!'

'It's gone now, Otto, there's nothing left for you to worry about!'

'Thank God! You do know, Anna, that I'm not afraid, but I don't want us to be discovered before our time. I want to be able to do this work as long as I can. If possible, I'd like to be around to see it all collapse. I would like to experience that. We've done our bit to make it happen!'

And this time it's Anna who consoles him. 'Yes, you will be around then, we both will. Think about it – what actually happened? Yes, we were both in great danger, but . . . you say our luck's turned? I think our luck stayed true to us; the danger's past, we're here.'

'Yes,' said Otto Quangel. 'We're here, we're at liberty. For the time being. And long may we remain so . . .'

41

The Old Party Member Persicke

Inspector Zott's agent, a certain Klebs, was given the task of combing Jablonski Strasse for old men living alone, that category of person the Gestapo was so interested in. He had a list in his pocket with the names of reliable Party comrades living in every house, and if possible in every back house too, and the name Persicke appeared on the list.

Prinz Albrecht Strasse might attach great importance to nabbing their man, but for Klebs it was just a run-of-the-mill job. Small, badly paid and badly nourished, bandy-legged, with bad skin and carious teeth, Klebs had about him something of a rat, and he went about his work much in the way a rat roots around in rubbish. He was always ready to snag a slice of bread, to cadge a drink or a smoke, and his plaintive, squeaky voice had something of a whistle about it, as though the unhappy creature was just on the point of expiring.

At the Persickes' flat, the old man opened the door. He looked dreadful, hair matted, face puffy, eyes red, and the whole man swaying and wallowing like a ship in a strong gale.

'Whaddaya want?'

'I'm just here to collect information, for the Party.'

Zott's spies had been instructed not to mention the Gestapo when they went about their business. The whole investigation was to have the appearance of a low-level search for some errant Party member.

But to old Persicke, even that harmless tag 'information for the Party' had the effect of a punch to the solar plexus. He moaned and leaned against the doorjamb. Some sort of thought process returned to his fogged brain, and with it, so did fear.

He pulled himself together and said, 'Come in!'

The rat followed in silence. It watched the old man with alert sliding eyes. Nothing escaped it.

The parlour was ravaged. Upset chairs, bottles of booze spilling their contents on the floor. A rumpled blanket. A table-cloth. Under the mirror, starred like a spider's web, a little heap of shards. One curtain drawn, the other pulled off. Everywhere cigarette ash, butts, half-open packets of smokes.

Klebs felt his fingertips twitch. He would have liked to reach out and help himself: drink, a cigarette, even the watch he could see in the pocket of a waistcoat draped over a chair. But for the time being he was just here on behalf of the Gestapo, or, as he should say, the Party. So he sat down politely on a little chair and squeaked happily: 'My, there's some collection of drinks and smokes you've got here! You're doing all right for yourself, Persicke!'

The old man looked at him with muddy eyes. Then he slid a half bottle of schnapps across the table to the visitor – Klebs grabbed it before it could tip over.

'And you can find yourself a cigarette!' muttered Persicke, looking round the room. 'There must be something to smoke somewhere here.' And he added in a thick voice, 'But I've not got a light.'

'Don't worry on that score, Persicke!' squeaked Klebs. 'I'll find what I need. You'll have gas in the kitchen, and a gas lighter.'

He behaved as if he and Persicke had known each other for ages. As though they were best buddies. With an air of entitle-ment he scuttled into the kitchen on his bandy legs it looked even worse in there than in the parlour, with smashed plates and overturned furniture – found the gas lighter amid the mess, and lit up.

He had pocketed three opened packs of cigarettes right off. One was drenched in schnapps, but that would dry out. On his way back, Klebs poked his nose into the other two rooms: everything looked wasted and shot to hell. As Klebs had sensed right away, the old man was all alone in the flat. The spy rubbed his hands contentedly and showed his blackish-yellow teeth. There was more to be got here than just some drink and a few ciggies.

Old Persicke was still sitting on the same chair beside the table, just as Klebs had left him. But wily Klebs knew the old man must have been up on his feet in the meantime, because in front of him was a full bottle of schnapps that hadn't been there before.

So he's got more stockpiled here. We'll have to see about that!

Klebs settled into his chair with a contented squeak, blew a cloud of smoke in his host's face, took a pull from the bottle, and asked innocently, 'So, what's on your conscience, Persicke? Come on, old fellow, make a clean breast of it! And remember, clean underpants for the firing squad!'

The old man trembled at those last words. He had missed the context in which they had appeared – he had only caught a reference to being shot.

'No, no!' he muttered anxiously. 'No firing squad, no firing squad. Baldur's coming, Baldur will fix everything.'

The rat disregarded the question of who this Baldur was who would fix everything. 'Well, so long as it's capable of being fixed, Persicke!'

He glanced at the other's face, which, he thought, was staring at him darkly and suspiciously. 'Mind you, once Baldur shows up . . .' he offered in a conciliatory tone.

The old man continued to stare at him in silence. Suddenly, in one of those lucid intervals that long-term drunks have from time to time, and no longer stammering, he said, 'Who are you, anyway? What do you want with me? I don't even know you!'

The rat looked cautiously into the face of the suddenly lucid man. In these intervals, drunks can get quarrelsome and aggressive, and there wasn't much of Klebs (and what there was was cowardly anyway), whereas old Persicke, even in this advanced state of decay, looked like a man who had given his Führer a couple of well-built SS men and a Napola student.

Klebs said mildly, 'I told you already, Herr Persicke. Maybe you missed it. My name is Klebs, and the Party sent me to get some information . . .'

Persicke's fist smashed down on the table. The two bottles teetered; moving quickly, Klebs managed to rescue them.

'How can a bastard like you say I missed something,' screamed Persicke. 'Are you any smarter than me, you skunk? You tell me in my own house, at my own table, that I'm not capable of grasping what you say. You're a skunk, a lousy skunk!'

'No, no, no, Herr Persicke!' burbled the rat soothingly. 'I didn't mean it that way. A little misunderstanding there. Everything in peace and harmony. Easy, easy – old Party hands like us!'

'Where's your membership card? How can you walk in here and not show me your card? You know the Party doesn't allow that!'

But on that point, there was nothing to worry Klebs: the Gestapo had furnished its men with excellent, valid, faultless identification.

'There you are, Herr Persicke, look at it, take your time. All correct. I'm entitled to obtain information, and you're under obligation to help me to the best of your ability!'

The old man stared mistily at the papers brandished in front of him – Klebs was careful not to let them leave his hand. The writing swam in front of his eyes; he jabbed the paper with his finger and asked, 'Is that you?'

'Can't you see that, Herr Persicke? Everyone says it's an excellent likeness!' And, vainly, 'Only I'm supposed to look ten years younger in actual life. I can't say, I'm not vain. I never look in the mirror!'

'Put that shit away!' growled the ex-publican. 'I'm not in the mood to read. Sit down, drink, smoke, but keep quiet. I need to think.'

The rat Klebs did as it was instructed, and kept a watchful eye on the man opposite, who seemed to have disappeared in a cloud of smoke.

Yes, old Persicke, after another long slug from his bottle, seemed abandoned by his clarity once more, drawn irresistibly back into the maelstrom of his inebriation; what he termed 'think' was a helpless anguished searching for something that had slipped his mind long ago. He didn't even know what it was.

He was in a bad way, the old man. First one son had been

sent to Holland, then the other to Poland. Baldur had gone on to a Napola school: the ambitious kid had achieved his first aim, and he was now among the best and brightest of the German nation, a special student of the Führer's! He was studying advanced subjects, such as discipline – not self-discipline, mind you, but the discipline of others, who hadn't done as well as he had.

The father and his wife and daughter had remained behind. He had always been fond of a drink – old Persicke had been his own best customer in the old days behind the bar. Once the boys were gone, and especially once he was away from Baldur's supervision, Persicke had begun to tipple, and from there he had progressed to heavy drinking. His wife hadn't been able to cope; small, timid, and tearful in her male-dominated household, where she had never been more than an unpaid and badly treated skivvy, she hated to think where her husband had got hold of the money to pay for all his drink. On top of that there was her fear of the drunkard's threats and abuse, and so she had taken refuge with relatives, leaving their daughter with her father.

The daughter, a real battleaxe, having been through the BDM – even been an official in the BDM – hadn't had the least inclination to tidy up after the old man and court his ill-treatment for doing so. Through connections, she got a job as a warder in the women's camp at Ravensbrück, and there, with the help of vicious dogs and a riding whip, began a new career, forcing old women who had never done physical labour in their lives to do more than their bodies could cope with.

Thus left alone, the father had swiftly degenerated. He called in sick at his office, no one brought him any food, he lived almost entirely on alcohol. In the early days he had at least gone out to buy bread with his food stamps, but he had lost the stamps or someone had stolen them, and Persicke hadn't had anything to eat for days.

The night before, he had been very ill, he could remember that. He no longer remembered rampaging through the flat, smashing dishes, knocking over cupboards, in his paranoia seeing persecutors everywhere. The Quangels and old Judge Fromm had stood at the door and rung and rung the bell. But he hadn't answered it; he wasn't about to admit his enemies. The people outside had to have been sent there by the Party, come to get the books from him, and there were more than three thousand marks missing (or it might be six, even in his more lucid moments he was unable to be precise about the sum).

The old judge had observed coolly, 'Well, we'll just let him carry on then. I've no interest myself in calling anyone . . .'

His generally friendly, mildly ironic face had looked very severe as he spoke. Then the old gentleman had gone back downstairs.

And Otto Quangel, with his usual profound aversion to being dragged into anything, had said, 'What should we get mixed up in this for? It'll only cause more trouble! You can tell he's drunk, Anna. He'll sober up sometime.'

But Persicke, who had forgotten all about the episode the next day, hadn't sobered up. In the morning he had felt rotten; he was shaking so hard he could hardly raise the bottle to his lips. But the more he managed to drink, the less he shook and the less often he lapsed into his amorphous dread. Yet the dark sense of having forgotten something vital still tormented him.

And now this rat was sitting opposite him, patient, cunning, greedy. The rat was in no hurry: it had spotted its opportunity and was determined to make the most of it. The rat Klebs was in no rush to write its report to Inspector Zott. You could always think of some reason to explain why progress had been unexpectedly slow. But this here was a splendid opportunity, not something to let slip.

And Klebs didn't let it slip, either. Old Persicke sank deeper into drunkenness, and if his words were all babble, even a babbled confidence was worth something.

After an hour Klebs knew everything there was to know about the old man's embezzlement, he knew where the schnapps bottles were, and the cigarettes, and what was left of the money was already in his pocket.

Now the rat has become the old man's best friend. It puts him to bed, and when Persicke yells, Klebs runs over to him and gives him enough schnapps to stop him yelling. In between times, the rat quickly packs a couple of suitcases with valuables. In this way the fine damask underwear of the late Frau Rosenthal once again changes owners, once again not entirely legally.

Then Klebs gives the old man one more hefty drink, picks up the suitcases, and tiptoes out of the flat.

As he opens the door, a tall, bony man with a grim expression comes up to him and says, 'What are you doing in the Persickes' apartment? What are you lugging away with you? You didn't have a suitcase when you walked in here! Come on, spit it out, or do you want to accompany me to the police?'

'Please, step closer,' whistles the rat meekly. 'I'm an old friend and Party comrade of Herr Persicke's. He will affirm it to you. You're the supervisor, aren't you? Herr Supervisor, you must know my friend Herr Persicke is a very sick man . . .'

42

Borkhausen is Rooked a Third Time

The two men sat down in the ravaged parlour; the 'super' is sitting where Klebs had sat and the rat is in Persicke's seat. No, old Persicke hadn't been in condition to give any information, but the serenity with which Klebs moved about the flat, the calm with which he addressed Persicke and gave him drink had sufficed to make the 'super' a little cautious.

Once more Klebs pulled out his worn imitation-leather wallet, which had once been black but was now reddish at the edges. He said, 'If I might show the supervisor my papers? Everything's legal, I have instructions from the Party . . .'

But the other declined to look at the papers, declined a drink, would agree to accept only a cigarette. No, he wasn't going to drink now, he could remember too clearly how Enno had fouled up the foolproof Rosenthal scheme by drinking. He wasn't going to fall for that again. Borkhausen – for it is none other – wonders how to get the better of Klebs. He has seen through him right away – whether he is actually an acquaintance of old Persicke's or not, whether he is here on Party business or not, it makes no difference: the fellow's a thief! The stuff in his suitcases has to be stolen goods – otherwise he wouldn't have got such a shock from the sight of Borkhausen, otherwise he wouldn't be so timid and fussy. No one on a legal errand would grovel so, as Borkhausen knows from personal experience.

'Perhaps a little shot of something now, Superintendent?'

'No!' Borkhausen all but roars back. 'Shut up, I'm trying to think . . .'

The rat shrinks back and doesn't speak any more.

Borkhausen has had a bad year. Yes, he missed out on the two thousand marks Frau Haberle had sent to Munich. In response to his request to have the money forwarded to him in Berlin, the post office had written back that the Gestapo had laid claim to the money as having been dishonestly come by; if he wanted to, he could take it up with them. Of course, Borkhausen had done no such thing. He wanted no more to do with that double-crossing Escherich, and Escherich for his part seemed to have had no more use for Borkhausen.

So that was a bust. But what was far worse was that Kuno-Dieter had failed to come home. At first, Borkhausen had thought, Ooh, just you wait! Once you get home! Had fantasized about various scenes of chastisement and rudely dismissed Otti's questions about where her precious darling might have got to.

But then, as week followed week, the situation without Kuno-Dieter had grown increasingly unbearable. Otti turned into a real snake, and made his life a misery. In the end he didn't care either way, let the bastard stay away for good if he liked – one less mouth to feed! But Otti was beside herself. It was as though she couldn't live for one more day without her precious darling, and yet when he was around, she had never stinted with beatings and scoldings.

Finally, Otti had gone completely nuts and had gone to the police and accused her own husband of murdering his son. The police didn't stand on ceremony with characters like Borkhausen. He didn't have a reputation unless it was a bad one, and they remanded him, pending a trial.

They kept him there for eleven weeks. While there, he had to pick oakum and sew his share of mailbags, otherwise they would have kept back his meals, which were pretty sparse as it was. Worst of all were the nights, when there were Allied bombing raids. Borkhausen had a healthy fear of bombing raids. Once he had seen a woman burning on Schönhauser Allee. She had been hit by a phosphorous bomb – he would never forget that as long as he lived.

So he was afraid of planes, and now they droned ever nearer, and the whole sky was full of their roar, and the first explosions were heard, and his cell wall was reddened by the flickering of fires near and far . . . no, they didn't allow prisoners to leave their cells, where they were securely held, those maggot wardens!

On such nights, the whole of Moabit prison grew hysterical, the prisoners clutched the bars of their cells and screamed – my God, how they screamed! And Borkhausen with them! He had wailed like a wild beast, he had buried his head in his mattress, and then he had battered his head against the cell door until he collapsed senseless on the floor . . . it was a sort of self-administered anaesthetic that helped him get through those nights.

When the eleven weeks were up and he was sent home, he was not in a very good frame of mind. Of course they hadn't been able to prove anything against him – how could they? But he could have been spared those weeks if Otti hadn't been such a bitch! And now he treated her like a bitch too, for living it up in his apartment (the rent for which she regularly paid) with her friends while he had picked oakum and gone half crazy from fear.

From that time on, blows were the regular currency chez the Borkhausens. At the least provocation, the man let rip. Whatever he had in his hand he flung at her, the bloody bitch who had brought him such misfortune.

And Otti fought back. Never was there anything for him to eat, never any money, never any smokes. Whenever he laid a finger on her, she would scream so loud that all the neighbours came running, and all of them sided with her against Borkhausen, even though they knew she was nothing better than a common whore. And then one day, after he had ripped fistfuls of hair from her scalp, she did the meanest thing of all: she disappeared for good, leaving him with the four remaining brats, none of whom he was at all sure he had fathered. Goddamnit, Borkhausen had had to go to work, regular work, otherwise they would have all starved, and ten-year-old Paula took over the household.

A bad year, it was a fucking rotten year! And he was still consumed with acid hatred of the Persickes, with whom he couldn't and didn't dare get even, oh, his helpless rage and envy when it became known in the house that Baldur had got into a Napola school, and finally the small, feeble spark of hope when he saw how old Persicke's drinking – maybe, maybe after all . . .

And now he was sitting in the Persickes' flat, and there on

the table under the window was the radio that Baldur had pinched from the old Rosenthal woman. Borkhausen was almost there; all he had to do now was discreetly remove the spy . . .

Borkhausen's eyes light up when he imagines Baldur's fury on seeing him seated at the table in his flat. Cunning devil, Baldur, but not cunning enough. Sometimes patience is worth more than cunning. And suddenly Borkhausen remembers what Baldur planned to do with him and Enno Kluge, that time they broke into the Rosenthal apartment – or rather, it wasn't even a break-in; they'd been set up . . . Borkhausen thrusts out his lower lip and looks thoughtfully at this other guy, who has become very fidgety during their long silence, and then he says: 'All right, why don't you just show me what you've got in those suitcases!'

'Hold on there,' the rat tries to resist, 'that's a bit much, isn't it? If my friend Herr Persicke has given me permission – that exceeds your rights as superintendent . . .'

'Cut the crap!' says Borkhausen. 'Either you show me what's in the suitcases, or else you and I are going to the police together.'

'I don't have to,' squeaks the rat, 'But I'll show you because I want to. The police always make trouble, and now that my Party comrade Persicke has become so ill, it might take days before he can confirm my statements.'

'Get on with it! Open up!' says Borkhausen suddenly furious, and he takes a swig from the bottle, too.

The rat Klebs looks at him, and suddenly a wicked smile comes over the spy's face. 'Get on with it! Open up!' With that cry, Borkhausen has betrayed his avarice. He has also betrayed the fact that he's not the super, and even if he is, then he's a super who has dishonest intentions.

'Well, chum?' says the rat suddenly in quite another tone of voice. 'What about fifty-fifty?'

A punch floors him. To be on the safe side, Borkhausen clouts him two or three times with a chair leg. There, that's the last of him for an hour or so!

And then Borkhausen starts unpacking and repacking. Once

again, old Frau Rosenthal's linens change owners. Borkhausen works swiftly and calmly. This time no one is going to come between him and success. He'd sooner kill them all, even if it means risking his own head. He won't be fooled again.

And then, a quarter of an hour later, there was only a brief scuffle with the two constables as Borkhausen left the apartment. A bit of tugging and stamping, and he was tied and cuffed.

'There!' says Judge Fromm. 'And that, I think, should spell the end of your time in this house, Herr Borkhausen. I won't forget to hand your children over to the welfare authorities. Though what happens to them probably won't interest you very much. Now, gentlemen, let's take a look inside. I do hope, Herr Borkhausen, you haven't been too rough with the little fellow who walked up the stairs before you. And then we should find Herr Persicke as well, Constable. Last night, I'm afraid, he suffered an attack of delirium tremens.'

43

Interlude: An Idyll in the Country

The ex-postie Eva Kluge is working in the potato fields, just as she had always dreamed of doing. It's a fine day in early summer, and already a little hot to be working; the sky is radiant and blue and there's almost no wind, especially in the sheltered corner of the field up against the forest. As she hoes, Eva takes off one garment after another; now she's only in a skirt and blouse. Like her face and arms, her strong, bare legs are golden brown.

Her hoe encounters orach, charlock, thistles, couch-grass – progress is slow; the field is choked with weeds. Often, too, the hoe strikes a stone, then it sings with a silvery clang – she likes the sound. Now, at the edge of the forest, Eva has found a clump of red willow herb – it's a damp little hollow, where the potatoes are small and mouldy but the willow-herb thrives. She had intended to eat her breakfast now – going by the sun, it's about the right time – but she wants to see off the willow herb before she allows herself to take a break. She hacks away vigorously, her lips pressed shut. She's learned to hate weeds, those useless, destructive things, and she chops away at them implacably.

Even if her mouth is tight shut, her eyes are clear and calm. Her expression no longer has that taut, concerned look it had two years earlier, in Berlin. She has grown calmer, she has survived. She knows that little Enno is dead, for her old neighbour Frau Gesch wrote to tell her so. She knows she has lost both her sons – Max fell in Russia, and she had already given up on Karlemann. She is just short of forty-five years old, and has a good bit of life still ahead of her, and she is not despairing; she is working. She doesn't just want to get through the remaining years, she wants to do something with them.

Also, she has something she looks forward to every day: her evening get-together with the village's substitute teacher. The regular teacher, Schwoch, is a rampant Nazi, a cowardly little yapper and denouncer, who must have declared a hundred times with tears in his eyes how much he regrets not being able to serve at the Front, but instead must follow the Führer's orders and accept his rural posting. Well, Schwoch finally was drafted into the Wehrmacht after all, in spite of his innumerable medical certificates. That was six months ago. But the war enthusiast has still not seen any action: Schwoch is currently serving in a secretarial capacity in a paymaster's office. Frau Schwoch regularly travels to her husband to supply him with ham and bacon, but her husband must have shared these tidbits with others: this had borne fruit, Frau Schwoch reported after her last bacon mercy mission, for her beloved Walter had been promoted to corporal. Corporal – when according to orders issued by the Führer in person only frontline troops were eligible for promotion. But in the case of fervent Party members with ham and bacon to disburse, exemptions clearly had to be made.

Well, Eva Kluge doesn't care about any of that. She knows all about it, has known ever since she quit the Party herself. Yes, she went back to Berlin; once she had recovered her composure, she returned to Berlin and confronted the Party court and the post office. Those were not pleasant days, anything but. They shouted at her, threatened her, and once, during her five-day arrest, beat her. She only just avoided being sentenced to concentration camp – but in the end they had let her go. Enemy of the state – that designation was punishment enough.

Then Eva Kluge had wound up her household. She had to sell a lot of her things – she had only been approved for one room in the village, but she was living alone now. And she wasn't working exclusively for her brother-in-law, who would have given her only board, and no money at all; she helped all the farmers. She worked in the fields and with the animals, but she was also in demand as nurse, seamstress, gardener, and sheep-shearer. She had deft hands, and she never felt that she was learning something new; it was more like the memory of some task she had known forever but just hadn't practised for a long time. Farmwork was somehow in her blood.

But this whole peaceful little existence she had established for herself after so much loss and collapse had only acquired focus and pleasure through the substitute teacher, Kienschaper. Kienschaper was a tall, slightly stooped man in his early fifties, who had white flapping hair and a deeply tanned face with youthfully shining blue eyes. The way he tamed the children of the village with those smiling blue eyes and led them away from the drills and rote memorizations of his predecessor into more human and humanist terrain, the way he walked through the farm orchards with his pruning shears, cutting away deadwood and wild shoots from neglected trees, cutting out cankers and applying carbolic to the wounds – in that same way he had healed Eva's wounds, soothed her bitterness, and brought her peace.

Not that he talked a lot – Kienschaper wasn't a great talker. But when he took her to his apiary and told her about the life of bees, which were creatures he loved with a passion, when he walked with her through the fields in the evening and showed her how untidily a certain field was sown and with how little effort it could be made far more productive, when Kienschaper helped a cow to calve or, unasked, righted a toppled fence, when he sat at the organ and improvised for the two of them, when everywhere he went looked tidy and at peace for his having been there – then that did more than any words could do for Eva's contentment. It was a life gently inclined toward its end, peaceful and bringing peace in a time full of hatred, blood, and tears.

Naturally, Frau Schwoch, an even more fervent Nazi than her warrior husband, took an instant dislike to Kienschaper, and did all her malicious brain could think of to hurt him. She had to provide bread and board for her husband's stand-in, but she did it with such precise calculation that Kienschaper never got breakfast before classes began, and his supper was always charred, and his room was never cleaned.

But she was powerless in the face of his unflappable cheerfulness. She might spit and rant and speak ill of him, press her ear to the classroom door and then go to the school governors to denounce him – he always spoke to her as though to a badly brought-up child that one day would come to see its naughtiness by itself. And in the end Kienschaper went to Eva Kluge for his meals, moved into the village, and the fat and furious Frau Schwoch was forced to conduct her campaign against him at a distance.

When the subject of marriage had first come up between Eva Kluge and the white-haired teacher was something neither of them quite knew. Perhaps they had never spoken about it. It had just presented itself, all by itself. They were in no hurry, either – one day, some day, it would happen. Two ageing people, unwilling to face the evening of their lives in solitude. No, no more children – Eva shuddered at the prospect. But friendship, love, intimacy, and above all, trust. She, who in her first marriage had never been able to trust, she, who had always had to take the lead, she now – trustingly – permitted herself to be led for the last stretch of her life. All was darkness, and she had been full of fear and apprehension, and then the sun had peeped through the clouds once more.

The red willow-herb lies piled up on the ground; it's been defeated for now. Yes, it will grow back, that's what weeds do, and really you should pick it up out of the loosened ground after ploughing, because each bit of individual root left underground will put forth new shoots. But Eva knows the place now; she'll keep an eye on it and she'll keep coming back until the willow-herb is gone for good.

She can stop for breakfast now; it's time, and her stomach is ready, too. But when she looks across to her bread and the coffee thermos she left on the sheltering edge of the forest, she can see she won't be having breakfast today, and starts shushing her stomach. Because there is someone there already, a boy of about fourteen, incredibly filthy and wild-looking, and he is gobbling down her bread as if he was close to starving.

The boy is so preoccupied with filling his belly that he hasn't even noticed that the hoe has stopped its work in the field. He gives a start when the woman draws up in front of him, and he stares at her with big blue eyes under a thatch of matted blond hair. Even though he's been caught red-handed and he can't run away, the boy doesn't look fearful or guilty; there is something challenging, almost taunting in his eye.

In the last few months in the village, Frau Kluge has got a little used to these children: the bombing raids on Berlin had intensified, and the populace was called upon to send their children out into the countryside. The provinces are inundated with these Berlin kids. It's a curious thing; some of these kids can't adjust to the quiet of rural life. Here they have peace and quiet, better food, undisturbed nights, but they can't stand it, they have to go back into the metropolis. And so they set off: barefoot, begging for scraps of food, with no money, hounded by rural constables, they make their way resolutely back into the city that almost every night is ablaze. Picked up and returned to their rural communities, they give themselves a little time to put some flesh on their bones, and then run away back home again.

This present specimen with the challenging eye who was eating Eva's breakfast had probably been on the road for quite some time. She couldn't remember ever having seen a figure quite as filthy and ragged as this. There were straws in his hair, and she felt she could have planted carrots in his ears.

'Well, is it good?' asked Frau Kluge.

'Sure!' he said, and the one word was enough to confirm his Berlin origins.

He looked at her. 'Are you going to beat me?' he asked.

'No,' she said. 'Go on eating. I can miss breakfast once in a while, and you're really hungry.'

'Sure!' he said. And then: 'Are you going to let me go?'

'I might,' she replied. 'But maybe you'll not mind if I wash you first, and sort out your clothes a little bit. Maybe I might find a decent pair of pants for you.'

'Oh, never mind that!' he said, dismissively. 'I'll only sell them off when I'm desperate. You'd be surprised at all I've sold off in the past year on the road! At least fifteen pairs of pants! And ten pairs of shoes!'

He looked at her proudly.

'Why are you telling me that?' she asked. 'It would have been more in your interest to take the pants and not say anything.'

'I don't know,' he said. 'Maybe because you didn't bawl me out for sneaking your breakfast. I don't like being bawled out.'

'So you've been on the road for twelve months?'

'That was a stretch. I had a job in the winter. Working for a publican in some burg. I fed the pigs and washed the beer glasses, I did all sorts. It wasn't a bad time,' he said reflectively. 'Funny guy, the publican. Always drunk, but he was on the level, talking to me as if I was no different to him, same age and all. That's where I learned to drink and smoke. D'you like schnapps yourself?'

For now Frau Kluge passed over the question whether drinking schnapps was advisable for fourteen-year-olds.

'But you ran away from there too? Are you going back to Berlin?'

'Nah,' said the boy. 'I'm not going back to my folks any more. They're too common for me.'

'But your parents will be worried about you – they don't even know where you are!'

'Them worry! They're pleased to be rid of me!'

'What does your father do?'

'Him? He's a bit of everything: a spy and a snoop, and he does a bit of stealing on the side. If he finds anything worth stealing. Only, he's a bit of a fool, and he doesn't often find anything.'

'I see,' said Frau Kluge, and her voice sounded a little less gentle after these revelations. 'And what does your mother say?'

'My mother? What would she ever say? She's just a hoor!'

Whap! In spite of her guarantees, he had got his slap.

'You should be ashamed to talk about your mother like that! Shame on you!'

The boy, not really changing his expression, rubbed his cheek.

'I felt that,' he said. 'I don't want any more like that, thank you very much.'

'You shouldn't talk about your mother like that! Do you understand?' she asked angrily.

'Why not?' he asked, and leaned back. He blinked contentedly at his hostess, perfectly replete now. 'Why wouldn't I! When that's what she is. She says so herself. "If I didn't go out on the

game," she often used to say, "then you'd all starve!" There's
five of us, see, all with different fathers. Mine is supposed to
have an estate in Pomerania. I was going to look him up. He
must be a queer fish – he's called Kuno-Dieter. There can't be
that many with such a silly name, so I'm sure I'll catch up with
him in the end . . .'

'Kuno-Dieter,' said Frau Kluge. 'So your name is Kuno-Dieter
as well?'

'Just Kuno will do; you can shove the Dieter!'

'All right then, Kuno, where were you evacuated to? What's
the name of the village where you got off the train?'

'I'm not an evacuee! I just ran away!'

He was lying on his side now, his dirty cheek propped on an
equally dirty fist. He blinked at her sleepily, all set for a little
gossip. 'I'll tell you what happened. My so-called father, it was
over a year ago now, he cheated me of fifty marks, and on top
of that he gave me a whipping. So I get together a few friends,
which is to say they weren't really friends, just kids, you know,
and we cornered him and gave him a bit of a hiding. That was
good for him; it taught him that it's not always the big ones that
can do the little ones! And then we stole the money out of his
pocket, too. I don't remember how much it was, the big kids
divvied it up among themselves. All I got was a twenty, and then
they said to me, You'd better scram now, your old man will
murder you or stick you in a Borstal. Get out in the countryside
and lay low with the farmers. And so I got out in the country
and hid out with the farmers. And I've led a pretty nice life ever
since, I'll say!'

He stopped and looked at her.

She looked at him silently. She was thinking of Karlemann.
This boy was three years younger than Karlemann and heading
the same way – no love, no belief, no ambition, only thinking
of himself.

She asked, 'And what do you think's going to become of you,
Kuno?' And she added, 'Are you planning to join the SA one day,
or the SS?'

And he, stretched out: 'Those guys? Not likely! They're even worse than my old man! Just shouting and barking orders all the time! No, thanks all the same, that's not where I'm headed.'

'But maybe you'd enjoy ordering other people around?'

'Why would I? No, I'm not like that. You know – what's your name?'

'Eva – Eva Kluge.'

'You know, Eva, what I'd really enjoy would be cars. I'd like to know everything there is to know about cars, how the engine runs, and what the carburettor does and the ignition – no, not what it does, I sort of half know that already, but why . . . I'd like to know all that, except I don't think I have the brains. When I was little they beat me about the head so much that I think it's gone soft. I can't even write properly!'

'But you don't look as stupid as all that! I'm sure you can pick it up, the writing, and later on the engines.'

'You mean learn it? Like at school? Naah, I'm too old for that. I've had a couple of girlfriends already.'

She shuddered. But she came back pluckily, 'Do you think one of your engineers or technicians has ever finished learning? They have to keep on learning, at the university or in evening classes.'

'I know! I know all that! That's up on the billboards. Evening courses for advanced electrotechnicians' – suddenly his German was rather fluent – 'the foundations of electronics.'

'Well then!' exclaimed Eva. 'And you think you're too old for that stuff! You don't want to go to school any more? Do you want to be a bum all your life, washing dishes and chopping wood to get through the winter? That's a nice life, and I wish you joy of it!'

He had opened his eyes wide, and looked at her questioningly, but also suspiciously.

'Are you saying I should go back to my people, and go to school in Berlin? Or do you want to hand me over to welfare?'

'Neither one. I want you to stay with me. And then I want to teach you myself, with a friend of mine.'

He remained suspicious. 'And what do you get for doing that?

I'd cost you a packet, what with food and clothes and books and everything.'

'I don't know whether you'll understand, Kuno. I used to have a husband and two sons, but I lost them all. I have a boyfriend now, but otherwise I'm all alone.'

'You can still have a baby!'

She blushed; the middle-aged woman blushed under the eye of the fourteen year-old boy.

'No, I can't have any more babies,' she said firmly. 'But it would make me happy if you made something of yourself, a car mechanic or an airplane designer or something. It would make me happy if I was able to make something of a boy like you.'

'I suppose you think I'm a poor bastard.'

'You know you've not got much going for you at the moment, Kuno!'

'You're right. Yeah, you've got a point, I guess.'

'And that's okay with you?'

'Well, not really, but . . .'

'But what? Wouldn't you want to come and live with me?'

'Sure I would, but . . .'

'What do you mean, *but?*'

'I think you'd have enough of me pretty quickly, and I don't want to be sent away – I'd rather leave by myself.'

'You can leave whenever you want, I'm not going to stop you.'

'Is that a promise?'

'Yes, that's a promise, Kuno. You're free to come and go as you please.'

'But, if I'm with you, then I'll have to be properly registered, and then my folks will find out where I am. They wouldn't let me stay with you another day.'

'If your home is the way you say it is, no one is going to make you go back. Maybe I'll be made your official guardian, and then you'll be my boy . . .'

For a moment they looked at one another. She thought she could make out a distant gleam in that indifferent blue gaze.

But then he said – dropping his head on his arm, and shutting his eyes again – 'All right then. I'm going to sleep now. You go back to your 'taters.'

'But, Kuno,' she cried. 'You haven't answered my question!'

'Must I?' he said sleepily. 'You can't make me.'

She looked down at him for a while musingly. Then, with a faint smile on her lips, she went back to her work.

She hoed, but she was hoeing mechanically now. Twice she caught herself about to decapitate a potato. Watch what you're doing, Eva! she said crossly to herself.

But it didn't help much. She thought maybe it was for the best if her scheme didn't come to anything. How much labour and love she had invested in Karlemann, who had been an unspoiled child – and what had happened to that? And now she wanted to take a fourteen-year-old layabout, who had a thoroughly jaundiced view of life and mankind, and transform him? Who did she think she was? Anyway, Kienschaper would never agree to it . . .

She looked round at the sleeping boy. But the sleeping boy was gone, and all that was left were her things in the shade, by the edge of the forest.

Well, have it your own way, she thought. He's made the decision for me. Run off! Good riddance!

And she went back to chopping angrily at the weeds.

Just a moment later she caught sight of Kuno-Dieter at the other end of the row, busily uprooting weeds and stacking them in piles along the edge of the field. She clambered over the furrows to him.

'Woken up already?' she asked.

'Couldn't sleep,' he said. 'I'm all confused because of you. I need to think!'

'Then think! But don't think you have to work for my sake!'

'For your sake!' It was impossible to describe the contempt bundled into those words. 'I'm pulling out weeds because it helps me think, and because I happen to enjoy it. Honestly! On your account! You mean in return for the sandwiches? Are you kidding!'

Once again, Frau Kluge went back to her work with a gentle smile playing about her lips. Whatever he might say, and even if he didn't know it himself, he was doing it for her. Now she no longer doubted that he would leave with her at noon, and from that moment on, all the urgent, warning voices in her head lost their influence.

She stopped work a little earlier than usual. She went back over to the boy and said, 'Okay, I'm going back for lunch now. If you want, you can come with me, Kuno.'

He pulled out a couple more weeds and then looked at the patch he had cleared. 'I've done quite a bit,' he said with satisfaction. 'Of course I've only done the worst of the weeds, you'll need to go after the little ones with the hoe, but I figure it'll be easier for you.'

'That's right,' she said. 'You take out the big weeds, I'm sure I can manage the little ones.'

He gave her another sidelong look, and she noticed that those blue eyes could also take on a roguish expression.

'Are you implying something?' he inquired.

'Whatever you think,' she said. 'Not necessarily.'

'Well, huh!'

On the way back, she stopped by a swiftly flowing little stream.

'You know, Kuno, I don't want to take you back into the village looking the way you do,' she said.

At once a furrow appeared in his brow, and he asked suspiciously, 'I expect you're ashamed to be seen with me?'

'Of course, if you want, you can come just as you are,' she said. 'But if you plan on living in the village for any length of time, you could be here five years and always be spic and span, but the farmers won't ever forget what you looked like when they first clapped eyes on you. Like a pig, they'll say in ten years' time. Like a dosser.'

'You're right,' he said. 'That's just what they're like. Well, you hurry off and get some stuff, and I'll start scrubbing myself.'

'I'll bring soap and a brush,' she called over her shoulder, and hastened off into the village.

Later that day, much later – in the evening, by which time they had had their first meal together, Eva, the white-haired Kienschaper and an almost unrecognizable Kuno-Dieter – later, then, Eva said, 'Tonight you'll sleep in the hayloft, Kuno. Starting tomorrow I'm going to have the little spare bedroom, they just need to clear the stuff out of it so you can move in. I'll make it nice for you. I've got a bed and a dresser.'

Kuno merely looked at her. 'You're telling me it's time to push off,' he said. 'The two of youse want to be alone together. All right then! But I'm not going to bed yet, Eva, I'm not a baby, you know. I'm going to have a look around the village first.'

'But don't let it get too late, Kuno! And don't smoke in the hayloft, either!'

'Bah! I'd never do that! I'd be the first to go. Okay then. Have fun, you young people, as the old man said . . . And he proceeded to put the old lady in the family way.'

And exit Kuno-Dieter.

Eva Kluge smiled a little worriedly. 'I don't know if I've done the right thing in inviting that scamp into our little family, Kienschaper! He's a bit of a caution!'

Kienschaper laughed. 'But Evi,' he said, 'surely you can see he's only trying to show off! He's trying to make an impression, and he doesn't really care if it's a good or a bad one! And because he's sensed you're a little prudish . . .'

'I'm not prudish!' she cried. 'But if a fourteen-year-old boy tells me he's already bedded a couple of women . . .'

' . . . Well, then as I say, you're just a bit prudish. And as far as him bedding those women, he certainly did nothing of the sort – at the very worst, they will have bedded him! That's nothing. I'll spare you tales of what the children in this simple, devout village get up to – compared to them, your Kuno-Dieter's a saint!'

'But the children don't go and talk about it!'

'That's because they feel guilty. He doesn't; to him, it's all perfectly natural, because it's all he's ever known. He'll settle down. There's a core of good in the boy; in six months' time, I imagine he'll blush when he remembers the stuff he said in his first few days here. He'll drop it, just like he'll drop his Berlin argot. Did you notice he's actually capable of speaking perfectly good German when he wants to? Only he doesn't want to.'

'I feel bad, especially toward you, Kienschaper.'

'You mustn't, Evi. I get a kick out of the boy, and there's one thing I can promise you: whatever he turns out like, he'll never be a common-or-garden Nazi. He might be an eccentric, but never a Nazi.'

'Oh, pray to God!' said Eva. 'That's all I want.'

And she had a faint sense that by rescuing Kuno-Dieter, she was in some way beginning to atone for the atrocities committed by Karlemann.

44

The Fall of Inspector Zott

The letter from the precinct supervisor was correctly addressed to Inspector Zott at Gestapo Headquarters, Berlin. But that didn't result in the letter landing in Zott's in-tray. Instead, it was his superior, SS Obergruppenführer Prall, who was clutching it as he walked into Zott's office.

'What's this all about, Inspector?' asked Prall. 'Here's another one of your Hobgoblin's cards, and this note pinned to it: "Prisoners released in accordance with phoned instructions from the Gestapo, Inspector Zott." What prisoners might those be? Why has none of this reached my ears?'

The inspector looked up over the rims of his spectacles at his superior. 'Oh, yes! I remember. It was yesterday, or maybe the day before. I've got it, it was on Sunday. Sunday evening. Sometime between six and seven, I would say, Obergruppenführer.'

And he looked up at the Obergruppenführer, proud of his excellent memory.

'And what precisely happened on Sunday between six and seven o'clock? What prisoners are you talking about? And why were they let go? And why has none of it been reported to me? It's profoundly comforting to hear that you know what it's about, but I'd like to know too, Zott!'

That 'Zott', spat out without any form of title, sounded like the opening salvo in a barrage.

'But it's a perfectly trivial matter!' The inspector made calming motions with his parchment yellow hands. 'There was some nonsense at the station. The police, bless them, pulled in a married couple as possible writers or distributors of the postcards, complete nonsense of course – we know the man lives by himself! Ah yes, and there was another thing, too: the man was a carpenter, when we know the Hobgoblin has something to do with the trams!'

'Are you trying to tell me, sir,' said the barely restrained Ober-gruppenführer (that 'sir' was the second, and far more dangerous, shot in this battle), 'are you trying to tell me that you authorized the release of these people without even having *seen* them, without even having *questioned* them, just because there were two of them rather than one, and because the man had a carpenter's ID on him? Sir!'

'Obergruppenführer,' replied Inspector Zott as he got to his feet, 'in our investigations, we detectives follow a specific plan and don't deviate from it. I am looking for a man who lives alone and works in public transport, not a married man who is a carpenter. I'm simply not interested in the latter. I wouldn't go a step out of my way for him.'

'As if a carpenter couldn't work for public transport – for instance, repairing carriages!' Prall screamed back at him. 'How stupid can you get!'

At first, Zott thought he should be offended, but his superior's apt remark gave him pause. 'You're right,' he said glumly, 'that didn't occur to me.' He collected himself. 'But I am still looking for a man living on his own,' he said again. 'And this man has a wife.'

'Have you any idea what vile bitches women can be!' growled Prall. But he had something else in his armoury: 'And did it not occur to you, *Inspector* Zott,' (this was the third and most lethal shot), 'that this card was dropped on a Sunday afternoon, near Nollendorfplatz! Did that minor or meaningless circumstance escape your schooled detective's attention?'

This time Inspector Zott was really stunned, his little goatee bobbed up and down, and it was as though a veil had been drawn over his dark, sharp eyes.

'I'm embarrassed, Obergruppenführer! How could something like this have happened to me? I got ahead of myself. I was thinking about tram stations; I was so proud of my discovery. Too proud . . .'

The Obergruppenführer looked angrily at the little man, who was confessing his shortcomings, not cringingly but with evident disappointment.

'It was a mistake on my part,' the inspector proceeded, 'to have taken over this inquiry in the first place. I am good for desk work, not a criminal investigation. Escherich is ten times better than I am. And now I've also had the misfortune that one of the men I asked to check out a house in the area, a certain Klebs, has beeñ arrested. He is alleged to have been involved in theft, the robbing of a dipsomaniac. He has been badly beaten up. A very unpleasant story altogether. The man will not keep quiet in court, he will say that we sent him . . .'

Obergruppenführer Prall trembled with rage, but Inspector Zott's dignity and utter lack of regard for his own fate held him in check.

'Do you have any views on how we should proceed in this matter, sir?' he asked coldly.

'I beg you, Obergruppenführer,' Zott beseeched him with raised hands, 'release me! Release me from this investigation, which is completely over my head! Get Escherich back out of the basement, he will do better than me . . .'

'I do hope,' Prall said, and it was as though he hadn't listened to a word of what Zott had just said, 'I do hope you've at least kept a record of the name and address of the two detainees?'

'I didn't! I didn't! I behaved with culpable negligence. I was blinded by my theory. But I will call the station, they will find the addresses, and we will see . . .'

'All right, call them!'

The conversation was very short. The inspector told the Obergruppenführer, 'No note was kept of the names and addresses.' And, in response to a furious gesture from his superior: 'I am to blame, only I! After calling me, they had no option but to view the incident as closed. I am completely to blame for there being nothing in writing!'

'So we have no lead?'

'No lead!'

'And what do you think about your conduct?'

'I ask that Inspector Escherich be brought up from the basement, and that I be confined in his place!'

Obergruppenführer Prall looked at the little man in silence.

Then, shaking with rage, he said, 'Do you know I'll have you put away in a concentration camp? You dare make such a suggestion to me, to my face, without wailing and shaking with fear? It's Communists and Bolsheviks that are made of the sort of stuff you're made of! You confess your shortcomings, but you still appear to be proud of them!'

'I'm not proud of my shortcomings. But I am ready to take the consequences for them. I hope I will do it without wailing and trembling!'

Obergruppenführer Prall sneered contemptuously at those words. He had seen too many illusions of dignity collapse under the punches and kicks of SS men. But he had also seen something in the eye of some victims, a look of cool, almost mocking superiority even as they were being tortured. And his memory of that look caused him not to scream and lash out, but merely to say, 'I want you to stay here at my disposal. I must first make a report.'

Inspector Zott inclined his head in agreement, and Obergruppenführer Prall walked out.

45

Inspector Escherich is Free Again

Inspector Escherich is back. The man who was written off as dead or good as dead has returned to life from the basements of the Gestapo. A little rumpled, a little in need of repair, but still, he is back at his desk, and his colleagues hasten to give him their sympathy. They had always gone on believing in him. They had been willing to do everything they could for him. 'Only, you know, when the top brass drops someone in it, there's nothing the likes of us can do about it. You just get your fingers burned. Well, you know all that anyway, Escherich, you understand.'

Escherich assures them he understands everything. He twists his mouth into a grin, but the grin looks a little sad, presumably because Escherich has not yet got the hang of grinning with a few teeth missing.

There were only two people who impressed him when he returned to work. One was Inspector Zott.

'Colleague Escherich,' he had said, 'I am not being sent down to the basement in your place, even though I deserve it ten times more than you ever did. Not just because of the mistakes I made, but because I behaved like a bastard to you. My only excuse is that I did really believe you'd done bad work . . .'

'Don't mention it,' Escherich had replied with his gap-toothed smile. 'None of us have come out of the Hobgoblin case with reputations enhanced, not you, not me, none of us. It's funny, but I'm quite excited to meet this man who has created such a lot of misfortune for his fellow men with these postcards. He must be a really odd bird . . .'

He looked thoughtfully at the inspector.

Zott extended his parchment-coloured hand. 'Please don't think too badly of me, Colleague Escherich,' he said quietly. 'And one other thing: I've got the idea that the culprit is something to do with the tram service. You'll find it written up in the files. Please don't lose sight of that in the course of your own investigations. It would make me very happy if at least in that one point my ideas proved to be correct! Just bear it in mind!'

And with those words Inspector Zott disappeared up to his own cubbyhole, there to devote himself entirely to his own theories.

The second, of course, was Obergruppenführer Prall. 'Has Escherich,' he said with raised voice, 'Inspector Escherich! How are you feeling?'

'Perfectly well!' replied the inspector. He was standing behind his desk, his thumbs pressed against his trouser seams, a drill he had picked up down in the cells. However much he tried not to, the inspector was trembling. He looked alertly at his superior, toward whom he felt nothing but fear, insensate fear that Prall might at any moment send him down to the basement again.

'If you feel perfectly well, Escherich,' Prall went on, perfectly aware of the effect his words were having, 'then you'll surely be able to work. Or not?'

'I am able to work, Obergruppenführer, sir!'

'And if you can work, Escherich, then you can catch the Hobgoblin? You can do that, can't you?'

'Yes, sir, I can!'

'In double-quick time, Escherich!'

'In double-quick time, Obergruppenführer, sir!'

'You see, Escherich,' drawled Obergruppenführer Prall, all the while gorging himself on his subordinate's obvious fear, 'you see what good a little spell in the basement does! That's how devoted I am to my men! You no longer feel terribly superior to me, Escherich?'

'No, Obergruppenführer, certainly not. At your orders, Obergruppenführer, sir!'

'You're no longer of the view that you're the cleverest little bastard in the entire Gestapo, and that nothing anyone else does is worth shit – you don't think that any more, do you, Escherich?'

'At your command, sir, Obergruppenführer, no, I don't think that any more.'

'Now, Escherich,' the Obergruppenführer went on, giving the flinching Escherich a playful but painful punch on the nose, 'whenever you next feel incredibly clever, or you undertake private initiatives, or you think that Obergruppenführer Prall is as thick as pigshit, well, just let me know in time. Then, before things get too bad, I'll put you down for another little rest cure. All right?'

Inspector Escherich stared helplessly at his superior. He was shaking so hard a blind man would have heard it.

'Well, Escherich, will you tell me in time, whenever you next feel incredibly clever?'

'At your orders, Obergruppenführer, sir!'

'Or if you're not getting on too well with the work, so that I can give you a little giddyap?'

'At your orders, Obergruppenführer, sir!'

'I think we understand each other, Escherich!'

The master suddenly and most unexpectedly put out his hand to the sufficiently humiliated man. 'Escherich, I'm glad to see you back at work. I hope for excellent collaboration. Where are you going to begin?'

'I'm going to get a detailed description of the man from the supervisor at the Nollendorfplatz station. It's time we got one! And maybe the officer who questioned the two suspects still has a sense of their names. Then I'll carry on with Zott's house-to-house inquiries . . .'

'All right, all right. That's a start. I want you to report to me every day . . .'

'At your orders, Obergruppenführer, sir!'

And that was the second conversation that made an impression on Inspector Escherich upon the resumption of his official duties. After a while, he bore no more visible traces of his experience; his teeth were fixed. His colleagues even found that Escherich had become a lot nicer. He seemed to have lost his air of superiority and condescension. There was no one he could feel superior to now.

Inspector Escherich works, makes inquiries, questions witnesses, collates descriptions, reads through files, makes telephone calls – Escherich is working much the way he always had. But even if no one notices anything different about him, and even if the man himself lives in hope of one day being able to face Prall, his superior, without shaking, Escherich knows he will never be his old self again. He is just a sort of robot now; what he does is routine. Along with his feeling of superiority, he has lost his pleasure in work – his old conceit was what fertilized, so to speak, the fruit the man bore.

Escherich once felt very secure. He once thought nothing could happen to him. He worked on the assumption that he was completely different from everyone else. And Escherich has had to give up these little self-deceptions. It happened basically in the few seconds after SS man Dobat smashed him in the face and he became acquainted with fear. In the space of a very few days, Escherich became so thoroughly acquainted with fear that now there is no chance of him forgetting it for as long as he lives. He knows it doesn't matter how he looks, what he does, what honours and praise he receives – he knows he is nothing. A single punch can turn him into a wailing, gibbering, trembling wretch, not much better than the stinking coward of a pickpocket who shared his cell for a few days and whose hurriedly rattled off last prayers are still ringing in his ears. Little better than that. No, no better at all!

There's one thing still keeping Inspector Escherich going, and that's the thought of the Hobgoblin. He's got to catch him; he doesn't care what happens afterwards. He has to look this man in the eye; he has to talk to this man who has been the cause of his downfall. He wants to tell that fanatic to his face what panic, ruin, and hardship he has brought to so many people. He wants to crush him, his secret enemy.

If only he had the man already in his grip!

46

The Fateful Monday

On the Monday that was to prove so fateful for the Quangels –

on this Monday, eight weeks after Escherich was reinstated in his job;

on this Monday, on which Emil Borkhausen was sentenced to two years in prison, the rat Klebs to one;

on this Monday, when Baldur Persicke – not before time – returned to Berlin from his Napola school and visited his father in the drying-out clinic;

on this Monday, when Trudel Hergesell fell down the steps at Erkner Station and suffered a miscarriage;

on this fateful Monday, then, Anna Quangel was in bed with a bad case of the 'flu. She had a high temperature. Otto sat by her bedside; the doctor had been and gone. They were having an argument as to whether he should drop the postcards today or not.

'You're not to go again, Otto, we agreed on that! The cards can wait till tomorrow or the day after. I'll be up and about by then!'

'I want the things out of the house, Anna!'

'Then I'll take them!' And Anna pulled herself upright in bed.

'You stay where you are!' He pushed her back on to the pillows. 'Anna, don't be silly. I've dropped a hundred, two hundred cards . . .'

Just then the doorbell rang.

They both jumped, as though caught red-handed. Quangel hurriedly pocketed the two postcards that had been lying on the bed.

'Who can it be?' Anna asked anxiously.

And he, too, 'Now? At eleven in the morning?'

She guessed, 'Maybe something's happened to the Heffkes? Or the doctor's come back?'

The bell went again.

'I'll go see,' he murmured.

'No,' she begged. 'Stay here. If we'd been off with the cards, they would have rung in vain.'

'I'll just have a look, Anna!'

'No, don't open the door, Otto! Please! I have a bad feeling that if you do, misfortune will come into the house!'

'I'll go very quietly, and ask you first.'

He went.

She lay there, angry and impatient. Why did he never give in, never do anything she asked? There was misfortune lurking outside, but now that it was really here, he couldn't sense it. And now he won't even keep his word! She can hear he's opened the door and is talking to a man. And he promised he would go back and ask her first.

'Well, what is it? Come on, Otto, talk to me! You can see I'm dying of impatience! Who is it? He's still in the flat, isn't he!'

'It's nothing to get excited about, Anna. Just a messenger from the factory. The foreman on the morning shift has had an accident – they want me to go and fill in for him.'

She drops her head back on the pillows, a little relieved, 'And you're going to go?'

'Of course!'

'You haven't had your lunch!'

'I'll get something at the canteen!'

'At least take a sandwich with you!'

'It's all right, Anna, don't worry. I feel bad about having to leave you alone here for such a long time.'

'You would have had to go at one o'clock anyway.'

'I'll do my own shift right afterwards.'

'Is the man still waiting?'

'Yes, I'm going to go in with him.'

'Well, come back soon, Otto. Take the tram today, why don't you!'

'I'll do that, Anna. Hope you feel better!'

He was on his way out when she called: 'Oh, Otto, will you come and give me a kiss?'

He came back, a little surprised, a little sheepish about this desire for affection that so rarely arose between them. He pressed his lips to her mouth.

She pulled his head down to her and kissed him hard.

'I am silly, Otto,' she said. 'I still feel frightened. It must be the fever. But now go!'

And they parted, never to see each other again in freedom. In the confusion of parting, neither of them thought of the cards in his pocket.

But the old foreman remembers them again, as he sits with the messenger in the tram. He feels them in his pocket – there they are! He is unhappy with himself; he really should have thought of that! He would rather have left them at home, even have got off the tram now and dropped them in some office building on the way. But he can't find a plausible pretext for the messenger. It means he'll have to take the cards into work with him, which is something he's never done before, never should have done – and now it's too late not to.

He's in a stall in the lavatory. He has the cards already in his hands, all set to rip them up and flush them away, when his eye lights on the words it took him so much time and trouble to write: They are powerful, he thinks, effective. It would be a shame to destroy such a weapon. His parsimony, his 'confounded miserliness' prevents him from destroying them, but also his respect for work; everything that constitutes work is sacred to him. The destruction of work is a sin.

But he can't leave the cards in his jacket, which he wears in the shop. So he puts them in his satchel, along with the bread, and the thermos of coffee. Otto Quangel is well aware that there is a split down the side of the satchel – he tried taking it to the saddler weeks ago to have it restitched, but the saddler was drowning in work, and muttered something about not getting to it for at least two weeks. Quangel hadn't wanted to be without his case for so long, and he's never lost anything out of it yet. So he drops the cards in there without a second thought.

He goes through the shop to the locker room. He walks slowly, already looking this way and that. It's a different crew; there are hardly any familiar faces. Occasionally he nods to someone, and once he lends a hand. The men look at him curiously: a lot of them know him by reputation. Oh, that's old Quangel, an odd bird, but his men never complain about him, he's fair, you have to say that for him. Rubbish, he's a slave driver, he always manages to get every last ounce of energy out of his men. But none of his men ever gripe. He looks odd all right. Is his head on hinges, because that would explain why he nods so stiffly? Ssh, he's coming back. He can't stand chatter – anyone caught chattering gets a stare and then an earful.

Otto Quangel has put his satchel in the locker, and the key is in his pocket. Okay, eleven hours, and then the cards will be out of the factory, and even if it's midnight then he'll find somewhere to get rid of them; he won't take them back to the house. He wouldn't put it past Anna to get up from her sickbed purely to post them somewhere.

With this different shift, Quangel can't do what he likes to do, which is take up a position in the middle of the room and keep an eye on things. He has to go from one group to the next, and they don't even understand what his silent glare signifies; some are even brazen enough to try and draw the foreman into conversation. It takes quite a while before the shop is humming in the way he likes, till they have quieted down and realized there's nothing to do here but work.

Quangel is just on his way to his usual observation post when his foot draws back. His pupils widen, and a shudder goes through him: on the ground in front of him, on the factory floor littered with sawdust and shavings, is one of his two postcards.

He feels a twitch in his hands, he wants to stoop and pick it up discreetly, when he sees the other one a couple of steps further along. Impossible to pick them both up without attracting notice. The eye of one of the workmen is riveted to him. My God, what women they are, staring at him as if they'd never seen a man in their lives.

Bah, I'll just pick it up, whether they see me or not. It's none of their business! No, I can't, it might have been lying there for fifteen minutes already – it's a miracle that someone else hasn't picked it up already! But perhaps someone has seen it, then dropped it when he saw the contents. What if he sees me pick it up and put it in my pocket!

Danger! Danger! screams the voice inside Quangel. Deadly danger! Leave the cards where they are! Pretend you never saw them, let someone else pick them up! Get back to your place!

But suddenly something strange comes over Otto Quangel. He's been writing and dropping these cards for two years now, and he's never had a chance to see the effect they have on people. He has gone on living quietly, in his gloomy cave, and the effect of the cards, the commotion they must produce, well, he's imagined it a hundred times, but he's never yet seen it.

But now I'd like to see it, just once! What can happen to me? I'm one of eighty men here, they're all as much under suspicion as I would be – more, because I am known to be an old and reliable worker, with no interest in politics. I'll risk it, I have to see it once.

And before he's finished thinking it through, he calls out to one workman, 'Hey, you! Pick those up! Someone must have dropped them. What are they? What are you staring at?'

He takes a card from the worker's hand and pretends to read it. But he can't read just at the moment, he can't read his own big block capitals. He's not able to divert his gaze from the face of the worker, who is staring at the card. The man isn't reading any more either, but his hand is shaking, and there is fear in his eye.

Quangel stares at him. So fear is the answer, nothing but fear. The man didn't even read to the end of the card; he barely got past the first line before being overwhelmed by fear.

Quangels hears sniggering. He looks up and sees that half the shift is staring at the two men standing around idly in the middle of the shift reading postcards . . . Or have they got some sense already that something terrible has happened?

Quangel takes the card out of the man's hand. He has to play this game on his own from now on; the other man is so terrified, he's no good for anything any more.

'Where's the Arbeitsfront representative here? The one in corduroys at the table saw? Okay! Get back to work, and don't you dare chat, otherwise you'll be in for a bad time!'

'Listen!' says Quangel to the man at the table saw. 'Can you step outside a minute, I have something to show you.' And when they are both standing outside: 'It's these postcards here! The man at the back picked them up. I saw them. I think you'd better take them to the management? Am I right?'

The other man reads. He, too, doesn't read more than a couple of sentences. 'What is this?' he asks in fear. 'Were these lying in the shop where we were working? Jesus, they could cost us our lives! Who was it picked them up? Did you notice anything about the way he looked at them?'

'I told you, it was me that told him to pick them up! I might have seen them before him! Might, mind!'

'God, what am I going to do with them? I'll drop them down the bog!'

'You're going to have to take them to management, otherwise you'll be making yourself responsible. The man who picked them up can't be relied upon to keep his mouth shut for ever. Hurry along, I'll fill in for you at the saw.'

Reluctantly, the man walks off. He holds the cards with the very tips of his fingers, as though they were terribly hot.

Quangel returns to the shop. But he can't go to the table saw right away: the whole shop is in uproar. No one knows anything for certain, but they all have a sense that something has happened. They put their heads together, they whisper and tsk, tsk, and this time the silent birdlike stare of the foreman is no use. He is forced to do what he hasn't done for years, curse them out loud, threaten punishment, play the wild man.

When quiet returns to one corner of the shop, the opposite corner grows all the noisier, and once things are running reasonably well, he notices that two or three of the machines are unmanned: the bunch have decamped to the lavatory! He chases them down there, and one of them has the nerve to ask, 'What was that you were reading a moment ago, boss? Was it really a British propaganda leaflet?'

'Just get back to your work!' growls Quangel, and drives them ahead of him back to the shop. Where everyone is once again chattering. They've formed up into little clusters and there is an unprecedented level of disorder. Quangel has to run back and forth, he has to yell, threaten, swear – the sweat is beading on his brow . . .

And all the while he continues to think, So that's the effect. Just fear. So much fear they that don't even read on! But maybe that doesn't mean anything. In here, they feel they're under observation. Most of my cards were found by individuals on their own. They could read them in peace, think about them – they would have a completely different effect under those conditions. This is a stupid experiment I'm conducting. Let's see how it goes. It's probably just as well that I, as foreman, found the cards and reported them – that will get me off the hook. No, I've not risked anything. Even if they search the flat, they won't find anything. Admittedly, Anna will get a shock – but no, before they do the search I'll be back and prepare Anna . . . Two minutes past two, the afternoon shift ought to be coming on, it's time for my regular shift to begin.

But there is no change of shift. No bell goes off in the shop, no relieving shift (which would have been Quangel's own) appears, and the machines continue to run noisily. Now the men are getting really restive; they put their heads together more and more frequently, and look at their watches.

Quangel is forced to give up his effort to stop their chatter: there is only one of him and eighty of them; he has no chance.

Then suddenly a gentleman comes down from the office, a smart-looking gentleman with sharp creases and a Party badge. He stands next to Quangel and shouts into the noise, 'Shift! Your attention, please!'

All faces turn in his direction – curious, expectant, gloomy, apathetic, hostile faces.

'Circumstances require the shift to continue working for the time being. Overtime will be paid!'

He stops, they all stare. Is that it? Circumstances require? They want a bit more than that!

But he merely yells, 'All right, back to work!'

And, turning to Quangel, 'I want you to keep them calm and focused! Who is the fellow who picked up the cards?'

'I think it was me that saw them first.'

'I know. That one? Okay, you know his name?'

'No, this isn't my shift.'

'Of course. Oh, and will you tell the shift that they're not able to use the lavatories for the time being, and no one is allowed to leave the workshop. There are two sentries posted outside every door!'

And the man with the sharp creases nods brusquely at Quangel and walks off.

Quangel walks down the assembly line. For a moment he studies the work, the hands of the men. Then he says, 'For the time being, no one is allowed to leave the workshop or go to the toilet. There are two sentries posted outside every door!'

And before they can ask him any questions, he's gone on to the next place on the line and repeats his message.

Now he doesn't need to drive them on or tell them to stop chatting. They are all working silently and doggedly. They all sense the threat hanging over each one of them. Because there is not one among the eighty men there who has not in some way opposed the present government, at least by a word or two! Each one is threatened. Each life is at risk. They are all terrified . . .

And they continue to turn out coffins. They pile up the coffins, which cannot leave the premises, in a corner of the workshop. To begin with there are only a few, but as the hours go by, there are more and more of them, piled up as high as the ceiling, and new piles have started up alongside them. Coffins and coffins, enough for everyone on the shift, enough for everyone in Germany! The men are still alive, but they are already making their own coffins.

In the midst of them stands Quangel. His head jerks this way and that. He can feel the danger, but it makes him laugh. He has taken a chance, he has thrown the whole machine into disarray, but still he's just silly old Quangel, the old miser. They'll never suspect him. He will fight on and on.

Then the door opens, and the man with the sharp creases walks in again. He is followed by a second man, a tall, gangling fellow with a sandy moustache that he keeps stroking.

Immediately all work stops.

And while the manager calls out, 'All right, everyone, knock off!'

while they put down their tools with a mixture of relief and disbelief;

while light returns to their dulled eyes;

while all this is happening, the tall man with the pale moustache says, 'Foreman Quangel, I'm arresting you on urgent suspicion of treason. I want you to leave the room quietly, I'll follow!'

Poor Anna, thought Quangel, and with his head and bird profile upraised, he slowly preceded Inspector Escherich out of the shop.

47

Monday, Inspector Escherich's Great Day

This time, Inspector Escherich had worked quickly and efficiently.

No sooner had news reached him that two postcards had been found in the eighty-man shop of the furniture makers Krause & Co. than he knew: this was the moment he had been waiting for for so long. At long last, the Hobgoblin had made a mistake. Now he was going to get him!

Within five minutes he had ordered up enough personnel to seal off the entire factory and he was rushing towards it in a Mercedes, with the Obergruppenführer himself at the wheel.

Once there, Prall was in favour of pulling all eighty men out of the shop immediately and questioning every one of them until they had established the truth, but Escherich said, 'First get me a list of all the employees with their addresses. How soon can I have that?'

'In five minutes. What about the men? They're due to knock off in five minutes' time.'

'At the end of their shift, tell them they have to carry on working. No explanations. I want two men on every door. No one leaves the room. I want it all done as discreetly as possible; I don't want the men to grow alarmed!'

The secretary comes back with the list. 'The author of the cards must live in one of three streets: Chodowiecki, Jablonski, or Christburger Strasse. Which of the eighty men lives there?'

They go through the list: None! Not one!

It seemed as though Otto Quangel's luck was holding. He was on the afternoon shift, so his name did not appear on the list.

Inspector Escherich thrust out his lower lip, quickly retracted it, and bit hard on his moustache, which he had just previously been stroking. He had been perfectly sure of himself, and he was now distinctly unnerved.

Apart from the assault on his dearly loved moustache, he showed no trace of his disappointment, saying coolly, 'All right, let's go through them one by one. Which of you can confirm information? Are you the head of personnel here? Okay, let's go, Abeking, Hermann . . . What about him?'

They proceeded incredibly slowly. After an hour and a quarter they had got to H.

Obergruppenführer Prall kept lighting cigarettes and immediately putting them out. He began whispered conversations that trailed off after a sentence or two. He drummed on the window-panes. Suddenly he burst out, 'This is stupid! Why don't I just . . .'

Inspector Escherich didn't even look up. His fear of his superior had finally left him. He was going to find his man, but admitted to himself that drawing a blank on the street addresses had set him back. He didn't care how impatient Prall got, he wasn't going to conduct a general questioning of everyone.

'Carry on!'

'Kampfer, Eugen – he's the foreman!'

'I'm sorry, but we can rule him out. This morning at nine he hurt his hand on the planer. We called in Otto Quangel to replace him . . .'

'Okay, carry on: Krull, Otto . . .'

'Excuse me again, but Foreman Quangel doesn't appear on the inspector's list . . .'

'Will you stop interrupting! How long are we going to sit here for? Quangel, that old donkey, we can forget about him!'

But Escherich, a spark of hope lighting up in him, asks, 'Where does this Quangel live?'

'We'll have to check; he's not on this shift.'

'Well, check him then, for God's sake! And get a move on! I thought I'd asked you for a comprehensive list!'

'Of course we'll check right away. But I can tell you, Inspector, Quangel's not your man. He's an almost senile old guy, who's worked here for ever. We know him inside out . . .'

The inspector gestured dismissively. He knew how many mistakes were made by people claiming to know someone inside out.

'Well?' he asked the returning office boy. 'Well!'

Not without a little ceremony, the young man intoned, 'Foreman Quangel lives at Jablonski Strasse number . . .'

Escherich jumped up. With wholly uncharacteristic excitement he shouted, 'It's him! That's our Hobgoblin!'

And Obergruppenführer Prall screamed, 'All right, bring the bastard in here, and we'll rough him up!'

Everyone was excited.

Quangel! Who would have thought it – Quangel? That old fool – it couldn't be. But then he was the first to pick up the postcards! No wonder, if he was the one who dropped them! But why would he be such a fool as to entrap himself? Quangel – no!

And above them all, Prall's hysterical screams, 'Get me the son of a bitch! I want him roughed up!'

Inspector Escherich was the first to recover his composure.

'If I might have a word with you, Obergruppenführer! Might I suggest that we first conduct a search of Quangel's apartment?'

'Why go to those lengths, Escherich? In the end the fellow will slip through our fingers again!'

'No one can get out of here! But what if we find some piece of evidence in his apartment that convicts him straight off, that makes it impossible for him to deny his guilt? That would save us a lot of work. And this is the moment for that! Now, while the man and his family have no idea that he's under suspicion . . .'

'I'd have thought it was simpler to twist the man's guts out of his body till he confesses. But do it your way: we'll pick up his wife at the same time. I tell you this, though, Escherich, if the man tries any funny business, if he throws himself into some machinery or something, then I'll have your guts for garters! I want to see the fellow strung up!'

'And so you shall! I'll have someone keep an eye on Quangel secretly through the door. The shift is to carry on, gentlemen, until we're back – I expect we'll be an hour or so . . .'

48

The Arrest of Anna Quangel

After Otto Quangel was gone, Anna Quangel lapsed into a state of dull stupor, from which she woke suddenly. She felt all over the cover for the two postcards and couldn't find them. She tried to think, but she couldn't remember that Otto had taken them with him. No, quite the opposite, now it was coming back to her, it was she who was going to drop them the next day or the day after – that was how they had left it.

So the cards had to be in the apartment still. And, alternately freezing and burning with fever, she starts looking for them. She turns the apartment upside down, she looks through the laundry, she crawls under the bed. She has trouble breathing, and sometimes she has to stop and sit on the side of the bed because she simply can't go on. She pulls the covers round her and stares into space, having forgotten the postcards again. Then she suddenly jumps up once more and starts looking.

She's been doing this for hours when the bell goes off. She stops. Was that the doorbell? Who can it be? Who wants something from her?

And she lapses into a further round of feverish thinking, which is interrupted by a second ring. This time it keeps going for a long time, insistently. And then there is the sound of fists banging on the door. She hears the cry: 'Open the door! Police! Open up immediately!'

Anna Quangel smiles, and smiling she goes back to bed, pulling the covers over her head. Let them shout and ring all they like! She's sick, she doesn't have to open. Let them come back another time, when Otto's home. She's not going to let them in.

More ringing, shouting, banging . . .

Idiots! As if I would pay any attention to their noise! They can all go to hell!

In her present feverish condition, she doesn't think of the missing postcards, or of the danger of this police visit. She is just pleased to be ill and not to have to answer the door.

Then they're inside the flat, five or six of them – they'd got hold of a locksmith, or used a skeleton key. She hadn't had the chain on; because she was sick she hadn't chained the door after Otto left. Today of all days – otherwise, she always puts the chain on.

'Are you Anna Quangel? Married to Foreman Otto Quangel?'

'Yes, that's right, sir. Have been for twenty-eight years now.'

'Why didn't you open the door when we rang and shouted?'

'Because I'm sick, sir. I've got 'flu!'

'Don't give us that!' yells a fat man in a black uniform. 'You're just pretending!'

Inspector Escherich makes a calming gesture in the direction of his superior. Any child could see the woman really is sick. And perhaps it's a good thing for them: after all, people sometimes blab when they have a temperature. While his men start searching the flat, the inspector turns to the woman again. He takes her hot hand and says sympathetically, 'Frau Quangel, I'm afraid I have some bad news for you . . .'

He pauses.

'Well?' asks the woman, but she seems quite relaxed.

'I've had to arrest your husband.'

The woman smiles. Anna Quangel smiles. Smiling, she shakes her head and says, 'No, my dear man, I don't believe you! No one would arrest Otto, he's a law-abiding citizen.' She bends over to the inspector and whispers, 'Do you want to know what I think? I think this is all a dream. I've got a temperature, you know. The doctor said it was 'flu, and if you have a temperature, you can dream all sorts of things. And you're all part of my dream: you and the fat man in the black uniform, and the man over by the chest of drawers, going through my clothes. No, my dear man, you haven't arrested Otto, I'm just dreaming.'

Inspector Escherich replies, also in a whisper, 'Frau Quangel, now you're dreaming about the postcards. You know, the postcards your husband always wrote?'

But Anna Quangel's senses are not so befuddled that the word *postcards* doesn't ring a bell. She gives a start. For an instant, the eyes with which she fixes the inspector are clear and alert. But then, smiling again and shaking her head, she says, 'What postcards? My husband doesn't write postcards! If there's any writing to be done, I'm the one to do it. But we haven't written to anyone for a long time. We haven't written to anyone since my son fell. You're just dreaming that, my dear man, that my Otto writes postcards!'

The inspector detected her start, but that's no proof as yet. So he says, 'Actually, it's like this: the moment your son fell is when you both began writing postcards. Both of you. Don't you remember your very first one?'

And with a certain ceremony, he recites, 'Mother! The Führer has murdered my son! Mother! The Führer will murder your sons too, he will not stop till he has brought sorrow to every home . . .'

She listens. She smiles. 'It took a mother to write that! My Otto could never have written it, you're just dreaming!'

And the inspector: 'You dictated it, and Otto wrote it! Admit it!'

But she shook her head. 'No, dear sir! I couldn't dictate something like that, I don't have the brains . . .'

The inspector gets up and leaves the bedroom. In the parlour he joins his men in the search for writing things. He finds a little bottle of ink, a pen and nibs, and a field postcard. Armed with those things, he returns to Anna Quangel.

In the intervening time, she has been questioned – after his fashion – by Obergruppenführer Prall. Prall is firmly convinced that all that stuff about 'flu and temperature is just pretend. Then again, even if he had thought she was really sick, it wouldn't have made the least difference in his methods. He grabs Anna Quangel by the shoulders, really hurting her, and starts shaking her. Her head slams against the wooden bedstead. He jerks her back and forth twenty or thirty times, and then presses her head down into the pillows, screaming venomously in her face: 'You're still lying to me, aren't you, Communist pig? When – will – you – learn – to – stop – lying! Stop – lying!'

'No!' wails the woman. 'Stop that!'

'Admit you wrote those postcards! Admit – it – right – now! Or – I'll – beat – your – brains – out, you Bolshevik pig!'

And with every word, he slams her head against the bedstead.

Inspector Escherich, standing in the doorway with the writing things in his hand, has a smile on his face. So that's what the Obergruppenführer means by interrogating a suspect! Another five minutes like that, and she'll be out of commission for the next five days. No amount of cunningly conceived torment will give her back her consciousness then.

But for a little while, it might not be such a bad idea. Let her feel a little fear and pain, and then throw herself all the more at him, the soft cop!

When the Obergruppenführer sees the inspector pop up beside the bed, he stops his maltreatment of the suspect and says, half apologetically, half reproachfully, 'Your touch is far too soft for women like this, Escherich! You have to squeeze them till the pips squeak!'

Prall turns to the invalid, who is lying in bed with her eyes shut, trying to breathe. 'Listen to me, Frau Quangel!'

She seems not to hear.

The inspector reaches out and gently pulls her upright. 'There,' he says, mildly. 'Now won't you open your eyes, please!'

She does so. Escherich was quite right: after the shaking and the threats, his friendly, polite voice is welcome to her.

'You just told me that no one here has had occasion to write anything for a long time? Well, look at this pen. It's been used very recently, yesterday or today; the ink on it is very fresh! You see, I can scratch it off with my nail!'

'I wouldn't know about that!' says Frau Quangel. 'You'd better ask my husband about that – I don't understand.'

Inspector Escherich looks at her attentively. 'You understand perfectly well, Frau Quangel!' he says, a little more harshly. 'But you don't want to understand, because you know you've already given yourself away!'

'No one here writes anything!' Frau Quangel repeats stubbornly.

'And I don't need to ask your husband any more,' the inspector continues, 'because he's already confessed. He wrote the cards, and you dictated them . . .'

'Well, if Otto's confessed, what are you worried about?' says Anna Quangel.

'Give the bitch a smack in the chops, Escherich!' the Obergruppenführer suddenly butts in. 'She's got a nerve to string us along like this!'

But the inspector doesn't give the bitch a smack in the chops; instead, he says, 'We caught your husband with two postcards in his pocket. There was nothing he could say.'

At the mention of the two postcards that she spent so long looking for in her fever, Frau Quangel gets another shock. So he did take them with him, even though they'd agreed that she was to drop them the next day or the day after. That was wrong of Otto.

Something must have happened with the cards, she thinks to herself. But Otto hasn't confessed anything; otherwise, they wouldn't be standing around here, questioning me. They would simply . . .

And out loud she asks, 'Why don't you bring Otto here, then? I don't know what you keep going on about postcards for. Why would he write postcards?'

She lies back in bed, mouth and eyes closed, resolved not to say another word.

For a moment, Inspector Escherich looks thoughtfully down at the woman. She is exhausted, he can see that. For the time being, there's nothing to be done with her. He spins round, calls a couple of his men, and gives the order: 'Move the woman to the other bed, and then search this one minutely! Obergruppenführer, if you please!'

He wants to get his superior out of the room, for fear of another Prall-style interrogation. It's very likely that he will need this woman in the course of the next few days, and he would prefer her to be clear-headed and strong. Besides, she seems to belong to the minority that respond to threats with increased obstinacy. There's nothing to be gained by knocking her about.

The Obergruppenführer is loath to leave her behind. He would only too gladly have shown the old cow what he thought of her. He would have vented his irritation with this whole never-ending Hobgoblin story on her. But with the two detectives in the room . . . and in any case, by nightfall the bitch would be safely in the Prinz Albrecht Strasse basement, and then he could do whatever he liked with her.

'You do mean to arrest the baggage, Escherich?'

'Certainly,' replied the inspector, as he watched his men meticulously unfold and refold every single piece of bed linen, drill through the sofa cushions with long pins, and feel along the walls. He added, 'But I need to see that I get her in a fit state to answer questions. In her fever she only half understands things that are put to her. She must be made to understand that her life is in danger. Then she will be frightened, and with fear . . .'

'I'll happily teach her what fear is!' growled the Obergruppenführer.

'Not in the way you mean – and anyway, she needs to be over her fever,' said Escherich, and then he exclaimed, 'What do we have here?'

One of his men had been working on the little shelf of books. He had shaken one of the books, and something white had fluttered to the ground.

The inspector was first to the spot. He picked up the piece of paper.

'A card!' he exclaimed. 'An unfinished draft of a card!'

And he read it out: 'FÜHRER, YOU GIVE THE ORDERS, WE OBEY! YES, WE HAVE BECOME A FLOCK OF SHEEP, FOLLOWING OUR FÜHRER TO THE SLAUGHTERHOUSE. WE HAVE GIVEN UP THINKING FOR OURSELVES . . .'

He lowered the card and looked about him.

All eyes were on him.

'We have the proof!' said Inspector Escherich, with a touch of solemnity. 'We have the culprit. We have clear proof of guilt, no need for a forced confession. This long, long campaign was worth it!'

He looked around, his dim eyes shining. This was his hour, the hour he had been looking forward to for so long. For a moment, he thought about the long, long way he had come to get here. From the first card, which he had taken receipt of with smiling indifference, to this one now in his hand. He thought of the great wash of cards and the red flags proliferating on his map, and he thought of little Enno Kluge.

Once again, he was with him in the police cell, and then above the dark surface of the Schlachtensee. A shot rang out, and he thought he was blind for life. He saw himself: two security men throwing him down the stairs, bleeding, finished, while a little pickpocket slithered about on his knees, appealing to his holy Virgin. Fleetingly, too, his thoughts took in Zott – poor man, his tram theory was dashed.

It was the zenith of Inspector Escherich's life. It had been worth it, worth the patience and the long-suffering. He had caught him at last, his Hobgoblin, as he had begun calling him in jest, though he had turned into a real one later: he had almost shipwrecked Escherich's life. But now they had him, and the chase was over, the game at an end.

Inspector Escherich raised his head like one awakening. He gave orders: 'I want the woman taken away in an ambulance. Two-man escort. You're in charge, Kemmel. There's to be no interrogation; in fact, I don't want anyone to speak to her. A doctor, right away. I want the fever gone in three days, tell him, Kemmel!'

'At your orders, sir!'

'The rest of you are to tidy up the flat, I want it impeccable. What book was the card in? Radio kit instructions? Okay! Wrede, put the card back where you found it! In one hour everything has to be shipshape, because that's when I'll be returning here with the culprit. I don't want to find anyone still here. No sentries, no one. Got it?'

'At your orders, sir!'

'Well, shall we be going then, Obergruppenführer?'

'Aren't you going to confront the woman with the postcard, Escherich?'

'What would be the point? In her fever we won't get a proper reaction out of her, and I'm only interested in the husband. Wrede, did you happen to see any spare keys?'

'In the woman's handbag.'

'Let's have them – thank you. All right then, let's be off, Obergruppenführer!'

Downstairs at his window, Judge Fromm watched them go. He waggled his head from side to side. Later on, he saw Frau Quangel being lifted on a stretcher into an ambulance, but from the look of the stretcher bearers, he could tell they weren't taking her to an ordinary hospital.

'One after the other,' Judge Fromm said softly. 'One after the other. The house is emptying. The Rosenthals, the Persickes, Borkhausen, Quangel – I'm almost on my own here. Half the population is set on locking up the other half. Well, it can't go on like this much longer. At any rate, I will remain here; no one is about to lock me up . . .'

He smiles and nods.

'The worse it gets, the better it will be. The sooner it will all be over!'

49

The Conversation With Otto Quangel

Inspector Escherich had not found it easy to persuade Obergrup-penführer Prall to let him conduct the first interview with Otto Quangel alone. But in the end, he had been successful.

When he accompanied the foreman up the steps to his flat, it had already grown dark. There was a light on in the stairwell, and Quangel turned on another light when they entered the flat. He made straight for the bedroom.

'My wife's ill,' he murmured.

'Your wife isn't here any more,' said the inspector. 'She's been taken away. Won't you come and join me here . . .'

'My wife has a high temperature – the 'flu . . .' Quangel murmured.

It was plain to see that he was shaken by the news that she had been taken away. The stolid indifference he had manifested so far was gone.

'A doctor's looking after her,' the inspector said soothingly. 'I think she'll be over the fever in two or three days. I ordered an ambulance.'

For the first time, Quangel took a closer look at the man opposite him. His beady bird's eye lingered on the inspector a long time. Finally Quangel nodded. 'An ambulance,' he said, 'a doctor – that's good. Thank you. That's right. You're not a bad man.'

The inspector took his opportunity. 'We're not so bad, you know, Herr Quangel,' he said, 'not as bad as we're painted. We do all we can to ease the conditions of inmates. All we want is to establish whether a crime has been committed or not. That's our business, just as your business is manufacturing coffins . . .'

'Yes,' said Quangel, 'that's right, the manufacture and supply of coffins.' There was an edge to his voice.

'Are you suggesting that I supply the contents for the coffins?' replied Escherich with faint irony. 'Is that really the view you take of your case?'

'There is no case!'

'Oh, yes, there is, a bit of one. I mean, here, take a look at this pen, Quangel. It's your pen, that's right. The ink is still quite fresh. What were you writing with it yesterday or today?'

'I had to sign something.'

'And what did you have to sign, Herr Quangel?'

'I had to sign a medical certificate for my wife. My wife's ill with the 'flu . . .'

'And your wife told me you never wrote anything. Everything that gets written in this household, she told me, is written by her.'

'That's quite right. She does all the writing. But yesterday I had to do it, because she has a fever. She doesn't know anything about that.'

'And Herr Quangel, did you notice this,' the inspector continued, 'the way the pen sticks! It's quite a new pen, but the nib is already splitting. It must be because you have such a heavy hand, Herr Quangel.' He laid the two postcards from the factory on the table. 'You see, the first of these cards is written quite smoothly. But on the second one, you see – here – here – and on the B – the nib stuck! Well, Herr Quangel?'

'Those are the cards,' said Quangel apathetically, 'that were on the floor in the factory. I told the man in the blue jacket to pick them up. He picked them up. I took one look at them and I handed them over to the representative of the Arbeitsfront. He took them away with him. That's the extent of my knowledge of the cards.'

Quangel spoke in a slow, monotonous drone, sounding like an old, rather dim man.

The inspector said, 'Now come on, Herr Quangel, can't you see that the end of the second card is written with a split nib?'

'I wouldn't know about that. I'm not a scribe or a learned man, as it says in the Bible.'

For a moment there was silence in the room. Quangel stared vacantly at the table in front of him.

The inspector looked at him. He was firmly convinced that this man wasn't as slow and lumbering as he pretended to be, but rather as sharp as his profile and as quick as his eye. His first duty was to get the man to betray some of that inner sharpness. He wanted to talk to the clever author of the postcards, not this ancient foreman, grown dull from decades of labour.

After a while Escherich asked, 'What are those books on the shelf?'

Slowly Quangel raised his head, looked at the inspector for a moment, and then jerked his head round till the shelf was in front of him. 'Those books? There's my wife's hymnal and her Bible. And the others are probably all books belonging to my son, who fell in the war. I don't read or own any books. I was never much good at reading . . .'

'May I see the fourth book from the left, Herr Quangel, the one with the red jacket?'

Slowly and carefully Quangel took the book from the shelf and set it down on the table in front of the inspector.

'*Otto Runge's Radio Assembly Kit*,' the inspector read out. 'Well, Quangel, and what does this book signify to you?'

'It's a book of my son Otto's, who fell in the war,' Quangel replied slowly. 'He loved radios. He was well known for it; the employers in the engineering companies all wanted him, he knew each and every . . .'

'And does nothing else occur to you, Herr Quangel, when you see this book?'

'Nope!' Quangel shook his head. 'Nothing. Like I say, I don't read books.'

'But perhaps you use it to keep things in? Why don't you open the book, Herr Quangel!'

The book fell open at the place where the card lay.

Quangel stared at the words: 'FÜHRER, LEAD – WE FOLLOW! YES, WE FOLLOW . . .'

When had he written that? It must have been long, long ago.

Right at the beginning. But why hadn't he finished it? And what was the card doing in Ottochen's book?

Slowly it came back to him: the first visit of his brother-in-law, Ulrich Heffke. He had had to put the card away in a hurry, and had taken up the carving of the bust of Ottochen instead. He'd put the card away and forgotten all about it – he had, and Anna had, too!

This was the danger he had always sensed! This was the unseen enemy whose presence had haunted him. This was the mistake he had made, the one he hadn't been able to remember . . .

They've caught you! said a voice within him. You've had it – and it's all your own fault. Your goose is cooked.

And – did Anna confess to anything? They must have shown her the card too. But Anna will have denied it, I know her, and that's what I'll do, too. Of course, she was feverish, so . . .

The inspector asked, 'Well, Quangel, cat got your tongue? When did you write the card?'

'I don't know anything about the card,' he replied. 'I wouldn't know how to write something like that, I'm too stupid!'

'Then what's the card doing in your son's book? Who put it there?'

'How would I know?' Quangel replied almost rudely. 'Maybe you put it in there yourself, or one of your men did! You hear about it being done, evidence being supplied where there is none!'

'The card was found in the presence of several excellent witnesses. Your wife was present, too.'

'Well, and what did she say?'

'When the card was found, she immediately confessed that she dictated the card and you wrote it. Come on, Quangel, don't be so obstinate. Just admit it. If you admit it now, you're not telling me anything I don't know. But you will make it easier for yourself and your wife. If you don't admit it, I will have to take you back to Gestapo headquarters, and the basement there is a pretty rough sort of place . . .'

The memory of what he himself had experienced there caused Escherich's voice to tremble slightly.

He got a grip on himself and went on, 'Whereas if you confess,

I can hand you over to the examining magistrate. And then you'll end up in Moabit, and you'll be well treated, like any other detainee.'

But try as Escherich might, Quangel stuck to his guns. Escherich had made a mistake after all, which the sharp-witted Quangel had spotted right away. Quangel's lumbering manner and the statements of his superiors had sufficiently impressed Escherich that he didn't think Quangel was the author of the cards, but merely the writer of what his wife dictated . . .

And the fact that he had now said it a second time proved to Quangel that Anna had not confessed. That was just a line the inspector was spinning.

He continued his denials.

Finally, Escherich broke off the unsuccessful interview in the apartment and took Quangel back to Prinz Albrecht Strasse. He hoped the change of ambience, the swarm of SS men, and the whole menacing apparatus would intimidate the man, and make him more amenable to persuasion.

They were in the inspector's office, and Escherich showed him the map of Berlin with the many red flags.

'Take a look at this, Herr Quangel,' he said. 'Each flag indicates where a postcard was handed in. The exact place. If you look closely,' he tapped with his finger, 'you'll see that there are flags all over this whole area, except in this spot. Because that's Jablonski Strasse, where you live. Of course you didn't drop any cards there, because you're too familiar a figure . . .'

But Escherich saw that Quangel wasn't even listening. At the sight of the map, a strange, inexplicable excitement had come over the man. His eyes were rolling, his hands shaking. Almost shyly, he said, 'That's a lot of flags you've got there – do you know how many there are?'

'I can tell you the exact number,' replied the inspector, now understanding why his man was so shaken. 'There are 267 flags, indicating 259 cards and eight letters. How many did you write, Quangel?'

The man said nothing, but this time it was not out of defiance, but from disappointment.

'And consider this as well, Herr Quangel,' the inspector continued, taking full advantage of the other's shock, 'all these letters and cards were freely handed in to us. We didn't find a single one of them. People came running to us as though they were on fire. They couldn't hand them in quickly enough, and most of them hadn't even read them all the way through . . .'

Quangel still did not speak, but his face was working. The man was in turmoil; his sharp, beady glance wavered: the eyelids flickered, the eyes wandered off, looked at the ground, then were drawn back to the little flags.

'And one other thing, Quangel. Did you ever stop to think how much misery and fear you brought upon people with those cards of yours? People were in terror, some were arrested, and I know of someone killing himself over one . . .'

'No! No!' Quangel cried out. 'I never wanted that! I never thought that would happen! I wanted things to get better, I wanted people to learn the truth, so that the war would end sooner and the killing stop – that's what I wanted! I didn't mean to sow terror and dread, I didn't want to make things worse than they were already! Those wretched people – and I made them even more wretched! Who was it who killed themselves?'

'Oh, a hustler and gambler, no great loss, don't worry yourself about him!'

'But everyone matters! I have his blood on my hands.'

'You see, Herr Quangel,' said the inspector to the man standing grim-faced beside him. 'You've confessed your crime, and you didn't even notice!'

'My crime? I never committed any crime, at least not in the way you mean. My crime was thinking myself too clever, wanting to do everything by myself, even though I know really that one man is nothing. No, I didn't do anything that I should be ashamed of, but the way I went about it was mistaken. That's why I deserve my punishment, and that's why I'll go gladly to my death . . .'

'Oh, it won't be as bad as that,' the inspector said consolingly.

Quangel ignored him. As if to himself, he said, 'I never had that high an opinion of people, otherwise I should have known what would happen.'

Escherich asked, 'Do you know how many letters and post-cards you wrote, Quangel?'

'Two hundred and seventy-six postcards, nine letters.'

'Which means that all of eighteen items were not handed in.'

'Eighteen items: that's the sum total of my work of two years, my hope. My life for those eighteen pieces of paper. Well, at least they were as many as that!'

'Don't flatter yourself, Quangel,' said the inspector, 'that those eighteen circulated from hand to hand. No, it's just that they were found by individuals so deeply compromised already that they didn't dare hand them in. Those eighteen cards were just as ineffectual as all the others. We've never heard anything from the public at large that leads us to think they had the least effect . . .'

'So I've accomplished nothing?'

'So you've accomplished nothing – certainly nothing that you would have wanted to accomplish! But you should be glad of that, Quangel, because it will certainly help to bring about a reduction in your punishment! Maybe you'll get off with fifteen or twenty years!'

Quangel shuddered. 'No,' he said. 'No!'

'What did you expect anyway, Quangel? You, an ordinary worker, taking on the Führer, who is backed by the Party, the Wehrmacht, the SS, the SA? The Führer, who has already conquered half the world and will overcome the last of our enemies in another year or two? It's ludicrous! You must have known you had no chance! It's a gnat against an elephant. I don't understand it, a sensible man like you!'

'No, and you will never understand it, either. You see, it doesn't matter if one man fights or ten thousand; if the one man sees he has no option but to fight, then he will fight, whether he has others on his side or not. I had to fight, and given the chance I would do it again. Only I would do it very differently.'

He turned his now steady gaze upon the inspector: 'By the way, my wife had nothing to do with all this. You must let her go!'

'Now you're lying, Quangel! Your wife dictated the postcards – you said so yourself!'

'Now *you* are lying! Do I seem like a man who would take dictation from his wife? Perhaps you'll go on to say she was the mastermind behind it all. But it was me, it was all my doing. I had the idea, I wrote the cards, I dropped them, I want my punishment! Not her, not my wife!'

'She confessed . . .'

'She confessed nothing! I don't want to hear any more lies about her! You shouldn't try to tell a husband lies about his wife!'

For a moment they confronted one another, the man with the sharp bird's head and the grey colourless inspector with his pale eyes and fair moustache.

Then Escherich lowered his gaze, and said, 'I'm going to send for someone to take down your statement. I hope you'll stand by it?'

'I stand by it.'

'And you fully understand what lies in store for you? A long jail sentence, or possibly death?'

'I know what I've done. And I hope you know what you're doing, too, Inspector!'

'Oh, and what's that, then?'

'You're working in the employ of a murderer, delivering ever new victims to him. You do it for money; perhaps you don't even believe in the man. No, I'm certain you don't believe in him. Just for money, then . . .'

Once again they confronted one another, and once again the inspector finally lowered his gaze, vanquished.

'Well, I'm going, then,' he said almost sheepishly. 'To get a stenographer.'

And he went.

50

The Death of Escherich

Midnight finds Inspector Escherich still, or more accurately, once again in his office. He's sitting there slumped, but however much he's had to drink, he is unable to wash from his mind the horrible scene in which he has just participated.

This time, his noble superior, Obergruppenführer Prall, didn't have an Iron Cross for his darling, hardworking, successful inspector, but he did invite him to a little SS victory celebration. Then they had sat together, they had drunk a lot of powerful Armagnac out of not such little glasses, they had bragged of their capture of the Hobgoblin, and, to general applause, Inspector Escherich had been forced to read out the statement that included Quangel's confession . . .

Arduous, painstaking detective work cast before swine!

And then, once they were all well sozzled, they had thought of yet more fun. Clutching bottles and glasses, they had decamped, the inspector included, to Quangel's cell. They wanted to see that odd bird for themselves in the flesh, the maniac with the audacity to take on the Führer!

They had found Quangel rolled up in his blanket on his cot, sound asleep. A strange face, thought Escherich, not even relaxed in sleep. Asleep and awake, it looked equally opaque and worried. In this instance the man had been sound asleep . . .

Of course they hadn't let him lie. They had jolted him awake, roused him from his cot. There he had stood before a lot of men in black and silver uniforms, in his much too short shift that didn't quite conceal his nakedness – a ludicrous figure, as long as you remembered not to look at the head!

And then someone had had the idea of baptizing the old Hobgoblin, and they had emptied a bottle of schnapps over his head. The Obergruppenführer had given a little, comically slurred speech on the Hobgoblin, that pig that was now on his way to the slaughter, and at the end of his speech he had smashed his brandy balloon over Quangel's head.

That was the signal for all the rest of them to smash their glasses over the old man's head. A mixture of Armagnac and blood ran down his face. But while all this was going on, Escherich had had the sense that through the rivers of blood and drink, Quangel was staring at him; he could have sworn he heard him saying, So that's the just cause in which you do murder! These are your henchmen! This is how you are. You know very well what you're about. But I will die for committing acts that were not crimes, and you will live – so much for the justice of your cause!

Then they had made the discovery that Escherich's glass was still intact, and ordered him to break it over Quangel's head as well. Prall had had to order him twice in the most explicit terms – 'Have you forgotten what happened to you before, Escherich, when you were disobedient?' – and so Escherich had smashed his glass over Quangel's head. He had to try four times, with trembling hand, before the glass broke, and all the while he'd had to face the mocking, challenging stare of Quangel. This ridiculous figure in his too-short shift was actually stronger and more dignified than all his tormentors. And with each blow that Inspector Escherich had brought down in terror and despair, he had had the sense that he was hitting out at himself, striking with an axe at the roots of the tree of his own life.

Then all at once Otto Quangel had collapsed, and they had let him lie on the bare floor, bleeding and unconscious. They had also told the guard to ignore the bastard, and had gone back upstairs to their boozy celebrations, as if they had won God knows what heroic victory.

And now Inspector Escherich is back at his desk. Up on the wall there is the map with the red flags. His body has crumpled, but his mind is still clear.

Yes, that map is finished. It can be taken down tomorrow. And the day after I'll put up a new one, and begin the chase of a new Hobgoblin. And then another. And another. What's it all for? Is that my purpose here on earth? I suppose it must be, but in that case, I don't understand the world, and nothing makes sense. It really doesn't matter what I do . . .

'I have his blood on my hands . . .' The way he said it! And his, in turn, on mine! No, there's Enno Kluge's as well – that wretched weakling I sacrificed in order to deliver this man to a gang of drunken thugs. He won't whimper the way that little runt did on the pier, no, he'll die with dignity . . .

And me? What about me? For me, it's on to the next case, and if the diligent Escherich isn't up to the expectations of Obergruppenführer Prall, I'll get another stint in the basement. Eventually, the day will come when I'll go down there never to come up again. Is that the day I'm living for? No, Quangel is right to call Hitler a murderer and me his henchman. I never cared who manned the tiller, or why this war was being fought, so long as I was able to go about my usual business, the catching of human beings. Then, once I'd caught them, I didn't care what became of them . . .

But now I do care. I've had it up to here with it; it disgusts me to keep those fellows supplied with fresh prey; from the moment I caught Quangel, it felt disgusting to me. The way he stood there and looked at me. Blood and liquor running down his face, but the stare! This is your doing, his eyes were telling me, you betrayed me! Oh, if only I could, I would sacrifice ten Enno Kluges for the sake of this one Quangel, I would give this entire building here for his liberty! If it were still possible, I would leave here, and I would start something, like Otto Quangel did – something better conceived, but I also want to fight.

But it's impossible, they wouldn't let me, they call that kind of thing desertion. They would catch me and throw me in the basement again. And my flesh screams when they torture it. I'm a coward. A coward like Enno Kluge, not a brave man like Otto Quangel. When Obergruppenführer Prall yells at me, I start to shake, and I do what he tells me. I smashed my glass over the head of the only decent man here, but each blow was like a sprinkling of earth on my coffin.

Slowly Inspector Escherich got to his feet. There was a helpless smile on his face. He went to the wall and pressed his ear against it. There was quiet now in the building on Prinz Albrecht Strasse, an hour after midnight. Only the pacing of the sentry in the corridor, back and forth, back and forth . . .

You have no idea why you're going back and forth, do you? thought Escherich. One day you, too, will understand that you have wasted your life . . .

He reached for the map and tore it off the wall. There was a flurry of little flags. Escherich scrunched up the map and dropped it on the floor.

'Finished!' he said. 'Over! The Hobgoblin case is over!'

He walked slowly to his desk, pulled open a drawer, and nodded.

'Here I am, probably the only man Otto Quangel converted with his postcard campaign. But I'm no good to you, Otto Quangel, I can't carry on your labour. I'm too much of a coward. Still, I'm your only disciple, Otto Quangel!'

Quickly he drew out the pistol and fired.

This time his hand hadn't trembled.

The sentry ran in to find an almost headless corpse behind the desk.

Obergruppenführer Prall raged. 'Desertion! All civilians are pigs! Everyone not in uniform belongs in a cell, behind barbed wire! But just you wait, whoever follows in the footsteps of that pig, Escherich, I'll have you from the start, so that you won't have a single thought in your head, just fear! I've always been too easygoing, that was my biggest mistake! Bring that pig, Quangel, upstairs! I want him to look at this mess, and clean it up!'

In this way, Otto Quangel's only convert put the foreman to the trouble of a couple of hours of grisly overtime.

PART IV
The End

51

Anna Quangel is Interrogated

It was two weeks after her arrest, at one of her first interrogations following her recovery from the 'flu, that Anna Quangel let slip that her son Otto had once been engaged to a certain Trudel Baumann. At that time, Anna had not yet understood that naming anyone would endanger the party concerned. Because with pedantic precision, the friends and acquaintances of all detainees were arrested, every trace was followed up, so that 'the cancer can be completely eradicated'.

Her interviewer, Escherich's successor, Inspector Laub, a short, compact individual who loved to slap the prisoner across the face with the back of his bony hand, had, as was his habit, initially passed over this detail without seeming to pay any attention to it. He grilled Anna Quangel long and exhaustively about her son's friends and employers, asked her things she couldn't possibly know but was supposed to know, asked and asked, and, every so often, slapped her across the face with his bony hand.

Inspector Laub was a past master in the art of interrogation. He was capable of going for ten hours without a break, and if he could do it, then the prisoner had to do it, too. Anna Quangel was swaying with exhaustion on her stool. Her recent illness, her anxiety about Otto, of whose fate she had heard nothing, the humiliation of being slapped like a naughty child, all this combined to make her confused, and then Inspector Laub struck her again.

Anna Quangel groaned softly and covered her face with her hands.

'Take your hands down!' shouted the inspector. 'Look at me! Will you do as you're told!'

She did so, and looked at him with fear in her eyes. It wasn't fear of him, though, but fear that she might weaken.

'When was the last time you saw your son's so-called fiancée?'

'That was such a long time ago. I can't remember. Before we started with the postcards. Two years . . . Oh, please don't hit me again! Think of your own mother! You wouldn't want anyone to hit your mother!'

A volley of two or three slaps hit her.

'My mother is no traitorous bitch like you! If you dare refer to my mother again, I'll hit you properly! Where did the slut live?'

'I don't know! My husband told me she had got married since. She will have moved away somewhere.'

'So your husband saw her! When was that?'

'I can't remember! It was when we were writing the cards.'

'And she was involved? She helped you?'

'No! No!' cried Frau Quangel. With terror she saw what she had done. 'My husband,' she hurriedly went on, 'bumped into Trudel on the street. That was when she told him she had got married and wasn't working in the factory any more.'

'Well – go on. What factory did she go to then?'

Frau Quangel named the uniform factory.

'And then?'

'That's all. That's everything I know about her. Really, Inspector!'

'Doesn't it seem odd to you that your son's so-called fiancée hasn't come to see her in-laws once more, not even after the death of her intended?'

'But that was what my husband is like! We never had dealings with other people, and once we began with the cards, he broke off relations with everyone.'

'You're lying again! You only took up with the Heffkes after you'd begun writing the cards!'

'Yes, that's true! I'd forgotten that. But Otto wasn't at all happy about that; he made an exception because Ulrich was my brother. Still, he hated family!' She looked sadly at the inspector. Shyly, she said, 'Can I ask you something now, Inspector?'

'Ask away!' growled Inspector Laub.

'Is it true . . .' She broke off. 'I thought I saw my sister-in-law in the corridor yesterday . . . Is it true that the Heffkes are under arrest as well?'

'You're lying again!' A slap, hard. And another. 'Frau Heffke's somewhere else. You couldn't have seen her. Someone told you. Who could have told you?'

Frau Quangel shook her head. 'No, no one told me. I saw her from a distance. I wasn't even sure it was her.' She sighed. 'And now the Heffkes are in prison as well, and they didn't do anything and didn't know anything. Poor people!'

'Poor people!' mocked Inspector Laub. 'Didn't know anything! That's what you all say! But you're all criminals, and as true as my name is Laub, I'll have you disembowelled if you don't tell me the truth! Who's in your cell with you?'

'I don't know her full name. I call her Berta.'

'How long has Berta been your cellmate?'

'Since last night.'

'Well, then she told you about the Heffkes. Just admit it, Frau Quangel, otherwise I'll have her brought up, and in your presence I'll keep on hitting her till she confesses.'

Anna Quangel shook her head again. 'It doesn't matter if I say yes or no, Inspector,' she said, 'you were going to bring Berta upstairs anyway, and hit her. All I can say is that I saw Frau Heffke in the corridor yesterday . . .'

Inspector Laub looked at her with a sardonic grin. Abruptly he screamed, 'You're all shit! Shit the lot of you! I won't rest until all you shits are in the ground! I've got to deal with you all! Orderly, bring Berta Kuppke upstairs!'

He spent the next hour beating and intimidating both women, even though Frau Kuppke admitted straight off that she had told Frau Quangel about Frau Heffke, with whom she had previously shared a cell. But that wouldn't do for Inspector Laub. He wanted to know every word that had passed between them, when all they had done was complain. He, though, sensed conspiracy and betrayal everywhere, and went on hitting and questioning them for a long time.

In the end, a crying Frau Kuppke was carted back downstairs, and Anna Quangel was once again the sole beneficiary of

Inspector Laub's attentions. She was so tired now that his voice seemed to come from far away, his figure swam before her eyes, and his blows no longer mattered.

'So what happened to make your son's so-called fiancée stop coming to see you?'

'Nothing happened. My husband didn't want visitors.'

'But you admitted he had no problem with the Heffkes.'

'The Heffkes were an exception, because of Ulrich being my brother.'

'Then why did Trudel stop coming to the house?'

'Because my husband didn't want her to.'

'When did he tell her?'

'I don't know! Inspector, I can't go on any more. Couldn't you let me rest for half an hour? A quarter of an hour?'

'Not until you've told me what I want to know. When did your husband tell the girl to stop coming to see you?'

'When my son died.'

'Well then! And where did he tell her?'

'In our apartment.'

'And what did he give as a reason?'

'Because he didn't want to see any more people. Inspector, please, I can't go on. Ten minutes!'

'Okay. We'll have a break in ten minutes. What did your husband give as a reason for Trudel to stop coming?'

'Because he didn't want to see anyone. We were about to begin with the postcards.'

'So the reason he gave was that he wanted to do the post-cards?'

'No, he didn't mention that to a soul.'

'So what reason did he give?'

'That he didn't want to see anyone. Oh, Inspector!'

'If you tell me the real reason, we'll stop for today!'

'But that is the real reason!'

'No, it's not! I can see you're lying! If you don't tell me the truth, I'll question you for the next ten hours. What did he say? Tell me the words he said to Trudel Baumann.'

'I can't remember. He was so furious.'

'Why was he so furious?'

'Because I let Trudel Baumann spend the night in our flat.'

'But he didn't ban her till the next day – or did he send her away immediately?'

'No, the following morning.'

'He banned her that morning?'

'Yes.'

'What made him so furious?'

Anna Quangel sighed. 'I'll tell you, Inspector. It's not going to hurt anyone any more. I had secretly hidden an old Jewish woman in our flat – Frau Rosenthal, who later jumped out of the window. That's what made him so furious, and he threw Trudel out at the same time.'

'What was Frau Rosenthal doing, hiding in your apartment?'

'She was afraid, all alone in her apartment. She lived upstairs from us. They took away her husband, and she got scared. Inspector, you promised you would let me . . .'

'In a minute. In a minute. So Trudel knew you were keeping a Jew hidden in your apartment?'

'But that's not against the law . . .'

'Of course it's against the law! A self-respecting Aryan doesn't take in a Jewish bitch, and a law-abiding girl would report something like that to the police. What did Trudel have to say about you keeping a Jewess in your flat?'

'Inspector, I'm not going to say anything any more. You twist every word I say. Trudel didn't break the law; she didn't know about anything!'

'But she knew you were giving refuge to Jews in your apartment!'

'That wasn't a bad thing!'

'We think differently. I'll have a word with Trudel tomorrow.'

'Oh my God, what have I done now!' Frau Quangel cried out. 'Now I've plunged Trudel into misfortune as well. Inspector, you mustn't do anything to hurt Trudel, she's expecting!'

'Oh, really, so you know that, after not seeing her for two years! How did you come to know that?'

'But I told you, Inspector, it was when my husband saw her in the street.'

'When was that?'

'That will have been a few weeks ago. Inspector, you promised I could have a break. Just a short break, please. I really can't go on.'

'Just a bit more! We're almost there. Who started talking, Trudel or your husband, considering there was bad blood between them?'

'There wasn't any bad blood between them, Inspector.'

'Well, your husband told her never to show her face again!'

'Trudel didn't mind about that. She knows what my husband's like!'

'Where did they bump into each other?'

'I think it was in Kleine Alexanderstrasse.'

'What was your husband doing in Kleine Alexanderstrasse? You told me he just went to work and back.'

'That's right.'

'So what was he doing in Kleine Alexanderstrasse then? Probably dropping off a postcard, ha, Frau Quangel?'

'No, no!' she cried out, and went pale with fear. 'It was always me that dropped the postcards! Always me on my own, never him!'

'I wonder why you turned so pale just now, Frau Quangel?'

'I didn't turn pale. Well, if I did, it was because I felt faint. You said we were going to have a break, Inspector!'

'Soon, as soon as we've straightened this out. Well now, your husband is dropping a postcard, and he runs into Trudel Baumann? So what did she have to say about the cards?'

'She didn't know about them!'

'Did your husband still have the card on him when he ran into Trudel, or had he already dropped it off?'

'He had already dropped it off.'

'There, you see, Frau Quangel, we're slowly getting there. Now I just need to hear from you what Trudel Baumann had to say about the card, and we're through for today.'

'But she can't have said anything, because he had already dropped the card.'

'Think about it, now! I can see from your face that you're lying. If you stick to your story, we'll still be here tomorrow morning. Why are you so set on needlessly tormenting yourself? I'll put it to Trudel directly tomorrow, that she knew about the postcards, and she'll admit it right away. So why make trouble for yourself, Frau Quangel? I imagine you'll be relieved to be able to crawl off to your cell. So, how about it then, Frau Quangel? What did Trudel Baumann say about the postcards?'

'No! No! No!' screamed Frau Quangel, jumping to her feet in desperation. 'I'm not going to say another word! I'm not giving anyone away! I don't care what you say, you can kill me if you like, I'm not saying any more!'

'Sit down,' said Inspector Laub, and struck the despairing woman a couple of times. 'I'll tell you when you're allowed to stand. And I'll tell you when the interrogation's over, too. Now let's get to the end of Trudel Baumann's role in all this. Following your confession that she perpetrated high treason . . .'

'I did not confess that!' cried the tormented, desperate woman.

'You said you didn't want to give Trudel away,' said the inspector evenly. 'And now I'm not going to rest until I hear from you what there is to be given away.'

'Never, I will never tell you that!'

'Very well! But understand, Frau Quangel, that you're being stupid. You should bear in mind that it will take me about five minutes to get what I want to know from Trudel Baumann tomorrow morning. A pregnant woman like her can't endure very much. Once I've slapped her round a bit . . .'

'You mustn't hit Trudel! You mustn't! Oh God, if only I hadn't told you her name!'

'But you did! And you'll make everything much easier for her if you admit everything! Well, how about it, Frau Quangel? What did Trudel say about the cards?'

And later: 'I could get this out of Trudel herself, but I feel like hearing it from you. And now I won't stop till I have! It's time you learned you're not worth shit to me. All your vows to stop talking are crap. All your talk of loyalty and not wanting to betray people is just hot air. You're nothing, all right? Now, Frau Quangel, do you want to bet that within an hour I'll have heard from your mouth all that Trudel had to do with the postcards?! Bet?'

'No! No! Never.'

But of course Inspector Laub heard it, and it didn't even take an hour.

52

The Downcast Hergesells

The Hergesells were taking their first walk together since Trudel's miscarriage. They followed the road out to Grunheide, then turned left down Frankenweg and followed the shore of Flakensee toward the lock at Woltersdorf.

They walked very slowly, and every so often Karl shot a look at Trudel, walking beside him with downcast eyes.

'Isn't it nice in the woods?' he said.

'Yes,' she replied, 'it's nice.'

A little later he exclaimed, 'Look at the swans on the lake!'

'Yes,' she answered, 'the swans . . .' And that was all.

'Trudel,' he asked in concern, 'why won't you talk? Have you lost all feeling for everything?'

'I keep thinking of our dead baby,' she whispered.

'Oh, Trudel,' he said. 'We'll have lots of children yet!'

She shook her head. 'I'm never going to have a child now.'

He asked anxiously, 'Did the doctor say something to you?'

'No, he didn't. But I can feel it.'

'No,' he said. 'You mustn't think like that, Trudel. We're young, we can have plenty of children.'

Again she shook her head. 'I sometimes think that was my punishment.'

'Your punishment! What for, Trudel? What have we done, that we deserve to be punished like that? No, it was just an accident, an awful, random accident!'

'It wasn't an accident, it was punishment,' she said obstinately. 'We weren't meant to have a baby. I keep having to think what would have happened to Klaus if he'd lived. Hitler Youth or SA or SS . . .'

'Goodness, Trudel!' he exclaimed, startled by the pessimistic thoughts that tormented his wife, 'if our baby Klaus had lived, all this Hitler stuff would be over. It can't last much longer, trust me!'

'Yes,' she said, 'but what have we done to secure a better future? Nothing at all! Worse than that: we abandoned the cause. I keep thinking about Grigoleit and Babyface . . . that's why we're being punished . . .'

'Ach, bloody Grigoleit!' he said irritably.

He was furious with Grigoleit, who still hadn't called to pick up his suitcase.

Hergesell had already had to extend the left-luggage ticket.

'I think Grigoleit must be in prison,' he said. 'Otherwise we would have heard from him.'

'If he's in prison,' she insisted, 'then it's our fault. We left him in the lurch.'

'Trudel!' he exclaimed. 'I won't have you think like that. We're not cut out to be conspirators. We had no option but to give it up.'

'Yes,' she said, 'but we're cut out to be shirkers and cowards! You say Klaus wouldn't have had to join the Hitler Youth. But if that's right, and if he had been allowed to live, we have to ask ourselves: What would we have we done to deserve his love and respect? What have we done toward a better future? Nothing!'

'We can't all play at being conspirators, Trudel!'

'No, but we could have done something else. If a man like my former father-in-law, Otto Quangel . . .' She stopped.

'Well, what about him? What do you know about him?'

'No, I'd rather not tell you. I promised him I wouldn't anyway. But if an old man like Otto Quangel finds it in himself to oppose this state, then I think us sitting on our hands is pathetic!'

'But what can we do, Trudel? Nothing! Think of all the power Hitler has, and the two of us are nothing at all! There's nothing we can do!'

'If everyone thought like that, then Hitler would stay in power for ever. Someone somewhere has to make a start.'

'But what can we do?'

'Everything! We could write appeals and put them up on trees!

You work in a chemical factory, as an electrician you have the run of the place. You just need to adjust a lever, or loosen a screw on a machine, and many days' work will be ruined. If you did something like that, and a few hundred others did the same, then pretty soon Hitler would start running out of armaments.'

'Sure, and the second time I did it, they'd haul me off and execute me!'

'As I say, we're cowards. We only think about the consequences for us, not for everyone else. Look, Karli, you've been excused military service because your job is so important for the war effort. But if you were a soldier, you'd be risking your life every day, and would find it perfectly natural.'

'Oh, the Prussians would find me a cushy job in their army!'

'And you'd let others die in your place! As I keep saying, we're cowards, we're worthless cowards!'

'Those damned stairs!' he started in. 'If you hadn't had your miscarriage, we would have had such a happy life together!'

'No, it wouldn't have been happy, not really, Karli! From the moment I knew I had Klaus inside me, I always wondered what would become of him. I wouldn't have been able to bear it if he'd extended his right arm in the Hitler salute, and I wouldn't have been able to look at him in a brown shirt. The next time there was some victory to celebrate, he would have seen his parents hang out the swastika bunting, and he would have known we were lying. Well, at least we've been spared that. We weren't meant to have our Klaus, Karli!'

He walked along beside her awhile in grim silence. They were on the way back now, but they had eyes for neither lake nor woods.

Finally he asked, 'So you really want us to get involved? You want me to do something in the factory?'

'I do,' she said. 'We must do something, Karli, to stop us feeling so ashamed of ourselves!'

He thought awhile, then he said, 'I can't help it, Trudel. Slinking around the factory sabotaging machines just isn't in me.'

'Well, think of something that is in you, then! You will. It doesn't have to be right away.'

'And what about you? Have you thought of something you'd do?'

'Yes,' she said. 'I know of a Jewish woman in hiding. She was supposed to be put on a transport already. But the people she's staying with are bad people, and every day she's afraid she might be betrayed. I'm going to take her in.'

'No!' he said. 'No! Don't do that, Trudel! The way we're spied on, it'll come out right away. And think about ration cards! She's not going to have one! We're not going to be able to feed an extra person on our two cards!'

'Don't you think? Don't you think we can starve ourselves a bit, if it means saving another person from death? Oh, Karli, if that's the truth of it, then Hitler will have an easy job. Then we really are all dirt, and whatever happens to us will serve us right!'

'But people will see her with us! You can't hide someone in a tiny flat like ours. I won't allow it!'

'I don't think I need your permission, Karli. It's my flat as much as yours.'

A quarrel broke out, the first really bad quarrel in their marriage. She said she would just bring the woman back while he was at work, and he told her he would throw the woman out of the house.

'Then why don't you throw me out while you're at it!'

They went as far as that. Both were angry, provoked, aggressive. They couldn't set the thing aside, no compromise was possible. She was desperate to do something against Hitler, against the war. In principle, he was too, but it mustn't carry any risk; he wasn't willing to run the least danger. The thing with the Jewish woman was just mad. He would never allow it!

They walked home in silence through the streets of Erkner. Their silence was so dense, so thick, that it seemed harder and harder to break. They were no longer arm in arm, but walked side by side, not touching. Once, when their hands happened to brush, each quickly pulled back, and then they increased the distance between them.

They didn't see the large car parked in front of their house. They walked up the stairs and didn't notice that at every door they were met by curious or angry glances. Karl Hergesell unlocked the door and let Trudel in first. Even in the corridor, they didn't notice anything. Only when they saw the little stout man in a green jacket standing in their parlour did they give a start.

'Hello?' said an indignant Hergesell. 'What do you think you're doing in my flat?'

'Allow me. Detective Inspector Laub, from the Gestapo, Berlin,' the man in the green jacket introduced himself. He had kept on his little huntsman's hat with the badger brush.

'Herr Hergesell? And Frau Gertrud Hergesell, née Baumann, likes to go by the name of Trudel? Excellent! I would like to have a few words in private with your wife, Herr Hergesell. Perhaps you could wait in the kitchen, if you don't mind.'

They exchanged fearful looks. Then Trudel suddenly broke into a smile. 'Well, goodbye then, Karli!' she said, and gave him a hug. 'I hope things get better. It was stupid of us to quarrel! You never know what's round the corner!'

Inspector Laub cleared his throat threateningly. They kissed, and Hergesell walked out.

'Why did you just take leave of your husband like that, Frau Hergesell?'

'I wanted to make up with him; we'd just had a quarrel.'

'What did you quarrel about?'

'About an aunt of mine coming to visit. He didn't want her to come; I did.'

'And the sight of me was enough to make you concede? Strange, you don't seem to have a very clean conscience. Wait a moment now! Stay where you are!'

She heard him talking to Karli in the kitchen. Karli was bound to say the quarrel had been about something else, and this thing had got off to the worst possible start. She had thought right away of Quangel. But it wasn't like Quangel to give someone away . . .

The inspector came back. Rubbing his hands with satisfaction, he said, 'According to your husband, your quarrel was about whether to adopt a child or not. That's the first lie I've caught you in. Now don't you worry, in the next half hour there'll be plenty more from you, and I'll catch you out in all of them! So, you had a miscarriage?'

'Yes.'

'I expect you probably helped things along a bit, eh? So that the Führer doesn't get any more soldiers?'

'Now you're lying! If I'd wanted to do something like that, I would hardly have waited till I was in my fifth month.'

A man came in, bearing a piece of paper.

'Inspector, Herr Hergesell tried to burn this in the kitchen a moment ago.'

'What is it? A left-luggage ticket. Frau Hergesell, tell us, has your husband deposited a suitcase in the station at Alexanderplatz?'

'A suitcase? I've no idea; my husband never mentioned it to me.'

'Bring Hergesell in here! I want a man to drive to Alexanderplatz right away and collect the suitcase.' Another man led Karl Hergesell in. The whole flat was jammed with policemen – and they had simply blundered into it.

'What's this suitcase you've left in storage at Alexanderplatz?'

'I don't know, I've never seen inside it. It belongs to an acquaintance. He said there were sheets and clothes in it.'

'Highly likely! And that would be why you tried to burn the receipt once you noticed there were police around!'

Hergesell hesitated, then, with a swift look at his wife, he said, 'I did it because I don't trust my acquaintance. There might be something else inside it. The suitcase is very heavy.'

'And what do you think it might actually contain, then?'

'Maybe printed leaflets. I always tried not to think about it.'

'Tell me about this strange acquaintance of yours, who can't leave his things in left-luggage by himself? His name wouldn't be Karl Hergesell by any chance?'

'No, his name is Schmidt, Heinrich Schmidt.'

'And how do you come to know him, this – Schmidt?'

'Oh, I've known him a long time, ten years at least.'

'Why did you think the suitcase might contain printed matter? What sort of man is this Emil Schulz?'

'Heinrich Schmidt. He was a Social Democrat or a Communist, even. That's what made me think they might be printed papers.'

'Where were you born, Herr Hergesell?'

'Me? In Berlin. In Moabit.'

'And when?'

'On the tenth of April, in 1920.'

'I see, and you're claiming to have known this Heinrich Schmidt for at least ten years, and to have been aware of his political views? You would have been around eleven at the time, Herr Hergesell! You mustn't play me for a fool, because then I get angry, and if I get angry, chances are you'll feel a sudden pain somewhere!'

'I wasn't playing you for a fool! Everything I said is true!'

'Name Heinrich Schmidt: lie number one! Never seen inside the suitcase: lie number two! Reason for giving it up: lie number three! No, my dear Herr Hergesell, every sentence you've spoken to me is a lie!'

'No, everything is true. Heinrich Schmidt was on his way to Königsberg, and because the suitcase was too heavy and he didn't need it where he was going, he asked me to hand it in for him. That's the whole story!'

'And he puts himself to the trouble of travelling out to Erkner to pick up the receipt, when he could carry it around quite comfortably in his pocket! Very likely, Herr Hergesell! Well, let's leave it there for the moment. We'll have occasion to return to it, I think, and you'll be kind enough to accompany me back to Gestapo headquarters. As far as your wife is concerned . . .'

'My wife doesn't know anything about this suitcase business!'

'Funny, that's what she says, too. But I'll get a chance to hear what she knows and doesn't know. But while I have you two

lovebirds together – you've known each other from the time you
worked in the uniform factory?'

'Yes . . .' they said.

'Well, and what was that like, what did you do there?'

'I was an electrician . . .'

'I cut uniform tunics . . .'

'What good, hardworking people you are, to be sure. But
when you weren't snipping material and pulling wires – what
were you up to then, my pretty ones? Could it be that you
formed a nice little Communist cell, the two of you, plus a
certain Jensch, known as Babyface, and one Grigoleit?'

They looked at him and the blood drained out of their faces.
How could he know? They exchanged bewildered looks.

'Yaha!' jeered Laub. 'That's got you rattled, sure enough. You
were under observation, all four of you, and if you hadn't broken
up as soon as you did, I might have made your acquaintance
before now. You're still under surveillance in your factory,
Hergesell!'

They were so bewildered, it didn't even occur to them to
contradict the man.

The inspector looked at them thoughtfully, and suddenly he
put a question. 'So which of them did the suitcase belong to,
Herr Hergesell?' he asked. 'Was it Grigoleit or Babyface?'

'To, uh – it hardly matters given you know everything – it
was Grigoleit who gave it to me. He was going to pick it up in
another week, but that's some time ago now . . .'

'He will have gone AWOL, your Grigoleit! Well, I'll catch up
with him – if he's still alive, that is.'

'Inspector, since my wife and I left the cell, we have not been
involved in any political activity. We even caused the cell to wind
up before it could do anything. We realized that we weren't cut
out for that sort of thing.'

'Hey, I realized that, too! Me!' jeered the inspector.

But Karl Hergesell went on: 'From that time, we've only
thought about our jobs, and we haven't undertaken anything
against the state.'

'Except to look after the suitcase; don't forget about the suitcase, Hergesell! Keeping Communist pamphlets, that's high treason, that'll cost you your neck, my dear fellow! Hey, Frau Hergesell! Frau Hergesell! What are you getting so hot about! Fabian, will you detach the young lady from her husband, but be sure to be very gentle, Fabian, for Lord's sake don't hurt the little poppet. She's recently had a miscarriage, the poor thing, she was so anxious not to give the Führer any more soldiers!'

'Trudel!' begged Hergesell. 'Don't listen to him! There might not be leaflets in the suitcase at all, I just sometimes thought that's what it might be. There might be just sheets and clothes in it. Grigoleit wasn't necessarily lying.'

'That's the way, young sir,' praised Inspector Laub. 'Give the young lady a bit of courage! Is that better, sweetheart? Can we carry on with our conversation? Well, let's change the subject from Karl Hergesell's treason to that of Trudel Hergesell, née Baumann . . .'

'My wife knew nothing about these matters! My wife has never done anything against the law!'

'No, no, quite, you were both good National Socialists, right?' Suddenly Inspector Laub was seized with fury. 'You know what you are? You're cowardly Commie swine! You're rats! But I'll expose you, I'll drag you both to the gallows! I want to see you both swing! You with your suitcase full of lies! And you with your so-called miscarriage! You jumped off the table till the bell rang! Isn't that right? Isn't that right? Tell me!'

He had seized the half-conscious Trudel and was shaking her.

'Leave my wife alone! Take your hands off my wife!' Hergesell grabbed hold of the inspector. He was struck on the jaw by Fabian. Three minutes later, handcuffed and guarded by Fabian, he was sitting in the kitchen and knew – wild despair in his heart – that Trudel was in the hands of her tormentor and there was nothing he could do.

And Laub continued to torment Trudel. Already half demented with worry for her Karli, she was now ordered to talk about Quangel's postcards. Laub didn't believe in the chance encounter on the street: no, she had remained in contact with the Quangels, cowardly Communist conspirators that they all were, and her husband, her Karli, had been in on it too!

'How many postcards did you drop then? What was written on them? What did your husband have to say about it?'

And so he went on tormenting her, hour after hour, and all the while Hergesell sat in the kitchen, with hell in his heart.

And finally: the return of the police car, the suitcase, the opening of the suitcase.

'Will you tickle the lock open for me, Fabian!' the inspector said. Karl Hergesell was back in the parlour, under guard. At opposite ends of the room, the Hergesells looked at one another, pale and anguished.

'A bit heavy for sheets and a change of clothing!' the inspector sneered, while Fabian jiggled a wire in the lock. 'Well, we're about to see the treasure! I'm afraid it might not turn out too well for you, eh – what do you think, Hergesell?'

'Inspector, my wife didn't know anything about the suitcase!' Hergesell proclaimed once more.

'Yes, and I suppose you didn't know anything about her dropping treasonable postcards in various staircases about town for Quangel! Each little traitor on his own! Call that a marriage!'

'No!' yelled Hergesell. 'You didn't do that, Trudel! Tell me you didn't!'

'I'm afraid she's already confessed to it!'

'Just once, Karli, and it was pure chance . . .'

'I'm not having you talking to each other! One more word, Hergesell, and you're going back in the kitchen! All right, at last – now, what's inside?'

He and Fabian stood in front of the suitcase so that the Hergesells were unable to see inside. The two detectives exchanged whispers. Then Fabian pulled out the heavy contents. A small machine, shiny screws, springs, gleaming blackness . . .

'Well, if it's not a printing press!' said Inspector Laub. 'A pretty little printing press – for Communist pamphlets. Well, that takes care of you, Hergesell. Once and for all!'

'I had no idea what was in the suitcase,' Karl Hergesell said, but it sounded utterly feeble.

'As if that mattered! You were obliged to report your meeting with Grigoleit, and to hand over the suitcase! That's enough, Fabian. Pack up. I know more than I need to know. I want the woman cuffed as well.'

'Farewell, Karli!' cried Trudel Hergesell with a strong voice. 'Farewell, my darling. You made me terribly happy . . .'

'Will you shut that bitch up!' yelled the inspector. 'What do you think you're playing at, Hergesell?'

Hergesell had broken away from his guard when, on the other side of the room, a punch on the mouth silenced Trudel. Even though he was handcuffed, he managed to knock over Trudel's abuser. They rolled about on the floor.

The inspector gestured to Fabian. He stood over the pair on the floor, watched for his moment, and then struck Karl Hergesell three or four times on the head.

Hergesell gave a groan, his limbs twitched, and then he lay still at Trudel's feet. She looked impassively down at him, her mouth bleeding.

During the long drive back to the city, she hoped in vain that he would come round so that she could look into his eyes again. But no, nothing.

They had done nothing. But they were doomed . . .

53

Otto Quangel's Heaviest Burden

Of the nineteen days that Otto Quangel spent in the basement of the Gestapo headquarters before being handed on to the examining magistrate at the People's Court, the interrogations of Inspector Laub were not the hardest thing he had to bear, even though Laub used all of his not inconsiderable resources to break, as he put it, Quangel's resistance. This meant, more or less, doing everything he could to turn the prisoner into a panicked, gibbering wreck.

Nor was it his steadily growing, tormenting anxiety about Anna that affected Otto Quangel so. He hadn't seen his wife and never heard anything directly about her. But when Laub in his interrogations dropped the name of Trudel Baumann, or rather Trudel Hergesell, he knew that his wife had been intimidated or outwitted, and that a name had escaped her lips that should never have been mentioned.

Later, as it became clearer that Trudel Baumann and her husband had been arrested, had given statements, and were caught up in the ongoing investigation, he spent many hours in his mind quarrelling with his wife. It had always been a source of pride to him in this life that he was an island unto himself, not needing others, and not a burden on them either, and now through his fault (because he took responsibility for Anna) two young people had been drawn into his affairs.

But the quarrel did not go on for very long, because soon his grief and worry for his wife came to dominate his thoughts. When left alone, he would dig his nails into his palms, shut his eyes, summon up all his strength – and think of Anna, try to imagine her in her cell, and transmit streams of energy to her to give her fresh courage, so that she would not lose her dignity, not humiliate herself in front of that miserable wretch Laub, who had so little that was human about him.

His worry for Anna was hard to bear, but still it wasn't the heaviest thing.

Nor was it the almost nightly incursions into his cell by drunken SS men and their officers, unleashing their rage and sadism on their helpless victims. They would tear open the cell door and teem in, wild with alcohol and intent on seeing blood, the twitching of humans in pain or death, the desire to feast their eyes on the weakness of the flesh. This too was very hard to bear, but it wasn't the hardest thing.

The hardest was the fact that he was not alone in his cell, that he had a cellmate, a fellow sufferer, someone guilty as himself. Worse, this was a person who caused Quangel to shudder: a wild, demented animal, heartless and cowardly, trembling and crude, a person whom Quangel could not so much as look at without feeling revulsion and yet was forced to be pleasant to, because the man had far greater physical strength than the old foreman.

Karl Ziemke – Karlchen to the warders – was a man of about thirty, with a Herculean build, a round, mastiff's head with tiny eyes, and long hairy arms and hands. His low, lumpy forehead under its fringe of matted hair was always creased with horizontal furrows. He spoke little, and what he did speak was crazed and murderous. As Quangel soon learned from the warders, Karlchen Ziemke had once been a prominent member of the SS, he had been given fairly spectacular missions to accomplish, and the number of people those hairy paws had killed would never be ascertained, as Karlchen hadn't bothered to keep count.

But for the professional killer Karl Ziemke, even these murderous times hadn't sufficed, and when he had no official employment he had taken to killing freelance. Though he never neglected to rob his victims of money and valuables, robbery had never been his motive, but rather the sheer love of killing. In the end he had drawn attention to himself, as he had been unwise enough to kill not only Jews and undesirables but also impeccable Aryans, among them a member of the Party. He had been consigned to the basement, and it was as yet uncertain what would become of him.

Karlchen Ziemke, who had sent so many others to an unnatural death, had become fearful for his own precious life, and in his brain, which was not much larger than a five-year-old boy's, only infinitely more depraved, the idea had surfaced that he might save himself from the consequences of his actions if he pretended insanity. His idea was to act like a dog – or this had been suggested to him by some comrades, which was likelier – and he played the part with considerable tenacity.

Usually he scrabbled around the cell on all fours, completely naked, ate out of his dish like a dog, and repeatedly tried to bite Quangel in the leg. Or else he demanded that the old foreman toss him a brush for hours on end, which he would then fetch in his jaws and be petted and praised for doing so. Or else Quangel would have to swing Karlchen's trousers round and round like a skipping rope for Karlchen to jump over.

If the foreman didn't show sufficient enthusiasm for these entertainments, the 'dog' would jump him, knock him to the ground, and go for his throat, and there was always the possibility that the game would turn serious. The warders took deep delight in Karlchen's antics. They would stand by the cell door for hours on end, spurring him on and making him angry, and Quangel had to take the consequences. But when they came to take their drunken fury out on the prisoners, then they would throw Karlchen to the ground, and he would spread his arms, begging them to kick the guts out of his bare body.

It was with this man that Quangel was condemned to share his life, day after day, hour upon hour, minute by minute. He, who had always lived as self-sufficient, now no longer had a quarter of an hour to himself. Even at night, when he sought the consolation of sleep, he wasn't safe from his tormentor. Suddenly the 'dog' would be squatting by his cot, with his paw on Quangel's chest, demanding water or a place on Quangel's bed. He would have to move aside, disgusted by the unwashed body, hairy as a beast's but without an animal's purity and innocence. Thereupon Karlchen would begin to bark quietly, and lick first Otto Quangel's face and then, by and by, the rest of him.

Yes, it was hard to bear, and often Otto Quangel would ask himself why he did bear it, given that the end was sure to be near. But he felt a reluctance to do away with himself, and to thus desert Anna, even though he wasn't able to see her. There was a reluctance in him to make it easier for them, to pre-empt their judgement. Let them take away his life with rope or axe, but they weren't to think that he felt any guilt in himself. No, he wanted to spare them nothing, and so he didn't spare himself Karlchen Ziemke.

And then a strange thing happened: as the nineteen days passed, the more devoted the 'dog' seemed to become to him. He didn't bite him any more, didn't knock him over, didn't go for his throat. If his SS chums had given him a better morsel for once, he would insist on sharing it with Quangel, and often the 'dog' would rest his gigantic round skull on the lap of the elderly man for hours, close his eyes, and yap softly to himself, while Quangel's fingers brushed his pelt.

The foreman wondered whether in the course of feigning madness this animal hadn't actually become mad. But if he was, then so were his 'free' comrades, and then it didn't matter, because along with their crazy Führer and the inanely grinning Himmler they were one brood that would have to be wiped off the face of the earth so that sensible people could live.

When it emerged that Otto Quangel was being shipped out, Karlchen was broken-hearted. He whimpered and yelped, he forced Quangel to take the whole of his bread ration, and when the foreman was made to step out into the corridor and press his face against the wall with upraised arms, the naked man slipped out of his cell, hunkered down beside him, and howled pitifully. That had the good effect that the SS men weren't quite as rough with Quangel as they were with other inmates: a man who had won the heart of a dog like that, this man with the cold, implacable bird face, impressed even the Führer's henchmen.

And when the order came to move out, when Karlchen the

dog was driven back into his cell, then Quangel's face was no longer cold and implacable, and in his heart he felt a slight pressure akin to regret. The man who all his life had only ever given his heart to one being, his wife, was sorry to see the multiple murderer, the beast of a man, pass out of his life.

54

Anna Quangel and Trudel Hergesell

Maybe it was just mismanagement that following Berta's death Anna Quangel was given Trudel Hergesell as a cellmate. Or maybe it was that Inspector Laub had nothing but contempt for them anyway. What they knew had been wrung out of them – whatever they had heard from their menfolk – and then that was it. The real criminals were always the men; the women were mere accomplices – which admittedly did nothing to save them from being executed along with the men.

Yes, Berta had died, the Berta who had innocently betrayed to Anna the presence of her sister-in-law and brought down the wrath of Inspector Laub upon her head. She had sputtered out like a light. With ever quieter voice she had kept imploring her cellmate not to send for anyone, and she finally died in Anna Quangel's arms. Berta – whatever her surname was, whatever she was in for – was suddenly no more. There was a strange rattle in her throat, she had struggled for breath, and then a wash of blood had come up, and her arms, round Anna's shoulders, had relaxed . . .

She had lain there, very pale and still – and Anna in anguish asked herself whether she was not partly to blame for this death. If only she hadn't mentioned her sister-in-law to Inspector Laub! And then she thought of Trudel Baumann, and she started to shake – there was someone she really had betrayed! Of course there were reasons, excuses. How could she have known what the consequences would be of mentioning Ottochen's bride? And then it had been got away from her, step by step by step, and in the end the betrayal was plain to see, and she had brought misery to a human being who was dear to her, and maybe to more than one.

When Anna Quangel imagined being confronted with Trudel

and having to repeat to her the perfidious words she had said, it made her shake all over. But when she thought of her husband, she felt true despair. Because she was convinced that this conscientious, diligent man would never forgive her for this betrayal, and that she had lost the only comrade she had ever had, even before her approaching death.

How could I have been so feeble, Anna Quangel upbraided herself, and each time she was fetched to an interrogation session with Laub, she didn't pray that he not torture her, she prayed for the strength not to incriminate others in spite of all the tortures he had ready for her. And this small, slight woman insisted on bearing her part, and more than her part: she insisted that it had been she, and she alone – with one or two exceptions – who had delivered the postcards, and that she alone had thought up their contents and dictated them to her husband. She was the only begetter of the postcards; once her son had fallen, that's when she had had the idea.

Inspector Laub, well aware that her statements were lies and that this woman was not capable of doing the things she claimed to have done – Inspector Laub ranted and raved and tortured her as much as he liked, but she would sign no other statements and refused to withdraw any of her confessions, even if he proved to her ten times over that they couldn't possibly be right. Laub had overwound the screw, and he was powerless. And when Anna was brought back to her cell after each such interrogation, she had a feeling of relief, as though she had atoned for a part of her guilt, as though Otto could be a tiny bit pleased with her. And the thought grew in her that by taking all the guilt upon herself, she might even be able to save Otto's life . . .

In accordance with the way things were done in the Gestapo prison, there was no hurry to remove the dead woman's body from Anna's cell. It might have been mismanagement, or again it could have been further, intentional torture – at any rate, Berta's corpse was on its third day in the repulsively sweetish-smelling cell when the door was unlocked and there was shoved into the cell the very woman whom Anna had been in such dread of seeing.

Trudel Hergesell advanced one step into the cell. Her eyes took in almost nothing; she was tired to death and almost insensate with fear for Karli, who had not come round and from whom she had just been brusquely separated. She gave a little scream of horror when she smelled the disgusting sweet reek and saw the dead woman, bloated and discoloured on her wooden pallet.

She moaned, 'I can't go on,' and Anna Quangel caught the woman she had betrayed as she keeled over.

'Trudel!' she whispered in her ear, 'Trudel, can you forgive me? I told them your name, because you were Ottochen's bride. And then he tortured me until he got everything out of me. I don't understand it myself any more. Trudel, don't look at me like that, I beg you! Trudel, weren't you going to have a baby? Have I destroyed that for you as well?'

While Anna Quangel was speaking, Trudel Hergesell had broken away from her embrace and retreated to the door of the cell. Now she leaned against the iron-studded door, and with a face gone pale looked over at the old woman, who was looking back at her from the opposite wall.

'It was you that did that, Mother?' she asked. 'You did it?'

And with a sudden outburst: 'Oh, it's not me that I care about! But they broke my Karli, and I don't know if he'll ever come round. Perhaps he's already dead.'

The tears spurted from her eyes as she cried, 'And I can't see him any more! I don't know what's being done to him, and maybe days and days will pass before I hear anything. He might be dead and buried, but he's still living in me. And I won't get to have his baby – how poor I have suddenly become! Only a few weeks ago, before I met Dad, I had everything I needed to be happy, and I was happy too! And now I've got nothing. Nothing! Oh, Mother . . .'

And she suddenly added, 'But the miscarriage wasn't your fault, Mother. That was before anything happened.'

Suddenly Trudel Hergesell rushed swaying through the cell, buried her head in Anna's bosom, and wailed, 'Oh, Mother, I'm so unhappy! Won't you tell me that Karli will make it!'

And Anna Quangel kissed her and whispered, 'He will live, Trudel, and so will you! You've not done anything bad, either of you!'

They embraced each other silently. Each rested in the other's love until a faint hope stirred.

Then Trudel shook her head and said, 'No, we won't make it out alive. They've found out too much about us. What you said is true: neither of us did anything bad. Karli kept a suitcase for someone without knowing what was in it, and I dropped a postcard for Dad. But according to them, that's high treason and will cost us our lives.'

'It must be that horrible Laub who said that to you!'

'I don't know his name, and I don't want to, either. They're all like that! The ones who bring you here are all the same. But maybe it's better this way: sitting in prison for years and years . . .'

'But they won't be in power for years and years, Trudel!'

'Who knows? And all the things they were able to do to the Jews and the other peoples – unpunished! Do you believe there is a God, Mum?'

'Yes, Trudel, I do. Otto was dead against it, but it's the one secret I kept from him: I still believe in God.'

'I never did, really. But it would be nice if He existed, because then I could be sure that Karli and I would be together after death!'

'And so you shall, Trudel. You see, even Otto doesn't believe in God. He says he's sure everything comes to an end after this life. But I know we will be together once we're dead, for ever and ever. I know it, Trudel!'

Trudel looked over at the cot with the motionless body on it, and fretted.

She said, 'That woman looks so awful! It scares me to look at her, all puffy and blotchy! I don't want it to be me, lying there like that!'

'It's her third day like that, Trudel – they won't take her away. She was beautiful when she died, quiet and dignified. But now the soul has flown from her, and she's just lying there like a piece of rotting meat.'

'They should take her away! I can't stand to look at it! I don't want to breathe the stink any more!'

And before Anna Quangel could do anything to stop her, Trudel had run over to the door. She drummed with her fists against the iron and shouted: 'Open up! Open up! Hey!'

That wasn't allowed. They weren't supposed to make any noise; in fact, even speaking was against the rules.

Anna Quangel dashed over to Trudel, seized hold of her hands, drew her away from the door, and whispered fearfully, 'You mustn't do that, Trudel! It's against the rules! They'll come in and beat you up!'

But it was too late. The lock cracked open, and a gigantic SS man dashed in with rubber truncheon upraised. 'What are you shouting about, you whores?' he yelled. 'Do you want room service?'

The two women looked at him in terror from a corner of the cell.

'It stinks like a morgue in here. How long has that been lying there?'

He was a young fellow, and his face had gone ghastly pale.

'The third day already,' said Anna. 'Oh, won't you be kind and get the dead woman out of here! We really can't breathe any more!'

The SS man mumbled something and left the cell. But he didn't lock the door behind him.

The two women snuck over to the door and pushed it open just a little, and drew in the smells of disinfectant and toilet from the corridor as if they were balm.

Then they retreated inside again, because the young SS man was coming back along the corridor.

'There!' he said. He had a piece of paper in his hand. 'Well, get on with it then! You, old woman, take the legs, and you, young one, take the head. Come on – surely you can manage a bundle of bones like that!'

For all its coarseness, his tone was almost cheery, and he helped them carry.

They went down a long corridor; then there was an iron door

in the way. Their escort showed the sentry his piece of paper, and they went down many flights of stone steps. It got damp, and the electric light grew dim.

'There!' said the SS man, opening a door. 'This is the morgue. Lay her down on the pallet there. But take the clothes off her. Clothes are in short supply. We need all we can get!'

He laughed, but it sounded forced.

The women gasped with horror. Men and women, all naked as the day they were born, lay there with smashed features and bloody welts, with twisted limbs encrusted with blood and dirt. No one had bothered to shut their eyes, and their dead stares seemed sometimes to blink, as if they were curious about the newcomer, or eager to welcome her.

While Anna and Trudel with shaking hands set about undressing Berta, they couldn't help looking around at this collection of the dead: a mother whose long-drooping breasts were now empty for all time; an old man who had looked forward to dying peacefully in bed at the end of a long, hardworking life; a young, pale-lipped girl, created to give and receive love; a youth with a shattered nose and a beautiful symmetrical body that looked as if it had been fashioned from yellow ivory.

It was quiet in the room except for the rustling of Berta's clothes in the hands of the two women. Then a fly buzzed, and everything went quiet again.

Hands in his pockets, the SS man stood and watched the two women at their work. He yawned and lit a cigarette, and he said, 'Well, that's life!' And then everything was quiet once more.

Once Anna Quangel had tied the clothes into a bundle, he said, 'Okay, let's go!'

But Trudel Hergesell laid her hand on his black sleeve and begged, 'Please, please – couldn't you let me look around here! It's my husband – in case he's down here somewhere . . .'

For a moment he looked at her. Suddenly he said, 'Girl! Girl! What are you doing here?' Slowly he moved his head this way and that. 'My sister back home in the village is about your age.' He looked at her again. 'Okay, you can check. But be quick about it.'

She walked quietly among the bodies, looking into all the extinguished faces. Many were disfigured by wounds, but the skin colour or physical marks on the bodies told her they couldn't be her Karli.

She came back, very pale.

'No. He's not here – not yet.'

The sentry avoided her eye. 'Okay, go!' he said, and let them precede him.

But as long as he was on duty that day, he kept opening their door, so that they might have slightly better air in their cell. He brought fresh sheets for the dead woman's bed, too – a mercy in this implacable hell.

That day, Inspector Laub didn't get much joy from his interrogation of the two women. They had been able to comfort one another, they had taken a little sympathy from one another and even from the SS man, and as a result they felt strong.

But there were many days ahead of them, and this particular SS man was never on duty in their corridor again. He had probably been dismissed as unsuitable – he was too human to do duty here.

55

Baldur Persicke Pays a Visit

Baldur Persicke, proud Napola student, the most successful scion of the Persicke clan, has wound up his affairs in Berlin. At last he can go back and resume his training in being a lord of creation. He has fetched his mother from her hiding place with her relatives and given her strict orders never to leave home again, otherwise she will face all sorts of consequences, and he has visited his sister at Ravensbrück concentration camp where he duly complimented her on her mistreatment of old women. In the evening, brother and sister, along with a few other Ravensbrück warders and some friends from Fürstenberg, celebrated a proper little orgy among themselves, with booze and cigarettes and 'love' . . .

But Baldur Persicke's principal efforts were directed at the resolution of serious business difficulties. His father, old Persicke, had done some stupid things in his drunkenness. There was said to be money missing from funds, and he was even supposed to be put in front of a Party tribunal. Baldur had pulled all the strings he could – he had used medical reports that described the old man as senile, he had cajoled and threatened, he had appeared by turns snappish and conciliatory, he had exploited the break-in, after which the money had gone missing again – and in the end he had succeeded in having the whole rotten business discreetly set aside. He hadn't even had to sell anything from the flat: the missing money was booked as stolen. Not stolen by old Persicke – oh, no! – but by Borkhausen and his accomplices, and so the Persicke honour remained unstained.

While the Hergesells were being threatened with violence and capital punishment for a crime they hadn't committed, Party member Persicke was forgiven for one he had.

All this has been quite skilfully accomplished by Baldur

Persicke, of whom nothing less would be expected. He can now go back to his Napola institution, but before doing so, he wants to fulfil his family duties by visiting his father in the drying-out clinic. Also, he wants to forestall any possible repetition of such events and reassure his timid mother that she can feel safe at home in the flat.

As he is Baldur Persicke, he is immediately given permission to call upon his father without the presence of doctors or other medical personnel.

Baldur finds the old man in pretty poor shape. In fact, he looks as shrivelled up as a pricked balloon.

Yes, the good days of the rowdy old publican are over. He is just a ghost, but a ghost that still has some bad habits. The father begs his son for something to smoke, and after the son has refused a couple of times ('You don't deserve it, you old crook') he breaks out a cigarette for the old fellow. But when old Persicke begs the son to smuggle in a bottle of schnapps – only once – Baldur just laughs. He smacks his father on his bony, shaky knee, and says, 'You'd better get used to it, Dad! You won't be getting any more schnapps to drink as long as you live, you've let the side down too badly!'

And while the father glowers angrily, his son complacently enumerates all the steps he's been forced to take to tidy up the mess the old man made.

Old Persicke was never much of a diplomat. He was always one to say what he thought straight out, and not to worry himself about what anyone else might feel. And so he now says, 'You always were a braggart, Baldur! I knew that the Party would never do anything against me, given that I've been part of Hitler's organization these past fifteen years! If you were put to any trouble, then it's your own silly fault. I would have settled it with a sentence or two, once I was out!'

Stupid father. Had he flattered the son, thanked and praised him, then Baldur Persicke would be in a more generous frame of mind now. Instead he is deeply offended, and says curtly, 'Yes, once you're out, Father! But you won't get out of this bin, not as long as you live!'

These pitiless words give the father such a shock that he begins trembling all over. But he manages to get a grip on himself, and says: 'I'd like to see the man that could pin me down here! For the moment I'm still a free man, and Dr Martens told me himself that if I keep off the sauce for six more weeks, I can leave. Cured.'

'You won't be cured, Father,' mocked Baldur. 'You'll never stay on the wagon. I've seen it often enough. I'll tell the doctor so myself when I go, and make sure you're committed.'

'He won't do that! Dr Martens is very fond of me; he says no one can tell stories like I can! He'll not do that to me! And anyway he promised to let me go in six weeks!'

'But if I tell him you were just trying to persuade me to smuggle in a bottle for you, he might think differently about your progress!'

'You won't do that, Baldur! You're my son, I'm your father . . .'

'Where does that get us? It stands to reason I'm someone's son, and I don't think I was exactly lucky in the father stakes . . .'

He looked contemptuously at his father. Then he added, 'No, Dad, I'd get used to it if I were you: you'll be staying here. If you get out, all you'd do is bring disgrace on the whole family!'

The old man is desperate. He says, 'Your mother will never permit that to happen, the thing with the committing, or me being detained here for ever!'

'Well, I don't think it'll be as long as all that, from the look of you!' Baldur laughs and crosses his legs, with their nicely fitted riding breeches. Approvingly he views the sheen – his mother's work – of his boots. 'Mother's so scared of you, she won't even come and visit you. Don't imagine she's forgotten the times you grabbed her by the throat and choked her! She'll not forget that!'

'Then I'll write to the Führer!' yelled old Persicke in a rage. 'The Führer won't abandon an old fighter like me!'

'What good are you to the Führer? The Führer doesn't give

a shit about you; he'll not waste his time looking at anything you scribble to him! Anyway, with your trembly old booze-hound's hands you're not capable of writing anything, and they won't allow any letter from you to leave these premises, I'll see to that! If I was you, I wouldn't waste the paper.'

'Baldur, take pity on me! You were a sweet little boy once! We used to go for walks together on Sundays! Do you remember we went up the Kreuzberg one time, and the water was so pretty, pink and blue? I always used to buy you sausages and sweets, and when you got into that trouble with the little girl when you were eleven, I made sure you didn't get thrown out of school and sent to a home! Where would you be without your old man, Baldur? You can't let them keep me in this loony bin!'

Baldur had listened indifferently to this long outpouring. Now he said, 'So you're trying to pull out a few emotional stops, eh, Dad? Good idea. Only that sort of thing doesn't work with me. You ought to know I don't care about emotions. I'd rather have a proper ham sandwich than all the emotion in the world! But I don't want to leave you without one more cigarette – hup, there you go!'

But the old fellow was too agitated to be able to think of smoking now, and the cigarette fell – to Baldur's irritation – unregarded to the floor.

'Baldur!' wailed the old man again. 'You don't know what it's like in here! They leave me to starve, and the warders keep on hitting me. The other inmates hit me as well. My hands are so shaky, I can't fight back, and they even take my little bit of food away from me . . .'

While the old man was pleading with him, Baldur made ready to leave, but his father clung to him, and went on, even faster now, 'And far worse things happen, too. Sometimes, if an inmate makes too much noise, a nurse will give him an injection with green stuff, I don't know the name of it. It makes you puke and puke, you end up puking the soul out of your body, and then you're gone. Just like that. Dead. Baldur, you wouldn't want your own father to die like that, puking the soul out of his body, not your own father! Baldur, be kind, help me! Get me out of here, I'm so frightened!'

But Baldur had heard enough of these lamentations. He broke free from old Persicke, pushed him down into a chair, and said, 'Well, so long, Dad! I'll give Mum your regards! Remember there's one more cigarette for you on the table. Don't waste it!'

And with that, the son of his father was gone.

But Baldur did not leave the clinic immediately. Instead, he had himself announced to Dr Martens. He was lucky: the doctor was present and available. He greeted his visitor politely, and for an instant the two men eyed one another warily.

Then the doctor said: 'You attend a Napola school, Herr Persicke, or am I mistaken?'

'No, you're quite right, I am at a Napola,' Baldur replied proudly.

'So much is being done for our young people nowadays,' said the doctor, nodding approvingly. 'I wish I might have enjoyed such preferential treatment in my youth. You haven't received your call-up yet, Herr Persicke?'

'I'd be surprised if the regular army bothered me,' said Baldur Persicke, with casual contempt. 'I'll probably be given a large estate to administer, in the Ukraine or Crimea. A few dozen square miles.'

'I see,' said the doctor.

'Are you in the Party, Dr Martens?'

'Unfortunately not. To be absolutely honest with you, a grandfather of mine committed a little folly, the er, little aberration. You understand?' And quickly going on, 'But it's all been sorted out, my superiors have given me their support, and I'm registered as purebred Aryan. I mean to say, that's what I am. So I hope to be permitted to wear the swastika before long.'

Baldur sat very erect. A pure Aryan himself, he felt vastly superior to the doctor, who needed to resort to such backstairs methods. 'I wanted to talk to you about my father, Doctor,' he said, his tone almost that of a superior.

'Oh, your father's doing fine, Herr Persicke! I think in six or eight weeks we'll be able to send him home cured . . .'

'My father is incurable!' Baldur Persicke brusquely interrupted him. 'My father has been drinking ever since I can remember. And if you release him in the morning as cured, he'll arrive at home in the afternoon drunk as a skunk. We've had these sort of cures before. It is the wish of my mother and my siblings that my father spend the rest of his life here. I share their wish, Doctor!'

'Of course, of course!' the doctor hurriedly assured him. 'I'll have a word with the professor . . .'

'No need. This can be settled between us. The consequence of my father ever turning up at our home will be the arrival, that same day, of a completely inebriated man on your premises! That's your so-called complete cure, Doctor, and I promise you that the consequences for you personally will not be pretty either!'

They eyed one another through their glasses. Unfortunately, the doctor was a coward: he lowered his eyes before the blatant impertinence of Baldur. He said, 'Of course there is always a danger with hardened drinkers, with dipsomaniacs, as we say, of a relapse. And if, as you tell me, your father has always been a drinker . . .'

'He drank up his pub when he had it. He drank everything my mother earned. He would drink up everything we four children earned, if we allowed him to. My father stays here!'

'Your father stays here. Until further notice. If at some later stage, when the war is over, you form the impression while visiting your father that his condition . . .'

Again, Baldur Persicke interrupted the doctor. 'My father will receive no visits, neither from me nor from my siblings, nor from my mother. We know he is in good hands here, and that's enough for us.' Baldur looked piercingly at the doctor, and kept his eyes raised. Having spoken thus far in a loud, almost peremptory tone, he now continued more quietly, 'My father mentioned a certain green injection, Doctor . . .'

The doctor gave a little twitch. 'Purely a control measure. Very occasionally used for young and difficult patients. The advanced age of your father prohibits . . .'

Again, he was interrupted. 'My father has already been given one of these green injections . . .'

The doctor exclaimed, 'Out of the question! I'm sorry, Herr Persicke, there must be some misunderstanding!'

Baldur said severely, 'My father told me about the injection. He told me it had done him good. Is there any reason why he cannot continue to receive such treatment, Doctor?'

The doctor was entirely confused. 'But, Herr Persicke! It's a control measure! The patient vomits for hours, sometimes for days!'

'Well, so what? Let him puke! Maybe he enjoys it! He assured me the green injection had done him good. He can't wait for the next one. Why do you refuse him the drug, if it helps his condition?'

'No, no!' put in the doctor hurriedly. And, deeply ashamed, he added, 'I really think there must be some misunderstanding. I have never once heard of a patient requesting . . .'

'Now, Doctor, who understands the patient better than his own son? And I'm my father's favourite son, at that. I would really be most obliged if you would instruct the chief orderly, or whoever's responsibility it is, to give my father an injection on the spot. It would mean my going home – so to speak – in a more tranquil frame of mind, having managed to satisfy the old man's wish!'

Very pale now, the doctor stared at the other man.

'You really mean it, don't you? Right now?' he murmured.

'Can you be in the least doubt as to what I mean, Doctor? I must say, for a senior practitioner, I find you rather, how shall I say, soft. You were quite right in what you said a moment ago, by the way: a spell at a Napola school would have developed your leadership qualities!' And he added maliciously, 'And as far as your genetic flaw goes, you must know that there are other control methods . . .'

After a long pause, the doctor quietly said, 'I'll go and administer an injection to your father . . .'

'Dr Martens, please, why go to the trouble personally? Why not leave it to the hospital orderly? Since it seems to be among his duties?'

The doctor was struggling with himself. There was silence in the room.

Slowly he got to his feet. 'Then I will tell the hospital orderly . . .'

'I don't mind accompanying you. Your enterprise here is fascinating to me. You know, the weeding out of those who are unfit for life, sterilizations, and so forth . . .'

Baldur Persicke stood by as the doctor gave the orderly his instructions. Patient Persicke was to receive such and such an injection . . .

'He means, a special puke jab, chum!' said Baldur ingratiatingly. 'How many cc's do you give, normally? A few more wouldn't hurt, in this case! Oh look, I have a few cigarettes over. Take the pack, senior orderly!'

The orderly thanked him and left, the syringe full of green liquid in his hand.

'Your senior orderly looks as strong as an ox! He's not one to take any nonsense from the patients! Muscles, muscles are half of life, I always say, Dr Martens! Well, my sincerest thanks, Doctor! I hope the treatment continues successfully! Heil Hitler, eh!'

'Heil Hitler, Herr Persicke!'

Back in his office, Dr Martens slumped down in a chair. He was trembling all over and could feel a cold sweat on his brow. But he couldn't calm down. He got up and went over to his medicine cabinet. Slowly he filled a syringe. But it wasn't the green liquid that he filled it with, however appropriate it might be to puke at the state of the world and of his own life in particular. Dr Martens preferred morphine.

He returned to his chair, stretched out pleasurably, and waited for the narcotic to take effect.

What a coward I am! he thought. It makes me sick. That ghastly impertinent punk – probably the only influence he has is his big mouth. And the way I kowtowed to him. I didn't need to. But there's always my bloody grandmother and the fact that I can't keep quiet about anything! And she was such a lovely old lady, and I was so fond of her . . .

His mind wandered: he saw the old lady with the fine features in front of him again. Her apartment smelled of seedcake and rose pot-pourri. She had such delicate hands, the hands of an old child . . .

And because of her I humiliated myself in front of that bastard! On second thoughts, Herr Persicke, I don't think I will join your Party. I think it's too late for that. It took you all too long.

He blinked, stretched. His breathing came easier, he felt better now.

I'll go and visit the old man afterward. At any rate he won't be getting any more of those jabs. I hope he survives this one. I'll go and see him in a minute; I want to enjoy my morphine first. But straight afterwards – that's a promise!

56

Otto Quangel's Second Cellmate

When Otto Quangel was brought by a warder to his new cell in the remand prison, a tall man got up from the table where he had been reading and stood under the cell window in the prescribed position, with his hands pressed against the seams of his trousers. Something about the way he executed this show of respect suggested he didn't think it very necessary.

The warder motioned to him to relax. 'It's all right, Doctor,' he said. 'I'm bringing you your new cellmate!'

'Good!' said the man, though in his dark suit, shirt and tie, he looked to Otto Quangel more like a gentleman than a cellmate. 'Good! Reichhardt's the name, musician. Accused of Communist activities. And you?'

Quangel felt a cool, firm hand in his own. 'Quangel,' he said hesitantly. 'I'm a carpenter. They're accusing me of high treason.'

'Oh, it's you!' exclaimed the musician Dr Reichhardt. And to the warder who was just about to shut the door, 'Two portions again from today, okay?'

'All right, Doctor!' said the warder, 'I won't forget!'

And the door closed behind him.

The two men looked at one another curiously. Quangel was doubtful; he almost wished he was back in the Gestapo basement with Karlchen the human dog. To be put with this fine gentleman, a doctor – it made him uneasy.

The 'gentleman' smiled. Then he said, 'Just behave as if you were on your own, if that's easier for you. I won't bother you. I read a lot, I play chess with myself. I do exercises to keep in shape. Sometimes I sing a little to myself, but only very quietly; it's forbidden, of course. Does any of that bother you?'

'No, it doesn't bother me,' replied Quangel. And almost in

spite of himself, he added, 'I've just come from the Gestapo cells, where I spent three weeks locked up with a madman who didn't wear clothes and thought he was a dog. I don't think there's much that would bother me any more.'

'Good!' said Dr Reichhardt. 'Of course I would have preferred it if music had been something you liked. The only way of finding a little harmony within these walls is to make your own.'

'I wouldn't know about that,' replied Otto Quangel. And he added, 'This is a pretty plush establishment compared to where I've just been.'

The gentleman had sat down at his table again and picked up his book. He answered amiably, 'I spent some time where you've just been. Yes, it's true, things are better here. At least they don't knock you about. The warders are usually dull, but not completely barbarous. But prison is prison, you know: that doesn't change. I have a couple of privileges. I'm allowed to read, smoke, get my own meals delivered from outside, use my own clothes and bed linen. But I'm a special case, and even with privileges, prison remains prison. You need to get to a point where you no longer feel the walls.'

'And have you?'

'Maybe. Most of the time. Not always. No, not always. When I think of my family, not then.'

'I just have a wife,' said Quangel. 'Is there a women's wing in this prison?'

'Yes, but we never see any of them.'

'I suppose not.' Otto Quangel sighed. 'They arrested my wife as well. I hope they brought her here today too.' And he added, 'She's too weak to last long in the cells.'

'Well, I hope she's here, too, then,' said the man kindly. 'We'll find out through the chaplain. Maybe he'll come this afternoon. By the way, now that you're here, you're allowed access to a lawyer.'

He nodded amiably to Quangel and added, 'There's lunch in an hour.' Then he put on his reading glasses and again began to read.

Quangel looked at him for a moment, but the gentleman was engrossed in his book and clearly did not want further conversation.

Queer, these fine gentlemen! he thought. I had a lot of questions for him still. But if he doesn't want to speak, that's okay as well. I don't want to be his dog and not leave him a moment's peace.

And, ever so slightly offended, he set about making up his bed.

The cell was clean and light. Nor was it all that small either: three and a half paces each way. The window was half open, and the air was fresh. It even smelled good, too; as Quangel was later to establish, the cause for this was Dr Reichhardt, with his soap and clean clothes. After the suffocating stink in the Gestapo basement, Quangel felt he had been transported to somewhere bright and cheerful.

Having made his bed, he sat down on it and looked across at his cellmate. The gentleman continued to read, turning the pages fairly rapidly. Quangel, who had no recollection of having read any book since his school days, thought to himself, What can he be reading? Why isn't he fretting? I could never sit and read like that! I keep thinking about Anna, how everything happened, and what will happen next and if I can continue to put a brave face on things. He says I can get a lawyer. But a lawyer costs money, and what good is he going to do me, seeing as I'll be sentenced to death anyway? I confessed everything! Everything's different for a gentleman like that. I saw it the moment I walked in, the warder calling him Sir and Doctor, as is only fit. He won't have a lot on his plate, I reckon – he can read all he likes . . .

Dr Reichhardt interrupted his pre-lunch reading only twice. The first time was to say, not raising his head, 'Cigarettes and matches are in the little cupboard – if you want to smoke?'

But when Quangel replied, 'I don't smoke. It costs too much money!' he was deep in his book again.

The second time, Quangel had clambered on to the stool and was trying to look out on the yard, where the regular rhythm of scraping feet could be heard.

'Best not now, Herr Quangel!' said Dr Reichhardt. 'It's exercise. Some of the warders make a note of the windows where inmates watch. Then it's solitary confinement with only bread and water. It's usually safe to look out the window in the evenings.'

Then lunch came. Quangel, who was used to the contemptuously thrown together grub in the Gestapo prison, was astonished to see two big bowls of soup and two plates with meat, potatoes and green beans. But he was even more astonished to see his cellmate pour a little water from the ewer and carefully wash and dry his hands. Then Dr Reichhardt poured fresh water into the basin, stepped aside and politely said, 'Herr Quangel!' and Quangel duly washed his hands, even though he hadn't touched anything dirty.

Then they ate the – for Quangel – unusually good lunch in near silence.

It took three days before the foreman understood that this wasn't the ordinary diet afforded by the People's Court to remand prisoners, but Dr Reichhardt's private food, which he shared without the least fuss with his cellmate. In the same way that he was completely ready to give Quangel whatever he had, whether that was cigarettes, soap, or books; all he had to do was ask.

It took a few more days for Otto Quangel to overcome the sudden surge of suspicion that was his instinctive reaction to all Dr Reichhardt's kindness. He was convinced that whoever enjoyed such incredible privileges had to be a spy for the People's Court. Whoever offered another man such favours must want something in return. Watch your step now, Quangel!

But what could the man want from him? Quangel's was an open-and-shut case, and he had repeated to the examining magistrate, coolly and succinctly, the statements he had previously given to Inspectors Escherich and Laub. He had said everything exactly as it was, and if the files still hadn't been passed on to the prosecution for the fixing of a date for proceedings, that was purely because of Anna's peculiar insistence that she had done everything and that her husband had merely been a sort of tool for her. But all that was no reason to shower Quangel with valuable cigarettes and good, clean food. The case was straightforward, there was no reason to spy on him.

Quangel only really got over his suspicion of Dr Reichhardt on the night that his cellmate, this superior, elegant gentleman, confessed to him in whispers that he was horribly afraid of death, whether by rope or axe; often he would think of nothing else for hours on end. Dr Reichhardt also admitted that often he only turned the pages of his books mechanically: before his eyes he saw not printer's ink but a grey concrete prison yard, a gallows with a noose swinging gently in the breeze that within three to five minutes would convert a strong, healthy man into a repulsive piece of dead meat.

But even more horrifying than the death that Dr Reichhardt foresaw (it was his firm conviction) coming closer with every new day, even more horrifying was his fear on behalf of his family. Quangel learned that Reichhardt and his wife had three children, two boys and a girl, the oldest eleven, the youngest only four. And Reichhardt was often desperately afraid that his persecutors, not content with murdering the father, would extend their vengeance to his innocent wife and children, would drag them into a concentration camp and slowly torture them to death.

Witnessing these agonies, not only did Quangel feel his suspicions swept aside, but he even came to regard himself as a relatively fortunate man. He had only Anna to worry about, and however foolish and contrary her reported statements were, he could see from them that she had fully recovered her courage and strength. One day, they would both have to die, but dying would be made easier for them, because it would take both of them: they weren't leaving anyone behind whom they would have to worry about in the hour of their death. The torments that Dr Reichhardt had to go through on behalf of his wife and three children were incomparably greater. They would accompany him to the last second of his dying. The old foreman understood that.

Quangel never learned quite what it was that Dr Reichhardt had done wrong and that made capital punishment seem so certain to him. As far as Quangel knew, his cellmate had not very actively opposed the Hitler regime, nor conspired with others, nor put up posters, nor plotted assassinations, but had simply lived in accordance with his principles. He had refused all the temptations that National Socialism had thrown his way, he had never contributed financially or by word or deed to their rallies, though he had often raised his voice in warning and had clearly stated how disastrous the course was that the German people were taking under their Führer. In a word, all the things that Quangel had laboriously written out on his postcards, Reichhardt had been happy to say to persons at home and abroad. Because even in the latter years of the war, Dr Reichhardt had gone on giving concerts abroad.

It took a very long time for the carpenter Quangel to form a reasonably clear picture of the sort of work that Dr Reichhardt had done in the world – and even then the picture never became completely clear, and in the depths of his soul he never quite saw Reichhardt's activity as work.

When he first learned, right at the beginning of their acquaintance, that Reichhardt was a musician, he had thought of dance musicians playing in cafés, and he had smiled a little contemptuously about that as not much of a job for a tall man with strong limbs. It was a little like reading: something superfluous that only high-up people went in for, people who did no proper work.

Reichhardt had to explain to the old man at some length and repeatedly what an orchestra was and what a conductor did. Quangel never tired of hearing about it.

'So you get up in front of your people with your little stick, and you're not even playing anything yourself . . . ?'

Yes, that was pretty much the way of it.

'And purely for showing an individual when you want him to start playing, and how loud – purely for that, you get paid a lot of money?'

Yes, Dr Reichhardt was afraid that was all he had done to come into so much money.

'But you're able to play music yourself, on a violin or a piano?'

'Yes, I am. But I don't do it, at least not in public. You see, Quangel, it's a bit like you: you can plane and saw and bang in nails. But that wasn't what you were doing; you were overseeing others doing it.'

'Sure, to make them work harder. Did your standing there make your people do their work any faster?'

'No, they didn't do that.'

Silence.

Then Quangel suddenly said: 'Anyway, music . . . You see, in the good years, the things we made weren't coffins, but furniture – sideboards, bookshelves, tables – and we could take pride in our work! First-class carpentry, pinned and glued, things that will last a hundred years. But music – the minute you stop playing, what have you got left?'

'There is something, Quangel. The joy in the people who hear good music, that's something enduring.'

But no, on this point they weren't able to agree, and Quangel was left with a quiet disdain for the work of the conductor Reichhardt.

But he could at least see that his companion was an upright, sincere man who went on living his life in the same way he had always lived it, despite all the threats and terrors he was confronted with, always friendly and helpful. With astonishment Otto Quangel saw that the kindnesses he received at Reichhardt's hands were not specifically directed at him, but would have been offered to any other cellmate, even, for instance, to the 'dog'. For a few days they had a small-time thief in their cell with them, a spoiled and deceitful creature, and this louse exploited the doctor's kindnesses to the full, smoking all his cigarettes, trading away his soap, stealing his bread. Quangel itched to beat him up – oh yes, the old foreman would have taught the creature a lesson he wouldn't have forgotten in a hurry. But the doctor wasn't having that, and he simply took the fellow under his wing – the thief who took his kindness for weakness.

When the man was finally taken away, it transpired that in his unfathomable wickedness he had taken a picture that Dr Reichhardt had, his only picture of his wife and children, and torn it up. As the doctor sat grieving before the scraps of the picture, which he was unable to put together again, Quangel angrily said, 'You know, Doctor, pardon my saying so, I think you're just too soft at times. If you had let me, I would have sorted the guy out right away, and something like that would never have happened.' The conductor replied with a rueful smile, 'Do you want us to be like the others, Quangel? They think they can convert us to their views by physical punishment! But we don't believe in force. We believe in goodness, love, and justice.'

'Goodness and love for a monster like that!'

'But do you know what turned him into such a monster? Are you sure he's not just resisting goodness and love because he's afraid his life would change if he were no longer evil? If we'd had him in our cell for four weeks, I think you would have seen a change in him.'

'But in life you need to be tough sometimes, Doctor!'

'No, you don't. And a saying like that is justification for every form of brutality, Quangel!'

Quangel shook his head, with its sharp, angular bird face, in dissent. But he did not continue the dispute.

57

Life in the Cell

They got used to one another and became friends, insofar as a hard, dry man like Otto Quangel could ever become friends with an open and kindly one. Their days were rigidly ordered – by Reichhardt. The doctor got up very early, washed all over with cold water, did exercises for half an hour, and then tidied the cell. After breakfast, Reichhardt would read for a couple of hours and then walk up and down the cell for a further hour, never forgetting to take off his shoes so that the other inmates would not be bothered by his continual pacing.

In the course of his morning walk, which lasted from ten to eleven, Dr Reichhardt would sing to himself. Generally he confined himself to humming softly, because a lot of warders wouldn't allow it, and Quangel got used to listening to this humming. Whatever his poor opinion of music, he did notice its effect on him. Sometimes it made him feel strong and brave enough to endure any fate, and then Reichhardt would say, 'Beethoven'. Sometimes it made him bafflingly lighthearted and cheerful, which he had never been in his life, and then Reichhardt would say, 'Mozart', and Quangel would forget all about his worries. And sometimes the sounds emanating from the doctor were dark and heavy, and Quangel would feel a pain in his chest, and it would be as though he was a little boy again sitting in church with his mother, with something grand – the whole of life – ahead of him, and then Reichhardt would say, 'Johann Sebastian Bach'.

Yes, while continuing to think poorly of music, Quangel was unable to avoid its influence, however basic the doctor's hummed vocal settings might be. He got accustomed to sitting on a stool and listening to him as he walked up and down, usually with eyes closed, because of course his feet knew every inch of the

short narrow path. Quangel would look at him, this fine
gentleman, whom he wouldn't have known how to talk to in
the outside world, and sometimes a doubt would come over
him; he wondered whether he had lived the right sort of life,
cutting himself off from everyone else in a voluntary self-isola-
tion. Sometimes Dr Reichhardt would say, 'We live not for
ourselves, but for others. What we make of ourselves we make
not for ourselves, but for others . . .'

Yes, there was no doubt: past fifty and facing death, Quangel
was changing. He might not like it – he even fought it – but he
noticed more and more clearly that he was changing, influenced
not only by the music but also, more generally, by the man who
hummed it. He, who had so many times told Anna to keep
quiet, who had taken silence for the best condition, would now
suddenly catch himself wishing that Dr Reichhardt would put
down his book and speak to him again.

And quite often he would. Once, the doctor looked up from
his reading and asked with a smile, 'What's going on, Quangel?'

'Hmm, nothing, Doctor.'

'You know you shouldn't sit and think so much. Don't you
want to give life a chance?'

'It's too late for that, surely.'

'Maybe you're right. What did you use to do after work? You
can't just have sat around idly at home after your shift, a man
like you!'

'I wrote my postcards.'

'And earlier, before the war?'

Quangel had to think quite hard what he had done then. 'I
suppose I used to enjoy carving things out of wood.'

The doctor said thoughtfully, 'Well, that's one thing they won't
allow us in here: knives. We mustn't cheat the executioner,
Quangel!'

To which Quangel hesitantly replied, 'What's chess like? You
can play against other people too, can't you?'

'Yes. Would you like to learn?'

'I think I'm probably not clever enough.'

'Nonsense! Let's get you started right away.'

And Dr Reichhardt shut his book.

And so Quangel learned to play chess. To his surprise, he learned very quickly and easily. And again he made the discovery that something he had thought before was completely wrong. He had always found it rather silly and childish when he'd seen two men sitting at a café table, pushing wooden figures back and forth: killing time, it was, something suitable for children at the most.

Now he learned that this back-and-forth of wooden figures could bring something like happiness, clarity in one's mind, a deep and honest pleasure in an elegant move, the discovery that it mattered very little if you won or lost, but that the pleasure of losing a closely contested match was much greater than that of winning through a blunder on the part of his opponent.

Now, while Dr Reichhardt read, Quangel would sit opposite him, the chessboard with the black and white figures in front of him, and open next to it a little paperback, Dufresne's *Guide to Chess*, and he would practise openings and endgames. Later on, he progressed to playing over famous matches in their entirety. His clear, sober brain could easily remember twenty or thirty moves, and before long the day came that he was the better player.

'Checkmate, Doctor!'

'You caught me again, Quangel!' said the doctor, and he laid down his king on its side in tribute to his conqueror. 'You could make a very good player.'

'I sometimes think now, Doctor, about the gifts I had no idea I had. It's only since meeting you, since coming to this death row, that I understand how much I've missed out on in my life.'

'It's like that for everyone. Everyone facing death, especially premature death, like us, will be kicking themselves about each wasted hour.'

'But it's different for me, Doctor. I always thought it was enough if I did my work properly and didn't mess anything up. And now I learn that there are loads of other things I could have done: play chess, be kind to people, listen to music, go to the theatre. You know, Doctor, if I were granted one wish before my death, it would be to see you with your baton conducting a big symphony orchestra. I'm so curious to see it, and find out my reaction to it.'

'No one can develop every side of themselves, Quangel. Life is so rich. You would only have spread yourself too thin. You did your job and were a man of integrity. When you were at liberty, Quangel, you had everything you wanted. You wrote your postcards . . .'

'Yes, but they didn't do any good, Doctor! I wished the earth would swallow me up when Inspector Escherich told me that of the 285 postcards I wrote, 267 went straight to him! Only eighteen not handed in! And those eighteen didn't do any good, either!'

'Who can say? At least you opposed evil. You weren't corrupted. You and I and the many locked up here, and many more in other places of detention, and tens of thousands in concentration camps – they're all resisting, today, tomorrow . . .'

'Yes, and then they kill us, and what good did our resistance do?'

'Well, it will have helped us to feel that we behaved decently till the end. And much more, it will have helped people everywhere, who will be saved for the righteous few among them, as it says in the Bible. Of course, Quangel, it would have been a hundred times better if we'd had someone who could have told us, such and such is what you have to do; our plan is this and this. But if there had been such a man in Germany, then Hitler would never have come to power in 1933. As it was, we all acted alone, we were caught alone, and every one of us will have to die alone. But that doesn't mean that we *are* alone, Quangel, or that our deaths will be in vain. Nothing in this world is done in vain, and since we are fighting for justice against brutality, we are bound to prevail in the end.'

'And what good will that do us, down in our graves?'

'Quangel, I ask you! Would you rather live for an unjust cause than die for a just one? There is no choice – not for you, nor for me either. It's because we are as we are that we have to go this way.'

For a long time there was silence.

Then Quangel began, 'This game, chess . . .'

'Yes, Quangel, what about it?'

'I sometimes think I'm doing wrong by playing. For hours on end, I have my head full of chess, but I have a wife still, and . . .'

'You think about your wife enough. You want to remain brave and strong; everything that keeps you brave and strong is good, just as everything that makes you weak and doubtful, such as brooding, is bad. What good is your brooding to your wife? What helps her is when Chaplain Lorenz is able to tell her that you're brave and strong.'

'But he can't speak to her openly, now that she's got her new cellmate. The chaplain is convinced she's a spy.'

'The chaplain will find a way of telling your wife that you're doing well and are feeling strong. A nod of the head or a look will do. Lorenz can take care of himself.'

'I wouldn't mind giving him a letter to take to Anna,' mused Quangel.

'I shouldn't, if I were you. He wouldn't refuse, but it would put his life in danger. You know yourself that he's under constant suspicion. It would be awful if our friend wound up in one of these cells. He risks his life every day, as it is.'

'Well, I won't write a letter then,' said Otto Quangel.

And he didn't, either, even though the chaplain brought him some terrible news the next day – terrible news in particular for Anna Quangel. The foreman begged him not to tell Anna the news just yet.

'Please not yet, reverend!'

And the chaplain promised not to.

'I shan't, then. You tell me when you think it's time, Herr Quangel.'

58

The Good Chaplain

Chaplain Friedrich Lorenz, who worked tirelessly in the prison, was a man in his prime, which is to say around forty, very tall, narrow-chested, forever coughing, a man marked by tuberculosis but who ignored his illness because his work left him no time to attend to and remedy his health. A pair of dark sideburns framed his pale face with its dark bespectacled eyes and fine sharp nose, but he was clean-shaven about the mouth, which was large and thin-lipped, and about his firm round chin.

This was the man for whom hundreds of inmates waited every day – their only friend in the building, and moreover a bridge to the world outside, to whom they could tell their fears and tribulations and who did all in his power to help them – far more, at any rate, than he was officially allowed to do. He went tirelessly from cell to cell, never desensitized to the sufferings of others, always oblivious to his own, and perfectly fearless where his own person was concerned. He was a true shepherd, never asking after the faith of the men and women coming to him for help, happy to pray with them when that was what they wanted, a brother to all.

Chaplain Friedrich Lorenz is standing before the director's desk, sweat beading on his brow, two hectic splotches of red on his cheeks, but he says perfectly calmly, 'This is the seventh case of death by neglect in the past two weeks.'

'It says pneumonia on the death certificates,' replies the director, not bothering to look up from whatever he is writing.

'The doctor is failing in his duty,' says the chaplain stubbornly, rapping gently on the desk with his knuckles, as though asking to be let in. 'It hurts me to have to say so, but the doctor is drinking too much. He is neglecting his patients.'

'Oh, the doctor's fine,' the director replies casually, and goes on writing. He refuses to admit the chaplain. 'I wish you were doing as good a job. Tell me, did you slip No. 397 a secret communication or didn't you?'

Finally, their eyes meet, those of the ruddy-faced director, with his face covered in duelling scars, and those of the cleric burning with fever.

'It's the seventh case in two weeks,' insists Chaplain Lorenz. 'The prison needs a new doctor.'

'I just asked you a question, Chaplain. Would you have the kindness to give me an answer?'

'Yes, I took No. 397 a letter, but no secret communication. It was a letter from his wife, telling him that his third son was not dead, as feared, but a prisoner of war. He has already lost two sons, and thought his third was also dead.'

'You always seem to find some justification to violate prison regulations, Chaplain. But I'm not going to stand for it much longer.'

'I request that the doctor be replaced,' repeats the chaplain, rapping softly on the desk.

'Bah, nonsense!' the red-faced director suddenly explodes. 'Don't bother me with your idiotic chatter! The doctor's a good doctor; he's staying! As for you, you should see to it that you obey prison rules occasionally, otherwise something will happen to you.'

'What could happen to me?' asks the chaplain. 'I can die. I shall die. Very soon. But I'm asking you to replace the prison doctor.'

'You're a fool, Chaplain,' said the director coldly. 'I'm assuming your illness has affected your mental powers. If you weren't such a harmless idiot – as I say, a bloody fool! – you'd have been strung up long ago! You're lucky I feel pity for you!'

'You should try a little pity on your prisoners,' the chaplain replied, just as coldly. 'And get hold of a decent doctor.'

'Close the door when you go, Chaplain.'

'Do I have your word that you'll get a new doctor?'

'No, goddamnit, no! Go to hell!'

Then the director lost his temper after all, jumped up behind his desk and took two steps toward the chaplain. 'Do you want me to throw you out by force? Is that what you want?'

'I don't think the prisoners working in your outer office would like that. It might destroy the last vestiges of authority you have over them. But do as you please, director!'

'Idiot!' said the director, but the chaplain's threat had cooled his blood sufficiently for him to sit down again. 'Now get lost. I've got work to do.'

'The most urgent work you have is the recruiting of a new doctor.'

'Do you suppose your pigheadedness makes the least difference? It's quite the opposite! I'm keeping the doctor if it's the last thing I do.'

'I can remember a day,' the chaplain said, 'when you yourself weren't quite so satisfied with the present doctor. It was night, and it was raining hard. You had called for other doctors, but they didn't come. Your six-year-old son Berthold had a middle ear infection and was howling with pain. His life was in danger. In answer to your pleas, I got the prison doctor. He was drunk. When he saw the dying child, he lost whatever composure he had. He looked at his shaking hands, which made any surgical incision impossible, and he burst into tears.'

'The filthy drunk!' murmured the director, with abruptly darkened brow.

'Your Berthold's life was saved by the intervention of another doctor. But what happened then could happen again at any time. You are proud not to be a Christian, Director, but I tell you: God is not mocked!'

Reluctantly, without looking up, the director said, 'All right, Chaplain, you can go now.'

'And the doctor?'

'I'll see what I can do.'

'Thank you, Director. Many people will thank you.'

The man of God walked through the prison, a bizarre figure in his worn black surplice out at elbows, his tattered black pants, his thick-soled boots, and his crooked black tie. Some of the warders greeted him; others turned away ostentatiously at his approach, only to peer after him suspiciously once he had gone. But all the prisoners who were busy in the corridors looked at him – they weren't allowed to greet him – with gratitude.

The man of God passes through many iron doors and down flights of iron steps, holding on to iron banisters. Hearing sobbing from a cell, he stops a moment, only to shake his head and quickly go on. He walks down an iron corridor, and on either side of him are the open doors of darkened cells, punishment cells, but there is a light on in the room in front of him. The chaplain stops and looks inside.

In an ugly, dirty room a fat man with a glowering grey face is staring at seven men, who are completely naked and trembling pathetically with cold under the eyes of two warders.

'Well, my beauties!' growls the man. 'What are you shaking like that for? Cold? Ach, come on, you don't know what cold is – you wait till you're in the basement, on bread and water, lying on bare cement . . .'

He stops. He has seen the quiet, observant shape in the doorway.

'Senior Warder,' he orders crossly, 'take them away! They're all healthy, and up to solitary. Here's your authorization.'

He scribbles a signature under a list of names and hands it to the official.

The prisoners file past the chaplain, not without directing pitiful, anxious glances at him.

The chaplain waits for the last of them to pass, and only then does he enter the room and say, 'I hear No. 352 is dead as well. And I'd asked you . . .'

'What can I do, Chaplain? I sat with the man myself for two hours, making cold compresses for him.'

'In that case I must have been asleep. I had the impression I'd been up all night with him. And there was nothing wrong with his lungs, either; it was No. 357 who had pneumonia. Hergesell in 352 had a fractured skull.'

'We should change places if you're such an expert,' the chubby man said sarcastically. 'I'll be the God bloke.'

'My only worry is you'd be an even worse chaplain than you are a doctor.'

The doctor laughed. 'I love it when you get fresh with me, Padre. Wouldn't you like me to check out your lungs some time?'

The chaplain persisted, 'No, I'll leave that to another doctor.'

'I don't need to look at you to tell you that you won't last another three months,' the doctor went on maliciously. 'I know you've been spitting blood since May – you won't have long to wait till your first haemorrhage.'

The chaplain might have turned a shade paler at this cruel news, but his voice didn't shake as he said, 'And how long till the prisoners you just showed into solitary in the blackout cell have their first haemorrhage, Medical Councillor?'

'The prisoners are all healthy and up to solitary – according to medical evidence.'

'They were never even examined.'

'Are you commenting on the way I do my job? I warn you! I know more about you than you think!'

'And with my first haemorrhage your knowledge becomes worthless! By the way, it's already behind me . . .'

'What? What have you got behind you?'

'My first haemorrhage – it was three or four days ago.'

The doctor stood up a little stiffly. 'Well, come along then, Padre, I'll examine you upstairs in my office. I'll see that you get sick leave right away. We'll write Switzerland on the application, and while they're making up their minds on that you can go to Thuringia.'

The chaplain, with the half-drunk doctor clutching his arm, stood there immobile. 'And what happens in the meantime to the men in solitary? Two of them are certainly in no condition to endure the damp, the cold, and the hunger, and all seven will receive permanent harm.'

The doctor replied, 'Sixty per cent of the people here will be executed. At least thirty-five of the remaining forty will be sentenced to long periods in jail. What do a couple of months matter either way?'

'If that's the way you think, you have no right to call yourself a doctor. I call on you to renounce your profession!'

'My successor's not going to think any differently! So why bother?' The medical councillor laughed. 'Come on, chaplain, let me examine you. You know I've got a soft spot for you, even though you're forever agitating against me. You're a complete Quixote!'

'I have just come from agitating against you. I asked the director to have you replaced, and got at least half-consent from him.'

The doctor started laughing. He clapped the chaplain on the back, and exclaimed, 'Oh, Padre, you are priceless, and I am deeply in your debt! If I am indeed replaced, it'll mean that they kick me upstairs, and I'll become senior medical councillor and won't have to do any more work. I can never thank you enough, Padre!'

'Why don't you show your gratitude then by taking Kraus and little Wendt out of solitary? They'll never survive it. Your negligence has contributed to seven deaths in the last fortnight.'

'Ooh, you do flatter me! But I find it impossible to turn you down. I'll fetch them out tonight. If I did it right away, just after signing them in, it would look a little too much like vacillation. Wouldn't you say, Padre?'

59

Trudel Hergesell, Née Baumann

The transfer to remand prison had parted Trudel Hergesell from Anna Quangel. It was hard for Trudel to do without her 'Mother'. She had long since forgotten that Anna was responsible for her arrest, or rather, she hadn't forgotten it, but forgiven it. More, she had understood that really there was nothing to forgive. No one could stand up to those interrogations – those wily inspectors could twist the most harmless incidentals into something that would cost you your neck.

Now that Trudel was without her mother, she had no one to talk to. She could only be silent about her former happiness, about her fears for Karli that were now consuming her. Her new cellmate was an elderly, wizened woman – the two of them had detested each other from the moment they saw each other, and this woman was forever whispering to the warders and overseers. When the chaplain was in the cell, she made sure she caught every word.

It was through the chaplain that Trudel had managed to get some news of her Karli, while Frau Hänsel, her cellmate, was paying a call on the administration – no doubt to plunge some other poor woman into misfortune with her relentless tale-bearing. The chaplain had told Trudel that her husband was in the same prison; he was sick, in and out of consciousness, but Lorenz was at least able to bring her a greeting from him.

From that time forth, Trudel had lived for visits from the chaplain. Even when Frau Hänsel was in attendance, the reverend was able to smuggle her some news, one way or another. Often they would sit close together under the window on two stools, and Chaplain Lorenz would read some verses from the New Testament while Frau Hänsel stood by the opposite wall, her sharp eyes fixed on the pair of them.

For Trudel the Bible was something completely new. She was a product of Hitler's educational system, and she had encountered no religion from that, and had never felt a religious urge in herself either. She had no sense of God. God for her was an exclamation: 'Oh my God!' and so forth. One might as well exclaim 'Great Scott!' – there was no real difference.

Even now that she was learning about the life of Christ from the Gospel according to Matthew, she told the chaplain that the term Son of God meant nothing to her. But Father Lorenz had merely smiled and said that didn't matter for now. She was to concentrate on the way Jesus Christ had lived his life here on earth, and on how he had loved mankind, including even his enemies. She should interpret the 'miracles' in any way that made sense to her, even as beautiful fairy-tales, but she should take account of the fact that a man had once lived in such a way that even two thousand years later, his influence was still unforgotten, an enduring proof of the fact that love was stronger than hate.

Trudel Hergesell, who was capable of hating as much as loving (and who, as she was being told about Jesus, was full of a violent hatred for Frau Hänsel standing not ten feet away), to begin with Trudel Hergesell had rejected such a doctrine. It struck her as too soft. It wasn't Jesus Christ who appealed to her heart, but Father Friedrich Lorenz. When she beheld this man, of whose grave illness no one could remain unaware, when she saw him taking on her fears as if they were his own, never thinking about himself, when she saw his courage as he slipped her a note with a message about Karli, and when she heard him go on to speak to the two-faced Hänsel just as kindly as he did to her, even though he knew the woman was capable of denouncing him at any moment to the hangman, then she would feel something akin to happiness, and the profound peace that emanated from this man who could not hate but only love, and loved even the very worst people.

This new feeling did not bring with it any softening of Trudel Hergesell's attitude toward the Hänsel woman, but perhaps she became a little more indifferent, a little less intent on her hatred.

Sometimes, in the course of pacing back and forth across the cell, she would suddenly stop in front of Frau Hänsel and ask her, 'What makes you do it? Why do you snitch on everyone? Do you hope to get a lesser punishment?'

When addressed this way, Frau Hänsel would keep her evil yellow eyes locked on Trudel's. Either she would not offer any reply or else she would say, 'Do you think I didn't notice you pressing your tits against the chaplain's arm? I think it's really low, to try to seduce a man who has only days to live! Just you wait, I'll catch you at it one day! You won't get away with it!'

What the chaplain and Trudel Hergesell weren't supposed to get away with remained unclear. All Trudel would offer by way of reply to such accusations was a brief, mocking laugh, and then she would set off on her endless tramping back and forth in the cell, always occupied in her mind with Karli. There was no getting around the fact that news of him was getting steadily worse, however discreetly and gently the chaplain tried to convey it. If he said there was no news, that his condition was unchanged, that meant that Karli had not sent her a greeting, which could only mean that he was unconscious. Because the chaplain would not lie – Trudel had learned that – he would not pass on a greeting when he had not been instructed to do so. He scorned the cheap consolation that one day would be unmasked as a lie anyway.

But Trudel also learned from the questions of the examining magistrate that her husband was in a bad way. There was never any reference to any new testimony from him. She was expected to give information about everything, and she really didn't know anything about the suitcase of Grigoleit's that had plunged both of them into their doom. Though the methods of the magistrate were not as deceitful and downright brutal as those of Inspector Laub, he had just as much stamina. Trudel always returned to her cell exhausted and demoralized. Oh, Karli, Karli! Just to see him one more time, to sit by his bedside, to press his hand, silently, without a word!

There had been a time when she had supposed she didn't

love him and would never be able to love him. Now she was full of him, the air that she breathed was him, the bread she ate, the blanket that kept her warm, all him. And he was so near, a couple of corridors, a couple of flights of steps, a door – but in the whole world there was no one so merciful as to conduct her to him, even once! Not even the tubercular chaplain!

They were all afraid for their lives, with no one willing to risk making a serious effort to help her in her helplessness. Then suddenly there swims into her memory the morgue in the Gestapo basement, the lanky SS man lighting his cigarette and saying, 'Girl! Girl!' to her, her search among the corpses after she and Anna had undressed the dead Berta – and now that strikes her as a mild and merciful hour, when she was allowed to look for Karli. And since then? Her beating heart locked up between iron and stone! Alone!

The door is unlocked, much more slowly and respectfully than the way the warders do it, and there is even a soft knock: the chaplain.

'May I come in?' he asks.

'Please, please come in, Chaplain!' cries a tearful Trudel Hergesell.

Meanwhile Frau Hänsel glares and mutters, 'What does he want this time?'

And then all at once Trudel rests her head against the bony, panting chest of the priest, her tears are flowing, she buries her head in his chest and implores him, 'Chaplain, I'm so afraid! You must help me! I've got to see Karli, just once! I'm sure it'll be the last time . . .'

And the harsh voice of Frau Hänsel: 'I'll report you! I'll report you right now!' while the chaplain strokes her head gently, and says, 'Yes, child, you shall see him once more!'

She is shaken by an ever stronger sobbing, and she knows Karli is dead, that she hadn't looked for him in the morgue for nothing, that she had had a foreboding, a presentiment.

And she wails, 'He's dead! Oh, Father, he's dead!'

And he answers, giving the only consolation he can to the

condemned woman, 'Child, his sufferings are over. It's harder for you.'

She hears it. She tries to think about it, understand what it means, but the light dims, then everything goes dark before her eyes. Her head slumps forward.

'Will you give me a hand, Frau Hänsel!' the chaplain pleads. 'I'm not strong enough to manage her on my own.'

And then it's night outside, night meets night, darkness meets darkness.

Trudel, the widowed Frau Hergesell, has woken up, and she knows that she isn't in her cell, and she knows too that Karli is dead. She can see him lying on his narrow cot in his cell, his face youthful and small and shrunken, and she thinks of the face of the child she was carrying, and the faces merge into one another, and she knows that she has lost everything there is to lose in this world, that she has lost husband and child, and that never will she love again, never will she conceive again, and all because she left a postcard on a windowsill for an old man, and that this has annihilated her whole life and Karli's with it, and there will never be sunshine and happiness and summer for her again, or flowers . . .

Flowers on my grave, flowers on your grave . . .

And with the intense pain she feels radiating out, chilling her like ice, she closes her eyes again and tries to return to night and oblivion. But night is outside, it remains there, it doesn't enter her, but suddenly heat courses through her . . . She leaps up out of bed, she wants to run away from this ghastly pain. But a hand reaches for her . . .

It grows light, and once more it's the chaplain who is sitting with her, holding her. Yes, it's a different cell, it's Karli's cell, but they've already taken him away, and the man who was in here with Karli has gone as well.

'Where has he gone?' she asks breathlessly, as though she had just run here.

'I will say my prayers at his grave.'

'What good will your prayers do him? You should have prayed for his life, while there was still time!'

'He is at peace, child!'

'I can't stay here!' says Trudel feverishly. 'Please, let me return to my cell, Chaplain! I have a picture of him there, I have to see it right away. He looked so different.'

And as she says this she knows quite well that she is lying to the good chaplain, deliberately, to deceive him. She doesn't own a picture of Karli, and she never wants to go back to the cell with Frau Hänsel again.

The thought rushes through her head: I'm out of my mind, but I must disguise myself well, so that he doesn't know it . . . I just need to keep my madness hidden for five more minutes!

The chaplain leads her carefully on his arm out of the cell, down many corridors and flights of steps, back into the women's prison, and from the passing cells she hears deep breathing – they are sleeping – and from others nervous pacing – they are fretting – and from still others the sound of crying – they are grieving, but no one has such grief as she does.

The chaplain is busy unlocking and then locking a door after her; she doesn't take his arm again, and the two of them walk silently down the unlit passage with the dark solitary cells, where the drunken doctor has broken his word and not released the two sick prisoners after all, and then they are climbing many flights of steps to Block V, where Trudel's cell is.

There on the top passage, a warder shuffles toward them, and she says, 'It's twenty to midnight, and you're only returning Hergesell now? What kept you so long, Chaplain?'

'She was unconscious for many hours. Her husband has died, you know.'

'I see – and you took it upon yourself to comfort the young widow, is that right, Chaplain? Nice – nice! Frau Hänsel has told me you take every opportunity of throwing yourself at her. A nice comfort session at the dead of night is even better, though, eh? I must make a note of it in my log!'

But before the chaplain can get out a word of reproach for her foul insinuation, they both see that Trudel, the widowed Frau Hergesell, has clambered over the iron railing on the corridor. For a moment she stands there, gripping the railing with one hand, her back toward them.

And they call out, 'Stop! No! Don't do it!'

They dash toward her, hands reaching out to grasp her.

But Trudel Hergesell has already dived into the void. They hear a rush of fluttering air and then a thump.

And then everything is deathly silent, while the two of them, pale-faced, lean down over the rail and see nothing.

They take a step toward the stairs.

And in that instant all hell broke loose.

It was as though the prisoners had been able to see what had happened through their cell doors. First, there might have been a single scream, but it went from cell to cell and from block to block, from one side of the corridor to the other and across the central atrium.

And on its way, the scream was augmented by yelling, howling, shrilling, keening, raging.

'You murderers! You killed her! Why don't you kill the lot of us, you butchers!'

And there were some who clung to their window bars and yelled it into the yard, so that the men's wing awoke from its troubled sleep and likewise began to rage, scream, yell, wail, and despair.

It accused, it accused with one, two, three thousand voices: the beast screamed its accusation from one, two, three thousand muzzles.

The alarm sounded, and they drummed their fists against the iron doors, then battered the doors with their stools. Iron bedsteads were picked up and dropped. Tin plates were kicked around the floors, bucket lids banged, and the whole establishment, the whole of the gigantic prison, suddenly stank like a latrine many hundreds of times multiplied.

The riot squads got into their uniforms and reached for their rubber truncheons.

Cell doors were unlocked: *click click*!

And the ripe smacking sound of rubber truncheons on skulls was heard, and the roar of fury rose, mixed with the scraping of fighting feet and the high bestial yells of epileptics and the enthusiastic yodelling of idiots and the shrill whistles of pimps . . .

Water was splashed in the faces of the attacking guards.

And in the morgue Karli Hergesell lay perfectly still, with a child's small and gentle face.

The whole thing was a wild, gruesome symphony, performed in honour of Trudel, née Baumann, and then the widowed Frau Hergesell.

Meanwhile she herself lay on the ground, half on the linoleum and half on the dirty grey cement of Block I.

She lay perfectly still, her small grey girlish hand half open. Her lips were flecked with blood, and her sightless eyes looked at some unknown world.

Her ears, though, still seemed to hear the wild infernal noise swelling and diminishing, and her brow was creased, as though pondering whether this could be the peace that the good chaplain had promised her.

In consequence of this suicide, it was the prison chaplain, Friedrich Lorenz, who was suspended from duty, rather than the drunken doctor. Charges were laid against the priest. Because it was a crime and the abetting of a crime to enable a prisoner to put an end to his own life: only the state and its servants were supposed to have that prerogative.

If a detective pistol-whips a man so badly that his skull is fractured, and if a drunken doctor allows the injured man to die, both are an example of due process. Whereas if a priest fails to hinder a suicide, if he allows a prisoner to exercise his or her will – that will that is supposed to have been taken away – then he has committed a crime and must be punished.

Unfortunately – rather like Frau Hergesell – Father Friedrich Lorenz cheated justice by dying of a haemorrhage just as he was about to be arrested. A suspicion had arisen that he had enjoyed immoral relations with some of those in his care. But he had found, to use his own word, peace, and he was spared much.

This was how it came about that until the trial Anna Quangel did not learn of the deaths of Trudel and Karl Hergesell, because the successor of the good chaplain was either too fearful or unwilling to pass messages among the prisoners. He confined himself to the cure of souls, in those instances where it was explicitly requested.

60

The Trial: A Reunion

The most perfectly constructed system is occasionally subject to malfunction. The People's Court in Berlin, which had nothing to do with the people and to which the people were not admitted even as silent spectators, for most of its sessions were held behind closed doors – this People's Court was an instance of a perfect system: before any accused person even set foot in the court-room, that person was for all intents and purposes already condemned, and there was no indication that he or she had anything to hope for in there.

That morning only one case was scheduled: the one brought against Otto and Anna Quangel for treason. The public gallery was only one-quarter full: a few Party uniforms, a few lawyers who for inscrutable reasons had chosen to attend these proceed-ings, and the rest law students, who wanted to learn how justice deals with people whose one crime was to love their country more than the judges did. All these people had come by tickets to the proceedings through 'influence'. How the little man with the white beard and the clever wrinkles around his eyes, how retired Judge Fromm had obtained his ticket was a mystery. At any rate, he was sitting unobtrusively with the others, a little apart from them, his face lowered, and regularly polishing his gold-rimmed spectacles.

At five minutes to ten, a guard led Otto Quangel into the courtroom. He had been put in the clothes he was wearing at the time of his arrest: a clean but much-mended pair of overalls, with dark blue patches standing out distinctly from the faded blue of the garment. His still-sharp eyes slid indifferently from the empty seats beyond the dock to the spectators, lighting up briefly on seeing the judge, before he sat down on the bench for the accused.

Just before ten o'clock, the second defendant, Anna Quangel, was led in by a second guard, and there now occurred the malfunction referred to above: no sooner did Anna Quangel catch sight of her husband than, perfectly naturally, without hesitating and without looking at the other people in the room, she made straight for him and sat down next to him.

Otto Quangel raised his hand and whispered, 'Don't say anything! Not now!'

But there was a light in his eye that told her how glad he was to see her again.

Of course it was no part of the plan of this exalted establishment that the two accused, having been kept apart for months, should sit together and enjoy a cosy chat a quarter of an hour before proceedings began. But whether it was that the two guards were new at their job, or that the state attached but slight importance to this case, or that the two poorly dressed, ordinary old people looked so wholly unthreatening – whatever it was, the court made no objection to Anna's choice of seat and for the next quarter of an hour left them to it. In the meantime, the two guards had got into a stimulating conversation about terms and conditions, some overtime pay for night work that they had been tricked out of, and a number of other unfair raids on their wages.

In the courtroom, no one – Judge Fromm excepted – noticed the malfunction. The attendants were sloppy and slovenly, and so no one picked up on this slip that worked to the disadvantage of the Third Reich and the advantage of the two traitors. A case against two old workers was of no great interest to anyone. Here, people were used to monster conspiracy cases with thirty or forty accused, who usually didn't know each other but who in the course of the proceedings learned that they had all been involved in something together and were accordingly all sentenced together.

So, after looking around carefully for a few seconds, Quangel was able to say, 'I'm glad to see you, Anna. Are you doing all right?'

'Yes, Otto, I'm better now.'

'They won't leave us sitting together for long. But let's make something of our few minutes. You know what's coming, I take it?'

Very softly, 'Yes, Otto.'

'It's the death sentence for us both, Anna. There's no other way.'

'But, Otto . . .'

'No, Anna, no buts. I know you tried to shoulder all the blame for everything . . .'

'They won't sentence a woman so heavily, and maybe you'll get away with your life.'

'No, no, you're mistaken. You can't lie well enough. You'll only succeed in drawing out the trial. Let's tell the truth, and then it will be over sooner.'

'But, Otto . . .'

'No, Anna, no buts. Think. No lies. Let's be truthful . . .'

'But, Otto . . .'

'Anna, please!'

'Otto, don't make it so hard for me!'

'Do you want us to lie to them? Quarrel? Put on a show for them? The simple truth, Anna!'

She struggled with herself. Then she gave in, as she always gave in. 'All right, Otto, I promise.'

'Thank you, Anna. I'm very grateful.'

They stopped speaking, and looked down at their feet. Both were ashamed to have grown so heated.

The voice of one of the policemen behind them became audible: 'And so I said to the lieutenant, "Lieutenant, I said, you can't treat me like that, I said, Lieutenant . . ."'

Otto Quangel concentrated. It had to be. If Anna learned of it in the course of the proceedings – which it was inevitable that she would – then it would be so much worse. The consequences were incalculable.

'Anna,' he whispered. 'You're brave and strong, aren't you?'

'Yes, Otto,' she replied. 'I am now. Now I'm with you again, I am. What is it?'

'There is something, Anna . . .'

'What is it, Otto? Tell it me, Otto! If you're scared of telling me, that's enough to make me scared.'

'Anna, did you hear anything more about Gertrud?'

'About what Gertrud?'

'Trudel, then!'

'Oh, Trudel! What about Trudel? No, I haven't had any news of her since I was transferred into remand. I've missed her very much; she was so good to me. She forgave me for betraying her.'

'You didn't betray her! At first I thought you did, too, but later I understood.'

'Yes, well, she understood, too. I was so confused during the early interrogations with that awful Inspector Laub, I didn't know what I was saying, but she understood. She forgave me.'

'Thank God! Now, Anna, be brave and strong: Trudel is dead.'

'Oh!' groaned Anna, and laid her hand on her heart. 'Oh!'

And, to get it all over with, he quickly added, 'And her husband is dead as well.'

No words came for a long time. She sat there, with her head in her hands, but Otto sensed that she wasn't crying, that she was still numb with the shock. Involuntarily he said the same words that Chaplain Lorenz had used when telling him: 'They're dead. They are at peace. They have been spared further pain.'

'Yes!' Anna said at last. 'Yes. She was so fearful for her Karli when there was no news, but now she is at peace.'

She didn't speak for a long time, and Quangel didn't press her, even though he sensed from some commotion in the hall that the court was about to go into session.

Softly Anna asked, 'Were they both – put to death?'

'No,' Quangel replied. 'He died from the after-effects of a blow he received when they were arrested.'

'And Trudel?'

'She took her own life,' Otto Quangel said quickly. 'She jumped from the railing on the fifth floor. She was dead on the spot, Father Lorenz said. She didn't suffer.'

'It must have happened that night,' Anna Quangel suddenly

said, 'when the whole prison was in uproar! I remember it, it was terrible, Otto!' And she buried her face in her hands again.

'Yes, it was terrible,' Quangel agreed. 'With us, too, it was terrible.'

After a while she raised her head again, and looked firmly at Otto. Her lips were still trembling, but she said, 'It's better this way. It would be so awful if they were both sitting here with us. Well, now they're at peace.' And, very quietly, 'You know, Otto, we could do the same.'

He looked at her firmly. And she saw in his hard, cutting glance a look she'd never seen before, a look of mockery, as though everything were just a game, the things she was saying, what lay ahead of them, and the inevitable finale. As though it weren't worthy of being taken seriously.

Then slowly he shook his head. 'No, Anna, we won't do that. We won't sneak away, like criminals caught red-handed. We won't make their judgement any easier for them. Not us!' And, in a different tone of voice, 'It's too late for all that. Don't they keep you in chains?'

'Yes,' she said. 'But when the guard walked me up to the door, he took them off.'

'You see!' he said. 'It wouldn't work.'

What he didn't tell her was that from the moment he'd been taken out of remand he'd been in handcuffs and leg irons connected by a steel rod. As with Anna, the guard had taken off these ornaments at the door to the court: the state wasn't to be cheated of its victim.

'All right,' she said, adjusting to the idea. 'But you do think they'll let us die together, don't you, Otto?'

'I don't know,' he replied. He didn't want to lie to her, but at the same time he was certain each of them would die alone.

'But they'll execute us at the same time?'

'Yes, Anna, I'm sure they'll do that.'

In fact, he wasn't so sure. He went on, 'But don't think about it now. Just remember that we have to be strong. If we plead guilty, everything will happen very quickly. If we don't lie and prevaricate, we might get our sentence as soon as in half an hour.'

'Well, let's do it like that, then. But, Otto, if it's so quick, then we'll be separated just as quickly, and we might never see each other again.'

'I'm sure we will – just before it happens, Anna. That's what they told me: we'll be allowed to say farewell. For definite, Anna!'

'That's good, then, Otto. Then I'll have something to keep looking forward to. And now we're sitting together.'

They sat together for only one more minute, and then the malfunction was discovered, and they were made to sit far apart. They had to crane their necks to see each other. Luckily, it was Frau Quangel's defence attorney who discovered the mistake – a friendly, grizzled, rather worried-looking man who had been chosen by the State to defend her, as Quangel had stuck to his original position of not wanting to waste money on something as useless as a defence.

Because it was the attorney who had discovered the mistake, it passed off without noise or fuss. The two guards had every reason to keep their mouths shut, and so the judge of the People's Court, Feisler, never got wind of the unpardonable thing that had happened. If he had, the trial would probably have gone on for much longer.

61

The Trial: Judge Feisler

The president of the People's Court, the senior judge in Germany at the time, Judge Feisler, looked like a cultured man.* He was, to use the terminology of Foreman Otto Quangel, a distinguished-looking gentleman. He wore his robe with style, and the cap gave his head dignity rather than looking merely stuck on, as it can on some heads. His eyes were clever, but cold. He had a high, smooth forehead and a mean little mouth, and it was the mouth, with its hard, cruel, sensual lips that gave the man away: he was a sybarite who sought all the pleasures of this world and left others to pay the bill.

The hands with the long, knotty fingers were mean, too, like vulture's claws, and each time he asked an especially hurtful question his fingers curled, as though to dig into the flesh of his victim. And his way of speaking was mean, too: this man was incapable of speaking coolly and dispassionately; he always hacked at his victim, abused him, talked with vicious sarcasm. A mean man, and a bad man.

Since Otto Quangel heard who was going to try his case, he had spoken about it a few times with his friend Dr Reichhardt. Clever Dr Reichhardt had also been of the view that since the outcome was a foregone conclusion, Quangel should admit everything, and not cover anything up or lie. That would take the wind out of their sails, and they wouldn't be able to go on abusing him for as long as they would have liked to. The trial

* Roland Freisler (Fallada's character is 'Feisler') was the president, or chief justice, of the People's Court (Volksgerichtshof), which was set up outside constitutional authority and was often the venue for show trials. Although possessor of a brilliant legal mind, Freisler was famous for screaming at defendants and personifying the Nazi concept of 'blood justice'. He represented the Reich Ministry of Justice at the Wannsee Conference, where the 'Final Solution' for the extermination of Jews was devised.

would be short, and they wouldn't even have to call witnesses.

It created a minor sensation when the judge asked how they pled, and both accused answered with a simple 'guilty'. That 'guilty' made them subject to the death penalty and rendered any further business superfluous.

Judge Feisler hemmed and hawed for a while, stunned by this almost unprecedented plea.

But then he recovered his grasp of the situation. He wanted his day in court. He wanted to see these two workers grovel, he wanted to see them writhe under his razor-sharp questioning. This 'guilty' plea betrayed pride. Judge Feisler could see recognition of it in the faces of the spectators in the courtroom, some of whom were astonished, and others pensive. He wanted to strip the accused of that recognition. He wanted them to leave these proceedings without a shred of dignity.

Feisler asked, 'Are you clear in your minds that you have just renounced your lives, that you have cut yourselves off from all decent people? That you are now a common criminal deserving to die, carrion that will be hanged by the neck? Are you quite clear about that? Now, are you still guilty?'

Quangel said slowly, 'I am guilty. I did what it says on the charge sheet.'

The judge leveled his beak at him: 'I want you to answer yes or no! Are you a common traitor, or not? Yes or no!'

Quangel looked hard at the distinguished-looking gentleman above him. 'Yes!' he said.

'Disgusting!' yelled the judge, and spat over his shoulder. 'Disgusting! And that sort of creature calls itself German!'

He looked at Quangel with deep contempt, then turned to Anna Quangel. 'What about you, woman?' he asked. 'Are you as common as your husband or not? Are you another loathsome traitor? Are you set on disgracing the memory of your son who fell on the field of honour? Yes or no?'

The worried-looking, grizzled attorney quickly got to his feet and said, 'Your Honour, may I have the court's permission to note . . .'

The judge struck him down with his beak. 'I warn you,

attorney,' he said, 'I warn you not to speak unless I ask you to! Sit down!'

The judge returned to Anna Quangel. 'Well, what about it? Can you summon up some last shred of decency in your breast, or are you intent on matching your husband, who, as we have heard, is a common traitor? Did you betray your people in their hour of need? Had you the heart to let down your son? Yes or no!'

Anna Quangel looked timidly across at her husband.

'Look at me! Not that traitor! Now, yes or no?'

Quietly, but distinctly, 'Yes.'

'Speak up! We all want to hear it, a German mother who feels no shame in staining the heroic death of her son with filth!'

'Yes,' said Anna Quangel loudly.

'Unbelievable!' cried Feisler. 'I have sat through many sad and hideous experiences, but I have never witnessed a disgrace like yours! It seems to me hanging would be too good for you; you should be quartered, like beasts!'

He was addressing the spectators more than the Quangels, as he took over the role of the prosecutor. Then he recovered himself (he wanted his day in court). 'But my heavy duty as judge obliges me not to be contented with your confessions. However loath I am to undertake it, and however hopeless it might appear to be, my duty obliges me to examine whether there might not be some grounds for clemency in your case.'

So it began, and it went on for seven hours.

Yes, sensible Dr Reichhardt had been mistaken, and Quangel with him. Never had it occurred to them that the highest-ranking judge in Germany would conduct the trial in a spirit of such bottomless, mean-spirited malice. It was as though the Quangels had offended him, Judge Feisler, personally, as though this unforgiving, rancorous little man had had his honour besmirched and had now set himself to wound his enemy to death. It was as though Quangel had seduced the man's daughter, so personal was it all, so infinitely wide of any impartiality. No, the two of them had made a colossal mistake. This Third Reich kept springing new surprises on its antagonists; it was vile beyond all vileness.

'Accused, witnesses – your law-abiding co-workers – have stated that you were driven by a positively squalid avarice . . . For instance, how much did you make in a week?' the judge asked.

'Latterly, I was taking home forty marks a week,' Quangel replied.

'I see, forty marks, and that was net of tax and medical insurance and contributions to the Winter Relief Fund?'

'Yes, net.'

'Doesn't that seem a decent sum for an older couple like yourselves?'

'We got by on it.'

'No, you didn't get by on it! You're lying again! You managed to save regularly! Is that correct or not?'

'That's correct. Most of the time we managed to put something by.'

'How much would you say you were able to put by in an average week, then?'

'I couldn't tell you. It varied.'

The judge lost his temper: 'I said in an average week! Average! Do you understand the meaning of the word, *average*? And you call yourself a foreman! Can't even do basic arithmetic! Wonderful!'

Judge Feisler didn't seem to think it all wonderful, however, because he looked at the accused indignantly.

'I'm over fifty years old. I've worked for twenty-five years. There were good years and not-so-good years. I was unemployed for a while. My son was ill. I can't give you an average.'

'Oh? You can't, can't you? I'll tell you why that is! It's because you don't want to! That's your filthy avarice, from which your decent colleagues recoiled. You're afraid we might find out how much you managed to scrape together! Well, how much did it come to? Or can't you tell us that either?'

Quangel struggled with himself. The judge had found his weak spot. Not even Anna knew how much they had saved. But then Quangel mastered himself. He got over it. There was so much he had got over in the course of the past few weeks, why not this too? He broke with the last thing that tied him to his old life, and said, 'It was 4,763 marks!'

'Yes,' drawled the judge, and leaned back in his high-backed judge's chair. 'It was 4,763 marks and 67 pfennigs!' He read the figure from a file. 'And are you not ashamed to fight a state that allowed you to save such a sum? To oppose the commonweal that cared for you to that degree?' He raised his voice. 'You don't know the meaning of gratitude. You don't know the meaning of honour. You're a disgrace, a blot. You need to be blotted out!'

And the vulture's claws closed, opened, closed again, as though ripping at prey.

'Almost half the money I saved before the Nazis came to power,' Quangel said.

There was a laugh in the auditorium, but it froze under a furious glare from the judge. A sheepish cough was all that remained of it.

'Silence in court! Absolute silence! And you, accused, if you think you can be insolent, you will be punished. Don't think you're safe from additional punishment, you're not! You'll take whatever I give you!' He looked piercingly at Quangel, 'Now, tell me, accused, what were you saving for?'

'For our old age.'

'Your old age? You don't say. How sweet that sounds! But it's just another lie. From the time you began writing your postcards you must have been damned sure you weren't going to experience any old age! You confessed yourself that you were always aware of the consequences of what you were doing. But even so, you carried on putting money aside and depositing it in the bank. What for?'

'I reckoned I would get away with it?'

'What do you mean, get away with it? Be acquitted?!'

'No, I never thought that. I thought I wouldn't be caught.'

'You see, you were wrong to think that. But I don't believe that's what you did think anyway. You're not so stupid as you like to pretend. You can't possibly have thought you could go on committing your crimes year after year.'

'I wasn't thinking about year after year.'

'What is that supposed to mean?'

'I don't think it's going to go on much longer, your Thousand-Year Reich,' said Quangel, inclining his sharp bird's head toward the judge.

The attorney shuddered.

There was another laugh in the listening gallery, followed by an ominous murmuring.

'The bastard!' someone yelled.

The guard behind Quangel adjusted his cap, and with his other hand reached for his holster.

The prosecutor had jumped to his feet, brandishing a piece of paper.

Frau Quangel was smiling at her husband, nodding enthusiastically.

The guard behind her grabbed her shoulder and squeezed it viciously.

She bit back the pain and didn't cry out.

An assistant judge was staring at Quangel open-mouthed.

The judge jumped up: 'You, criminal! Idiot! Cretin! How dare you . . .'

He stopped, mindful of the impression he was creating.

'Take the accused away, Sergeant! Get him out of here! The court will come up with a suitable punishment . . .'

A quarter of an hour later, the trial resumed.

It was widely noticed that the accused seemed to have difficulty walking. People thought, They will have given him a good going-over. Fearfully, Anna Quangel thought the same.

Judge Feisler announced: 'The accused Otto Quangel is sentenced to four weeks in solitary on bread and water, with enforced fasting every third day. In addition,' Judge Feisler went on, by way of explanation, 'the defendant has had his braces taken from him, since, during the interval, he was seen behaving suspiciously with them. There is a view that he may have intended to attempt suicide.'

'I only had to be excused.'

'Silence, accused! He might have attempted suicide. The

accused will have to get along from now on without braces. He has no one to blame but himself.'

There was a further outbreak of laughter in the court, but this time the judge shot an almost grateful look at the gallery, evidently pleased with his own little joke. The accused stood there looking cramped up, having to keep one hand on his trousers to stop them from sliding down.

The judge smiled. 'Now, let's get on with the case.'

62

The Trial: Prosecutor Pinscher

If Judge Feisler's proceedings suggested to an unprejudiced viewer those of a bad-tempered bloodhound, the prosecutor played along as a little yapping terrier, only waiting to give the bloodhound's quarry a nasty little nip in the calf while his big brother had him by the throat. Once or twice in the course of proceedings thus far, the prosecutor had tried to get in a yap, only to be silenced by the bloodhound's barking. What need was there for his yapping, in any case? The judge had assumed the duties of the prosecution from the first minute; from the first minute, Feisler had violated the basic duty of any judge, which is to establish the truth. He had been utterly partisan.

But following a break for lunch, during which the judge had eaten a large and rich meal requiring no ration cards and including wine and schnapps, Feisler felt a little tired. Why go to so much trouble? The pair of them were dead anyway. In any case, it was the wife's turn – and from a judicial point of view, certainly, women were of no great interest to him. They were stupid and did what their menfolk told them. Other than that, they were only good for one thing.

So Feisler was indulgent, and allowed Pinscher to come forward and yap a little. With half-closed eyes, he leaned back in his judge's chair, head propped on his hand, giving the appearance of listening, when in reality he was entirely busy with his digestive processes.

'Accused, is it true you were fairly advanced in age when your present husband married you?'

'I was almost thirty.'

'And before that?'

'I don't understand.'

'Don't play the innocent: I want to hear about your relation-
ships with men before your marriage. Out with it!'

The crudity of the question made Anna Quangel first blush,
then turn pale. Seeking help, she looked over at her ageing
defence attorney, who got to his feet and said, 'Please your
Honour, the question is not relevant to the case!'

To which the prosecutor: 'My question is highly relevant. We
have heard it claimed that the wife of the accused was the mere
accomplice of her husband. I will prove to you that she was a
deeply immoral person in her own right, raised in the gutter,
and capable of any crime.'

The judge, bored, gave his opinion: 'The question is
allowed.'

Pinscher yapped again. 'Well, how many men did you sleep
with before your marriage?'

All eyes were on Anna Quangel. A few of the students in the
listening gallery licked their lips, and someone gave a mock
groan of pleasure.

Quangel looks at Anna in some concern – he knows how
sensitive she is about such matters.

But Anna Quangel has made her mind up. Just as Otto dropped
all his anxiety about the money he had saved up, so she is now
willing to face these shameless men with utter shamelessness
herself.

The prosecutor asked, 'Well, how many men did you sleep
with before your marriage?'

And now Anna Quangel replies, 'Eighty-seven.'

Someone in the gallery explodes into laughter.

The judge awakens from his slumbers and looks down with
something approaching interest at the little working-class
woman, with her red cheeks and full bust.

Quangel's dark eyes had lit up; now, the lids have fallen almost
shut. He doesn't look at anyone.

The prosecutor, though, wholly confused, stammers, 'With
eighty-seven? Why eighty-seven?'

'I don't know,' says Anna Quangel coolly. 'I suppose because
that's all there were.'

'I see,' says the prosecutor sullenly, 'I see!'

He is thoroughly annoyed, because he has suddenly turned the accused into an interesting person, which was in no way what he intended. Also, like most of those present, he is convinced that she is lying, that it was only two or three lovers, and quite possibly none at all. It might be possible to haul her off for making fun of the court. But who could prove her intention?

Finally he settles. Unhappily, he says, 'I am quite sure you are exaggerating, accused. A woman who has had eighty-seven lovers would hardly be able to remember the figure. She would say a great many. Your reply demonstrates the depths of your degradation. You rejoice in your shamelessness! You are proud to be a whore. And from having been a whore, you became what all whores eventually become, you became a procuress. You procured for your own son.'

And now Pinscher has got his teeth into Anna Quangel.

'No!' cries Anna Quangel, and raises her hands imploringly. 'Don't say that! I never did anything like that!'

'You never did that?' yaps Pinscher. 'So what do you call it when you put up the so-called fiancée of your son overnight not once, but on numerous occasions? Do we take it you took your son to bed with you on those occasions? Eh? Or where did Trudel sleep? You know she's dead now, don't you? Otherwise that harlot, that whore who helped your husband commit his crimes, would be here in the dock with you!'

The mention of Trudel, though, gives Frau Quangel fresh courage. She says, not to the prosecutor, but to the court at large: 'Yes, thanks be to God that Trudel is dead, that she isn't alive to witness this degenerate . . .'

'Watch your language, accused, I warn you!'

'She was a lovely, decent girl . . .'

'Who aborted her five-month-old baby, because she didn't want to give the government any soldiers!'

'She didn't abort it at all, she was miserable after it died!'

'She admitted it herself!'

'I don't believe you.'

The prosecutor screams, 'Do you think we care what you do

or don't believe! I warn you to change your tone, accused, otherwise you will experience something extremely unpleasant! Frau Hergesell's statement was taken by Inspector Laub. A Gestapo inspector does not tell lies!'

Pinscher glowered menacingly round the courtroom.

'Now I ask you again to tell me, accused: Did your son have relations with the girl or not?'

'I'm not a snoop. That's not what a mother does.'

'But you had a duty to care! If you tolerated your son's immoral behaviour within your four walls, you were making yourself guilty of procuring; that's what the law says.'

'I wouldn't know about that. What I do know is that there was a war, and there was a chance my son would die. In our circles that's the way it works: if a couple are engaged or as good as engaged, and there's a war, then we might turn a blind eye.'

'Aha, so you admit it, accused! You knew about the immoral relations, and you tolerated them! And then you call it turning a blind eye. The law calls it procuring for immoral purposes, and a mother who tolerates such a thing deserves our condemnation!'

'Oh, does she? Then I should like to know,' says Anna Quangel quite fearlessly, and with a steady voice, 'what the law has to say about the goings-on at the *Bubi-drück-mich-verein*?'*

General laughter . . .

'And what the SA get up to with their girls . . .'

The laughter dies.

'And the SS – we hear the SS violates Jewish women before shooting them . . .'

Deathly silence . . .

And then pandemonium breaks loose. People start yelling. Some of the spectators clamber into the dock to assault the accused.

Otto Quangel has jumped to his feet, ready to run to the aid of his wife.

---

* Irreverent popular nickname for the 'Bund Deutscher Mädel' (BDM); see note on page 95. The 'Baby, Do Me' Club would be an approximation.

His guard and his missing braces hinder him.

The judge stands and motions wildly for silence.

The assistant judges talk among themselves.

The prosecutor Pinscher is yapping away, but no one can hear a word.

Finally, Anna Quangel is dragged out of the court, the noise abates, and the judges withdraw to consult.

Five minutes later, they return.

'The accused Anna Quangel is excluded from participation in the trial against her. She will remain shackled from now on, and under solitary confinement until further notice. A regimen of bread and water, and only every other day.'

The trial continues.

63

The Trial: The Witness Ulrich Heffke

The witness Ulrich Heffke, technician and hunchbacked brother of Anna Quangel, had been through some hard months. The industrious Inspector Laub had arrested him along with his wife immediately after the Quangels, for no very good reason, other than that they were related to the Quangels.

From that moment on, Ulrich Heffke had lived in fear. This gentle man with his simple nature, who all his life had avoided strife, had been arrested by the sadistic Laub, had been tortured, yelled at and beaten. He had been starved and humiliated. In short, he had been tortured by all the rules of the art.

Finally, something had swung in his hunchback's mind. He had listened fearfully for what his tormentors wanted to hear from him and then given them the most incriminating statements – insanely incriminating, as was immediately demonstrated to him.

And then the tortures had begun all over again, in the hope that the hunchback might spill the beans on some further crime. Inspector Laub followed the watchword of the times: Everyone is guilty. You just need to probe for long enough, and you'll find something.

Laub simply refused to believe that he had stumbled upon a German citizen, not a member of the Party, who never listened to enemy radio, or indulged in defeatist whisperings, or fiddled his rations. Laub accused Heffke directly of having delivered postcards around Nollendorfplatz for his brother-in-law.

So Heffke confessed – and three days later, Laub was able to prove to him that he, Ulrich Heffke, could not possibly have delivered any postcards.

Now Inspector Laub was accusing Heffke of having sold industrial secrets at the optics factory where he was employed. Heffke confessed, and after a week of painstaking questioning, Laub was able to establish that there were no secrets to betray at the factory; no one even knew what weapon the parts they made there were destined for.

Heffke paid dearly for each false confession he made, but that only intimidated him more. He admitted anything, merely to be left alone. To avoid further questioning, he signed whatever was put in front of him. He would have signed his own death warrant. He was a quivering jelly, a bundle of fear ready to start trembling at the first word he heard.

Inspector Laub was unprincipled enough to have the poor man remanded along with the Quangels, even though there was no evidence of any involvement on Heffke's part in the Quangels' 'crimes'. Better err on the safe side, and let the examining magistrate see if he couldn't get anything incriminating out of Heffke. Ulrich Heffke took advantage of the slightly more generous accommodation in remand by promptly hanging himself. He was found in the nick of time, cut down, and returned to a life that had become completely unbearable to him.

From that moment on, the little hunchback was forced to live under much more onerous conditions: the light in his cell was left on all night, a special sentry peered in at him through a peephole every few minutes, his hands were manacled, and he was taken for questioning almost every day. Though the examining magistrate was unable to find anything incriminating against Heffke, he remained firmly convinced that the hunchback was covering a crime of some sort, why else would he have tried to kill himself? That wasn't the way an innocent person behaved! The positively imbecilic way that Heffke agreed with every charge against him put the examining magistrate to the trouble of adopting the most wearisome procedures and strategies, all of which only revealed that Heffke hadn't done anything.

So it happened that, barely a week before the beginning of the trial, Ulrich Heffke was released from remand. He went back to his tall, dark, tired wife, who had been released before him. She received him in silence. Heffke was too disturbed to be able to work; he would kneel for hours in a corner of his room, singing hymns in his light, pleasing falsetto. He barely spoke, and cried a great deal at night. They had money put by, so the woman did nothing to spur the man to go back to work.

Three days after his release Ulrich Heffke received a further summons, to appear as a trial witness. His enfeebled brain could not make the distinction between witness and accused. His trepidation increased by the hour, he ate almost nothing, and his bouts of singing grew ever longer. He was tormented by the fear that his only recently suspended sufferings would recommence.

On the eve of the trial he hanged himself again, and this time it was his wife who saved his life. As soon as he was able to breathe, she gave him a sound thrashing. She didn't think much of his new hobby. The next day she took him under her arm and delivered him to the servant of the court at the door of the witnesses' room, with the words, 'You'd better keep an eye him! He's gone crazy!'

As the witnesses' waiting room was already fairly full – for the most part with colleagues of Quangel's, the directors of the factory, and the two women and the senior clerk who had seen him drop his postcards – as there were already quite a number of witnesses present when Anna Heffke gave her warning, not only the servant of the court but also the whole body of witnesses eagerly kept an eye on the little hunchback. Some tried to while away the tedious wait with teasing him, but it didn't really catch on: he was too patently terrified, and most of them were too kindhearted to torment him too much.

The hunchback got through the questioning by Judge Feisler fairly well, in spite of being so terrified, simply because he spoke so softly and was shaking so hard that the highest judge in the land scorned to question such a scaredy-cat for very long. Then the hunchback returned to the witnesses' bench, hoping that that was it for him.

But by then he had been forced to witness Pinscher's attack on his sister. He had had to listen to the scurrilous questions that were put to Anna, and his heart waxed indignant. He had wanted to step forward, to speak for his dearly loved sister, to bear witness that she had always led an honest and respectable life – but his fear had forced him down, made him lie low in silence.

So now, almost beside himself with a mixture of fear and cowardice and sudden surges of bravery, he followed the course of the trial up to the moment when Anna Quangel attacked the BDM, the SA, and the SS. He witnessed the ensuing riot, and he himself with his ridiculous little figure created a bit of a riot by climbing up on the bench for a better view. He saw two guards drag Anna from the court.

He was still standing on the bench when the judge finally restored order. His neighbours had forgotten him; they were huddled together, whispering.

Then the eye of Prosecutor Pinscher fell on Ulrich Heffke, and he looked at him with astonishment, and called, 'Hey, you there . . . ! You're the brother of the accused, aren't you? What's your name again?'

'Heffke, Ulrich Heffke!' supplied the prosecutor's assistant.

'Witness Heffke, that was your sister! I call upon you now to tell the court about Anna Quangel's previous life! What can you tell us about it?'

And Ulrich Heffke opened his mouth – he was still standing up on the bench – and for the first time his eyes looked out without dread. He opened his mouth, and in his pleasing falsetto he sang:

> Adieu to you, you wicked world
> Whose evil doings I abhor
> I yearn to be in heaven above
> Which God reserves for those he loves!

Everyone was so startled that they let him sing. A few enjoyed the plain manner of the singing, and moved their heads foolishly from side to side with the tune. One of the assistant judges gaped. Some of the law students gripped the rails hard and watched intensely. The grizzled, anxious defence attorney picked his nose abstractedly. Otto Quangel turned his sharp features toward his brother-in-law, and for the first time he could feel his cool heart beating a little for the poor chap. What punishment would they have in store for him?

> Hide my soul in Thy wounded side
> Keep it there from grievous plight.
> Admit me to Thy celestial home,
> For e'er to dwell in Thy bosom.

While he sang the second verse, the court once again became a little unruly. The judge was distracted by a whispered consultation with the prosecutor, who passed a note to the guard.

But the little hunchback didn't pay any regard to any of this. His gaze was directed toward the ceiling of the courtroom. Then, in ecstatically transfigured tones, he called out, 'I'm coming!'

He spread his arms, pushed off from the bench, and flew . . .

And he fell clumsily among the witnesses sitting in front of him, who quickly got out of the way, and he rolled among the benches . . .

'Get that man out of here!' the judge barked to the once again unruly court. 'He needs medical attention!'

Ulrich Heffke was escorted from the court.

'Plainly a family of criminals and madmen,' the judge declared. 'They will all be exterminated.'

And he darted a threatening look in the direction of Otto Quangel, who, holding his pants up with his hands, was still looking at the door through which his little brother-in-law had disappeared.

The hunchback Ulrich Heffke was indeed duly exterminated. Physically and mentally he was found to be unfit for life, and after a brief spell in an asylum, was given an injection that saw to it that he really did bid adieu to this wicked world.

64

The Trial: The Defence Team

Anna Quangel's attorney, the grizzled, careworn, elderly man appointed by the court to defend her, who had a habit of picking his nose at moments of excitement and who was thoroughly Jewish-looking (but against whom nothing could be proved, because his papers proclaimed him a purebred Aryan), rose to make his plea.

He said it was much to his regret that he was forced to speak in the absence of his client. Certainly, her outbursts against such pillars of the Party as the SA and the SS were regrettable . . .

'Criminal!' – an intervention from the prosecutor.

Yes indeed, his colleague for the prosecution was perfectly right, such outbursts were criminal. But as could be seen from the brother, his client could not be described as wholly *compos mentis*. The case of Ulrich Heffke had been further, living proof of religious mania in the family. Without venturing to second-guess the medical experts, he was sure that this was an instance of schizophrenia, and as schizophrenia was a genetic condition . . .

At this point the grizzled defence attorney was interrupted for a second time by the prosecutor, who asked the court to make him come to the point.

Judge Feisler instructed the attorney to come to the point.

The attorney objected that this was the point at issue.

No, it wasn't. This was about high treason, not schizophrenia and madness.

Again, the defence attorney objected: If the prosecutor was entitled to make the case for the moral turpitude of his client, then he was as entitled to speak about schizophrenia. He asked the court for a judgement.

The court withdrew to consider the defence attorney's

petition. Then Judge Feisler announced: 'Neither during the preliminary investigation nor in today's hearing have there been any indications of mental frailty in Anna Quangel. The behaviour of her brother Ulrich Heffke cannot be used in evidence, as the court has no medical reports on the witness's condition. It is quite possible that Ulrich Heffke is a dangerous faker, who hopes to give his sister some assistance. The defence is instructed to stick to the matter of treason, which is the issue before the court today . . .'

Triumphant look from Prosecutor Pinscher at the worried defence attorney.

Meek look back from the attorney.

'As the high court prevents me,' Anna Quangel's lawyer began again, 'from speaking of my client's mental state, I will pass over all those points that bespeak her diminished responsibility: her fury with her own husband following the death of her son, her often eccentric, almost deranged behaviour here . . .'

Pinscher yaps, 'I protest in the strongest terms against the way the counsel is circumventing the instruction of the court. While claiming to pass over his points, he brings them up repeatedly. I demand a ruling!'

Again, the court withdraws, and when it reconvenes Judge Feisler angrily announces that the attorney is sentenced to a fine of 500 marks for disregarding a prohibition of the court. In the event of any repetition, he will be barred from taking further part in the trial.

The grizzled attorney bows. He looks anxious, as though troubled by the question of where to come up with those 500 marks. For the third time, he begins to speak. He endeavours to describe Anna Quangel's youth, her years as a housemaid, and then her marriage to a man who was a cold-blooded fanatic: 'Nothing but work, worry, self-denial, subjugation to an implacable man. Then all at once this man starts to write highly treasonable postcards. The proceedings have clearly established that this was the husband's idea, not the wife's. All claims to the contrary on the part of my client during preliminary inquiries should be seen as a misguided self-sacrifice . . .' He cries,'What was Anna Quangel to do against the criminal desire of her husband? What could she do? She had a lifetime of service behind her, she had learned nothing but obedience – never resistance. She was a creature of her husband, a cypher, she was besotted . . .'

The prosecutor sits there with ears pricked.

'High court! Criminal action, or being accessory to such action, cannot be laid at the door of such a woman. You don't punish a dog for catching rabbits on someone else's land on his master's instructions: this woman is not fully responsible for her role. For which reason also, she throws herself upon the mercy of Paragraph 51, Subhead 2 . . .'

The prosecutor interrupts. The defence has once again disregarded the orders of the court, he yaps.

The defence denies this.

The prosecutor reads from his notes. 'According to the stenographer's records, the defence spoke as follows: "For which reason also, she throws herself upon the mercy of Paragraph 51, Subhead 2." The words "For which reason also" make clear reference to the alleged insanity in the Heffke family. I invoke the judge's ruling!'

Judge Feisler asks the defence attorney what the words 'For which reason also' were intended to refer to.

The attorney explains that the words referred to arguments yet to be elaborated in his plea.

The prosecutor yells that no one can base an argument on things he hasn't said yet. A reference can be made only to something already existing – it is absurd to claim that one might refer to things yet unsaid! The defence attorney's words are mere prevarication.

The defence protested against the charge of prevarication. Furthermore, one might very well refer in the course of an argument to something still to be said; that was a widely used rhetorical ploy – Cicero, for instance, in the third of his *Philippics* says . . .

Anna Quangel had been forgotten; Otto sat there open-mouthed, looking from side to side at this ping-pong match.

A heated dispute was in progress. Greek and Latin quotations were bandied back and forth.

Finally, the court withdrew once more to consult, and Judge Feisler returned to announce to general surprise (for in the course of the learned argument, most people had forgotten what it was actually about), that on account of repeated violations the defence attorney was now barred from further speaking. The role of official state-appointed defence counsel was transferred to Assistant Ludecke, who happened to be among those present.

The grizzled defence attorney bowed and left the court, looking more worried than ever.

Assistant Ludecke, who 'happened to be among those present', now got up and spoke. He didn't have much experience, hadn't been listening very closely, was intimidated by the court; moreover, he was in love at the time, and so was powerfully distracted. He spoke for three minutes, asked for mitigating factors to be taken into consideration (didn't say what they were, and in case the court disagreed with him, he asked that his plea be disregarded), and then sat down, looking hot and flustered.

It was now Otto Quangel's designated defence attorney's turn to speak.

He got up, very blond and full of himself. He had not spoken in the trial thus far, had not taken a note, and the table in front of him was empty. During the hours and hours of the hearing, he had busied himself by rubbing together and examining his pink and beautifully manicured fingertips.

But now he spoke, his gown half open, one hand in his trouser pocket and the other economically gesturing. This attorney could not stand his client, he found him loathsome, stupid, ugly and generally repulsive. And Quangel had done everything in his power to heighten the man's revulsion by ignoring Dr Reichhardt's urgent advice and withholding all information from him – he needed no attorney.

So now Defence Attorney Stark spoke. His nasal drawl was in stark contrast to the words he used.

He said, 'Rarely can we who are assembled here have been

presented with such a specimen of human degradation as we have had before us today. Treason, prostitution, procuring, abortion, miserliness – is there a vice anywhere that my client does not exemplify or has not participated in? Gentlemen of the court, you see me unable to defend such a criminal. In a case like this one, I am obliged to lay aside the role of defender and join ranks with the prosecution, for whom I raise my voice: I say, let justice take its natural course. Varying the famous sentence, I say, *Fiat justitia, pereat mundus!* No mitigation for this criminal, who doesn't deserve to be called a human being.'

With that the defender bowed and, to general surprise, sat down, carefully pulling his trouser creases up over his knees. He looked down attentively at his fingertips and began rubbing them together gently.

After a short pause, the judge asked the accused if he had anything to say for himself. If so, then he advised him to keep it short.

Clutching his trousers with both hands, Otto Quangel said, 'I have nothing to say in my favour. But I would like to thank my attorney for his defence. At last I understand what the law is for.'

And Quangel sat down amidst a general uproar. The attorney interrupted his fingertip-rubbing, got up, and added casually that he was personally and professionally finished with his client, who had once more given proof of what a hardened criminal he was.

It was then that Quangel laughed for the first time since his arrest, the first time in a very long time. He laughed with whole-hearted gusto. The preposterous comedy of this gang of criminals branding everyone else as criminals was suddenly too much for him to take.

The judge attacked the accused for his unseemly mirth, and considered imposing further punishments on him, but then he remembered he had already burdened him with everything in his power. The only remaining thing he could do was banish him from the courtroom, and that struck him as counterproductive. He therefore opted for temporary leniency.

The court withdrew to consider its verdict.

Long interval.

As at the theatre, most people went out to smoke a cigarette.

65

The Trial: The Verdict

According to standard practice, the two guards who were now in charge of Otto Quangel should have taken him down to a little holding cell during the break in proceedings. But the court had almost completely emptied, and moving the prisoner up and down many corridors and flights of stairs – and he with his trousers forever slipping down – was a cumbersome process, so they took it upon themselves to disregard standard practice, and let him stay where he was, while they stood chatting a few feet away him.

The old foreman propped his head in his hands and sank into a doze. The seven-hour-long proceedings, during which he had remained riveted in concentration, had exhausted him. Shadowy images played in his head: the clawlike hands of Judge Feisler opening and closing; Anna's attorney with his finger up his nose; the little hunchback Heffke trying to fly; Anna, pink-cheeked, saying 'Eighty-seven', her eyes as merry and serene as he had ever seen them; these and many others . . . many . . . others . . .

His head weighed more heavily in his hands – he was so tired, he simply had to sleep, even if only for five minutes . . .

So he dropped his arm on the table, and his head on his arm. He drew a deep breath. Five minutes of deep sleep, a little spell of oblivion.

But he awoke again with a start. There was something in the courtroom, still, that disturbed his longed-for rest. He stared all round the room, and his eyes came to rest on Judge Fromm, who was standing beside the railing of the public gallery, apparently gesturing to him. Quangel had noticed the old gentleman earlier – nothing seemed to have escaped his attention – but on such a crowded day he had paid little heed to his former neighbour from the house on Jablonski Strasse.

Now the judge was standing by the rail, motioning to him.

Quangel darted a look at the two guards. They stood about three paces away from him, engrossed in a lively conversation. Quangel picked up the words, 'And so I grab the guy by the throat . . .'

The foreman stood up, snatched up his trousers, and shuffled across the courtroom toward the judge.

The latter stood by the rail, his eyes lowered now, as though he didn't want to see the prisoner slowly drawing nearer. Then – Quangel at this stage was only a couple of steps away – the judge rapidly turned on his heel and walked down the aisle to the exit. But he had left behind on the railing a small white package a little smaller than a spool of thread.

Quangel took the last few steps, reached out, and grabbed the little package, concealing it first in the palm of his hand, then in his trouser pocket. It had a firm feeling. He turned round and saw that the guards hadn't remarked his absence. A door shut at the back of the public gallery, and the judge was gone.

Quangel started to wander back to his place. He was excited and his heart was pounding. It was so unlikely that this adventure was going to end well. What had seemed so important to the judge that he had risked so much in slipping it to him?

Quangel was only a few yards from his place when one of the guards finally noticed him. He gave a jump, looked in confusion at Quangel's seat as though to confirm that the accused wasn't actually sitting in it, and then he almost shouted in alarm, 'What are you doing wandering around?'

The other guard spun round, too, and stared at Quangel. They both stood there, rooted to the spot in bewilderment; it didn't even occur to them to lead the prisoner back.

'I want to be excused, officer!' said Quangel.

But while the guard growled, 'Well, kindly ask, the next time! You don't just go shuffling off by yourself!' – while the guard was still talking, Quangel suddenly thought that he didn't want to be any better off than Anna. Let them announce their verdict without the presence of the two principals – it would spoil their fun. He, Quangel, wasn't in the least curious; he knew what was coming. But he was curious to learn what the judge had slipped him.

The guards had come up alongside Quangel and taken his arms, while he held up his trousers.

Quangel looked at them icily, and said, 'Fuck Hitler!'

'What?' They were stunned, didn't believe their ears.

And Quangel, very fast and very loud, 'Fuck Hitler! Fuck Göring! Fuck Goebbels, you piece of shit! Fuck Streicher!'

A punch on the jaw prevented him from continuing with this litany. The two policemen lugged the unconscious Quangel out of the court.

And so it came about that Judge Feisler ended up passing sentence on the two accused in absentia. In vain had he ignored Quangel's insulting behaviour to his defence attorney. And Quangel was right: Feisler didn't enjoy passing sentence without being able to look into the faces of the accused. He had thought up such fine insults.

Feisler was still speaking in court when Quangel opened his eyes in his cell. His chin hurt, his whole head hurt, he could barely remember what had happened. His hand slid into his trouser pocket. Thank God, the little package was still there.

He heard the footfall of the sentry in the corridor, and then it stopped, and there was a quiet scraping sound from the door: the peephole cover being slid aside. Quangel shut his eyes and remained stretched out as though still unconscious. After a seemingly endless interval, there was a second scraping sound, and then the renewed footfall of the sentry . . .

The peephole was shut; the sentry wouldn't be looking in for another two or three minutes.

Quangel reached into his pocket and pulled out the little package. He slipped off the thread that tied it and unfolded the piece of paper to find a glass vial. On the paper was a typed note: 'Cyanide, kills painlessly in seconds. Hide it in your mouth. Your wife will be similarly provided for. Destroy this note!'

Quangel smiled. The good old man! The lovely old man! He put the note in his mouth, chewed it until it was sodden with spittle, then swallowed it.

He gazed curiously at the vial, with its clear contents. Swift, painless death, he mused. Oh, if they knew! And Anna provided for as well. He really does think of everything. Good old man!

He put the glass vial in his mouth. After trying various places, he found he could best lodge it in his cheek beside his jawbone, like a plug of tobacco – many of the workers in the furniture factory had chewed. He felt his cheek. No, there was no bump there. And if they did spot something, he would crunch the glass and swallow before they could take it from him.

Quangel smiled again. Now he felt really free. Now they had no more power over him!

66

The Death House

The death house in Plötzensee is now Otto Quangel's home. The solitary cell in the death house is his last address on earth.

Yes, he is in solitary now. There are no more cellmates for those sentenced to death, no Dr Reichhardt, not even a 'dog'. The only companion for those sentenced to death is Death: that's the way the law wants it to be.

From the ghosts in the cells there isn't a sound to be heard. The condemned are so quiet! Brought together from all corners of Europe: Germans, French, Dutch, Belgians, Norwegians, some of them little more than boys, and good characters, weak characters, bad characters – every temperament is represented, from sanguine to choleric to melancholic. In this establishment, distinctions are blurred, for everyone is so quiet; these men are no more than shadows of their former selves. Only rarely does Quangel hear someone sobbing at night, and then silence, silence . . . Silence . . .

He has always loved silence. These past few months, he has been forced to live a life against his own bent: never alone, continually forced to speak, when more than anything he hated speech. Now for one last time he is allowed to return to his own element: silence, patience. Dr Reichhardt is a good man, he learned a lot from him, but now, so close to death, it is better to be without Dr Reichhardt.

He has established (based on what he learned from Dr Reichhardt) a regular routine here in the cell. Everything at the prescribed time: careful washing, a few calisthenics picked up from his former cellmate, an hour's walk in the morning and one in the afternoon, thorough cleaning of the cell, eating, sleeping. There are books to read here too; each week he is allowed six books in his cell. But he hasn't changed as much as all that, and he never looks at them. He is not about to start reading in the twilight of his life.

But there is one other thing he has picked up from Dr Reichhardt: while he walks he hums to himself. He remembers nursery rhymes and folk songs from his school days and before. They well up in him from forgotten depths, verse after verse – what a brain he must have, remembering those things after forty years! And then the poems: 'The Ring of Polycrates', 'The Pledge', 'The Ode to Joy', 'The Erlking'. Only for 'The Bell' he can't quite remember all the stanzas. Maybe he never had them all memorized in the first place; he can't remember now . . .

A quiet life, with work, as ever, at the core of his day. Yes, he has to work here too. He has to sort batches of dried peas and pick out the wormy ones, the broken ones, stray seeds of this or that, blackish grey balls of vetch. He likes the work; his busy fingers sort peas hour after hour.

And it's good, too, that he's landed this particular job, because it keeps him fed. The good days when Dr Reichhardt shared his meals with him are now well and truly over. What they give him in his cell now is poorly cooked, watery swill – glutinous bread with potatoes to stretch it – and it sits heavy in his gut.

But the peas help. He can't take many because they're weighed, but enough to satisfy his appetite. He takes the peas and softens them in water, and when they've swelled up he drops them in his soup to warm them through, and then he mashes them. This way he improves his food, of which it would have been true to say not enough to live on and too much to die on.

He senses that the warders know what he's up to, but they don't say anything. And the reason they don't is not because they want to make life easier for the condemned man, but because they've witnessed so much misery it has dulled their feelings.

They don't talk themselves, lest their charges should. They don't want to listen to any complaints; there's nothing they can do about them anyway. Everything here takes its rigid course. They are cogs in a machine, iron cogs, steel cogs. If an iron cog happened to soften, it would have to be replaced, and the cogs don't want to be replaced – they want to be just the way they are.

They don't provide any comfort because they don't want to. They are as they are, which is to say indifferent, cold, lacking empathy.

When Otto Quangel was first brought to this cell from the solitary confinement to which Judge Feisler had sentenced him, he thought it would be for a day or two. He thought they would be in a hurry to carry out his sentence, and that would have been fine by him.

But gradually he comes to realize that it can take weeks or months for a sentence to be carried out, even a whole year. There are people sentenced to death who have been waiting for fully a year, who every night go to bed and don't know whether they will be rudely awakened by the executioner; any night, any hour – while they are chewing their food, while they are sorting peas, while they are slopping out – at any moment the door might open, a hand beckon, a voice say, 'All right! It's time!'

There is a monstrous cruelty in the way fear is spun out over days, weeks, months. Nor is it just because of some legal formalities: it's not just pleas for clemency waiting to be settled one way or another that cause this delay. Some people say the executioner has too much to do; he can't keep up. The executioner only works here on Mondays and Thursdays. All the other days, he's on the road; his services are in demand all over Germany; the executioner takes his work with him. But how can it be that in the case of, say, two men sentenced for the same thing at the same time, one is punished seven weeks before the other? No, it's a question of cruelty, of sadism, of barbarism. They don't beat you up in this establishment, don't torture you physically; here the poison is dribbled imperceptibly into you. They don't want to let your soul out of the clutches of death for a single minute.

Each Monday and Thursday there is commotion on death row. The night before, the ghosts begin to stir; they hunker in doorways, shaking; they listen to the sounds from the corridor. The sentry is still pacing back and forth; it's only two in the morning. But soon . . . Maybe today. And they beg and pray, Just these three more days, or these four more days till the next scheduled executions, and I'll go willingly, but not today, please! And they beg and pray and cajole.

The clock strikes four. Footfall, clank of tin dishes, murmurs. The sounds come closer. Your heart starts to beat; sweat breaks out all over your body. Suddenly a key grinds in the lock. Easy, easy, it's next door – no, two doors away! Not your turn yet. A stifled 'No! No! Help!' Feet scraping. Silence. The sentry's regular pacing back and forth, back and forth. Silence. Waiting. Terrified waiting. I can't stand it . . .

And after an endless delay, after a gulf of fear, an unendurable period of waiting which nonetheless has to be endured, the murmurs, the noise of feet, the rattle of the key . . . Coming closer, closer, closer. O God, not today, not me! Just three more days. Clank! The keys – that's my cell. No, yours! It's next door, a few murmured words, they came for my neighbour. They get him out, the sound of footsteps receding . . .

Time here crumbles into myriad tiny pieces. Waiting. Nothing but waiting. And the footsteps of the sentries in the corridor. O God, today they're just going from cell to cell, and I'm next. My – turn – next! In three hours I'll be a corpse, this body will be stiff, these legs that can still carry me will be pegs, this hand that knew work, caresses, tenderness, sin, will be a rotting piece of meat! It can't be, but it is!

Waiting – waiting – waiting! And suddenly the condemned man sees the gleam of light outside the window, he can hear the bell saying it's time to get up. The day is at hand, another working day – and he's been spared once more. He has another three days' grace – or four, if it's a Thursday. Fortune has smiled on him! He breathes more easily; at last he can breathe again – perhaps they'll just let him live. Perhaps there'll be a great victory and an amnesty and maybe his punishment will be commuted to life imprisonment!

An hour of breathing more easily!

And then fear begins again, and poisons these three days, or four: last time they stopped right outside my door. Next Monday, they'll begin with me. Oh, what can I do? Nothing . . .

And always anew, always anew, culminating twice a week, but every day of the week, fear, every second, fear!

Month after month: deadly fear!

Sometimes Otto Quangel asks himself how he knows all this. He hasn't talked to anyone, and no one has talked to him. A few mean words from the sentry: 'Come! Get up! Work faster!' Perhaps while his tin dish was being filled, something like 'seven this week', more mouthed than whispered, and that was the size of it.

His senses had become preternaturally acute: they guessed whatever he couldn't see. His ears picked up every sound in the corridor: the scraps of conversation as sentries clocked on and off, a curse, a scream – everything revealed itself to him, nothing remained a secret. And then at night, in the long nights that according to regulations went on for thirteen hours but that were never nights at all because a light was kept burning in each cell, then he would sometimes dare to clamber up to the window and hang there listening to the night outside. He knew that the sentries in the yard with their dogs had orders to shoot at any face that appeared in the window – and he heard shots, fairly regularly – but he did it anyway.

He stood there on his stool, sniffing the pure night air (the air alone made the risk worthwhile), and he heard the whispering going from window to window: 'Karl's been beaten again!' or 'The woman in No. 347 spent the whole day standing downstairs,' and in time he was able to puzzle things out. In time he knew that the man in the cell next to his had worked in counterintelligence and was supposed to have sold secrets to the enemy; twice already he had tried to kill himself. And in the cell behind his was a worker in a power plant who had allowed the dynamos to fry. And one of the guards, Brennecke, would get you paper and pencil stubs and smuggle letters out, if someone on the outside bribed him with money or, better yet, food. And so on and so on. News and more news. Even death row speaks, breathes, lives. Even on death row, the deep-seated urge to communicate cannot be extinguished.

But even though Otto Quangel – occasionally – put his life

on the line to listen at the window, even though his senses never tired of picking up on each little change, still he was not like the others. Sometimes they sensed that there was someone at the window in his cell; once someone whispered, 'Well, what's with you, Otto? Got the answer to your appeal yet?' (They knew all about him.) But he never answered; he never admitted that he, too, was listening. He didn't belong to them; even though he was facing the same sentence they were, he was different.

And the thing that made him different wasn't his cussedness, as before, nor the love of peace and quiet that had always set him apart, nor his dislike of speaking that had enjoined him to silence, but the little glass vial that Judge Fromm had slipped into his possession.

The vial of cyanide had made him free. The others, his companions in suffering, had to walk to the end of their designated road; he had a choice. He could die at any minute of his choosing. He was free. In the death house, behind bars and high walls, in chains and irons, he – Otto Quangel, erstwhile master carpenter, husband, father, troublemaker – was free. They had done it, they had made him free as he had never in his life been free before. He, the possessor of the vial, did not fear death. Death was with him at all hours; Death was his friend and intimate. He, Otto Quangel, had no need to wake early on Mondays and Thursdays and listen gibbering at the door of his cell. He was not with them, or not of them, not quite. He didn't have to torment himself, because the end of all torments was in his possession.

It was a good life he was leading. He loved it. He wasn't even quite sure he would ever need his glass vial. Perhaps it was better to wait till the very last moment? Perhaps he would be able to see Anna once more? Wasn't it right to spare them no trouble, no shame?

Let them kill him, that was better! He wanted to know how it felt – it was as though he had an entitlement, a duty to know how they went about it. Up until the moment when they put a noose round his neck, or a block under his head, he wanted to know. And then, at the very last minute, he could still play his trick on them.

Then, in the certainty that nothing could happen to him, that – perhaps for the very first time in his life – he could be just himself, as he was, in that certainty he found calm, serenity, even cheerfulness. His ageing body had never felt so well as during these weeks. His beady bird's eye had never looked as friendly as it did now in the death cell in the Plötze. His spirit had never been able to roam as easily as here.

A good life it was!

He hoped Anna was doing well, too. Old Fromm was a man of his word. Anna, too, would be beyond chicaneries and torments; Anna, too, would be free, imprisoned and free . . .

67

The Pleas For Clemency

Otto Quangel had spent only a few days – in accordance with the order of the People's Court – lying in the dark cell in solitary, freezing miserably in the little iron cage that most resembled a scaled-down version of the monkey house at the zoo, when the door opened, a light came on, and there in the doorway stood his lawyer, Dr Stark, looking at him.

Quangel slowly stood up and looked back.

So that suited and booted gent with his rosy fingernails and his casual drawl had taken it upon himself to pay him a call. Probably to see him suffer.

But even then Quangel had lodged in his cheek the vial of cyanide, his talisman that allowed him to endure cold and hunger. And so, despite being in rags and shaking with cold and with hunger burning his stomach, he stared back calmly, even with a mocking cheerfulness, at the 'distinguished-looking gentleman'.

'Well?' Quangel finally asked.

'I'm bringing you the verdict,' said the lawyer, drawing a piece of paper out of his briefcase.

Quangel didn't take it. 'I'm not interested,' he said. 'I know it's death. And my wife?'

'Your wife as well. And there's no appeal.'

'Good,' he replied.

'But you can petition for clemency,' said the lawyer.

'To the Führer?'

'Yes, to the Führer.'

'No, thanks.'

'So you want to die?'

Quangel smiled.

'Are you not afraid?'

Quangel smiled.

For the first time, the lawyer studied his client's face with a trace of interest. He said, 'In that case, I'll submit the petition myself.'

'After first calling for me to be sentenced!'

'It's the way things happen. Following the death sentence, there's the petition for clemency. It's among my duties.'

'Your duties. I understand. Like defending me. Well, I expect your petition won't have much effect, so why don't you just forget it.'

'I'll submit it anyway, regardless of what you say.'

'I can't stop you, I suppose.'

Quangel sat down on his cot again. He was waiting for the other man to stop his stupid chatter and leave.

But the lawyer didn't leave, and after a long pause he said, 'Can I ask you what made you do it?'

'Do what?' asked Quangel coolly, without looking at the elegant lawyer.

'Write those postcards. They didn't accomplish anything, and now they'll cost you your life.'

'Because I'm stupid. Because I didn't have any better ideas. Because I thought they would accomplish something, as you put it. That's why!'

'And don't you regret it? Aren't you sorry to lose your life over a stupid stunt like that?'

Quangel cast a sharp glare at the lawyer, his proud, old, tough bird-glare. 'At least I stayed decent,' he said. 'I didn't participate.'

The lawyer took a long look at the man sitting there in silence. Then he said, 'I have to say, I think my colleague who defended your wife was right: you are both mad.'

'Do you think it's mad to be willing to pay any price for remaining decent?'

'You didn't need the postcards for that.'

'That would have been a kind of tacit agreement. What was your price for turning into such a fine gentleman, with creased trousers and polished fingernails and deceitful concluding speeches? What did you have to pay?'

The lawyer said nothing.

'You see!' said Quangel. 'And you will continue to pay more and more, and maybe one day, like me, you will pay with your life, but you will have done it for your indecency!'

Still the lawyer said nothing.

Quangel stood up. 'There,' he laughed. 'You know perfectly well that the man behind bars is the decent one, and you on the outside are a scoundrel, that the criminal is free, and the decent man is sentenced to death. You're no lawyer. And now you want to ask for clemency for me – why don't you just get out of here?'

'I will appeal for clemency for you,' said the lawyer.

Quangel remained silent.

'Well, I'll be seeing you!' said the lawyer.

'Hardly – that is, unless you want to come to my execution. You're cordially invited!'

The lawyer left.

He was coarse and insensitive, and a bad man. But even so he was able to admit to himself that Quangel was the better man.

The clemency plea was drawn up, and insanity was suggested as grounds on which the Führer might be merciful, but the lawyer knew full well that his client was not mad.

A petition for clemency was sent to the Führer on Anna Quangel's behalf as well, but it didn't come from Berlin; it came from a small poor village in Brandenburg, and the name of the sender on the envelope was Heffke.

Anna Quangel's parents had received a letter from their daughter-in-law, that is, from the wife of their son, Ulrich. The letter contained only bad news, and it was couched in short, harsh, unsparing sentences. Ulrich was in an asylum in Wittenau, and it was Otto and Anna Quangel who were to blame. They had been sentenced to death for betraying their Führer and Fatherland. So much for your children! The name of Heffke brings disgrace to all who wear it!

Speechless, afraid even to look at one another, the two old people sat in their wretched little parlour. The letter, the terrible news, lay on the table between them. They didn't dare look at it again.

They had had to scrape by all their lives, humble farmworkers on a large estate under rough stewards. It had been a tough life for them: hard work and few joys. Their pride had been in the children, and the children had turned out well. They had done better for themselves than the parents, and they hadn't had to work quite as hard – Ulrich became a technician in an optics factory, and Anna was married to a master carpenter. The fact that they hardly ever wrote and never visited, that barely bothered the old people: that was the way of the world, birds flew the nest. At least the children were doing well for themselves.

And now this pitiless, pitiless blow! After a time, the bony, exhausted hand of the old farmworker reaches across the table: 'Mother!'

And suddenly tears well up in the old woman's eyes. 'Oh, Father! Our Anna! Our Ulrich! And now they're said to have betrayed our Führer! I can't believe it, not for the life of me!'

For three days they were too bewildered to do anything. They didn't set foot outside the house; they didn't dare look anyone in the eye, for fear that their shame might already have been broadcast everywhere.

Then, on the fourth day, they asked a neighbour to keep an eye on their hens, and they set off for Berlin. As they walked down the windswept avenue, the man ahead, the woman in country fashion a step or two behind, they resembled two children who had wandered out into the big wide world, where everything – a gust of wind, a falling branch, a passing car, a crude word – menaced them. They looked so defenceless.

Two days later, they trekked back down the same windswept avenue, even smaller, more bowed and disconsolate.

They had achieved nothing in Berlin. Their daughter-in-law had called them a load of names. They hadn't been allowed to see Ulrich because they had come outside 'visiting hours'. Anna and her husband – no one could even tell them what prison they were in. They hadn't found their children. And the Führer, to whom they had looked for help and comfort, and whose chancellery they had gone to, the Führer wasn't in Berlin at the time. He was in his principal HQ – Hitler Quarters – busy killing sons, and he had no time to help parents who were in the process of losing their children.

Why didn't they file a petition for clemency? someone at HQ had suggested.

But they didn't dare entrust their case to anyone. They were afraid of humiliation. They had a daughter who had betrayed the Führer. They couldn't continue to live there, if that got out. And they had to stay alive to save Anna. No, they couldn't get help from anyone with the petition – not the teacher, not the mayor, not even the minister.

Laboriously, after hours of discussion, agonizing, and writing with trembling hands, they drew up a petition themselves. They copied it out, and then copied it out again. It read:

Dearly beloved Führer, a wretched mother is begging you on her knees for the life of her daughter, who committed a grave sin against you, but you are so great, you will surely show her mercy. You will forgive her . . .

Hitler apotheosized, Hitler in excelsis, lord of the universe, all-powerful, all-seeing, all-forgiving! Two old people – the war rages on, slaughtering millions, but still they believe in him – even as he delivers their daughter into the hands of the executioner they believe in him, no doubt creeps into their hearts; it is their own daughter who is evil, not their Divine Führer!

They don't dare deliver the letter in the village, so together they trek to the local town to post it themselves. The envelope is addressed: 'To our dearly loved Führer – personal . . .'

Then they return home to their parlour and wait faithfully for their god to grant his forgiveness . . .

He will be merciful!

The post takes receipt of both petitions, the perfunctory, hypo-critical one of the lawyer and the desperate one from the two grieving parents, and conveys them both, but not to the Führer. The Führer doesn't care to see such petitions; they don't interest him. What interests him is war, destruction, and killing – not the avoidance of killing. The petitions go to the Führer's chan-cellery, where they are numbered, registered and stamped: TO BE FORWARDED TO THE MINISTRY OF JUSTICE. Only to be returned if the condemned is a Party member, which is not stated in the petition . . .

A double standard. Clemency is for Party members, not for members of the public.

In the Ministry of Justice, the appeals are again registered and numbered, and are given another stamp: TO THE PRISON ADMINISTRATION FOR ASSESSMENT.

The post conveys the appeals a third time, and for the third time they are numbered and logged. A secretary scrawls the same formulaic words on Anna and Otto Quangel's appeals: 'Conduct in custody was acceptable. No case for clemency. Return to Reich Ministry of Justice.'

Once again, a double standard: those who transgress against the prison rules, or even merely follow them, do not qualify for mercy; those others who have distinguished themselves by betraying, abusing, or snooping on a fellow prisoner just might.

In the Ministry of Justice, they register the returned appeals and stamped them REJECTED, and a pert young lady types from morning till night, Your appeal was declined . . . was declined . . . declined . . . declined . . . declined . . . all day and every day.

Then one day an official tells Otto Quangel, 'Your appeal was declined.'

Quangel, who never made any appeal, doesn't say anything. It's not worth it.

But the post conveys the other rejection to the old people, and the village is abuzz with gossip: 'The Heffkes got a letter from the Ministry of Justice.'

And even if the old couple keep adamantly, fearfully, shakingly silent, a mayor has ways of finding out the truth, and soon sorrow turns into humiliation for two old people . . .

The ways of clemency!

68

Anna Quangel's Most Difficult Decision

It was harder for Anna Quangel than it was for her husband: she was a woman. She longed for speech, kindness, a little tenderness – and now she was always alone, from morning till night, busy with the unpicking and rolling up of sackfuls of knotted string that were delivered to her cell. While she had been used to little in the way of intimacy and regard from her husband, even that little now struck her as paradise, and the presence of a mute Otto would have been a blessing under her present circumstances.

She cried a lot. The long, hard period in solitary had robbed her of the little strength that had suddenly come back to her when she had seen her Otto again and that had made her so brave and strong during the trial. She had been so cold and hungry in the chilly cell in solitary that the cold was still in her bones. Unlike her husband, she couldn't improve her diet with dried peas, and she hadn't learned, as he had, to divide the day into meaningful activities, a rhythm that allowed for change and something like enjoyment: an hour's walking after work, or the pleasure in one's own freshly washed body.

Anna Quangel had learned to listen at her cell window at night. But she didn't just do it occasionally, she did it night after night. And she whispered, she talked at the window, she told her story, she kept asking after Otto, Otto Quangel . . . O God, did no one know where Otto was, how he was doing, Otto Quangel, yes that's right, an elderly foreman, but still fit and healthy, such and such a description, fifty-three years old – someone must know!

She didn't notice, or she didn't want to notice, that she bothered the others with her incessant questions, her lack of restraint. They all had their own worries here.

'Can't you shut up, No. 76, we've heard it all before!'

Or else, 'Oh, it's her and her Otto again, Otto this, Otto that!'

Or, bitterly, 'If you don't shut up, we'll denounce you! Let someone else get a word in!'

When Anna Quangel finally crawled off to bed late at night, she couldn't sleep for a long time, and she had trouble getting up the following morning. The guard told her off and threatened her with further punishment. She was late getting started on her work. She had to hurry, and then she undid whatever good her hurrying did when she thought she heard a noise in the corridor and got up to listen at the door – for half an hour, an hour. She, who had once been calm, kind and motherly, was so transformed by her experience in solitary that she got on everyone's nerves now. And because the guards always had trouble with her, they were rough with her, and she would start quarrelling with them; she would claim she was given less food than the others, and of poorer quality, and the most work. Once or twice she had become so heated in the course of these arguments that she'd started screaming, just screaming her head off.

Then she would stop in surprise at herself. She thought about the distance she had come to be in this barren death cell. She remembered her home on Jablonski Strasse, which she would never see again, and she remembered her son Otto as he grew up, his childish babble, the first troubles at school, the little pale hand that reached up to her face to caress it – the child's hand that had grown in her belly, that her blood had made into flesh, flesh now long since consigned to earth and for ever lost to her. She thought of the nights that Trudel had lain in bed with her, whispering, the young, blooming body next to hers, talking for hours and hours about the strict husband in the bed across the way, about Ottochen and their prospects for the future. Trudel, of course, was gone as well.

And then she thought of her work with Otto, their silent struggle waged over the past two years. She remembered the Sundays sitting together in the parlour – she on the sofa, he on a chair, writing – formulating sentences together, sharing dreams of spectacular success. Lost and gone, all of it, lost and gone! Alone in her cell, facing certain death, with no word of Otto, maybe never to see his face again – to die alone, to lie in her grave alone . . .

She paces back and forth in her cell for hours; it's all more than she can bear. She neglects her work: the knotted twine lies there on the ground, she kicks it away impatiently, and when the guard comes in the evening, she has done nothing. There are harsh words for her, but she doesn't listen – they can do what they want with her; why don't they just put her to death right away, the sooner the better!

'Listen, I'm telling you,' the female guard says to her colleagues. 'She's going off the rails; you should keep a straitjacket ready. And look in on her regularly – she's perfectly capable of stringing herself up. One day you'll look in and see her swinging from a beam, and we'll have nothing but trouble!'

But the guard is wrong: Anna Quangel is not thinking of hanging herself. What keeps her alive, what makes even this starkly reduced form of life seem liveable to her, is the thought of Otto. She can't just sneak away from here, she has to wait – perhaps there'll be a message from him one day, perhaps they'll even allow her to see him once more before she dies.

And then, one day in this endless succession of grim days, fortune seems to smile on her. A guard suddenly opens the door: 'Come along, Quangel! You've got a visitor!'

Visitor? Who's going to visit me here? I don't have anyone who would visit me. It can only be Otto! It must be Otto! I can feel it, it's Otto!

She glances at the warder; she would so like to ask her who the visitor is, but it's the warder she always has arguments with, so she can't ask her. She follows, trembling, not knowing where they're going. She has forgotten that she must shortly die – all she knows is that she's on her way to Otto, the only person in the whole world . . .

The warder hands No. 76 to a guard, and she is led into a room divided in two by steel bars. On the other side stands a man.

All joy leaves Anna Quangel when she sees who the man is. It isn't Otto at all; it's old Judge Fromm. There he is, looking at her with his blue eyes wreathed in wrinkles, and he says, 'I wanted to see how you were, Frau Quangel.'

The guard on duty stands next to the bars. He looks at them both carefully, then turns away and goes over to the window.

'Quick!' whispers the judge, and pushes something through the bars to her.

Instinctively she takes it.

'Hide it!' he whispers.

And she hides the small paper-wrapped tube.

A note from Otto, she thinks, and her heart starts pounding again. She has got over her disappointment.

The guard has turned round and is looking at them from the window.

At last Anna finds words. She doesn't say hello to the judge, she doesn't thank him, she simply asks the only thing that still interests her in the world: 'Judge, have you seen my Otto?'

The old gentleman moves his wise head this way and that. 'Not recently,' he says. 'But I've heard from friends that he's doing well, very well. He's keeping his chin up beautifully.'

He thinks for a moment, and adds, as though reluctantly, 'I think I can greet you on his behalf.'

'Thank you,' she whispers. 'Thank you very much.'

His words have triggered many sensations within her. If he hasn't seen him, he can't have a letter from him, either. But no, he spoke of friends; couldn't these friends have conveyed a letter through him? And the words 'He's keeping his chin up beautifully' fill her with pride and happiness . . . And the greeting from him, the greeting passed through granite walls and iron bars, like a breath of spring! Oh lovely, lovely, lovely life!

'You're not looking at all well, Frau Quangel,' says the old man.

'No?' she asks absently, a little surprised. 'But I'm feeling well. Very well. Tell Otto. Please tell him so! Don't forget to greet him from me. You will see him, won't you?'

'I think so,' he says evasively. He is so scrupulous, the pedantic old gentleman. The least untruth spoken to this doomed woman pains him. She has no idea what ruses, what intrigues he has had recourse to in order to get permission to see her! He has had to pull all the strings he knows! In the eyes of the world, Anna Quangel is dead – and how can you visit the dead?

He doesn't dare tell her that he will never see Otto Quangel again in this life, that he has no news of him, that he lied when he said Quangel sent her his regards, just to give this weak old woman a little courage. Sometimes it's necessary to lie to the dying.

'Oh!' she suddenly says, with a little animation, and – lo! – her pale sunken cheeks show a little colour. 'Tell Otto when you see him that I think about him every day, every hour, and I'm sure we'll see each other again before I die . . .'

The guard looks in momentary bewilderment at the elderly woman who's speaking like a besotted little girl. Old straw burns fiercest! he thinks to himself, and goes back to the window.

She fails to notice, and continues feverishly, 'And tell Otto I have a nice cell all to myself. I'm doing fine. I'm always thinking of him, and that makes me happy. I know nothing can part us, not walls, not bars. I'm with him, every hour of the day and night. Tell him that!'

She's lying, oh, how she's lying, just to be able to say something good to her Otto! She wants to give him ease, ease that she hasn't felt for a moment, not since she came into this building.

The judge glances across at the guard, who is staring out the window. He whispers, 'Look after the thing I gave you!' because Frau Quangel looks so distracted, as if she's forgotten everything in the world.

'Yes, I will, Judge.' And then, quietly, 'What is it?'

And he, still more quietly, 'Poison. Your husband has his.'

She nods.

The official at the window turns round. He warns them, 'No whispering in here, otherwise that's it. Anyway,' he consults his watch, 'the visit's over in a minute and a half.'

'Yes,' she says pensively. 'Yes,' and suddenly she knows what

to say. She asks, 'And do you think Otto will travel anywhere –
before his big trip? What's your sense?'

Her face is full of such agonized unrest, even the thick-witted
guard realizes that this is a conversation about something else.
For an instant he thinks about stepping in, but then he looks at
the ageing woman and the gentleman with the white goatee,
who, according to the form, is a judge – and the guard has a
change of heart and looks out the window again.

'Well, it's hard to say,' replies the judge cagily. 'Travel's a
complicated business nowadays.' And then, very quickly, in a
whisper, 'Wait till the very last minute, and maybe you'll see
him one last time. All right?'

She nods once, twice.

'Yes,' she says aloud. 'Yes, that's probably the way to do it.'

And then they stand facing each other in silence, each suddenly
feeling there is nothing more to say. Over. Done.

'Well, I think I'd best be going,' says the old judge.

'Yes,' she whispers back, 'I think it's time.'

And suddenly – the guard has turned round again, and with
watch in hand gives them both a warning look – Frau Quangel
is overcome. She presses her body against the bars, and with her
head between the bars, she whispers, 'Please – maybe you're the
last decent person I'll see in this world. Please, Judge, would
you give me a kiss. I'll shut my eyes, I'll imagine it's Otto . . .'

Man-crazy, thinks the guard. About to be executed, and still
only one thing on her mind. An old biddy like that . . .

But the old judge says with a mild, friendly voice, 'Don't be
afraid, child, there's nothing to be afraid of . . .'

And his old thin lips gently brush her dry, cracked mouth.

'Don't be afraid, child. You have peace with you . . .'

'I know,' she whispers. 'Thank you very much.'

Then she's back in her cell, and the twine is a tangled bundle
on the floor, and she paces back and forth, kicking it into the
corners as on her very worst days. She has read the note, and
understood. She knows that she and Otto now have a weapon,
that they can throw away this wretched life at any moment,
when it becomes too unendurable. She doesn't have to let herself

be tormented further; she can, if she wants, end it this minute, while there's still a last bit of happiness in her from her visit.

She walks around, talks to herself, laughs, cries.

They are listening outside the door. They say, 'She's lost it now. Is the straitjacket ready?'

The woman inside doesn't notice. She is fighting the hardest struggle of her life. She pictures old Judge Fromm standing in front of her, his expression terribly serious as he tells her to wait till the very last minute, and maybe she would get to see her husband one last time.

And she agrees with him. Of course that's the right answer: she has to wait, be patient, it might take months yet. But even if it's just weeks, it's so hard to wait. She knows what she's like. She will fall into despair again, cry for hours, be despondent. And they are all so rough with her, never a good word or a smile. The time will be hard to get through. She just needs to toy with it, with her tongue and her teeth, she doesn't even have to mean it, just practise, and it will have happened. It's so easy for her now – too easy!

That's it. Some time she will be weak and do it, and in the instant that she's done it, the tiny instant between life and death, she will be sorry, more sorry than for anything in her life: by her weakness and her cowardice she will have robbed herself of the chance of maybe seeing Otto once more. He will be told the news of her death, and he will learn that she has stopped waiting for him, that she betrayed him, that she was cowardly. And he will despise her – he, whose respect is the only thing that matters to her in the whole world.

No, she must destroy this awful glass vial right away. If she waits till tomorrow it might be too late – who knows what mood she'll wake up in tomorrow?

But on the way to the bucket she stops.

And again she starts pacing. Suddenly she has remembered that she must die, and how she is to die. She learned in the course of her window conversations at night that it isn't the gallows that await her but the guillotine. They described it to her, how she will be made fast to the table, face down, staring into a bucket half filled with sawdust, and a few seconds later her head will fall into the sawdust. They will bare her neck, and her neck will sense the chill of the blade even before it comes down. Then the roaring in her ears will get louder and louder, it will be like the sound of the last trump, and then her body will just be a quivering something, the neck spewing thick gouts of blood, while the head in the basket might still be looking at the bloody neck, still able to see, to feel, to hurt . . .

So they told her, and so she has pictured it many hundreds of times to herself, and sometimes she has dreamed of it too. And now she can free herself of all these terrors with a single bite on a glass tube! And she's expected to give it up, give up this deliverance of her own accord! A choice between an easy and a horrible death – and she's expected to choose the horrible death, just because she's afraid of weakening and dying before Otto?

She shakes her head: no, she won't weaken. She can manage to wait until the very last moment. She wants to see Otto again. She endured the fear that always seized her when Otto went delivering the postcards, she endured the shock of the arrest, she endured the torments of Inspector Laub, she got over Trudel's death – she will be able to wait now, for a few weeks or months! She has endured everything – she will endure this as well! Of course she has to keep the poison safe till the last minute.

She paces back and forth, back and forth.

But her new resolve doesn't ease her. Doubt begins all over again, and all over again she wrestles with it, and again she decides to destroy the poison right away, on the spot, and again she doesn't do it.

In the meantime, evening has fallen, night. They've come and collected the unsorted string from her cell and told her that for her laziness she will have her mattress taken away for a week and be put on bread and water. But she hardly listens. What does she care what they say?

Her soup is on the table, untouched, and still she paces back and forth, dead tired now, unable to think straight, a prey to doubt: Should I – shouldn't I?

Now her tongue is playing with the vial in her mouth, without her even knowing, and without her wanting to, she rests her teeth on the glass gently, and cautiously, ever so gently bites down . . .

Hurriedly she pulls the vial out of her mouth. She paces and practises, she no longer knows what she's doing – and outside the straitjacket is waiting . . .

Then suddenly, late at night, she discovers she's lying on a cot, on bare boards, covered with the thin blanket. She is shaking with cold. Did she fall asleep? Is the vial still there? Did she swallow it? It's not in her mouth any more!

She sits up in panic – and smiles. There it is – it's in her hand. She had it in the hollow of her hand while she was asleep. She smiles, rescued once more. She won't have to die that other, terrible death . . .

And while she sits there shivering, she thinks that from now on she will have to fight this terrible battle on every day that dawns, the battle between will and weakness, courage and cowardice. And how uncertain the outcome is . . .

And through doubt and despair, she hears a gentle, kindly voice: Don't be afraid, child, there's nothing to be afraid of . . .

Suddenly Anna Quangel knows: Now my mind is made up! Now I have the strength!

She creeps to the door and listens for sounds in the corridor. The step of the warder is coming nearer. She stands by the facing wall, and then, when she notices she is being observed through the peephole, she starts pacing back and forth slowly. Don't be afraid, child . . .

Only when she is completely sure the warder has passed does she climb up to the window. A voice asks, 'Is that you, seventy-six? Did you have a visitor today?'

She doesn't answer. She won't answer again, ever. With one hand she clings to the dead light while she sticks the other hand out, with the little vial in her fingers. She scrapes it against the stone wall and feels its thin neck snap. She lets the poison fall into the depths of the yard.

When she is back in her cell, she can smell it on her fingers, the bitter-almond smell. She washes her hands and lies down on her bed. She is deathly tired, and she has the feeling she has escaped a grave danger. She falls asleep immediately. She sleeps deeply and dreamlessly and wakes up refreshed.

From that night forth, No. 76 gave no more cause for complaint. She was quiet, cheerful, industrious, friendly.

She hardly gave any more thought to her horrible death. All she thought about was that she must do honour and credit to Otto. And sometimes, in her dark hours, she heard the voice of old Judge Fromm again: Don't be afraid, child, there's nothing to be afraid of.

She wasn't. Not ever again.

She had got over it.

69

It's Time, Quangel

It's still night when a guard unlocks the door to Otto Quangel's cell.

Quangel, awakened from deep sleep, blinks his eyes at the large black-clad figure that has entered his cell. The next moment, he is wide awake, and his heart is beating faster than usual, because he has grasped what this large figure, standing there silently in the doorway, means for him.

'Is it time, Reverend?' he asks, reaching for his clothes.

'It's time, Quangel!' replies the minister. And he asks, 'Are you ready?'

'I'm always ready,' replies Quangel, and his tongue bumps against the little vial in his mouth.

He begins to get dressed, quietly, without fluster.

For a moment the two of them look at each other silently. The minister is a raw-boned young man, with a simple, even slightly foolish face.

Not too much going on there, thinks Quangel. Not like the good chaplain.

The chaplain in turn sees before him a tall man, exhausted from a lifetime of work. He takes against the face with its sharp, birdlike profile, he takes against the expression of the dark, strangely beady eyes, he takes against the narrow blood-less mouth with the pinched lips. But the reverend makes an effort, and inquires with as much compassion as he can, 'I hope you have made your peace with the world, Herr Quangel?'

'Has this world made peace, Reverend?' replies Quangel.

'Unfortunately not yet, Quangel, not yet,' replies the reverend, and his face tries to express a sorrow that he doesn't feel. He skips that point and moves on: 'But have you made your peace with the Almighty, Quangel?'

'I don't believe in any Almighty,' replies Quangel truculently.

'What?'

The reverend appears almost shocked by the brusque declaration. 'Well,' he continues, 'if you don't believe in a personal god, you will at least be a pantheist, won't you, Quangel?'

'What's that?'

'Well, it's quite simple . . .' The chaplain tries to explain something that he himself doesn't find simple. 'It's the world soul, you know? Your own immortal soul will return to the great world soul, Quangel!'

'Everything is God?' asks Quangel. He has finished dressing, and is standing in front of his bed. 'Is Hitler God? Is all the killing out there God? Are you God? Am I?'

'You misunderstand me, presumably on purpose,' the minister replies irritably. 'But I'm not here to discuss doctrinal questions with you, Quangel. I've come to prepare you for death. You must die, Quangel, in a few hours. Are you ready?'

Instead of answering, Quangel asks, 'Did you know Father Lorenz in the remand prison?'

The minister, rattled again, answers irritably, 'No, but I've heard of him. I may say the Lord summoned him at the right time. He has done some disservice to our calling.'

Quangel looked alertly at the clergyman. He said, 'He was a very good man. A lot of prisoners remember him with gratitude.'

'Yes,' cried the minister with unfeigned annoyance. 'Because he did your bidding! He was a weak man, Quangel. The man of God must be a fighter during these times of war, not a flabby compromiser!' He recovered himself. Quickly he looked at his watch and said, 'I only have another eight minutes with you, Quangel. I still have to see some of your companions in travail, to provide spiritual solace to others who, like you, will take their last walk today. Now let us pray . . .'

The priest, that rough, raw-boned peasant, pulled a white

cloth from his pocket and spread it carefully on the ground.

Quangel asked, 'Do you provide solace to the women who are to be executed as well?'

His mockery was so obscure that the minister failed to register it. He spread out his snow-white cloth and answered rather distantly, 'No executions of women are scheduled for today.'

'Can you remember,' Quangel persisted, 'if you've visited one Frau Anna Quangel?'

'Frau Anna Quangel? Your wife, I take it? No. I haven't. I would remember if I had. I have an exceptional memory for names . . .'

'Can I ask you a favour, Father . . .'

'Well, out with it, Quangel! You know my time's limited!'

'I would ask you not to tell my wife that I've been executed before her, when her time comes. Please tell her we'll be dying at the same time.'

'But that would be a lie, Quangel, and as a man of God I cannot violate His eighth commandment.'

'So you never lie, Reverend? Have you never lied in your life?'

'I would hope,' said the minister, a little confused by the mocking scrutiny of the other, 'I would hope I've always done my utmost to keep God's commandments.'

'So God's commandments call upon you to deny my wife the comfort of believing that she is dying at the same hour as me?'

'I may not bear false witness to my neighbour, Quangel!'

'That's really too bad! You're not the good shepherd, are you?'

'What?' exclaimed the clergyman, half confused, half threatening.

'Father Lorenz was always known as the good shepherd,' Quangel explained.

'No, no, no,' cried the minister angrily, 'I have no desire for any honorifics from the likes of you! They would have the opposite meaning, so far as I am concerned!' He calmed down. With a smack he dropped to his knees right on the white handkerchief.

He pointed to a spot on the grimy floor next to him (the cloth was only large enough for him). 'Kneel down with me, Quangel, and let us pray!'

'Who do I kneel down to?' Quangel asked coldly. 'Who do I pray to?'

'Oh!' the minister exclaimed petulantly, 'don't start that again! I've wasted too much time on you already!' From his kneeling position, he looked up at the man with the angry, beaky face. He muttered, 'Never mind, I'll do my duty. I'll pray for you!'

He lowered his head, folded his hands, and shut his eyes. Then he thrust his head forward, opened his eyes wide, and suddenly shouted so loud that Quangel jumped, 'O my Lord and Christ! All-powerful, all-knowing, beneficent and just God, Judge of good and evil! A sinner lies before you in the dust, I beg you to turn your eyes in mercy upon this man who has committed many misdeeds, to freshen him in body and soul and to forgive him all his sins in your grace . . .'

The kneeling minister yelled louder still, 'Accept the sacrifice of Jesus Christ, your dearly loved Son, in recompense for his misdeed. He is baptized in the same name, and washed and cleansed with the same blood. Save him from the body's pain and torment! Curtail his agonies, sustain him against the accusation of his conscience! Give him blissful transport to eternal life!'

The minister lowered his voice to a mysterious whisper: 'Send your holy angels here, that they may accompany him to the assembly of the elect in Christ, our Lord.'

Then again at the top of his voice, the minister shouted, 'Amen! Amen! Amen!'

He got up, folded the white cloth carefully and put it away, and asked, without looking at Quangel, 'I take it there's no point in asking if you want to receive the last rites?'

'No point whatever, Reverend.'

The minister hesitantly stretched out his hand toward Quangel.

Quangel shook his head and put his hands behind his back. 'There's no point in that either, Reverend!' he said.

The minister walked to the door without looking at him. He turned back, shot a quick look at Quangel, and said, 'Take these words with you to your place of execution, Philippians 1:21 – "For me to live is Christ, and to die is gain."'

The door clacked open, and he was gone.

Quangel sighed.

70

The Last Walk

No sooner was the chaplain gone than a short, stocky man in a pale grey suit walked into the cell. He threw a quick, astute look at Quangel, then went up to him and said, 'Dr Brandt, prison doctor.' He had shaken Quangel's hand, and now he kept hold of it as he asked, 'May I take your pulse?'

'Help yourself!' said Quangel.

The doctor counted slowly. Then he let Quangel's hand go and said approvingly, 'Very good. Excellent. You're a man.'

He cast a quick look at the door, which was still half open, and asked in a whisper, 'Can I give you something? An anaesthetic?'

Quangel slowly shook his head. 'Thank you, doctor. I'll be okay without.'

His tongue nudged the vial in his cheek. He wondered for a moment whether to ask the doctor to take a message to Anna. But no, that minister would tell her whatever was needed . . .

'Anything else?' asked the doctor in a whisper. He had noticed Quangel's hesitation. 'A note to someone?'

'I've nothing to write with – ach, no, leave it. Thank you, doctor, you're a good man! At least not everyone in this institution is bad.'

The doctor nodded gloomily, shook hands with Quangel again, and said quickly, 'All I can say is, keep your courage up.'

And he was gone.

A guard walked in, followed by a trusty carrying a bowl and a plate. The bowl was full of steaming coffee, and on the plate were pieces of bread and butter. On the rim of the plate were a couple of cigarettes, two matches and a piece of emery board.

'There,' said the guard. 'You see, we don't spare any expense. And all without ration cards!'

He laughed, and the trusty laughed dutifully along. One could tell he had heard the 'joke' many times before.

In a sudden surprising fit of anger, Quangel said, 'Get that stuff out of here! I don't need your last meal!'

'I don't need a second invitation!' said the guard. 'By the way, the coffee's made from acorns, and the butter's margarine . . .'

And Quangel was alone again. He straightened his bed, stripped the sheet, dropped it by the door, propped the pallet against the wall. Then he started washing.

He hadn't finished yet when a fourth man, followed by a couple of others, entered his cell.

'No need to wash like that,' said the man boisterously. 'We'll give you a first-class shave and trim! Okay, boys, get a move on, we're running late!' And apologetically, to Quangel, 'The man before held us up, I'm afraid. Wouldn't see sense and realize there's nothing anyone can do. I'm the Berlin executioner . . .'

He held out his hand to Quangel.

'Well, you'll see, I'm not one to make you wait, or make you suffer unnecessarily. If you don't kick up, I won't either. I always say to my lads, "Lads," I say, "if someone plays up, and throws himself on the floor and kicks and screams, then you can play up, too. Grab him anywhere you can, even if it's his nuts!" But with sensible people like yourself, it's always "Easy does it!"'

As he continued to talk, a clipper criss-crossed over Quangel's head, and his hair lay on the floor. The other assistant had worked up a lather and was shaving Quangel's beard. 'There!' said the executioner with satisfaction. 'Seven minutes! We're caught up. A couple more sensible customers like yourself, and we'll be as punctual as the railways.' Then, to Quangel, 'Would you help us out and sweep the floor yourself? There's no obligation, but we are short of time. The director and prosecutor could be along at any moment. Don't chuck the hair in the pail; I've got a sheet of newspaper here: Wrap it up in that and leave it by the door. It's a little racket I've got going on the side, see?'

'What will you do with my hair?' asked Quangel.

'Sell it to a wigmaker. Wigs will always be in demand. Not

just for actors, but for everyday use too. You're a gent. Heil Hitler!'

Then they, too, were gone. A spirited bunch, really: they knew their business, and you couldn't slaughter hogs more calmly. And yet Quangel decided that these rough heartless types were more to his liking than the reverend of a moment ago. He had shaken hands with the executioner as if it were the most natural thing in the world.

Quangel had just done what the executioner had asked him to do in regard to tidying the cell when the door opened again. This time there walked in, accompanied by a uniformed escort, a fat, pasty-faced man with a red moustache – the prison governor, as immediately became apparent – and an old friend of Quangel's, the prosecutor from the trial, the yapping Pinscher.

Two guards seized Quangel and thrust him roughly against the wall, forcing him to stand to attention. Then they stood on either side of him.

'Otto Quangel!' one of them yelled out.

'Aha!' yapped Pinscher. 'I thought I remembered the face!' He turned to the director. 'I got him his sentence!' he said proudly. 'A shameless piece of work. Thought he could sass the court and me. But we showed you, son!' he yapped, facing Quangel now. 'Eh, didn't we show you! How are you feeling now? Not so fresh any more, ha?'

One of the men flanking him elbowed Quangel in the ribs. 'Answer!' he whispered.

'Oh, take a walk!' said Quangel, bored.

'What? What?' The prosecutor was jigging from one foot to the other in his excitement. 'Director, I demand . . .'

'Ach, never mind!' said the governor, 'lay off him! You can see he's a perfectly quiet chap. That's right, isn't it?'

'Of course!' said Quangel. 'I just want to be left in peace. If he leaves me in peace, then I'll leave him in peace, too.'

'I protest! I call for . . . !' yelled Pinscher.

'What?' said the director. 'What more can you want? We can't do any more than execute the man. Go on and read him the sentence!'

At last Pinscher calmed down, unfolded a document, and started to read from it. He read hastily and unclearly, skipped sentences, got tangled up, and came to a sudden stop. 'There, now you know!'

Quangel said nothing.

'Take him down!' said the red-bearded director, and the two sentries grabbed Quangel tightly by the arms.

He freed himself angrily.

They grabbed him again, harder.

'Let the man walk!' ordered the director. 'He won't make any trouble.'

They stepped out into the corridor. A lot of people were standing around, in uniforms and civvies. Quickly, a column formed, with Otto Quangel at its middle. Prison guards led the way. There followed the minister, now wearing a gown with a white collar, mumbling inaudibly to himself. Behind him went Quangel, in a cluster of guards, but the little doctor in the pale suit was close at hand, too. Then came the director and prosecutor, followed by more men in uniforms and suits, and some of those in suits had cameras.

So the column passed through the ill-lit corridors and down the iron staircases, over the slippery linoleum flooring of the death house. And wherever he passed, a groan went up from the cells, a muffled sigh from the depths of prisoners' chests. In one cell a cry went up: 'Farewell, comrade!'

And quite mechanically Otto Quangel responded, 'Farewell, comrade!' and only a moment later did it strike him how absurd that 'Farewell' was, addressed to one about to die.

One more door was unlocked, and they stepped out into a courtyard. Night-time darkness hung between the walls. Quangel looked left and right, and nothing escaped his attention. At the windows of the cells he saw a ring of pale faces – his comrades, like himself sentenced to death, but still living. A loudly barking Alsatian approached the column, was whistled back by the sentry, and retreated growling. The gravel crunched underfoot. It was probably yellowish by day; now, bled of colour by the harsh electric lighting, it looked grey-white. Looming over the wall were the bare limbs of a winter tree. The air was chilly and damp. Quangel thought, In a quarter of an hour, I won't feel cold any more – strange!

His tongue felt for the glass vial. But it was still too soon . . .

Strange, to be able to see and hear so clearly, and yet it all felt so unreal. It was like something he had heard about once. Or he was lying in his cell, dreaming it. Yes, it was quite impossible that he was physically walking here among all these people, with their indifferent or crude or evil or sad expressions – they were none of them real. The gravel was dream gravel, the crunching of stones underfoot was a sound in a dream . . .

They passed through a door and entered a room that was so garishly lit that at first Quangel saw nothing at all. His guards suddenly pulled him forward, past the kneeling chaplain.

The executioner approached him with his two assistants. He held out his hand again.

'No hard feelings!' he said.

'Nah, why would I?' replied Quangel, and mechanically shook his hand.

While the executioner helped Quangel out of his jacket and cut off the collar of his shirt, Quangel looked back on those who had accompanied him on this last walk. In the dazzle, all he saw was a ring of white faces, all turned toward him.

It's all a dream, he thought, and his heart began to pound.

One form detached itself from the gaggle of onlookers, and as it came closer, Quangel recognized the helpful little doctor in the pale grey suit.

'Well?' asked the doctor with a watery smile. 'How are you doing?'

'Keeping calm!' said Quangel, while his hands were made fast behind his back. 'Just at the moment, my heart's going a bit, but I expect it'll settle down in a minute or two.'

And he smiled.

'Wait a minute, I'll give you something!' said the doctor, and reached into his bag.

'Don't worry, doctor,' replied Quangel. 'I'm provided for . . .'

And he put out his tongue with the glass vial on it . . .

'Oh!' said the doctor, looking a little confused.

They turned Quangel round. Now he faced the long table, which was covered with a sleek black material like oilcloth. He saw buckles and straps, but above all he saw the broad blade. It seemed to him to hang very high over the table, menacingly high. Silvery-black it winked at him; it looked at him duplicitously.

Quangel heaved a little sigh . . .

Suddenly the director was standing beside him, exchanging a few words with the executioner. Quangel stared at the blade. He listened with only half an ear: 'I hand over to you, the executioner of the city of Berlin, this man, Otto Quangel, that you may with your axe separate the head from the body in accordance with the legal judgement of the People's Court . . .'

The voice was unbearably loud. It was too bright . . .

Now, thought Quangel. Now . . .

But he didn't do it. A terrible, tormenting curiosity tickled him . . .

A couple minutes more, he thought. I must know what it feels like to lie on the table . . .

'All right, old boy!' said the executioner. 'No fuss. It'll be done in two minutes. Did you remember about the hair?'

'Behind the door,' replied Quangel.

A moment later, Quangel was on the table, and he could feel them tying his ankles. A steel rod was lowered on to his back, and pressed his shoulders down on to the oilcloth surface . . .

It stank of chalk, of wet sawdust and disinfectant . . . But more than anything, more than all of that, it smelled disgustingly sweet, of something . . .

Blood . . . thought Quangel. It stinks of blood . . .

He heard the executioner softly whisper, 'Now!'

But however softly he whispered it, and no one could whisper any more softly, still Quangel heard it, that 'Now!'

And he heard a humming sound . . .

Now! he thought, too, and his teeth made to bite down on the vial of cyanide . . .

Then he felt nausea, a stream of vomit filled his mouth, washed the vial away . . .

O God, he thought, I waited too long . . .

The humming had turned into a rushing, the rushing had become a piercing scream that must be audible up in the stars, to the throne of God . . .

Then the edge bit through his neck.

Quangel's head lands in the basket.

For an instant he lay there perfectly still, as though the headless trunk were puzzled about the trick that had been played on it. Then the trunk arced up, it pushed against straps and steel stirrups, and the executioner's assistants hurled themselves on it to hold it down.

The veins in the dead man's hands grew thicker and thicker, and then everything collapsed in on itself. All that could be heard was blood – hissing, rushing, falling blood.

Three minutes after the axe had fallen, the pallid doctor with trembling voice pronounced the prisoner dead.

They cleared the body away.

Otto Quangel no longer existed.

71

Anna Quangel's Reunion

The months came and went, the seasons changed, and still Anna Quangel sat in her cell, waiting to be reunited with her Otto.

Sometimes the warder, whose favourite Anna Quangel had become, said to her, 'I think they must have forgotten about you, Frau Quangel.'

'Yes,' replied No. 76 mildly. 'It would appear so. Me and my husband. How is Otto?'

'Fine!' the warder replied quickly. 'He sends his love.'

They had all agreed not to tell the kind, hardworking woman about the death of her husband. They always sent regards from him.

Yes, this time fortune really was smiling on Frau Anna: no needless chitchat, no conscientious chaplain destroyed her belief that Otto Quangel lived.

Almost all day she sat at her little knitting machine and knitted socks – socks for soldiers; she knitted them day in, day out.

Sometimes she sang softly to herself. She was firmly convinced that not only would she and Otto see each other again but that they would go on living together for a long time. Either they really had been forgotten, or else they had secretly been amnestied. Not much longer, and they would be free.

Because however little the warders talked about it, Anna Quangel had picked up on it: the war was going badly, and the news was getting worse from week to week. She noticed it from the rapid deterioration in the food, the regular shortages of material to work with, the broken part in her knitting machine, which took many weeks to replace – everything seemed to be in short supply. But if the war was going badly, then things must be going well for the Quangels. Soon they would be free.

So she sits and knits. She knits dreams into the socks, wishes doomed never to come true, hopes she had never previously entertained. She composes an Otto quite unlike the real one, a serene, contented, tender Otto. She has become a young woman again, seeing the whole of life beckoning to her. Doesn't she even dream sometimes of having more children? Oh, children . . . !

Ever since Anna Quangel destroyed the cyanide, when she decided after a dreadful struggle to hold on till she saw Otto again, come what may – ever since that time she has been free and youthful and joyful. She has conquered herself.

Yes, now she is free. Fearless and free.

She is fearless, too, during the ever more terrible nights that the war has brought upon the city of Berlin, when the sirens wail, the planes move over the city in ever denser swarms, the bombs fall, the high explosives howl as they detonate, and fires burst out all over.

Even on such nights, the prisoners must stay in their cells. The authorities don't dare move them to bomb shelters in case they stage an uprising. They scream in their cells, they rage, they beg and plead, they go mad with fear, but the corridors are empty, no sentry stands there, no merciful hand unlocks the cell doors, the guards are all hunkered down in the air-raid shelters.

But Anna Quangel has no fear. Her little machine clatters and rattles, adding row after row of loops. She makes use of these hours when she can't sleep anyway to knit. And as she knits, she dreams. She dreams of her reunion with Otto, and it is during one such dream that a bomb comes down and turns that part of the prison into ash and rubble.

Anna Quangel had no time to awaken from the dream of her reunion with Otto. She is already reunited with him. She is where he is. Wherever that may be.

The Boy

But we don't want to end this book with death, dedicated as it is to life, invincible life, life always triumphing over humiliation and tears, over misery and death.

It is summer, early summer in 1946.

A boy, almost a young man, crosses an old farmyard in Brandenburg.

He runs into an elderly woman. 'Well, Kuno,' she asks. 'What are you doing today?'

'I'm going into town,' the boy replies. 'I'm to collect the new plough.'

'Well,' she says, 'I'll write down some things you can pick up for me – if you find any of them!'

'If they're there, I'll find them, Mother!' he calls, laughing. 'You know that!'

They look at each other, smiling. Then she goes inside to her husband, the old schoolmaster who has long since reached pensionable age but who – as much as the youngest – is still teaching.

The lad takes Toni the horse, their pride and joy, out of his stable.

Half an hour later, Kuno-Dieter Borkhausen is on his way to town. But he is no longer called Borkhausen; he has been adopted, with all the legal formalities by the Kienschapers, back when it became clear that neither Karl nor Max Kluge would return alive from the war. Incidentally, the Dieter also fell casualty in this renaming: Kuno Kienschaper has a ring to it, and it's quite enough of a name.

Kuno whistles cheerfully to himself while the chestnut Toni ambles along the well-marked path. Let Toni take his time, they'll be back by lunch anyway.

Kuno eyes the fields on either side, assessing them, professionally gauging the state of the crop. He has learned a lot here in the country, and – thank God – he's forgotten just as much. The back-tenement with Otti he hardly ever thinks of any more, nor of the thirteen-year-old Kuno-Dieter who used to be a kind of hoodlum, no, none of that exists any more. But the dreams of engineering have been postponed, and for the time being it's enough for the boy to drive the tractor for the ploughing, in spite of his youth.

Yes, they've made progress together, Father, Mother and himself. They are no longer dependent on relatives, because the previous year they were given some land. They are independent people, with Toni, a cow, a pig, a couple of sheep and seven hens. Kuno can mow and plough; his father taught him how to sow, and his mother how to hoe. He likes the life, and he'll certainly help to build up the farm, oh yes!

He's whistling.

By the side of the road, a tall wasted-looking spectre suddenly looms up: ragged clothes, ravaged face. He's not one of the desperate war refugees; he's a wastrel, a layabout, a scoundrel. His sodden voice wheezes, 'Hey there, boy, will you take me into town with you!'

The sound of the voice makes Kuno Kienschaper jump. He feels like asking the cosy old sofa Toni to break into a gallop, but it's too late for that, and so, with lowered head, he says, 'A ride? Not up front with me! You can sit in the back if you like!'

'Why not with you?' wheezes the man challengingly. 'Not good enough for you, huh?'

'Idiot!' shouts Kuno with feigned roughness. 'It's because you'll sit softer in the straw!'

The man agrees grumblingly, crawls up on to the wagon, and Toni breaks into a canter of his own accord.

Kuno has got over his initial shock at having to help his father Borkhausen out of the gutter into the wagon. But perhaps it was no accident; perhaps Borkhausen has been waiting for him and knows exactly who this is, giving him his ride.

Kuno squints over his shoulder at the man.

He is stretched out in the straw and now says, as though he had seen the boy's look, 'Do you know a boy hereabouts, a Berliner, must be sixteen or so? He must live somewhere here . . .'

'There's loads of Berliners live round here!' replies Kuno.

'So I noticed! But the boy I'm referring to, he's a special case – he wasn't evacuated in the war, he ran away from his parents! D'you ever hear of a boy like that?'

'Nah!' lies Kuno. And after a pause he asks, 'You wouldn't know a name for him, would you?'

'Yes, he's called Borkhausen . . .'

'There's no Borkhausens anywhere round here, mister; I'd know it if there was.'

'Funny!' says the man, forcing a laugh, and hits the boy hard between the shoulder blades. 'I'd have sworn it was a Borkhausen driving this cart!'

'You'd be making a mistake then!' answers Kuno, and now that he's sure what's going on, his heart is beating solidly and coolly. 'My name's Kienschaper, Kuno Kienschaper . . .'

'Well, there's a coincidence!' says the man in mock astonishment. 'The boy I'm looking for's Kuno, Kuno-Dieter in fact . . .'

'No, my name's plain Kuno. No Dieter. Kuno Kienschaper,' says the boy. 'Plus if I knew I had any Borkhausen on my cart, I'd turn my whip around and hit him till he got off my cart!'

'No! No! Surely not!' says the tramp. 'A boy who whips his own father off a cart?'

'And once I'd whipped Borkhausen off my cart,' Kuno Kienschaper continues mercilessly, 'then I'd go straight to the police in town and tell them to look out. There's a man around who's no good for anything except lazing around and stealing and doing damage; he's got a jail record, he's a criminal, you'd better get hold of him!'

'You wouldn't do that, Kuno-Dieter,' calls Borkhausen in real alarm now. 'You won't set the police on me! Now that I've got out of jail and am on my way to recovery. I've got a letter from the padre saying that I've bettered myself, and I don't touch stolen goods any more, I swear! But I was just thinking now that you've got a farm and are living off the fat of the land, you wouldn't mind letting your father rest up a bit with you! I'm not well, Kuno-Dieter, I've got something wrong with my chest, I need a break . . .'

'Now you give me a break!' cries the boy bitterly. 'I know if I let you into our house for one day, you'd take root there, and it'd be impossible to get rid of you, and with you we'll have unhappiness and bad luck in the house. No, you get right off my cart, or I really will give you a taste of the whip!'

The boy had stopped the cart and jumped down. Now he stood there, whip in hand, prepared to do anything to defend the peace of his newly acquired home.

The eternal loser Borkhausen said miserably, 'You wouldn't do that! You wouldn't hit your own father!'

'You're not my father! You told me that often enough before!'

'That was meant as a joke, Kuno-Dieter, don't you understand!'

'I've got no father!' shouted the boy, wild with anger. 'I've got a mother, and I'm starting afresh. And if people come from long ago and say this and that, then I'll whip them until they leave me alone! I'm not letting you ruin my life!'

He stood there so threateningly with whip upraised that the old man was really frightened. He crept down from the wagon and stood on the road, fear contorting his face.

He came back with the cowardly threat: 'I can do you a lot of harm . . .'

'I was waiting for that!' cried Kuno Kienschaper. 'First you beg, then you threaten – that was always your way! But I'm telling you, I swear, I'm going straight to the police, and I'm going to accuse you of threatening to set fire to our home . . .'

'But I never said that, Kuno-Dieter!'

'Nah, but you thought it, I could see it in your eyes! That's the way you are! Remember, in an hour the police will be on your tail! So, you get away from here.'

Kuno Kienschaper stood on the road until the ragged shape had disappeared into the cornfields. Then he patted Toni on the neck and said, 'Come on, Toni, are we going to let someone like that make a mess of our lives a second time? We started afresh. When Mother put me in the water and washed the dirt off me with her own hands, that's when I swore to myself: From now on I'm going to keep clean all by myself! And so I shall!'

Over the next few days, Mother Kienschaper had occasion to wonder several times why she couldn't get the boy out of the house. Usually he was always the first to volunteer for fieldwork, and now he didn't even want to play with the cow in the pasture. But she said nothing, and the boy said nothing, and when the days lengthened into summer, and the rye harvest came due, then at last the boy headed out with his scythe . . .

Because it is written that you reap what you sow, and the boy had sown good corn.

Afterword

Rudolf Ditzen

Early on the morning of 17 October 1911, eighteen-year-old Rudolf
Ditzen and his friend Hanns Dietrich von Necker armed themselves,
walked out into the countryside around the Thuringian town of
Rudolstadt (where they were attending school), and fired on each
other in the manner of duellists. Like many other young men in
imperial Germany, Ditzen and von Necker had struggled to recon-
cile their developing sexuality with the prevailing social conventions,
and were seeking escape in a suicide pact, but they staged it as a
duel (purportedly to uphold the honour of a young woman) to
protect the reputations of their families. Von Necker missed, but
was fatally wounded by Ditzen, who then used his friend's revolver
to shoot himself in the chest. Miraculously, Ditzen survived, and he
was charged with von Necker's murder. However, Ditzen was
declared unfit for trial on psychological grounds, and committed to
a private sanatorium for the mentally ill in February 1912. Although
Ditzen had been studying for his university-entrance exams in
Rudolstadt, upon his release from the sanatorium in September 1913
his parents and doctors decided that he should pursue an agricultural
career, and he spent the next several years working mainly on farms
and for farming organizations. These years were also characterized
by the intermittent dependence on various drugs against which
Ditzen struggled for all of his adult life. No single factor or incident
can be isolated as the immediate cause of his addictions, which at
different times encompassed alcohol, sleeping drugs, cocaine and
morphine – though Ditzen often relied simply on whatever was
most readily available: for example, he was sometimes prescribed
sleeping drugs for insomnia and nervous complaints, and morphine

was particularly accessible during and immediately after the two World Wars.

But neither his legal problems, nor the abandonment of his formal education, nor his recurrent substance abuse could extinguish the interest in writing which Ditzen first showed during his schooldays, and in 1920 the Ernst Rowohlt publishing house issued his debut novel, *Young Goedeschal*, which deals with the sexual and psychological tribulations of the eponymous male protagonist. Rudolf Ditzen's father Wilhelm, a retired justice of the German Supreme Court, had urged him to publish *Young Goedeschal* under a pseudonym, to avoid reviving public memories of how he had killed von Necker. So Rudolf chose the *nom de plume* 'Hans Fallada', and adhered to it throughout his literary career. The name was inspired by two Grimm fairy tales, 'Hans in Luck' and 'The Goose Girl'. In the first tale, Hans retains his naïve optimism while losing the wages of seven years' labour in a series of bartering deals with smooth-tongued strangers: he starts with a lump of gold, and ends with two stones, which he lets fall into a well before continuing happily on his way. In the second tale, a talking horse called Falada saves a dispossessed princess from her lowly work tending geese by testifying to her true identity. Rudolf Ditzen's choice of a literary pseudonym in 1920 reflected both his protracted struggle to come to grips with the realities of the world around him, and his defiant conviction that he would still somehow succeed in asserting himself against it. That struggle and that conviction persisted for the remainder of his life, and were embodied in many of the characters he created.

Hans Fallada

Neither *Young Goedeschal* nor its successor *Anton and Gerda* (1923), which also deals with adolescent sexuality, attracted much critical or popular attention, and Hans Fallada – as I shall now call him – continued his agricultural career. He was twice convicted of embezzling from employers, serving prison sentences in 1924 and 1926–8, and after the second sentence he settled in the north German town of Neumünster, where he worked on a local newspaper and married Anna Issel, a woman of working-class background from Hamburg. In 1930 Fallada took a clerical position with his publisher Rowohlt in Berlin, where he also completed a novel about provincial politics which was based on his experiences in Neumünster, and appeared in 1931 under the title *Farmers, Functionaries and Fireworks*. Although this third novel was a modest literary and financial success, the Rowohlt firm was placed in receivership a few months after it was published, and employees were then asked to continue working at reduced salaries. Fallada refused, and instead negotiated a contract that guaranteed five modest monthly payments which were to support him while he wrote his next novel, and to be treated as advances against his earnings from it.

That novel was *Little Man, What Now?* (1932), the story of how the sales clerk Pinneberg struggles to provide for his wife and their baby during the Great Depression, though finally he joins the ranks of the long-term unemployed. *Little Man, What Now?* was a major hit, and restored the Rowohlt firm's finances. Forty-eight thousand copies were issued before the end of the year, serializations were printed in dozens of newspapers, translation rights were sold in numerous languages, a film version was made in Germany, and a stage version was performed in Denmark. In the US, the novel was published by Simon & Schuster (with Richard Simon describing it as 'perilously close to a masterpiece' in a letter to Fallada on 2 March 1933), and selected as the Book of the Month Club's choice for June 1933. It was also filmed by Universal Pictures, with Douglass Montgomery and Margaret Sullavan in the lead roles, premiering in New York on 31 May 1934. The reviews of *Little Man, What Now?* were mostly positive, and scores of readers wrote fan letters to Fallada. On the evidence of the reviews and fan letters, the novel's success was based not on its intermittent and unsystematic attempts to analyse the Pinnebergs' predicament in economic or political terms, but on its emotional affirmation of their family life as a refuge from their material difficulties. This is the aforementioned combination of struggle and self-assertion that recurs often in Fallada's works. The Pinnebergs do not so much resolve their problems as defy them, so that in the last paragraphs of the novel, even after months of poverty and humiliation, the despairing Pinneberg is consoled by his wife's insistence that 'You're with me, we're together', and they feel elevated 'higher and higher, from the tarnished earth to the stars'.

Fallada and Nazi Germany

Although the Nazis' accession to power in January 1933 prompted many authors to leave Germany, Fallada remained, partly because – as he told his parents in a letter on 6 March 1933 – his next novel would be 'a quite unpolitical book which can't give offence'. He was also preoccupied by more immediate personal problems, because among other things he had resumed his habit of heavy drinking. Fallada sought refuge from political and personal hazards in what he hoped was the obscurity and tranquillity of the countryside by buying a house in Berkenbrück, on the outskirts of Berlin. However, at Easter 1933 Fallada was denounced as an anti-Nazi conspirator by the previous owner of the house, who hoped to regain possession of it, and he was arrested by a local storm-trooper unit, and spent several days in prison. The denunciation was of course spurious, and Fallada gained his release in a similarly irregular manner, after Ernst Rowohlt engaged a prominent lawyer with connections in the German National People's Party (which had long collaborated with the Nazi Party) that he exploited on Fallada's behalf. Several months later – in what seemed to have been an effort at 'out of sight, out of mind', as well as to escape the recurrence of his heavy drinking after the success of *Little Man, What Now?* – Fallada acquired a smallholding in the village of Carwitz, about fifty miles north of Berlin, where he lived for most of the next twelve years. But Carwitz was not immune from Nazism either, as was exemplified by its virulently pro-Hitler schoolteacher. Fallada's experiences in Berkenbrück and Carwitz have obvious echoes in *Alone in Berlin*. When Trudel Baumann and Karl Herge-sell move just outside Berlin to start their life together after their resistance cell is disbanded, they make 'the painful discovery that recrimination, eavesdropping, and informing were ten times worse in the small towns than in the big city' (p. 305). And when Eva Kluge settles in a village after leaving her post-office job and the Nazi Party, she finds that the local schoolteacher is 'a rampant Nazi, a cowardly little yapper and denouncer' (p. 371), though he is later drafted, and replaced by the humane Kienschaper.

The political hostility which Fallada encountered in Nazi Germany was not confined to his everyday life, but extended to his literary work. His fifth and supposedly 'quite unpolitical' novel, *The World Outside* (which he began before 1933 but did not complete and publish until 1934), was viciously attacked by Nazi critics for its comparatively sympathetic portrayal of convicts. Fallada's literary career in the decade following *The World Outside* developed a remarkable diversity, as he searched for genres in which he could avoid political controversy, retain his artistic integrity, and earn a sufficient income. More than anything else, he wrote light novels with non-contemporary settings, often designed partly for magazine serializations, and sometimes commissioned by film studios. But he also produced short stories for children, fictionalized autobiographies about his childhood and his life in Carwitz, the first part of a projected medieval mock epic (which was not published until 1995), and translations of Clarence Day's *Life With Father* and *Life With Mother*. And he planned books based on journeys to France, Spain and the Czech town of Mimoň which had been sponsored by the Reich Labour Service, and on a financial scandal of the 1920s which had involved Jewish stockbrokers, but no manuscripts of these have survived.

By the time of the Nazi defeat, Fallada had completed only one work that stands comparison with the novels about contemporary society which he published in the early 1930s. This is *Wolf Among Wolves* (1937), an intricately detailed but tightly plotted panorama of life in Berlin and the countryside during the hyperinflation of 1923. The main characters, Wolfgang Pagel and Petra Ledig, echo the Pinnebergs by adhering defiantly to their own conceptions of love and morality while the ever-deepening financial crisis threatens the social contract no less than the economic foundations of postwar Germany. Fallada's next novel, *Iron Gustav* (1938), is the most notorious of his Nazi-era works. It was commissioned as the basis for a major film featuring star actor Emil Jannings, and traces the fortunes of the Berlin-based Hackendahl family from shortly before the Great War. Fallada's original manuscript ended the Hackendahls' story in the late 1920s, but he was induced – partly, he claimed later, by Joseph Goebbels' reported comment that if Fallada still didn't know what he thought of the Nazi Party, then the Nazi Party would know what it thought of Fallada – to continue the action into the 1930s. The novel was then published in this extended form, with the final section showing first one of Hackendahl's sons as a stormtrooper, then Hackendahl himself – hesitantly, at first, then firmly – accepting the extended hand of his son's senior officer in the book's last lines. However, the film was abandoned. In a letter to his friend Nico Rost on 19 September 1946, Fallada wrote candidly that he had agreed to revise *Iron Gustav* in fear of the concentration camp, though 'nevertheless the guilt of every line I wrote then still weighs on me today'. In a letter to Ernst Rowohlt on 20 March the same year, he had said somewhat less candidly that: 'Apart from the ending of *Iron Gustav*, I can be accused of nothing at all.' Fallada's opinion of Jannings can perhaps be inferred from his portrayal in Chapter 19 of *Alone in Berlin* of the film actor Harteisen, who is obsessed by regaining the friendship which Goebbels has capriciously granted and then capriciously withdrawn.

The constant threats to Fallada's individual liberty and artistic integrity after 1933 prompted him to reconsider his decision to remain in Germany, but not to reverse it. According to an account which Anna gave decades afterwards, in late 1938 the Putnam publishing firm arranged transport to England for the couple and their children, and the family had literally packed their bags and were about to set off when Fallada decided to take a farewell walk to one of the lakes around Carwitz, and declared when he returned that he could not leave. The restrictions on Fallada's literary creativity adversely affected his personal life, in his recurring abuse of alcohol and sleeping drugs, and in a growing deterioration of his relationship with Anna, from whom he was divorced in July 1944, although the exigencies of wartime meant that they both continued living on the smallholding. On 28 August 1944, Fallada threatened Anna with a gun. She disarmed him easily, hit him over the head with the gun, then called the local doctor. The doctor in turn called the police, who committed Fallada to a psychiatric hospital in nearby Alt-Strelitz for observation; a court document confirming the committal stated that he had drunk twelve bottles of wine from 26 to 28 August. On 28 November Fallada was sentenced to three months and two weeks in prison, but he remained in the psychiatric hospital until that sentence expired on 13 December.

It was during his incarceration in Alt-Strelitz that Fallada, having secured permission to work on his novel about the financial scandal, wrote a deliberately almost illegible manuscript – writing in a very small hand, and first filling the pages, then writing upside down in the spaces between the lines, then writing in any remaining spaces, so that the manuscript was not deciphered until some years after his death, when it was found to consist of several different texts. In addition to some uncontroversial short stories, it contained both his politically sensitive account of his clashes with the Nazi authorities, and his novel *The Drinker*, which was not deciphered and published until 1950. *The Drinker* describes how a provincial merchant called Sommer succumbs to alcoholism, is confined to an asylum, and finally tries to commit suicide by infecting himself with tuberculosis in the asylum's infirmary. Thus in one sense the novel reverses the pattern which I have identified in some of Fallada's works by showing how Sommer – in contrast to figures like the Pinnebergs or Pagel or Petra – is resoundingly defeated by his problems. But in an autobiographical sense *The Drinker* shows Fallada's characteristic defiance, not simply by thematizing and criticizing his own substance abuse, but also by daring to do so in Nazi Germany, where eugenic and cultural policy encompassed extreme sanctions (including physical abuse or sterilization or death) both for alcoholics and for authors who wrote about them (whether privately or for publication) with any degree of empathy.

There is no simple concept which adequately describes Fallada's career in Nazi Germany: he was neither an eager collaborator nor a resistance fighter. In his life as an author, Fallada cooperated with the Nazi regime, most obviously by accepting officially sanctioned commissions and writing or revising with the official ideology in mind, but he also challenged the regime, among other things by reasserting his humane values in a novel such as *Wolf Among Wolves* and attempting anti-Nazi allegory in ostensibly light fiction like *Old Heart Goes A-Journeying* (1936). In his life as a citizen, Fallada complied with most of the Nazi system's demands, for example by enrolling his oldest son in the Hitler Youth, but he also gave financial and legal support to some of the system's outcasts, particularly authors and publishers' employees who suffered discrimination on political or racial grounds. And there were contradictions in the way the Nazis treated Fallada, sometimes promoting his work and sometimes censoring it, sometimes sending him on propaganda tours and sometimes imprisoning him. It is not overly generous to point out, however, that what resistance he made put him in actual, deadly jeopardy, and what compromises he made were in the same context.

While the debate about the justifications for emigrating from or remaining in Nazi Germany which has not ceased since 1933 is too complex to recapitulate here, it is worth noting that the conflicting currents in Fallada's story are not untypical of the stories of those who remained: collaboration was not necessarily prompt, uncoerced or unconditional, and resistance was not always immediate, impassioned or uncompromising. The only certainty for Fallada, as for all those who remained, was that even moderate acts of resistance carried the threat of imprisonment or death.

Fallada and Occupied Germany

In February 1945 Fallada married Ursula Losch, a widow of working-class background whose first husband had been a wealthy businessman. However, neither Fallada's new marriage nor the Nazi defeat a few months later significantly reduced the personal and political pressures on him. Ursula had weaknesses for alcohol and morphine which matched, and encouraged, Fallada's own. And in May 1945 the Soviet military authorities appointed him mayor of the district around Carwitz, evidently because he was a nationally known figure who had demonstrated some independence from the

Nazi regime. Fallada then faced such daunting tasks as securing food and medical supplies for the local population, assisting the flood of refugees from hitherto German-occupied areas further east, dealing with demands that alleged Nazis be handed over to the Soviet secret police, and curbing the numerous Red Army soldiers who were literally raping and pillaging their way across Germany. He proved unequal to the job, perhaps partly because – as he later claimed in a letter to Johannes R. Becher on 15 October 1945 – the local Soviet commandant deliberately overworked him with the aim of 'destroying me, in order to get his hands on my 24-year-old wife'. In August, after Fallada had resumed his morphine habit and Ursula had attempted suicide, they were admitted to hospital in nearby Neustrelitz, and when they were discharged in early September they moved to Berlin, where Ursula owned a badly damaged apartment in what was now the US sector of the city.

It was in Berlin that Fallada met Johannes R. Becher, a German author of his own generation who had returned from a decade of exile in the USSR and was now a leading figure in the Soviet military administration. Among other things, Becher was president of the Cultural Association for the Democratic Renewal of Germany, in which he was attempting – in accordance with the USSR's overall political policy immediately after the war – to create a wide-ranging alliance of intellectuals who were committed to revitalizing culture in Germany on a broadly antifascist basis. Becher provided Fallada with a comparatively comfortable house in the Soviet sector of Berlin, procured him additional rations of food and fuel, arranged for him to make some public speeches and radio broadcasts, and put him in contact with the newspaper founded by the Soviet administration, the *Daily Survey*, in which Fallada began publishing a variety of short pieces.

Becher also encouraged Fallada to write novels again, suggesting that he fictionalize the story of Otto and Elise Hampel, a middle-aged couple who began leaving handwritten anti-Nazi missives in buildings around Berlin after Elise's brother was killed during the invasion of France, and who were arrested in October 1942, tried in January 1943, and executed eleven weeks later. Fallada examined some of the documents in the Hampels' case, and in October 1945 he signed a contract for a novel about it with the Reconstruction publishing firm, which had recently been established by the Soviet authorities, and which was to reissue *The World Outside* in March 1946. Although Fallada wrote a short and largely factual account of the Hampels' story which appeared in a Soviet-sponsored magazine (also called *Reconstruction*) in November 1945, he did not then start work on the book, which he had undertaken to deliver by 1 January 1946. He spent much of the first seven months in 1946 undergoing hospital treatment for substance abuse and failing general health, but by September he had completed *The Nightmare* (1947), a novel in which an author called Doll struggles both to acknowledge his complicity in the Nazi regime and to overcome his dependence on morphine and sleeping drugs, but ultimately – and with the assistance of the Soviet administration – rededicates his literary career to helping build a new antifascist Germany. Fallada returned to the Hampels' case in late September 1946, and finished the first draft of the novel before the end of October, and the final revisions before the end of November. In early December he was admitted to the Charité hospital, where he wrote various letters which expressed his satisfaction with *Alone in Berlin*, sometimes comparing it to his last major published work, *Wolf Among Wolves*. He described *Alone in Berlin* to his mother on 22 December as 'a truly great novel'; he repeated to his sister Margarete on 27 December that it was 'a real one . . . a great novel . . . somewhat along the lines of my *Wolf*'; and he also told his sister Elisabeth on the same day that he had produced 'a great novel . . . You could say that, after *Wolf*, at last I've got one right.'

Fallada was transferred to another hospital in early January 1947, and died there on 5 February, before *Alone in Berlin* could be published.

Alone in Berlin

There was substantial and heroic resistance to the Nazi regime at all levels of German society, from aristocratic officers in the army to brutalized inmates of concentration camps. But all this resistance was unsuccessful, in the sense that the regime was destroyed by the foreign armies which conquered it rather than by internal rebels who overthrew it. Otto and Elise Hampel's resistance was particularly unsuccessful, in that (as the files in their case indicate) almost all the subversive materials which they distributed were handed to the Nazi authorities. I mean no disrespect to the Hampels' memory in adding that their resistance was unspectacular and unsophisticated if their localized propaganda effort is compared to (say) von Stauffenberg and his associates' attempted *coup d'état* in July 1944, or if their sometimes ungrammatical and inarticulate missives are compared to (say) the literate and cultivated leaflets written by the university-educated dissidents of the 'White Rose' group in 1942–3. Fallada knew that the German resistance was ineffectual before he even learned of the Hampels' existence as, for example, Anna Seghers could not know when she described the Communist underground in *The Seventh Cross* (1942), or as Klaus Mann could not know when he invoked a Communist uprising in the final pages of *Mephisto* (1936). And when Fallada read about the Hampels' resistance, he found their story uninspiring. In the article published in *Reconstruction* he described the couple as 'two insignificant individuals . . . without particular skills', noted that they were 'faithful supporters of the Führer' until 1940, commented that their postcard propaganda was 'poorly spelt' and 'clumsily expressed', speculated that such few cards as were not taken to the police were 'read hastily and fearfully and destroyed immediately', and emphasized that 'the sound of their protest died away unheard'.

Fallada transfers this almost bathetic characterization of the Hampels to their counterparts in *Alone in Berlin*, Otto and Anna Quangel. The fictional couple initially approve of the Nazi regime, believing after the failure of Otto's business during the Great Depression that 'Hitler was the one who had pulled their chestnuts out of the fire' (p. 15). Although the Quangels subsequently feel some reservations about the regime, their active rebellion against it originates in the purely personal grief of their son's death in 1940, and only develops a broader ethical dimension – for example in a postcard decrying 'the persecution of the Jews' (p. 166) – as it continues. The couple's eventual capture is pronounced inevitable not only by Inspector Escherich, with the authority of his professional experience, but also by Otto, who feels that chance must defeat them sooner or later. When the Quangels are arrested, Otto accepts Escherich's statement that the Gestapo 'never heard anything from the public at large that leads us to think they [the postcards] had the least effect' (p. 417), and Anna incautiously draws an interrogator's attention to her son's former fiancée, Trudel Baumann, who is then arrested and later commits suicide in prison.

The Quangels' lack of intellectual sophistication and political impact is paralleled by the numerous other dissidents in *Alone in Berlin*, who sometimes act from idiosyncratic motives, and almost always fail to thwart or damage the regime. Karl Hergesell joins the resistance cell in his factory primarily as a pretext to spend time with Trudel, the cell disbands after Trudel reveals its existence to Otto, and it subsequently emerges that the authorities had the group under observation in any case. Hetty Haberle is not really 'interested in politics' (p. 231), but rather is sheltering Enno Kluge from the Gestapo because they persecuted her husband, and she is unable to prevent Enno's death. Of the four Communist dissidents, Walter Haberle is murdered in a concentration camp, his associate Anna Schonlein is arrested for helping Hetty and Enno, Grigoleit – the third member of Karl and Trudel's cell – is eventually presumed to have 'gone AWOL' (p. 440), and Jensch – the fourth member – is described very fleetingly and vaguely as 'carrying on' (p. 313) after the cell breaks up. Among those who challenge the Nazis on ethical grounds, the retired Judge Fromm invokes his lifelong commitment to 'Justice' (p. 76) when giving refuge to his Jewish neighbor Frau Rosenthal, only for her to reject his stringent safety precautions and immediately fall victim to the Gestapo (while Fromm himself later dies in an air raid); Trudel also decides to hide a Jewish woman, but Karl determines to stop her, and the couple are arrested before she can act on her resolve; and the orchestral conductor Reichhardt makes repeated public statements about 'how disastrous the course was that the German people were taking under their Führer' (p. 470), for which he is imprisoned and condemned to death. With the possible minor exceptions of Grigoleit and Jensch, the only dissident who is neither incarcerated nor dead by the end of *Alone in Berlin* is Eva Kluge, and even this is essentially a matter of chance, in that the Nazi state – which Eva defies openly by resigning from the Party and her government job – decides on lesser sanctions:

She only just avoided being sentenced to concentration camp – but in the end they had let her go. Enemy of the state – that designation was punishment enough. (p. 371)

Thus Fallada goes to considerable lengths to create a large number of anti-Nazi dissidents who in practical terms fail almost completely. It is the sound not just of the Quangels' protest, but of many other protests, which dies away unheard, to repeat Fallada's phrase from the article about the Hampels which I quoted above. However, after using that phrase Fallada wrote that the couple

sacrificed their lives in a purposeless battle, apparently in vain. But perhaps not entirely purposeless, after all? Perhaps not entirely in vain, after all?

I, the author of an as yet unwritten novel, I hope that their battle, their suffering, their deaths were not entirely in vain.

And when the novel was written, it did suggest that the dissidents had not lived or died in vain. The fact that they achieve very little material success against the Nazi regime is portrayed as secondary to the idea that they defeat the regime in ideal and even metaphysical terms, by preserving their moral integrity both as individuals, and as representatives of a better Germany who justify the nation's survival. This means that *Alone in Berlin* examines for one final time the recurring tension in Fallada's works between how people struggle with – or, as in *The Drinker*, are destroyed by – the world around them, and how they still assert themselves against it in some meaningful way.

That the Quangels' objectively largely ineffectual resistance nevertheless has an ethical significance is emphasized when Otto first tells Anna that he intends to write the postcards. She protests that this initiative is 'a bit small', but he points out that 'if they get wind of it, it'll cost us our lives', prompting her to reflect that 'no one could risk more than his life', and that 'the main thing was, you fought back' (p. 140). Later the couple promise each other that they will stand by their criticisms of the regime even under threat of death, so that – as Otto says – they will 'be able to die properly, without moaning and whimpering' (p. 324). Like the Quangels, Eva recognizes that she is planning an individual and dangerous rebellion, but goes ahead in the conviction that through it 'she will keep her self-respect. Then that will have been her attainment in life, keeping her self-respect' (p. 43). And Reichhardt assures Otto that even though their and others' resistance will have no concrete result, 'it will have helped us to feel that we behaved decently till the end' (p. 476). I should perhaps note here that in the German text of the novel, Otto's 'properly', Eva's 'self-respect' and Reichhardt's 'decently' are all expressed by the adjective-cum-adverb '*anständig*', which refers primarily to what is 'decent' or done 'decently' in a moral sense, and moreover that '*anständig*' and its related forms are key words in many of Fallada's novels. *Little Man, What Now?*, in particular, can be understood partly as an examination of the strains which the Great Depression imposes on human decency.

Fallada reinforces the significance of the Quangels' moral integrity through Escherich. Initially the Inspector regards himself simply as a police detective, a servant of the state, whose work pursuing dissidents for the Gestapo has no more complex ethical implications than a clerk's work selling stamps for the post office. However, the brutality of his superior Prall gradually shows Escherich that he has assimilated to a corrupt system. Under pressure from Prall to demonstrate progress towards catching 'the hobgoblin', Escherich first falsely incriminates Enno Kluge and then murders him to conceal the deception, an action for which 'he will never be able to exonerate himself' (p. 283). When Prall later has Escherich himself arrested and mistreated, the Inspector becomes 'thoroughly acquainted with fear' (p. 390), and realizes that it is the driving principle of the regime. And when Escherich (who is eventually released) finally captures the Quangels, he concedes that their resistance was legitimate and that he has forfeited his integrity, returning no answer when Otto takes responsibility for his own actions and challenges the Inspector to accept responsibility for his:

You're working in the employ of a murderer, delivering ever new victims to him. You do it for money; perhaps you don't even believe in the man. No, I'm certain you don't believe in him. Just for money, then . . . (p. 418)

Escherich shoots himself that night, reflecting as he pulls the trigger that he is Otto's 'only disciple' (p. 422). While Escherich's suicide is unlikely to damage the Gestapo substantially, Otto clearly and literally gains a moral victory. Incidentally, there is nothing in the extant files in the Hampels' case which indicates that either Otto or Elise exercised any particular influence on the chief investigating officer, Willy Püschel, and Manfred Kuhnke's masterly study of the continuities and discontinuities between the Hampels' and the Quangels' stories has demonstrated that Püschel survived until at least 1947. That Fallada creates a more complex relationship between Otto Quangel and Inspector Escherich, which culminates in the latter's dramatic acknowledgement of his own inhumanity, highlights the emphasis that the novel places on the Quangels' steadfast decency.

Alone in Berlin characterizes the dissidents not only in ethical terms, as upholding profound ideals, but also in more metaphysical terms, as the conscience of the nation. This idea is introduced when Trudel tells Otto that the members of her factory cell see themselves as being 'like good seeds in a field of weeds. If it wasn't for the good seeds, the whole field would be nothing but weeds' (p. 29). The motif is repeated when Eva clears a potato paddock which is 'choked with weeds' (p. 370), and varied when Otto must 'sort batches of dried peas and pick out the wormy ones, the broken ones, stray seeds of this or that' (p. 527) while on death row. These references recall the biblical parable of the wheat and the tares (Matt. 13: 24–30 and 36–43), suggesting that those who oppose the Nazis embody Christian virtues which will ensure Germany's eventual salvation from the regime. This suggestion becomes stronger when Anna and Trudel are reunited in prison, and Anna says that 'I still believe in God' (p. 425), and it becomes explicit in Reichhardt's evaluation of his and the Quangels' and others' resistance, which I quoted in part above:

Well, it will have helped us to feel that we behaved decently till the end. And much more, it will have helped people everywhere, who will be saved for the righteous few among them, as it says in the Bible. (p. 476)

Reichhardt is invoking Genesis 18: 26–32, which begins: 'And the Lord said, If I find in Sodom fifty righteous within the city, then I will spare all the place for their sakes.'

The dissidents' significance as 'the righteous few' who redeem the nation is reinforced by the association between their rebellion and their children, who symbolize the nation's future. The Quangels of course begin writing their postcards when their only son is killed during the invasion of France. Eva's revolt is triggered by the news that one of her sons has murdered Jewish children in Poland. And Trudel forms her plan of sheltering the Jewish woman after she becomes pregnant, and starts thinking about how her son would grow up in the Nazi system. That Fallada is particularly concerned to establish the dissidents as the metaphorical parents of a better Germany born after 1945 is underlined by the fact that the Quangels' and Trudel's and Eva's children are all his own invention. For the Hampels turned against the regime when Elise's brother died in France, and had no children of their own, while Fallada's acquaintance Alfred Schmidt – who was executed in April 1943 for possessing duplicating machines which had been used for anti-Nazi propaganda, and who probably influenced Trudel and Karl's story – had no children either, and no one involved in the Hampels' case or known to Fallada personally was an obvious counterpart to the fictional Eva or either of her children. It is perhaps also worth noting that Trudel's miscarriage in the fifth month of her pregnancy and her renewed (if unfulfilled) commitment to opposing Nazism can be interpreted as repudiating the

Pinnebergs' belief, in *Little Man, What Now?*, that their love for each other and for their son provides a safe haven from the deeply flawed society around them.

All the elements which invest the dissidents' actions with ideal and transcendent meanings are combined in the brief final chapter of *Alone in Berlin*. The opening sentence replaces the third-person narration which has preceded it with an authorial 'we' in order to emphasize that the novel has shown the dissidents' moral victory:

But we don't want to end this book with death, dedicated as it is to life, invincible life, life always triumphing over humiliation and tears, over misery and death. (p. 564)

The chapter then moves forward to summer 1946, and describes how Eva remained in the countryside, married Kienschaper, civilized and adopted the delinquent teenager Kuno (without realizing that he was the son of her dead husband's criminal associate Emil Borkhausen), and is now building up a smallholding. The redemptive quality of Eva's – and by extension of the other dissidents' – actions is highlighted by the baptismal imagery in Kuno's recollection of how Eva 'put me in the water and washed the dirt off me with her own hands' (p. 568) when she first took him into her home, as well as by a final invocation of the parable of the wheat and the tares in the novel's closing sentence: 'Because it is written that you reap what you sow, and the boy had sown good corn.' (p. 568; see also Gal. 6: 7–10) And Eva's and the others' metaphorical status as the parents of a humane post-Nazi Germany is underlined literally by Eva's formal adoption of Kuno, and more figuratively both by her quasi-baptismal washing of him and by his rejection of his unreformed ex-convict father Emil, who reappears unexpectedly and tries to claim or extort a share of Kuno's comparative prosperity: '"I've got no father!" shouted the boy, wild with anger. "I've got a mother, and I'm starting afresh."' (p. 567)

It could be argued that Fallada's affirmative portrayal of the anti-Nazi resistance in *Alone in Berlin* is somewhat unconvincing, especially in his use of Christian symbolism. Some of the religious references which I have noted are contested elsewhere in the narrative. For example, when Anna tells Trudel that she still has faith in God, she goes on to say that Otto thinks 'everything comes to an end after this life' (p. 452), and minutes before his execution Otto insists to the prison chaplain that: 'I don't believe in any Almighty' (p. 551). The narrative then seems to challenge Otto's unbelief as the guillotine blade falls – 'the rushing had become a piercing scream that must be audible up in the stars, to the throne of God . . .' (p. 561) – but the subsequent description of Anna's death in an air raid concludes more equivocally: 'She is . . . reunited with him. She is where he is. Wherever that may be' (p. 563). This uncertain treatment of Christian motifs is entirely congruent with Fallada's previous career. And Fallada's personal relationship to Christianity may be judged from the letter to the Rowohlt firm on 15 January 1934, in which he mentioned a biblical quotation that might serve as an epigraph to *The World Outside*, and sought advice about 'where it is in the Bible (I don't own one to look in)'. Thus it is arguable that in seeking – as foreshadowed by his article in *Reconstruction* – to demonstrate that the dissidents had not lived or died in vain, Fallada adopts a metaphysical framework with which he is rather uncomfortable and unfamiliar. Similarly, the opening of the final chapter ('But we don't want to end this book with death . . .') can be read as suggesting that the author is still trying to convince himself that the resistance's failures were nevertheless meaningful. And that chapter's comment about how the Kienschapers 'were given' their smallholding 'the previous year' (p. 565) – which refers to the Soviet military administration's program of expropriating large agricultural properties – is also interesting in possibly indicating that Fallada is unduly eager to establish continuities between the dissidents and the postwar promises of a better Germany. But even assuming that Fallada does not entirely establish his case for the resistance's ultimate historical significance, these minor hesitations and exaggerations are hardly surprising in a novel written barely eighteen months after the Nazi defeat, and by a man who had struggled to survive artistically and psychologically under the Nazi regime, as he had struggled to survive in German society all his life. They are unlikely to obscure the novel's particular achievement, which is perhaps best characterized by a comparison with a later, purely factual and more celebrated examination of Nazi oppression: whereas Hannah Arendt's *Eichmann in Jerusalem* (1963) dissects and analyses 'the banality of evil', Hans Fallada's *Alone in Berlin* comprehends and honours the banality of good.

Editorial Note

All quotations from *Little Man, What Now?* are from the Melville House edition (New York, 2009).

All quotations from Fallada's letters are from the copies held by the Hans Fallada Archive in Carwitz. All translations are my own.

All quotations from Fallada's essay about the Hampels are from Fallada, 'Über den doch vorhandenen Widerstand der Deutschen gegen den Hitlerterror' in *Wir haben nicht nur das Chaos, sondern wir stehen an einem Beginn: Hans Fallada 1945–1947*, ed. Sabine Lange (Neubrandenburg: Literaturzentrum Neubrandenburg, 1988) pp. 45–56. All translations are my own.

All references to the Bible are to the King James Version.

The extant files in the cases of the Hampels and Alfred Schmidt are held by the 'Stiftung Archiv der Parteien und Massenorganisationen der DDR' of the Federal Archive in Lichterfelde, Berlin. The files on the Hampels are NJ36/2, NJ36/3, NJ36/4, and ZC12614; the files on Schmidt are NJ1705/1, NJ1705/2, NJ1705/4 and NJ5110/1.

Manfred Kuhnke's study of the factual Hampels and the fictional Quangels is *Die Hampels und die Quangels: Authentisches und Erfundenes in Hans Falladas letztem Roman* (Neubrandenburg: Literaturzentrum Neubrandenburg, 2001).

Geoff Wilkes
University of Queensland
Brisbane, Australia

The True Story Behind
Alone in Berlin

Alone in Berlin is based upon the case of Elise and Otto Hampel, a poorly educated working-class couple living in Berlin with no history, prior to this case, of political activity. After Elise's brother was killed early in the war, the couple commenced a nearly three-year propaganda campaign that baffled – and enraged – the Berlin police, who eventually handed the case over to the Gestapo. The Hampels' campaign consisted, quite simply, of leaving hundreds of postcards calling for civil disobedience and workplace sabotage all over Berlin. They were particularly insistent in urging people not to give to the Winter Fund, which was essentially a false-front charity the Nazis pressured citizens to contribute to, which was actually used to fund the war.

Many of the cards were quickly turned in to the police, but the Hampels blanketed the city so thoroughly, and eluded capture so successfully, that the Gestapo and other units of the Nazi police forces came to assume that they were dealing with a large, sophisticated underground resistance.

Hans Fallada was given their Gestapo file by Johannes R. Becher, a poet friend of his who had become what was essentially the cultural minister in the post-war government set up by the Soviets in Eastern Germany. Fallada had barely survived the war after a long stint in a Nazi insane asylum (in most instances, a death sentence), which, upon his release, had in turn contributed to a relapse of his drug and alcohol problems. At war's end he was a shattered man, and in an effort to get him back on his feet, Becher gave him the Hampels' Gestapo file and suggested he use it as the basis of a novel. Fallada wrote the book in twenty-four days, but did not live to see its publication.

What follows is material from the Gestapo file given to Hans Fallada by Johannes Becher. It includes documents from the initial police investigation as well as from the Gestapo's own investigation. It was the main basis for the case against Elise and Otto Hampel presented in the People's Court – where the Nazis held their show trials – before the President of the Court, Roland Freisler. The Hampels were found guilty and sentenced to death, and executed by beheading in Plotenzee Prison in March 1943.

Geheime Staatspolizei   C. 2   20. 10.
Staatspolizeistelle Berlin   Berlin-   , den

                                                              72

Geschäftszeichen: IV A 1c.-

                xxxxxxxxxxxx   Vom Unterzeichneten
                Auf Anordnung de

als Hilfsbeamten der Staatsanwaltschaft wurde bei Gefahr im Verzuge vor heute
um 9,00 Uhr in den Wohnräumen*) Geschäftsräumen*) — de   10
N. 69, Amsterdamer   XX
           Berlin   Straße — Platz Nr.

eine Durchsuchung von dem Unterzeichneten vorgenommen.

        Die Durchsuchung ei:

        KOA. Zilian und Laur,

        Dr. Büttner, sämtlich IV A 1c

Es wurden die umseitig aufgeführten Gegenstände aufgefunden und beschlagnahmt, da sie — als
Beweismittel von Bedeutung sein können*) — der Einziehung unterliegen*) —.

        Gegen die Beschlagnahme wurde seitens de
                                xxxxxxx
                — kein*) — ausdrücklich*) — Widerspruch erhoben.

                        Ks.   IV A 1c.

Name des Beamten   Amtsbezeichnung   Dienststelle

1. The Gestapo report of a search of the Hampels' apartment.
Their final report documented the entire case from start to finish,
including the investigation of not only the Hampels but their
family, friends and neighbours, and people at Otto Hampel's
employer (including a supervisor who seems to have been on the
Gestapo payroll, and who denounced Hampel).

Sicherheitsdienst des Reichsführers ☩☩

SD-Leitabschnitt Berlin
Außenstelle Berlin VI

Berlin N 65, den 12 1 42

Müllerstraße 135
Fernsprecher 46 28 21

Aktenzeichen: II B 4 - SA 994/39 Hg/Ro.

Geheime Staatspolizei
Staatspolizeistelle Berlin
15 JAN 1942

IV A1c S. 31/46

An die
Staatspolizeileitstelle Berlin
über den
SD-Leitabschnitt Berlin.

Betr.: Gegnerische Flugblattpropaganda
Vorg.: Hies. Schrb. v. 9.12.41
-.-.-.-.-.-.-.-.-.-.-.-.-.-.-.-.-.-.

In der letzten Zeit mehren sich die Meldungen über gegnerische
Propaganda in Wort und Schrift. Vor allem die bereits laufend übe
sandten Hetzschriften in der gleichen imitierten Druckschrift
werden in verstärktem Masse im hiesigen Bereich verteilt. Aller-
dings werden die wenigsten Exemplare dieser Art abgegeben.
Es scheint, als ob diese Sudeleien doch in nicht wenigen Kreisen
Anklang finden, zumindest werden sie als Beweis für eine rühri-
ge und bestehende Gegenorganisation betrachtet. In vielen Fällen
scheuen sich die Volksgenossen auch aus Angst vor irgendwelchen
persönlichen Nachteilen, diese Schreibereien abzugeben, bezw.
diesbezügliche Beobachtungen der NSDAP oder der Polizei oder son-
stigen Stellen anzuzeigen, vor allem wollen sie nie als Zeugen
auftreten müssen.
Eine schwache Möglichkeit, einen der Täter oder auch den Täter
selbst ausfindig zu machen, ist durch die Meldung der Ortsgruppe
Fehmarn der NSDAP gegeben. Der beiliegende gelbliche Doppelbo-
gen wurde am 27.12.41 um etwa 15 Uhr von der Volksgenossin Frau
Kempin, Berlin N 65, Samoastr. 8, im gleichen Hause gefunden.
Frau Kempin sowie die Vgn. Frau Beck, wohnhaft im gleichen Hause, gaben der Ortsgruppe gegenüber an, dass sie den Verteiler
gesehen hätten und genau beschreiben könnten. Es sei nur in der
Nähe kein Mann oder ein Schutzpolizist gewesen, sonst hätten sie
die betreffende Person festnehmen lassen.
In offenbar derselben Schrift sind die anliegenden Postkarten,
die der Vg. Zunke, Berlin N 65, Müllerstr. 133 B, am 21.12.41
um etwa 11 Uhr sowie dem Vgn. Schwabe, Berlin N 65, Kameruner
Str. 2, fanden, geschrieben.

---

2. The investigation begins: one of the first police reports on the
case, which notes, 'In the last week, there have been more reports
of anti-Nazi propaganda.'

S t a p o IV A l c   Berlin, den 13.4.42   53

B e r i c h t .

Betrifft: Hetzschriften "Freie Presse"

Die Mitteilungen über das Auftreten des Verbreiters der "Freien
Presse" und das bisher angefallene Material wurden zur Ermittlung
von Anhaltspunkten über den Täter einer genauen Durchsicht unter-
zogen:
Bisher liegen 2 Personenbeschreibungen des vermutlichen Täters vor;
die Ehefrau Lill fand in der Müllerstr. 54 gegen 22 Uhr auf der
Treppe ihres Hauses, in den sie die Hauswartsarbeiten verrichtet,
ein Exemplar der Flugschrift. Sie bezeichnete als vermutlichen
Verbreiter dieser Schrift einen Mann, der kurz vor dem Auffinden
der Schrift das Haus verlassen hat und beschreibt ihn wie folgt:

> 40 bis 50 Jahre alt, 1,80 m groß,
> grauer Anzug, dunkler Hut,
> (Personenbeschreibung stammt vom
> Juni 1941).

Der Betreffende war der Frau Lill, welche die im Hause wohnenden
Personen sonst naturgemäß gut kennt, völlig unbekannt. Da um 22 Uhr
in den Häusern kaum noch Publikumsverkehr herrscht, kann angenommen werden, daß es sich bei dem von Frau Lill gesehenen Mann
tatsächlich um den Verbreiter der "Freien Presse" gehandelt hat.
Am 27.1.1942 trat der Verbreiter im Hause Samoastr. 8 auf.
Er ist vermutlich mit der Person identisch, die von der im gleichen Hause wohnhaften Frau Lisbeth B e c k gegen 14.45 gesehen
worden ist. Frau Beck beschreibt den Mann wie folgt:

> 35 bis 40 Jahre alt, etwa 1.75
> groß, schlank, ovales, längliches
> Gesicht, gestutzten dunklen Schnur-
> bart, bläulichen Unterton (zwar
> gut rasiert aber starken Bartwuchs,
> dunkelgrauen vorn heruntergeschla-
> genen Haarhut, dunklen Paletot
> zweireiher vermutlich Handschuhe.

Den Umständen nach kann angenommen werden, daß der Hetz-
schriftenverbreiter auch in diesem Falle mit der beschriebenen Person identisch ist.

---

3. A police report citing an eyewitness account of a man dropping
a card, noting it was left in the stairwell of a residential building.
A second eyewitness account would also describe a man, but the
two descriptions were so different police had to discount them.

Original an H-Stuf Günde, Br.9 gür
Fahndung
57

Betrifft: Verbreiter der Hetzschriften "Freie Presse".
(Es handelt sich um handgeschriebene Postkarten oder auch Bogen.)

Täter tritt seit 2.9.1940 auf.

Vermutliches Aussehen:

Etwa 35 bis 45 Jahre alt, 1,75 bis 1,80 groß, schlank längliches ovales Gesicht, gestutzten dunklen Schnurrbart, bläulicher Unterton (starker Bartwuchs). Gut gekleidet, kein ungepflegter äußerer Eindruck (dürfte etwa wie ein mittlerer Angestellter wirken.)

Wohnung: Vermutlich die Gegend Schönhauser Allee, südlich des Straßenzuges Seestr./Wisbyerstr., mehr nach Westen zur Müllerstraße hin als nach Osten.

Bildungsgrad: Wenn der Täter ein Deutscher ist, lassen seine schriftlichen Ausführungen auf ein niederes Bildungsniveau schließen.

Familienstand: vermutlich ledig oder verwitwet.

Arbeitsweise: Sucht sich mit Vorliebe Häuser aus, in denen ein starker Publikumsverkehr herrscht (Häuser mit Praxisräumen). Legt die Schriften zumeist in den unteren Stockwerken auf den Fensterbrettern der Flure nieder. Der Täter scheint das Wochenende für seine Arbeit zu bevorzugen.

Täter tritt in der Hauptsache in der Gegend Müllerstraße (zwischen der Belfareter und der Reinickendorferstraße) auf. Hier ist er zu fast allen Tageszeiten in Erscheinung getreten. Neben den Bezirk Müllerstraße hat der Täter aber auch noch in verschiedenen anderen Stadtbezirken Blätter verbreitet, die ziemlich genau abgegrenzt werden konnten. So ist er in der Gegend Schönhauser Allee/Danzigerstraße in Erscheinung getreten.

Ferner trat der Verbreiter in folgenden Bezirken auf: Bezirk Moabit (Pudlitzstraße bis zur Wittstockerstraße). An folgenden Tagen :

19.1.41, sonntags
2.3.41   14 Uhr , sonntags
3.3.41   18 "   , montags
7.3.41   10.55   , freitags
11.3.41   9 u.18 , dienstags
1.5.41   18.30   , donnerstags
7.6.41   17.30   , sonnabends
12.8.41   20.00   , dienstags
3.10.41   17.   , sonntags

4. A police report detailing the growing list of cards turned in so far, including the dates and locations of the findings.

'Hitler's regime will bring us no peace!'

5. A sampling of cards turned in to the police. The cards included numerous misspellings and grammatical errors, and were clearly laboriously written by someone with little education. Messages were often somewhat disjointed, too, with disconnected phrases such as 'free press!' thrown in.

'Free Press! Why suffer war and
death for the Hitler plutocracy?'

'Hitler's war is the worker's death!'

'German people wake up!'

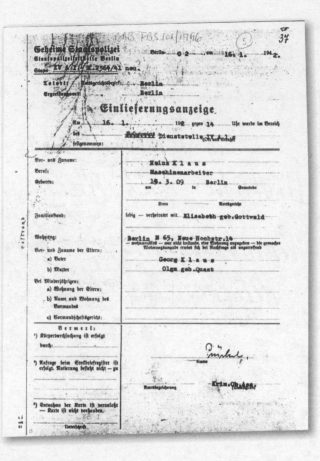

6. The cover sheet of the arrest report for Heinz Klaus – the model for the character Enno Kluge in *Alone in Berlin*. Klaus was a gambler who left his home frequently and at odd hours, making the police suspicious. Klaus was suspected of dropping cards that were found in stairwells and hallways outside a doctor's office, a lawyer's office and some residences. He was arrested after a card was found outside a dentist's office. The dentist's nurse pointed him out to police and said he'd been acting suspiciously in the waiting room, going frequently back and forth to the lavatory. He was eventually released when his description did not match that of either of the two eyewitnesses and police realized gambling was behind his suspicious behaviour.

1

Perſonalbogen

Perſonalien des politiſch — ſpionagepolizeilich*) — in Erſcheinung getretenen:

1. a) **Familienname: (bei Frauen auch Geburtsname)** <u>H a m p e l</u>

   b) **Vornamen: (Rufname unterſtreichen)** Otto Hermann

2. **Wohnung: (genaue Angabe)** Bln. N. 65, Amsterdamer Str. 10., I. Aufg
   2 Tr.

3. a) **Deckname:** —

   b) **Deckadreſſe:** —

4. **Beruf:** Einrichter in der Metallbranche

5. **Geburtstag, -jahr** 21.6.97 **Geburtsort:** Mühlbock bei Züllichau

6. **Glaubensbekenntnis und Abſtammung:** ev. Auch früher, ar. Abst.

7. **Staatsangehörigkeit:** R.D.

8. **Familienſtand: (ledig, verheiratet, verwitwet, geſchieden) *)** verh.

   a) **Nationale und Wohnung der Ehefrau:** Elise, geb. Lemme,27.10.03 Bismarck §

   b) **Nationale und Wohnung des Vaters:** Gustav Hampel,10.8.72 Mühlbock geb.
   Berlin, Antwerpener Str. 47 wohnhaft

   c) **Nationale und Wohnung der Mutter:** Pauline geb. Krause, 7.1.60 Krossen
   beim Vater wohnhaft

   d) **Nationale und Wohnung ſonſtiger Auskunftsperſonen:** ---

9. **Arbeitsdienſtverhältnis:** bestand nicht

   Muſterung: (Ort) — am 19

   Ergebnis: —

   Angehöriger des Reichsarbeitsdienſtes von: nein 19 **bis:** 19

   Abteilung: **Standort:**

10. **Militärverhältnis: (Wehrpflicht, Dienſtpflicht, früheres Militärverhältnis) *)**

    Muſterung: (Ort) Bln.-Wedding am 1940 19

    Ergebnis: Kv.

    für: (Waffengattung) .... **als Freiwilliger eingetreten?**

    Wehrbezirkskommando, Wehrmeldeamt *) Wedding

    Dienſtzeit: von: 11.10.16 **bis:** Januar 19 19

    als: Schütze

    Truppenteil: Landst. Rgt. 77. **Standort:** Brandenburg

---

*) Zutreffendes unterſtreichen. B. St. Rt. 163

8. The mug shots of Otto and Elise Hampel.

zu beeinflussen. Inwieweit unsere Arbeit unter dem Volke
Schaden angerichtet hat, kann ich nicht ermessen, ich
sehe aber ein, dass bei der grossen Auflage derartiger
Schriften manches Unheil angerichtet worden ist. Heute
bedauere ich, dass ich mich auf diese Weise zum Staats-
feind stempelte und mich in dieser schweren Zeit gegen
Volk und Staat verging. Wenn ich mir auch bewusst bin,
dass meine Handlungsweise durch Strafe gesühnt werden
muss, so bitte ich hiermit um milde Beurteilung. Zum
Teil ist doch der Krieg und seine Folgen für unsere
jetziges Unglück verantwortlich zu machen. Ich bitte
bei mir zu berücksichtigen, dass ich vor unserer
staatsfeindlichen Betätigung selbst positiv für den
nationalsozialistischen Staat mitarbeitete und auch sonst
ein einwandfreies Leben führte. Ich möchte auch nochmals
auf meinen Seelenzustand hinweisen. Durch die Todesfälle
in unserer Verwandtschaft im letzten Kriege, wie auch in
diesem Kriege, bin ich seelisch etwas xxxxxxxxxxxxxx
zerrüttet worden.

selbst gelesen: genehmigt: unterschrieben:

[signature]
Geschlossen:

[signature]
KS.

9. The signed confession of Elise Hampel: Elise made one statement
after her arrest, probably indicating less interrogation than Otto
seems to have undergone. She explained her motivation by saying,
'My soul was devastated by the losses of the war, particularly of
my brother.' She also said, 'My husband wrote all the cards because
I cannot write in print well,' and further claimed that he delivered
all the cards, although she said they shared culpability. Note the
signature that appears below Elise's of someone named 'Püschel'.
It is a name that appears on many of the reports, including Otto
Hampel's confession, and belongs to the chief investigating officer,
Willy Püschel – the model for the character Gestapo Inspector
Escherich in *Alone in Berlin*.

2 ~~gewesen sein.~~ Keinesfalls ~~waren~~ es aber mehrere oder ein
ganzer Stoß gewesen.

Als Motiv zu meiner Handlung kann ich nur eine innere Ver-
stimmung, die durch den Tod meines Schwagers entstanden ist,
anführen. Ich bin dadurch in meiner inneren Haltung schwach
geworden und habe aus Verärgerung heraus diese Hetzkarten
geschrieben. Irgendwie wollte ich meinem Herzen Luft machen
und tat dies in dieser weniger freundlichen Form. Das gleiche
war auch bei meiner Frau der Fall. Auch sie war durch den
Verlust ihres Bruders sehr verbittert und in ihrer guten
Gesinnung schwach geworden. Ich selbst übernehme aber die
alleinige Verantwortung für die Herstellung und Verbreitung
der Hetzkarten. Zur besseren Beurteilung meiner Person weise
ich auf meinen früheren einwandfreien Lebenswandel hin."

Durchgelesen und unterschrieben:

Otto Hampel

[signature]

10. Otto Hampel's signature on one of his three confessions, indicating that he seems to have undergone at least three interrogations.
The first statement is on his motivation, which he said was inspired
by the death of his brother-in-law. The second is a detailed description of how he wrote and disseminated the cards, which he says
was mostly improvisational. The third goes back to motive. In it,
he says he realizes his actions made him an enemy of the state,
and insists he acted alone and that his wife was not involved.